PRAISE FOR JAMES LEE BURKE

"James Lee Burke is the reigning champ of nostalgia noir."

—*The New York Times Book Review*

"A gorgeous prose stylist."

—Stephen King

"James Lee Burke is the heavyweight champ, a great American novelist whose work, taken individually or as a whole, is unsurpassed."

—Michael Connelly

"Burke's evocative prose remains a thing of reliably fierce wonder."

—*Entertainment Weekly*

"America's best novelist."

—*The Denver Post*

"Burke can touch you in ways few writers can."

—*The Washington Post*

"For five decades, Burke has created memorable novels that weave exquisite language, unforgettable characters, and social commentary into written tapestries that mirror the contemporary scene. His work transcends genre classification."

—*The Philadelphia Inquirer*

"Burke's writing [is] Faulkner-esque in its beauty, its feel on the ear like a southern breeze blowing through magnolia blossoms and oil fields."

—*Missoulian*

CREOLE BELLE

A DAVE ROBICHEAUX NOVEL

JAMES LEE BURKE

SIMON & SCHUSTER PAPERBACKS

New York   London   Toronto   Sydney   New Delhi

SIMON & SCHUSTER PAPERBACKS
An Imprint of Simon & Schuster, Inc.
1230 Avenue of the Americas
New York, NY 10020

This Simon & Schuster trade paperback edition October 2018

SIMON & SCHUSTER PAPERBACKS and colophon are registered trademarks
of Simon & Schuster, Inc.

For information about special discounts for bulk purchases,
please contact Simon & Schuster Special Sales at
1-866-506-1949 or business@simonandschuster.com.

The Simon & Schuster Speakers Bureau can bring authors
to your live event. For more information or to book an event,
contact the Simon & Schuster Speakers Bureau at
1-866-248-3049 or visit our website at www.simonspeakers.com.

Manufactured in the United States of America

3   5   7   9   10   8   6   4

The Library of Congress has cataloged the hardcover edition as follows:

Burke, James Lee.
Creole belle / James Lee Burke.
p. cm.
1. Robicheaux, Dave (Fictitious character)—Fiction.
2. Police—Louisiana—Fiction.
3. New Iberia (La.)—Fiction. I. Title.
PS3552.U723C74   2012
813'.54—dc23   2012002542

ISBN 978-1-9821-0030-8
ISBN 978-1-4516-4815-7 (ebook)

*In memory of Michael Pinkston,
Martha Hall, and David Thompson*

CREOLE BELLE

CHAPTER 1

FOR THE REST of the world, the season was still fall, marked by cool nights and the gold-green remnants of summer. For me, down in South Louisiana, in the Garden District of New Orleans, the wetlands that lay far beyond my hospital window had turned to winter, one characterized by stricken woods that were drained of water and strung with a web of gray leaves and dead air vines that had wrapped themselves as tightly as cord around the trees.

Those who have had the following experience will not find my descriptions exaggerated or even metaphorical in nature. A morphine dream has neither walls nor a ceiling nor a floor. The sleep it provides is like a warm bath, free of concerns about mortality and pain and memories from the past. Morpheus also allows us vision through a third eye that we never knew existed. His acolytes can see through time and become participants in grand events they had believed accessible only through history books and films. On one occasion, I saw a hot-air balloon rising from its tether in Audubon Park, a uniformed soldier operating a telegrapher's key inside the wicker basket, while down below other members of the Confederate Signal Corps shared sandwiches and drank coffee from tin cups, all of them as stately and stiff as figures in a sepia-tinted photograph.

I don't wish to be too romantic about my experience in the recovery facility there on St. Charles Avenue in uptown New Orleans.

While I gazed through my window at the wonderful green streetcar wobbling down the tracks on the neutral ground, the river fog puffing out of the live oak trees, the pink and purple neon on the Katz & Besthoff drugstore as effervescent as tentacles of smoke twirling from marker grenades, I knew with a sinking heart that what I was seeing was an illusion, that in reality the Katz & Besthoff drugstore and the umbrella-covered sno'ball carts along St. Charles and the musical gaiety of the city had slipped into history long ago, and somewhere out on the edge of my vision, the onset of permanent winter waited for me.

Though I'm a believer, that did not lessen the sense of trepidation I experienced in these moments. I felt as if the sun were burning a hole in the sky, causing it to blacken and collapse like a giant sheet of carbon paper suddenly crinkling and folding in on itself, and I had no power to reverse the process. I felt that a great darkness was spreading across the land, not unlike ink spilling across the face of a topographic map.

Many years ago, when I was recovering from wounds I received in a Southeast Asian country, a United States Army psychiatrist told me that my morphine-induced dreams were creating what he called a "world destruction fantasy," one that had its origins in childhood and the dissolution of one's natal family. He was a scientist and a learned man, and I did not argue with him. Even at night, when I lay in a berth on a hospital ship, far from free-fire zones and the sound of ammunition belts popping under a burning hooch, I did not argue. Nor did I contend with the knowledge of the psychiatrist when dead members of my platoon spoke to me in the rain and a mermaid with an Asian face beckoned to me from a coral cave strung with pink fans, her hips spangled with yellow coins, her mouth parting, her naked breasts as flushed with color as the inside of a conch shell.

The cult of Morpheus is a strange community indeed, and it requires that one take up residence in a country where the improbable becomes commonplace. No matter what I did, nor how many times I disappeared out my window into the mists along St. Charles Avenue, back into an era of rooftop jazz bands and historical streetcars filled with men in bowler hats and women who carried parasols, the watery gray rim of a blighted planet was always out there—intransigent and corrupt, a place where moth and rust destroy and thieves break in and steal.

IN THE EARLY A.M. on a Friday, I asked the black attendant to open the windows in my room. It was against the rules, but the attendant was an elderly and kind man who had spent five days on a rooftop after the collapse of the levees during Hurricane Katrina, and he wasn't given to concerns about authority. The windows reached to the ceiling and were hung with ventilated green shutters that were closed during the heat of the day to filter the sun's glare. The attendant opened both the glass and the shutters and let in the night smell of the roses and camellias and magnolia and rain mist blowing through the trees. The air smelled like Bayou Teche when it's spring and the fish are spawning among the water hyacinths and the frogs are throbbing in the cattails and the flooded cypress. It smelled like the earth may have smelled during the first days of creation, before any five-toed footprints appeared along the banks of a river.

Or at least I think the black man opened the windows. Even to this day I cannot be sure of what I said and saw and heard that night. Like the drunkard who fears both his memory and his dreams, I had become cynical about my perceptions, less out of fear that they were illusions than a conviction that they were real.

After the black man had left the room, I turned my head on the pillow and looked into the face of a Cajun girl by the name of Tee Jolie Melton.

"Hi, Mr. Dave," she said. "I read all about the shooting in the papers. You was on television, too. I didn't know you was here in New Orleans. I'm sorry to see you hurt like this. You was talking French in your sleep."

"It's nice to see you, Tee Jolie. How'd you get in?" I said.

"T'rew the front door. You want me to come back another time?"

"Can you get me a glass of water?"

"I got you better than that. I brought you a Dr Pepper and a lime

I cut up, 'cause that's what you always drank when you came into the club. I brought you somet'ing else, too. It's an iPod I filled wit' music. I loaded 'Beat Me Daddy, Eight to the Bar' on it, 'cause I knew how you always liked that song."

Her eyes were blue-green, her hair long and mahogany-colored with twists of gold in it that were as bright as buttercups. She was part Indian and part Cajun and part black and belonged to that ethnic group we call Creoles, although the term is a misnomer.

"You're the best," I said.

"Remember when you he'ped me with my car crash? You was so kind. You took care of everyt'ing, and I didn't have no trouble at all because of it."

It wasn't *a* car crash. As I recalled, *it* was at least three car crashes, but I didn't pursue the point. The most interesting aspect of Tee Jolie's auto accidents were her written explanations at the scene. To the best of my memory, these were her words:

"I was backing up when this light pole came out of nowhere and smashed into my bumper.

"I was turning left, but somebody was blocking the lane, so, trying to be polite, I switched my turn indicator and cut through the school parking lot, but I didn't have no way of knowing the chain was up on the drive at that time of day, because it never is.

"When the transmission went into reverse, Mr. Fontenot was putting my groceries in the backseat, and the door handle caught his coat sleeve and drug him across the street into the gas pump that blew up. I tried to give him first aid on the mouth, but he had already swallowed this big wad of gum that the fireman had to pull out with his fingers. I think Mr. Fontenot almost bit off one of the fireman's fingers and didn't have the courtesy to say he was sorry."

Tee Jolie fixed a glass of ice and Dr Pepper with a lime slice and stuck a straw in it and held it up to my mouth. She was wearing a long-sleeve shirt printed with purple and green flowers. Her skirt was pale blue and fluffy and pleated, and her shoes looked tiny on her feet. You could say that Tee Jolie was made for the camera, her natural loveliness of a kind that begged to be worshipped on a stage or hung on a wall. Her face was thin, her eyes elongated, and her hair full of waves, as though it had been recently unbraided, although that was the way it always looked.

"I feel selfish coming here, 'cause it wasn't just to give you a Dr Pepper and the iPod," she said. "I came here to ax you somet'ing, but I ain't gonna do it now."

"You can say anything you want, Tee Jolie, because I'm not even sure you're here. I dream in both the day and the night about people who have been dead many years. In my dreams, they're alive, right outside the window, Confederate soldiers and the like."

"They had to come a long way, huh?"

"That's safe to say," I replied. "My wife and daughter were here earlier, and I know they were real. I'm not sure about you. No offense meant. That's just the way it is these days."

"I know something I ain't suppose to know, and it makes me scared, Mr. Dave," she said.

She was sitting in the chair, her ankles close together, her hands folded on her knees. I had always thought of her as a tall girl, particularly when she was onstage at the zydeco club where she sang, an arterial-red electric guitar hanging from her neck. Now she looked smaller than she had a few moments ago. She lifted her face up into mine. There was a mole by the corner of her mouth. I didn't know what she wanted me to say.

"Did you get involved with some bad guys?" I said.

"I wouldn't call them that. How come you to ax me that?"

"Because you're a good person, and sometimes you trust people you shouldn't. Good women tend to do that. That's why a lot of us men don't deserve them."

"Your father was killed in a oil-well blowout, wasn't he? Out on the Gulf when you was in Vietnam. That's right, ain't it?"

"Yes, he was a derrick man."

As with many Creoles and Cajuns, there was a peculiarity at work in Tee Jolie's speech. She was ungrammatical and her vocabulary was limited, but because of the cadence in her language and her regional accent, she was always pleasant to listen to, a voice from a gentler and more reserved time, even when what she spoke of was not pleasant to think about, in this case the death of my father, Big Aldous.

"I'm wit' a man. He's separated but not divorced. A lot of people know his name. Famous people come to the place where we live. I heard them talking about centralizers. You know what they are?"

"They're used inside the casing on drilling wells."

"A bunch of men was killed 'cause maybe not enough of those centralizers was there or somet'ing."

"I've read about that, Tee Jolie. It's public knowledge. You shouldn't worry because you know about this."

"The man I'm wit' does bidness sometimes with dangerous people."

"Maybe you should get away from him."

"We're gonna be married. I'm gonna have his baby."

I fixed my gaze on the glass of Dr Pepper and ice that sat on the nightstand.

"You want some more?" she asked.

"Yes, but I can hold it by myself."

"Except I see the pain in your face when you move," she said. She lifted the glass and straw to my mouth. "They hurt you real bad, huh, Mr. Dave?"

"They shot me up proper," I replied.

"They shot your friend Mr. Clete, too?"

"They smacked both of us around. But we left every one of them on the ground. They're going to be dead for a long time."

"I'm glad," she said.

Outside the window, I could hear the rain and wind sweeping through the trees, scattering leaves from the oaks and needles from the slash pines across the roof.

"I always had my music and the piece of land my father left me and my sister and my mama," she said. "I sang wit' BonSoir, Catin. I was queen of the Crawfish Festival in Breaux Bridge. I t'ink back on that, and it's like it was ten years ago instead of two. A lot can change in a short time, cain't it? My mama died. Now it's just me and my li'l sister, Blue, and my granddaddy back in St. Martinville."

"You're a great musician, and you have a wonderful voice. You're a beautiful person, Tee Jolie."

"When you talk like that, it don't make me feel good, no. It makes me sad."

"Why?"

"He says I can have an abortion if I want."

"That's his offer to you?"

"He ain't got his divorce yet. He ain't a bad man. You know him."

"Don't tell me his name," I said.

"How come?"

Because I might want to put a bullet between his eyes, I thought. "It's not my business," I said. "Did you really give me this iPod?"

"You just saw me."

"I can't trust what I see and hear these days. I truly want to believe you're real. The iPod is too expensive a gift."

"Not for me. He gives me plenty of money."

"My wallet is in the nightstand drawer."

"I got to go, Mr. Dave."

"Take the money."

"No. I hope you like the songs. I put t'ree of mine in there. I put one in there by Taj Mahal 'cause I know you like him, too."

"Are you really here?" I asked.

She cupped her hand on my brow. "You're burning up, you," she said.

Then she was gone.

NINE DAYS LATER, a big man wearing a seersucker suit and a bow tie and spit-shined shoes and a fresh haircut and carrying a canvas bag on a shoulder strap came into the room and pulled up a chair by the bed and stuck an unlit cigarette in his mouth.

"You're not going to smoke that in here, are you?" I asked.

He didn't bother to answer. His blond hair was cut like a little boy's. His eyes were bright green, more energetic than they should have been, one step below wired. He set his bag on the floor and began pulling magazines and two city library books and a box of pralines and a carton of orange juice and a *Times-Picayune* from it. When he bent over, his coat swung open, exposing a nylon shoulder holster and the blue-black .38 with white handles that it carried. He removed a pint bottle of vodka from the bag and unscrewed the cap and poured at least three inches into the carton of orange juice.

"Early in the day," I said.

He tossed his unlit cigarette end over end into the wastebasket and drank out of the carton, staring out the window at the robins fluttering in the oak trees and the Spanish moss stirring in the breeze. "Tell me if you want me to leave, big mon."

"You know better than that," I said.

"I saw Alafair and Molly getting in their car. When are you going home?"

"Maybe in a week. I feel a lot stronger. Where have you been?"

"Running down a couple of bail skips. I still have to pay the bills. I'm not sleeping too good. I think the doc left some lead in me. I think it's moving around."

His eyes were bright with a manic energy that I didn't think was related to the alcohol. He kept swallowing and clearing his throat, as though a piece of rust were caught in it. "The speckled trout are running. We need to get out on the salt. The White House is saying the oil has gone away."

He waited for me to speak. But I didn't.

"You don't believe it?" he said.

"The oil company says the same thing. Do you believe *them*?"

He fiddled with his fingers and looked into space, and I knew he had something on his mind besides the oil-well blowout on the Gulf. "Something happen?" I said.

"I had a run-in two nights ago with Frankie Giacano. Remember him? He used to burn safes with his cousin Stevie Gee. He was knocking back shots with a couple of hookers in this joint on Decatur, and I accidentally stepped on his foot, and he says, 'Hey, Clete, glad to see you, even though you probably just broke two of my toes. At least it saves me the trouble of coming to your office. You owe me two large, plus the vig for over twenty years. I don't know what that might come to. Something like the national debt of Pakistan. You got a calculator on you?'"

Clete drank again from the carton, staring at the birds jittering in the trees, his throat working, his cheeks pooling with color as they always did when alcohol went directly into his bloodstream. He set the carton down on the nightstand and widened his eyes. "So I told him, 'I'm having a quiet beer here, Frankie, and I apologize for stepping on your needle-nose stomps that nobody but greaseballs wears these days, so I'm going to sit down over there in the corner and order a po'boy sandwich and read the paper and drink my beer, and you're not going to bother me again. Understood?'

"Then, in front of his skanks, he tells me he peeled an old safe owned by his uncle Didi Gee, and he found a marker I signed for two grand, and all these years the vig was accruing and now I owe the principal and the interest to him. So I go, 'I think a certain kind of social disease has climbed from your nether regions into your brain, Frankie. Secondly, you don't have permission to call me by my first name. Thirdly, your uncle Didi Gee, who was a three-hundred-pound tub of whale shit, died owing me money, not the other way around.'

"Frankie says, 'If you'd be a little more respectful, I would have worked something out. But I knew that was what you were gonna say. For that reason, I already sold the marker to Bix Golightly. By the way, take a look at the crossword puzzle in your newspaper. I was working on it this morning and couldn't think of a thirteen-letter word for a disease of the glands. Then you walked in and it hit me. The word is "elephantiasis." I'm not pulling your crank. Check it out.'"

"You think he was lying about selling the marker to Golightly?" I asked.

"Who cares?"

"Bix Golightly is psychotic," I said.

"They all are."

"Put away the booze, Clete, at least until afternoon."

"When you were on the hooch, did you ever stop drinking because somebody told you to?"

It was Indian summer outside, and the sunlight looked like gold smoke in the live oaks. At the base of the tree trunks, the petals of the four-o'clocks were open in the shade, and a cluster of fat-breasted robins were pecking in the grass. It was a fine morning, not one to compromise and surrender to the meretricious world in which Clete Purcel and I had spent most of our adult lives. "Let it go," I said.

"Let what go?" he asked.

"The sewer that people like Frankie Giacano and Bix Golightly thrive in."

"Only dead people get to think like that. The rest of us have to deal with it."

When I didn't answer, he picked up the iPod and clicked it on. He held one side of the headset close to his ear and listened, then smiled in recognition. "That's Will Bradley and Freddie Slack. Where'd you get this?"

"From Tee Jolie Melton."

"I heard she disappeared or went off someplace. She was here?"

"It was about two in the morning, and I turned on the pillow and she was sitting right there, in the same chair you're sitting in."

"She works here?"

"Not to my knowledge."

"After ten P.M. this place is locked up like a convent."

"Help me into the bathroom, will you?" I said.

He set the iPod back on the nightstand and stared at it, the driving rhythms of "Beat Me Daddy, Eight to the Bar" still rising from the foam-rubber pads on the earphones. "Don't be telling me stuff like this, Streak," he said. "I'm not up to it. I won't listen anymore to that kind of talk."

He lifted the orange juice carton and drank from it, fixing one eye on me like a cyclops who was half in the bag.

CLETE MAINTAINED TWO private investigative offices, one on Main Street in New Iberia, over in the bayou country, and one in New Orleans, on St. Ann in the French Quarter. After Katrina, he bought and restored the building on St. Ann that he had formerly rented. With great pride, he lived on the second floor, above his office, with a fine view from the balcony of St. Louis Cathedral and the oak trees and dark green pike-fenced garden behind it. As a PI, he did scut work for bondsmen and liability lawyers, wives who wanted their unfaithful husbands bankrupted in divorce court, and cuckolds who wanted their wives and their lovers crucified. On the upside of the situation, Clete hired out at nearly pro bono rates to bereaved parents whose missing children had been written off as runaways, or to people whose family members may have been railroaded into prison and even placed on death row.

He was despised by many of his old colleagues at NOPD and the remnants of the Mob. He was also the bane of the insurance companies because of the massive amounts of property damage he had done from Mobile to Beaumont. He had skipped New Orleans on a murder beef after shooting and killing a federal witness, and he had fought on the side of the leftists in El Salvador. He had also been a recipient of the Navy Cross, the Silver Star, and two Purple Hearts. When a private plane loaded with mobsters crashed into the side of a mountain in western Montana, the National Transportation Safety Board's investigation determined that someone had poured sand in the fuel tanks. Clete threw a suitcase in the back of his rusted-out Caddy convertible and blew Polson, Montana, like it was burning down. He dropped a corrupt Teamster official upside down from a hotel balcony into a dry swimming pool. He poured a dispenser of liquid soap down the throat of a button man in the men's room of the New Orleans airport. He handcuffed a drunk congressman to a fireplug on St. Charles Avenue. He opened up a fire hose on a hit man in the casino at the bottom of Canal Street and blew him into a toilet stall like a human hockey puck. He destroyed a gangster's house on Lake Pontchartrain with an earth-grader, knocking down the walls, troweling up the floors, and crushing the furniture into kindling, even uprooting the shrubbery and flowers and trees and grading them and the lawn furniture into the swimming pool.

An average day in the life of Clete Purcel was akin to an asteroid bouncing through Levittown.

Child molesters, pimps, dope dealers, and men who abused women got no slack and feared him as they would the wrath of God. But Clete's role as the merry prankster and classical trickster of folklore had a price tag. A succubus lived in his breast and gave him no respite. He had carried it with him from the Irish Channel in New Orleans to Vietnam and to the brothels of Bangkok and Cherry Alley in Tokyo and back home to New Orleans. In Clete's mind, he was not worthy of a good woman's love; nor did he ever measure up in the eyes of his alcoholic father, a milkman who took out his anger and low self-esteem on his confused and suffering firstborn son.

His two visitors had parked their car on Decatur and walked up Pirates Alley, past the small bookshop that once was the apartment of William Faulkner, then had mounted the stairs of Clete's building, where one of them banged loudly on the door with the flat of his fist.

It was evening, and Clete had just showered after an hour of lifting barbells by the stone well in his courtyard. The sky was mauve-colored and filled with birds, the banana plants in his courtyard rattling in the breeze that blew from Lake Pontchartrain. He had just dressed in new slacks and white socks and Roman sandals and a Hawaiian shirt, his skin still glowing with the warmth of the shower, his hair wet-combed, all the time whistling a tune and looking forward to sitting down at his table over a bowl of crawfish gumbo and loaf of hot buttered French bread. It was the kind of timeless evening in Louisiana when spring and fall and winter and summer come together in a perfect equinox, so exquisite and lovely that the dying of the light seems a violation of a divine ordinance. It was an evening that was wonderful in every way possible. Street musicians were playing in Jackson Square; the air smelled of beignets baking in Café du Monde; the clouds were ribbed like strips of fire above a blue band of light that still clung to the bottom of the sky. Maybe there was even a possibility of turning around in a café and unexpectedly seeing a beautiful woman's smile. It was an evening that would have been good for anything except an unannounced visit by Bix Golightly and a pimple-faced part-time killer and full-time punk named Waylon Grimes.

Clete opened the door. "I'm closed for the day. You got business with me, call the office tomorrow and make an appointment," he said.

Bix Golightly still had the sloping shoulders and flat chest and vascular forearms and scar tissue around his eyes that had defined him when he boxed at Angola, breaking noses, busting lips and teeth, and knocking his opponents' mouthpieces over the ropes into the crowd on the green. His face was all bone, the bridge of his nose crooked, his haircut tight, his mouth a mirthless slit. Some people said Bix shot meth. Others said he didn't have to; Bix had come out of his mother's womb with a hard-on and had been in overdrive ever since.

Three tiny green teardrops were tattooed at the corner of his right eye. A red star was tattooed on his throat, right under the jawbone. "I'm glad to see you looking so good," Bix said. "I heard you and your buddy Robicheaux got shot up. I also heard you capped a woman. Or was it Robicheaux who did the broad?"

"It was me. What are you doing here, Bix?"

"Frankie Gee told you about me acquiring your marker?" he said.

"Yeah, I know all about it. With respect, this business about a marker is bogus," Clete said. "I think Frankie took you over the hurdles. I hope you didn't get burned too bad."

"If it's bogus, why is your name signed on it?" Bix asked.

"Because I used to play bourré with the Figorelli brothers. I lost some money in a pot, but I covered it the following week. How that marker ended up in Didi Gee's safe, I don't know."

"Maybe because you were stoned out of your head."

"That's a possibility. But I don't know and I don't remember and I don't care."

"Purcel, 'I don't know' and 'I don't care' don't flush."

"It'd better, because that's as good as it's going to get. What's Waylon doing here?" Clete said.

"He works for me. Why do you ask?"

"He killed a four-year-old child, is why," Clete replied.

"That was during a robbery. Waylon was the victim, not the guy doing the robbery," Bix said.

"He backed up over a kid and made the parents testify that a car-jacker did it," Clete said.

"That's news to me," Bix said, looking at his friend. "What's this stuff about intimidating the parents, Waylon?"

"You got me," Waylon Grimes said. He was a small-boned man with a concave chest and a wispy red pencil mustache and hair that hung like string over his ears. He wore his shirt outside his slacks, the sleeves buttoned at the wrists the way a 1950s hood might, a chain hooked to a wallet in his back pocket. He lit a cigarette, his hands cupped around his lighter. "Want me to go downstairs?"

"No, stay where you're at," Bix said. "Purcel, I'm not greedy. I checked out your finances. You got about fifty grand equity in this place. You can borrow on the equity and give the check to me, since I know you don't have any cash. But no matter how you cut it, I want thirty large from you. I want it in seven working days, too. Don't try to stiff me on this, man."

"I want a retroactive patent on the wheel, but that doesn't mean I'm going to get one," Clete replied.

"Can I use your bathroom?" Waylon said.

"It's broken," Clete said.

"You got a broad back there?" Waylon said.

Clete stepped forward, forcing the two visitors backward onto the landing, a brass marching band coming to life in his head. "You listen, you little piece of shit," he said. "If you ever come here again, I'm going to start pulling parts off you. That's not a metaphor. I'm going to rip your arms and legs off your body and kick them up your ass. You want to crack wise? I hope you do, because I'm going to bust your spokes right now, head to foot."

Waylon took a deep puff off his cigarette, letting the smoke out slowly, like balls of damp cotton rising from his mouth. He dropped the cigarette on the landing and ground it out flatly under his shoe and glanced at Bix Golightly, his expression contemplative. "I'll be down at the Vietnamese grocery," he said.

"No, we're gonna iron this out," Bix said. "You don't talk to my employees like that, Purcel. Besides, we got a lot of commonalities. Did you know we used to ball the same broad, the one with the king-size jugs?"

"This guy is a jerk and a welcher, Bix," Waylon said. "Why waste your time talking to him? You know how it's gonna play out." He walked down the stairs, as indifferent to his employer as he was to Clete's threat. He paused at the bottom, the wind blowing through the brick foyer, ruffling his clothes. He looked up the stairs at Clete. "About that kid who got himself crunched under the car? He was a Mongoloid and still wearing diapers, even though he was four years old. The only reason his parents kept him around was the state aid they got. He was also playing in the driveway, where he wasn't supposed to be, primarily because his parents weren't watching him. If you ask me, he's better off now."

Before Clete could respond, Bix Golightly stepped closer to him, blocking Clete's view of the foyer, his body heat and the astringent smell of his deodorant rising into Clete's face. "Can you read my ink?" he said.

"What about it?"

"Tell me what it says."

"The teardrops mean you popped three guys for the Aryan Brotherhood. The red star on your carotid tells ambitious guys to give it their best shot. You're a walking fuck-you to every swinging dick on the yard."

"You think you're a tough guy because you ate a couple of bullets on the bayou? 'Tough' is when you got nothing to lose, when you don't care about nothing, when you don't even care if you're going to hell or not. Are you that tough, Purcel?"

"I'm not following you."

"I'm gonna send an appraiser out to look at your property. We got a small window of opportunity here. Don't let this thing get out of control."

"Don't blow your nose too hard, Bix. I think your brains are starting to melt."

Bix took a folded piece of lined notebook paper from his shirt pocket and handed it to Clete. "Check out the addresses there and see if I got them right."

Clete unfolded the piece of notebook paper and stared at the letters and numbers penciled on it, his scalp shrinking. "What if I shove this down your throat?" he said.

"Yeah, you can do that, provided you don't mind Waylon knowing where your sister and your niece live. Smells like you're cooking gumbo in there. Have a nice evening. I love this neighborhood. I always wanted to live in it. Don't get your dork stuck in the lamp socket on this."

CHAPTER 2

AFTER THE SHOOTING behind my house on Bayou Teche in New
Iberia, I underwent three surgeries: one that saved my life at Our Lady
of Lourdes in Lafayette; one at the Texas Medical Center in Houston;
and the third in New Orleans. A solitary .32 bullet had struck me between the shoulder blades. It was fired by a woman neither Clete nor I
had believed was armed. The wound was no more painful and seemed
no more consequential than the sharp smack of a fist. The shooter's
motivation had been a simple one and had nothing to do with survival,
fear, greed, or panic: I had spoken down to her and called her to task
for her imperious treatment of others. My show of disrespect enraged
her and sent her out my back screen door into the darkness, walking
fast across the yellowed oak leaves and the moldy pecan husks, oblivious to the dead men on the ground, a pistol extended in front of her
with one arm, her mission as mindless and petty as they come. She
paused only long enough to make a brief vituperative statement about
the nature of my offense, then I heard a *pop* like a wet firecracker, and
a .32 round pierced my back and exited my chest. Like the dead man
walking, I stumbled to the edge of the bayou, where a nineteenth-
century paddle wheeler that no one else saw waited for me.

Though my description of that peculiar moment in my career as a
police officer is probably not of much significance now, I must add a
caveat. If one loses his life at the hands of another, he would like to

16

believe his sacrifice is in the service of a greater cause. He would like to believe that he has left the world a better place, that because of his death at least one other person, perhaps a member of his family, will be spared, that his grave will reside in a green arbor where others will visit him. He does not want to believe that his life was made forfeit because he offended someone's vanity and that his passing, like that of almost all who die in wars, means absolutely nothing.

One day after Clete's visit, Alafair, my adopted daughter, brought me the mail and fresh flowers for the vase in my window. My wife, Molly, had stopped at the administrative office for reasons I wasn't aware of. Alafair's hair was thick and black and cut short on her neck and had a lustrous quality that made people want to touch it. "We've got a surprise for you," she said.

"You going to take me sac-a-lait fishing?"

"Dr. Bonin thinks you can go home next week. He's cutting down your meds today."

"Which meds?" I said, trying to hold my smile in place.

"All of them."

She saw me blink. "You think you still need them?" she said.

"Not really."

She held her eyes on mine, not letting me see her thoughts. "Clete called," she said.

"What about?"

"He says you told him Tee Jolie Melton came to see you at two in the morning."

"He told you right. She left me this iPod."

"Dave, some people think Tee Jolie is dead."

"Based on what?"

"Nobody has seen her in months. She had a way of going off with men who told her they knew movie or recording people. She believed anything anyone told her."

I picked up the iPod off the nightstand and handed it to Alafair. "This doesn't belong to the nurses or the attendant or any of the physicians here. Tee Jolie bought it for me and downloaded music that I like and gave it to me as a present. She put three of her songs on there. Put the headphones on and listen."

Alafair turned on the iPod and tapped on its face when it lit up. "What are the names of the songs?"

"I don't remember."

"What are they categorized as?"

"I'm not up on that stuff. The songs are in there. I listened to them," I said.

The headphones were askew on her ears so she could listen to the iPod and talk to me at the same time. "I can't find them, Dave."

"Don't worry about it. Maybe I messed up the iPod."

She set it back on the nightstand and placed the headphones carefully on top of it, her hands moving slowly, her eyes veiled. "It'll be good having you home again."

"We'll go fishing, too. As soon as we get back," I said.

"That depends on what Dr. Bonin says."

"What do these guys know?"

I saw Molly smiling in the doorway. "You just got eighty-sixed," she said.

"Today?" I asked.

"I'll bring the car around to the side entrance," she said.

I tried to think before I spoke, but I wasn't sure what I was trying to think about. "My meds are in the top drawer," I said.

FIVE DAYS HAD passed since Clete was visited by Bix Golightly and Waylon Grimes, and gradually he had pushed the pair of them to the edge of his mind. Golightly had taken too many hits to the head a long time ago, Clete told himself. Besides, he was a basket case even as a criminal; he'd made his living as a smash-and-grab jewelry-store thief, on a par with gang bangers who had shit for brains and zero guts and usually victimized elderly Jews who didn't keep guns on the premises. Also, Clete had made innocuous calls to his sister and to his niece, who was a student at Tulane, and neither of them mentioned anything of an unusual nature occurring in their lives.

Forget Golightly and Grimes, Clete thought. By mistake, Golightly once put roach paste on a plateful of Ritz crackers and almost croaked himself. This was the guy he was worrying about?

On a sunny, cool Thursday morning, Clete opened up the office and read his mail and answered his phone messages, then told his secretary, Alice Werenhaus, he was going down to Café du Monde for beignets and coffee. She took a five-dollar bill from her purse and put it on the corner of her desk. "Bring me a few, will you?" she said.

Miss Alice was a former nun whose height and body mass and gurgling sounds made Clete think of a broken refrigerator he once owned. Before she was encouraged out of the convent, she had been the terror of the diocese, referred to by the bishop as "the mother of Grendel" or, when he was in a more charitable mood, "our reminder that the Cross is always with us."

Clete picked up the bill off the desk and put it in his shirt pocket. "Those two guys I had trouble with have probably disappeared. But if they should come around while I'm not here, you know what to do."

She looked at him, her expression impassive.

"Miss Alice?" he said.

"No, I do not know what to do. Would you please tell me?" she replied.

"You don't do anything. You tell them to come back later. Got it?"

"I don't think it wise for a person to make promises about situations that he or she cannot anticipate."

"Don't mess with these guys. Do you want me to say it again?"

"No, you've made yourself perfectly clear. Thank you very much."

"You want café au lait?"

"I've made my own. Thank you for asking."

"We've got a deal?"

"Mr. Purcel, you are upsetting me spiritually. Would you please stop this incessant questioning? I do not need to be badgered."

"I apologize."

"Thank you."

"You're welcome."

Clete walked down the street in the shade of the buildings, the scrolled-iron balconies sagging in the middle with the weight of potted roses and bougainvillea and chrysanthemums and geraniums, the wind smelling of night damp and bruised spearmint, the leaves of the philodendron and caladium in the courtyards threaded with humidity that looked like quicksilver in the shadows. He sat under the colonnade at Café du Monde and ate a dozen beignets that were white with powdered sugar, and drank three cups of coffee with hot milk, and gazed across Decatur at Jackson Square and the Pontalba Apartments that flanked either side of the square and the sidewalk artists who had set up their easels along the piked fence that separated the pedestrian mall from the park area.

The square was a place that seemed more like a depiction of life in the Middle Ages than twenty-first-century America. Street bands and mimes and jugglers and unicyclists performed in front of the cathedral, as they might have done in front of Notre Dame while Quasimodo swung on the bells. The French doors to the big restaurant on the corner were open, and Clete could smell the crawfish already boiling in the kitchen. New Orleans would always be New Orleans, he told himself, no matter if it had gone under the waves, no matter if cynical and self-serving politicians had left the people of the lower Ninth Ward to drown. New Orleans was a song and a state of mind and a party that never ended, and those who did not understand that simple fact should have to get passports to enter the city.

It was a bluebird day, the flags on the Cabildo straightening in the breeze. Clete had gone to bed early the previous night and his body was free of alcohol and the residue of dreams that he sometimes carried through the morning like cobweb on his skin. It seemed only yesterday that Louis Prima and Sam Butera had jammed all night and blown out the walls at Sharkey Bonano's Dream Room on Bourbon, or that Clete and his partner from New Iberia had walked a beat with nightsticks on Canal and Basin and Esplanade, both of them recently back from Vietnam, both of them still believers in the promise that each sunrise brought.

He bought a big bag of hot beignets for Miss Alice that cost him twice the amount she had given him. He listened to one song played by a string-and-rub-board band at the entrance to Pirates Alley, then walked back to St. Ann, his mind free of worry.

As soon as he turned the corner on St. Ann, he saw a large black Buick with charcoal-tinted windows parked illegally in front of his building. By the time he reached the foyer that gave onto his office, he had little doubt who had parked it there. He could hear the voice of Alice Werenhaus in the courtyard: "I told the pair of you, Mr. Purcel is not here. I also told you not to go inside the premises without his permission. If you do not leave right now, I will have you arrested and placed in the city prison. I will also have your automobile towed to the pound. Excuse me. Are you smirking at me?"

"We didn't know we were gonna get a show," the voice of Waylon Grimes replied.

"How would you like your face slapped all over this courtyard?" Miss Alice said.

"How'd you know I'm a guy who likes it rough? You charge extra for that?" Grimes said.

"What did you say? You repeat that! Right now! Say it again!"

"You promise to hit me?" Grimes said.

Clete walked through the shade of the foyer and into the courtyard, squinting in the glare at Grimes and a bald man who wore a suit and carried a clipboard in his hand.

"What do you think you're doing, Waylon?" Clete said.

"Mr. Benoit here is our appraiser. Bix is thinking of buying you out, less the principal and the vig on your marker," Grimes replied. "But this place looks like it has some serious problems. Right, Mr. Benoit?"

"You have some settling, Mr. Purcel," the appraiser said. "You see those stress cracks in the arch over your foyer? I notice the same tension in the upper corners of your windows. I suspect you have trouble opening them, don't you? That's because your foundation may be sinking, or you may have Formosan termites eating through the concrete. There's a possibility here of structural collapse."

"The roof is caving in? People will be plunging through the floors?" Clete said.

"I don't know if it would be that bad, but who knows?" Benoit said. He was smiling, his pate shiny in the sunlight. He seemed to be clenching his back teeth to prevent himself from swallowing. "Have you seen any buckling in the floors?"

"This building has been here for over a hundred and fifty years," Clete said. "I renovated it after Katrina, too."

"Yeah, it's old and storm-damaged. That's why it's falling apart," Grimes said.

"Get out of here," Clete said.

"It don't work that way, Purcel," Grimes said. "Under Louisiana law, that marker is the same as a loan agreement signed at a bank. You fucked yourself. Don't blame other people."

"Watch your language," Clete said.

"You worried about the bride of Frankenstein, here? She's heard it before. You killed a woman. Who are you to go around lecturing other people about respect? I heard you blew her head off in that shootout on the bayou."

Clete never blinked, but his face felt tight and small and cold in the wind. There was a tremolo in his chest, like a tuning fork that was out of control. He thought he heard the downdraft of helicopters and a sound like tank treads clanking to life and grinding over banyan trees and bamboo and a railed pen inside which hogs were screaming in panic. He smelled an odor that was like flaming kerosene arching out of a gun turret. His arms hung limply at his sides, and his palms felt as stiff and dry as cardboard when he opened and closed his hands. His shirt and tie and sport coat were too tight on his neck and shoulders and chest; he took a deep breath, as though he had swallowed a chunk of angle iron. "I killed two," he said.

"Say again?" Grimes asked.

"I killed two women, not just one."

Waylon Grimes glanced at his wristwatch. "That's impressive. But we're on a schedule, here."

"Yes, we should be going," the appraiser added.

"The other woman was a mamasan," Clete said. "She was trying to hide in a spider hole while we were trashing her ville. I rolled a frag down the hole. There were kids in there, too. What do you think about that, Waylon?"

Grimes massaged the back of his neck with one hand, his expression benign. Then a short burst of air escaped his mouth, as though he were genuinely bemused. "Sounds like you got issues, huh?" he said.

"Is that a question?"

"No. I wasn't in the service. I don't know about those kinds of issues. What I was saying is we're done here."

"Then why did you make it sound like a question?"

"I was trying to be polite."

"The mamasan lives on my fire escape now. Sometimes I leave a cup of tea on the windowsill for her. Look right over your head. There's her teacup. Are you laughing at me, Waylon?"

"No."

"If you're not laughing at me, who are you laughing at?"

"I'm laughing because I get tired of hearing you guys talk about the war. If it was so fucking bad, why did you go over there? Give it a rest, man. I read about a guy at the My Lai massacre who told a Vietnamese woman he was gonna kill her baby unless she gave him a blow job. Maybe that was you, and that's why your head is fucked up. The truth is, I don't care. Pay your marker or lose your building. Can you fit that into your head? You killed a mamasan? Good for you. You killed her kids, too? Get over it."

Clete could feel a constriction in one side of his face that was not unlike an electric shock, one that robbed his left eye of sight and replaced it with a white flash of light that seemed to explode like crystal breaking. He knew he had hit Waylon Grimes, but he wasn't sure where or exactly how many times. He saw Grimes crash through the fronds of a windmill palm and try to crawl away from him, and he saw the appraiser run for the foyer, and he felt Alice Werenhaus trying to grab his arms and wrists and prevent him from doing what he was doing. All of them were trying to tell him something, but their voices were lost in the squealing of the hogs and the Zippo-track rolling through the hooches and the downdraft of a helicopter blowing a rice paddy dry while a door gunner was firing an M60 at a column of tiny men in black pajamas and conical straw hats who were running for the tree line.

Clete picked up Waylon Grimes by the front of his shirt and shoved him through a cluster of banana plants into the side of the building, pinning him by his throat against the wall, driving his fist again and again into the man's face, saliva and blood stringing across the plaster.

He dropped Grimes to the ground and kicked at him once and missed, then steadied himself with one hand against the wall and brought his foot down with all his weight on Grimes's rib cage. It was then that Clete knew, perhaps for the first time in his life, that he was not only capable of killing a man with his bare hands but he could literally tear him into pieces with no reservation or feeling whatsoever. That was what he commenced doing.

Out of nowhere, Alice Werenhaus pushed past him, her feet sinking to the ankles in the mixture of black dirt and coffee grinds and guano that Clete used in his gardens, dropping onto all fours and forming a protective arch over Grimes's body, her homely face terrified. "Please don't hit him anymore. Oh, Mr. Purcel, you frighten me so," she said. "The world has hurt you so much."

OUR HOME WAS located on a one-acre lot shaded by live oak and pecan trees and slash pines on East Main in New Iberia, right up the street from the Shadows, a famous antebellum home built in the year 1831. Even though our house was also constructed in the nineteenth century, it was of much more modest design, one that was called "shotgun" because of its oblong structure, like a boxcar's, and the folk legend that one could fire a bird gun through the front door and the pellets would exit the back entrance without ever striking a wall.

Humble abode or not, it was a fine place to live. The windows reached all the way to the ceiling and had ventilated storm shutters, and in hurricane season, oak limbs bounced off our roof without ever shattering glass. I had extended and screened the gallery across the front, and hung it with a glider, and sometimes on hot afternoons I would set up the ice-cream freezer on the gallery and we would mash up blackberries in the cream and sit on the glider and eat blackberry ice cream.

I lived in the house with my daughter, Alafair, who had finished law school at Stanford but was determined to be a novelist, and with my wife, Molly, a former nun and missionary in Central America who had come to Louisiana to organize the sugarcane workers in St. Mary Parish. In back, there was a hutch for our elderly raccoon,

Tripod, and a big tree above the hutch where our warrior cat, Snuggs, kept guard over the house and the yard. I had been either a police officer in New Orleans or a sheriff's detective in Iberia Parish since I returned from Vietnam. My history is one of alcoholism, depression, violence, and bloodshed. For much of it I have enormous regret. For some of it I have no regret at all, and given the chance, I would commit the same deeds again without pause, particularly when it comes to protection of my own.

Maybe that's not a good way to be. But at some point in your life, you stop keeping score. It has been my experience that until that moment comes in your odyssey through the highways and byways and back alleys of your life, you will never have peace.

I had been home from the recovery unit nine days and was sitting on the front step, cleaning my spinning reel, when Clete Purcel's restored Cadillac convertible with the starch-white top and freshly waxed maroon paint job pulled into our driveway, the tires clicking on the gravel, a solitary yellow-spotted leaf from a water oak drifting down on the hood. When he got out of the car, he removed the keys from the ignition and dropped them in the pocket of his slacks, something he never did when he parked his beloved Caddy on our property. He also looked back over his shoulder at the one-way traffic coming up East Main, fingering the pink scar that ran through one eyebrow to the bridge of his nose.

"You run a red light?" I asked.

He sat down heavily next to me, a gray fog of weed and beer and testosterone puffing out of his clothes. The back of his neck was oily, his face dilated. "Remember a guy name of Waylon Grimes?"

"He did some button work for the Giacanos?"

"Button work, torture, extortion, you name it. He came to my place with Bix Golightly. Then he came back with a property appraiser. That's after he was warned."

"What happened?"

"He said some stuff about Vietnam and killing women and kids. I don't remember, exactly. I lost it."

"What did you do, Clete?"

"Tried to kill him. Alice Werenhaus saved his life." He took a breath and lifted one arm and placed his hand on top of his shoulder, his face flinching. "I think I tore something loose inside me."

"Have you been to a doctor?"

"What can a doctor do besides open me up again?"

"Has Grimes filed charges?"

"That's the problem. He told the ambulance attendants that he fell from my balcony. I think he plans to square it on his own. I think Golightly has given him the addresses of my sister and niece."

"How do you know?"

"Because Golightly told me he was going to do it unless I paid him for the marker. You know the word about Bix. He's a nutjob, and he'd gut and stuff his own mother and use her for a doorstop, but he's straight up when it comes to a debt, either collecting or paying it. What do you think I ought to do?"

"Talk to Dana Magelli at NOPD."

"What should I tell him? I tried to beat a guy to death, but I'm the victim, and now I need a couple of cruisers to follow my family around?"

"Find something else to use against Grimes," I said.

"Like what?"

"The death of the child he ran over."

"The parents are scared shitless. They're also both junkies. I think Grimes was delivering their skag when he killed their kid."

"I don't know what else to offer."

"I can't let my sister and niece take the fall for what I did. This is eating my lunch."

"You stop having the thoughts you're having."

"What else am I going to do? Grimes should have been cycled through a septic tank a long time ago."

I heard the front door open behind me. "I thought I heard your voice, Clete. You're just in time for dinner," Molly said. "Is everything okay out here?"

CLETE TURNED DOWN the invitation, claiming he was meeting someone for supper down the street at Clementine's, which meant he would close the bar there and probably sleep in the back of his car that night or in his office on Main or perhaps at the motor court down the bayou, where he rented a cottage. Regardless of how the evening ended, it was obvious Clete had returned to his old ways, mortgaging tomorrow for today, holding mortality at bay with vodka and weed and a case of beer he kept iced down in the back-seat of the Caddy, and in this instance maybe toying with the idea of premeditated murder.

After we ate supper, I tried to read the paper and put Clete's problems with Waylon Grimes and Bix Golightly out of my mind. I couldn't. Clete would always remain the best friend I'd ever had, a man who once carried me down a fire escape with two bullets in his back, a man who would give up his life for me or Molly or Alafair.

"I'm going to take a walk," I said to Molly. "You want to go?"

She was baking a pie in the kitchen, and there was a smear of flour on her cheek. Her hair was red and cut short, her skin powdered with freckles. Sometimes her gestures and expressions would take on a special kind of loveliness, like a visual song, without her being aware of it. "You're going to talk to Clete?" she said.

"I guess."

"Why are you looking at me like that?"

"No reason."

"Clete won't talk openly if I'm there."

"I'll be back soon," I said. "You look beautiful."

I picked up the iPod given to me by Tee Jolie Melton and strolled down East Main under the canopy of live oaks arching over the street. The streetlamps had just come on, and fireflies were lighting in the trees and bamboo along Bayou Teche. I walked out on the drawbridge at Burke Street and looked down the long dark tidal stream that eventually dumped into the Gulf. The tide was coming in, and the water was full of mud and sliding high up on the banks when a boat passed, the lily pads in the shallows rolling like a green carpet. For me, Louisiana has always been a haunted place. I believe the specters of slaves and Houma and Atakapa Indians and pirates and Confederate soldiers and Acadian farmers and plantation belles are still out there in the mist. I believe their story has never been adequately told and they will never rest until it is. I also believe my home state is cursed by ignorance and poverty and racism, much of it deliberately inculcated to control a vulnerable electorate. And I believe many of the politicians in Louisiana are among the most stomach-churning examples of white trash and venality I have ever known. To me, the fact that large numbers of people find them humorously picaresque is mind-numbing, on a level with telling fond tales about one's rapist.

But these are dismal thoughts, and I try to put them aside. As I gazed down the Teche, I clicked on the iPod and found one of Tee Jolie's recordings. She was singing "La Jolie Blon," the heartbreaking lament that you hear once and never forget for the rest of your life. Then I remembered that Alafair had said she had not been able to find Tee Jolie's songs in the contents. How was that possible? There on the bridge, in the gloaming of the day, while the last of the sunlight blazed in an amber ribbon down the center of the bayou, while the black-green backs of alligator gars rolled among the lily pads, I listened to Tee Jolie's beautiful voice rising from the earphones that rested on the sides of my neck, as though she were speaking French to me from a bygone era, one that went all the way back to the time of Evangeline and the flight of the Acadian people from Nova Scotia to the bayou country of South Louisiana. I did not realize that I was about to relearn an old lesson, namely that sometimes it's better to trust the realm of the dead than the world of the quick, and never to doubt the existence of unseen realities that can hover like a hologram right beyond the edges of our vision.

When I went into Clementine's, Clete was standing at the bar, a tumbler of vodka packed with shaved ice and cherries and orange slices and a sprig of mint in front of him. I sat down on a stool and ordered a seltzer on ice with a lime slice inserted on the glass's rim, a pretense that for me probably disguised thoughts that are better not discussed. "You want me to go back to New Orleans with you?" I said.

"No, I put my sister on a cruise, and my niece is visiting a friend in Mobile, so they're okay for now," he said.

"How about later on?"

"I haven't thought it through. I'll let you know when I do," he said.

"Don't try to handle this on your own, Clete. There're lots of ways we can go at these guys," I said.

"For instance?"

"Go after Grimes for vehicular homicide of the child."

"Using what for evidence? The testimony of his junkie parents who already flushed the kid down the drain for their next fix?"

The bar was crowded and noisy. Inside the conversation about football and subjects that were of no consequence, Clete's face seemed to float like a red balloon, estranged and full of pain. "I grew up around guys like Golightly and Grimes. You know how you deal with them? You take them off at the neck." He put two aspirins in his mouth and bit down on them. "I've got this twisted feeling high up in my chest, like something is still in there and it's pushing against my lung." He took a deep drink from his vodka, the ice making a rasping sound against the glass when he set it down on the bar. "You know the biggest joke about all this?" he said.

"About what?"

"Getting shot. Almost croaking. I would have bought it right there on the bayou if the bullet hadn't hit the strap on my shoulder holster. I got saved by my holster rather than by my piece. That's the story of my fucking life. If anything good happens to me, it's because of an accident."

"Sir, would you hold down your language, please?" the bartender said.

"Sorry," Clete said.

"Let's get out of here," I said.

"No, I like it here. I like the bar and the food and the company, and I have no reason to leave."

"Meaning I do?" I said.

"You know anybody who goes to a whorehouse to play the piano?" He thought about what he had said and smiled self-effacingly. "I'm just off my feed. I'm actually very copacetic about all this. Is that the iPod you had at the recovery unit?"

"Yeah, I was listening to Tee Jolie Melton's songs. 'La Jolie Blon' is on there."

"Let me see." He picked up the iPod from the bar and began click-ing through the contents. "There're only a few songs on here: Will Bradley and Taj Mahal and Lloyd Price."

"Tee Jolie's songs are on there, too."

"They're not, Dave. Look for yourself."

I took the iPod back and disconnected it from the headphones and put it in my pocket. "Let's take a ride up to St. Martinville," I said.

"What for?" he asked.

"I know where Tee Jolie's house is."

"What are we going to do there?"

"I don't know. You want to stay here and talk about football?"

Clete looked at the bartender. "Wrap me up an oyster po'boy sandwich and a couple of Bud longnecks to go," he said. "Sorry about the language. I've got an incurable speech defect. This is one of the few joints that will allow me on the premises."

Everybody at the bar was smiling. Tell me Clete didn't have the touch.

CHAPTER
3

I T WAS RAINING when we drove up the two-lane highway through the long tunnel of trees that led into the black district on the south end of St. Martinville. A couple of nightclubs were lit up inside the rain, and flood lamps burned in front of the old French church in the square and shone on the Evangeline Oak in back, but most of the town was dark except the streetlamps at the intersections and the warning lights on the drawbridge, under which the bayou was running high and yellow, the surface dancing with raindrops.

Tee Jolie had grown up in a community of shacks that once were part of a corporate plantation. The people who lived there called themselves Creoles and did not like to be called black, although the term was originally a designation for second-generation colonials who were of Spanish and continental French ancestry and born in New Orleans or close proximity. During antebellum times, there was another group of mixed ancestry called "free people of color." During the early civil rights era, the descendants of this group came to be known as Creoles, and some of them joined whites in resisting court-ordered school integration, a fact that always reminds me elitism is with us for the long haul.

Tee Jolie had lived with her mother and younger sister in a two-bedroom cypress house on the bayou, one that had a rust-stained tin roof and pecan and hackberry trees and water oaks in front and clusters of banana plants that grew above the eaves and a vegetable garden in back and a dock on the bayou. When Clete and I drove into the yard, I didn't know what I expected to find. Maybe I wanted proof that Tee Jolie was all right and living in the New Orleans area and that she actually visited me in the recovery unit on St. Charles Avenue. I didn't think my visit was self-serving. I wanted to know that she was safe, that she was not among dangerous men, that she would have the baby her lover had told her she could abort, that he would turn out to be a decent man who would marry her and take care of their child, and that all good things would come to Tee Jolie Melton and her new family. That was what I sincerely wished, and I didn't care whether others thought I was delusional or not.

Clete and I stepped up on the gallery. The wind was blowing in vortexes of rain across the property and on the trees and the great green shiny clusters of flooded elephant ears that grew along the bayou's banks. When the door opened, we were not prepared for the person silhouetted against a reading lamp in the background. He walked with two canes, his spine so bent that he had to force his chin up to look directly at us. His hands were little more than claws, his skin disfigured by a dermatological disease that sometimes leaches the color from the tissue of black people. It would not be exaggeration to say he had the shape of a gargoyle. But his eyes were the same color as Tee Jolie's, a blue-green that had the luminosity you might see in a sunlit wave sliding across a coral pool in the Caribbean.

I introduced myself and showed him my badge. I told him I was a friend of Tee Jolie and had recently seen her in New Orleans, and I wondered if she was all right. He had not invited us inside. "You seen her, suh?" he said.

"Yes, she visited me when I was recovering from an injury. Are you her relative?"

"I'm her grandfather. After her mama died, she went away. That was maybe t'ree months ago. Right there on the dock, a man picked her up in a boat, and we ain't seen or heard from her since. Then her little sister, Blue, went away, too. You ain't seen Blue, have you?"

"No, sir, I'm afraid not. May we come in?"

"Please do. My name is Avery DeBlanc. You'll have to excuse the place. It ain't very neat. Y'all want coffee?"

"No, thank you," I said. Clete and I sat down on a cloth-covered couch while Mr. DeBlanc continued to stand. "Did you report Tee Jolie's disappearance?"

"Yes, suh. I talked to a deputy sheriff. But wasn't nobody interested."

"Why do you think that?"

"'Cause the deputy tole me Tee Jolie's got a reputation. This is the way he said it: 'She got a reputation, and let's face it, ain't none of it is good.' He said she run off in high school and she hung out wit' young people that sells dope. I axed him which one of them *don't* sell dope. I called him twice more, and each time he said there ain't any evidence a crime was committed. I got to sit down, me. I cain't stand up long. Y'all sure you don't want coffee?"

"Sir, do you have someone here to help you?" I asked.

"There ain't no he'p for what I got. I was at Carville eighteen years. I t'ink I scared that deputy. He wouldn't shake hands wit' me."

"You have Hansen's disease?" I said.

"*That* and everyt'ing else." For the first time he smiled, his eyes full of light.

"Tee Jolie told me she was living with a man I know," I said. "She mentioned centralizers. I think this man might be in the oil business. Does any of this sound familiar?"

"No, suh, it don't." He had sat down in a straight chair, a photograph of a World War I doughboy hanging behind him. A framed color picture of Jesus, probably cut from a magazine, hung from the opposite wall. The rug was frayed into string along the edges; a moth swam in the glow of the reading lamp. Outside, in the rain, I could see the green and red running lights on a passing barge, the waves from the bow slapping into the elephant ears. He added, "She had a scrapbook, though."

"Sir?" I said.

"In her room. You want me to get it? It's got a mess of pictures in there."

"Don't get up, sir. With your permission, I'll go into her room and get it."

"It's there on her li'l dresser. She was always proud of it. She called it her 'celebrity book.' I tole her, 'There ain't no celebrities down here, Tee Jolie, except you.' She'd say, 'I ain't no celebrity, Granddaddy, but one day that's what I'm gonna be. You gonna see.'"

He looked wistfully into space, as though he'd said more than he should have and had empowered his own words to hurt him. I went into Tee Jolie's bedroom and found a scrapbook bound in a thick pink plastic cover with hearts embossed on it. I sat back down on the couch and began turning the pages. She had cut out several newspaper articles and pasted them stiffly on the pages: a story about her high school graduation, a photograph taken of her when she was queen of the Breaux Bridge Crawfish Festival, another photo that showed her with the all-girl Cajun band called BonSoir, Catin, a picture of her with the famous Cajun fiddler Hadley Castille.

Among the back pages of the scrapbook was a collection of glossy photographs that she had not mounted. Nor were they the kind that one finds in a small-town newspaper. All of them appeared to have been taken in nightclubs; most of them showed her with older men who wore suits and expensive jewelry. Some of the men I recognized. Two of them were casino people who flew in and out of New Jersey. One man ran a collection agency and sold worthless insurance policies to the poor and uneducated. Another man operated a finance company that specialized in title loans. All of them were smiling the way hunters smiled while displaying a trophy. In every photo, Tee Jolie was dressed in sequined shirts and cowboy boots or a charcoal-black evening gown with purple and red roses stitched on it. She made me think of a solitary flower placed by mistake among a collection of gaudy chalk figures one takes home from an amusement park.

In one photograph there was a figure I did not expect to see in Tee Jolie's scrapbook. He was standing at the bar behind the main group, wearing a dark suit with no tie, the collar of his dress shirt unbuttoned, a gold chain and gold holy medal lying loosely around his neck, his scalp shining through his tight haircut, his eyebrows disfigured by scar tissue, his mouth cupped like a fish's when it tries to breathe oxygen at the top of a tank. I handed the photo to Clete for him to look at. "Do you know who Bix Golightly is?" I asked Mr. DeBlanc.

"I don't know nobody by that name."

"He's in this photo with Tee Jolie and some of her friends."

"I don't know none of them people, me. What's this man do?"

"He's a criminal."

"Tee Jolie don't associate wit' people like that."

But she does associate with people who use other people, I thought. I took the photo from Clete and showed it to Mr. DeBlanc. "Take a good look at that fellow. Are you sure you haven't seen him?"

"No, suh, I ain't seen him, and I don't know him, and Tee Jolie never talked about him or any of these men. What kind of criminal are we talking about?"

"The kind of guy who gives crime a bad name," I replied.

His face became sad; he blinked in the lamplight. "She tole me she was falling in love wit' a man. She said maybe she'd bring him home to meet me. She said he was rich and had gone to col'letch and he loved music. She wouldn't tell me nothing else. Then one day she was gone. And then her sister left, too. I don't know why this is happening. They left me alone and never called and just went away. It ain't fair."

"What isn't fair?" Clete asked.

"Everyt'ing. We never broke no laws. We took care of ourself and our place on the bayou and never hurt nobody. That's my father's picture up there on the wall. He fought in France in the First World War. His best friend was killed on the last day of the war. He had eight children and raised us up against ever fighting in a war or doing harm to anybody for any reason. Now somebody taken my granddaughters from me, and a deputy sheriff tells me ain't no evidence of a crime been committed. That's why I say it ain't fair." He struggled to his feet with his two walking canes and went into the kitchen.

"What are you doing, sir?" I asked.

"Fixing y'all coffee."

"You don't need to do that."

"Yes, suh, I do. I ain't been a good host. I cain't find the sugar, though. I couldn't find it this morning. I cain't concentrate on t'ings like I used to."

I had followed him into the kitchen to dissuade him from putting himself out. The cupboards, which had curtains on them rather than doors, were almost bare. There were no pots on the stove, no smell of cooked food in the air. He pulled a coffee can off a shelf, then accidentally dropped it on the drainboard. The plastic cap popped loose, spilling the small amount of coffee that was inside. "It's all right. We still got enough for t'ree cups," he said.

"We have to go, Mr. DeBlanc. Thank you for your courtesy," I said.

He hesitated, then began scooping the coffee back in the can. "Yes, suh, I understand," he replied.

Clete and I walked out into the rain and got into the Caddy. Clete didn't start the engine and instead stared through the windshield at the lamplight glowing in the front windows of the house. "His kitchen looked pretty bare," he said.

"I suspect he's in the Meals On Wheels program," I said.

"You ever see the stuff those old people eat? It looks like diced rabbit food or the kind of crap Iranian inmates eat."

I waited for him to continue.

"You think Mr. DeBlanc might like a warmed-up po'boy and a cold brew?" he said.

So we took Clete's foot-long sandwich, which consisted of almost an entire loaf of French bread filled with deep-fried oysters and baby shrimp and mayonnaise and hot sauce and sliced lettuce and tomatoes and onions, and carried it and the two longneck bottles of Bud inside. Then we fixed a pot of coffee and sat down with Mr. DeBlanc at his kitchen table and cut the po'boy in three pieces and had a fine meal while the rain drummed like giant fingers on the roof.

ALICE WERENHAUS LIVED in an old neighborhood off Magazine, on the edges of the Garden District, on a block one might associate with the genteel form of poverty that became characteristic of mid-twentieth-century New Orleans. Even after Katrina, the live oaks were of tremendous dimensions, their gigantic roots wedging up the sidewalks and cracking the curbs and keeping the houses in shadow almost twenty-four hours a day. But gradually, the culture that had defined the city, for good or bad, had taken flight from Alice's neighborhood and been replaced by bars on the windows of businesses and residences and a pervading fear, sometimes justified, that two or three kids dribbling a basketball down the street might turn out to be the worst human beings you ever met.

Out of either pride or denial of her circumstances, Alice had not installed a security system in her house or sheathed her windows with bars specially designed to imitate the Spanish grillwork that was part of traditional New Orleans architecture. She walked to Mass and rode the streetcar to work. She shopped at night in a grocery store three blocks away and wheeled her own basket home, forcing it over the broken and pitched slabs of concrete in the sidewalks. On one occasion, a man came out of the shadows and tried to jerk her purse from her shoulder. Miss Alice hit him in the head with a zucchini, then threw it at him as he fled down the street.

Her friends were few. Her days at the convent had been marked by acrimony and depression and the bitter knowledge that insularity and loneliness would always be her lot. Ironically, the first sunshine in her adult life came in her newly found career as a secretary for an alcoholic private investigator whose clientele could have been characters lifted from Dante's *Inferno*. She pretended to be viscerally offended by their vulgarity and narcissism, but there were occasions on an inactive day when she caught herself glancing through the window in hopes of seeing a betrayed wife headed up the street, out for blood, or one of Nig Rosewater's bail skips about to burst through the door in need of secular absolution.

These moments of introspection made her wonder if a thinly disguised pagan might not be living inside her skin.

On the day after Clete Purcel went to New Iberia to tend his office, a sudden thunderstorm had swept ashore south of the city, bringing with it the smell of brine and sulfa and a downpour in her neighborhood that flooded the streets and filled the gutters and yards with floating leaves. The clouds were bursting with electricity when she got off the streetcar on St. Charles and walked toward Magazine, the thunder booming over the Gulf like cannons firing in sequence. The air was cool and fresh and had a tannic odor that made her think of long-standing water poured from a wood barrel. She felt an excitement about the evening that she couldn't quite explain, as though she were revisiting her childhood home in Morgan City where the storm clouds over the Gulf created a light show every summer evening, the wind straightening the palms on the boulevard where she had lived, a jolly Popsicle man in a white cap driving his truck down to the baseball diamond in the park.

When she walked up on the gallery of her small house and unlocked the door, her cat, Cedric, was waiting to be let in. He was a pumpkin-size orange ball of fur with white paws and a star on his face who left seat smears all over her breakfast table and was never corrected for it. He ran ahead of her into the house and attacked his food bowl while she turned on the television in the living room and filled the house with the sounds of CNN and a family she didn't have.

She filled a teakettle with water and lit the gas range and set the kettle to boil, and put a frozen dinner in the microwave, and glanced out the side window at a man in a hooded raincoat walking down the alley, his shoulders rounded, his hands stuffed in his pockets, his red tennis shoes splashing in the puddles. He disappeared from her line of vision. She picked up her cat, cradling him heavily in one arm, and tugged playfully on the furry thickness of his tail. "What have you been doing all day, you little fatty?" she said.

Cedric pushed against her grasp with his hind feet, indicating that he wanted to be bounced up and down. For some unaccountable reason, he changed his mind and twisted in her arms and jumped onto the breakfast table, staring out the rear window at the alley. Alice peered out the window and saw a neighbor lift the top of his Dumpster and drop a vinyl sack of garbage inside.

"You're a big baby, Cedric," Alice said.

She heard the microwave ding and took the preprepared container of veal and potatoes and peas out and fixed a cup of tea and sat down and ate her supper. Later she lay back on a reclining chair in front of the television and watched the History Channel and fell asleep without ever realizing she was falling asleep.

When she woke, the thunderstorm had passed and flashes of electricity were flaring silently in the clouds, briefly illuminating the trees and puddles of floating leaves in her yard. Cedric was on the rear windowsill, flicking a paw at a raindrop running down the glass. Then someone twisted the mechanical bell on the front door, and she slipped off the night chain and pulled open the door without first checking to see who her visitor was.

He was black, perhaps eighteen or nineteen, with a goatee that looked like wire protruding from his chin. He wore a dark rain jacket, the hood hanging on his back. Through the screen, she could smell his body odor and unbrushed teeth and the unrinsed detergent in his clothes. Under one arm he was clutching a cardboard box that had no top.

"What do you want?" she said.

"I'm selling chocolate for the Boys Town Fund."

"Where do you live?"

"In St. Bernard Parish."

She tried to see his shoes, but her line of vision was obstructed by the paneling at the bottom of the door. "There's a white man who picks up you kids in the Lower Nine and drops you off in neighborhoods like mine. You have to pay him four dollars for each chocolate bar you don't bring back, and the rest is yours. Is that correct?"

He seemed to think about what she had said, his eyes clouding. "It's for the Boys Town Fund."

"I can't give you any money."

"You don't want no candy?"

"You're working for a dishonest man. He uses children to deceive and cheat people. He robs others of their faith in their fellow man. Are you listening to me?"

"Yes, ma'am," he said, turning toward the street, his gaze shifting off hers.

"If you need to use the bathroom, come in. If you want a snack, I'll fix you one. But you should get away from the man you're working for. Do you want to come in?"

He shook his head. "No, ma'am. I ain't meant to bother you."

"Were you in my alleyway a while ago? What kind of shoes are you wearing?"

"What kind of shoes? I'm wearing the kind I put on this morning."

"Don't be smart with me."

"I got to go. The man is waiting for me on the corner."

"Come see me another time and let's talk."

He looked at her warily. "Talk about what?"

"Anything you want to."

"Yes, ma'am, I'll do that," he said.

After she closed the inside door, she looked through the side window and watched him walk up the street under the overhang of the trees. He did not stop at any of the other houses. Why had he stopped at only hers? She stepped out on the gallery and tried to see down the sidewalk, but the boy was gone. Maybe he had gone up a driveway to a garage apartment. That was possible, wasn't it? Otherwise . . . She didn't want to think about otherwise.

As she chained the door, she heard a Dumpster lid clang in the alley and the subdued thunder of rap music from inside a closed vehicle and a tree limb scraping wetly across the side of her house. She heard Cedric run across the linoleum in the kitchen.

"Where are you going, you fat little pumpkin head?" she said.

She glanced in her hallway and in her bedroom and in her clothes closet, but Cedric was nowhere to be seen. Then she felt a coldness in the wall that separated the guest room from the bath. She opened the door and stared numbly at the curtains blowing from the open window, one from which the screen had been removed.

She turned around in the hallway, her heart beating hard, just as a man in a purple ski mask and black leather gloves and red tennis shoes stepped out of the bathroom and swung his fist into the middle of her face. "You're sure a stupid bitch," he said. "You live in a neighborhood like this without a security system?"

WHEN SHE WOKE up, she didn't know if she had been knocked unconscious by the blow of her assailant or by her head striking the floor. All she knew was that she was in her kitchen, stretched out on the linoleum, her wrists wrapped with duct tape and the duct tape wrapped through the handle on the oven door. The only light in the kitchen came from the gas flame under the teakettle and the glow around the edge of the blinds from a streetlamp in the alley.

Her attacker was standing above her, breathing through the mouth hole in his mask, his gloved hands opening and closing at his sides. "You like opera?" he said. His pronunciation was strange, as though the inside of his mouth had been injured or he were wearing dentures that didn't fit. "Answer my question, bitch."

"Who are you?" she said.

"A guy who's gonna turn you into an opera star. I'll put you on the phone so you can yodel to a friend of yours. I heated up your teapot for you."

"I know who you are. Shame on you."

"That's a dumb thing to say. Why do you think I'm wearing this mask?"

"Because you're a coward."

"It means you got a chance to live. But the odds of that happening aren't as good as they were a few seconds ago. Your cat is hiding under the bed."

She tried to read the expression in his eyes inside his mask, to no avail.

"Has the kitty got your tongue?" he said.

"Leave him alone."

He looked over his shoulder at the microwave. "I think he might make a nice fit."

"Friends are coming over anytime. You'll be punished for whatever you do here. You're a nasty little man. I should have let Mr. Purcel have his way with you."

He leaned over her, looking straight down into her face. "You don't have friends, lady. Nothing is gonna help you. Accept that. You're totally in my power, and you're gonna do everything I say. I think I'm gonna alter my plan a little bit. What do they call that place in Kentucky where people take vows of silence?" He snapped his fingers, his glove making a whispering sound. "Gethsemane? I said I was gonna make an opera singer out of you, but that's not a good idea. You'd wake up the whole neighborhood. I'm gonna give you my own vow of silence. Open wide."

When she refused, he clenched the bottom of her chin and stuffed a dishrag in her mouth and pressed a strip of tape across her cheeks and lips. "There," he said, standing erect. "You look like a balloon that's about to pop. That's not far from wrong."

He turned off the flame on the stove and picked up a hot pad from the drainboard and lifted the teakettle off the burner. "Where do you want it first?" he asked.

She felt sweat popping on her brow, her throat gagging on the dishrag and her own saliva, her shoes coming off her feet as she thrashed against the linoleum. He tipped the spout of the teakettle down and slowly scalded one of her legs and then the other. "How's that feel? That's just for openers," he said.

It became obvious that he was not prepared for what came next. Alice Werenhaus flexed both of her upper arms and her massive shoulders and tore the handle out of the oven door, rising to her feet like a behemoth emerging from an ancient bog. She ripped the tape from her face and pulled the dishrag from her mouth and drove her fist into a spot right between her assailant's eyes.

The blow sent him crashing into the wall. She picked up a bread box and smashed it over his head, then opened the door to the pantry and pulled a Stillson pipe wrench loose from a washtub full of tools. The Stillson felt as heavy as a shot put, its serrated grips mounted on a long shaft. Her assailant was getting to his feet when she caught him across the buttocks. He screamed and arched his back in an inverted bow, as though it had been broken, one hand fluttering behind to protect himself from a second blow. Alice swung again, this time across his shoulders, and a third time high up on his arm, and a fourth time on the elbow, each blow thudding into bone.

He stumbled through her living room and jerked open the front door, his nose bleeding through his mask. She hit him again, this time across the spine, knocking him through the screen onto the gallery. She followed him outside, catching him in the rib cage, knocking him onto the sidewalk, beating him across the thighs and knees as he picked himself up and began running down the street, careening off balance, like a bagful of broken sticks trying to reassemble itself.

Her ears were roaring with sound, her lungs screaming for air, her heart swollen with adrenaline. The black kid with the box of chocolate candy was staring at her in disbelief.

"What are you looking at?" she said.

"I done what you tole me. I quit my job. I ain't give back the chocolate bars, either."

She wanted to say something to him, but she couldn't catch her breath or even remember what she had planned to say.

"Your cat just run out the door. I'll go catch him."

"No, he'll come back."

"You ain't gonna hit nobody else wit' that wrench, are you?"

The world was spinning around her, and she had to hold on to a tree limb so she would not fall down. Nor could she find breath enough or the right words to answer the boy's question.

I WENT BACK to work at the Iberia Parish Sheriff's Department on a half-day schedule the morning after the thundershower, primarily because we needed the income. But in all honesty, I loved my job and the place where I worked. The department had been consolidated with the city police and had moved from the courthouse to a big brick colonial-style building behind the library, with a lovely view of a tree-shaded religious grotto and Bayou Teche and City Park on the far side of the water. It was a sunny, cool, rain-washed morning my first day back, and the sheriff, whose name was Helen Soileau, and some of my colleagues had placed flowers on my desk, and as I sat down in my swivel chair and looked at the glaze of sunlight on the bayou and the wind blowing hundreds of arrowpoints across the water's surface, I felt that perhaps Indian summer would never end, that the world was a grand place after all, and that I should never let the shadows of the heart stain my life again.

Then Clete Purcel came in at ten A.M. and told me he had just gotten a phone call from Alice Werenhaus and that she had been attacked in her house by a masked intruder she believed was Waylon Grimes.

"How does she know it was Grimes?" I said.

"He scalded both of her legs with a teakettle and talked about stuffing her cat in the microwave. Know a lot of guys with an MO like that?" He was pacing up and down, breathing through his nose.

"What are you planning to do?" I asked.

"Guess."

"Clete, something isn't adding up here. One, there's no explanation for your marker being found in a safe owned by Didi Giacano. Didi has been dead for almost twenty-five years. Where has the safe been all this time? His office was on South Rampart, but I thought it caught fire or something."

"It did. Some PR or marketing guy restored it. He's from around here. Pierre something. Look, that's not the point. Alice Werenhaus was tortured by a degenerate who has already killed a child and done four or five contract hits I know of. Waylon Grimes and Bix Golightly have been on the planet far too long."

My office door was closed. Through the glass, I saw Helen Soileau smile and pass in the corridor. "I won't be party to this," I said.

"Who asked you to?"

"Then why are you here?"

"Because I don't know what to do. Grimes couldn't get to my sister or niece, so he went after an old woman, an ex-nun, for Christ's sakes, the same woman who stopped me from tearing him apart. You think Golightly or Grimes is going to be shaken up by NOPD? That's like warning the devil about his overdue library books."

"We were born in the wrong era, Cletus."

"What's that supposed to mean?"

"We don't get to blow up their shit at the O.K. Corral."

"That's what you think," he replied.

I wished I hadn't heard that last remark.

CHAPTER 4

I COULDN'T SLEEP that night. Clete had gone off to New Orleans on his own, leaving me with the choice of either dropping the dime on him with my boss or NOPD or letting him founder in the chaos and trail of destruction that had come to be his logo across the entire state. I slipped on my khakis and sat on the back steps and drank a glass of milk in the dark. Tripod, our pet raccoon, was sleeping under a big live oak in a hutch we had recently rain-proofed. His buddy Snuggs, our unneutered warrior cat, lay on his side next to me, his thick white short-haired tail flopping up and down on the wood step. His ears were chewed, his neck thick and hard as a fire hydrant, his body rippling with sinew when he walked. He was fearless in a fight, took no prisoners, and would chase dogs out of the yard if he thought they were a threat to Tripod. It was no accident that he and Clete were great pals.

I'm not being completely honest here. Clete's problems were not my only concern. I was off the morphine drip, and every cell in my body knew it. Withdrawal from booze and pharmaceuticals is a bit like white-knuckling your way through a rough flight in an electric storm. Unfortunately, there's another element involved, a type of fear that doesn't have a name. It's deep down in the id and produces a sense of anxiety that causes hyperventilation and night sweats. You don't get to leave your fear on the plane. Your skin becomes your prison, and you take it with you everyplace you go. You walk the floor. You hide your thoughts from others. You eat a half gallon of ice cream in one sitting. You crosshatch the tops of your teeth in your sleep. Every mistake or misdeed or sin in your life, no matter how many times you've owned up to it, re-creates itself and takes a fresh bite out of your heart the moment you wake.

That's why mainline cons say everybody stacks time; it depends on where you stack it, but you stack it just the same.

When the house finally comes down on your head, you conclude that ice cream is a poor surrogate for that old-time full-throttle-and-fuck-it rock and roll, and there's nothing like four fingers of Jack in a mug filled with shaved ice and a beer on the side or maybe a little weed or a few yellow jackets to really light up the basement.

For those who don't want to run up their bar tab or put themselves at the mercies of a drug dealer, there's another recourse. You can go on what is called a dry drunk. You can stoke your anger the moment you open your eyes in the morning and feed it through the day, in the same way that someone incrementally tosses sticks on a controlled fire. Your anger allows you to mentally type up your own menu, with many choices on it. You can become a moralist and a reformer and make the lives of other people miserable. You can scapegoat others and inflame street mobs or highjack religion and wage wars in the name of a holy cause. You can spit in the soup from morning to night and stay as high as a helium balloon in a windstorm without ever breaking a sweat. When a drunk tells you he doesn't have a problem anymore because he has quit drinking, flee his presence as quickly as possible.

As I looked out at the reflection of moonlight on the bayou, I thought of Tee Jolie Melton and the music that no one heard except me. Had I become delusional? Maybe. But here's the rub. I didn't care. Long ago I had come to believe that the world is not a rational place and that only the most self-destructive of individuals convince themselves that it is. Those who change history are always rejected in their own era. As a revolutionary people, we Americans won an improbable victory over the best and biggest army in the world because we learned to fight from the Indians. You can do a lot of damage with a Kentucky rifle from behind a tree. You don't put on a peaked hat and a red coat and white leggings and crossed white bandoliers with a big silver buckle in the center of the X and march uphill into a line of howitzers loaded with chain and chopped-up horseshoes.

Somehow I knew with absolute certainty that not only had Tee Jolie visited me in the recovery unit on St. Charles Avenue but that now, right at this moment, she was out there in the darkness beckoning, her mouth slightly parted, her mahogany tresses flecked with the golden glow of the buttercups that grew along the levees in the Atchafalaya Swamp. Our wetlands were cut by over eight thousand miles of channels that allowed a constant infusion of saline into freshwater marsh; our poorest communities were dumping grounds for chemical sludge trucked in from other states; and the Gulf Stream waters of Woody Guthrie's famous song were strung with columns of oil that were several miles long. But I believed I could hear Tee Jolie's voice rising out of the mists, her Acadian French lyrics as mournful as a dirge. Maybe all my perceptions and convictions were the stuff one expects of a dry drunk or, in this instance, a drunkard who had to wet his lips each time he thought about the slow seep of a translucent tube into his veins. No matter how it played out, my vote would always remain with those who'd had their souls shot out of a cannon and who no longer paid much heed to the judgment of the world.

I would like to say that all my cerebral processes gave me a solution to my problems. The opposite was true. At sunrise, when steam rose off the bayou and the tidal current reversed itself and I heard the drawbridge at Burke Street clanking into the air, I still had no answer to two essential questions: What had happened to Tee Jolie Melton, and how had a collection of low-rent gumballs gotten their hands on a bourré marker that Clete Purcel paid off two decades ago?

AT 7:45 A.M. I walked down East Main and up the long driveway past the city library and the shady grotto dedicated to Jesus' mother and entered the side door of the sheriff's department and knocked on Helen Soileau's door. Helen had started her career as a meter maid with NOPD and had worked herself up to the level of patrolwoman in a neighborhood that included the Desire Projects. Later, she became a detective with the department in New Iberia, the town where she had grown up. For several years she had been my partner in our homicide unit, overcoming all the prejudices and suspicions that people have toward women in general and lesbians in particular. She had been the subject of an Internal Affairs investigation and brought to task because of her romantic involvement with a female confidential informant. She had received three citations for bravery and meritorious service. She had been Clete Purcel's lover. Last, there had been occasions when Helen looked at me with an androgynous light in her eyes and I found it necessary to leave the room and devote myself to other duties in the building.

I told her about Clete's problems with Waylon Grimes and Bix Golightly and about Grimes's invasion of Alice Werenhaus's home. I also told her about the disappearance of Tee Jolie and her sister, Blue Melton, in St. Martin Parish.

"Dave, no matter what Clete does or does not do, Ms. Werenhaus is going to file charges with NOPD against Grimes," she said. "Let them do their job."

"There's no evidence it was Grimes," I replied.

"Maybe they'll create some."

"Things have changed since you and I worked there."

She picked up a ballpoint pen and stuck the end between her teeth while she stared flatly into my face. "What Clete does in New Orleans is his business. I don't want to hear about it again. Got it?"

"No. What do you think happened to Tee Jolie?"

"I don't know," she said, her exasperation barely constrained. "You say you saw her at your recovery unit. Why do you think *anything* happened to her?"

I didn't have an adequate answer for that one.

"Hello? Are there two of us in the room, or did you just take flight?" she asked.

"Tee Jolie was afraid. She was talking about centralizers."

"About what?"

"She said she was scared. She said she was around dangerous people."

"If we're talking about the same person, she has a promiscuous reputation, Dave. Bad things happen to girls who drop their panties for bad guys."

"That's a rotten thing to say."

"Too bad. It's the truth. Didn't she sing in that zydeco dump by Bayou Bijoux?"

"So what?"

"It's a place where guys in suits and ties hunt on the game farm."

"What you're suggesting is that she deserved her fate."

"It's a real pleasure to have you back on the job."

"You're dead wrong about Tee Jolie."

She tapped her ballpoint on the desk blotter, her eyelids fluttering, her gaze focused on neutral space. "How should I say this? Tell you what, I won't even try. Thank you for all this information that has nothing to do with crimes committed in Iberia Parish. In the future, bwana put it in writing so I can look at it and then file it in the trash basket. That way bwana and I can both save loads of time."

Before I could speak, she jiggled her fingers at me and widened her eyes and silently mouthed, *Get out of here.*

BIX GOLIGHTLY DIDN'T like the way things were going. Not with the squeeze on Purcel, not with this nutcase kid Grimes attacking an ex-nun, not with the general state of cultural collapse in New Orleans. If you asked him, Katrina was a blessing in disguise, hosing out the projects when nothing else worked. This artsy-fartsy renaissance stuff needed to get washed off the streets, too. What did poets and sidewalk painters and guys blowing horns on the corners for pocket change have to do with rebuilding a city? "It's a publicity scam run by these Hollywood actors whose careers are washed up," he told his friends. "We shipped out the boons and got hit with half the panhandlers in San Francisco. You ever been to San Fran? I went into a steam room in a part of town named after Fidel Castro, which shows you what kind of neighborhood it is, and there were two dozen guys having a Crisco party. The door was jammed or something, and it took me almost half an hour to fight my way out of there."

For Bix, the city was a safe and predictable place when it was under the supervision of the Giacanos. Everybody knew the rules: Tourists got what they wanted; any vice was acceptable in the Quarter except narcotics; jackrollers had their sticks broken, by either the Giacanos or NOPD; no bar operator double-billed a drunk's credit card; the hookers were clean and never rolled a john; pimps didn't run Murphy scams; street dips or anybody washing Jersey money at a cardhouse or the horse track got their thumbs cut off; no puke from the Iberville Projects would strong-arm a tourist in the St. Louis cemeteries unless he wanted to see the world through one eye; and child molesters became fish chum.

What was wrong with any of that?

Before Katrina, Bix owned a corner grocery store on the edge of the Quarter, a seafood business across the river in Algiers, and a car wash in Gentilly. The grocery was looted and vandalized and the car wash buried in mud when the levees burst, but to Bix these were not significant losses. His seafood business was another matter. The gigantic plumes of oil from the blowout in the bottom of the Gulf had fanned through the oyster beds and shrimping grounds all along the Louisiana and Mississippi and Alabama coastline. Not only had Bix seen his most lucrative business slide down the bowl, he'd lost his one means to declare his illegal income, such as the two big scores he'd pulled off in Fort Lauderdale and Houston, one jewelry heist alone amounting to eighty grand, less the 40 percent to the fence.

How do you end up with that much money and nowhere to put it besides a hole in your backyard? Now Waylon Grimes had busted into the house of an ex-nun and poured scalding water on her, and the *Times-Picayune* had put the story on the front page. The more Bix thought about Grimes, the angrier he got. He picked up his cell phone from the coffee table and went out on the balcony of his apartment, dialing Grimes's number. The evening sky was pink, the wind warm and cool at the same time, the palm trees on the apartment grounds rattling drily. He should be out on the town, dialing up a lady or two, having a dinner in a café on St. Charles, not dealing with all this grief. What had he done to deserve it? Out of the corner of his eye, he thought he saw a maroon Caddy with a starch-white top pass through the intersection.

Grimes picked up. "What do you want?" he asked.

"Guess."

"Who is this?"

"*Who* is this? Who do you think, asshole?" Bix said.

"In case it's escaped your attention, I'm not feeling too good, and I've already told you what happened, and I don't need any more of your bullshit, Bix."

"Did I hear right? You don't need *my* bullshit. If an elephant is sleeping, you don't take a dump on its head and wipe your ass with its trunk and stroll off down the street."

"What are you talking about?"

"I think I just saw Purcel's car go through the intersection."

"It was you who threatened Purcel's family, not me."

"The point is, I wasn't gonna do anything."

"How is Purcel supposed to know that? Most people around here think you got brain damage."

"Where are you?" Bix asked.

"What do you care?"

"I want to give you your cut on the Houston job. Are you at that fuck pad you got?"

"You said the fence hadn't paid you."

"He just did."

"It's true you bit off the nose of the psychiatrist at Angola?"

"No, it's not true, you little bitch. My cellmate did. You want to know what I'm gonna do if you don't clean up this mess?"

"Speak slower, will you? I'm taking notes on this so I can send Purcel a kite and tell him what you got planned for his family."

Bix's hand was opening and closing on the cell phone, his fingers sticking to the surface. "You got twenty large coming. You want it or not?"

"Change your twenty large into nickels and shove them up your nose. While you're at it, go fuck yourself, because no broad is gonna do it. I heard some guys in the AB say you were queer bait and on the stroll at Angola. Is that why you never get laid?"

Before Bix could reply, the connection went dead, and he found himself squeezing the cell phone so tightly he almost cracked the screen. There was a pain behind his eyes as if someone had hammered a nail into his temple. He tried to concentrate and rid his head of all the energies that seemed to devour him from dawn to dusk. What was that word people were always using? Focus? Yeah, that was it. Focus. He heard the wind in the palm trees and the sound of the streetcar reversing itself for the return trip up St. Charles Avenue. Music was playing in a café over on Carrollton. Then a Hispanic guy who looked like a pile of frijoles came roaring around the side of the building on a mower that didn't have a bag or muffler on it, the discharge chute firing a steady stream of grass clippings and ground-up palm fronds and dog turds against the walls. *Screw focus,* Bix thought.

"Hey, you! The greaseball down there! Yeah, you!" Bix shouted. "Hey, I'm talking here!"

The driver, who was wearing ear protectors, smiled stupidly at the balcony and kept going.

"Think that's funny?" Bix said. He waited until the mower had made a turn and was passing under the balcony again. The flower-pot he picked up was packed with dirt and a root-bound palm and felt as heavy as a cannonball. Bix gripped the pot solidly with both hands, judging distance and trajectory like a bombardier, and lobbed it into space.

He couldn't believe what happened next. He not only missed the gardener and the mower; just as he let fly, the neighbor's poodle, whom Bix called the Barking Roach, ran out from the patio below and got knocked senseless by the pot. Then the driver swung the mower in a circle to cut another swath in the opposite direction and crunched over the broken pot and the compacted dirt and the palm plant and its exposed roots and shredded all of them without ever noticing that Bix had just tried to brain him. The only break Bix got was the fact that the Barking Roach ran back into its apartment and, unless it knew Morse code, wouldn't be able to report him.

Before Bix could reload for a second shot, he saw the maroon Caddy come around the corner and park in front of a refurbished double-shotgun house called the Maple Street Bookstore. Maybe it wasn't Purcel, Bix thought. What would an albino ape be doing in a bookstore, particularly one named Purcel, unless it sold porn or bananas? Time to stop messing around and get to the bottom of things. He Velcro-strapped a .25 auto on his ankle, pulled his trouser cuff over the grips, and headed downstairs.

He crossed the street and took up a position in front of the bookstore, leaning back on the Caddy's fender, his arms folded comfortably on his chest. Five minutes later, Purcel came out with a couple of books in a plastic sack, wearing cream-colored pleated slacks and oxblood loafers and a pale blue long-sleeve shirt and a straw hat that had a black band around the crown, like he was some kind of planter in the islands instead of an alcoholic bail-skip chaser for Nig Rosewater and Wee Willie Bimstine. "You dogging me?" Bix said.

"Get off my car."

"I asked you a question."

"If I was following you around, would I park my car next to your crib?"

"It ain't a crib. It's a condo. You want Waylon Grimes, or do you just want to look through people's windows?"

"What I want is your germs off my fender."

"Relax. We go back, right? Old school. I didn't sic Grimes on your secretary."

"Who said it was Grimes?" Clete asked.

"Maybe it wasn't. What I'm saying is I didn't have anything to do with it."

Clete unlocked the driver's door and threw his books on the seat. "You threatened to harm my sister and niece. You think you're going to walk off from that?"

Bix stepped up on the curb, away from the car, flexing his neck the way he used to before he came out of his corner in the first round, both gloves flying into his opponent's face. "You're a bum and your word don't mean anything, Purcel. Sorry your secretary got hurt, but it's on you, not me." He squeezed his penis and pulled it taut against his slacks. "You don't like that, bite my stick."

"Here's what doesn't make sense, Bix. Why is it that after all these years you guys end up with an old marker you think you can use to steal my home and my office? Who could think up a harebrained scheme like that?"

"I told you. Frankie Giacano opened up Didi Gee's safe as a favor for somebody."

"For who?"

"I don't know."

"Where was the safe?"

"At the bottom of Lake Pontchartrain. How would I know? Ask Frankie Gee."

"I think you're lying. Didi Gee kept a two-thousand-pound safe right by his aquarium, the one that was full of piranhas. I don't think that safe went anywhere. I did some checking on the ownership of Didi's old building. It's owned by a guy named Pierre Dupree. Is that the guy y'all got the marker from?"

"This is all over my head."

"You look a little uncomfortable, Bix. You don't have a meth problem, do you?"

"I don't have *any* kind of problem," Bix said, leaning forward, pointing his stiffened fingers into his own chest. "It's you who's got the problem, Purcel. You were a dirty cop. Everybody laughed at you behind your back. Why do you think our whores slept with you? It's because Didi Gee told them to. I put you in a cab once outside the Dos Marinos. You had puke on your clothes and cooze on your face. Why are you staring at me like that?"

"I think you're scared."

"Of you?"

"No, of somebody else. I think you and your lamebrain friends went out on your own and ended up stepping in your own shit. Now you've gotten somebody else jammed up, and they're about to clamp jumper cables on your ears. That's it, isn't it, or something close to it?"

"What gave you this brilliant idea?"

"All this time you haven't said anything about money. Every one of you guys has got only one thing on the brain, and it's money. Y'all never talk about anything else. Not sex, not sports, not politics, not your families. You talk about money from morning to night. You never get enough of it, you don't give five cents of it away, and you don't tip in restaurants unless you can make a production out of it. For you guys, greed is a virtue. But there hasn't been one peep out of you about the money you say I owe you. Are you hooked up with some kind of new action in the city? Something besides smash-and-grab scores on old people?"

"Maybe I'm willing to let bygones be bygones. You want Grimes, I'll give you Grimes."

"I didn't think AB guys did that."

"So I'm making an exception. Grimes deserves anything that happens to him. Also, I'm tearing up your marker."

"You already missed your opportunity. I'll find Grimes on my own. If I discover you told him to hurt Miss Alice, I'm going to cancel your whole ticket. In the meantime, you might start thinking about giving back your ink."

"Say again?"

Clete Purcel pulled a small recorder from his pants pocket and rewound it until he isolated the moment when Bix had said he was making an exception to the code of the Aryan Brotherhood and was willing to rat out Waylon Grimes. "By tomorrow this will be on several Aryan-supremacist message boards."

"You can't do that, man."

"Get on the Internet in the morning. You're going to be a celebrity. Maybe I can get some pics from your jacket and post them on there." Clete Purcel got in the Caddy and turned the ignition, an unlit Lucky Strike in his mouth. "Look, go to a psychiatrist. Get some help. Getting over on you is like cruelty to animals. It's really depressing."

"Don't talk to me like that, man. Hey, come back here. Come on, Purcel, we always got along. Hey, man, you don't know what you're doing. We're old school, right?"

IT WAS ALMOST ten P.M. when Clete called me at the house. "I creeped Bix Golightly's crib. His toilet seat is inlaid with silver dollars. His interior decorator must do the decor for cathouses."

"You broke into Golightly's apartment?"

"I got into his phone records and listened to all the messages on his machine. I also got into his computer. He's a degenerate gambler. He must have half a dozen bookies and shylocks after him. That's why he was trying to squeeze me. I think he's been trying to fence some stolen paintings, too. Or forgeries. He had written some e-mails about an Italian painter. What does a guy like Golightly know about art?"

"Where are you now?"

"Over in Algiers. Golightly is parked by an old brick apartment building. I think that's where Grimes is holed up."

"Get out of there."

"No, I'm going to take the pair of them down."

"That's really dumb, Clete."

"So is letting one of them pour scalding water on my secretary."

"Why'd you call me?"

"In case it doesn't go right, I want you to know what happened. This is what I think is going on. Golightly is working for somebody he's afraid of. He and Frankie Giacano got ahold of my marker and decided to score a few easy bucks, then somebody else came down on their case. Now Golightly is sweating marbles on several fronts. The old-time Giacanos always behaved like family men and lived in the suburbs and didn't draw attention to themselves. Golightly and Frankie and Grimes broke the rule."

"Are you carrying a drop?"

"I always carry one."

"Don't do what you're thinking."

"I don't let myself know what I'm thinking. So how can I do what I'm thinking if I don't know what I'm thinking? Lighten up, big mon."

Try arguing with a mind-set like that.

CLETE FOLDED HIS cell phone and set it on the passenger seat of the Caddy. He was parked behind a truck on a tree-lined street in an old residential neighborhood of Algiers that had gone to seed and been rezoned for commercial development. Across the Mississippi, he could see the lights of the French Quarter and the black outline of the docks on the Algiers side and a greasy shine on the surface of the river. Bix Golightly's van was parked just beyond the streetlamp at the corner, in the lee of a two-story purple brick building, Bix puffing on a cigarette behind the wheel, the window half down, smoke drifting in the wind.

Why didn't Bix go in? Clete wondered. Was he waiting for Grimes to go to bed? Was he planning to pop him? It was possible. Bix usually hired button men, homicidal morons like Grimes, to do payback for him, but now his voice was on tape blowing off the AB, and in the meantime he'd probably brought some extra heat down on himself for queering somebody else's action. Would Bix cap a guy like Grimes to wipe at least part of the slate clean?

Would anybody who knew Bix Golightly even ask the question?

Clete reached into his glove box and removed a .32 auto that was one cut above junk. The numbers were acid-burned, the wood grips wrapped with electrician's tape, the sight filed off. He dropped it in his coat pocket and got out of the Caddy and walked up the street in the shadows of the buildings. He saw Bix take a final hit off his cigarette and flick it sparking onto the asphalt. *Showtime,* Clete thought.

Then he realized why Bix had remained in his van. Two city cops came out of a corner café on the side street and got in their cruiser and drove through the intersection and on down toward the river. Ironically, they paid no attention to the van, but the cop in the passenger seat looked directly at Clete. The cruiser's brake lights went on briefly, then it turned at the next intersection, and Clete knew he had not only been made, but by cops who considered him an adversary.

He reversed direction, got in the Caddy, throwing the drop in the glove box, and backed all way through an alley until he popped out on the next street, one block away, his mouth dry, his heart beating. He turned off his engine, his breath coming hard in his chest, and knew with no doubt what he had been planning for Bix Golightly and Waylon Grimes.

Just rein it in, he thought. *You can still take them down. It doesn't have to be for the whole ride.*

Right?

Right, he answered himself.

He waited until he was sure the cruiser had left the neighborhood, then he got out of the Caddy and began walking up the alley toward the street where Golightly's van was parked.

THE INSIDE OF the apartment building was poorly lighted and smelled of old wallpaper and carpet that hadn't been vacuumed in months. Bix climbed the stairs to the second floor, taking them three at a time, pulling on the banister with the elasticity of a simian swinging through the trees. He felt a sense of anticipation he hadn't experienced in years. The blood-pounding rush of a big score had long ago faded into a memory, like the joys of sex or flashing money at the track. Intravenous drugs once were a great source of pleasure and secret comfort, but they no longer got him high and he shot up only to maintain, as they said in the trade. Which meant he was a zero plugged into the end of a needle. The vices he could easily afford had become bland and uninteresting, and there were days when Bix felt that someone had done a smash-and-grab on his life.

He walked down a hallway that was lit by low-wattage bulbs inside fluted shades gray with dust, the wallpaper stiff from water seepage, the fire escape framed against the glow of the Quarter across the river. He paused in front of a door that had a metal number seven on it and slipped a credit card from his wallet and started to wedge it between the lock and the doorjamb, then realized the door was unlocked. He replaced the card in his wallet and put his wallet in his side pocket and peeled the Velcro strap off the .25 auto strapped to his ankle. He twisted the knob a second time and stepped quickly inside the room.

It was almost totally dark. A digital clock glowed on top of a stereo; a television set was playing in the bedroom, the sounds of a woman in orgasm bleating from the speakers. Bix held the .25 behind him, staring into the darkness, waiting for his eyes to adjust. "Waylon?" he said.

There was no response.

"It's Bix. I got a little hotheaded on the phone. I'm getting too old and don't know how to hold my water sometimes."

The only sound in the room came from the porn film.

"Hey, Waylon, what's going on?"

Bix felt on the wall for the light switch, the .25 flat against his thigh. Then his hand froze on the switch. He stared at the silhouette of a man sitting in a cloth-covered chair, the red glow of the clock reflecting a nickel-plated revolver the man was holding casually in his lap.

"Jesus Christ, Waylon!" Bix said. "You trying to give me a coronary?"

He eased the .25 into his back pocket, successfully concealing it from Grimes. He wiped his palm on his trousers. "This is your fuck pad? Where do you pick up your broads? At the Lighthouse for the Blind?"

Bix waited for Waylon to speak. Then he said, "You want to put your piece away? Let's have a drink, then we'll go down to my van and I'll give you the twenty large you got coming. We'll forget about Purcel and the nun. Are you listening? Somebody slip you a hot shot?"

Bix hooked his thumb under the light switch, paused briefly, then flicked it on.

Waylon Grimes did not move, not an inch. His right hand rested on the frame and cylinder of a Vaquero .357. His head was tilted back slightly into the upholstery, his mouth partly open. One eye seemed to be fixed on Bix, as though he had been taking a nap and been disturbed by an unwelcome visitor. The other eye had been blown back into the socket, the lid hanging halfway down.

Bix let out his breath. "Hey, who screwed the pooch?" he said, turning in a circle, his piece held out in front of him. "Is there anybody else here? If there is, I got no beef with you. I was here to pay a debt, that's all. You heard me say it."

He felt like a fool. Was he losing his guts? He went into the bedroom and the bath and the kitchen, but there was no sign of a burglary. He replaced the .25 in its holster and pulled a hand towel from the rack in the kitchen and wiped the inside doorknob, then stepped out in the hallway and wiped the outside doorknob and stuck the towel in his pocket. Had he missed anything? He couldn't think. He had touched the doorknobs and nothing else. He was sure of that.

Time to boogie and think through complexities after he was clear of Grimes's pad.

He went back down the stairs and exited the building without being seen, the wind cool on his face and hair, the smell of the river balm to his soul. *How lucky can a guy get?* he thought. Somebody else had snuffed Grimes, and now Bix was home free, not only on the Purcel scam but on the invasion of the nun's house and the twenty grand he owed Grimes. He could use the money to square his debts and maybe get into a program for his addiction. *Thanks, Waylon. I never thought you could do me so many favors. I hope you enjoy your ride in a body bag to the mortuary.*

But who had popped him? That one was up for grabs. Plenty of people hated the punk, including Purcel and the parents of the kid Grimes had killed. *Yeah, it could have been Purcel,* Bix thought. Grimes must have known the killer, because there was no forced entry. Grimes always had two or three guns stashed around his crib and must have tried to make a play with his .357. It was probably hidden under the chair cushion; he had gone for it, and Purcel had parked one in his eyeball. If that was true, maybe Bix could squeeze a few bucks out of Purcel after all, or see him go down on a murder beef. How sweet could it get?

Or maybe one of Grimes's broads did it. There were stories that he liked to hang them up on a hook and work them over with leather gloves or make them play Russian roulette. Grimes was definitely not into long-term female relationships. Who cared, anyway? It was a great night. Time to celebrate, have a few champagne cocktails with a lady friend or two, maybe shoot craps at Harrah's. This was still his city. Then he had a thought. What would make this whole caper perfect? What if he planted evidence implicating Purcel? He had plenty of time. Nobody would find Grimes until he started rotting into the chair. Bix knew a house creep who would steal something out of Purcel's office and plant it in the apartment for a few lines of unstepped-on blow.

Bix walked down to the van, tossing his keys in the air and catching them, a song in his heart. He opened the door and got in and peeled the Velcro-strapped holster off his ankle and locked it in the glove box. It was no time to get stopped and frisked in Algiers. He inserted the key in the ignition, lighting a cigarette, blowing the smoke at an upward angle out the window, like a dragon that could breathe fire.

He had paid no attention to a figure standing in a doorway across the street. The figure stepped into the light and walked toward the van, wearing a red windbreaker and a Baltimore Orioles baseball cap and tight-fitting jeans tucked inside suede boots. The figure's hands were in plain view. Bix started the engine but did not shift into gear, his cigarette hanging from his mouth, his grin stretched as tight as rubber.

"Is that you, Caruso?" he said. "I didn't know you were back in town."

The figure did not speak.

"I took a wrong turn off the bridge," Bix said. "I ought to know better, growing up here and all. You want to get coffee or something? I'm supposed to close a couple of deals tonight. It's part of a charity drive with the chamber of commerce, can you believe that?"

The figure leaned down as though determining if anyone else was in the van, then stepped back, glancing up and down the street.

"You can come along if you like," Bix said. "I belong to an all-night health club. We can play some handball. I'm trying to get off of cigarettes and lose some other bad habits I got. Funny seeing you in Algiers. I always lived in the Quarter or uptown and never really dug the lifestyle over here. If it's not in the Quarter or up St. Charles, it's not New Orleans. It's like Muskogee, Oklahoma, you know, downtown Bum Fuck with Merle Haggard singing songs about it. Jump in and we'll take a spin across the bridge. From the bridge, the lights of the city are beautiful. When you visit New Orleans, you ought to call me. I know all the famous places you won't find on any map. You want to see the house where that vampire novelist used to live? I can show you the rooftop where the sniper killed all those people in the Quarter. I was born and bred in this city. I'm your man. Believe me, Caruso, Algiers sucks. Why the fuck would you want to hang out here?"

Bix stuck another cigarette in his mouth without ever missing a beat, forgetting he had left one in the ashtray, the cigarette in his mouth bouncing on his bottom lip while he talked on and on, his dignity draining through the soles of his shoes.

Then he felt an engine inside him wind down and stop. He looked at the glove box where he had locked his .25 auto and became silent. He lifted his eyes to the figure standing by the window and removed the unlit cigarette from his mouth. He started to speak, but the words would not come out right. He sucked the moisture out of his cheeks and swallowed and tried again. When he heard his own words, he was surprised at the level of calm in them: "You ought to come here during Mardi Gras. Like Wolfman Jack used to say, it's a toe-curlin' blast," he said.

The figure lifted a silenced .22 auto and pointed it with both hands and fired three times into Bix Golightly's face, hitting him twice in the forehead and once in the mouth, clipping his cigarette in half, the ejected casings tinkling like tiny bells on the asphalt.

The shooter bent over and picked up the ejected rounds as dispassionately and diligently as someone recovering coins dropped on a beach. From the edge of the alleyway, Clete watched the figure walk down the street through a cone of light under a streetlamp and disappear inside the darkness. The shooter's windbreaker reminded him of the one worn by James Dean in *Rebel Without a Cause*. Then the shooter reversed direction and came back toward the streetlamp and seemed to stare momentarily at the alleyway, uncertain or bemused. Clete edged deeper into the alley. His .38 was clenched in his right hand, the grips biting into his palm, his pulse jumping in his neck. He pressed himself into the brick wall, his own body odor climbing into his nostrils, a vaporlike coldness wrapping itself around his heart. His blood was pounding so loudly in his ears that he couldn't be sure if the shooter spoke or not. Then he heard the shooter walk away, whistling a tune. Was it "The San Antonio Rose"? Or was he losing his mind?

CHAPTER
5

Clete's Caddy pulled into my drive at five the next morning, the windows and waxed finish running with moisture. I heard him walking on the gravel through the porte cochere and into the backyard. When I disarmed the alarm system and opened the back door, he was sitting on the steps. The oak and pecan trees and slash pines were barely visible inside the fog rolling off Bayou Teche. He told me everything that had happened in Algiers.

"You went into Grimes's apartment after Golightly got it?" I said.

"I didn't touch anything."

"Grimes died with a .357 in his hand?"

"Yeah, he probably let the wrong person in and didn't realize his mistake until it was too late."

"Why'd you go into his apartment?"

"Grimes tortured my secretary. I shouldn't go into his apartment?"

"You didn't call the shooting in?"

"I called in a shots-fired from a pay phone."

"You did that later?"

"Yeah."

"There's something not coming together here, Clete. You had your piece out when you were in the alley?"

"That's what I said."

"But you didn't try to stop the shooter?"

63

"Would you eat a round for Bix Golightly?"

Clete was staring into the fog, his big hands cupped on his knees, his porkpie hat low on his forehead, his stomach hanging over his belt. He picked up Snuggs and started wiping the mud off the cat's paws with his handkerchief, smearing mud and fur on his slacks and sport coat.

"You're leaving something out," I said.

"Like what?"

"You're telling me you froze?"

"I didn't say that. I just left Golightly to his fate, that's all. He was born a bad guy, and he went out the same way. The world is better off without him."

"You're a witness to a homicide, Clete."

"What else do you want me to say? I told you what happened. You don't like what I've told you, so you put the problem on me. You got anything to eat?"

"Yeah, I guess."

"You guess?" he said, putting Snuggs down.

"Come inside. I'll get some eggs and bacon started."

He took off his hat and rubbed his forehead as though he could smooth the wrinkles out of it. "Just coffee," he said. "I don't feel too hot."

"You pull something loose inside?"

"No, that's not it."

"How can I help you if you won't be square with me?"

"I thought this fall we'd be fishing again. Like the old days, when we caught green trout north of Barataria Bay. New Orleans is the only place in the world where people call bass 'green trout.' That's pretty neat, isn't it?"

"Who was the shooter, Clete?"

AT 7:45 A.M. I went to the office, and Clete went to the cottage he rented at a motor court down the bayou. At eleven A.M. I called Dana Magelli at the NOPD. I asked him what he had on a double shooting in Algiers. "How do you know we have anything?" he replied.

"Word gets around," I replied.

"Bix Golightly got it. So did a kid by the name of Waylon Grimes. So far no brass, no prints. It looks like a contract hit. Somebody called in an anonymous shots-fired from a public phone."

"Why do you think it was a contract job?"

"Aside from the fact that the shooter recovered his brass, he probably used a twenty-two or a twenty-five with a suppressor. The pros like small-caliber guns because the round bounces around inside the skull. Who told you about the shooting, Dave?"

"I got a tip."

"From who?"

"Maybe from the same guy who called in the shots-fired. He said the shooter was wearing a red windbreaker and a Baltimore Orioles baseball cap and jeans stuffed in suede boots. He said Golightly called the shooter Caruso."

"We've already been to Golightly's condo. A neighbor says a guy who sounds a whole lot like Clete Purcel was hanging around the condo last night. What are you guys up to?"

"Nothing of consequence. Life is pretty boring on the Teche."

"I think you're lying."

"You're a good man, but don't ever talk to me like that again," I said.

"You're holding back information in a homicide investigation," he said.

"You ever hear of a hitter named Caruso?"

"No. And if I haven't, nobody else around here has, either."

"Maybe there's a new player in town."

"Sometimes when people have a near-death experience, they think they don't have to obey the same rules as the rest of us. You tell Purcel what I said."

"He's the best cop NOPD ever had."

"Yeah, until he killed a federal informant and fled the country rather than face the music."

I hung up the phone. At noon my half-day shift was over. I walked home under the canopy of live oaks that arched over East Main, the sunlight golden through the leaves, the Spanish moss lifting in the wind, the autumnal Louisiana sky so hard and perfectly blue that it looked like an inverted ceramic bowl. Molly was at her office down the bayou, where she worked for a relief agency that helped fisher-people and small farmers build their own homes and businesses. Alafair was proofreading the galleys of her first novel at our redwood picnic table in the backyard, Tripod and Snuggs sitting like bookends on either side of the table. I fixed ham-and-onion sandwiches and a pitcher of iced tea and carried them outside and sat down next to her.

"Did Pierre Dupree find you?" she said.

"He called?"

"No, he was here about an hour ago."

"What did he want?" I asked.

"He didn't say. He seemed in a hurry."

"Dupree owns a building in New Orleans that used to be the headquarters of Didoni Giacano. There was a safe in the building that contained an old IOU from a card game Clete was in. Clete had paid the debt, but a couple of wiseacres got their hands on the marker and tried to take his office and apartment away from him. What do you know about Dupree?"

"I've met him at a couple of parties. He seems nice enough," she said. She took a bite of her sandwich and avoided my eyes.

"Go on," I said.

"He's had a lot of commercial success as an artist. I think he's a marketing man more than a painter. There's nothing wrong in that."

"There isn't?"

"He owns an ad agency, Dave. That's what the man does for a living. Not everybody is Vincent van Gogh."

"When was the first time you wrote a dishonest line in your fiction?"

She drank from her iced tea, her expression neutral, her galley pages fluttering when the wind gusted.

"The answer is you never wrote a dishonest line," I said.

Her skin was unblemished and dark in the shade, her hair as black as an Indian's, her features and the luster in her eyes absolutely beautiful. Men had trouble not looking at her, even when they were with their wives. It was hard to believe she was the same little El Salvadoran girl I pulled from a submerged airplane that crashed off Southwest Pass. "There's Pierre Dupree," she said.

A canary-yellow Humvee with a big chrome grille had just pulled into the driveway. Through the tinted windshield, I could see the driver talking on a cell phone and fooling with something on the dashboard. I walked through the porte cochere until I was abreast of the driver's window. Pierre Dupree had thick black hair that was as shiny as a raven's wing. He also had intense green eyes with a black fleck in them. He was at least six feet seven and had a face that would have been handsome except for the size of his teeth. They were too big for his mouth and, coupled with his size, they gave others the sense that in spite of his tailored suits and good manners, his body contained physical appetites and energies and suppressed urges that he could barely restrain.

"Sorry I missed you earlier, Mr. Robicheaux," he said through the window.

"Get down and come in," I replied.

He thumbed a breath mint loose from a roll and put it in his mouth and dropped the roll back on the dashboard. "I've got to run. It's about Mr. Purcel. He's called my office twice regarding a betting slip of some kind. His message said the betting slip was in a safe I inherited from the previous tenant of a building I own. I got rid of that safe years ago. I just wanted to tell Mr. Purcel that."

"Then tell him."

"I tried. He doesn't pick up. I've got to get back to New Orleans. Will you relay the message?"

"Do you know a guy named Bix Golightly?"

"No, but what a grand name."

"How about Waylon Grimes or Frankie Giacano?"

"Everybody in New Orleans remembers the Giacanos. I never knew any of them personally. I really have to go, Mr. Robicheaux. Stop by the plantation in Jeanerette or my home in the Garden District. Bring Alafair. I'd love to see her again. Is she still writing?"

While he was speaking the last sentence, he was already starting his engine. Then he backed into the street, smiling as though he were actually listening to my reply. He drove past the Shadows and into the business district.

I tried to assess what had just occurred. A man who indicated he wanted to deliver a message had gone to my home earlier but had not bothered to go to my office, although he had been told that was where I could be found. Then he had bounced into my driveway and delivered his message, all the while explaining that he didn't have time to be there. Then he had left, communicating nothing of substance to anyone except the fact that he owned two expensive homes to which we were invited on an unspecified day.

I decided that Pierre Dupree definitely belonged in advertising.

HELEN SOILEAU CALLED me at home on Saturday morning. "We've got a floater down at the bottom of St. Mary Parish," she said.

"A homicide?" I asked.

"I don't know what it is. I'm getting too old for this job. Anyway, I'm going to need you there."

"Why not let St. Mary handle it?"

"One of the deputies recognized the victim. It's Blue Melton, Tee Jolie's sister."

"Blue drowned?"

"She may have frozen to death."

"*What?*"

"Blue Melton floated into the marsh inside a block of ice. The water temperature is seventy degrees. The deputy said her eyes are open and she looks like she's trying to say something. I'll pick you up in ten minutes."

The trip down to the watery southern rim of St. Mary Parish didn't take long. But the geographic distance between St. Mary Parish and other parishes had little to do with the historical distance between St. Mary Parish and the twenty-first century. It had always been known as a fiefdom, owned and run by one family with enormous amounts of wealth and political power. Its sugarcane acreage and processing plants were the most productive in the state. Its supply of black and poor-white labor was of a kind one would associate with an antebellum economy and mind-set. The oil and natural gas wells punched into its swamps and marshlands brought in unexpected revenues that seemed to be a gift from a divine hand, although the recipients did not feel a great Christian urgency to share their good fortune. The have-nots lived in company houses and did and thought as they were told. No court, clergyman, police official, newspaper publisher, or politician ever challenged the family who ran St. Mary Parish. Any historian studying the structure of medieval society would probably consider St. Mary Parish a model teleported from the thirteenth century.

We drove in Helen's cruiser down a long two-lane road through flooded gum and willow and cypress trees, the sunlight spangling through the canopy on water that was black in the shade or filmed with a skim of algae that resembled green lace. The road dead-ended on a cusp of oil-streaked beach and a shallow saltwater bay that bled into the Gulf of Mexico. The St. Mary Parish sheriff, two deputies, a crime scene investigator, the coroner, and two paramedics were already at the scene. They were standing in a circle with the blank expressions of people who had just discovered that their vocational training and experience were perhaps of no value. When they glanced up at us in unison, they reminded me of late-night drinkers in a bar who stare at the front door each time it opens, as though the person coming through it possesses an answer to the hopelessness that governs their lives.

The sheriff of St. Mary Parish was not a bad man, but I would not call him a good one. He was trim and tall and wore cowboy boots and western-cut clothes and a short-brim Stetson. He gave the impression of a law officer from a simpler time. However, there was always a cautious gleam in his eyes, particularly when someone was making a request of him, one that might involve the names of people he both served and feared. One person he obviously did not like was Helen Soileau, either because she was a lesbian or because she was a female administrator. There were razor nicks on his jaw, and I suspected the discovery of Blue Melton's body had robbed him of his day off. The sheriff's name was Cecil Barbour.

"Thanks for contacting us," Helen said.

"No thanks are necessary. I didn't contact you. My deputy did that without my permission," Barbour replied. The deputy was looking out at the bay, his arms folded across his chest.

"I didn't know that," Helen said.

"My deputy is a relative of the girl's grandfather and says Detective Robicheaux was asking about her. That's how come he contacted you," Barbour said. "Look down in the ice. Is that Blue Melton, Detective Robicheaux?"

"Yes, sir, it is," I replied. "How about putting a tarp over her body?"

"Why should we do that?" Barbour asked.

"Because she's naked and exposed in death in a way no human being should be," I replied.

"We have to defrost her before we take her in. Do you object to that?" he said.

"It's your parish," I said.

I walked down to the water's edge, my eyes on the southern horizon, my back to the sheriff. I did not want him to see my expression or the thoughts that probably showed in my eyes. The tide was out, and a dead brown pelican, the Louisiana state bird, was rolling in the frothy skim along the shoals, its feathers iridescent with oil. I could feel my right hand opening and closing at my side. I picked up a pebble and threw it underhanded into a swell. My mouth was dry in the way your mouth is dry when you come off a bender, my heart was beating, and the wind was louder than it should have been, like the sound a conch shell makes at your ear. I turned around and looked at Barbour. His attention had shifted back to the body of Blue Melton. She had been frozen nude inside a block of ice that must have been the size of a bathtub. The salt water and the sun and stored heat in the sand had reduced the block to the size and rough shape of a footlocker. Her blond hair and her blue eyes and her small breasts and nipples seemed protected by only an inch or so of frosted glass. The sheriff was smoking a cigarette, the ash dripping off the end onto the ice.

"Dave's right," the coroner said. He was a taciturn man who wore straw gardener's hats and firehouse suspenders and long-sleeve blue shirts buttoned at the wrists. "This poor girl has been exposed to enough abuse. Bust off some of that ice and get her on the gurney and cover her up, for God's sake."

A few moments later, I was alone with the coroner. "You ever see anything like this?"

"Never," he replied.

"What do you think we're looking at?" I asked.

"She was in a big subzero locker of some kind. Maybe on a freighter. There's no way to know how long she was in the water. Ice creates its own environment and temperature zones. Maybe I can come up with an estimate of when she died, but I don't know how dependable it will be."

"Y'all better look at this," a female paramedic said. She wiped her gloved hand across the ice barely covering Blue's face, cleaning the melt and ice crystals away like someone brushing powdered snow off a windshield. The sun's rays had probably magnified inside the ice block and created an air bubble and a pool of water that wobbled around Blue Melton's head, like Jell-O. "There's something in her throat. It looks like a piece of red rubber."

SECRETLY, I WAS glad Blue Melton's body had washed ashore in St. Mary Parish and not in Iberia Parish, because I would not have to notify the grandfather of her death. The rest of the day I tried to forget the images of Blue's face and hair and embryonic-like arms and tiny feet locked inside a block of ice that could have been sawed out of a glacier. She could not have been over seventeen. What kind of human could do something like that to a young woman? Unfortunately, I knew the answer. There were misogynistic sadists in our midst, in greater numbers than most people could guess at. And how did they get there? Answer: Our system often gives them a free pass.

I prayed that she had not died of drowning or hypothermia. I prayed that the angels had been with her in the moments that led up to her death. I prayed that she heard the echo of a kind and loving voice from her childhood before someone stole her life away. I prayed most of all that one day she would have justice and that a better man than I would find it for her, and perhaps for her sister, because I feared I was no longer up to doing the job that I had done for most of my adult life.

I RECEIVED A call from the coroner Sunday afternoon. "I'm at Iberia Medical. I've just finished the postmortem. I'd like for you to come down here," he said.

"What is it you want to tell me?"

"It's what I want to show you, not tell you."

"I appreciate your deference, but your first obligation is to Sheriff Barbour."

"Two weeks ago my wife and I were having supper in Lafayette. Barbour happened to be sitting at the table next to us. He was wearing a Rolex watch. I suspect it cost in excess of a thousand dollars. I was trying to figure how I could afford a fine watch like that on my salary. Unfortunately, I couldn't come up with an answer. Are you coming down here or not?"

Iberia Medical Center was only ten minutes away, located behind oak and palm trees, not far from the turn-bridge where Nelson Canal empties into Bayou Teche. On that same spot in April 1863, Louisiana's boys in butternut set up a skirmish line in a failed attempt to stop General Banks's sweep across the southern part of the state. The Episcopalian church on Main was turned into a field hospital for the wounded and the dying, and Union soldiers vandalized and looted the town and were given sanction to rape black women. Up the bayou in St. Martinville, a Catholic priest who tried to shelter women in his church was almost beaten to death by these same soldiers. These events happened, but they are seldom if ever mentioned in history books that deal with the War Between the States.

The coroner was waiting for me in the room where he performed autopsies, a nonabsorbent apron not unlike a butcher's looped around his neck and tied about the waist. Blue Melton lay on a stainless steel table, one that had a gutter and a drain and a flushing mechanism. She was covered by a sheet, but the side of her face and one eye and a lock of hair were exposed. Her skin had turned gray or pearly where the tissue was pressed against the bones. "She didn't die from hypothermia or asphyxiation or blunt trauma. Cause of death was a massive heroin overdose," the coroner said. "I don't think she was an intravenous addict. There is only one puncture mark on her body and only one drug in her system. I think she was injected while she was in water, or she was put in water immediately after she was injected. I suspect she was alone when she died."

"Why?"

The coroner picked up a tray from the counter behind him and held it out so I could see its contents. "I removed this red balloon from her mouth," he said. "There are traces of heroin in it. There was also this slip of paper inside the balloon. The ink has run badly, but I think you can make out the letters."

He lifted the strip of paper from the tray with a pair of tweezers and laid it out wetly on the corner of the autopsy table. My eyes filmed when I read the words that Blue Melton had written.

"Can you give me a time frame?" I asked.

"I'd say she's been dead at least three weeks. That's a guess. This was a brave girl. I don't know how she pulled off what she did."

My eyes were locked on the message Blue had left: *My sister is still alive.* I couldn't concentrate on what the coroner was saying. "Would you repeat that?"

"It's hard to say what happened, but chances are the heroin she was injected with came from the balloon she tried to swallow. Considering the amount of heroin that went into her heart, it must have taken an enormous effort to write those words on a piece of paper and place it in the balloon and then conceal it in her mouth. When people are dying, particularly under her circumstances, they don't usually think about the welfare of others. Did you know her?"

"I used to see her at the convenience store where she worked. I knew her sister, Tee Jolie."

"The singer?"

"She was more than that."

"I don't get your meaning," he said.

I started to explain, then decided to keep my thoughts to myself. I drove back home in my pickup and sat for a long time on a folding chair in the shadows down by the bayou. I watched a cottonmouth moccasin curl out of the water into a cypress tree four feet away, its coils slithering and tightening around the branch, its eyes as small as BBs, its tongue flickering. I picked up a pinecone and tossed it at the snake's head. But the snake ignored me and drew its tail out of the water and secured itself inside the cypress tree's branches, the leaves already turning from green to yellow in anticipation of winter.

CHAPTER
6

THERE ARE THREE essential truths about law enforcement: Most crimes are not punished; most crimes are not solved through the use of forensic evidence; and informants produce the lion's share of information that puts the bad guys in a cage.

I couldn't help Blue or Tee Jolie Melton, but perhaps I could do something about the shooting death of Bix Golightly and the fact that Clete Purcel had been a witness to it and would probably be hounded by the NOPD. I was convinced that Clete was concealing the identity of the shooter, although I had no idea why. Where does a person go in New Orleans for the type of information you can't find in the Yellow Pages?

The best source I ever had in New Orleans was a former spieler at a strip club on Bourbon Street known as Jimmy the Dime. Jimmy's nickname came from the fact that with one phone call, he could connect you with any action you were looking for, maybe a card game or access to counterfeit money that sold for twenty cents on the dollar or a brick of Acapulco gold. In terms of underworld activity, he was a minor offender and never a rat. His troubles usually came about from his bizarre and anachronistic frame of reference, which in his case was that of a Depression-era Irish tenement kid for whom dysfunction and living on the rim were as natural as the rising and setting of the sun.

Jimmy had a house in the Holy Cross section of the Ninth Ward when Hurricane Katrina struck the city. Rather than pay attention to the evacuation order or even listen to the news, Jimmy had watched a porn film on cable the morning the storm made landfall. When a tidal wave blew his house into rubble, Jimmy climbed onto a giant inner tube in polka-dot boxer shorts, with an umbrella and two six-packs of Bud and a Walkman and half a dozen joints in a Ziploc bag, and floated on the waves for thirty-six hours. He was fried to a crisp and almost run down by a Coast Guard boat and ended up in the branches of a tree down in Plaquemines Parish.

Jimmy's eccentricities, however, were nothing compared to those of his full-time podjo and part-time business partner, Count Carbona, also known as Baron Belladonna. The Count wore a black cape and a purple slouch hat and had a face like a vertical chunk of train rail. The Count shaved off his eyebrows and was obsessed with the female rock-and-roll singers he believed lived under Lake Pontchartrain. If anyone asked how he knew about the women under the lake, the Count explained that he communicated with them daily through the drain in his lavatory. The Count's current underwater drainpipe pal was Joan Jett.

After I finished work at noon on Monday, I drove to New Orleans and visited Jimmy and the Count at their book and voodoo store down by Dauphine and Barracks. In spite of Katrina, the windows looked like they had not been washed since the fall of the city to Union forces in 1862. The shelves and the array of worthless books on them stayed under a patina of dirt that Jimmy moved from place to place in the shop with his feather duster. In back were cartons of hand-painted tortoise shells and mason jars that contained pickled lizards and snakes and birds' eggs and alligators' feet. On the back wall was a garish painting of Marie Laveau, the voodoo queen of New Orleans.

"You know anything about Bix Golightly getting capped, Jimmy?" I said.

"There's not a lot of mourning going on about that," he replied. He was drinking a bottle of soda behind the counter, next to a beautiful antique brass cash register, his face florid, his hair as white as meringue, his stomach draped over his belt. "Remember that Louis Prima song, how's it go, 'I'll be standing on the corner plastered when they bring your body by'?"

"Any rumors about why he got capped?"

"He was in the AB. The AB is for life. Maybe he made the wrong guys mad about something."

"Waylon Grimes got popped the same night, probably by the same hitter. Grimes wasn't in the AB."

"The word was Bix was into a new racket, something that was more uptown. Also that he was out of his depth, that him and Frankie Giacano and Waylon Grimes decided they were gonna get even with Clete Purcel and make a few bucks at the same time. You talk to Purcel?"

"Clete didn't do it, Jimmy."

"Who filled up a guy's convertible with concrete? Or packed a cue ball into a guy's mouth? Or dragged a guy's mobile home onto a drawbridge and set it on fire? Let me think."

"Have you heard of a new button man in town, somebody named Caruso?"

"There's always new talent floating around. You read vampire books? I just bought a shitload of them. Vampire lit is in, muff-diver lit is out. I'm ahead of the curve."

"Where's the new talent from?" I asked.

"Someplace that begins with M. Miami or Memphis. Maybe Minneapolis. I don't remember. This is stuff I don't need to know about."

I looked toward the back of the store. The Count was sweeping a cloud of dust through the door into a courtyard that was green and dark with mold and cluttered with junk.

"He's on his meds and doing good. Leave him alone, Dave," Jimmy said.

"The Count is what is called an autistic savant, Jimmy. Everything he hears and sees goes onto a computer chip."

"Yeah, I know all that, and I don't like people giving him names like 'autistic savant.' He did too many drugs, but that don't mean he's retarded."

"You want to ask him, or do you want me to?" I said.

Jimmy poured the rest of his soda into a sink and put a matchstick in his mouth. "Hey, Count, you hear anything about a new mechanic in town?" he said.

The Count stopped sweeping and stared downward at his broom. Rain was swirling inside the courtyard, blowing in a fine mist across his cape and small pale hands. He lifted his eyes to mine, puzzled about either the question or my identity.

"It's Dave Robicheaux, Count," I said. "I need your help. I'm looking for a hitter by the name of Caruso."

"Caruso? Yes. I know that name," said the Count. He smiled.

"In New Orleans?"

"I think so."

"Where?" I asked.

The Count shook his head.

"Who's he work for?" I asked.

He didn't speak and instead continued to look into my face, his irises tinged with the colors you expect to see only in a hawk's eyes.

"How about the name Caruso? Is that an alias?" I said.

"It means something."

I waited for him to go on, but he didn't. "It means what?" I asked.

"Like the opera singer."

"I know who the opera singer is. But why is this guy called by that name?"

"When Caruso sings, everybody in the theater gets quiet. When he leaves, they stay in their seats."

"Where do you think I might find him? This is real important, Count."

"They say he finds you. I heard what you said about me. I'm the way I am because I'm smart. People say things in front of me that they won't say in front of anyone else. They don't know I'm smart. That's why they make fun of me and call me names."

He swept a cloud of dust out into the rain, then followed it into the courtyard and shut the door behind him.

I deserved his rebuke.

• • •

THE HOUR WAS three P.M., and I had time to make another stop before returning to New Iberia, which was only a two-hour drive if you went through Morgan City. The old office of Didi Giacano, the one where he kept an aquarium full of piranha, was on South Rampart, outside the Quarter, just across Canal. The building was two stories and constructed of soft, variegated brick and had an iron balcony and a colonnade, but one of the side walls had been scorched by fire and the building had a singed, used look that the potted bougainvillea and caladium and philodendron on the balcony did little to dispel.

The inside of the office had been completely redone. The beige carpet was two inches thick, the off-white plastered walls hung with paintings of Mediterranean villages and steel-framed aerial color photos of offshore oil platforms, one of them flaring against a night sky. The receptionist told me that Pierre Dupree was at his home in Jeanerette but that his grandfather was in his office and perhaps could help me.

"Actually, I was interested in a safe that used to be here," I said. "I collect all kinds of historical memorabilia. It was a huge box of a thing right over there in the corner."

"I know the one you mean. It's not here anymore. Mr. Pierre took it out when we installed the new carpets."

"Where is it?" I asked.

She was an attractive blond woman in her early twenties, with an earnest face and eyes that seemed full of goodwill. Her forehead wrinkled. "I'm sorry, I don't remember. I think some movers took it out."

"How long ago was that?"

"About five or six months ago, I think. Did you want to buy it?"

"I doubt that I could afford it. I just wanted to look at it."

"What's your name again?"

"Dave Robicheaux, with the Iberia Parish Sheriff's Department."

"I'll tell Mr. Alexis you're here. That's Mr. Pierre's grandfather. I'll bet he can tell you all about the safe."

Before I could stop her, she went into the back of the building and returned with a man I had seen once or twice in New Iberia or Jeanerette. For his age, he was remarkable in his posture and his bearing. He was even more remarkable for the story associated with his name. I couldn't remember the specific details, but people who knew him said he had been a member of the French Resistance during World War II and had been sent to an extermination camp in Germany. I couldn't recall the name of the camp or the circumstances that had spared his life. Was it Ravensbrück? He was dressed in slacks and a long-sleeve white shirt rolled to the elbows. When he shook my hand, the bones in his fingers felt hollow, like a bird's. A chain of numbers was tattooed in faded blue ink on the underside of his left forearm. "You were asking about an old safe?" he said.

"I collect old things. Antiques and Civil War artifacts and that sort of thing," I replied.

"There was a safe here that came with the building, but it was taken out a long time ago, I think."

His face was narrow, his eyes as gray as lead, his hair still black, with a few strands of white. There was a pronounced dimple in his chin. On his left cheek were two welted scars. "Would you like coffee or perhaps a drink?"

"No, thank you. I didn't mean to disturb you. Do you know a fellow by the name of Frankie Giacano or his friend Bix Golightly?"

"Those names aren't familiar. Are they antique dealers?" He was smiling when he spoke, the way an older man might when he's showing tolerance of his listener.

"No, they're bad guys, Mr. Dupree. Pardon me, the use of the present tense isn't quite accurate. Frankie Giacano is still around, but somebody over in Algiers parked three rounds from a semi-auto in Bix Golightly's face."

"That's a graphic image, Mr. Robicheaux. Why are you telling me this?"

"It's probably just the ambience. I remember when Didi Gee used to hold a person's hand in an aquarium over by that wall. I came in here once when the water was full of blood."

"I'm not one who needs convincing of man's inhumanity to man."

"I meant you no offense."

"Of course you did," he said. "Good day to you, sir."

I started to leave. He was an elderly man. The tattoo on his left arm was of a kind that only a visitor to hell could have acquired. Sometimes there are occasions when charity requires that we accept arrogance and rudeness and deception in others. I didn't feel this was one of them. "You lied to me, sir."

"How dare you?" he replied, his eyes coming to life.

THE NEXT MORNING at work, Helen Soileau called me into her office. She was watering the plants on her windowsill with a tin sprinkler painted with flowers. "I just got off the phone with Alexis Dupree. You called an eighty-nine-year-old man a liar?" she said.

"I said he lied to me. There's a difference."

"Not to him. My ear is still numb. What were you doing in his office?"

I explained to her about Didoni Giacano's old safe and the marker that supposedly was found inside it. "The receptionist said the safe was taken out five or six months ago. The old man said otherwise. In front of her. Her face turned red."

"Maybe Dupree was confused. Or maybe the receptionist was."

"I think he was lying. I also think he was mocking me."

"What happens in New Orleans is not our business."

"I went there on my own time."

"You identified yourself at Dupree's office as a member of this department. That's why he called here and yelled in the phone for five minutes. I don't need this kind of crap, Pops."

"That old man is corrupt."

"Half the state is underwater, and the other half is under indictment. Our own congressional representative said that."

"What was the name of the death camp Dupree was in?" I asked.

"What difference does it make?"

"Was it Ravensbrück?"

"Did you hear what I just said?"

"I'm almost sure it was Ravensbrück. I read a feature on Mr. Dupree in the *Advocate* about two years ago."

"Why do you care which camp he was in? Dave, I think you're losing your mind."

"Ravensbrück was a women's camp, most of them Polish Jews," I said.

"I'm about to throw a flowerpot at your head," she said.

"I don't think the problem is mine," I replied.

I went back to my office. Ten minutes later, Helen buzzed my extension. "I Googled Ravensbrück," she said. "Yes, it was primarily a women's extermination camp, but a camp for male prisoners was right next to it. The inmates were liberated by the Russians in 1945. Does this get World War Two off the table?"

"That old man is hinky, and so is his grandson," I replied.

I heard her ease the receiver into the phone cradle, the plastic surfaces clattering against each other.

IT STARTED RAINING again that night, hard, in big drops that stung like hail. Through the back window, I could see leaves floating under the oaks and, in the distance, the drawbridge at Burke Street glowing inside the rain. I heard Molly's car pull into the porte cochere. She came through the back door, a damp bag of groceries clutched under one arm, her skin and hair shiny with water. "Did you see my note on the board?" she asked.

"No," I said.

"Clete called," she said, putting down her groceries on the breakfast table.

"What did he want?"

She tried to smile. "I could hear music in the background."

"He was tanked?"

"More like his boat left the dock a little early."

"Was he in town or phoning from New Orleans?"

"He didn't say. I think Clete is trying to destroy himself," she said.

When I didn't reply, she began putting away the groceries. She had the arms and shoulders of a countrywoman, and when she set a heavy can on a shelf, I could see her shirt tighten on her back. She pushed a strand of hair out of her eyes and looked at me. "I don't want to see you lying on a gurney in an emergency room with a bullet hole in your chest again. Is that wrong?" she said.

"Clete's in serious trouble, and he doesn't have many friends."

"Don't get mixed up in it."

"All of us would be dead if it wasn't for Clete."

"You can be his friend without making the same kinds of choices he does. You've never learned that."

"I see."

"No, you don't," she said.

She went into the bathroom and closed the door behind her and turned the lock.

I PUT ON my raincoat and hat and drove to Clete's motor court down the Teche. His cottage was the last one on a driveway that dead-ended in a grove of live oaks by the bayou. His Caddy was parked by the trees, the rain clicking loudly on the starched top. The cottage was dark, and pine needles had clotted in the rain gutters, and water was running down the walls. I knocked, then knocked again harder, with the flat of my fist. A lamp went on inside, and Clete opened the door in his skivvies, the unventilated room sour with the smell of weed and beer sweat and unchanged bed linens. "Hey, Dave, what's the haps?" he said.

"You ever hear of opening a window?" I said, going inside.

"I nodded out. Is it morning?"

"No. Molly said you called."

"Yeah?" he said, rubbing his hand over his face, moving toward the breakfast table, where a manila folder lay open. "I forgot why I called. I was drinking doubles at Clementine's, and a switch went off in my head. It's not morning?"

"It's not even ten P.M."

"I guess I was having some kind of crazy dream," he said. He closed the folder and moved it aside, as though straightening things so we could have a cup of coffee. His nylon shoulder holster and blue-black snub-nosed .38 were hanging on the back of a chair. A huge old-style blackjack, one teardropped in shape and stitched with a leather cover and mounted on a spring and wood handle, lay by the manila folder. "I dreamed some kids were chasing me through the Irish Channel. They had bricks in their hands. What a funny dream to have."

"Why don't you take a shower, and then we'll talk."

"About what?"

"Why you called me."

"I think it was about Frankie Giacano. He called me up and begged me to help him."

"Frankie Gee begged?"

"He was about to shit his pants. He thinks he's going to get capped like Bix Golightly and Waylon Grimes."

"Why?"

"He won't say."

"Why does he think you can get him off the hook?"

"He mentioned your name. He said, 'You and Robicheaux won't let this thing die.'"

"What's he talking about?" I asked.

"Who knows? Did you roust him or something?"

"I went to Pierre Dupree's office on South Rampart yesterday. I talked with the grandfather. He lied to me about the safe. What's in the manila folder?"

"Nothing."

"You want to level with me, or should I leave?"

"It's a file on a kid in Fort Lauderdale. I got it from a friend in the state attorney's office in Tallahassee."

"Who's the kid?"

"Just a kid. One who was abused."

"Abused how?"

"As bad as it gets. So bad you don't want to know. Dave, don't look at that."

I took my hand away from the folder. Clete pulled out a drawer under the table and removed a clear plastic bag of weed and a sheaf of cigarette papers.

"Lay off that stuff," I said.

"I'll do what I please."

"No, you won't." I pulled the bag from his hand and opened the front door and shook the weed into the rain. I threw the bag and the papers into a waste can.

"Even my ex didn't do that."

"Too bad. What's in the folder?"

"Let it slide, big mon."

I picked up the folder regardless and looked at the black-and-white photographs of a small child. I read the medical report written by an emergency room physician. I read the statements of a social worker who threatened to quit her agency if the state didn't remove the child from the home. I read the report of a Broward County sheriff's detective detailing the arrest of the mother's live-in boyfriend and the condition in which he found the child upon his last visit to the mother's apartment. Most of the photos and the paperwork were almost twenty-five years old. The photos of the child were of a kind you never want to see or remember or discuss with anyone. "Who's the mother?" I asked.

"A junkie."

"You knew her?"

"She used to strip and hook out of a joint on Bourbon. She was from Brooklyn originally, but she'd moved to New Orleans, and she and her pimp were running a Murphy game on conventioneers. They blew town on an assault warrant. The john got wise to the scam when the pimp showed up as the outraged husband, because the same pimp had shown up on the same john six months earlier. So the pimp busted up the john with a pair of brass knuckles. How about that for a bunch of geniuses?"

"The pimp is the one who did this?" I was holding one of the photos, the paper shaking slightly in my fingers.

"No, Candy would screw anybody who'd give her heroin. There were always different guys living with her."

"That's when you were in Vice?"

"Yeah, and on the grog and pills and anything else I could cook my head with."

"You got it on with her?"

"Big-time."

"What's going on, Cletus?"

He got a beer out of the icebox and ripped the tab and sat down at the table. The scar that ran through his eyebrow and touched the bridge of his nose had flushed a dark pink. He drank from the can and set it down and took his hand away from it and looked at the prints his fingers had left on the coldness of the can. "The kid in those photos had a miserable life."

"Who is she?"

"You already know."

"Tell me."

"Let it go, Dave."

"Say it, Cletus."

"It won't change anything."

"Is she alive?"

"You'd better believe it." He was breathing harder, through his nose, his face shiny under the overhead light.

"Come on, partner."

"She's my daughter."

"What's the rest of it?"

"Her name is Gretchen." His hands were propped on his knees, his big shoulders bent forward. He looked like a man experiencing vertigo aboard a pitching ship. "I made some calls to people around Miami and Lauderdale. In Little Havana people talk about a hitter they call Caruso. The old Batistiano and Alpha 66 crowd don't mess with her. The greaseballs in Miami Beach say she's like the Irish button men on the west side of New York: all business, no passion, a stone killer. They say maybe she's the best on the East Coast. I think Caruso might be my daughter, Dave. I feel like somebody drove a nail in my skull."

CHAPTER
7

CLETE TOOK A shower and dressed and sat down again at the table, his hair wet-combed, his eyes clear. "I didn't know I had a daughter until Gretchen was fifteen," he said. "Her mother called collect from the Dade County stockade and said Gretchen was in juvie and I was her father. I don't think Candy could have cared less about her daughter; she wanted me to bail her out of the can. I got a blood test done on Gretchen. There was no doubt she was mine. In the meantime she'd been transferred from juvie to foster care. Before I could get the custody process in gear, she disappeared. I tried to find her two or three times. I heard she was a hot walker at Hialeah, and she started hanging with some dopers and then got mixed up with some Cuban head cases, guys who think a political dialogue is blowing up the local television station."

"Why didn't you tell me any of this?".

"Think I'm proud I fathered a child who was left in the hands of a sadist? I'm talking about the guy who did what's in those pictures."

I waited for him to go on. His beer can was empty, and he was staring at it as though unsure where it came from. He crunched it and tossed it in the trash, his eyes looking emptily into mine.

"What happened to her abuser?" I asked.

"He moved down to Key West. He had a small charter boat business. He used to take people bone fishing out in the flats."

"Where is he?"

"He's still there," Clete said.

I looked at him.

"He's going to be there a long time," Clete said.

I didn't acknowledge the implication. "How can you be sure she's the one who shot Golightly?"

"Candy sent me pictures showing the two of them together only two years ago. Candy is back on the spike and says Gretchen comes and goes and drops out of sight for a year at a time. She doesn't know what Gretchen does for a living."

"You know who killed Bix Golightly. You can't hold back information like that, Clete."

"Nobody at NOPD wants to see me anywhere near a precinct building. When is the last time they helped either one of us in an investigation? You were fired, Dave, just like me. They hate our guts, and you know it."

"Does Gretchen know you're her father?"

"I'm not sure. I saw her for maybe five minutes when she was in juvie."

"Does she know you live in New Orleans?"

"Maybe. I can't remember what I told her when we met. She was fifteen. How many fifteen-year-old girls are thinking about anything an adult says?"

"Who do you think she's working for?"

"Somebody with a lot of money. The word is she gets a minimum of twenty grand a hit. She's a pro and leaves no witnesses and no money trail. She has no bad habits and stays under the radar."

"No witnesses?" I repeated.

"You heard me."

"Did she see you?"

"After she left, she came back and looked at the alleyway where I was standing," he said. "Maybe she thought she saw something. Maybe she was just wondering if she picked up all her brass. She was whistling 'The San Antonio Rose.' I'm not making this up. Stop looking at me like that."

HELEN SOILEAU COULD be a stern administrator. She also had a way of forgetting her own lapses in professional behavior (straying arbitrarily into various romantic relationships, whipping her baton across the mouth of a dope dealer who was chugalugging a bottle of chocolate milk after he insulted her), but no one could say she was unfair or afraid to take responsibility when she was wrong.

On Wednesday morning I had a doctor's appointment and didn't arrive at work until ten A.M. I was going through my mail when Helen buzzed my extension. "I just got off the phone with Tee Jolie Melton's grandfather," she said. "He tried to get ahold of you first, then he called me."

"What's the deal?"

"He says there's a witness to Blue Melton's abduction. He says St. Martin Parish won't do anything about it."

"We're out of our jurisdiction," I said.

"Not anymore. If the witness's account is accurate, we just became players. It's not something I wanted, but that's the way it is, bwana. I suspect you couldn't be happier. Check out a cruiser, and I'll meet you out front."

We drove up the two-lane state road to the home of Avery DeBlanc in St. Martinville, up the bayou from the drawbridge and the old cemetery, one that was filled with white crypts. He was waiting for us in a rocking chair on his gallery, both of his walking canes propped across his thighs. He stood up when we approached him, lifting his crippled back as straight as he could. "T'ank y'all for coming," he said.

I introduced Helen, then helped him sit down. "Can you tell us again what this little boy told you, Mr. DeBlanc?" I said.

"Ain't much to it. The boy lives yonder, down where them pecan trees is at. He said he looked out the window. He said it was night, and a white boat come up the bayou and parked at my li'l dock, and two men got out and went to my house. He said the boat had a fish wit' a long nose painted on the bow. He said the men went into my house and came back out wit' Blue. He said he could see all t'ree of them in the porch light. They had a big green bottle and some tall glasses, and they was all drinking out of the glasses and laughing."

"When did this happen?" Helen interrupted.

"The boy ain't sure. Maybe a mont' ago. Maybe more. He's only eleven. He said Blue was walking wit' the men toward the bayou, and then she wasn't laughing no more. The two men took her by the arms, and she started fighting wit' them. He said they took her down to the dock, and he t'inks one of them hit her. He said he couldn't see good when they was on the dock. The only light come from the nightclub across the bayou. He t'inks the man hit Blue in the face and put her on the boat. He said she cried out once, then didn't make no more sounds."

"The boy didn't try to tell anybody or call 911?"

"He was home alone. That li'l boy don't do nothing wit'out permission," Mr. DeBlanc said.

"Where did the boat go? In which direction?" Helen asked.

"Sout', back toward New Iberia."

"Why is the boy telling you this only now?" I asked.

"He said his momma tole him it ain't his bidness. He said his momma tole him my granddaughters ain't no good. They're on dope and they hang out wit' bad men. But it bothered him real bad 'cause he liked Blue, so he tole me about it."

"And you told this to the deputy sheriff?" I said.

"I went to his office. He wrote it down on his li'l pad. He said he'd check it out. But he ain't come to see me or returned my phone calls, and the boy said ain't nobody talked to him, either."

Helen and I walked down to the dock. The planks were weathered gray, the wood pilings hung with rubber tires. The bayou was high and dark from the rain, the surface wrinkling like old skin each time the wind gusted. I tried to squat down and examine the wood, but a burst of pain, like a nest of tree roots, spread through my chest. For a moment the bayou and the live oaks on the opposite bank and the whitewashed crypts in the cemetery went in and out of focus.

"I got it, Dave," Helen said.

"Give me a minute. I'm fine."

"I know. But easy does it, right?"

"No, I'm going to do it," I said. I eased down on one knee, swallowing my pain, touching the dock with the tips of my fingers. "See? Nothing to it."

"There's no telling how many times it's rained on those planks," she said.

"Yeah, but the kid didn't make up that story."

"Maybe not. Anyway, let's have a talk with the deputy or whoever this guy is who can't get off his ass."

"Look at this." I took my pocketknife from my slacks and opened the blade. The tops of the planks in the dock were washed clean and uniformly gray and free of any residue, but between two planks, I could see several dark streaks, as though someone had spilled ketchup. I cut a splinter loose and wrapped it in my handkerchief.

"You think it's blood?" Helen said.

"We'll see," I replied.

We drove to the St. Martin Parish Sheriff's Annex, next to the white-columned courthouse past which twenty thousand Union troops had marched in pursuit of Colonel Mouton's malnourished Confederate troops in their unending retreat from Shiloh, all the way to the Red River parishes of central Louisiana.

The plainclothes sheriff's deputy was Etienne Pollard. He wore a beige suit and a yellow tie and blue shirt, and he looked tan and angular and in charge of the environment around his desk. By his nameplate was a Disney World souvenir cup full of pens with multicolored feathers. While we explained our reason for being there, he never blinked or seemed disturbed by thoughts of any kind. Finally, he leaned back in his swivel chair and gazed at the traffic passing on the square and the tourists entering the old French church on the bayou. His forehead knitted. "What do you want me to do about it?" he asked.

He used the word "it," not "abduction," not "assault," not "homicide." Blue Melton's fate had become "it."

"We have the impression you haven't interviewed the boy who saw Blue Melton abducted," I replied.

"The old man called y'all?" he said, grinning at one corner of his mouth.

"You mean Mr. DeBlanc?" I said.

"That's what I just said."

"Yes, Mr. DeBlanc did. He's a little frustrated," I said.

Pollard pinched his eyes. "Here's the deal on that. Blue Melton was a runaway. She was suspended from school twice, once for smoking dope in the restroom. She and her sister had a reputation for loose behavior. The old man wants to think otherwise. If it'll make everybody feel better, I'll look into this boy's story about somebody dragging the girl onto a boat."

"You'll *look* into it?" Helen said. "In a homicide investigation, you'll *look* into an eyewitness account of an assault on the victim and her possible abduction?"

"Homicide?" Pollard said.

"What did you think we were talking about?" Helen said.

"What homicide?"

"Blue Melton floated ashore in St. Mary Parish inside a block of ice," Helen said.

"When?"

"Four days ago."

"I've been on vacation. We were in Florida. I just got back Monday," Pollard said.

"Today is Wednesday," Helen said.

Pollard took one of the pens from his souvenir cup and twirled it with his thumb and index finger, studying the colored feathers. His skin was as unlined as wet clay turned on a potter's wheel. The grin returned to the corner of his mouth. I tried to ignore the vacuous glint in his eye.

"We found what appears to be blood on the DeBlanc dock," I said.

Pollard glanced out his office door into the corridor, as though looking for someone hiding just outside the doorway. "She was in a block of ice?" he said. "That's what y'all are saying? In this kind of weather?"

"That's correct," I said.

"You had me going. The sheriff put y'all up to this, didn't he?" he said. He shook his head, an idiot's grin painted on his mouth, waiting for us to acknowledge our charade.

We interviewed the eleven-year-old who had seen Blue Melton forced onto a boat that had an emblem of a fish painted on the bow. He said the fish looked like it was smiling, but he could add little to what he had already told the grandfather. His time reference was not dependable, and it was obvious he was afraid and wanted to tell us whatever he thought would please us. People wonder how justice is so often denied to those who need and deserve it most. It's not a mystery. The reason we watch contrived television dramas about law enforcement is that often the real story is so depressing, nobody would believe it.

WHEN WE GOT back to New Iberia, I went to the office of our local newspaper, *The Daily Iberian*. The previous month the drawbridge at Burke Street had been stuck three nights in a row, jamming up barge and boat traffic north and south of the bridge. Each night a staff photographer had taken many photographs from the bridge, although the paper had run only a few of them. He sat down with me and showed me all his pictures on a computer screen. The photographer was an overweight, good-natured man who wheezed when he bent forward to explain the images. "The moon was up, so I had some nice lighting," he said. "The small boats could get under the bridge without any problem, but some of them got behind the barges and had to wait longer than they planned. You see the boat you're looking for?"

"No, I'm afraid not," I said.

He cleared the screen and brought up another set of photos, then another. "How about these?" he said.

"Behind the tugboat. Can you blow up that image?" I said.

"Sure," he replied. "It's funny you noticed that particular boat. The guy driving it was impatient and got out of line and worked his way past a barge full of shale that had been waiting two hours."

The boat was sleek and white and constructed of fiberglass, with a deep-V hull and a flared bow and outriggers for saltwater trolling. I suspected it was a Chris-Craft, but I couldn't be sure. "Can you sharpen the bow?" I asked.

"Probably not a whole lot, but let's see," the photographer replied.

He was right. The image was partially obscured by another boat, but I could make out the shape of a fish, thick through the middle, cartoonish in its dimensions. It seemed to have a snout. Maybe a marlin or a bottlenose dolphin? The image was like one I had seen somewhere, as though in a dream. I tried to remember, without success.

"You have any other photos?" I asked.

"No, that's it, Dave," the photographer said.

"Did you see a girl on board?"

"I'm sorry, I just wasn't paying that much attention. Maybe there were two guys in the cabin. The only reason I remember them is because they were pretty rude about pushing their way ahead of the other boats."

"Do you remember what they looked like?"

"No, I'm sorry."

"How about the painting of the fish on the bow? You remember any details about it?"

"Yeah, it was like the paintings you see in photographs of World War Two bomber planes, like Bugs Bunny or Yosemite Sam."

I thanked him for his time and went back to my office. It was past noon, and officially I was off the clock. I checked my mail and returned a couple of phone calls and thumbed through my in-basket. For the first time in years, there seemed to be no pressing matters on my desk. So why was I standing in the middle of my office rather than walking out the front door and down the street to my house, where I would fix ham-and-onion sandwiches and eat with Alafair?

There was only one answer to my question: Clete Purcel had told me he'd seen his out-of-wedlock daughter cap Bix Golightly. I wanted to go into Helen Soileau's office and tell her that. Or call Dana Magelli at the NOPD. What was wrong with making a clean breast of it?

Answer: Clete Purcel would be in the cook pot; he had not seen his daughter since she was fifteen, and his identification of her as Golightly's killer was problematic; last, the NOPD and the Orleans Parish district attorney were in the process of investigating and prosecuting New Orleans cops who had shot and killed innocent people during Katrina, in one instance trying to hide their guilt by burning the victim's body. Other than exploiting the opportunity to ruin Clete's career, how much time would the DA be willing to invest in finding the killer of men like Bix Golightly and Waylon Grimes?

My conscience wouldn't let go of me. I went down to Helen's office, perhaps secretly hoping she wouldn't be there and the issue would be set in abeyance and would somehow resolve itself. When she saw me through the glass, she waved me inside. "Did you have any luck at *The Daily Iberian*?"

"I was going to write you a memo in the morning. The photographer has a shot of a white fiberglass boat that has a fish painted on the bow. I suspect the guys on board are the ones who abducted Blue Melton."

"Can you see them in the photo?"

"Not at all."

"You wanted this case, Dave. The boat's presence at the bridge gives us jurisdiction. What are you down about?"

I repeated everything Clete had told me about his daughter, about her status as a killer, about the fact that the woman Bix had called Caruso before he died was, in Clete's opinion, his errant daughter, Gretchen. Helen sat motionlessly in the chair while I spoke, her chest rising and falling, unblinking, her hands resting on her desk blotter. When I finished, there was complete silence in the room. I cleared my throat and waited. No more than ten seconds passed, but each of those seconds was like an hour. Her gaze locked on mine. "I'm not interested in thirdhand information about a street killing in New Orleans," she said. I started to speak, but she cut me off. "Did you hear me?"

"Yes, ma'am."

"My office is not a confessional, and I'm not a personal counselor. Do you copy that?"

"I do."

"You tell Clete Purcel he's not going to drag his problems into my parish."

"Maybe you should do that."

"What if I twist your head off and spit in it instead?"

"I'm going to ask that you not speak to me like that."

She stood up from her desk, her face tight, her breasts as hard-looking as cantaloupes against her shirt. "I was your partner for seven years. Now I'm your supervisor. I'll speak to you in any fashion I think is appropriate. Don't push me too far, Dave."

"I told you the truth. You didn't want to hear it. I'm done."

"I can't begin to tell you how angry you make me," she said.

Maybe I had handled it wrong. Maybe I had been self-serving in dumping my problems of conscience on Helen's rug. Or maybe it was she who was out of line. Regardless, it wasn't the best day of my life.

CLETE PURCEL WAS determined to find the shooter Bix Golightly had called Caruso just before he ate three rounds fired directly into his face. But if Caruso was the pro Clete thought she was, she would avoid the mistakes and geographical settings common to the army of miscreants and dysfunctional individuals who constitute the criminal subculture of the United States. Few perpetrators are arrested during the commission of their crimes. They get pulled over for DWI, an expired license tag, or throwing litter on the street. They get busted in barroom beefs, prostitution stings, or fighting with a minimum-wage employee at a roach motel. Their addictions and compulsions govern their lives and place them in predictable circumstances and situations over and over, because they are incapable of changing who and what they are. Their level of stupidity is a source of humor at every stationhouse in the country. Unfortunately, the pros—high-end safecrackers and jewel thieves and mobbed-up button men and second-story creeps—are usually intelligent, pathological, skilled in what they do, middle class in their tastes, and little different in dress and speech and behavior from the rest of us.

In the 1980s, out by Lake Pontchartrain, Clete Purcel nailed a home invader who had warrants on him in seventeen states and had only one conviction, for check forgery, on his sheet. He had not only escaped from custody three times, he had successfully passed himself off as a minister, a Dallas oil executive, a stockbroker, a self-help author, a psychotherapist, and a gynecologist. When Clete later transported him to Angola, he asked the home invader, who was hooked to the D-ring in the backseat of the cruiser, how he had acquired all his knowledge, since he had no formal education.

The home invader replied, "Easy. I get a public library card in every city I live in. Everything in every book in that building is free. I also read every story and every column in the morning newspaper, from the first page to the last. Pretty good deal for two bits."

"How does that help you?" Clete asked.

"Where you been, man? Most kinds of work are based on appearance, not substance. Stick a bunch of ballpoints in your shirt pocket and carry a clipboard and you can play it till you drop."

Clete believed Caruso was in New Orleans, primarily because Frankie Giacano, the third member of the triad who had tried to scam Clete, was alive. But where would Caruso hole up? Not in the black areas, where there was a high police presence. Nor anyplace where there were hookers or dealers working the corners. No, she'd be in a guesthouse uptown, or in a white working-class neighborhood, or maybe around Tulane and Loyola, where a lot of college kids lived and hung out. Or she might be strolling the streets of the French Quarter in the morning, when the revelers had been replaced by family people who gazed through the windows of the antique stores on Royal or visited St. Louis Cathedral in Jackson Square or enjoyed coffee and hot milk and beignets under the pavilion at Café du Monde.

So far the only person who had shown any knowledge about Caruso was Count Carbona, aka Baron Belladonna, who had freeze-dried his head with Owsley purple at the Stones concert in Altamont, where the decade of the flower children ended and the music flew away in a helicopter, leaving a dead man on the stage and outlaw bikers beating concertgoers with pool cues.

Clete left his Caddy parked inside the courtyard at his office and walked to the store operated by the Count and Jimmy the Dime. As soon as he entered the store and the tiny bell over the door rang,

Clete realized some sea change had taken place in his relationship with Jimmy and the Count. "What's the haps?" he said.

"What it is, Purcel?" Jimmy replied, not looking up from his cash register.

"I've got a couple of tickets to WrestleMania at the arena for the Count, because I know he digs it," Clete said. "I caught these same guys in Lafayette once. A South American dwarf shot Mr. Moto in the crotch with a blowgun."

The Count was busying himself in the back of the store, whipping a feather duster across a row of capped jars filled with mushrooms and herbs and pickled amphibians. "I'm looking for a hitter named Caruso," Clete said. "I think maybe the Count can be of great help to me."

"Stow it, Purcel," Jimmy said.

"This one is personal. Don't you guys stonewall me on this."

"I got news for you. Everything is personal. Like us getting mixed up in a homicide is personal," Jimmy said. "Like another nickel in Angola is personal."

"Did I get Nig and Wee Willie off your case when you couldn't pay the vig on your bond?" Clete said.

"I burned a candle for you at the cathedral," Jimmy replied. "I paid for the candle, too."

"I'm about to arrange your funeral service there unless you stop cracking wise," Clete said.

"She came in here yesterday," Jimmy said.

"How did you know it was her?"

"The Count's seen her. But where, I don't know, and he ain't saying."

"What'd she want?"

"A book on Marie Laveau. Then she saw my cash register and wanted to buy it. She said she has an antique store in the Keys."

"How about it, Count? Is that straight?" Clete said.

The Count was not answering questions.

"I'm jammed up on this one, you guys. I really need y'all's help," Clete said.

Neither man answered. "I'm going to tell y'all something I haven't told anybody but Dave Robicheaux. I think Caruso is my daughter.

She's had a lousy life and, in my opinion, deserves a better shake than the one she's had."

His entreaty was to no avail. He removed two admission tickets to the New Orleans Arena from his wallet and placed them by the cash register. "You might really dig this, Count," he said. "I once saw the Blimp. He had a curtain of fat hanging down to his knees so he looked like six hundred pounds of nakedness when he climbed into the ring. Plus he had BO you could smell ten rows into the seats. He'd get his opponent in a bear hug and fall on him and smother him in sweat and blubber and GAPO from hell until the guy was screaming for the ref. Nobody can equal the Blimp in terms of gross-out potential, but see what you think."

"What's GAPO?" Jimmy said.

"Gorilla armpit odor," Clete replied.

He went back outside and lit a cigarette by a parking meter and tried to think. A man in a split-tail coat and tattered top hat rode by on a unicycle. A man in a strap undershirt was watering his plants with a hose on a balcony across the street, an iridescent mist blowing from the palm and banana fronds into the sunlight. On the corner, under the colonnade, a lone black kid with iron shoe taps was dancing on the sidewalk, a portable stereo blaring out "When the Saints Go Marching In."

Wrong time of day, wrong place, wrong tune, wrong century, kid, Clete thought, then tried to remember when he had been this depressed. He couldn't.

He felt someone touch him on the shoulder. He turned and looked into the hawklike glare that constituted Count Carbona's gaze. "Good earth," the Count said.

"What are you saying?"

"You know."

"No, I don't. Are you talking about the name of a book?"

The Count continued to stare into Clete's face. "I'm no code breaker, Count," Clete said.

The Count pressed a book of paper matches into Clete's palm. The cover had a satin-black finish with words embossed in silver letters.

"This joint is in Terrebonne Parish?" Clete said. "That's what you're telling me? Caruso left this in your store?"

The Count's cheeks creased with the beginnings of a smile.

CLETE WAITED IN his office until sunset, then drove deep into Terrebonne Parish, south of Larose, almost to Lake Felicity, down where the wetlands of Louisiana dissolve into a dim gray-green line that becomes the Gulf of Mexico. The sun was an orange melt in the west, veiled with smoke from a sugar refinery or a grass fire, the moss in the dead cypress trees lifting in the breeze. The nightclub and barbecue joint advertised on the book of matches was located in a clearing at the end of a dirt road, right at the edge of a saltwater bay, the trees strung with multicolored Japanese lanterns. Clete thought he could hear the sounds of an accordion and fiddle and rub-board drifting out of a screened pavilion behind the nightclub.

He had put on his powder-blue sport coat and gray slacks and had shined his oxblood loafers and bought a new fedora with a small feather in the band. Before he got out of the Caddy, he gargled with a small amount of Listerine and spat it out the window. He also took off his shoulder holster and put it under the seat, along with his heavy spring-loaded leather-wrapped blackjack shaped like a darning sock. When he entered the nightclub, the refrigeration was set so low, the air felt like ice water.

He sat at the bar and laid out his cigarettes and his Zippo lighter in front of him and ordered a Bud and gazed out the back window at the last spark of sun on the bay and at the band inside the screened pavilion. He salted his beer and drank it slowly, enjoying each moment of it in his mouth, letting its coldness slide down his throat, lighting places inside him that only the addicted know about. He didn't have long to wait before he knew she was in the room. How or why he knew she was there, he couldn't explain. He felt her presence before he saw her in the bar mirror. He smelled her perfume before he turned on the stool and watched her drop a series of coins in the jukebox. He saw her midriff and exposed navel and the baby fat on her hips and resented its exposure to other men in a way that was completely irrational. He looked at the fullness of her breasts and the tightness of her jeans and the thickness of her reddish-blond Dutch-boy haircut and felt protectiveness rather than erotic attraction. He felt as though someone else had slipped into his skin and was thinking thoughts that were not his.

He ordered another Bud longneck and two fingers of Jack. The girl sat down at the bar, three stools from him, and idly tapped a quarter on the bar's apron, as though she had not made up her mind. Clete looked at the mirror and tossed back his Jack, a great emptiness if not a balloon of fear swelling in his chest. The Jack went down like gasoline on a flame. He began opening and closing his Zippo, his heart racing, an unlit cigarette between his fingers.

She tilted her head forward and massaged the back of her neck, her fingers kneading deep into the muscle. Then she turned and gazed at the side of his face. "You eyeballing me in the mirror, boss?" she said.

"Me?" he said. When she didn't reply, he asked, "You talking to me?"

"Is someone else sitting on your stool?"

"You had some tats removed from your arms, maybe. I guess I noticed that. I know what that can be like."

"I never had tats. Would you put a needle in your arm that an AIDS patient has used?"

"So where'd you get the scars?"

"I was in an accident. My mother's diaphragm slipped, and I was born. Is that your come-on line?"

"I'm over the hill for come-on lines. On a quiet day, I can hear my liver rotting. For exercise, I fall down."

"I get what you're saying: Old guys are rarely interested in getting in a girl's pants. That would be strange, wouldn't it?"

"Where'd you learn to talk like that?"

"At the convent." The bartender brought her a drink in an oversize glass without her having ordered one. She used both hands to pick it up and drink. She took a cherry out of it and broke it between her teeth.

"Why not order your next one in a bathtub and put a straw in it?" Clete said.

"Not a bad idea," she said. Her cheeks had taken on a deeper color, and her mouth was glossy and red with lipstick. "I've seen you around."

"I doubt it. I'm a traveling man, mostly."

"You're a salesman?"

"Something like that."

"You're a cop."

"I used to be. But not anymore."

"What happened?"

"I had an accident, too. I popped a government witness."

"'Popped,' like made him dead?"

"Actually, getting snuffed was the noblest deed in his career. The DA's office here made a lot of noise about it, but the truth is, nobody cared."

She picked a second cherry out of her drink by its stem and sucked on it. "Maybe I shouldn't be talking to you."

"Suit yourself."

"Are you from New Orleans?"

"Sure."

"Say 'New Orleans.' Say it like you regularly say it."

"'Neu Or Luns.'"

"It's not 'Nawlens'?"

"Nobody from New Orleans uses that pronunciation. TV news-people do it because it gives the impression they know the city."

She turned her stool toward him, her thighs slightly spread, her eyes roving over his face and body. She pursed her lips. "What are you looking for, hon? An easy lay out here in the swamps? I don't like people who make comments about the scars on my arms. None of my scars look like they came from tattoo removal."

"I was just making conversation."

"If that's your best effort, it's a real dud."

"I think you're beautiful. I wouldn't say something to offend you."

He hadn't meant to say that. Nor did he know why he had. His face was burning. "Sometimes I say things the wrong way. I bet you like baseball and outdoor dance pavilions and barbecues and stuff like that. I bet you're a nice girl."

"You go around saying things like that to people you don't know?"

"You look like an all-American girl, that's all."

"If you're determined to pick up girls in bars, this is what I suggest: Call Weight Watchers, don't let your swizzle stick do your talking for you, and change your deodorant. You'll get a lot better results."

Clete poured his glass full but didn't drink. He felt a sensation similar to a great spiritual and physical weariness seeping through his body.

"I was kidding. Brighten up," she said. "Your problem is you're a bad actor."

"I'm not following you on that."

"I've seen you before." She fixed her eyes on his and held them there until he felt his scalp tighten. "Are you an Orioles fan?"

"Yeah, I like them. I go to baseball games everywhere I travel."

"You ever go to exhibition games in Fort Lauderdale?" she asked.

"They call it Little Yankee Stadium, because the Yankees trained there before the Orioles."

"That's where I bet I saw you," she said. She moved a strand of hair off her cheek. "Or maybe I saw you somewhere else. It'll come to me. I don't forget very much."

"Yeah, you look smart, the way you carry yourself and all."

"Jesus Christ, you're a mess," she said.

"What do you mean?"

"You want to dance?"

"I'm clumsy when it comes to stuff like that. What do you mean, I'm a mess?"

"You're too innocent for words."

She went to the jukebox and began feeding coins into it. In spite of the air-conditioning, he was sweating inside his clothes, blood pounding in his temples. He walked out onto the dance floor and stood inches behind her. He could smell the heat in her skin and the perfume in her hair. She turned around and looked up into his face, her eyes violet-colored in the light. "Something wrong?" she asked.

"I got to go," he said.

"Buy me a drink?"

"No, I got to take care of some stuff. I'm sorry. It's been good meeting you," he said.

"You better get yourself some high-octane tranqs, boss," she said.

"I really like you. I'm sorry for the way I talk," he said.

His hands were shaking when he got to his car.

CLETE THOUGHT THE drive back into the city would calm his heart and give him time to think in a rational manner, but he was wired to the eyes when he pulled into the driveway of the garage apartment down by Chalmette that Frankie Giacano was using as a hideout. He didn't even slow down going up the stairs. He tore the screen door off the latch and splintered the hard door out of the jamb. Frankie was sitting stupefied in a stuffed chair, a sandwich in his hand, food hanging out of his mouth. "Are you out of your mind?" he said.

"Probably," Clete said.

"What are you gonna do with that blackjack?" Frankie said, rising to his feet.

"It's part of my anger-management program. I hit things instead of people. When that doesn't work, I start hitting people," Clete said. "Let's see how it goes."

He smashed a lamp in half and the glass out of a picture frame on the wall and the glass in a window overlooking the side yard. He went into the kitchen and turned the drying rack upside down and broke the dishes across the edge of the counter and began feeding a box of sterling silverware into the garbage grinder.

With the grinder still roaring and clanking, he grabbed Frankie by the necktie and dragged him to the sink. "One of your skanks told me your nose is too long," he said. "Let's see if we can bob off an inch or two."

"Who pissed in your brain, man?"

"When'd you peel Didi Gee's safe?"

"I don't know. Maybe a couple of months ago."

"Where?"

"In Didi Gee's old office."

"Who hired the shooter to cap Golightly and Grimes?"

"How would I know?"

"You're lying."

"Yeah, but let me finish."

"You think that's cute?" Clete swung Frankie in a circle by his tie and threw him over a chair and against the wall, then whipped the blackjack across the tendon behind one knee. Frankie fell to the floor as though genuflecting, his eyes watering, his bottom lip trembling. "Don't do this to me, man," he said.

"Get up!"

"What for?"

"So I don't start stomping you into marmalade."

When Frankie didn't move, Clete pulled him erect by his shirtfront and swung him into the bedroom, knocking his head against the doorjamb and a bedpost. "Pack your suitcase," he said. "You're taking the first bus to either Los Angeles or New York, you choose."

"Why are you doing this?"

"What do you care? You get to live."

"I don't get it."

"Because you're stupid."

"You're trying to save my life? You beat me up so you can save my life?"

"Yeah, the world can't afford to lose a person of your brilliance. You've got three minutes."

Frankie lifted a suitcase from a shelf in the closet and opened it on the bed and began pulling clothes off the hangers and laying them inside the case. "I got a piece in my sock drawer. I'm gonna take it with me."

"No, you're not," Clete said. He moved between the dresser and Frankie and opened the top dresser drawer and reached inside and lifted out a black semi-automatic pistol. "Where you'd get a German Luger?"

"At a gun show."

"You're not a collector, and guys like you don't buy registered firearms."

"It was a gift. A guy owed me. So I took it. It's mine. You don't have any right to it. Look at the Nazi stamps on it. It was used by the German navy. It's worth at least two thousand bucks."

"When you get situated in your new rathole, drop me a card and I'll mail it to you."

Frankie looked emptily into space, like a child whose alternatives had run out. "You're really taking me to the bus station? 'Cause I heard a story about a guy you took out by the lake, a guy nobody saw again."

"I'm doing you a favor, Frankie. Don't blow it." Clete dropped the Luger's magazine from the frame and pulled back the slide to clear the chamber. He stuck the Luger in his belt. "Time to catch the Dog."

"How about the airport?"

"The person who put the hit on you has probably broken into your credit cards. So I'm paying for your ticket out of my own pocket. That means you're riding the Dog."

"Bix had a new scam going. It was bringing in a lot of cash. But I don't know what it was. I'm being honest here."

"The day you're honest is the day the plaster will fall from the ceiling of the Sistine Chapel," Clete said.

"Why you got to run me down, man?"

Clete thought about it. "You've got a point," he replied. "Come on, Frankie. Let's see if we can't get you on an express to L.A. You might even dig it out there. Here, wipe your nose."

CHAPTER
8

Have you ever been told, either by friends or by a therapist, that you're obsessive? If the answer is yes, I suspect that you, like most people of goodwill, had to accept one of two alternatives. You humbled yourself and ate your feelings and tried to change your emotional outlook, or you realized with a sinking of the heart that you were on your own and the problem you saw was not imaginary and others did not want to hear or talk about it or be reminded of it in any fashion, even though the house was burning down.

My obsession was Tee Jolie Melton. I could no longer be sure she had visited me in the recovery unit on St. Charles Avenue in New Orleans, but I had no doubt her message to me was real, transmitted perhaps in ways that are not quite definable. Many years back I gave up all claim to a rational view of the world and even avoided people who believed that the laws of physics and causality have any application when it comes to understanding the mysteries of creation or the fact that light can enter the eye and form an image in the brain and send a poetic tendril down the arm into a clutch of fingers that could write the Shakespearean sonnets.

There were only three leads in the disappearance of Tee Jolie, and all were tenuous: I had seen a group photo in her scrapbook taken at a zydeco club, with Bix Golightly in the background; at the recovery unit, she had indicated she feared for her life because of knowledge she had about the oil-well blowout in the Gulf; the boat that abducted her sister may have been a Chris-Craft, with a thick-bodied fish painted on the bow.

I had left out one other element in the story: She was unmarried and pregnant, and the undivorced father of her child had asked if she wanted an abortion.

Where do you start?

Answer: Forget morality tales and all the fury and mire of human complexity, and follow the money. It will lead you through urban legends about sex and revenge and jealousy and the acquisition of power over others, but ultimately, it will lead you to the issue from which all the other motivations derive—money, piles of it, green and lovely and cascading like leaves out of a beneficent sky, money and money and money, the one item that human beings will go to any lengths to acquire. Let's face it, it's hard to sell the virtues of poverty to people who have nothing to eat. In Louisiana, which has the highest rate of illiteracy in the union and the highest percentage of children born to single mothers, few people worry about the downside of casinos, drive-through daiquiri windows, tobacco depots, and environmental degradation washing away the southern rim of the state.

Oil and natural gas, for good or bad, comprise our lifeblood. When I was a boy, my home state, in terms of its environment, was an Edenic paradise. It's not one any longer, no matter what you are told. When a group of lawyers at Tulane University tried to file a class action suit on behalf of the black residents whose rural slums were used as dumping grounds for petrochemical waste, the governor, on television, threatened to have the lawyers' tax status investigated. The same governor was an advocate for the construction of a giant industrial waste incinerator in Morgan City. His approval ratings remained at record highs for the entirety of his administration.

In Louisiana, refined or extracted oil is everywhere, sometimes in barrels buried in the 1920s. Working-class people display bumper stickers that read GLOBAL WARMING IS BULLSHIT. Former vice president Al Gore is mocked and denigrated with regularity for his warnings about arctic melt.

Last spring, when the wind was out of the south, I could stand in our front yard and smell oil. It was not buried in the ground, either. It was pouring in thick columns, like curds of smoke, from a blown casing five thousand feet below the Gulf's surface.

This particular blowout has been referred to again and again as a "spill." A spill has nothing to do with the events that occurred southeast of my home parish. A spill implies an accident involving a limited amount of oil, one that will seep from a tanker until the leak is repaired or the ship's hold is drained. The oil leaking from the tanker is not pressurized or on fire and incinerating men on the floor of a drilling rig.

Even when a well is completed under normal circumstances, there is a cautionary tale buried inside the sense of accomplishment and prosperity that everyone on the rig seems to experience. At first you smell the raw odor of natural gas, like the stench of rotten eggs, then the steel in the rig seems to stiffen, as though its molecular texture is transforming itself into something alive; even in hundred-degree heat, the great pipes running out of the hole start to sweat with drops of moisture that are as cold and bright as silver dollars. The entire structure seems to hum with the power and intensity of forces whose magnitude we can only guess at. The driller touches a flaming board to a flare line to burn off excess gas, and a ball of fire rises into the blackness and snaps apart in the clouds and makes us wonder if our pride in technological success isn't a dangerous presumption.

When a drill bit hits what is called an early pay sand, punching into an oil or natural gas dome unexpectedly, with no blowout preventer in place, the consequences are immediate. An unlimited amount of fossil decay and oceanic levels of natural gas that are hundreds of millions of years old are released in seconds through one aperture, blowing pipe, drilling mud, salt water, and geysers of sand up through the rig floor, creating havoc among the men working there and a cacophony of sound similar to a junkyard falling piece by piece out of the sky. The first spark off the wellhead ignites the gas. The explosion of flame is so intense in velocity and temperature that it will melt the spars of a rig and turn steel cable into bits of flaming string. In minutes the rig can take on the appearance of a model constructed from burned matchsticks.

My father, Big Aldous, was a fur trapper on Marsh Island and a commercial fisherman who, in the off-season, worked the monkey board high up on a rig in the Gulf of Mexico. He was illiterate and irresponsible and spoke English poorly and had never traveled farther from home than New Orleans. He also had no understanding of how or why the Cajun world of his birth was coming to an end. My mother's infidelities filled him with shame and anger and bewilderment, just as she in turn could not understand his alcoholism and barroom violence and apparent determination to gamble away their meager income at bourré tables and racetracks.

Big Al died in a blowout while I was in Vietnam. His body was never recovered, and I spent a great deal of time wondering whether he suffered greatly before his death. Sometimes I dreamed I saw him standing knee-high in the surf, giving me the thumbs-up sign, his hard hat tilted on his head, the swells around him denting with rain. I didn't know what kind of death he died, but I knew one thing for sure about my old man: He was never afraid. And I knew in my heart, when the pipe came out of the hole on that windswept night decades ago, Big Al clipped his safety belt onto the Geronimo line and jumped into the black with the courage of a paratrooper going out the door of a plane, and I also knew that as he plummeted toward the water with the tower coming down on top of him, his last thoughts were of me and my half brother, Jimmy, and my mother, Alafair Mae Guillory. He died so we could have a better life. And that's what I will always believe.

It seems to me a "spill" is hardly an adequate term to describe the fate of men who die inside a man-made inferno.

MY INTROSPECTION WASN'T taking me any closer to solving the disappearance of Tee Jolie and the abduction and murder of her sister, Blue. When I came home from work on Thursday, Alafair was reading a glossy magazine at the kitchen table, both Snuggs and Tripod sitting in the open window behind her. Tripod was wearing a diaper. "What's up, Alfenheimer?" I said.

"Dave, can you get rid of the stupid names?" she said without looking up from her magazine.

"I will. Someday. Probably. What are you reading?"

"There's a showing of Pierre Dupree's work in Burke Hall at UL. You want to drive over?"

"Not really."

"What do you have against him?"

"Nothing. He's just one of those guys who seems to have someone else living inside him, someone he wants none of us to meet."

"His paintings aren't bad. Look," she said, handing me the magazine.

I glanced indifferently at the images on one page and started to return the magazine to her. Had I followed through, perhaps none of the events that would happen in the next days and weeks and months would have occurred, and maybe we all would have been the better for it. I'll never know. I stared at the photograph of a painting on the second page of the article. In it a nude woman was reclining on a reddish-brown sofa, a white towel draped across her vagina. She wore a mysterious smile, and her hair was tied behind her head and touched with tiny pools of yellow, like buttercups. Her neck was swanlike, her eyes elongated, her nipples as dark as chocolate; because of her position, her breasts had flattened against her chest, and her body seemed to possess the warm softness of browned bread dough.

"Dave, your face is white," Alafair said.

"Take a look at the woman on the sofa," I said, handing back the magazine.

"What about her?"

"It's Tee Jolie Melton."

She shook her head and started to speak, then stopped. She rubbed the ball of one finger on her brow, as though a mosquito had bitten it, as though somehow our conversation could be diverted from the direction it was about to take. "The figure looks like one of Gauguin's Tahitian natives," she said. "The portrayal is almost generic. Don't make it into something it's not."

"I think you're wrong."

"I know Tee Jolie. That's not her."

"How do you know that?" I said.

"I can't prove it isn't, but something else is going on in our lives that you won't acknowledge."

"Would you like to tell me what?"

"You're imagining things about Tee Jolie Melton. Molly knows it and so do I and so does Clete."

"Why would I imagine things about Tee Jolie?"

"To you, she represents lost innocence. She's the Cajun girl of your youth."

"That seems frank enough."

"You asked me."

"You're mistaken."

"You hear songs on an iPod that no one else can hear."

"I'm going to fix a ham-and-onion sandwich. Do you want one?"

"I already made some. They're in the refrigerator. I made some deviled eggs, too."

"I appreciate it."

"Are you mad?"

"I've never been angry at you, Alf. Not once in your whole life. Is that a fair statement?"

"I didn't mean to hurt you."

"You didn't."

"You want to talk to Pierre Dupree?" she said.

"If I can find him."

"I saw him this morning. He's at his home in Jeanerette. I'll go with you."

"You don't need to do that."

"I think I do," she replied.

"You don't like him, do you?"

"No, I guess I don't."

"Why not?"

"That's what bothers me about him. I don't know why I don't like him," she replied.

THE HOME OF Pierre Dupree outside Jeanerette had been built on the bayou in 1850 by slave labor and named Croix du Sud Plantation by the original owners. Union forces had ransacked it and chopped up the piano in the chicken yard and started cook fires on the hardwood floors, blackening the ceilings and the walls. During Reconstruction, a carpetbagger bought it at a tax sale and later rented it to a man who was called a free person of color before the Emancipation. By the 1890s, Reconstruction and the registration of black voters had been nullified, and power shifted back into the hands of the same oligarchy that had ruled the state before the Civil War. Slavery was replaced by the rental convict system, one established by a man named Samuel James, who turned Angola Plantation—named for the origins of its workforce—into Angola Penitentiary, which became five thousand acres of living hell on the banks of the Mississippi River.

The home of Pierre Dupree was reacquired by the same family who had built it. Unfortunately for the family, one of the descendants was insane and sealed herself inside the home while the grounds turned into a jungle and Formosan termites reduced the walls and support beams to balsa wood.

Then the house was purchased by the Dupree family, who not only restored it and rebuilt the foundation and cleaned up the grounds and terraced the slope but turned the entire environment into artwork, even reconstructing the slave quarters, relying solely on antique wood and brick from historical teardowns, going all the way to France to buy eighteenth-century square nails. I had called ahead and had been surprised by Pierre Dupree's generosity of spirit when I asked if Alafair and I could visit him at his home that afternoon. "I'd be delighted, Mr. Robicheaux," he had said. "I'm due at my exhibition at UL this evening, but I'd love to have y'all for an early supper. Something simple out on the terrace. I'll tell cook to put something together. I'm sure y'all will enjoy it. We'll see you then."

He hung up before I could reply.

He was waiting for us on the front porch when we turned off the old two-lane road into his drive. His lawns and gardens were already in shadow, the camellias blooming, the sunlight dancing on the tops of oak trees that were easily two hundred years old. He was dressed in a dark suit with a vest and a luminescent pink tie and a watery blue shirt with a diamond design stamped into the fabric.

He opened the car door for Alafair and in all ways was everything a gentleman should be. But something continued to bother me about him besides the physicality that emanated from his tailored clothes; I just couldn't put my finger on it. "Would you like the grand tour?" he asked.

"We don't want to take up too much of your time," I said. "I just wanted to ask a question or two of you."

"Did you know that ghosts live here? Five rebellious slaves and a white instigator were hanged right on that tree by the side of the house. Sometimes people see them in the mist."

I knew the story well. But the event had taken place outside St. Martinville, not Jeanerette. I wondered why he had appropriated the story, because the details of the execution and the level of inhumanity it involved were sickening.

He looked at me, then at Alafair, and seemed to realize we were not entertained. "I already have food on the terrace. Cook has created a new recipe, shrimp deep-fried in a mushroom batter. Have you ever tried it?"

"No, I haven't," I replied.

"I think you might find yourself addicted," he said.

He was smiling, but I wasn't sure at what. Had he chosen the word "addicted" deliberately? I heard a sound above me and looked upward into the glaze of sunlight on the tree branches and saw Alexis Dupree peering down at us from the second-story veranda.

"My grandfather told me about your visit to our office in New Orleans," Pierre Dupree said. "Don't worry about it, Mr. Robicheaux. *Gran'père* gets things confused sometimes. Rather than admit it, he becomes defensive. Please, let's sit down."

I did not want to sit down, and I was becoming less and less inclined to be polite. Alafair intervened. "I'd love some shrimp, Pierre," she said.

I gave her a look, but she refused to acknowledge it. So the three of us sat down at his table on the terrace in the cooling of the day and the glimmer of the late sun on Bayou Teche. The four-o'clocks were opening in the shade, and I could smell the horse stables and see the wind blowing plumes of cinnamon-colored dust out of the cane fields. In the middle of our table was a silver tray set with a decanter of brandy and several crystal glasses. Close by the French doors was an artist's easel with a partially completed painting propped on it. I asked permission to look at it.

"Why, certainly," Dupree said.

On the canvas was a peculiar scene, one that seemed to draw its meaning from outside itself: a weathered wood home with cornices and gables, a vegetable garden by a stream, oak trees pooled with shadow, a Victrola in the yard, a guitar leaning against the steps that led up to the gallery. There were no people or animals in the painting.

I sat back down. Alafair had accused me earlier of obsession. I wondered if she was right.

"Does something bother you about my painting?" Dupree said, his eyes bursting with so much goodwill that they were impenetrable.

"Yes, it does bother me," I replied. Before I could continue, my cell phone chimed. I started to silence it, then saw who the call was from. "I'm sorry, I have to take this call."

I got up from the table and walked through the trees and down the slope toward the bayou. "Where are you?" Helen asked.

"At Pierre Dupree's home in Jeanerette."

"Is Clete Purcel with you?"

"No, I haven't seen him."

"Dana Magelli just called from NOPD. Frankie Giacano got popped last night in the men's room of the Baton Rouge bus depot. Three rounds in the head inside a toilet stall. Giacano's neighbors say he left his garage apartment with a man in an antique Cadillac convertible. The ticket seller at the New Orleans depot identified Giacano's photo and said a man fitting Clete's description bought a ticket for him to Los Angeles."

"Did Clete get on the bus with him?"

"No, he just paid for the ticket."

"So why should Clete be a suspect for a homicide committed in Baton Rouge?"

"Ask Dana Magelli. Listen, Dave, if you see Clete Purcel, you tell him to get his big fat ass into my office."

"Copy that," I said.

"Don't be clever. I'm really pissed off."

"About what?"

"What are you doing at the Dupree house?"

"I'm not sure."

She made a sound that wasn't quite a word and hung up. When I got back to the table, Alafair and Pierre Dupree were eating jumbo shrimp that had been fried in a thick golden batter. "Dig in, Mr. Robicheaux," he said. "What were you about to say about my painting?"

"It reminds me of a song by Taj Mahal. It's called 'My Creole Belle.' Mississippi John Hurt wrote it, but Taj sings it. There's mention of a house in the country and a garden out back and blues on a Victrola."

"Really?" he said.

Out of the corner of my eye, I saw Alafair watching me.

"A Cajun singer named Tee Jolie Melton gave me a recording of it when I was in a hospital in New Orleans."

He nodded pleasantly, his gaze as radiant as the sunlight filtering through the trees. Then I realized what it was that had bothered me most about him. His eyes performed a constant deceit. I believed he could look endlessly into the face of another human being with a lidless, almost ethereal curiosity, giving no hint about his inner thoughts while he simultaneously dissected the other party's soul.

"Today I saw a photo of one of your paintings at the UL exhibition. The nude woman on the sofa is Tee Jolie, isn't she?"

"I'm afraid I don't know this person," he said, biting into a shrimp and chewing, leaning over his plate, his gaze never leaving mine.

"Her sister was the girl who floated up on a sand spit in a block of ice south of here."

He wiped his mouth with a napkin. "Yes, I heard about that. How does someone end up in a block of ice in the Gulf of Mexico?"

"That beats all, doesn't it?" I said. "Tee Jolie used to sing in a couple of clubs by Bayou Bijoux. You ever go to clubs on Bayou Bijoux?"

"I haven't had the pleasure," he replied.

"Boy, that's a lot for coincidence, isn't it?" I said.

"What is?"

"You paint a woman who looks like Tee Jolie. You paint a scene that seems to derive from a song she gave me on an iPod. But you've never heard of her. The phone call I just received was in regard to Frankie Giacano. You bought your office building from his uncle Didi Gee. Somebody splattered Frankie's grits in a toilet stall at the Baton Rouge bus station last night."

Dupree set his shrimp back on his plate. He seemed to gather his thoughts. "I don't understand your level of aggression, Mr. Robicheaux. No, that's not quite honest. Let me offer a speculation. The whole time we've been talking, your eye has kept drifting to the decanter. If you'd like some brandy, you can pour yourself one. I won't. No offense; your history is well known. I admire the fact that you've rebuilt your life and career, but I don't like the implications you've made here."

"Dave's questions were put to you in an honest fashion. Why don't you answer them?" Alafair said.

"I thought I did," Dupree said.

"Why not just say where you got the concept for your still life if it wasn't from a song? Why should that be a problem?" Alafair said.

"I didn't know you were an art critic," he said.

Just then Alexis Dupree opened the French doors and came out on the terrace. His mouth was downturned at the corners, his long-sleeve gray shirt buttoned at the wrists and throat, even though the afternoon was warm. His posture was an incongruous mix of stiffness and fragility, the parallel scars on one cheek like half of a cat's whiskers. "Why are you here?" he said.

"A mistake in judgment," I said.

"Who is *she*?" the grandfather said to Pierre, his eyes narrowing in either curiosity or suspicion.

"That's my daughter, sir. Show her some respect," I said.

Alexis Dupree raised his finger. "You'll not correct me in my home."

"Let's go, Alfenheimer," I said.

"What was that? You said Waffen?"

"No, *Gran'père*. He was calling his daughter a pet name. It's all right," Pierre said.

Alafair and I got up from the table and began walking toward her car. Behind us, I heard footsteps in the leaves. "I can't believe you have the nerve to speak to a Holocaust survivor like that. My grandfather was in an extermination camp. His brother and sister and his parents were killed there. He survived only because he was chosen for medical experiments. Or did you not know any of that?" Dupree said.

"Your grandfather's age or background doesn't excuse his rudeness," I said. "I don't think he's an impaired man, either. In my opinion, the suffering of other people is a sorry flag to operate under."

"You may not drink anymore, but you're still a drunkard, Mr. Robicheaux, and white trash as well. Take yourself and Miss Alafair off our property. I think only a special kind of fool—I'm talking about myself—could have invited you here."

"What did you just call me?" I said.

"What I called you has nothing to do with your birth. The term 'white trash' references a state of mind," he replied. "You hate people who succeed or who have money and who force you to admit you're a failure. I don't think that's a difficult concept to understand."

"Open your mouth like that again, and you're going to have the worst experience in your life," Alafair said.

"I'd listen. She has a black belt. She'll take your head off," I said.

Pierre Dupree turned his back on us and returned to the terrace and went into the house with his grandfather, as though they were leaving behind an odious presence that, through chance or accident, had drifted across the moat and gotten inside the castle walls.

As we drove away, I tried to figure out what had happened. Had I reached a point in life when insults no longer bothered me? Years ago, my response to Pierre Dupree would have been quite different, yet I thought it would have been preferable to the passivity I had shown. "I won't call you those stupid names anymore, Alafair, particularly around other people," I said.

"What was the word that set off the grandfather?"

"He thought I said Waffen. The Waffen SS were elite Nazi troops. They were known for their fanaticism and lack of mercy. They executed British and American prisoners and worked in some of the death camps. GIs usually shot them whenever they got their hands on them."

"You think we leaned on them too hard back there?" she said. "The old man's family was sent to an oven."

"Pierre Dupree not only enjoyed telling me a story about the hanging of black men and a white abolitionist on his property, he lied in order to tell the story. Then he used his grandfather's ordeal to instill feelings of guilt in others. Don't fall for this guy's rebop."

We passed a sugarcane field whose stalks were thrashing in the wind, the dust rising out of the rows, a tractor and cane wagon emerging suddenly onto the highway in front of us. Alafair swerved right, blowing her horn, scouring gravel out of the road shoulder. She looked in the rearview mirror, her nostrils dilating, her eyes wide. "Jesus," she said. "I was talking and didn't see that guy coming."

We seldom do, I thought. But who wants to be a prophet in his own country?

CHAPTER
9

CLETE SAT IN a metal chair inside the interview room, forty feet from the holding cell where he had spent the last three hours. Dana Magelli was not in a good mood. He was standing across the table from Clete, his right hand on his hip, his coat pushed back. His breath was audible, his groomed appearance and normal composure at odds with the anger he was obviously experiencing. "We have your prints inside the homes of two homicide victims," he said. "We have witnesses that put you with Frankie Giacano right before his murder. We have a tape you made of a conversation between you and Bix Golightly hours before he was shot in his vehicle in Algiers."

"Yeah, and you searched my apartment and my office without a warrant," Clete said.

"Do you deny driving Frankie Gee to the bus depot and buying him a ticket?"

"Getting a safecracker out of New Orleans is a crime?"

"You paid cash for his ticket to L.A. When did you start doing financial favors for sociopaths?"

"I saw Frankie give a quarter to a homeless guy once. So I figured he couldn't be all bad. Of course, he threw the quarter into the homeless guy's eye and blinded him."

"There are people I work with who want to see you hung by your colon from an iron hook."

"That's their problem. By the way, do you know Didi Gee actually did that to a guy?"

"I know you didn't follow the bus to Baton Rouge so you could shoot Frankie in a toilet stall. But some of my colleagues think you're irrational enough to do anything. When I leave this room, I have to convince these same people you're the wrong guy. Why did you buy Frankie his ticket out of town?"

"Bix Golightly and Waylon Grimes are both dead because they tried to run a scam on me. Frankie was their partner. I figured he was next. Enough is enough. Frankie was a shitbag, but he didn't deserve getting his brains blown all over a toilet bowl."

"You were protecting Frankie out of the goodness of your heart?"

"Characterize it any way you want, Dana."

"Who do you think killed Grimes and Golightly?"

"I chase bail skips and take pictures of husbands porking the maid."

"I'm going to square with you. The only thing preventing the prosecutor's office from charging you with murder is the fact that somebody much smaller than you and wearing western clothes was seen leaving the men's room right after Frankie was left in a pool of blood. You ought to learn who your friends are, Clete."

"I can go now?"

"No, you can't. You're under arrest."

"For what?"

"Possession of stolen property. The German Luger under your car seat."

"I took the Luger off of Frankie Gee. I didn't want him parking one in my brisket."

"Well, Frankie screwed you from inside a body bag. How do you like that?"

"Where was the Luger stolen from?"

"See what your lawyer can find out before you enter your plea."

"Why are you doing this?"

"We can hold you as a material witness indefinitely. The possession charge is a bone for my colleagues. They'll accuse me of doing favors for you and Dave, but eventually, they'll forget about it. No, no need to thank me. I like taking the heat for you two."

"You had my Caddy towed. You rousted me on a phony beef. Your colleagues are bums. I'm supposed to be grateful?" Clete rubbed the fatigue from his face and looked wanly out the window. "Put me in an isolation unit, will you? I'm not up to the tank."

"You were protecting Frankie Gee from somebody."

"Yeah, from whoever was trying to smoke him."

"Who?"

Clete seemed to think for a long time, his forehead propped on the heel of his hand. Then he looked up at Dana Magelli as though he had just come to a profound conclusion. "I saw the trusty headed down to the tank with the food cart. If I don't go to the tank, can I still have a sandwich and coffee?" he said.

IN CLETE'S VIEW, few people understood what jails represented or what it was like to be confined in one, regardless of the duration. People were not locked in jails simply because they had committed crimes. The commission of the crime was secondary to the larger issue, namely, that jails provide a home for defective and often hapless people who can't cut it on the outside. In an era when minor offenders have to get on a waiting list to serve their sentences, almost anyone stacking serious time in a parish, state, or federal prison is not only pathological or brain-dead but would not have it any other way, at least in the gospel according to Clete.

He knew from his own life that in many ways, a jail is like a late-hour low-bottom bar, one with no windows or clocks or direct lighting. Once you are safely inside, time stops, and so do all comparisons. No matter how much damage you have done to your life, no matter how shameful and degrading and cowardly and depraved your conduct has become, there is always somebody on the tier who has been dealt a worse hand or committed worse deeds than you.

The biggest downside of incarceration, however, isn't stacking the time. It's the realization that you are in the right place and you put yourself there so someone else could feed and take care of you. Titty-babies come in all stripes, many of them with tats from the wrist to the armpit. It isn't coincidence that mainline recidivists usually have a heavy commitment to topless bars.

Clete didn't have all of these thoughts, but he had some of them, and each applied to him. He no longer kept tally of the holding cells and booking rooms he had been in or the times he had been hooked on a chain and transported from jail to morning court, the professional miscreants on the chain eyeing him cautiously. Was it accident that again and again he found himself in their midst, trying to rationalize his behavior, staring at a urine-streaked drainhole in the floor while a night-count man went down the corridor, raking his baton across the bars on the cells? Miscreants broke into the slams, not out of them. They all knew one another, shared needles and women the way ragpickers share clothes, passing their diseases around without remorse or recrimination. The die had been cast for most of them the day they were born. What was Clete's excuse?

The light fixture outside his holding cell was defective and kept flickering like a damaged insect, causing him to blink constantly, until his eyelids felt like sandpaper. The paint in the cell was a yellowish-gray and still bore the watermarks and soft decay from five days of submersion during Katrina, when the inmates were left by their warders to slosh about in their own feces until they were rescued by a group of deputies from Iberia Parish. Drawings of genitalia were scratched on the walls, and the names of inmates had been burned onto the ceiling with twists of flaming newspaper, probably during the storm. The toilet bowl had no seat, and the rim was encrusted with dried matter that Clete didn't want to think about. As he lay on the metal bench against the back wall, his arm across his eyes, he wondered why people always felt compassion toward political prisoners. A political prisoner had the solace of knowing he had done nothing to deserve his fate. The miscreant knew he had ferreted his way into the belly of the beast deliberately, in the same way a tumblebug burrows its way into feces. Could a person have worse knowledge about himself?

At eight-fifteen A.M. a screw unlocked Clete's cell door. The screw was a dour lifetime employee of the system, with creases as deep as

124 JAMES LEE BURKE

a prune's in his face and five o'clock shadow by ten in the morning. "You just got sprung," he said.

"Nig Rosewater is out there?" Clete said.

"Nig Rosewater hasn't been up this early since World War Two."

"Who bailed me out?"

"A woman."

"Who?"

"How would I know? Why don't you take your problems somewhere else, Purcel?"

For some reason, the remark and the flatness of the screw's tone bothered Clete in a way he couldn't define. "I do something to set you off?"

"Yeah, you're here," the screw said.

THE GIRL HE had met in the nightclub way down in Terrebonne Parish was standing in the foyer on the other side of the possessions desk, her chestnut hair backlit by the sunlight out on the street. "You went my bail?" Clete said.

"You're good for it, aren't you?"

"How'd you know my name? How'd you know I was in the can?"

"A friend of mine at Motor Vehicles ran your tag. I called your office, and your secretary told me where you were."

"That doesn't sound right. Miss Alice doesn't give out that kind of information."

"I kind of lied when I said I was your niece and it was an emergency." A pale blue cloth purse embroidered with an Indian design hung from her shoulder. She opened it and removed Clete's Zippo lighter. "You left this on the bar at the club. It has the globe and anchor on it. I thought you'd want it back."

"You bet," he said.

"Why'd you go charging out of the club? You hurt my feelings."

"I didn't mean to. I'm sorry."

"You're pretty easy to jerk around. Maybe you should take some happy pills."

"I used to. That's why I don't take them anymore."

"I'm waiting," she said.

"On what?"

"Are you gonna invite me to breakfast or not?"

"Let's go to Café du Monde. I love it there in the morning. It's entirely different from the crowd you see there at night. The whole Quarter is that way. Do you know why I was in the can?"

"Suspicion of theft or something?"

They were out on the street now, in the freshness of the morning and the noise of the city. "They were looking at me for a homicide," he said.

She was unlocking the passenger door of her rental Honda, her gaze fixed on the traffic, not seeming to listen. "Yeah?" she said.

"A guy by the name of Frankie Giacano got clipped in the Baton Rouge bus terminal. Somebody came up behind him in a toilet stall and put three rounds in his head," he said.

When they got in her Honda, she put the keys in the ignition but didn't start the engine. "Say that again?"

"A safecracker, a guy by the name of Frankie Gee, got shot and killed in Baton Rouge. NOPD wanted to put it on me," Clete said.

In the silence, he held his eyes on hers, barely breathing, studying every aspect of her face. He could feel his lungs tighten and his heart start to swell, as though no oxygen were reaching his blood, as though a vein might pop in his temple. She moistened her lips and returned his stare. "If we go to breakfast, you won't run off on me again, will you?"

"No."

"Good. Because I really wouldn't like that."

If there was a second meaning in her words, he couldn't tell. All the way to Café du Monde, he watched the side of her face as though seeing part of himself, not necessarily a good one, that he had never recognized.

THEY GOT A table under the pavilion with a fine view of Jackson Square and the cathedral and the Pontalba Apartments. The sky was blue, the myrtle bushes and windmill palms and banana plants in the square covered with sunshine. It was the kind of crisp green-gold late-fall day in Louisiana that seems so perfect in its dimensions that winter and even mortality are set at bay. "So you're a private investigator?" she said.

"I used to be with the NOPD, but I messed up my career. It's my fault, not theirs. I started over, know what I mean?"

"Not really."

"I worked for some mobbed-up guys in Reno and Montana. But I got clear of them. I have a friend named Dave Robicheaux. He says it's always the first inning. You get up one morning and say fuck it and start over."

"Why are you telling me this?"

"What kind of work do you do?"

"Antiques, collectibles, that kind of stuff. I've got a little store in Key West, but most of my sales are on the Internet."

"You didn't know my name, but you ran my tag and traced me to the jail and got me back on the street. You even brought me my cigarette lighter. Not many people could pull that off. Maybe you have a gift."

"My mother said my father was a marine who got killed in the first Iraqi war, so that's why I brought you your lighter. I was never sure if my mother was telling me the truth. She should have had a turnstile on her bedroom door."

"What I'm saying is I could use an assistant," Clete said.

"Are you having hot flashes or something?" she asked, biting into a beignet.

"I didn't get a lot of sleep last night. I have blood pressure issues."

"You ought to take better care of yourself," she said. "This junk we're eating isn't helping either your blood pressure or your cholesterol count."

"I've got two offices, one here and one in New Iberia. That's on Bayou Teche, about two hours west. How long are you going to be in town?"

"I'm not big on clocks and calendars."

"You think you could work for a guy like me?"

"You married?"

"Not now. Why do you ask?"

"You act strange. I don't think you're on the make, but I can't quite figure you."

"What's to figure?"

"You never asked my name. It's Gretchen Horowitz."

"Glad to meet you, Gretchen. Come work for me."

"I never saw you at Little Yankee Stadium. It was somewhere else, wasn't it?"

"Who cares?" he said.

"What did you do in the Crotch?"

"Tried to stay alive."

"You kill any people while you were staying alive?"

"I did two combat tours in Vietnam. Who told you the Corps was called the Crotch?"

"I get around. I picked up some of my mother's habits. Mostly the bad ones."

"It doesn't have to be like that now," he said.

She gazed at him without replying. He realized her eyes were violet in the daylight as well as in the evening shadows, and they engendered feelings in him that he could not deal with.

"Thanks for the beignets. You don't mind walking to your office, do you?" she said. "It's across the square and about a block down, right? See you around, big boy. Keep it in your pants."

She left five dollars under her plate for the waitress. After she was gone, he pressed his fingers against his temples and tried to put together what she had just said. How did she know where his office was, and how did she know the exact distance? Had she followed the Greyhound to Baton Rouge and popped Frankie Gee in the stall? Had his seed produced a psychopath? Even though a breeze was blowing off the river, the scent of her perfume seemed to hang on every surface she had touched.

THAT SAME NIGHT in New Iberia, the southern sky was filled with strange lights, flashes of electricity that would ignite inside a solitary black cloud and in seconds ripple across the entirety of the heavens without making a sound. Then a rain front moved across the marshlands and drenched the town and overflowed the gutters on East Main and covered our front yard with a gray and yellow net of dead leaves. At four in the morning, amid the booming of thunder, I thought I heard the telephone ring in the kitchen. I had been dreaming before I woke, and in the dream, large shells fired from an offshore battery were arching out of their trajectory, whistling just before they exploded inside a sodden rain forest.

I felt light-headed when I picked up the phone, part of me still inside the dream that was so real I could not shake it or think my way out of it. "Hello?" I said into the receiver.

At first I could hear only static. I looked at the caller ID, but the number was blocked. "Who is this?" I said.

"It's Tee Jolie, Mr. Dave. Can you hear me okay? There's a bad storm where I'm at."

Through the window, I could see fog rolling off the bayou into the trees, pushing against the windows and doors. I sat down in a chair. "Where are you?" I said.

"A long ways from home. There's a beautiful beach here. The sea is green. I wanted to tell you everyt'ing is all right. I scared you at the hospital in New Orleans. I wish I ain't done that."

"Nothing is right, Tee Jolie."

"Did you like the songs I left on your iPod? I dropped it before I gave it to you. It don't always work right."

"You said everything is all right. Don't you know about your sister?"

"What about her? Blue is just Blue. She's sweet. To tell you the troot', her voice is better than mine."

"Blue is dead."

"What's that?"

"She was murdered. Her body floated up in St. Mary Parish."

"You're breaking up, Mr. Dave. What's that you said about Blue? The storm is tearing up the boathouse on the beach. Can you still hear me, Mr. Dave?"

"Yes."

"I cain't hear you, suh. This storm is terrible. It scares me. I got to go now. Tell Blue and my granddaddy hello. Tell them I couldn't get t'rew."

The line went dead, and the words "blocked call" disappeared from the caller identification window. Molly was awake when I got back into bed and lay back on the pillow. "Were you fixing something in the kitchen?" she said.

"No, that was Tee Jolie Melton on the phone."

Molly raised herself up on one elbow. Each time lightning flashed in the clouds, I could see the freckles on her shoulders and the tops of her breasts. "I didn't hear the phone ring," she said.

"It woke me up."

"No, I was awake, Dave. You were talking in your sleep."

"She said she was sorry for making me worry about her. She doesn't know her sister is dead."

"Oh, Dave," Molly said, her eyes filming.

"These are the things she said. It was Tee Jolie. You think I could forget what her voice sounds like?"

"No, it was not Tee Jolie."

"She told me she dropped the iPod. That's why other people can't hear the songs she put on there."

"Stop it."

"I'm telling you what she said. I didn't imagine it."

"You're going to drive us all crazy."

"You want me to lie to you instead?"

"I almost wish you were drinking again. We could deal with that. But I can't deal with this."

"Then don't," I said.

I returned to the kitchen and sat in the darkness and looked through the window at the Teche rising over its banks. A pirogue was spinning in the current—empty, with no paddle, rotating over and over as it drifted downstream toward a bend, filling with rainwater that would eventually sink it in the deepest part of the channel. I could not get the image of the sinking pirogue out of my head. I wished I had asked Tee Jolie about the baby she was carrying. I wished I had asked her many things. I felt Molly's hand on my shoulder.

"Come back to bed," she said.

"I'll be along directly."

"I didn't mean what I said."

"Your feelings are justified."

"I thought you were dreaming about Vietnam. I heard you say 'incoming.'"

"I don't remember what I was dreaming about," I lied, my gaze fixed on the pirogue settling in a frothy whirlpool beneath the current.

UNLESS A FELON walks into a police station and confesses his crime, or unless he is caught in the commission of the crime, there are only two ways, from an evidentiary point of view, that the crime is solved and given prosecutable status. A detective either follows a chain of evidence to the suspect, or the detective begins with the suspect and, in retrograde fashion, follows the evidence back to the crime. So far I had no demonstrable evidence to link Pierre Dupree to Tee Jolie Melton or her sister, Blue. But there was one thing I knew about him for certain: He was a liar. He had denied knowing Tee Jolie, even though his painting of the reclining nude looked very much like her; second, he had claimed that years ago he had gotten rid of the safe from which Frankie Giacano had taken Clete Purcel's IOU.

So where do you start when you want to find out everything you can about a man whose physical dimensions and latent anger give most men serious pause?

His ex-to-be might be a good beginning.

Varina Leboeuf Dupree had once been known as the wet dream of every fraternity boy on the LSU campus. By the time she was twenty-five, she had proved she could break hearts and bank accounts and succeed at business in a male-oriented culture in which women might be admired but were usually thought of as acquisitions. She was certainly nothing like her father, a retired Iberia sheriff's detective, the mention of whose name would cause black people to lower their eyes lest they reveal the fear and loathing he instilled in them. Jesse Leboeuf had named his daughter for Jefferson Davis's wife, I suspect in hopes that it would allow her to occupy the social station that would never be his or his wife's. Unfortunately for him, Varina Leboeuf did things her own way, couldn't have cared less about her social station, and made sure everyone knew it. In college she wore her dark brown hair in braids wrapped around her head, some-times with Mardi Gras beads woven in. She wore peasant dresses to dances, jeans and pink tennis shoes without socks to church, and once, when her pastor asked her to greet a famous televangelical leader at the airport, she arrived barefoot and braless at the Lafay-ette concourse in an evening gown that looked like sherbet running down her skin.

She was scandalous and beautiful and often had a pout that begged to be kissed. Some condemned her as profligate, but she always seemed to enter into her affairs without anger or need and depart from them in the same fashion. Even though she broke hearts, I had never heard one of her former lovers speak ill of her. In the American South, there is a crude expression often used to define the plantation-bred protocol of both conjugal and extramarital relation-ships. The statement is offensive and coarse and is of the kind that is whispered with a hand to the mouth, but there is no question about its accuracy inside the world in which I grew up: "You marry up and you screw down." I heard some women say Varina married up. I didn't agree. By the same token, I didn't understand why she had married into the Dupree family or why she had taken up residence in St. Mary Parish, a place where convention and sycophancy and Shintoism were institutions.

On Monday morning I signed out of the office and drove in my pickup down to Cypremort Point, a narrow strip of land extending into West Cote Blanche Bay, where Varina's father lived among cy-press and oak trees in a beachfront house elevated on pilings. Jesse Leboeuf was a Cajun but originally from North Louisiana and the kind of lawman other cops treat with caution rather than respect, in the same way you walk around an unpredictable guard dog, or a gunbull whose presence in the tower can make a convict's face twitch with anxiety, or a door gunner who volunteers for as much trigger time as possible in free-fire zones. Jesse had abused himself with whiskey and cigarettes for a lifetime but showed no signs of physical decay. When I found him on his back porch, he was smok-ing an unfiltered cigarette, gazing at the bay, his outboard boat rock-ing against his small dock. He rose to greet me, his hand enveloping mine, his face as stolid as boilerplate, his hair flat-topped and boxed and shiny with butch wax. "You want to know where my little girl is at?" he said.

I had left a message on his phone and wondered why he had not simply called me back. But Jesse was not a man whose motivations you openly questioned. "It's a nice day to take a drive, so I thought I'd stop by," I said.

He pushed a chair toward me. "You want a drink?" he said.

"I just wanted to ask Miss Varina a couple of questions about her husband."

"If I was you, I'd leave him alone. Unless you're planning to shoot him."

"I have reason to believe he might have ties to the Giacano family."

He puffed on his cigarette and laughed behind the smoke. "Are you serious?"

"You don't think Pierre would associate with criminals?"

"The Duprees don't associate with minorities of any kind, particularly New Orleans dagos. My daughter had all of it she could take."

"All of what?"

"The fact that the Duprees think their shit don't stink. The only time they make allowances for other groups of people is when a piece of tail floats by that one of them might be interested in."

"You're talking about Pierre?"

"My daughter is getting shut of them, that's all that counts." He watched a boat with outriggers cutting across the chop. He took a last hit on his cigarette and flicked it out on the water. "Isn't this oil spill enough to worry about? Yesterday afternoon my crab traps was loaded to the top of the wire. When I put them in the boiler, every one of them had oil inside the shell. I hear it's the same with the oyster beds. They say there's shitloads of sludge plumb to the continental shelf." He lit another cigarette and puffed on it, the smoke leaking slowly from his mouth.

"I think Pierre Dupree is dirty," I said.

"Dirty for what?"

"I'm not sure."

"Sounds like you got a problem."

"You ever see a boat around here with the emblem of a fish on the bow? A Chris-Craft with a white hull?"

"Doesn't ring a bell."

I was getting nowhere. I asked for his daughter's phone number.

"Why not just leave her alone?" he said.

"I think Pierre Dupree may know something about the murder of the girl who floated up inside a block of ice in St. Mary Parish."

"Then go talk to Pierre. He's a son of a bitch. I don't like cluttering up my day talking about a son of a bitch. My daughter don't need to be talking about him, either. Why don't y'all let us be, Robicheaux?"

"I'd appreciate it if you'd call me Dave."

"You're on my property, and I'll call you what I goddamn please."

"Do you want somebody who respects Miss Varina to interview her or some young guy who just got kicked up to plainclothes?"

"You're a hardtail. You always were. That's why you got where you are. That's not meant as a compliment." He wrote a telephone number on a scrap of newspaper and handed it to me. "She's in Lafayette." Then he raised his index finger at me, the nail as pointy as a piece of horn. "Treat her right. If you don't, you and I will talk again."

"Tell you what. I've got one more question for you, Mr. Jesse. You said the Duprees are snobs and they don't associate with minorities of any kind. The grandfather is Jewish and a survivor of a Nazi extermination camp. Does it make sense to say the Duprees don't associate with minorities? Didn't Pierre buy his office building from a member of the Giacano family? Or are Italian-Americans not minorities? I have a little trouble tracking your thought processes."

Jesse's skin was brown and deeply lined, like the skin on a terrapin's neck, an ugly purple birthmark buried in his hairline. He got up from his chair, taller than I, unstooped by age, an odor of tobacco and dried sweat emanating from his clothes. He looked me in the face with a glower that made me want to step back from him. He rubbed his jaw, his eyes never leaving mine, and I could hear the sound of his whiskers against the calluses on his palm. I wanted him to speak, to indicate what he was thinking; I wanted him to be more than an emotional condition that was impossible to read or understand. More succinctly, I wanted him to be human so I did not have to fear him. But not another word passed from his lips. He climbed the stairs that led into his screened porch and closed and latched the door behind him, never looking back, his shoulders stiff with hatred of his fellow man.

There was a Japanese tulip tree by the edge of the water. A hard gust of wind blew a shower of pink and lavender petals on top of the waves sliding in with the tide. I thought about Blue Melton's body inside the block of ice and the fact that Jesse Leboeuf had shown no reaction when I mentioned that his son-in-law might be involved with her death. Was he simply obtuse and insensitive? Or was it no accident that his skin was reminiscent of an early reptilian creature cracking its way out of the egg?

I drove back up the road through a corridor of oak and gum trees strung with Spanish moss and caught the four-lane to Lafayette.

THE TRUTH WAS, I had no idea what kind of investigation I was pursuing. I knew that three low-wattage gangsters had tried to run a scam on Clete Purcel and cheat him out of his apartment and office building. I also knew that Clete had creeped Bix Golightly's condo in the Carrollton district and found e-mails that indicated Golightly was fencing stolen or forged paintings. Was that all I was looking at, a gumball like Golightly selling hot or copied artwork for twenty cents on the dollar at best?

The sugarcane crop was in full harvest, and the highway was ribbed with dried gumbo strung from the fields by tractors and cane wagons. Traffic was backed up from the Lafayette city limits, and I got stuck behind an empty cane wagon blowing dirt and lint all over my windows. I clamped my emergency flasher on the roof of my pickup, but the driver of the tractor either couldn't see me or didn't care. I swung around him and tried to stay in the left lane but got caught in another jam after I crossed the bridge over the Vermilion River and entered the city.

I had already called Varina on my cell phone and told her I was on my way. I hit the redial. "I'm delayed, but I'll be there in ten minutes," I said.

"Don't worry about it, Dave. I'll be by the pool," she replied. "You said this is about Pierre?"

"You could say that."

"Y'all must not have much to do in New Iberia," she said, and hung up. Two minutes later, she called back. "I'm having some ice cream and strawberries. You want some?" Then she hung up again.

I wondered how many young men had wakened in the middle of the night, trying to sort out Varina's mood swings and the conscious or unconscious signals she sent regarding her affections. I also wondered how many of them woke in the morning throbbing with desire and went to their jobs resenting themselves for emotions they couldn't control. I thought Varina caused her lovers heartbreak because they believed there was nothing false or manipulative in her nature. They saw a loveliness and innocence in her that reminded them of dreams they'd had in adolescence about an imaginary girl, one who was so pretty and decent and good that they never told others about her or allowed themselves to think inappropriately of her. At least those were the perceptions of an aging man whose retrospective vision was probably no more accurate today than it was when he was young.

I had just turned in to Bendel Gardens, an old upscale apartment neighborhood shaded by live oaks and filled with tropical plants and flowers, when a freezer truck pulled alongside me in the left lane, trapping me behind an elderly driver in a gas-guzzler. I realized the battery had gone out on my flasher when I started to pull around. The freezer truck, the kind with big lockers that delivers frozen steaks and vegetables and pizzas to residential subscribers, inched forward, blocking me in. There were two men in the cab, both smoking and talking, their windows up. "How about it?" I said out my window.

They didn't hear me. I opened my badge and held it out the window. "Iberia Parish Sheriff's Department," I said.

The freezer truck dropped slightly behind me, and I thought I could swing out to pass. Except now I was only half a block to the

entrance of the two-story white stucco apartments where Varina Leboeuf lived. *Time to dial it down,* I told myself.

The freezer truck pulled abreast of me again, the side panels closer
than they should have been. Above me, the sun was shining through
the oak limbs that arched over the street, creating a blinding effect
on my windshield. I saw the two men in the truck talking to each
other, their hands moving in the air, as though they were reaching a
humorous conclusion to a joke or a story. Then the passenger turned
toward me, rolling down the window, his profile as sharp as razored
tin against a shaft of sunlight, his mouth breaking into a grin. "Eat
this, shit-for-brains," he said.

I stomped on the brake. The cut-down shotgun was wrapped in a
paper bag. The passenger pulled the trigger, and a load of buckshot
blew out my windshield and patterned across the hood and the top
of the dashboard and covered me with splinters of glass. My right
wheel slammed into the curb, throwing me against the safety belt. I
saw the freezer truck stop by the corner while other vehicles veered
around it. The passenger got out on the swale and walked toward
my pickup, evidently oblivious to the terror he was instilling in
others, the bottom of the paper bag curling with flame. I got my .45
loose from the holster clipped to my belt and opened the passenger
door on my pickup and rolled off the seat onto the swale.

My choices were simple. I could shoot from behind the truck
at my assailant and, with luck, drop him with the first shot. In all
likelihood, that would not happen, and I would end up firing into
the traffic and hitting an innocent person. So I crashed through the
hedge into the parking lot below Varina Leboeuf's apartment. In
seconds, my assailant was gone, the freezer truck grinding down the
speedway that led into Lafayette's commercial district.

I put away my .45 and realized my face and arms were bleeding.
Cars and SUVs were trying to work their way around my pickup,
in the way that people work their way around a fender-bender. The
sun was bright through the tree limbs overhead, the wind ruffling the
hydrangeas and caladiums in the gardens around me, the ebb and
flow and normalcy of the day somehow undisturbed for those who
had someplace to be. I sat down on a stone bench by a gate that gave

onto the apartment swimming pool and I got out my cell phone, my hands shaking so badly that I had to use my thumb to punch in a 911 call.

In the background, I heard the voice of Jimmy Clanton singing "Just a Dream." I saw Varina Leboeuf walk toward me in a swimsuit, her elevated sandals clacking on the flagstones. She went to one knee and brushed the broken glass off my face and arms. Then she looked up at me in the same way that I was sure she had melted the defense mechanisms in many a suitor. Her eyes were brown and warm and lustrous and charged with energy all at the same time, her expression so sincere, showing such concern for your welfare, that you would do anything for her. "Oh, Dave, they'll kill their own mothers. They have no boundaries. I think it involves millions. Don't be such a foolish man," she said.

A stereo was playing by the pool, the wind ruffling the water and the palm and banana fronds and the bloom on a potted orchid tree. Jimmy Clanton's voice had risen out of the year 1958, and for just a moment I believed I was back there with him, in an era of sock hops and roadhouse jukeboxes when the season seemed eternal and none of us thought we would ever die. I removed a sliver of glass from my eyebrow and felt a rivulet of blood on the side of my face. Varina caught my blood on a paper napkin and pushed my hair out of my eyes. "One day your luck is going to run out, Dave," she said.

"You wouldn't try to put the slide on a fellow, would you?" I replied.

CHAPTER
10

I WENT BACK through the hedge and started my truck and got it out of the traffic and into the parking lot. I knew I had no more than five minutes before the Lafayette Police Department would be at the apartment and all my opportunities to interview Varina would be lost. She had put on a robe and was sitting at a table by the pool, a carton of ice cream melting on the glass tabletop.

"Who shot at me?" I said.

"I have no idea," she replied.

"Don't tell me that."

"You scared my father. You had no right to do that."

"Nobody scares your father. It's the other way around. His whole career was invested in terrifying people who have no power."

"I don't mean *you*. I mean what you're doing. Pierre got mixed up with the Giacano family. On what level, I don't know. But I know he's afraid, just like my father is."

"The Giacanos slid down the pipe when Didi Gee died. The rest of the family are nickel-and-dime lamebrains who couldn't operate a pizza oven without a diagram. Your father has his vices, but I don't think fear of the Giacanos is one of them."

"My lawyer is in the middle of working out a divorce settlement with Pierre. I'm not sure of all the things he's involved in. My lawyer says maybe I should be careful about what I pray for, meaning what I end up with."

"Don't you and Pierre already own an electronic security service of some kind?"

"Not exactly. Pierre and I and my father own half of it together. An international conglomerate bought the rest of the stock a few years ago. I actually got into the business to create a job for my father."

What she was telling me didn't coincide with her history. Varina had been an electrical engineering major at LSU and had been involved with high-tech electronic security work since she graduated. "So your lawyer thinks Pierre's business enterprises might be toxic?" I said.

"At least some of them. He grew up in St. Mary Parish. Back in the 1970s, his mother's family evicted people from their company homes for even talking to a union representative. The funny thing about them, and this includes Pierre, is they've never felt they did anything wrong. They feel no guilt about anything, including infidelity." She let her eyes shift onto mine.

"You're talking about Pierre?"

"So you don't get the wrong idea, I did it back to him. I owned up to it at my church. It was embarrassing, but I'm glad I got it off my chest."

"Is the grandfather a player in any of this?"

"I don't know what he is. I always stayed away from him."

"What's the problem?"

"Everything. His eyes. The way his teeth show behind his lips when he looks at you. Once he came up behind me and touched the back of my neck. He said, 'You must be still. There's a bee in your hair.' Then he pushed his body against me. It was disgusting. I told Pierre about it, but he said I was imagining things."

I really didn't want to hear any more about the grandfather or Varina's problems with him. "Do the names Tee Jolie and Blue Melton mean anything to you?"

"No, who are they?"

"Girls from St. Martinville. One is missing, and one was found in a block of ice."

"I read about that." She shook her head, refocusing her concentration. "What does this have to do with me or Pierre or his grandfather?"

"I think Pierre used Tee Jolie as a model in one of his paintings."

"I don't think he uses models. I don't think he paints anybody. He's a fraud."

"Pardon?"

"His talent is like flypaper. Little pieces of other people's work stick in his head, and he puts them on a canvas and calls the painting his. Every time there's a real artist in the area, you can see Pierre's tail disappearing inside his hidey-hole. He's a sex addict, not an artist. Why would he stay down here if he's an artist? Wouldn't he be in New York or Paris or Los Angeles? There's an art gallery in Krotz Springs, Louisiana?"

"Say that again?"

"Pierre is a freak. I won't go into detail except to say our bed should have been cruciform in shape. I don't know why I'm telling you this. None of it seems to register."

I stared at her blankly, a bit in awe of her ability to control and manipulate a conversation. The first Lafayette PD cruiser to arrive at the crime scene turned in to the parking lot, followed by a sheriff's cruiser and a second city department vehicle that parked by the curb, on the other side of the hedge. While I still had my thoughts together—which was not easy after a conversation with Varina Leboeuf—I tried to remember everything she had told me. She was intelligent and lovely to look at. Her fine cheekbones and the softness of her mouth and the earnestness in her expression were of a kind that made both the celibate and the happily married question the wisdom of their vows. I also realized that she had managed to deflect the conversation away from specifics about her husband's criminality to how wretched it was to be married to him. I didn't know if her depiction of her husband's sexual habits was true, but I had to hand it to her: Varina could weave a spiderweb and sprinkle it with gold dust and lure you inside and wrap it around both your eyes and your heart, all the while making you enjoy your own entrapment.

"When you get finished with the local cops, hang around and we'll have some ice cream," she said.

"Will I learn anything else?"

"There are always possibilities."

"Would you repeat that?"

Her gaze lingered longer on my face than it should have. "You look picaresque with that cut over your eye." She touched the side of my face and studied my eyes.

I felt my cheeks coloring. "You always knew how to leave your mark," I said.

IT WAS RAINING when I walked to work the next morning. Helen Soileau caught me before I could take off my coat. "In my office," she said.

I was ready for a harangue, but as was often the case in my dealings with Helen, I had misjudged her. "You walked to work in the rain?" she said.

"My pickup is at the glazier's in Lafayette."

"The Lafayette PD found the freezer truck burning in a coulee. It was boosted from behind a motel early yesterday," she said. "You never saw the shooter before?"

"Not to my knowledge."

"Give me your coat."

"What's going on?"

She took my raincoat from my hand and shook it and hung it on a rack by the door. "Sit down," she said. "Why did you go to Lafayette without informing me or checking in with Lafayette PD?"

"I was off the clock, and I didn't think it was a big deal."

"What are we going to do with you, Pops?"

"How about a pay raise?"

"I don't know why I put up with you. I really don't. I have a fantasy: You're the sheriff and I'm you, and I get to do to you what you do to me."

"I can't blame you."

She was sitting behind her desk now, biting on the corner of her lip. I had always been convinced that several distinct and separate people had taken up residence inside her. I was never sure to which of them I would be speaking. She was a genuinely mysterious woman, probably the most complex I had ever known. Sometimes she would pause in midsentence and stare directly into my eyes in a way that made her features sharpen, her cheeks pool with shadow, as though she were having thoughts that the Helen Soileau who came to work that morning would not allow herself to have. All of us believe we have boundaries we won't cross. I believed Helen had boundaries, too. But I wasn't sure that either of us knew what they were. I cleared my throat and focused my attention on the raindrops running down the windows.

"You're supposed to be on the desk and off duty at noon," she said. "You're supposed to go home and take naps and throw pinecones in the bayou. Obviously, that's not what you have in mind. You prefer stirring up the wrong people in New Orleans and going to Lafayette and eating a load of buckshot."

"I didn't plan any of this. What do you want me to say?"

"I advise you to say nothing."

I sighed and raised my hands and dropped them in my lap.

"I think it's time to put you back on full-time status, bwana," she said. She narrowed one eye. "It's the only way I can keep your umbilical cord stapled to the corner of my desk."

How do you reply to a statement like that? "Thank you," I said.

"Lafayette PD thinks the shooter was some guy with a personal hard-on," she said. "They're looking at a parolee who just got off Camp J, a guy you put away years go. He was staying at the motel where the freezer truck got boosted. You remember a guy by the name of Ronnie Earl Patin?"

"Child molestation, strong-arm robbery, he hurt an elderly man with a hammer about ten years back?" I said.

"That's the baby."

"Ronnie Earl was a fat slob. I'm almost certain I've never seen either one of the guys in the freezer truck."

"People can change a lot in ten years, particularly if they're hoeing out a bean field."

"The shooter had features like the edge of an ax. The driver was short. Ronnie Earl wasn't."

"Could Pierre Dupree be behind this?"

"Maybe, but it doesn't seem his style. I wouldn't rule out Jesse Leboeuf."

"You don't think that's a stretch?" she said.

"When I was a pin boy at the bowling alley out on East Main, Jesse was one of the older boys who bullied the rest of us in the pits. He'd made a slingshot with a hand-carved wood frame and elastic medical tubing and a leather pouch to fit a marble in. On Saturday nights he and his buds would go nigger-knocking down on Hopkins."

"That was bad stuff, but it was a long time ago," she said.

"I knew a number of kids like him. Some of them are still around. Know what's interesting about them? They're as mean as they were when they were kids. They just know how to hide it better."

"How long did it take you to get from Jesse Leboeuf's place to Varina's apartment?"

"Maybe an hour."

"Bring Leboeuf in," she said.

CLETE PURCEL HAD poured three jiggers of sherry into a glass of milk and gone to sleep before eleven P.M. In his dream, he was standing on a dock under a velvet-black sky on the southernmost tip of Key West, music from a marimba band drifting on the wind behind him, the smoky-green glow of nameless organisms lighting under waves that slid through the pilings without capping. The dream was one he'd had many times and was a safe place to be, but even in his sleep, he knew he had to keep it inviolate and not let it be invaded and destroyed by a milkman who departed for work at four A.M. and often returned home by ten A.M., drunk and unpredictable, sometimes pulling his belt out of his pant loops as soon as he entered the house.

In the dream, the wind was balmy and smelled of salt spray and seaweed and shellfish that had been stranded on the beach by the receding waves. It also smelled of a Eurasian girl who spoke French and English and lived on a sampan in a cove on the edge of the South China Sea, her skin like alabaster traced with the shadows of palm fronds, her nipples as red and inviting as small roses. He could see her walking nude into the water, her hair floating off her shoulders, her teeth white when she smiled at him and extended her hand.

But Clete's dead father had long ago devised ways of breaking into his inner sanctum, throwing back the bedroom door, his scowl as scalding as an openhanded slap. Sometimes the father poured a sack full of dry rice on the floor and made Clete kneel on the kernels until sunrise; sometimes he sat on the side of the bed and gently touched Clete's face with a hand that was as callused as a carpenter's; sometimes he lay down beside Clete and wept as a child would.

Clete could feel himself losing the dream, the marimba music and the salt wind disappearing out an open window, the palm fronds collapsing against their trunks, the Eurasian girl turning her attentions elsewhere. He realized he was hearing the sounds of the street, which he never heard above the hum of his air conditioner. He sat up in bed and reached for the nine-millimeter Beretta he kept between his mattress and box spring. It was gone.

A figure was sitting in a chair by his television set. "Who are you?" he asked.

The figure made no reply.

"You're about to get the shit kicked out of you," Clete said. He pulled open the drawer of his nightstand, where he kept a blackjack. The drawer was empty. He put his feet on the floor and adjusted himself inside his skivvies. "I don't know why you're here, but you've creeped the wrong house."

In the glow from a streetlamp on the corner, he could see the hands of the figure pick up his Beretta and release the magazine from the frame and pull back the slide and eject the round in the chamber. The figure leaned forward and one by one tossed the Beretta and the magazine and the ejected round on his bed. "I can see why you need some help," a female voice said. "Your security service has been out of date since Alexander Graham Bell died."

"Gretchen?"

"That offer you made me, that was on the level?" she said.

"Sure, if you don't mind working cheap. I work on commission most of the time for Nig Rosewater and Wee Willie Bimstine."

"You're not trying to get in my bread?"

"I would have told you."

"I get it. You tell girls up front when you're planning to get it on with them? I bet you get a lot of action that way."

"You need to stop talking like that."

"Why were you asking about the scars on my arms?"

"Because you've got scars, that's all. I've got lots of them. They mean a person has been around. No, they mean a person has probably paid some dues."

"You want to know how I got them? It happened before I was supposed to be able to remember anything. But I still have dreams about a man who comes into my room with fingertips that glow with light. You know what the light is?"

"You don't need to talk about this, Gretchen."

"You figured it out?"

"Maybe."

"What kind of man would do that to a baby?"

"A sadist and a coward. A guy who doesn't deserve to live. Maybe a guy who already got what he deserved."

"What was that last part?"

"They all go down. It's just a matter of time. That's all I was saying. It takes a while, but they go down."

"I can't figure you out."

"You want to work for me or not?"

"Why are you doing this?"

"I like you. I need the help, too."

"I know where I saw you before."

"Oh yeah?" he said, his heart seizing up.

"Remember Boog Powell? He played first base for Baltimore. He used to own a boatyard in the Keys. I used to take a charter out of there to Seven Mile Reef. Boog always said mermaids lived under the reef. He was a big kidder."

"That was probably it."

"You're a piece of work," she said.

"I'm not sure how to take that."

"It's a compliment," she said. "Sometimes I have to travel. Are you cool with that?"

"No, if you work for me, you work for me."

She shrugged. "And eBay is killing my antique business, anyway. You got anything to eat? I'm starving."

BEFORE I LEFT the office to bring in Jesse Leboeuf, Helen told me to bring along a black female deputy named Catin Segura. "What for?" I asked.

"Because she's about to be promoted to detective, and I want her around a good influence."

"What's the real reason?"

"What I said." When I continued to look at her, she added, "If Jesse Leboeuf gives you trouble, I want a witness."

Catin Segura was a single mother and had a two-year degree in criminal justice from a community college in New Orleans. Like Helen, she had started her career in law enforcement at the NOPD as a meter maid, then had gone to work for the Iberia Parish Sheriff's Department as a 911 dispatcher. She owned a modest home in Jeanerette and lived there with her two children and was a pleasant and decent and humble woman who was conscientious about her job and the care of her family. In the five years she had been a patrolwoman, no complaint of any kind had ever been filed against her. As we headed down to Cypremort Point in her cruiser, I knew that Helen had made a mistake in assigning Catin to accompany me. There is an old lesson a police officer learns soon or learns late: Evil does not rinse itself out of the human soul. Catin Segura had no business around the likes of Jesse Leboeuf.

The rain had stopped, and through the cruiser's windshield, I could see a waterspout on the bay, its funnel as bright as spun glass, bending and warping in the sunlight. The cypress trees that stood in freshwater ponds on either side of us were turning gold with the season, and there was a smell in the wind like shrimp or trout schooling up in the coves.

"What's the story on this guy?" Catin asked.

"He's just an old man. Don't pay too much attention to what he says or does."

She took her eyes off the road. "He's got some racial issues?" "He's one of those guys whose head is like a bad neighborhood. It's better not to go into it."

She didn't speak the rest of the way to Jesse's house. When we pulled into his yard, he was standing by a barbecue pit under a pecan tree, wrapping a sheet of aluminum foil around a large redfish. He had filled the aluminum foil with sauce piquante and sliced onions and lemons and had perforated it with a fork so the fish could absorb the smoke from the coals. He glanced at us and then picked up a can of beer from a wood table and drank from it, his attention focused on the waterspout on the bay. His shoulders looked as wide as an ax handle. The wind was blowing steadily out of the south, rustling the leaves on the tree limbs above us.

"Sheriff Soileau wants you to help her out with something, Mr. Jesse," I said. "If you have a few minutes to spare, we can drive you into town."

"You're talking about the hermaphrodite?" he said.

"Bad choice of words," I replied.

"He'p with what?" he asked.

"Better take it up with her. She doesn't always share everything with me," I said.

"You're a goddamn liar."

"That's not a good way to talk to a fellow officer," I said.

"Who's *this*?" he asked, looking at Catin.

"Deputy Sheriff Segura, sir," she said.

Jesse's eyes traveled up and down her person as though he were examining a side of beef. "I'm fixing to eat," he said to me. "Tell the hermaphrodite I'll come in when I've got a mind to."

"No, sir, you need to come in now," Catin said.

"Did I address you?" Jesse asked.

"Jesse, you know the drill. It's not up for grabs," I said.

"I asked this girl a question," Jesse said.

"Sir, you can go in as a friend of the process or in cuffs," Catin said.

"You need to do something about this, Robicheaux."

"Here's the way I see it, Mr. Jesse," I said. "There are ponds on both sides of your road that are full of sunfish and goggle-eye perch. You're surrounded by palm and oak trees and a saltwater bay with schools of both white and speckled trout. You can sail a boat from your yard to Key West, Florida. How many men get to live in a place like that? Sheriff Soileau probably needs about twenty minutes of your time. Is that too much to ask of you, sir?"

"After I'm done with my dinner and washing my dishes and cleaning out my fire pit, I'll give it some thought," he replied. "Then I'll call Sheriff Soileau and take care of the matter. In the meantime, I want y'all out of here."

Catin stepped closer to him, her thumbs hooked on the sides of her belt. "No, you will get in the back of the cruiser, Mr. Leboeuf. You will also lose the attitude. If you don't like a female deputy or a black female deputy standing on your grass, that's too bad. I'm going to put my hand on you now and escort you to the cruiser. If you do not do as you are told, you are going to be charged with resisting."

"You get this bitch off my property," Leboeuf said to me.

"That's it," Catin said. She spun him around and shoved him between the shoulder blades into the side of the cruiser. Then she pulled out her handcuffs and reached for his left wrist, as though the situation had been resolved. That was a mistake. Jesse Leboeuf turned around and stiff-armed her in the chest, his face bitten with disdain.

She stumbled backward, then pulled her can of Mace from her belt. I stepped between her and Leboeuf and held my hands up in front of him, not touching him, moving side to side as he tried to advance toward her. "I'm hooking you up, Jesse," I said. "You're under arrest for resisting and assault on a police officer. If you touch my person, I'm going to put you on your knees."

His eyes looked hot and small and recessed in his sun-browned face. I could only guess at the thoughts he was having about Catin and the images he carried from a lifetime of abusing people who had no power: black women in the three-dollar cribs on Hopkins; a hobo pulled off a boxcar; a New Orleans pimp who thought he could bring his own girls to town and not piece off the action; an illiterate Cajun wife whose body shrank when he touched her. I could hear Catin breathing next to me. "I need to finish this, Dave," she said.

"No, Mr. Jesse is going to be all right," I said. "Right, Mr. Jesse? This bullshit is over. Give me your word to that effect, and we'll all go into town and work this out."

"Don't you do this," Catin said to me.

"It's over," I said. "Right, Jesse?"

He looked hard at me, then nodded.

"Shame on you," Catin said to me.

We rode in front with Leboeuf in back, unhooked, behind the wire-mesh screen. We didn't speak until we were at the department, and then it was only to get Leboeuf into a holding cell.

CATIN WENT IN to see Helen first, then I did. "Catin says you wouldn't back her up," Helen said.

"Call it what you want," I replied. "I didn't see too many alternatives at the time."

"Nobody is going to knock my deputies around."

"What would you have done?"

"You don't want to know."

"You'd bust up an old man and involve one of your deputies in a liability suit? That's what you're saying?"

She picked a pen up from her desk blotter and dropped it in a can full of other pens. "Talk to her. She thinks highly of you."

"I will."

"While you were gone, I pulled Leboeuf's phone records," she said. "I haven't charged him so far because I don't want him lawyered up."

"What did you find?"

"He's made some suspicious calls, put it that way. You think he's capable of putting a hit on a cop?"

"Jesse Leboeuf is capable of anything."

"Get him in here," she said.

On the way to the holding cell, I saw Catin in the corridor. "Walk with me," I said.

"Why should I?"

I rested my hand on her shoulder. "When I was a young second lieutenant in the United States Army, I reported a major who was drunk on duty. Nothing was done about it. Later, this same major sent us down a night trail strung with Bouncing Betties and Chinese toe-poppers. We lost two men that night. I know how it feels when somebody doesn't back your play. That wasn't my intention when I stepped in front of Jesse Leboeuf. The real problem was not you but me. The truth is, I hate men like Jesse Leboeuf, and when I deal with them, I sometimes go across lines I shouldn't."

She stopped walking and turned toward me, forcing me to drop my hand from her shoulder. She looked up at me, her eyes searching mine. "Forget it," she said.

"Sheriff Soileau wants Leboeuf in her office in a few minutes. I think he's dirty on some level, but right now we're not sure what. I wonder if you can do a favor for me."

After she and I talked, she walked by herself down to the holding cell while I took a seat in a chair around the corner.

"I have to clear up something between us, Mr. Leboeuf," she said through the bars. "I don't like you or what you represent. You're a racist and a misogynist, and the world would be better off without you. But as a Christian, I have to forgive you. The reason I'm able to do that is I think you're a victim yourself. It appears you were loyal to people who are now ratting you out. That must be a terrible fate to live with. Anyway, that's your business, not mine. Good-bye, and I hope I never see you again."

It was a masterpiece. I waited five minutes, then unlocked Leboeuf's cell door. "The sheriff wants to see you," I said.

"I'm getting out?" he said, rising from the wood bench where he had been sitting.

"Are you kidding?" I said. I cuffed his wrists behind him and made sure as many people as possible witnessed his humiliation while I escorted him to Helen's office.

"Y'all don't have the right to do this to me," he said.

"I don't want to tell you how to think, but if I were you, I wouldn't be the fall guy on this one," I replied.

"Fall guy on what?"

"Suit yourself," I said. I opened the door to Helen's office and sat him down in a chair.

Helen was standing by the window, backlit by the sun's glare off Bayou Teche. She smiled pleasantly at him. She was holding half a dozen printouts from the phone company. "Did you know that prior to Dave Robicheaux's visit to your home yesterday, you hadn't used your landline or your cell phone in two days?"

"I wasn't aware of that," he replied, his hands still cuffed behind him, the strain starting to show.

"Immediately after Detective Robicheaux left your house, you made three calls: one to the home of Pierre Dupree, one to a boat dock south of New Orleans, and one to a company called Redstone Security. Forty-five minutes later, someone tried to kill Detective Robicheaux."

"I called Pierre because him and me and my daughter own half of Redstone. I'm retired, but I still consult for them. I wanted Pierre to know that I'll sell him my shares in the company at the stock option price if he'll treat my daughter right in their divorce settlement. The phone call to the boat dock was a misdial. What difference does any of this make, anyway?"

"You dialed the wrong number?" she said.

"I guess. I didn't give it any thought."

"Your phone records show you called that same boat dock four times in the last month. Were those all misdials?"

"I'm old. I get confused," he said. "You're talking too fast and trying to trip me up. I want my daughter here."

"Lafayette PD was on the shooter from the jump," Helen said. "He's a guy you know, Mr. Leboeuf. He doesn't want to go back to Camp J. Are you going to take his weight? At your age, any sentence can mean life."

Leboeuf stared into space, his unshaved cheeks threaded with tiny purple veins. I realized we had been foolish in thinking we could take him over the hurdles. He belonged to that group of people who, of their own volition, eradicate all light from the soul and thereby inure themselves against problems of conscience and any thoughts of restraint in dealing with the wiles of their enemies. I cannot say with certainty what constitutes a sociopath. My guess is they love evil for its own sake, that they chose roles and vocations endowing them with sufficient authority and power to impose their agenda on their fellow man. Was Jesse Leboeuf a sociopath? Or was he something worse?

"I don't like you staring at me like that," he said to me.

"Did you ever think about the emotional damage you did to the people you tormented with your slingshot years ago?" I asked.

"I don't know what you're talking about."

"When you and your friends went nigger-knocking in the black district."

He shook his head. "I have no memory of that," he replied.

"Get him out of here," Helen said.

I unlocked Leboeuf's cuffs. He stood up, rubbing his wrists. "You charging me on the beef with the black woman?"

"You're free to go, sir," I replied.

Leboeuf huffed air out his nose and left Helen's office, trailing his cigarette odor like a soiled flag. But it wasn't over. Five minutes later, I was standing by the possessions desk when a deputy handed Leboeuf the manila envelope that contained his wallet and keys and pocket change and cigarette lighter. I watched him put each item back in his pockets, gazing indolently out the window at the oak-shaded grotto dedicated to Jesus' mother.

"Mind if I have a look at your key chain?" I said.

"What's so interesting about it?" he asked.

"The fob. It's a sawfish. It's like the one I think was painted on the bow of the boat that abducted Blue Melton."

"It's a goddamn fish. What kind of craziness are you trying to put on me now?"

"I remember where I saw that emblem painted on another boat many years ago. It was in sixty feet of water, south of Cocodrie. The sawfish was on the conning tower of a Nazi submarine. It was sunk by a Coast Guard dive-bomber in 1943. That's quite a coincidence, isn't it?"

"Give your guff to the devil," he replied.

Later, I made two calls to the boat dock whose number Helen had pulled from Leboeuf's phone records. In each instance the man I spoke with said he knew nothing of a white boat with a sawfish painted on the bow.

CHAPTER
11

THAT EVENING, CLETE Purcel pulled his Caddy to the curb one house down from ours and walked back across our yard to the front door, tapping softly, as though preoccupied about something. When I answered the door, I could see the Caddy in the shadows, a solitary spark of red sunlight showing through the live oaks that towered over it. The air was humid and warm, the trees along the bayou pulsing with birds. Clete untwisted the cellophane on a thin green-striped stick of peppermint candy and put it in his mouth. "Where'd you get the cuts on your face?" he asked.

"A situation in Lafayette. Why'd you park up the street?"

"I've got an oil leak."

"I thought you were in New Orleans. Come inside."

"I think NOPD still wants to hang Frankie Giacano's murder on me. I'll be at the motor court. I'll see you later. I just wanted to tell you I was back in town."

Through the gloom, I could see someone sitting in the passenger seat, even though the top was up. "Who's with you?"

"A temp I put on."

"What kind of temp?"

"The kind that does temporary jobs."

"A guy tried to take my head off with a cut-down yesterday. He was using double-aught bucks. Lafayette PD thinks it was a guy I helped send away about ten years ago. A retired plainclothes named Jesse Leboeuf may have sicced him on me."

"Why didn't you call me?"

"Who's in the Caddy, Clete?"

"None of your business. Is this guy Leboeuf connected to Pierre Dupree or any of this stuff with Golightly and Grimes and Frankie Gee?"

"Leboeuf is Pierre Dupree's father-in-law."

"This guy is like a stopped-up toilet that keeps backing up on the floor. I think maybe we should do a home call."

"Better listen to the rest of it," I said.

We sat down on the gallery steps, and I told him about the shooting by Varina Leboeuf's apartment in Bendel Gardens, the heisted freezer truck that the shooter and his driver had used, the connection between the Leboeufs and Pierre Dupree and a group called Redstone Security, and the key-chain fob cast in the miniature shape of a sawfish carried by Jesse Leboeuf.

"And there was a sawfish on that old wreck that used to drift up and down the continental shelf?" Clete said.

"I'm sure of it."

"Leboeuf is a crypto-Nazi or something?"

"I doubt if he could spell the word," I said.

"This isn't connecting for me, Dave. We're talking about the emblem on a Chris-Craft that kidnapped the Melton girl and now about a sawfish on a submarine and a key chain? And the guy with the key chain is the father-in-law of a guy who's part Jewish?"

"That pretty much sums it up."

"The shooter suspect, this guy Ronnie Earl Patin, is not in custody, right?"

"Right."

"You make him for the shooter?"

"I saw him for maybe two seconds before he fired into my windshield. The Ronnie Earl Patin I sent up the road was a blimp. The guy in the freezer truck wasn't. Who's in the Caddy, Clete?"

"My latest squeeze. She works for the Humane Society and adopts pathetic losers like me."

I laid my arm across his shoulders. They felt as hard and solid as boulders in a streambed. "Are you getting in over your head, partner?"

"Will you stop that? I'm not the problem here. It's you that almost caught a faceful of buckshot. Listen to me. This deal has something to do with stolen or forged paintings. They go into private collections owned by guys who want power over the art world. They not only want to own a rare painting, they want to make sure nobody ever sees it except them. They're like trophy killers who hide the cadavers."

"How do you know all this?"

"It's no secret. There's a criminal subculture that operates in the art world. The clientele are greedy, possessive assholes and are easy to take over the hurdles. Golightly had e-mails from well-known art fences in Los Angeles and New York. I confirmed the names with NYPD and a couple of PIs in L.A."

"It's not just stolen artwork. It's bigger than that," I said.

"Like what?"

"What do you know about this Redstone Security group?"

"They're out of Galveston and Fort Worth, I think. They did a lot of government contract work in Iraq. I've heard stories about their people indiscriminately killing civilians."

"Can I meet your temp?"

"No, she's tired. What's this obsession over my temp?"

"Jimmy the Dime called me. He told me Count Carbona gave you a lead on your daughter."

"Jimmy the Dime should keep his mouth shut."

"What are you up to, Clete? You think you can change the past?"

"You got to ease up on the batter, Streak. In this case, the batter is me."

"If that's the way you want it," I said.

He crunched down on the peppermint stick and chewed a broken piece in his jaw, making sounds like a horse eating a carrot, his eyes never leaving mine. "We almost died out there on the bank of the bayou, where we used to have dinners on your picnic table. Know why? Because we trusted people we shouldn't. That's the way it's always been. We turned the key on the skells while the white-collar crowd kicked a railroad tie up our ass. That's not the way this one is going down. Got it, big mon?"

• • •

EARLY THE NEXT morning Clete and Gretchen ate a breakfast of bis-
cuits and gravy and fried pork chops and scrambled eggs at Victor's
Cafeteria on Main and then drove to Jeanerette down the old two-
lane state road that followed Bayou Teche through an idyllic stretch
of sugarcane and cattle acreage. Her window was down, and the
wind was blowing her hair over her forehead. There was a thin gold
chain around her neck, and she was fiddling with the icon attached
to it. "It's beautiful here," she said.

"The fishing is good, too. So is the food, maybe even better than
New Orleans."

"You sure you want to 'front this guy at his house?"

"Stonewall Jackson used to say 'Mislead, mystify, and surprise the
enemy.'"

"That's great stuff as long as you have fifty thousand rednecks
stomping ass for you."

"Is that the Star of David?" he asked.

"This?" she said, fingering the gold chain. "My mother is Jewish,
so I'm at least half. I don't know what my father was. He could have
been a Mick or a Swede, because neither my mother nor anybody in
her family has reddish-blond hair."

"You go to temple?"

"Why are you asking about the Star of David?"

"Barney Ross and Max Baer both wore it on their trunks. I don't
know if they went to temple or not. Maybe they wore it for good
luck. Is that why you wear it? That's all I was asking."

"Who are Max Baer and Barney Ross?" she said.

"Never mind. Look, we're going into St. Mary Parish. Pierre
Dupree owns another home in the Garden District in New Orleans. I
suspect he's here. This place looks like the United States, but it's not.
This is Dupree turf. The rest of us are tourists. You don't want to get
pinched here. I have to ask you something."

"Go ahead."

"You know what 'wet work' is?"

"I've heard of it."

"I've had people ask me to do it."

"Did you?"

"No. I run an honest business. I don't work for dirtbags, and I don't jam the family of a skip in order to bring him in. What I'm asking you is did you know some bad guys in Little Havana, maybe some guys who got you into the life? Did you maybe do some stuff you don't feel good about?"

"I didn't know who Ernest Hemingway was until I moved to Key West and visited his house on Whitehead Street," she said. "Then I started reading his books, and I saw something in one of them I never forgot. He said the test of all morality is whether you feel good or bad about something the morning after."

"I'm listening," he said.

"The only time I felt bad about anything was when I didn't get even for what people did to me," she said. "By the way, I don't like that term 'in the life.' I was never 'in the life.'"

Clete passed a plantation on the Teche that had been built miles downstream in 1796 and brought brick by brick up the bayou in the early 1800s and reassembled on its present site. Then he entered the spangled shade of live oaks that had been on the roadside for over two hundred years, and passed a second antebellum plantation, one with enormous white columns. He crossed the drawbridge and drove by a trailer slum and entered the small town of Jeanerette, where time seemed to have stopped a century ago and the yards of the Victorian homes along the main street were bursting with flowers, the lawns so blue and green and cool in appearance that you felt you could dive into them as you would into a swimming pool. Clete approached the home of Pierre Dupree and turned in to the gravel lane that led to the wide-galleried entrance of the main house, the gigantic oak limbs creaking above.

"Every time I visit a place like this, I always wonder how things would have worked out if the South had won the war," Clete said.

"How would things have worked out?" Gretchen asked.

"I think all of us, white and black, would be picking these people's cotton," he replied.

They stepped out of the Caddy onto the gravel, the trees swelling with wind, a few yellow oak leaves tumbling through the columns of sunlight. In back they heard a dog bark. Clete rang the chimes on the front door, but no one answered. He motioned to Gretchen, and the two of them walked through the side yard to the rear of the house, where a gazebo stood on a long stretch of green lawn that sloped down to the bayou. An elderly man was training a yellow Lab down the slope, a reelless fishing rod clenched in his hand. By the corner of the house, inside a cluster of philodendron, Clete noticed a stack of wire tender traps. "May I help you?" the elderly man said.

"I'm Clete Purcel, and this is my assistant, Miss Gretchen," Clete said. "I'd like to talk to either Alexis or Pierre Dupree about a man who claimed to have taken a betting marker out of an office safe that used to belong to Didoni Giacano."

"Did Mr. Robicheaux send you here?"

"I sent myself here," Clete said. "Frankie Giacano and his friends tried to extort me with that same betting marker. Are you Alexis Dupree?"

"I am. It's customary to phone people in advance when you plan to visit their home."

"Sorry about that. Frankie Gee got himself capped, Mr. Dupree. But I don't think he got capped over this business with the marker. I think it has to do with stolen or forged paintings that a guy named Bix Golightly was fencing. You know anything about that?"

"I'm afraid I don't. Would you like to sit down? Can I get you something to drink?" Alexis Dupree said. His gaze shifted from Clete to Gretchen.

"We're fine," Clete said.

Dupree picked up a pie plate from a redwood table and a small sack of dry dog food. He walked down the slope as though Clete and Gretchen were not there and set the pie plate on the grass and sprinkled several pieces of dog food in it. He carried the fishing rod in his left hand. The Labrador retriever was sitting in the sunlight on the opposite side of the lawn but never moved. "Come," Alexis Dupree said.

The dog started across the grass. "Stop," Dupree said. The dog immediately sat down. "Come," Dupree said. The dog took another few steps, then stopped again upon command. "Come," Dupree said.

When the dog advanced, its attention remained upon Dupree and not the pie plate. "Stop," Dupree said. He looked up the slope at Clete and Gretchen, then at the white clouds drifting across the sky, then at a flock of robins descending on a tree. His lips were pursed, his regal profile framed against a backdrop of oaks and flowers and Spanish moss and a tidal stream and a gold-and-purple field of sugarcane. "Come," he said again. This time he let the dog eat.

"Is he telling us something?" Gretchen whispered.

"Yeah, don't let a guy like that ever get control of your life," Clete said.

From out front, Clete heard the sound of a car coming up the gravel drive, then a car door slamming.

"Mr. Dupree, somebody tried to kill my friend Dave Robicheaux," Clete said. "It was right after he left the home of Jesse Leboeuf. Your family and Jesse Leboeuf are mixed up with a group called Redstone Security, Inc. These guys have the reputation of stink on shit. You know who I'm talking about?"

"Your passion and your language are impressive, but no, I know nothing about any of this," Dupree said. He approached Gretchen with a fond expression, the fishing rod still in his hand, his gaze drifting to her throat. "Are you Jewish?"

"What's it to you?" she said.

"It's a compliment. You come from a cerebral race. I also suspect you're part German."

"What she is, is one hundred percent American," Clete said.

"Clete says you were in a death camp," Gretchen said.

"I was at Ravensbrück."

"I never heard a Jew call his religion a race," she said.

"You seem like a very perceptive young woman. What is your name?"

"Gretchen Horowitz."

"I hope you'll come by again. And you don't need to call in advance."

"Mr. Dupree, we didn't come out here to talk about religious matters," Clete said. "People you and your grandson are associated with may be involved in several homicides, including a girl who floated up in a block of ice a little south of here. Are you reading me on this, sir?"

Before Dupree could answer, Clete heard footsteps behind him. He turned around and looked at perhaps one of the most beautiful women he had ever seen. She did not seem to notice either his or Gretchen's presence; instead, she was staring at Alexis Dupree with a level of anger Clete would never want directed at him. "Where's Pierre?" she said.

"In Lafayette at his art exhibit. He'll be so sorry he missed you," Dupree said.

"Who are you?" the woman said to Clete.

"A private investigator," he replied.

"You came to the right place." She started to speak to Dupree, then she turned again to Clete. "You're Dave Robicheaux's buddy, aren't you?"

"That's right."

"I'm Varina Leboeuf. You tell Dave if he ever humiliates my father again like he did yesterday, I'm going to beat the shit out of him."

"If Dave Robicheaux busted your old man, he had it coming," Clete said.

"What are y'all doing here?" she said.

"You need to butt out, ma'am," Gretchen said.

"*What* did you say?"

"We're having a conversation with Mr. Dupree. You're not part of it," Gretchen said.

"I'll tell you what, young lady. Why don't you and this gentleman ask Mr. Dupree about these wire traps stacked in the flower bed? Alexis places them all over the property every two or three weeks. The madwoman who used to own this wretched dump fed every stray cat in the parish. Alexis hates cats. So he baits and traps them and has a black man drop them at night in other people's neighborhoods. Most of them will starve to death or die of disease."

"Did you mention we don't have a local animal refuge?" Dupree said.

"I just left the office of Pierre's lawyer. If your grandson tries to fuck me on the settlement, I'm going to destroy all of you," Varina said.

"You've certainly arrived here in a charming mood," Dupree said.

"What are you doing with my dog? Pierre said he'd run away."

"He did. But he came back home. He's a brand-new dog now," Dupree said.

"Come here, Vick," Varina called.

The dog rested its jowls on its paws and did not move.

"Vick, come with Mommy. Come on, fella," she called.

The dog seemed to shrink itself into the grass. Alexis Dupree was smiling at her, the fishing rod trembling slightly with the palsy that affected his hand. His gaze moved back to Gretchen and the lights in her hair and the thin gold chain. "Please accept my apologies for the behavior of my grandson's wife," he said. "Did your family emigrate from Prussia? Few people know that Yiddish is a German dialect. I suspect you're aware of that, aren't you?"

Gretchen looked at Clete. "I'll wait in the car," she said.

"Did I say something wrong?" Dupree asked, his eyes dropping to Gretchen's hips and thighs as she walked away.

"Don't let that old guy get to you," Clete said to her in the Caddy.

"I felt like he wanted to peel off my skin."

"Yeah, he's a little strange."

"*He's* a little strange? How about the broad?"

"She seemed pretty normal to me."

"She has a broom up her ass."

"So?"

"You couldn't keep your eyes off her. That's the kind of woman you're attracted to?"

"You work for me, Gretchen. You're not my spiritual adviser."

"Then act your fucking age."

"I can't believe I'm listening to this," Clete said.

She stared at the rusted trailers in the slum by the drawbridge and the children in the dirt yards and the wash flapping on the clotheslines. The Caddy rumbled across the steel grid on the drawbridge. "I don't know why I said that. I feel confused when I'm with you. I don't understand my feelings. You really aren't trying to put moves on me, are you?"

"I already told you."

"You don't think I'm attractive?"

"I know my limitations. I'm old and overweight and have hypertension and a few drinking and weed issues. If I was thirty years younger, you'd have to hide." He accelerated the Caddy toward New Iberia, lowering his window, filling the inside of the car with the sound of wind. "We're going to get you a badge," he said.

"A badge for what?"

"A private investigator's badge. At a pawnshop and police-supply store in Lafayette," he said. "Anybody can buy a PI badge. They're bigger and shinier and better-looking than an authentic cop's badge. The trick to being a PI is gaining the client's confidence. Our big enemy is not the skells but the Internet. With Google, you can look down people's chimneys without ever leaving your house. Most reference librarians are better at finding people and information than I am."

"Yeah, but you don't just 'find' people."

"Here's the reality of the situation. I've got certain powers not because I'm a PI but because I run down bail skips for two bondsmen. I'm not a bondsman, but legally, I'm the agent and representative of people who are, so the powers given them by the state extend to me, which allows me to pursue fugitives across state lines and kick down doors without a warrant. I have legal powers an FBI agent doesn't have. For example, if a husband and wife are both out on bond and the husband skips, Wee Willie and Nig can have the wife's bond revoked in order to turn dials on the husband. I don't do stuff like that, but Wee Willie and Nig do. You starting to get the picture?"

"You don't like what you do?"

"I want to wear a full-body condom when I go to work. Pimps and pedophiles and dope dealers use my restroom and put their feet on my office furniture. They think I'm their friend. I try not to shake hands with them. Sometimes I have to. Sometimes I want to scrub my skin with peroxide and a wire brush."

"It's a job. Why beat up on yourself?"

"No, it's what you do after you've flushed your legitimate career. The only time you actually help out your clients is in a civil suit. The justice system doesn't work most of the time, but civil court does. This guy Morris Dees broke the Klan and a bunch of Aryan Nation groups by bankrupting them in civil court. I don't catch many civil cases. If you work for me, you deal with the skells. That means we've got two rules: We're honest with each other, and we never hurt anybody unless they deal the play. Can you live with that?"

"This is the big test I'm supposed to pass?"

He pulled to the side of the road under a shade tree, next to a pasture where black Angus were grazing in the sunlight.

"What are you doing?" she said.

"I like you a lot, and I think the world has done a number on you that no kid deserves. I want to be your friend, but I don't have much to offer. I'm a drunk, and almost everything I touch turns to shit. I don't care what you did before we met. I just want you to be straight with me now. You want to tell me some things down the track, that's copacetic. If you don't want to tell me anything down the track, that's copacetic, too. You hearing me on all this? I back your play, you back mine. The past is past; now is now." He brushed a strand of hair from her eye.

"I don't get you," she said.

"What's to get? I love movies and New Orleans and horse tracks and Caddy convertibles with fins and eating large amounts of food. My viscera alone probably weighs two hundred pounds. When I go into a restaurant, I get seated at a trough."

"You really like movies?"

"I go to twelve-step meetings for movie addiction."

"You have cable?"

"Sure. I've got insomnia. I watch movies in the middle of the night."

"James Dean's movies are showing all this week. I think he was the greatest actor who ever lived."

He restarted the Caddy and turned back onto the road, his brow furrowed, remembering the red windbreaker worn by the person he watched murder Bix Golightly. "What do you know about guns?"

"Enough so I don't want to be on the wrong side of them."

"We'll stop at Henderson Swamp. I want to show you a few things about firearms."

"I found your Beretta and disarmed it on your premises. I don't need a gun lesson, at least not now. I'm a little tired, okay? The numbers tattooed on that old man's forearm, they're from the death camp?"

"Yeah, I guess. Why?"

"He made me feel dirty all over. Like when I was a little girl. I don't know why," she replied. "I'm not feeling too good. Can we go back to the motor court? I need to take a nap and start the day over."

THE ONLY LEAD I had on the men who had tried to kill me outside Bendel Gardens was the name of Ronnie Earl Patin, a strong-arm robber I had helped put away a decade ago. Though there are instances when a felon goes down for some serious time and nurses a grudge over the years and eventually gets out and does some payback, it's very rare that he goes after a cop or judge or prosecutor. Payback is usually done on a fall partner or a family member who snitched him off. Ronnie Earl was a sweaty glutton and a porn addict and a violent alcoholic who knocked around old people for their Social Security checks, but he had been jailing all of his adult life, and most of his crimes grew out of his addictions and were not part of vendettas. That said, would he do a contract job on a cop if the money was right? It was possible.

The driver of the freezer truck was too short to have been Ronnie Earl, and the shooter who had almost taken my head off with the cut-down had an ascetic face similar in design to a collection of saw blades. Could ten years in Angola, most of it on Camp J, have melted down the gelatinous pile that I helped send up there?

I called an old-time gunbull at Angola who had shepherded Ronnie Earl through the system for years. "Yeah, he was one of our Jenny Craig success stories," the gunbull said. "He stayed out of segregation his last two years and worked in the bean field."

"He went out max time?"

"He earned two months good time before his discharge. This was on a ten-bit. He could have been out in thirty-seven months."

"What kept him in segregation?"

"Making pruno and raping fish and being a general shithead. What are you looking at him for?"

"Somebody tried to pop me with a shotgun."

"It doesn't sound like Ronnie Earl."

"Why not?"

"He's got two interests in life: sex and getting high. The guy's a walking gland. The only reason he got thin was to get laid when he got out. Cain't y'all send us a higher grade of criminals?"

"You think he's capable of a contract hit?"

"You ever know a drunkard who wasn't capable of anything?" Then he evidently thought about what he had just said. "Sorry. You still off the juice?"

"I go to a lot of meetings. Thanks for your time, Cap," I said.

I began making phone calls to several bars in North Lafayette. A person might wonder how a sheriff's detective in Iberia Parish would be presumptuous enough to believe he could find a suspect in Lafayette, twenty miles away, when the local authorities could not. The answer is simple: Every alcoholic knows what every other alcoholic is thinking. There is only one alcoholic personality. There are many manifestations of the disease, but the essential elements remain the same in every practicing drunk. CEO, hallelujah-mission wino, Catholic nun, ten-dollar street whore, academic scholar, world boxing champion, or three-hundred-pound blob, the mind-set never varies. It is for this reason that practicing alcoholics wish to avoid the company of drunks who have sobered up, and sometimes even get them fired from their jobs, lest there be anyone in proximity who can hear their most secret thoughts.

One bartender told me Ronnie Earl had been in his place two months back, right after his release from Angola. The bartender said Ronnie Earl looked nothing like the fat man the court had sent up the road.

"But he's the same guy, right?" I said.

"No," the bartender said. "Not at all."

"What do you mean?"

"He's worse. You know how it works," the bartender said. "A sick guy like that gets even sicker when he doesn't drink. When he gets back on the train, he's carrying a furnace with him instead of a stomach."

The bartender had not seen Ronnie Earl since and did not know where he had gone.

The last bartender I called had picked me up out of an alley behind a B-girl joint in Lafayette's old Underpass area, a one-block collection of buildings that was so stark and unrelieved, whose inhabitants were so lost and disconnected from the normal world, that if you found yourself drinking there, you could rest assured you had finally achieved the goal you long ago set for yourself: the total destruction of the innocent child who once lived inside you. The bartender's name was Harvey. For me, Harvey had always been a modern-day Charon who turned me away from the Styx. "Every afternoon there's a guy who comes in here who goes by Ron," he said. "He drinks like he's making up for lost time. One mug of beer, four shots lined up. Same order every time. He likes to flash his money around and invite the working girls over to his table. The whole rainbow, know what I mean?"

"I'm not sure."

"He's definitely multicultural."

"What does Ron look like?"

"Neat dresser, good haircut. Maybe he's been working outdoors. I remember him telling a joke. It was about Camp J or something. Does that mean anything?"

"A lot."

"He just walked in. He's got three broads with him. What do you want me to do?"

I glanced at my watch. It was a quarter to five. "Keep him there. I'm on my way. If he leaves, get his tag and call the locals."

"I don't need a bunch of cops in here, Dave."

"Everything is going to be fine. If you have to, give Ron and his friends an extra round or two. It's on me."

My truck was still at the glazier's. I checked out an unmarked car and tore down the two-lane past Spanish Lake toward Lafayette, a battery-powered emergency light clamped on the roof.

THE CLUB WAS a windowless box with a small dance floor and vinyl booths set against two walls. The light from the bathrooms glowed through a red-bead curtain that hung from a rear doorway. Outside, the sky was still bright, but when I entered the bar, I could barely make out the people sitting in the booths. I saw Harvey look up from the sink where he was rinsing glasses. I didn't acknowledge him but went to the corner of the bar, in the shadows, and sat down on a stool. I was wearing my sport coat and a tie, and the flap of my coat covered the holstered .45 clipped onto my belt. The duckboards bent under Harvey's weight as he walked toward me. His face was round and flat, his Irish mouth so small it looked like it belonged to a goldfish. "What are you having?" he asked.

"A Dr Pepper on ice with a lime slice." Out of the corner of my eye, I saw a black woman in a short skirt and a low-cut white blouse sitting on a barstool. I looked back at Harvey. "You still serve gumbo?"

"Coming up," he said. He began fixing my drink, letting his gaze rest on a booth by the entrance. I glanced over and saw a blade-faced man and three females. Harvey placed my drink in front of me and picked up a stainless steel dipper and lowered it into a cauldron of chicken gumbo and filled a white bowl and set it and a spoon and a paper napkin in front of me. He picked up the twenty I had placed on the bar. "I'll bring your change back in a minute. I got an order waiting over here."

He took a frosted mug from the cooler and filled it until foam ran over the lip, then poured four shot glasses to the brim and placed the mug and all the glasses on a round tray. The work Harvey did behind a bar was not part of a mystique or of a kind most normal people would notice. But I could not take my eyes off his hands and the methodical way he went about filling the glasses and placing them on the cork-lined tray; nor could I ignore the smell of freshly drawn beer and whiskey that had not been cut with ice or fruit or cocktail mix. I could see the brassy bead in the beer, the strings of foam running down through the frost on the mug. The whiskey had the amber glow of sunlight that might have been aged inside yellow oak, its wetness and density and latent power greater than the sum of its parts, welling over the brim of the shot glasses as though growing in size. I felt a longing inside me that was no different from the desire of a heroin or sex addict or a candle moth that seeks the flame the way an infant seeks its mother's breast.

I drank from my Dr Pepper and swallowed a piece of shaved ice and tried to look away from the tray Harvey was carrying to the booth by the front door.

"You ever see a li'l boy looking t'rew the window at what he cain't have?" the black woman in the short skirt said.

"Who you talking about?" I said.

"Who you t'ink?"

"This is my job," I said. "I check out dead-end dumps that serve people like me."

"Ain't nothing that bad if you got a li'l company."

"You're too pretty for me."

"That's why you looking at them other ladies in the mirror? They ain't pretty?"

"You want a bowl of gumbo?" I asked.

"Honey, what I got don't come in no bowl. You ought to try some."

I winked at her and lifted a spoonful of gumbo to my mouth.

"Darlin'?" she said. Her stool squeaked as she turned toward me. She *was* pretty. Her skin was as darkly brown as chocolate and unmarked with scars or blemishes, her hair thick and black and freshly washed and blow-dried. "Your slip is showing."

I pulled the flap of my coat over my .45, my eyes still on the reflections in the bar mirror.

"One of the girls in the boot' you're looking at is my li'l sister. I'm gonna walk over there and ax her to go outside wit' me. We ain't gonna have no trouble over that, are we?"

"What's your name?"

"Lavern."

"You need to stay where you are, Miss Lavern. I'm going to speak to an old acquaintance over there. You and your friends are going to be just fine. Maybe I can buy y'all a drink a little later. But right now y'all need to take your mind off world events. That's Ronnie Earl Patin in the booth, isn't it?"

"You ain't wit' Lafayette PD."

"You've got that right."

"Then why you come in here making t'ings hard for people who ain't done you nothing?"

In reality, her question was not an unreasonable one. But wars are not reasonable, and neither is most law enforcement. In Vietnam, we killed an estimated five civilians for every enemy KIA. Law enforcement is not much different. The people who occupy the underside of society are dog food. Slumlords, zoning board members on a pad, porn vendors, and industrial polluters usually skate. Rich men don't go to the injection table, and nobody worries when worker ants get stepped on.

I picked up a loose chair from a table and carried it and my drink to the booth where the man named Ron was sitting with a young white woman and one black woman and one Hispanic girl who probably wasn't over seventeen. "What's the haps, Ronnie Earl?" I said, setting down the chair hard.

"You've mistaken me for somebody else. My name is Ron Prudhomme," the man said. He was smiling, his cheekbones and chin forming a V in his lower face, his eyes warm with alcohol.

"No, I think you and I go back, Ron. Remember when you bashed that old man with a hammer for his veteran's check? You put a hole in his skull. I don't think he was ever right again."

"I don't know who you are," he said.

"I'm Dave Robicheaux," I said to the two women and the girl. "I think Ronnie put a load of buckshot through my windshield."

The man who called himself Ron Prudhomme picked up a shot glass and drank it slowly to the bottom, savoring each swallow, his expression sleepy. He took a sip from his beer mug, a sliver of ice sliding across his thumb. "If I'd done something like that, would I be hanging around town?" he asked.

"Yeah, I have to admit that one doesn't fit," I replied.

"It doesn't fit because I'm not your guy."

"Oh, you're my huckleberry, all right. I just haven't figured out if you're doing contract hits now or if you're a minor player in a group that includes Jesse Leboeuf, a retired homicide roach. You know Jesse Leboeuf? He used to put the fear of God in guys like you."

He eased one of his full shot glasses toward me. "You want a beer back on that? If I remember, you got the same kind of taste buds I do. I think we got eighty-sixed from the same joints. The only reason you were allowed in some of the clubs was because you carried a shield."

"I think I figured out why you're hanging around, Ronnie. You didn't blow town because you weren't the hitter in the freezer truck. But you boosted the truck at the motel where you were staying. Which means you boosted it for somebody else. It seems to me you had a brother, but y'all didn't look alike. You looked like a helium balloon with stubs for arms and legs, but your brother was trim. The way you look now. Have I got my hand on it?"

"This is all Greek to me. Unless you're that cop who lied on the stand and sent me up the road for a ten-bit I didn't deserve."

"No, I'm the cop who made sure there was a short-eyes notation in your jacket," I said. "Ladies, y'all should be especially careful about this man. His weight loss is huge, and it occurred in a very short amount of time. I suggest you make him use industrial-strength condoms, or you stay completely away from him and spread the word to your sisters. He was both a predator and a cell-house bitch in Angola and stayed in lockdown for years because he was involved in at least two gang rapes. Do y'all get tested regularly for AIDS?"

The white woman and the black woman looked at each other, then at the Hispanic girl. The three of them rose from the booth and, without speaking a word, went out the front door of the club.

"I guess this means we're not gonna be drinking buddies," Ronnie Earl said.

"I can hook you up now and take you to the Lafayette PD. Or I can call them and have them pick you up. Or you can give up the hitter in the freezer truck. I think the hitter was your brother."

"I haven't seen my brother since I went inside. I heard he was dead or living in western Kansas. I cain't remember which it was."

"Stand up and put your hands behind you."

"No problem. I'll be out in two hours. I read about that shooting. I was playing bridge in Lake Charles the day it happened. I've got twenty witnesses you can call."

"I've got a flash for you, Ronnie Earl. It's not me who wants to hang you out to dry. It's Lafayette PD. They've got a special hard-on for child molesters around here. They don't care how they put you away. What you're doing is five-star dumb," I said.

"So is everything in my life. Do what you're gonna do, but one thing I want to clear up: I never harmed a child. The other stuff I did. The short-eyes charge was a bum beef. Y'all sent me up wit' a bad jacket. I paid a big price for that, man."

"That's the breaks, Ronnie."

"How'd you know I got AIDS?"

"I didn't."

"I got a cut on my wrist. When a cut doesn't heal, does that mean something?"

My hands froze.

"Got you, motherfucker," he said.

Sometimes the perps, even the worst of them, have their moments.

A strange phenomenon occurred while I was hooking up Ronnie Earl Patin and patting him down for weapons and jailhouse contraband. I saw the entirety of the club as though it had been freeze-framed inside a camera lens. I saw my friend Harvey, beetle-browed and head-shaved, his big arms propped on the bar, looking wanly at an Iberia cop he had picked up from a greasy pool of water, a cop who might now cost him his job; I saw the prostitute in the low-cut blouse and short skirt talking on her cell phone as she went out a side exit; I saw a handicapped man whose arms were too short for his truncated body trying to push coins into the jukebox, his fingers as inept as Vienna sausages; I saw all the sad burnt-out ends of the days and nights I had spent in bars from Saigon's Bring Cash Alley to the backstreets of Manila to a poacher's community in the Atchafalaya Basin, where I traded my army-issue wristwatch, one that survived the detonation of a Bouncing Betty, for a half-pint bottle of bourbon and a six-pack of hot beer. I saw all the detritus and waste and wreckage of my misspent life laid out before me, like a man flipping through his check stubs and realizing that the reminders of one's moral and psychological bankruptcy never go away.

"You gonna bust me or not?" Patin said.

"Right now I'm not sure what I'm going to do with you," I said. "It's not a time for you to shoot off your mouth."

"I've still got two full shot glasses on the table. You drink one, I'll drink the other. Who's the wiser? Come on, you know you want it. You're just like me. I've cut my intake in half by getting laid every day. What do you do? And don't lie to me. You're one thirsty son of a bitch."

I pushed him through the front door into the parking lot and took out my cell phone. The battery was dead. "Is your cell phone in your car?"

"I walked here. And I don't have a cell phone. I think they're for people who need to beat off more. I cain't believe this is happening. You got to bum a phone off the guy you're busting?" He started laughing uncontrollably, tears running down his cheeks.

I unlocked the manacle on one of his wrists. The sun was red and as big as a planet and starting to set behind the trees on the western side of the highway that led to Opelousas. I threaded the loose manacle through the rear bumper on my unmarked car and relocked it on Ronnie Earl Patin's wrist, forcing him to kneel on the asphalt. "I'm going to use the phone inside. I'll be back in a few minutes," I said.

"You're leaving me out here?"

"What does it look like?"

"Take me in."

"You did eight years in Camp J, Ronnie. You probably could have snitched your way out, but you didn't. Not many guys can say that. You're a stand-up guy, but for me that means you're probably a dead end. So now you're Lafayette PD's problem."

"I got bad knees. I used to do floor work without pads," he said.

"I believe it," I said. I got my raincoat off the back floor and folded it into a square and squatted down and slipped it under his shins.

He looked up at me, his mouth twisted with discomfort. "You gonna drink my booze?"

"You never can tell," I said.

I went back inside the club. Maybe I should have transported him down to Lafayette PD in the back of the unmarked car, even though there was no D-ring on the back floor. Maybe I should have kicked him loose and tried to follow him to his next destination. Maybe I should have pulled in the three hookers. Maybe I shouldn't have let my cell phone battery go down, even though I later discovered the recharger problem lay in the dash-lighter connection. I dialed 911 on a pay phone and watched the handicapped man dancing with an imaginary woman in front of the jukebox. I looked for the prostitute I had offered to buy a bowl of gumbo, but she was nowhere in sight. I watched Harvey washing glasses in a sink of dirty water and wondered what would have happened if he had left me lying behind the B-girl joint at the Underpass. Would I have been a feast for jackals? Would I have been jackrolled or even beaten to death? Would I have begged for my life if someone had pointed a switchblade under my chin? All of these things were part of the menu when you were a gutter drunk.

I lifted my hand in a silent thank-you to Harvey as my 911 call was transferred to a Lafayette PD detective. The low ceiling and painted-over cinder-block walls of the club and the stink of cigarettes and urine from the restrooms seemed to squeeze the oxygen out of the room. I pulled loose my tie and unbuttoned my collar and took a deep breath. I closed and opened my eyes, the veins shrinking across one side of my head, my old problems with vertigo returning for no apparent reason. My gaze wandered to the shot glasses of whiskey that had been abandoned on Ronnie Earl's table. Then I stared at the cigarette burns on the floor. All of them looked like the calcified bodies of water leeches. My hand made a wet noise against the phone receiver when I squeezed it.

My 911 call to the dispatcher and my conversation with the detective could not have taken over three minutes. The handicapped man was dancing to the same song that had been playing on the jukebox when I entered the club. But I knew I had swung on a slider, one that had Vaseline all over it. The black prostitute at the bar had been too cool after making me for a cop. She had realized it, too, and had become petulant and turned herself into a victim in order to muddy my perception of her behavior. *You dumb bastard,* I said to myself. I hung up the phone and flung open the front door.

The shot came from far down the street, from either the backseat of an automobile on the corner or a shut-down filling station behind it, one whose broken windows and empty bays lay deep in the shadow of a giant live oak. The report was a single loud crack, probably that of a scoped, high-powered rifle. Maybe the bullet struck another surface before it found its target, or maybe the powder was wet or old and had degraded in the casing. Regardless of the cause, the pathologist would later conclude that the round had started to topple when it cut a keyhole through Ronnie Earl Patin's face and ripped out part of his skull and spilled most of his brains onto the trunk of the unmarked car.

When I got to him, my .45 in my hand, the cooling of the late afternoon marred by dust and road noise and the smell of rubber and exhaust fumes, he was slumped sideways on his knees, like a child who fell asleep while at prayer. I stared at the traffic and at the smoke from trash fires rising into the red sun and wondered if Ronnie Earl Patin's soul had taken flight from his body. I also wondered if his life would have been different had I not made sure he went up the road with a short-eyes in his jacket. The answer was probably no. But it's hard to hate the dead, no matter what they have done. That's the power they hold over us.

CHAPTER
12

Clete gave his bed to Gretchen and made a bed for himself on the sofa in his cottage at the motor court. "I can get my own place," she said.

"All the cottages are rented up. A decent motel here is at least sixty a night. You want to watch James Dean, don't you? Maybe the motel service doesn't have the same selections. I have all the channels."

To say she wanted to watch James Dean was an understatement. After she had watched *Giant,* Clete thought she would turn off the set and go to sleep. Instead, she used the bathroom and went immediately back to the bed, lying on her stomach, her head at the foot of the mattress, her chin propped up on both hands. Clete tried to stay with *East of Eden,* then pulled two pillows over his face while the patriarchal voice of Raymond Massey seemed to thud inside his head with the regularity of stones falling down a well. When he woke at four A.M., the bed was empty, the volume on the set barely audible. The bathroom door was open, the light off, the chain in place on the front door. He gathered the sheet around him and stood up so he could see on the far side of the bed. Gretchen lay on the floor in front of the set like a little girl, still on her stomach, her arms hooked around a pillow, her chin raised, the soles of her bare feet in the air. She was watching the last scene in *Rebel Without a Cause,* a glazed look in her eyes. He sat down in a stuffed chair, the sheet wadded in his lap. As he watched her, he knew he should not speak, in the same way you know not to speak to someone during certain moments inside a church.

"You know why the title of this movie is wrong?" she said.

"I never thought about it a lot," he replied.

"It's not about rebelling against anything. It's the other way around. The movie comes together in the scene at the observatory. Natalie Wood and James Dean and Sal Mineo are hiding from the police and the bullies. James Dean believes he's responsible for killing Buzz when they played chicken on the bluffs with the stolen cars. When he tries to turn himself in, the bullies hunt him down. James and Natalie and Sal want to be a family because they don't have families of their own. They're like the Holy Family inside the manger. They're not rebels at all. They want to be loved. The only heavens that are real to them are the stars in the top of the planetarium."

"Did you know there's a slipup in that film?" Clete said. "Sal Mineo goes out in the dark with the semi-automatic. James Dean has already taken out the magazine. He tries to tell the cops the gun's empty, but they shoot Sal anyway. The truth is, the gun wasn't empty. Sal Mineo fired it earlier, which means a shell was in the chamber."

"That's all you got out of the film? That a great director like Nicholas Ray didn't know anything about guns? That the cops did what they were supposed to do? Maybe James Dean had already cleared the chamber. It just wasn't on camera. Or maybe a piece of footage hit the cutting room floor. Many of the people on the set were veterans of World War Two or Korea. You don't think they knew how to clear a semi-auto?"

"I was just making an observation."

"Don't pass it on to anyone with a brain. You'll embarrass yourself."

"You know a lot about firearms," he said.

"Duh," she replied.

He bent behind the TV and pulled out the plug and turned off the overhead light. Even with the pillows packed down on his head and his face shoved into the sofa cushions, he couldn't get Gretchen's words out of his head. What had he expected? For Gretchen to turn out to be someone other than the figure in the Orioles baseball cap and red windbreaker he had watched raise a semi-auto eye level to Bix Golightly's face and pump three rounds into his head and mouth? Gretchen not only knew about guns, she was the kind of person whose residual anger was so great that, given the chance, she would burn out the rifling in the barrel of an automatic weapon and stay high as a kite on it.

He didn't fall asleep until the first gray light of dawn touched the eastern sky and the fog from the bayou billowed through the trees and surrounded the walls of his cottage and closed him off from the rest of the world.

WHEN CLETE AND Gretchen woke, he fixed cereal and coffee for both of them, then fried four eggs and several pieces of bacon and slathered eight slices of bread with mayonnaise and made sandwiches that he wrapped in foil. He went outside and picked a handful of mint leaves from a wet spot below the water hydrant in the flower bed, then washed the leaves and sprinkled them inside a quart bottle of orange juice. He put the sandwiches and orange juice and a sack of frozen shrimp in his ice chest.

"Want to tell me what you're doing?" she said, flipping through the pages of a *Newsweek* magazine.

"We're going fishing."

"We traded the French Quarter for an Okie motel so we could go fishing in water that smells like the grease pit at the Jiffy Lube?"

"You know what my favorite line is in *Rebel Without a Cause*?" he asked. "After James Dean and Buzz have made friends, Buzz says they still have to play chicken with the stolen cars on the cliffs. James Dean asks him why, and Buzz says, 'You gotta do something for kicks.' Did I make you mad last night?"

"No. The only people who ever made me mad are dead or doing hard time," she replied.

"Say again?"

"I'm talking about some of my mother's boyfriends. One way or another, they got cooled out. The guy who burned me with cigarettes got his out in the flats somewhere. That's on the back side of Key West. They say his bones and some of his skin got washed out of a sandbank in a storm. Whoever did him stuffed his cigarette lighter down his throat."

"How do you feel about that?"

"It couldn't have happened to a more deserving guy. I just have one regret," she said.

"What's that?"

"I wish I'd been there for it."

They drove to a rental dock and boathouse on East Cote Blanche Bay where Clete kept an eighteen-foot boat mounted with a seventy-five-horsepower Evinrude engine he'd bought at a repo auction. He loaded his saltwater rods and tackle box and ice chest and a big crab net into the boat, and a plastic garbage bag containing six empty coffee cans capped with plastic lids, then hit the starter button and drove the boat out of the slip and into the bay. The sun was hot and bright on the water, the waves dark and full of sand when they crested and broke on the beach. Gretchen was sitting on the bow, wearing cutoff blue jeans and shades and a V-neck T-shirt, without a hat or sunblock.

"You need to get behind the console and sit next to me," he said.

"Why?"

"I can't see."

She turned her face into the breeze, her hair blowing. Then she took off her shades and rubbed her eyes and put the shades on again. She slid her rump along the bow and stood up in the cockpit and finally sat down on the cushions. "What do you catch out here?" she asked.

"A lobster-red sunburn, if you're not careful."

"How many times have you been married?"

"Once."

"Where's your ex?"

"Around."

"Therapy, the methadone clinic, electroshock, that sort of thing?"

"You got a mouth on you, you know that?"

"You have some sunblock?" she asked.

"Under the seat."

She retrieved a bottle of lotion and unscrewed the cap and began rubbing it on her calves and knees and the tops of her thighs. Then she spread it on her face and the back of her neck and her throat and the top of her chest. Clete opened up the throttle, cutting a trough across the bay, heading southeast toward open water. In the distance, he could see a line of black clouds low on the horizon, electricity forking silently into the water. He made a wide arc until he entered a long flat stretch between the swells. Then he cut the engine and let the boat slide forward on its own wake. "There's a school of white trout right underneath us," he said.

"That's not why we're here, is it?" she said.

"Not really."

"What are the coffee cans for?"

"You see how calm the water is here? It's because of the shift in the tides. High tide was two hours ago. The tide is on its way back out." He opened the garbage bag and lifted out three capped coffee cans and set them one by one in the water. "We're going to see where these guys drift."

"Did you ever think about making movies?"

"Are you listening to me?"

"No, I mean it. You're always thinking. You could be a better movie director than most of the guys around now. I read this article in *Vanity Fair* on how easy it is to make a successful movie today. You sign on Vin Diesel or any guy with a voice like a rust clot in a sewer pipe, then you blow up shit. You don't even have to use real explosives. You can create them with a computer. The actors don't even have to act. They stand around like zombies and imitate Vin Diesel and blow up more shit. I can't reach my back."

He couldn't track her conversation or line of thought. She turned around in the seat and worked her T-shirt up to the strap on her halter and handed him the bottle of lotion. "Smear some on between my love handles."

"*What?*"

"I always burn right above my panty line. It hurts for days."

"I need you to listen to me and keep your mind off movies a minute, as well as other kinds of distractions."

"Are you gay or something? Is that the problem? Because if it's not, you're deeply weird."

"You need to learn some discretion, Gretchen. You can't say whatever you feel like to other people."

"*This* from you? Have you checked out your rap sheet recently? You have more entries on it than most criminals."

"What do you know about rap sheets?"

"I watch *CSI*. Cops in neon shitholes like Las Vegas have billions of dollars to spend on high-tech labs staffed by Amerasian snarfs. In the meantime, hookers and grifters and the casinos are fleecing the suckers all over town."

"What's a snarf?"

"A guy who gets off on sniffing girls' bicycle seats."

"I can't take this," Clete said. He reached into the ice chest and retrieved one of the fried-egg-and-bacon sandwiches, wiped the ice off the bread, and bit into it.

"Can I have one?" she asked.

"By all means," he replied, chewing with his eyes wide, like a man trying to keep his balance while standing in front of a wind tunnel.

"Tell me the truth—you're not a closet fudge-packer, are you?" she asked.

He tossed his sandwich over the side. "I'm going to bait our hooks and set up our outriggers. Then we're going to drift and watch where those cans float. In the meantime, no more movie talk, no more insults, no more invasion of somebody else's space. Got it?"

"Where the fuck do you get off talking to me like that?"

"This is my boat. I'm the skipper. Out at sea, the skipper's word is absolute." He looked at her expression. "Okay, I apologize."

"You should. You're a one-man clusterfuck." When he didn't reply, she said, "How many times have you seen *Rebel Without a Cause*?"

"Four, I think. I saw Paul Newman in *The Left Handed Gun* six times."

"I knew it. You're like me. You just don't want to admit it."

"Could be, kid."

"I don't usually let any man call me that," she said, "but for you I might make an exception." She removed her shades, revealing the violet and magical intensity of her eyes. Her forehead was popping with sweat, her nostrils dilated. "I don't understand my feelings about you. You're a nice guy. But every nice guy I've ever known ended up wanting something from me. For some of them, that didn't work out too good. What do you have to say to that?"

"I'm a used-up jarhead and alcoholic flatfoot with no tread left on his tires. What's to say?"

TWENTY MINUTES LATER, Clete drove the boat through a bay that was copper-colored and flecked with a dirty froth when the wind blew. When the keel struck bottom, Gretchen dropped off the bow into the water and waded through the shallows and threw the anchor up on dry sand. Clete stood up in the cockpit and gazed through a pair of binoculars at the line of plastic-capped coffee cans disappearing in the south.

"I don't understand what we're doing," Gretchen said.

Clete eased himself over the gunwale and dropped heavily into the shallows and walked up on the beach beside her, the water darkening his khakis up to the knees. "This is the place where the body of Blue Melton floated up," he said. "If you look to the southeast, you'll see a channel that flows through the bay and into the Gulf. It's like an underground river that flows in and out with the tides. I think the guys who dumped her overboard didn't know much about tidal currents. I believe they intended for her body to sink and be eaten by sharks or crabs. If the body was found, it would look like she fell off a boat and drowned. Because the ice hadn't melted, I think they were in pretty close to shore. What I'm saying is I think these guys were on a big boat, one with a freezer unit, but they're not seafarers, and they're probably not from around here."

"Why are rich guys hanging around with a poor Cajun girl from St. Martinville?" Gretchen said.

"Try sex."

"She had a balloon in her mouth?"

"It probably held the same skag she was injected with. There was a message in it that said her sister was still alive. After she was abducted, somebody decided she knew more than she was supposed to and had her killed. Somebody gave her a hotshot and let her die in a freezer."

"Why are we talking about this now?"

"My buddy Dave keeps insisting that we're up against some big players. I told him we were dealing with the same collection of lamebrains we've been locking up for thirty years. I was wrong." Clete looked at the giant trunk of an uprooted cypress that had washed up onto the beach in a storm, now lying sun-bleached and worm-scrolled and polished by wind and salt next to a stand of gum and persimmon trees. "Sit down a minute, Gretchen."

"What for?"

"Because I asked you to. I don't know how to say this. Three New Orleans lowlifes who tried to scam me out of my office building and apartment got whacked. The mechanic who did the job was probably an out-of-towner, maybe somebody who's been mobbed up for a while. These three guys were criminals and knew the rules of the game. They made their bet and lost. The girl who floated up here wasn't a player. She was an innocent girl that a bunch of real cocksuckers got their hands on and murdered. Her sister, Tee Jolie Melton, may be in the hands of those same guys. You smell that?"

Gretchen turned her face into the breeze. They were sitting in the shade on the cypress trunk, the metallic reflection of the bay as bright and eye-watering as the arc from an electric welding torch. "It smells like a filling station," she said.

"You can't see it yet, but it's oil. Nobody knows how much of it is out there. The drilling company sank it with dispersants so there would be no way to accurately calculate how many barrels they'd be held responsible for spilling. Tee Jolie Melton said something to Dave about her boyfriend being mixed up with some guys who were talking about centralizers. Dave thinks the boyfriend is Pierre Dupree. Maybe the blowout was caused because there weren't enough centralizers in the casing. But everybody already knows that, so that's not the issue."

"Yeah, I think I got all that. Go back to what you said about the three guys who messed with you and got shot."

"They're dead. End of story. Maybe the person who smoked them did the world a favor, know what I'm saying?"

"No, I don't. Not at all."

"The hitter was somebody who goes by the name Caruso."

"Like the singer?" she said.

"Yeah, when Caruso sings, everyone else becomes silent. Permanently."

"Sounds like urban-legend Mafia bullshit to me. You ever go to Miami in the winter? The whole beach is littered with greaseballs. They have physiques like tadpoles. Before they leave New York, they get chemical tans. Their skin looks like orange sherbet with black hair. My mother used to turn tricks in a couple of big hotels on the beach. She said some of these guys wore prosthetic penises inside their Speedos. Most of these pitiful fucks have day jobs on sanitation trucks. If they weren't in the union, they'd be on welfare."

Clete hung his head, his hands folded between his knees, his eyes unfocused. The wind was cool inside the shade, the leaves of the gum trees rustling overhead. His boat was rocking in the small waves sliding back off the beach.

"Did I say the wrong thing?" she asked.

"No," he replied.

"What are you thinking about?"

"I love Louisiana."

She rested her hand on the back of his neck, her fingernails touching his hairline and the pockmarks in his skin. He felt her nails move back and forth inside his hair, as though she were stroking a cat. "Under it all, you're a tender man," she said. "I don't think I've ever known anybody like you."

As I sat in Helen's office on Thursday afternoon, less than twenty-four hours after the shooting death of Ronnie Earl Patin, I wondered how things might have worked out if I had gotten Patin into custody at Lafayette PD. But if my perceptions were correct, a black hooker at the bar had notified someone that Patin was hooked to my bumper in cuffs and about to be housed in the city jail. Which meant the people behind his death and behind the attempt on my life and probably behind the deaths of Blue Melton and Waylon Grimes and Bix Golightly and Frankie Giacano had influence and power and control that went far beyond the crime families that once operated out of Galveston and New Orleans. In other words, Ronnie Patin had been DOA no matter what I did or didn't do.

Or was I falling into that category of people who saw conspiracies at work in every level of society?

"Let's see if I've got this right, Dave," Helen said. "You think Patin's brother was the shooter in the freezer truck?"

"I'm not sure. I think Ronnie Earl boosted the truck. I think the shooter in it looked like Ronnie after he'd lost a hundred pounds. Ronnie said his brother was dead or living in Kansas."

"Patin didn't know which?"

"I wouldn't call him a family-values kind of guy."

"I just talked to the chief of police in Lafayette. He said no one heard the shot or saw who killed Patin. There were no shell casings and no outside surveillance cameras at any building on the street. The chief wonders why you didn't coordinate with him before you went to the club."

"I wasn't sure the guy there was Ronnie Earl."

"You should have let Lafayette handle it."

Maybe she was right. When I didn't reply, she said, "Second-guessing others is a bad habit of mine. Maybe Lafayette PD would have sent a couple of uniforms and spooked the guy out the back door. What a crock, huh, bwana?"

I was standing by her window, with a fine view of Bayou Teche and the lawn that sloped down to the water and the camellia bushes growing on the far bank and the shady grotto dedicated to the mother of Jesus. I saw a black Saab convertible turn off East Main and come up the long curved driveway past the grotto and park below our building, its waxed surfaces glittering like razor blades. A woman got out and walked across the grass through the side entrance. I could not see her face, only the top of her head and her figure and the martial fashion in which she walked. "Are you expecting Varina Leboeuf?" I asked.

"She's here?" Helen said.

"Her vehicle is parked in the yellow zone. She just came through the restricted entrance."

"That girl needs her butt kicked."

"I think I'd better get back to my office."

"I think you should stay right where you are. Let's see what our hypocritical little cutie-pie is up to."

"Maybe she's a bit hot-tempered, but I wouldn't call her a hypocrite."

"You know why I love you, Dave? When it comes to women, you're hopeless." She waited for me to speak, but I wasn't going to. "You think she's the rebel, the reckless and passionate woman who'll always risk her heart if the right man comes into her life?"

"How about we drop it?"

But I had stepped into it. Like many people who are made different, either in the womb or because they grew up in a dysfunctional home, Helen had spent a lifetime puzzling through all the reasons she had been arbitrarily rejected by others. Therapists often identify this particular behavioral syndrome with individuals who are weak and obsessed with concerns that are of no consequence. Nothing could be further from the truth. The only reason most of these individuals become survivors and not suicides or serial killers is because they finally figure out that the world did a number on them and their rejection is undeserved and is on the world and not on them.

"Run the tape backward," Helen said. "She's rebellious over issues nobody cares about. She attends a church where most of the people are poor and uneducated and where she's a superstar. But in politics and business, she's always on board with the majority and puckering up her sweet mouth to the right people. Let me rephrase that. She's always squatting down for her nose lube."

"That's kind of rough," I said.

"When she was about fifteen, I was an instructor at the gun range. Varina's summer church camp was sponsoring a rifle team. They'd come shoot for an hour or so every morning. One morning just after a rainstorm, Varina set up at a shooting table under the shed with her bolt-action twenty-two. Nobody had fired a round yet. I was getting some paper targets out of the office when I saw her loading her rifle. I never let the kids load until I had gone downrange and tacked up the targets and returned to the shed. She knew that. She was loading anyway, pushing one shell after another into the magazine, all the time looking downrange. I said, 'Varina, you don't load until I tell you.' But she locked down the bolt as though she hadn't heard me and raised the stock to her shoulder and let off two rounds before I could get to the table and shut her down. There was a possum in a persimmon tree about thirty feet on the far side of the plywood board we tacked the paper bull's-eyes on. The possum had three babies on her back. Varina put one round through her side and one through her head."

"Sometimes kids don't think," I said.

"That's the point. She *did* think. She knew the rules, and she heard me tell her to stop loading, but she went ahead and, with forethought, shot and killed a harmless creature. Speak of the devil."

Varina Leboeuf opened Helen's door without knocking and came inside. She was dressed in jeans and low-topped boots and an orange cowboy shirt. Her mouth was bright with lip gloss, her chest visibly expanding when she breathed, her cheeks streaked with color. "Good, I caught you both," she said.

"Ms. Leboeuf, you need to go back downstairs and out the side door and move your vehicle and then come through the front entrance and ask at the reception desk if Detective Robicheaux and I are here," Helen said. "Then someone will buzz my extension, and I will probably tell that person I'm here and to send you up. Or maybe not."

"My attorney is filing a civil suit against your department and the female deputy Catin Whatever. I wanted to tell you that in person, since y'all have a way of assigning secret plots to everyone who doesn't go along with your agenda."

"Suing us for what?" Helen asked.

"Harassment of my father. Knocking him against the side of a cruiser. Falsely accusing him of whatever you can think up. You know what your problem is, Dave?"

"Tell me," I said.

"You're intelligent, but you work for people who aren't. I think that creates a daily struggle for you."

"Out, Ms. Leboeuf," Helen said.

"I'm glad to see my tax money being used so wisely," Varina said. "Yuck."

She went back out the door and did not close it behind her. I followed her down the stairs and out the side exit. She was walking fast, her eyes flashing. "You're not going to get off that easy, Varina."

"Say whatever it is you're going to say. I'm late."

"For what?"

"To meet with my father's cardiologist. He keeled over this morning."

"Why didn't you say that upstairs?"

"You'll hear a lot more in court."

"After that guy almost killed me in front of your apartment, you cleaned the blood and glass off my face and were genuinely concerned about my welfare. You said there were millions of dollars involved in the case I was pursuing. You also indicated that the people who had tried to kill me had no boundaries. You said I should not be such a foolish man."

"That has nothing to do with the ill treatment of my father."

"I think it does. I think your father is a brutal and violent man who is capable of doing anything he believes he can get away with. I think this civil suit is meant to be a distraction."

"My father was raised in poverty in a different era. Do you think it's fair to look back from the present and judge people who never traveled outside the state of Louisiana in their entire life?"

"I always admired you, Varina. I hate to see you hurt the female deputy. She didn't treat your father unjustly. That civil suit will bankrupt her and probably ruin her life and the lives of her children. You want that on your conscience?"

The top was down on her convertible. She placed her palm on the door, then removed it when she realized how hot the metal had grown in the sun. Her face was pinched, her eyes full of injury.

"I have to ask you a question," I said. "I've known you since you were a kid and always thought you were a big winner. Someone told me you shot a possum out at the gun range when you were fifteen. The possum was carrying babies."

"That's a damn lie."

"Maybe you didn't mean to. Maybe you saw some leaves moving and meant to hit a branch. Kids do things like that. I did. I shot a big coon like that once, and it still bothers me."

"I never shot an animal in my life, and you tell the liar who told you that, who I'm sure is Ms. Bull Dyko of 1969, Helen Soileau, she had better keep her lying mouth shut, because sheriff or no sheriff, I'm going to catch her in public and slap her cross-eyed."

"I wouldn't recommend that."

The sun went behind a cloud, dropping the bayou and City Hall and the oak trees and the long curved driveway into shadow. Then I saw the heat go out of Varina's face. "None of this has to happen, Dave. Don't you see? We live our lives the best we can. The people who make the decisions don't care about us one way or another. Why give up your life for no reason? When all this is over, nobody will even remember our names."

"We'll remember who we were or who we weren't," I replied. "The box score at the end of the game doesn't change."

I expected her to drive away. That wasn't what she did. She clenched my left hand in hers and shook it roughly, her little nails biting into my palm, almost like an act of desperation. Then she got in her car and drove away, smoothing her hair, her radio playing as she passed the religious grotto, a single column of sunlight splitting her face as though she were two different people created by a painter who could not decide whom he was creating.

CHAPTER

13

THAT EVENING AT twilight, I saw Clete's Caddy pull to the curb in front of our house, a woman behind the wheel. Clete got out on the passenger side and walked up to the gallery. The woman pulled away into the traffic and turned the corner just beyond the Shadows, the blue-dot taillights on the Caddy winking in the gloom. I met Clete on the steps. "Was that your temp?" I asked.

"She went to get some aspirin. She got sunburned this morning. I just heard about this guy Patin getting shot outside a club in Lafayette. He's the guy who tried to pop you with the cut-down?"

"I doubt it. He would have blown town. My guess is he stole the freezer truck at the motel where he was staying and gave it to his brother. But I'm just guessing."

"You know what's weird about this, Dave? Why steal a freezer truck to use as a getaway vehicle in a contract hit?"

"You think it wasn't stolen?" I said.

"It's a possibility."

"Varina Leboeuf is suing the department. I think she knows more about this stuff than she pretends."

He sat down on the steps. The air was filled with the drone of cicadas, fireflies glowing briefly in the trees, then disappearing in curlicues of yellow smoke. "I wonder if she digs older guys," he said.

"Will you stop that? Go on about the freezer truck."

190

"Why drive yourself nuts? You were right from the outset. We're dealing with some big players. But back to this gal Varina. A woman can only be so beautiful. If your twanger doesn't go on autopilot when a broad like that walks by, you need to get a refund on your equipment. Don't tell me your flopper doesn't have a memory bank. When you were loaded, you racked up some heavy mileage. Don't pretend you didn't."

"I can't believe you. We're talking about multiple homicides, and you can't get your mind off your johnson."

"I was talking about yours, not mine. But okay, let's talk about mine. I think it has X-ray eyes. It sees through my pants. What am I supposed to do, cover it with concrete?" Clete glanced behind him through the screen door. His scalp constricted and his face turned hot pink, the blood draining out of the scar that ran through his eyebrow. "Hi, Molly," he said. "I didn't see you there."

"Hi, Clete," she said. "Enjoying the evening?"

"I was going to ask Dave to take a walk." He stood up. "Would you like to go?"

"Bring me some ice cream," she said.

"Sure," he said. "I was going to suggest that. Dave and I were just shooting the breeze. I was talking about myself, not anybody else."

"We always love having you over, Clete," she said.

I walked with him down the street, toward the Shadows. He looked back at the house. "How long was she there?" he said.

"Forget it. Who was driving your car?"

"That's what I want to talk to you about. Gretchen and I were over on East Cote Blanche Bay today. I think I know where the body of Blue Melton was dropped into the water. I think the guys who killed her were on a big yacht and don't know much about nautical science. How many yacht basins are there along the Louisiana coast, at least the kind that berth boats big enough to accommodate walk-in subzero freezers? Not many. That's where we need to start, Streak. Looking at people like Ronnie Earl Patin isn't going to take us to the top."

"Don't try to change the subject. You said Gretchen? As in Gretchen Horowitz, your daughter?"

We had walked out on the drawbridge at Burke Street, the water flowing dark and high through the pilings below, the sun descending in a burst of orange flame beneath clouds that resembled piled fruit. "I'm telling you this because I think maybe she's not Caruso," Clete said.

"How can you say that? You recognized her when she clipped Bix Golightly."

"Maybe it wasn't her. There's something I didn't tell you. Since we almost bought it on the bayou, I've had all this guilt about everything I ever did wrong in my life. I was obsessing about Gretchen and her mother and the fact that I used her mother like a whore, and the fact that Gretchen grew up in a home where a guy burned her with cigarettes when she was a baby, for Christ's sake. I had these pictures Candy sent me of Gretchen, and I was always looking at them and wondering where she was and how I could undo all the pain I'd caused her. Then I saw this person in a red windbreaker and ball cap splatter Bix Golightly's buckwheats, and maybe I transposed Gretchen's image onto the shooter."

"Is that likely?"

"Yeah, it's possible," he said, undeterred in his attempt to avoid conclusions he could not deal with. "She talks rough, but she's a sweet girl. The problem I got now is she doesn't know who I am, and she's getting a little bit too close to me emotionally, in definitely the wrong way, get my drift, and she doesn't need any more psychological damage done to her because she's getting the hots for her own father."

"You can clear all this up by telling Gretchen who you are. Why haven't you done that?"

It was a mean question to ask. Saint Augustine once said we should not use the truth to injure. In this case, my best friend was experiencing the kind of angst that no one should have to endure. The truth was not going to set Clete free. Instead, it would force him to choose between aiding and abetting several homicides or sending his daughter to the injection table at Angola. I had become his grand inquisitor, and I hated myself for it.

"What am I going to do, Dave?" he asked.

I said something I didn't plan to say. I said it out of a frame of reference that had nothing to do with reason, justice, right or wrong, legality, police procedure, or even common sense. I said it in the same way the British writer E. M. Forster once said that if he had to make a choice between his friend and his country, he hoped he would have the courage to choose his friend. I said, "Let it play out."

"You mean that?"

"It's another one of those deals where you have to say the short version of the Serenity Prayer. You have to step back and let all the worry and complexities and confusion in your life blow away in the wind. You have to trust that the sun will rise in the east and the race will not be to the swift and the rain will fall upon both the just and the unjust. You have to say fuck it and mean it and let the dice roll out of the cup as they will."

"We're both going to end up in Angola."

"That's what I mean. Fuck it. Everybody gets to the barn," I said.

"My liver is screaming. I got to have a beer with a couple of raw eggs in it. A couple of shots of Jack wouldn't hurt, either."

"Molly wants some ice cream."

"Clementine's sells sorbet to go. 'Let it play out.' I totally dig that. I think that also includes seriously stomping some ass and taking names. 'Let it play out.' Fuckin' A." He began churning his big fists as though hitting a speed bag, his teeth like tombstones when he grinned.

He had sucked me in again.

No one likes to be afraid. Fear is the enemy of love and faith and robs us of all serenity. It steals both our sleep and our sunrise and makes us treacherous and venal and dishonorable. It fills our glands with toxins and effaces our identity and gives flight to any vestige of self-respect. If you have ever been afraid, truly afraid, in a way that makes your hair soggy with sweat and turns your skin gray and fouls your blood and spiritually eviscerates you to the point where you cannot pray lest your prayers be a concession to your conviction that you're about to die, you know what I am talking about.

This kind of fear has no remedy except motion, no matter what kind. Every person who has experienced war or natural catastrophe or man-made calamity knows this. The adrenaline surge is so great that you can pick up an automobile with your bare hands, plunge through glass windows in flaming buildings, or attack an enemy whose numbers and weaponry are far superior to yours. No fear of self-injury is as great as the fear that turns your insides to gelatin and shrivels your soul to the size of an amoeba.

If you do not have the option of either fleeing or attacking your adversary, the result is quite different. Your level of fear will grow to the point where you feel like your skin is being stripped off your bones. The degree of torment and hopelessness and, ultimately, despair you will experience is probably as great as it gets this side of the grave.

Seven hours after I had said good night to Clete, I heard dry thunder in the clouds and, in my sleep, thought I saw flashes of heat lightning inside our bedroom. Then I realized I had forgotten to turn off my cell phone and it was vibrating on top of the dresser. I picked it up and walked into the kitchen. The caller ID was blocked. I sat down in a chair at the breakfast table and stared down the back slope at the bayou, where the surface of the water was wrinkling like curdled milk, the flooded elephant ears along the banks bending in the wind. "Who is this?" I said.

At first I heard only a deep breathing sound, like that of a man who was either in pain or whose anxiety was so intense that blood was starting to pop on his brow. "You Dave Robicheaux?" a male voice said.

"That's right. It's four in the morning. Who is this, and what do you want?"

"I'm Chad Patin. Ronnie Earl was my brother."

I thought the caller planned to make an accusation against me, but that was not the case. He must have been using a landline, because his voice was rasping against a larger surface than a cell phone's. I heard him take a gulp of air, like a man whose head had been held for a long time underwater.

"You still with me, bub?" I said.

"It was me who tried to take you out," he replied.

"How'd you get my number?"

"They got a file on you. Everything about you is in there."

"Who is 'they'?"

I waited and heard liquid being poured into a glass. I heard him drinking from the glass, swallowing sloppily, a man who didn't care whether Johnnie Walker or brake fluid was sliding down his throat.

"I'm jumping out into space on this one," he said.

"You were the shooter? Not your brother?"

"I agreed to do it. I wish I hadn't."

"You *agreed*? Can you translate that?"

"They were gonna send Ronnie Earl back inside. They weren't gonna give me any more gigs. I got to make a living."

"We ran you through the NCIC computer. You don't have a sheet."

"I was a transporter, girls and sometimes a little skag. I drove the girls up from Mexico. I wasn't full-time on any of this. One night on the border, I did something. Some people were crowded too tight into the back of the truck. When it went into the ditch, I ran away. The back was locked. It was over a hundred degrees, even at night. Maybe you read about it."

"No, I didn't. Why did you call me?"

"I need to get out of the country."

"And you want me to help you?"

"I got a few hundred dollars, but it's not enough. I need at least five t'ousand."

"You're asking this of the man you tried to kill?"

"The person running all this is named Angel or maybe Angelle. In French, *ange* means 'angel.'"

"I know what it means."

"You're not listening. This is bigger than all of us. They ship women from all over the world. Bosnia, Romania, Russia, Africa, Thailand, Honduras, any shithole where things are coming apart. A guy makes a call and gets any kind of woman or combination of women he wants. That's just part of it."

"What else are they into?"

"Everything. They own part of everything there is."

"Who hired you to kill me?"

"You're not listening. We're nothing down here, just ants running around on a wet log. I've heard about an island they got." His voice started to break, as though he were afraid to look at the images his mind was creating. "They do stuff to people there you don't want to know about. They got this big iron mold. I saw a photo of what they did to a guy."

"Take this to the FBI."

"I'll go inside on attempted murder. I'll be dead in a week. You saw what they did to Ronnie Earl. The guy who showed me the photo played a tape for me. I heard somebody being put into this iron thing they got. The guy going inside was talking in a language I didn't understand. I didn't have to understand it. He was begging and crying, then I heard them closing the door on him. It took a long time for them to close the door. He was screaming all the while. I got to hide someplace, man. Five t'ousand dollars, that's all it'll take. I'll give you all the information I got."

"It doesn't work that way, partner. Why'd you guys use a freezer truck?"

"Ronnie Earl said nobody would pay attention to it. Why you axing about the truck we drove? I'm telling you about people who aren't like anybody you ever knew, and you're worried about a truck? There's a girl involved, a singer, a Creole girl who was on that island. That's what Ronnie Earl said. She was big stuff in the zydeco clubs. I don't remember her name."

"Tee Jolie Melton," I said.

"Yeah, that's it. Her sister got grabbed, too. You gonna help me or not?"

"Where can we meet?"

"You'll get me the money?"

"We have funds to help out confidential informants or friends of the court," I said, wondering at my own willingness to make promises that perhaps I couldn't keep. "One way or another, we'll get you out of this."

"What's that iron thing? What do they call it? It's like from the

Middle Ages. I could see part of it in the photo. I could see pieces of the guy on it. It's got big spikes inside the door. What do they call that, man?"

"The iron maiden."

I heard wind in the receiver, as though he had taken the phone from his ear and mouth.

"Are you there, Chad?" I said.

"Oh, man," he said, the register in his voice suddenly dropping.

"What's happening?" I said.

"They're here. Those motherfuckers are here."

"Stay with me, podna. *Who's* there?"

"It's *them*," he said. *"Them."*

I heard him drop the phone and sounds of scuffling and furniture being knocked over, and then I heard Chad Patin squealing like a pig on its way to slaughter.

ALAFAIR ENTERED CLETE'S New Iberia office on Main at nine A.M. on Friday, expecting to see Clete's regular receptionist, Hulga Volkmann, behind the desk in the waiting room. Instead, she saw a thick-bodied woman in her mid- or late twenties, with reddish-blond hair cut Dutch-boy-style, sitting behind the desk in jeans, with one foot propped on an open drawer and cotton balls wedged between the toes while she painted lavender polish on each nail. The floor was unswept and littered from the previous day, newspapers and auto-mechanic magazines spilling off the metal chairs. "Mr. Purcel is across the street at Victor's Cafeteria," the woman said without looking up. "You need something?"

"Yeah, who are you, and where is Miss Hulga?"

"She's on vacation, and I'm her replacement. Who are you?"

"Alafair Robicheaux."

"Great." The woman at the desk straightened up in her chair and capped the nail polish and pulled the cotton balls from between her toes and dropped them one at a time into the wastebasket. "That saves me from calling up your father." She glanced at the top page on a yellow legal pad. "Tell Detective Robicheaux a stolen-vehicle report on the freezer truck was phoned in two hours before Ronnie Earl Patin tried to kill him. Or maybe not tell him that, since he was probably already aware, considering he was the guy who was almost killed. But if it will make your father happy, you can tell him the company that owns the truck doesn't have any apparent connection to the Patin brothers. Also tell your father that his department should do its own work. End of message." She looked up at Alafair. Her eyes were the color of violets and didn't seem to go with the rest of her face. "Anything else?"

"Yeah, who the fuck are you?"

The young woman's eyelashes fluttered. "How do I put this? Let's see, I guess I'm the fuck Gretchen Horowitz. I understand you graduated from Stanford Law. I've always wondered what Stanford was like. I went to Miami Dade College. In case you never heard of it, it's in Miami."

"This place is a mess."

"Tell me about it."

"Why don't you clean it up?"

"Should I start with the puke on the restroom floor or the apple core floating in the toilet bowl?"

"You might start with getting your feet off the furniture," Alafair said.

Gretchen folded back the pages on the legal pad until she reached a clean one, then set the pad and a felt pen on the forward edge of the desk. "Write down whatever you want to tell Mr. Purcel, and I'll give it to him. Or you can go across the street and help him with his hangover. I don't think he'd have one if it wasn't for your father."

"My father doesn't drink."

"I know that. He only takes Mr. Purcel to the bar and gets high watching *him* drink."

"Excuse me, miss, but I think you're probably an idiot. I don't mean that as an insult. I mean it in the clinical sense. If that's true, I'm sorry for the way I spoke to you. I'm sure you have many qualities. I love the vampiric shade of polish on your toenails."

Gretchen put two Chiclets in her mouth and slowly chewed them, her mouth open, her eyes indolent. "Can you tell me why people with degrees from Stanford live in a mosquito factory? There must be a reason."

Alafair picked up the trash can. "Are you through with this?" she asked.

"Morning sickness?"

"No, just doing your job for you." Alafair began straightening the metal chairs in the waiting room and picking up newspapers and Styrofoam cups from the floor and dropping them in the can.

"Don't do that," Gretchen said.

"I majored in janitorial studies at Reed. You've heard of Reed, I'm sure. It's in Portland, the home of John Reed the socialist writer, although he was not related to the family who endowed Reed. Did you see the movie *Reds*? It's about John Reed. He was a war correspondent during the Mexican Revolution in 1915. Portland is in Oregon. That's the state between California and Washington."

"Listen, Al-a-far, or whatever your name is, I don't need a horse's ass making my day any harder than it already is. Put down the trash can and kindly haul your twat out of here. I'll tell Mr. Purcel you came to see him. I'll also tell him I passed on the information your father needed. *Okay?*"

"I don't mind," Alafair said.

"Don't mind what?"

"Helping you clean up. Clete shouldn't have left you with this. He's a good guy, and everybody around here loves him. But as my father says, Clete has the organizational skill of a scrapyard falling down a staircase."

Alafair bent over to pick up a magazine from the floor. She heard Gretchen suppress a laugh. "Something funny?" Alafair said.

"I didn't say anything," Gretchen said. She took a mop and a bucket and a plumber's helper and a pair of rubber gloves out of the closet and went into the restroom. A moment later, Alafair heard the sloshing sounds of the plumber's helper at work, then the toilet flushing. Gretchen opened the door wider so she could see into the waiting room, her body still bent over the commode.

"*Reds* was Warren Beatty's best movie, better even than *Bonnie and Clyde*," she said. "Henry Miller did a cameo in there. Did you know he stayed here in New Iberia at that place called the Shadows? You ever see *Shampoo*? Warren Beatty is one of my all-time favorite actors, second only to James Dean."

THE REPORTS ON the denouement of Chad Patin, whose name the witnesses did not know at the time, had begun coming in to a 911 dispatcher in St. Charles Parish at 4:18 A.M. To whatever degree the abductors were lacking in sophistication, they compensated in terms of due diligence.

At a small settlement outside Des Allemands, down toward New Orleans, a woman called in a noise complaint. She said her neighbor, who lived in a garage apartment behind an abandoned stucco house encased in dead vines and banana stalks, was having a fight with a woman. When asked how she knew this, she answered that she could hear glass and furniture breaking and someone shrieking like a woman. At least that was her impression, she added.

At 4:23 A.M. a different caller in the same community reported a burglary in progress at the garage apartment. From his window, he said he could see three men carrying a rolled carpet down the garage apartment stairs. He said a light was attached to the power pole by the apartment, and he was certain he was watching an invasion of his neighbor's home. Then he realized he was not watching the theft of a carpet but a far more serious crime in progress. "They're carrying a guy wrapped up with rope. It looks like something is stuffed in his mouth. I think maybe it's a tennis ball."

At 4:26 A.M. the first caller reported in again. "They just drove a SUV t'rew my li'l garden. There's still one man out there. He's getting something out of the back of his car. When y'all coming?"

At 4:31 A.M. the second caller made his next report on his cell phone. So far he had not identified himself, but he did not seem to consider that a problem. "This is me," he said. "I'm in my car and following them guys up the dirt road. I'm gonna fix their ass, me."

"Disengage from what you're doing, sir," the female dispatcher said. "Do not try to stop these men. Help is on the way."

"What's gonna happen to that po' man?" the caller said.

At 4:33 A.M. the woman caller was back on the line. "The man getting something out of the back of his car? What name they got for that? The thing he was getting, I mean. Soldiers wear it on their back. He walked right up to the garage apartment and pointed it just like you do a hose. There ain't nothing left. Even the trees are burning. The leaves are coming down on my li'l house."

"You're not making sense, ma'am. Unless you're talking about a flamethrower," the dispatcher said.

The last 911 call on the tape was from the man who had followed the abductors in his car. "They got on a white boat just sout' of Des Allemands," he said. "I'm standing here on the dock. They're headed down toward the Gulf. It was a tennis ball. It's right here by my foot. A toot' is stuck in it, and there's blood on the toot'. Where was y'all?"

I HAD REPORTED my call from Chad Patin ten seconds after the intruders broke into his garage apartment, but my best efforts had not saved him. After Helen and I finished listening to the 911 recordings transmitted to us by the St. Charles Parish Sheriff's Department, she stared out her office window, her thumbs hooked in her belt. Her back looked as hard as iron against her shirt. "The guy running this operation is named Angelle?"

"Or Angel."

"And living on an island somewhere?"

"That's what Chad Patin said."

"And one of his guys has a flamethrower? This stuff is from outer space. What do you think it's really about?"

"Money. A lot of it. Drugs, prostitutes, maybe stolen or forged paintings. At least those things are part of it."

"The perps don't pop cops over drugs and girls and stolen property," she replied.

"I think it has some connection to neo-Nazis."

"I don't believe that for a minute. That's just crazy, Dave."

"Okay, let's look at another angle. What is the one subject around here that nobody brings up in a negative way, that no local journalist goes near? A subject so sensitive that people will walk away from you if they sense the wrong words are about to come out of your mouth? What enterprise could that possibly be?"

"Tell me."

"No, you tell me," I said.

She manufactured an expression that was meant to be dismissive. I didn't like to look at it. It made me feel embarrassed for Helen, and it caused me to think less of her, a person I had always admired.

"You're too hard on people, bwana," she said. "This is a poor state with a one-resource economy. Would you really like to go back to the good old days? I don't think any of us would like living under the old lifestyle of 'tote that barge and lift that bale.'"

"What's the word we're avoiding here? What is the sacred space that none of us track our irreverent shoes into?"

"The country wants cheap gasoline. They don't care how they get it. So the state of Louisiana is everybody's fuck. What else do you want me to say?"

"Nothing. You just said it all. You know what this case is about, so stop pretending you don't."

"You're not going to talk to me like that," she said.

"Ask yourself why this conversation offends you. Because I insulted you or I pissed on the sacred cow."

"Get out, Dave."

She had never spoken to me like that, at least not in that tone. I didn't care. I was angrier than she was. No, that's the wrong word. I was disappointed in Helen, and I felt let down in a way I couldn't describe. I couldn't shake the funk I was in for the rest of the day.

CHAPTER
14

THAT SAME AFTERNOON, Clete Purcel sat in his swivel chair in his office and through the back window watched the rain dimple the bayou and the fog puff in clouds from under the bridge and the lights of cars crossing the steel grid. His office was housed inside a nineteenth-century two-story building constructed of soft brick, with an iron colonnade over the sidewalk and a patio in back that he had decorated with potted banana plants and a bottlebrush tree and a spool table inset with a beach umbrella under which he often ate his lunch or read his mail in the morning.

The drizzle was unrelenting, and he was confined to his office and the endless flow of squalor and chicanery that went across his desk blotter, not to mention the worm's-eye view of the world that was the operational raison d'être of almost every client who came through his door.

With an occasional exception.

Gretchen stepped inside his office and closed the door behind her. "Little Miss Muffet would like to see you. She's got a guy with her who looks like he has a wig stapled to his scalp," she said. "Want me to blow them off?"

He shut and opened his eyes. "I'm trying to translate what you just said."

"The broad at the Dupree place with the broom up her ass. The guy didn't introduce himself. He's got a Roman collar on. I can tell them they need to make an appointment."

"Varina Leboeuf is out there?"

"Who'd you think I was talking about?"

"Send her in."

Gretchen opened her mouth wide and put her finger in it, as though trying to vomit.

"Lose the attitude," he said.

A moment later, Varina Leboeuf came into Clete's office, followed by a man in a black suit and lavender collar whose thick silver hair was bobbed in the style of a nineteenth-century western rancher. He had a high, shiny forehead, and turquoise eyes that were recessed in the sockets, and hands like those of a farmer who might have broken hardpan prairie with a singletree plow. His eyes stayed glued on Clete.

"Hello, Mr. Purcel," Varina said, extending her hand. "I want to apologize for my abruptness at my father-in-law's house. I'd had an absolutely terrible day, and I'm afraid I took it out on you and your assistant. This is Reverend Amidee Broussard. He has advised me to hire a private investigator. I understand you're pretty good at what you do."

"Depends on what it is," Clete said. He had risen when she entered the room and was standing awkwardly behind his desk, wishing he had put on his sport coat, his fingertips barely touching his desk blotter, his blue-black .38 strapped across his chest in its nylon holster. "If this is about divorce work, the expense sometimes outweighs the benefits. What we used to call immorality is so common today that it doesn't have much bearing on the financial settlement. In other words, the dirt a PI can dig up on a spouse is of little value."

"See, you're an honest man," she said.

Before Clete could reply, the minister said, "Mr. Purcel, may I sit down? I'm afraid I was running to get out of the rain and got a bit winded. Age is a peculiar kind of thief. It slips up on you and steps inside your skin and is so quiet and methodical in its work that you never realize it has stolen your youth until you look into the mirror one morning and see a man you don't recognize."

"Would y'all like some coffee?" Clete said.

"That would be very nice," the minister said. When he sat down, a tinge of discomfort registered in his face, as though his weight were pressing his bones against the wood of the chair.

"Are you all right?" Clete said.

"Oh, I'm fine," he said, breathing through his mouth. "What a magnificent view you have. Did you know that during the War Between the States, a Union flotilla came up the bayou and moored right at the spot by the drawbridge? The troops were turned loose on the town, mostly upon Negro women. It was a deliberate act of terrorism, just like Sherman at the burning of Atlanta."

"I didn't know that," Clete said.

"Unfortunately, history books are written by the victors." The minister's cheeks were soft and flecked with tiny blue and red capillaries, and his mouth formed a small oval when he pronounced his *o*'s. The cadences of his speech seemed to come from another era and were almost hypnotic. "Do you know who wrote those words?"

"Adolf Hitler did," Clete replied.

"It's very important that you help Ms. Leboeuf. Her husband is not what he seems. He's a fraudulent and perhaps dangerous man. I think he may have had dealings with criminals in New Orleans, men who are involved in the sale of stolen paintings. I'm not sure, so I don't want to treat the man unjustly, but I have no doubt he wants to make Ms. Leboeuf's life miserable."

Varina had sat down, smoothing her dress, her gaze fixed on the rain falling on the bayou. Every few seconds, her eyes settled on Clete's, unembarrassed, taking his measure.

"What do you base that on?" Clete asked.

"I'm Ms. Leboeuf's spiritual adviser." The minister hesitated. "She's confided certain aspects of his behavior to me that normally are difficult to talk about except in a confidential setting."

"I can speak for myself, Amidee," Varina said.

"No, no, this was my idea. Mr. Purcel, Pierre Dupree is a dependent and infantile man. In matters of marital congress, he has the appetites of a child. If the implication has unpleasant Freudian overtones, that's my intention. Do you understand what I'm saying, sir?"

"I don't think I need an audiovisual, Reverend," Clete said. "Why is Dupree a threat to Ms. Leboeuf?"

"Because he has the business instincts of a simpleton and is teetering on bankruptcy. He sees Ms. Leboeuf as the source of all his troubles and believes she's out to cause him financial ruin. He's a weak and frightened man, and like most frightened men, he wishes to blame his failure on his wife. Last night she went out to the Dupree home to get her dog. Pierre told her he'd had it put down."

"The dog named Vick?" Clete said to Varina.

"Pierre said Vick had distemper," she said. "That's a lie. You saw him. He was fine. Either Pierre or his grandfather did something to him, maybe hurt him in some way, then had him injected. I feel so bad about Vick, I want to cry. I hate Pierre and his hypocrisy and his arrogance and his two-thousand-dollar suits and his greasy smell. I can't stand the thought that I let him kill my dog."

"No good comes of blaming ourselves for what other people do," Clete said. "I understand you're filing a civil suit against the sheriff's department over an incident at your father's place. The incident involved Dave Robicheaux. That creates a conflict of interest for me, Ms. Leboeuf. I'd like to help you, but in this instance, I don't think I can."

"I've already dropped the suit. It's not worth the trouble," she replied.

Don't do what you're about to do, a voice in Clete's head told him.

"My husband is a pervert. I will not discuss the kinds of things he has asked me to participate in," she said. "He wasn't drunk when he did it, either. Frankly, I feel sick at the mention of this. The fact that he's considered a great artist locally is laughable. He has no understanding of intimacy or mutual respect inside a relationship. That's why he studied commercial art. It has no emotion. If he ever painted what was on his mind, he'd be put in a cage." Her eyes were moist, her small fists knotted in her lap.

"Maybe I can recommend a couple of PIs in Lafayette," Clete said.

"I'm going to be staying at my father's house at Cypremort Point. I'm at the end of my rope, Mr. Purcel. I have to take care of my father, and I can't be looking over my shoulder in fear of my husband. If you'd rather I go somewhere else, I will. I've made my livelihood in electronic security, but that will not protect me from a man who would euthanize a loving pet who was part of our household for five years. I feel such rage right now, I can't express it. If you want us to leave, please say so. But don't try to push me off on some seedy private investigator in Lafayette."

Clete could feel a strand of piano wire tightening along the side of his head. "You dropped the suit against the Iberia Parish Sheriff's Department?"

"I already told you that."

"What if I give you my cell phone number and the number of my answering service? Plus, I can have a talk with your husband about your dog."

"It's a bit late for that. Furthermore, I'd like more than talk when it comes to Pierre."

"Pardon?" Clete said.

"That's wishful thinking on my part. Don't pay attention to what I just said."

"Ms. Leboeuf sometimes speaks sharply, but she's a religious woman, Mr. Purcel, even though she might get mad at me for saying that," the minister said.

"My fee is seventy dollars an hour plus expenses," Clete said.

"You've been very kind," Varina said, her eyes crinkling.

"You'll probably find you don't need me, Ms. Leboeuf," Clete said. "In this kind of situation, a little time passes, and the lawyers agree on division of the assets, and both parties walk away and start new lives. At least the smart ones do."

"You sound like a man of the world," she said.

"Dave Robicheaux and I were plainclothes detectives at NOPD. Neither of us is now. That says more than I like to think about," he replied.

When they had gone and Clete had shut the door behind them, he remained standing in the center of the room, as though he couldn't remember where he was or what had just transpired in his life. The wind was whipping the rain against his window, obscuring the

bayou and the drawbridge and smudging the lights on the cars crossing the steel grid. His stomach was churning, and pinpoints of sweat
were breaking on his forehead. He wondered if he was coming down
with the flu.

Gretchen opened the door without knocking. "Why did you let
her do that to you?"

"Do what?"

"She's a cunt."

"Don't use that word."

"That's what she is."

"That word is never used in this office. Not by me, not by the skells,
not by you, not by anyone in our acquaintance. That one doesn't
flush. Do you understand that?"

"All right, she's the C-word from head to toe, from the way she
points her boobs at you to the way she crosses her legs to give you
a little preview of what might be waiting. You don't know how mad
you make me."

"I'm your employer, Gretchen, and you're my employee. I think
you're really a good kid, but while we're on the job, you need to
show some respect."

"Don't you call me a kid. You don't know what I'm capable of."
Her cheeks were wet, her bottom lip trembling. Her down-in-the-ass
jeans hung low on her hips, exposing her navel; her broad shoulders
were rounded, her eyes filled with sorrow. In that moment, she looked
more like a man than a woman. She sat down in the chair the minister
had occupied and stared into space.

"I'd never deliberately hurt you," Clete said.

"If you want to be a dildo, go be a dildo. Don't let on like you're
a man, though."

"Gretchen, I've been with a lot of women. I liked them all, but
there was only one I really loved. What I'm saying is I feel a special
kind of affection for you. We're kindred spirits, know what I mean?
Let me take you to dinner."

"Who was the one you loved?"

"She was a Eurasian girl. She lived on a sampan on the edge of the
South China Sea."

"What happened to her?"

"The VC killed her because she was sleeping with the enemy. Come on, let's go down to Bojangles."

Gretchen wiped her nose on the back of her wrist. "Call up your new douchebag and ask *her*. She's more your style."

FRIDAY EVENING MOLLY and I had people over for a crab boil in the backyard. The sky had turned from gold and purple to green as the sun descended into a bank of thunderheads in the west. The breeze smelled of rain falling from clouds that had drawn water out of the Gulf and fish eggs out of the wetlands; it smelled of newly mowed grass and sprinklers striking warm concrete and charcoal starter flaring on a grill; it smelled of chrysanthemums blooming in gardens dark with shadow, telling us that the season was not yet done, that life was still a party and should not be surrendered prematurely to the coming of night. Molly had strung Japanese lanterns through the live oaks and set the redwood table with bowls of potato salad and dirty rice and chopped-up fruit and corn on the cob, and I had lit the butane burner under the crab boiler, right next to an apple crate crawling with blue crabs. Across the bayou in City Park, the electric lights were blazing above the baseball diamond, where boys who had refused to accept the passing of summer were chasing line drives smacked by a coach at home plate. It was the kind of evening that people of my generation associate with a more predictable era, one that may have been unjust in many ways but possessed a far greater level of civility and trust and shared sense of virtue that, for good or bad, seemed to define who we were. It wasn't a bad way to be, having drinks in one's backyard, watching the sunset or a paddle wheeler passing on the bayou, couples dancing to a band on the upper deck. At a certain time in one's life, the ebb and flow of a tidal stream and the setting of the sun are not insignificant events.

As our guests began arriving, I looked around for Alafair, who I had assumed was joining us.

"Alafair is going to a movie with a new friend she's made," Molly said, apparently reading my thoughts.

"She has a date?" I asked.

"Clete has a new assistant. Alafair just met her this morning. They must have hit it off."

"Where is Alafair?" I said.

"She was looking for her car keys a minute ago. You don't want her to go?"

I went inside, then saw Alafair getting into her used Honda out front. I went through the front door, waving at her to stop, trying at the same time to be polite to the guests coming up the walk. In the meantime, Alafair pulled away from the curb. I walked down the street, still waving my arms. Her brake lights went on, and she turned out of the traffic and parked by the Shadows. She leaned down so she could see me through the passenger window. "Didn't Molly tell you where I was going?" she said.

I got in the front seat and closed the door. "You're seeing a movie with Gretchen Horowitz?"

"Yeah, I kind of had an argument with her this morning at Clete's office. But she turned out to be a nice person. I asked her to go to a show. Is there something wrong?"

"That's hard to say. I haven't met her. I have the sense she comes from a pretty rough background. Maybe she knew some bad guys in Miami."

"Which bad guys?"

"Mobbed-up Cubans, for openers."

"She works for Clete. He must think she's okay."

"Alafair, I'm not sure who this girl is. Clete believes she's his daughter. What he doesn't want to believe is that she may be a contract killer, one who's known in the life as Caruso. She might have capped two or three members of the old Giacano crowd, two in New Orleans, one in the Baton Rouge bus depot."

"This can't be the same person."

"Yeah, it can," I said.

Alafair stared straight ahead at the deepening shade under the live oaks. The wind was blowing off the Gulf, and the wall of bamboo that grew in front of the Shadows rattled against the piked fence. "Are you certain about any of this?" she said.

"No, I only know what Clete has told me."

"Does Helen Soileau know?"

"More or less."

"Why doesn't she want to do something about it?"

"Because sometimes neither she nor I trust Clete's perceptions. Because you don't give up your friends, no matter what they do."

"Thanks for the heads-up."

"You're still going to the movies with her?"

"Gretchen is waiting for me at the motor court. She's pretty angry at Clete."

"What for?"

"Something about Varina Leboeuf. Clete was driving down to Cypremort Point to see her tonight."

"Do you have any aspirin?" I asked.

"In the glove box. Is Gretchen involved somehow with the Dupree family?"

"It's possible."

"You believe Gretchen will give you a lead into the disappearance of Tee Jolie Melton and the death of her sister, don't you?"

"Maybe."

"If y'all are still in the backyard later, can I invite Gretchen to join us?"

"I don't think that's a real good idea."

"I don't believe she's a killer. I think she has no friends and she's lived a hard life and she feels betrayed because Clete is seeing Varina Leboeuf. Is that the kind of person our family shuts the door on? Look me in the face and tell me that, Dave. When did we start being afraid of someone who is friendless and alone?"

I felt sorry for the litigators who would have to face Alafair in a courtroom.

IN THE DARKNESS of the theater, Gretchen Horowitz sat totally still, enraptured by every detail of the film from the opening scene until the fade-out, never taking her eyes off the screen. Alafair had never seen anyone watch a film with such intensity. Even when the credits had finishing rolling, Gretchen waited until the trademark of the studio and the date of production had trailed off the screen before she allowed herself to detach. The film was *Pirates of the Caribbean.*

"Do you know what John Dillinger's last words were?" she asked.

"No," Alafair replied.

"It was in Chicago, at the Biograph Theater. He had just come out of seeing *Manhattan Melodrama* with the two prostitutes who sold him out to the feds. You've heard about the lady in red, right? Actually, she was wearing orange. Anyway, John Dillinger said, 'Now, that's what I call a movie.' Did you see *Public Enemies?* Johnny Depp played Dillinger. God, he was great. The critics didn't understand what the film was about, though. That's because a lot of them are stupid. It's a really a love story, see. John Dillinger's girlfriend was an Indian named Billie Frechette. She was beautiful. In the last scene, the fed who shot Dillinger goes to see Billie in jail and tells her that Johnny's last words were 'Tell Billie bye-bye blackbird.' That scene made me cry."

"Why were you holding your cell phone all during the movie?" Alafair asked. "You expecting a call?"

"A guy I know in Florida is making a nuisance of himself. Did you hear what I said about Dillinger and Billie Frechette?"

"Yeah, sure."

They were outside the theater now, not far from one of the bridges over the Teche. The air had cooled and smelled of the bayou, and on the horizon giant clouds of smoke were rising from the sugar refinery, which was lit as brightly as a battleship. "You like it here?" Gretchen asked.

"It's where I grew up," Alafair said. "I was born in El Salvador. But I don't remember much of life there, except a massacre I saw in my village."

Gretchen stopped walking and looked at her. "No shit. You saw something like that?"

"A Maryknoll priest flew my mother and me into the country. We crashed by Southwest Pass. Somebody had put a bomb on board. My mother was killed. Dave dove down without enough air in his tank and pulled me from the wreck."

"Is that in your book, the one that's about to come out?"

"Some of it."

"I wish I could write. I'd like to be a screenwriter. I have an associate's degree and fifteen hours at Florida Atlantic. You think I could get into film school at the University of Texas?"

"Why would you not be able to?"

"I wasn't the best student in the world. I think half the time my male professors were grading my jugs. I kind of had a way of choosing almost all male professors for my classes. Oops, there goes my phone. I'll be just a minute."

Gretchen walked across the parking lot and began speaking into the phone as she rounded the corner of the theater. Some middle-school kids cutting through from the street to the parking lot passed her, then looked back and started laughing. "What's so funny, you guys?" Alafair asked.

"That lady over there dropped her phone in the mud puddle. She knows some cuss words, yeah," one boy said.

Alafair looked at her watch, then walked to the corner of the building. She could hear Gretchen's voice in the darkness. Perhaps secretly, she hoped to hear a profane tirade at a lover or a family member. Or a confession of need or an attempt at reconciliation or an argument over money. But the voice she heard was not one dependent on profanity to intimidate the listener. Nor was it the voice of the Gretchen Horowitz enamored by the love story of Billie Frechette and John Dillinger.

"Here's what it is, and you'd better get it right the first time," Gretchen said. "I'm out. Don't leave anything in the drop box. The last deal was on the house. No, you don't talk, Raymond. You listen. You take my number out of your directory, and do not make the mistake of contacting me again." There was a pause. "That's the breaks. Go back to Cuba. Open a beans-and-rice stand on the beach. I think you're worrying about nothing. The people who pay us pay us for one reason: They're not up to the job themselves. So *adiós* and *hasta la cucaracha* and have a good life and stay away from me."

Gretchen closed her phone and turned around and looked into Alafair's face. "Didn't see you there," she said.

"Who was that?" Alafair asked.

"A guy I was in the antique business with in Key West. He's a *gusano* and always spotting his drawers about something."

"A worm?"

"A Batistiano, an antirevolutionary. Miami is full of them. They love democracy as long as it's run by brownshirts." She smiled awkwardly and shrugged. "We brought in some antiquities from Guatemala that were a little warm, like freshly dug up next to some Mayan pyramids, the kind of stuff that private collectors pay a lot of money for. I'm out of it now. You said something about going to your house for boiled crabs?"

"It's kind of late."

"Not for me."

"How about a drink at Clementine's?" Alafair said.

"You were looking at me a little funny. What did you think I was talking about?"

"I wasn't sure. It's not my business."

"You had a real funny look on your face."

"You have mud in your hair. You must have dropped your phone."

Gretchen touched her ear and looked at her fingers. "You think I could fit in at a place like the University of Texas? I hear a lot of rich kids go there. I'm not exactly a sorority girl. Tell me the truth. I'm not sensitive."

CLETE PURCEL TURNED the Caddy south on the two-lane and headed down the green tree-lined strip of elevated land that led to Cypremort Point. The surface of the bay was the color of tarnished brass, the waves capping close to the banks, the late sun as red and angry and unrelenting as a stoplight at a railroad crossing. He pulled down the visor but could not keep the brilliance out of his eyes. He had to drive with one hand and shield himself from the glare, as though the sun had conspired with the voices in his head that told him to desist, to cut a U-turn and scour grass and mud out of the swale, to floor the Caddy back to New Iberia and find a bar with a breezy deck by Bayou Teche and quietly sedate his head for the next five hours.

But omens and cautionary tales had never been an influence in the life of Clete Purcel. The sunset was splendid, the oil that lurked in the Gulf quiescent or even biodegrading, as the oil companies and government scientists had claimed. He and his best friend had eluded death on the bayou and left their enemies blown into bloody rags among the camellias and live oaks and pecan trees and elephant ears. How many times in his life had he been spared a DOA tag on his toe? Maybe it was for a reason. Maybe his attendance at the big dance was meant to be much longer than he had thought. Perhaps the world was not only a fine place and well worth the fighting for; perhaps it was also a neon-lit playground, not unlike the old Pontchartrain Beach, where the admission was free and the Ferris wheel and the aerial fireworks on the Fourth of July stayed printed against the evening sky forever.

Varina Leboeuf had called and said she'd found a photo she thought he should see. Should he have ignored her call and not driven out to Cypremort Point? Was there something inherently bad in his level of desire or the fact that he admired the way a woman walked and glanced back over her shoulder at a man? Was it wrong that he was fascinated by the mystery that hid in women's eyes and the way they kept their secrets to themselves and dressed for one another rather than for men? Why should age stop him from being who he was? The seventh-inning stretch was just the seventh-inning stretch. The game wasn't over until the last pitch in the bottom of the ninth. And sometimes the game went into extra innings.

He was almost home free in his thought processes, ready to get back on that old-time boogie-woogie, when he looked out at the bay and the flooded cypress trees strung with moss and a green rain cloud that had moved across the sun. Where had he seen all this before? Why did this seascape make his heart twist? Why couldn't he accept loss and life on life's terms? Why did he always have to seek surrogates for a girl who had not only been taken irrevocably from him but who was irreplaceable? Unfortunately, he knew the answer to his own question. When death stole the love of your life, no amount of revenge ever healed the hole in your heart. You lived with anger and physical yearnings that were insatiable, and you went about dismantling yourself on a daily basis, tendon and joint, for the rest of your days, all the time wearing the mask of a court jester.

He clicked on his radio and turned up the volume full-blast and kept it there until he saw the house on stilts that Varina Leboeuf had described to him. The house was constructed of weathered, unpainted cypress and had a peaked, synthetically coated fireproof roof that blended with the surroundings. She had set up a badminton net in the yard and was batting a shuttlecock back and forth with two little black girls dressed in pinafores that were threaded with ribbons.

He pulled onto the grass and got out of the Caddy. Varina was wearing shorts rolled high up on the thigh and a sleeveless blouse that exposed her bra straps. Her face was flushed and happy, her brown eyes electric, like light trapped inside a barrel of dark water. "Get a racket," she said.

He removed his porkpie hat and seersucker coat and put them in the Caddy, conscious of his shirt pulling loose from his slacks and the way his love handles hung over his belt. "Is your father back from the hospital?" he asked, already knowing the answer.

"He'll be at Iberia Medical Center for at least two more days. The twins here have been keeping me company. Their grandmother used to work for my father. He's their godfather."

"Really?" Clete said.

"Yeah, really. Did you hear some bad stories about him?"

"If I did, I don't remember them."

She hit the shuttlecock at him, whizzing it past his head. "Come on, I bet you can really sock it," she said.

But Clete was a hog on ice, slashing the racket into the net, tumbling over a lawn chair, batting the shuttlecock into a tree, almost stepping on one of the little girls. "I better quit," he said.

"You did great," Varina said. "Girls, let's have our ice cream and cake, then y'all had better run along home. Mr. Clete and I have some business to take care of."

"It's somebody's birthday?" Clete said.

"Tomorrow is. I'm going to take them to the zoo in the morning."

"I didn't mean to disturb y'all," he said.

"No, you're not disturbing anything. Come inside. Go wash your hands, girls. Let's hurry up now."

"I need to make a couple of calls," he lied. "I'll wait out here and have a cigarette."

He watched Varina escort the two girls into the back of the house. Through the window, he could see them gathered around a cake and a carton of ice cream at the kitchen table. He lit a cigarette and smoked it in the wind, unable to dispel his sense of discomfort. Why did the children have to leave? They obviously dressed for the occasion. They could have played in the yard while Clete looked at a photograph Varina had said would be of interest to him.

The twins came out the back door and walked up the road holding hands. Varina waved him inside.

"Think it's all right for those kids to walk home by themselves?" he asked.

"They don't have far to go." There was a smear of ice cream on her mouth. She wiped it away with her wrist. "I was watching you through the window. You looked wistful."

"South Louisiana makes me think of Southeast Asia sometimes. I'm an odd guy, probably one of the few who dug it over there."

"You were in Vietnam?"

"Two tours. I was in Thailand and the Philippines. Cambodia, too. But we weren't supposed to talk about that. I'd go back to Vietnam if I had the chance."

"What for?"

"I had a girl there. Her name was Maelee. I always wanted to find her family. I think they got sent to a reeducation camp by the VC. But I'm not sure."

"What happened to her?"

"She was killed."

"By who?"

"What difference does it make? We used snake and nape on their villes. The NVA buried people alive on the banks of the Perfume River. I helped dig up some of the bodies. When I was in Saigon, there was a place called the Stake where the public executions took place. The French could be nasty, too. The tiger cages and stuff like that. A lot of the Legionnaires were German war criminals. The whole country, north and south, was a moral insane asylum. The people got fucked by the Communists, then by us."

There was no expression on her face. She opened the icebox door and took out a bottle of tequila and a Carta Blanca and a white bowl of lime wedges. She set the tequila and the Mexican beer and the bowl of limes on the table and took two shot glasses from a cabinet and set them next to the tequila. "I'm sorry to hear about the girl you lost," she said. "I'll be back in a minute. Pour yourself a drink."

"I'm not sure I want one."

"*I'd* like one. I'd like for you to join me. Did I say something wrong?"

"No."

"Because you give me that impression."

"Why'd you send the little girls home?"

"I told their mother they'd be home before dark. They only have to walk two hundred yards, but if I had thought they were in danger, I would have driven them to their house. I've known their family since I was a small child."

Clete unscrewed the cap on the tequila and poured the two shot glasses full. The bottle felt cold and hard and full in his palm. "Can you show me that photo now?" he asked.

"I'll be right back," she replied.

He sat down at the table and salted a lime and took a hit off the tequila, then knocked back the whole shot and chased it with the Carta Blanca. The rush made him close his eyes and open his mouth, as though his body had just been lowered into warm water. *Wow,* he said to himself, and sucked on a salted lime. He heard the shower running in the back of the house.

He filled his shot glass again, until it brimmed, then sipped from the rim and gazed out the window at the long expanse of the bay, the brasslike color in the water fading to pewter, the sun no more than a spark on the horizon. Varina appeared in the doorway, wiping the back of her neck with a towel. She had changed into blue jeans and beaded moccasins and a cowboy shirt that glittered like a freshly sliced pomegranate. "Come in here," she said.

"I poured you a shot," he said. "Do you have another beer?"

"No, that one is for you. Here's the photo I wanted to show you." The next room had no windows and was furnished with only a couch and a rollaway bed covered by a beige blanket with an Indian design. On the couch was a big brown teddy bear that she had propped up against the cushions, as though to surveil the room. Above the couch were two shelves filled with antique Indian dolls, stone grinding bowls, a tomahawk, a trade ax strung with dyed turkey feathers, and pottery whose discernible markings looked hundreds of years old. She pulled a scrapbook from under the rollaway and sat down on the mattress and began turning the stiffened pages in the book, never glancing up at him.

He sat down next to her. It was only then that she turned to the back pages of the scrapbook and removed an envelope filled with photos. "These pictures were taken with a camera Pierre and I both used," she said. "I think he forgot about a couple of photos he took in a nightclub. I had them developed a couple of years back but never paid particular attention to them. I went to the house in Jeanerette yesterday and picked up a few things, including this scrapbook."

She removed a photo from the envelope and handed it to him. In it, Pierre Dupree was standing in front of a bandstand festooned with strings of Christmas wreath and tinsel. A young Creole woman with cups of gold in her hair stood next to him. She wore a magenta evening gown, an orchid pinned to one strap. Neither person was touching the other.

"Is that the girl you and Dave Robicheaux were looking for?" Varina asked.

"That's Tee Jolie Melton."

"And Pierre denies knowing her?"

"According to Dave. I haven't had the pleasure of meeting your husband."

"I no longer think of him as my husband."

"You think Mr. Dupree and Tee Jolie were an item?"

"I'm afraid you didn't hear me the first time. In my mind, Pierre is not my husband. That means I quit tracking his extracurricular activities years ago. He inherited the worst traits on both sides of his family. His grandfather is an imperious aristocrat who thinks he's genetically superior to others. His mother's family made most of their money on the backs of rental convicts. They literally worked those poor devils to death. I hated going out in public with any of them."

"Why?" Clete asked.

"They think the rest of the world is like St. Mary Parish. They expect waiters to grovel wherever they eat. They're boorish and loud and never read a book or see a film or talk about anything except themselves. They never once invited my father to dinner. I'm sorry, I can't stand them. I don't want to talk about this anymore. Was your marriage a great success? Is that why you're single? You *are* single, right?"

Trying to follow her train of thought was exhausting. "My wife dumped me for a Buddhist guru in Boulder, Colorado. This was a guy who made people take off their clothes in front of the commune he ran. She also gave him most of our savings account. It took three years for the divorce to go through. By that time I was hiding out in El Salvador on a murder beef. You want to go for a walk?"

"You committed a murder?"

"Not exactly. I thought the guy had a piece in his hand. Anyway, he was a sorry sack of shit and had it coming. I need a drink."

"Go ahead."

"You want to go in the kitchen?" he asked.

"No, I want to stay here. This was my room when I was a child. It was always my room, even after I left home. What should I do with the photo?"

"Give it to Dave. If I take it, I might create a problem with the chain of evidence."

"There's a tray on the drainboard. Will you bring the drinks and the limes in? I'll put the photo in my desk."

"It's pretty nice out. We can have our drinks outside, if you want."

"No, I don't want to go outside. The mosquitoes are terrible tonight. Would you rather not be here?"

Clete propped his hands on his knees and studied the far wall and the Indian artifacts on the shelves and the teddy bear staring back at him from the couch. "I shouldn't be calling somebody else a sorry sack of shit, even the guy I popped in the hogpen. His name was Starkweather, like the kid who killed all those people in Nebraska. What I'm saying is I have a history. For a while I was mobbed up with some guys in Reno and on Flathead Lake in western Montana. These guys happened to be on a plane that crashed into the side of a mountain. I heard they looked like fricasseed pork when they were raked out of the fir trees. The shorter version is I've got a jacket that's probably three inches thick."

"Are you trying to scare me off?"

He pressed his fingers against his temples. "Hang on a minute. There are some things I can't talk about without a drink in my hand, otherwise my gyroscope spins out of control and I fall down." He went into the kitchen and put the shot glasses and the Carta Blanca and the bottle of tequila and the bowl of limes and a salt shaker on the tray and brought them back to the rollaway. He drank his shot glass empty and sipped on the beer and felt it go down cold and bright and hard in his throat. He sucked on a lime and poured another shot, blowing out his breath, gin roses blooming in his cheeks. "I guess I'm going through some kind of physiological change. Hooch seems to go straight into my bloodstream these days, kind of like I'm mainlining. Or throwing kerosene on a fire. Sometimes I feel like I've got a dragon walking around in my chest. My nether regions get out of control, too."

"Maybe you shouldn't drink."

"That's like telling the pope he shouldn't work on Sundays."

"You shouldn't belittle yourself."

"Yeah?"

"The world beats up on everybody and breaks most of us," she said. "Why should we do it to ourselves when it's going to happen anyway? The only things we take with us are the memories of the good times we had and the good people we knew along the way."

"I never figured any of that stuff out."

"You're a lot more complicated than you pretend." When he didn't reply, she said, "It's almost dark. I'm going to turn on the floor lamp. I don't like the dark."

"Why tell me about it?"

"Because I don't hide anything I do." She walked to the lamp and clicked it on, then faced him. "Do you like me?"

"I get in trouble, Miss Varina. Lots of it, on a regular basis. I think you've had enough trouble in your life already."

She unbuttoned her shirt and the top of her jeans. "Tell me if you like me."

"Sure I do."

"You like the way I look now? Am I too forward? Tell me if I am."

"I don't have any illusions about my age and the way I look and the reasons I wrecked my career. I'd better hit the road. I showed bad judgment in coming here. You're a nice lady, Miss V. It would be an honor to get involved with a lady like yourself, but you're still married, and this won't be good for either one of us."

"If you call me 'Miss' again, I'm going to hit you. No, don't get up. Let me do this for you. Please. You don't know how important the love of a good man can be. No, not just a good man but a strong man. You are a good man, aren't you? Oh, Clete, you sweet man. Clete, Clete, Clete, that's so good. Oh, oh, oh."

He felt as though a great wave had just curled out of the ocean and knocked him backward into the sand.

CHAPTER
15

I LOOKED OUT our back bedroom window early Saturday morning and saw Clete Purcel slouching through the fog like a medieval penitent headed for the side door of the cathedral, hoping no one would see the load of guilt he was carrying. He stared at the house, looking for signs of life, then picked up a folding chair and walked down to the bayou, past Tripod's hutch, where both Tripod and Snuggs sat on the roof, watching him. Clete's seersucker coat was sparkling with damp, his wilted necktie and porkpie hat and rumpled shirt as incongruous as formal dress on a hippopotamus.

Molly was still asleep. I slipped on a pair of khakis and a sweater and lit the kitchen stove and set a pot of coffee on the burner and picked up a folding chair from the mudroom and walked down to the bayou. I could barely make out Clete's shape in the fog. He was leaning forward in his chair, studying the cattails and elephant ears and the water sliding over the cypress knees that marbled the bank. Somewhere deep inside the fog, I heard the giant cogged wheels lifting the drawbridge into the air.

"Did I wake you up?" he said.

"You know me. I'm an early riser," I replied. I unfolded my chair and sat down beside him. I could smell the booze and weed and the odor of funk and stale deodorant trapped inside his clothes. "Rough night?"

"I guess it depends on how you read it. Varina Leboeuf has a photo of her husband with Tee Jolie Melton. It was taken in a club, maybe one of those zydeco joints up by Bayou Bijoux. I told her to give it to you."

"I'm glad you did," I replied, waiting for him to get to the real reason he had come to the house.

"Think it's enough to get him in the box?"

"It's not proof of a crime, but it's a start."

"Varina came across it by accident. She wanted to do the right thing with it." He kept his attention fixed on the water and the bream starting to feed among the lily pads. "I agreed to take her on as a client."

"She wants you to get the gen on her husband?"

"She came into the office yesterday with a minister. She thinks she's in danger. What should I have done? Kicked her out?"

"That's all that's bothering you?"

"More or less."

"It's just another gig. If it doesn't work out, let it go."

"That's the way I figured it."

"I've got some coffee on. How about some Grape-Nuts and milk and blackberries?"

"That'd be nice. I didn't want to wake you up, that's all. So that's why I thought I'd sit on the bank awhile and watch the sun come up."

"What happened last night, Clete?"

He turned and looked at me sideways. He grimaced. "I went out to her old man's place on Cypremort Point. The old man is in Iberia General."

I nodded, trying to show no expression.

"We played badminton," he said. "Then I knocked back a few shots of tequila, and she showed me the photograph. She collects Indian artifacts, all kinds of junk from Santa Fe and around Mesa Verde and other places out west. She goes on archaeological digs. She found some ancient pottery in a cave, bowls that go back to the thirteenth century. That's when there was a big drought in the Southwest. She knows all about that kind of stuff."

"People who go on archaeological digs don't get to keep their artifacts, Clete."

"Yeah, I brought that up a little later."

"Later than when?"

"After we got it on."

"You were in the sack with Varina Leboeuf?"

"In the sack, on a chair, standing up, against the wall, you name it. I think we might have broken some of her old man's furniture. She's like a portable volcano. About four A.M. she was ready to rock again. We fell on top of her teddy bear."

"Her what?"

"She has this teddy bear on a couch under all her Indian artifacts."

"Varina Leboeuf keeps teddy bears in the room where she gets it on with guys our age?"

"Come on, Streak, I already feel like somebody ran over me with a garbage truck. I don't mean about her. I'm talking about me. I'm old and fat, and all I think about is getting my ashes hauled. It's the way I am, but having somebody else tell me that about myself doesn't make me feel any better."

"Go over it again."

"What for?"

"Just do it. Don't leave out one detail."

He squeezed his eyes shut and opened them again, his hands splayed on his knees, and repeated everything. I cupped my hand on the back of his neck. It felt as hard as iron, the pockmarks in his skin oily and hot and as coarse as pig hide on the edges. He looked at the water, his face wan, his coat almost splitting on his back. "I feel awful," he said.

"The teddy bear, did it look like an old one?"

"Now that you mention it, no."

"Think about it, Cletus. What doesn't fit in the story you just told me?"

"I can't follow you," he said. "I feel like the Tijuana Brass is doing a Mexican hat dance inside my head."

"Varina has a long history with men. She never asks for quarter and never gives it. She's not a sentimentalist. If Wyatt Earp ever had a female counterpart, it's Varina Leboeuf."

"The teddy bear?" he said.

"It doesn't belong in the picture, does it?"

"Why would she want to trap me with a nanny-cam? Who cares if a guy like me can't keep his stiff red-eye under control?"

"The better question is how many guys around here are in stag films they don't know about?" I said.

A HALF HOUR later, Gretchen Horowitz could barely contain her anger as she began dissecting Clete inside the cottage they were sharing at the motor court down the Teche. "You stay out all night and don't bother to call or leave a message?"

"I'm sorry, Gretchen. I was in the bag. I was doing tequila shots and mixing it with beer, then somebody ripped the hands off the clock."

"That's not all you were doing." She fanned at her face with a magazine.

"What's that supposed to mean?"

"Get in the shower. I'm going to open up some windows. Why don't you show some discretion? Who was the broad?"

Clete was taking off his shoes on the edge of the bed. "These things are none of your business," he said.

"It was Varina Leboeuf, wasn't it?"

He dropped a shoe on the floor and stood up and took off his shirt. Lipstick was smeared on the collar, and the underarms were dark with sweat. He threw the shirt in the corner. "She had a photo of Pierre Dupree with Tee Jolie Melton. That's why I went to her place. It was supposed to be business."

"They're playing you, Clete."

"Who's *they*?"

"She and her husband."

"Varina hates his guts."

"Use your head. From a legal perspective, that photo doesn't mean squat. Dupree knows you and Dave Robicheaux will eventually find out he knew Tee Jolie. So she provides you with a photo that he can claim he doesn't remember, and then both of them are off the hook. In the meantime, she gets you on a leash and gains access to everything you and Dave Robicheaux are doing. You'd see that if your brains weren't in your putz. Get undressed and give me your clothes. I'm going to take them to the Laundromat."

"Say that again about the two of them working together?"

"Not until you get in the shower," she said, throwing open a window, flooding the inside of the cottage with sunlight and fresh air. After she heard the water beating on the sides of the tin stall, she went into the bathroom and picked up his underwear and stuffed it in a dirty-clothes bag. Then she went through his slacks and the top shelf of his closet and his dresser drawers. She opened the bathroom door and leaned inside, steam billowing around her head. "I took your car keys, your sap, and your Beretta," she said. "Take a nap. While I'm gone, I'll do your laundry. In the meantime, you keep your harpoon in your tackle box. I'll be back this evening."

She got in the Caddy and drove to the McDonald's on East Main and used the pay phone so there would be no personal record of her calls. Then she bought a fish sandwich and a milk shake to go and rolled down the top on the Caddy. The trip to New Orleans on the four-lane, going through Morgan City, would take only two hours. The sky was a hard blue, the sun so bright she couldn't look directly at it, but there was a dark border of clouds low on the southern horizon, and the trees were starting to swell with wind. She burned rubber going down East Main, the unchecked power of the engine throbbing through the steering wheel into her hands.

SHE PARKED THE Caddy on a side street off St. Charles, not far from a restaurant that recently was redone in art deco. After she used the electric motor to put up the top, she tied a scarf on her head and removed a pair of sunglasses from her tote bag and put them on and looked at herself in the rearview mirror. She reached in the bag again and removed a tube of lipstick and rubbed it on her mouth. She could see the old iron green-painted streetcar coming up the neutral ground from the Carrollton district, its bell clanging. The sun had gone behind a rain cloud, and the homes along the avenue, most of them built in the 1850s, had fallen into deep shade, the white paint on them suddenly gray, the only touch of color in the yards from the camellia bushes that bloomed year-round. The barometer had dropped precipitously, the wind had started to gust, and the air was colder and smelled of dust and the advent of winter. Some of the restaurant's patrons were eating outdoors on a patio covered by a green-and-white-striped nylon awning. The streetcar stopped at the corner, discharging several passengers, then clanged its bell again and lumbered down the tracks through the tunnel of live oaks that extended almost to the Pontchartrain Hotel, near downtown. Gretchen studied the patrons at the tables and tried with no success to see through the smoked-glass windows in the side of the building. When the passengers who had been on the streetcar walked by her, she concentrated on locking the Caddy's doors, her face angled down. She adjusted the strap of her tote bag on her shoulder and entered the restaurant through a side door.

The maître d' approached from his station at the front of the restaurant, a menu under his arm. "Would you like a table?" he said.

"I'm supposed to meet Pierre Dupree here. But I don't see him," she replied.

"Mr. Dupree and his party have a private room. Please follow me," the maître d' said.

Gretchen did not remove her sunglasses or her scarf. When she entered the private dining area in back, she saw an elegantly dressed, tall, black-haired, handsome man sitting at a table with two other men, neither of whom wore a jacket. She pulled up a chair and sat down. The tall man was eating a shrimp cocktail, chewing in the back of his mouth, the fork dwarfed by his big hand. He had tucked a napkin into the top of his shirt. "Are you sure you have the right table, miss?" he said.

"You're Pierre Dupree, aren't you?" she said.

"I am."

"Then I'm in the right place. My name is Gretchen Horowitz. I've met your wife and your grandfather, so I thought it was time I meet you."

"How thoughtful. But I have no idea who you are or how you would know my whereabouts," he said.

"I called your answering service and explained to the woman there that I was from the Guggenheim Museum in New York. She was going to take a message, but I told her I had to catch a plane this afternoon and I wanted to see you before I left. She was very helpful."

"You're with the Guggenheim?"

"I went there once. But I don't work there. I work for Mr. Purcel. You know Clete Purcel?"

"I haven't had the pleasure. Your name is Horowitz?"

"That's right. Do you know Tee Jolie Melton?"

"You lied to my answering service, and now you want to sit down at my table and question me about whom I do or do not know?"

"You mind if I order? I haven't eaten yet."

"This is a put-on, isn't it?"

"You wish."

"The name is *Horowitz*, emphasis on the first syllable?"

"Any way you want to say it."

He set down his fork and removed a granule of crushed ice from the corner of his mouth. He studied her face, his eyes vaguely amused. The two men with him were smiling. One man wore his hair combed straight back, the sideburns buzzed off. There was a thick bump in the top of his nose; his eyes were wide-set and not in line with each other and gave the impression that he saw everything and nothing. The other man was fleshy, too big for his clothes, his neck chafing against a starched collar, his coat flecked with dandruff. He had a small, cruel mouth and wore a big ring on his right hand, inset with a sharp-edged emblem rather than a stone.

"How can I help you, Ms. *Horo*witz?" Dupree said.

"Here's the gen on your wife's situation," Gretchen said. "She—"

"The what?" Dupree said.

"The gen. That means the 'background,' the 'information.' Here's the gen on your wife. She's sending us signals that she's trying to screw you on your divorce settlement. So out of nowhere, she comes up with a photo that shows you with Tee Jolie Melton. That's the singer you told Dave Robicheaux you didn't know. But your wife has evidence proving that you're a liar. Except I don't believe Varina

Leboeuf is trying to screw you. I think she and you are working in concert in order to rat-fuck Mr. Purcel."

"I see," Dupree said, snapping his fingers for the waiter.

"You gonna have me eighty-sixed?"

"Oh, no, no. Andre, bring me some more hot water. Ms. Horowitz, all my dealings with my wife are through a lawyer. The other thing she and I work on together is staying out of each other's way. That's about all I can tell you, so let's call this business quits."

The fleshy man whose collar was biting into his neck said something to his friend. The friend's hair was greased and as shiny as wire against his scalp. "Sorry, I didn't catch that," Gretchen said.

"It was nothing," the fleshy man said.

"Something about lipstick?" she said.

The fleshy man shook his head, grinning broadly at his friend. The waiter arrived with a stainless steel teapot, a damp cloth wrapped around the handle; he set it in front of Pierre Dupree and went away.

"I wear lipstick when I work," Gretchen said. "I wear shades sometimes, too. Sometimes a scarf. Know why that is?"

"No," the man with the greased hair said. "Clue us in on that."

"It depersonalizes. Certain things shouldn't be personal. That's the way I look at it. What was that about a pig?"

"Don't know what you mean," the fleshy man said.

"You said something about lipstick on a pig. That's what I look like, a pig wearing lipstick?"

"Who would think that?" the fleshy man said.

Gretchen pulled off her shades and set them on the tablecloth, then untied her scarf and shook out her hair. "Now you can get a better idea of what I look like," she said. "Except now it's gotten kind of personal. I hate it when that happens."

Dupree rolled his eyes like a man reaching the limits of his patience. He pulled his napkin from the top of his shirt and dropped it on the table. "Ms. Horowitz," he said, the Z sound hissing off his teeth, "we have to say good-bye to you now. Say 'ta-ta' to everyone and squeeze your way through the dining room and out the door. I'll ask the waiter to help if you need assistance."

Another thought besides his own cleverness was obviously on

Pierre Dupree's mind. He suppressed an obvious laugh by coughing on his hand. "I'm going to take a guess. Miami, right? Family originally from Coney Island? How do y'all say it, 'Me-ami'?"

"I went over to Burke Hall at UL and checked out some of your artwork. I thought it was pretty keen," she said. "What I didn't understand was why all the figures look like they're made of rubber. They made me think of ectoplasm or maybe spermicide being squeezed out of a tube. My favorite painting was the abstract, the one that's all smears and drips, kind of like a big handkerchief someone with a brain hemorrhage blew his nose on."

Pierre Dupree reached out and took her hand in his. "You have eyes that are like violets. But they don't fit in your face or with the rest of your coloration," he said. "Why is that? You're a woman of mystery."

She felt his hand tighten on hers, squeezing her fingers into a cluster of carrots.

"No answer?" he said. "No more cute one-liners from our clever little kike from 'Me-ami'?"

The pain in her hand traveled like a long strand of barbed wire up her wrist and into her arm and shoulder and throat. She felt her eyes water and her bottom lip begin to tremble.

He tightened his grip. "Are you trying to tell me something?" he said. "Did you think perhaps you fucked with the wrong people? Have you experienced a change of heart? Nod if that's the case."

With her left hand, she fumbled the top off the teapot and threw the scalding water in his face. A cry rose from Dupree's throat as if he were being garroted. He jabbed the heels of his hands into his eyes, pushing back his chair, his shrimp cocktail spraying in a pulpy red shower on the tablecloth.

"Waste not, want not. Here's the rest of it," she said, and emptied the pot on top of him.

Dupree crashed backward on the floor, his arms wrapped around his head, his legs thrashing. Both of his friends had kicked back their chairs and were headed for her, their faces twisted with rage. She pulled Clete Purcel's blackjack from her tote sack, the wood handle clenched tightly in her palm. The blackjack was weighted at the large end with a

lump of lead the size of a golf ball, snugged tight inside stitched leather
and mounted on a spring that generated a level of torque and velocity
that could knock an ox unconscious. She swung it backward across
the mouth of the fleshy man and heard his teeth break against his lips.
The man with the greased-back hair got one hand on her shirt, but she
whipped the blackjack down on his collarbone and saw his mouth
open and his shoulder drop as though it had been severed from a string.
She was wearing alpine shoes with lug soles, and she kicked him in the
groin so hard the blood drained from his face and his knees buckled
and he took on the appearance of a griffin crouched in the middle of
the room. She whipped the blackjack across his ear and knocked him
sideways into a stack of chairs.

She shut the door that gave onto the main restaurant, her heart
pounding. When Pierre Dupree tried to pull himself up, she swung
the blackjack down on his neck and shoulders, then hit him across
the forearm and the point of one knee.

The fleshy man was trying to raise himself by holding on to the
table and had pulled the tablecloth onto the floor. His teeth were
broken off at the gums, and a string of blood and saliva hung from
his chin. She swung the blackjack across the side of his face and
heard the bone crack. "Treat this as a positive, a great opportunity
for weight loss. I've heard soup tastes lovely when it's sucked through
a straw," she said.

She surveyed the room, catching her breath, the blackjack hanging
loosely from her hand. "If you're thinking about dropping the dime
on me, ask yourself if you want a repeat performance," she said.
"I hate to tell you this, but you guys aren't the first team. Maybe
you should think about a career change. Maybe jobs in a Pee-wee
Herman theme park."

She walked back to Pierre Dupree and squatted down at eye level
with him, tapping the end of the blackjack on his nose. His eyes were
out of focus, his face mottled with burns. "Think this was bad? I've
had men do things to me with their penises that make this look like a
cakewalk. Next time I'm going to turn you into a quadriplegic." She
nudged one of his eyes wider with the tip of the blackjack. "One other
thing: Your grandfather is Jewish, but you called me a kike. You're

a puzzle, Pierre. I might have to look you up again. Enjoy the rest of your day."

She wiped off her blackjack on his necktie and put it in her tote bag, then slipped on her shades and tied her scarf on her head and went out the side exit and crossed the street to the Caddy. A soft rain was blowing along the avenue, and the pink neon glow of the restaurant inside the mist made her think of the cotton candy her mother once bought her on a visit to Coney Island.

CLETE PURCEL HAD spent most of the afternoon lying on a recliner under the live oaks by his cottage in his scarlet knee-length Everlast boxing trunks, a cooler packed with ice and five brands of foreign beer by his side, a pork roast turning on the rotisserie, the smoke drifting through the trees onto the bayou. He had self-medicated to the point where he had almost forgotten his wall-to-wall tryst with Varina Leboeuf and the fact that he had probably gone on tape and may have joined the great American porn pantheon of people like Johnny Wadd Holmes. The latter conclusion was one he could not deal with in the midst of a hangover that was already of monstrous proportions. *Time to cauterize the head with a little more flakjuice,* he thought. He cracked another bottle of St. Pauli Girl and chugged it to the bottom, upending it until every ounce of foam had drained down his throat.

Even when rain began to patter on the leaves overhead, he could not make himself get off the recliner and go inside. So he stayed under the trees throughout the shower, the rain hissing on the grill, the smoke wrapping itself around him, a tugboat on the bayou blowing its horn as though in mockery.

Then he saw his Caddy turn off East Main and bounce over the dip in the motor-court driveway and approach his cottage and parking space. He dropped his empty bottle on the grass and stood up, the trees and rooftops tilting, the Saint Augustine–like carpet nails under his bare feet. Gretchen got out of the car and locked the door and swung her tote bag over her shoulder.

"I need to have a word with you," he said.

"What about?"

"Other than you boosting my car and my sap and my nine-Mike, no problem at all," he replied.

"You got some Lysol?"

"Under the lavatory. What do you want it for?"

"To tidy up. What's for eats?"

"I don't believe you."

"Come inside. It's raining," she said. "Are you getting drunk again?"

She left the front door of the cottage open. When he went inside, she was spraying his blackjack with disinfectant and cleaning the leather cover with a wad of paper towels.

"Care to tell me where you went in my car?" he said.

"To New Orleans. I had a chat with Pierre Dupree and a couple of guys he was having lunch with. Did Alafair Robicheaux call?"

"*Alafair?* What does Alafair have to do with this?"

"Nothing. She was going to download a bunch of information for me on film schools. I want to make movies. I don't want to write them or act in them, I want to make them."

He was stabbing his finger in the air. "What happened with Dupree and these other guys?"

"I beat the living shit out of them. What did you think?"

"Where?"

"In a joint up St. Charles. Don't make a big deal out of it. They had it coming."

"You just walked in and walked out and left three guys with their sticks broken?"

"Yeah, I'd say that covers it. No, I take that back. Something else happened. Dupree called me a kike. His grandfather is a Jew. But he uses anti-Semitic language?"

"That's not the point."

"You're right. The point is you need somebody to take care of you."

"Kicking the shit out of a client's husband is not a caring activity."

"I wouldn't call Varina Leboeuf a client. An easy lay is more like it. Or a one-night punch. Or a sport fuck. Don't get me started."

"Get *you* started?"

She began brushing her hair. "Is there something you're not telling me, Clete?"

"Not telling you *what*? I can't begin to understand what's in your head. It's like having a conversation with a hurricane."

"Whatever it is you're hiding. I see it in your eyes when you don't think I'm looking."

"I like you in a special way. That's all. We're a lot alike."

"'Special way'? What is that, Sanskrit for 'deeply weird'? Are you carrying around a lot of guilt about Vietnam and working it out on me? Because if you are, I don't like it."

"I don't want to see you hurt. You went after these guys because of me. You've got to choose your battlefields more carefully, Gretchen. From this point on, these guys will know where you are, but you won't know where *they* are. You don't walk around in plain view while your enemy is wearing camouflage and setting up an L-shaped ambush. You know what an L-shaped ambush is? It's a meat grinder. We had an expression in Vietnam. We'd say, 'It's Vietnam.' Like the rules there were different and whatever happened didn't count. The truth is, the whole world is Vietnam. You either use your head and carry your own water and take care of yourself and stay true to your principles, or you walk into a meat grinder."

"What's the zip code on Mars?"

"Why?"

"Because that should be your zip code."

He sat down on the bed and gazed at the design in the rug. His skin was beaded with rainwater, his hair pasted on his scalp. "The two guys with Dupree, they tried to take you down?" he said.

"They weren't art dealers."

"And you busted up all three of them? Just with the sap? You never pulled your piece?"

"I didn't need to. They're amateurs, and they fell in their own shit."

"In what way?"

"They made fun of me because I'm a woman, even though they had no idea who I was. They have the judgment of people who abuse restaurant employees who cook and serve their food."

"They'll be coming after you."

"Too bad for them."

"I'll bring in the roast and fix you a sandwich. Don't ever run off with my car or mess with my stuff again."

"Whatever," she said. She was sitting in a straight-back chair. She rubbed the back of one wrist in her eye and gazed wanly out the window at the rain blowing off the rooftops. "Alafair told me about a 1940s musical revue that's coming up here in December. I thought about doing a documentary on it. It'd be a start, wouldn't it? Maybe something I could use to get into film school?"

He started to redirect the conversation back to the problem at hand but gave it up. "I don't know much about universities."

"I was just asking. I never went to many people for advice. My mother was always in and out of rehab. More out than in. I stopped calling her about a year ago. Do you think I have it? I mean the talent or the brains or whatever. You know stuff about history and business and the military that most college-educated people don't. Do you think somebody like me could make it in Hollywood?"

"You like Burt Reynolds?"

"Do I? Did you see *Deliverance*?"

"I met him once. Another guy asked him how he got into the film business. Reynolds said, 'Why grow up when you can make movies?' I bet they'd name a boulevard after you."

"Clete?"

He turned around, his hand on the doorknob, the mist drifting into the room.

"Lay off the hooch," she said. "There're certain kinds of behavior I can't deal with, not even when the person is somebody I'm really fond of. I'm sorry if I talked harsh to you."

CHAPTER
16

I DIDN'T LEARN of the incident in the art deco restaurant from Clete. I heard about it Monday morning when I got a phone call from Dana Magelli at NOPD. A patrolwoman had responded to the 911 at the same time the paramedics did. The private dining area was a wreck; blood and at least two teeth were splattered on a tablecloth. But the victims of the attack had helped one another out the back door and driven away in an SUV without making a report.

"You're sure one of them was Pierre Dupree?" I said.

"He's a regular. The charges were on his AmEx," Dana said. "Plus, the maître d' said Dupree had reserved the private room where the attack took place."

"Why are you calling me about it?"

"Because a witness said the assailant drove away in a maroon Cadillac convertible. Because I think this involves Clete Purcel or somebody associated with him. Because we don't have time for this crap."

"A woman beat up these guys?"

"That's what a busboy says."

"Why don't you talk to Pierre Dupree?" I asked.

"He left town. I suspect he's back in St. Mary Parish. But I don't think you're hearing me, Dave. We have the highest homicide rate in the United States. The same people who spread crack cocaine all over

South Los Angeles have had a field day here. You tell Clete Purcel he's not going to wipe his ass on this city again."

"The Giacanos got a free pass from NOPD for decades. The only guy who took a few of them down was Purcel. Save the bullshit for somebody else, Dana."

"Why is it I thought you'd take that attitude?"

"Because you're wrong? Because you're particularly wrongheaded when it comes to Clete?"

He hung up. I called Clete's office. He wasn't in, but Gretchen Horowitz was. "He doesn't always say where he goes. Want to leave a message?" she said.

"No, I want to talk to him, Ms. Horowitz."

"Call his cell phone. You have the number?"

"Can you take the chewing gum out of your mouth?"

"Hang on," she said. "Does that make it all better?"

I decided to take a chance. "If you're going to bust up somebody in a New Orleans restaurant, why drive a vehicle that every cop in the city recognizes?"

"I need a fresh stick of gum. Hang on again," she said. "If you're talking about Pierre Dupree, here's how it went down. He tried to break a woman's hand at his table. He also called her a kike. He also had two mooks with him who attacked her. So all three of them underwent sensitivity training."

"Pierre Dupree called you a kike?"

"I didn't say he called *me* anything."

"I haven't met you formally yet, but I'm looking forward to it," I said.

"Get yourself a better dialogue writer, Jack. And while you're at it, go fuck yourself," she said.

I eased the phone down into the cradle and signed out a cruiser and followed the back road down Bayou Teche into St. Mary Parish.

I'VE ACQUIRED LITTLE wisdom with age. For me, the answers to the great mysteries seem more remote than ever. Emotionally, I cannot accept that a handful of evil men, none of whom ever fought in a war, some of whom never served in the military, can send thousands of their fellow countrymen to their deaths or bring about the deaths or maiming of hundreds of thousands of civilians and be lauded for their deeds. I don't know why the innocent suffer. Nor can I comprehend the addiction that laid waste to my life but still burns like a hot coal buried under the ash, biding its time until an infusion of fresh oxygen blows it alight. I do not understand why my Higher Power saved me from the fate I designed for myself, while others of far greater virtue and character have been allowed to fall by the wayside. I suspect there are answers to all of these questions, but I have found none of them. I think Robert E. Lee was not only a good man but a heavily burdened one who debated long and hard over his decision to take Cemetery Ridge at a cost of eight thousand men. I think that's why he wrote at the end of his life that he had but one goal, "to be a simple child of God," because the contradictions of his life were so intense they were almost unbearable.

For me, the greatest riddle involves the nature of evil. Is there indeed a diabolic force at work in our midst, a satanic figure with leathery wings and the breath of a carrion eater? Any police officer would probably say he'd need to look no further than his fellow man in order to answer that question. We all know that the survivors of war rarely speak of their experience. We tell ourselves they do not want to relive the horror of the battlefield. I think the greater reason for their reticence lies in their charity, because they know that the average person cannot deal with the images of a straw village worked over by a Gatling gun or Zippo-tracks, or women and children begging for their lives in the bottom of an open ditch, or GIs hanged in trees and skinned alive. The same applies to cops who investigate homicides, sexual assaults, and child abuse. A follower of Saint Francis of Assisi, looking at the photographs of the victims taken at the time of the injury, would have to struggle with his emotions regarding abolition of the death penalty.

Regardless, none of this resolves the question. Perhaps there's a bad seed at work in our loins. Were there two groups of simian creatures vying for control of the gene pool, one fairly decent, the other defined by their canine teeth? Did we descend out of a bad mix, some of us pernicious from the day of our conception? Maybe. Ask any clinician inside the system how a sociopath thinks. He'll be the first to tell you he doesn't have a clue. Sociopaths are narcissists, and as such, they believe that reality conforms to whatever they say it is. Consequently, they are convincing liars, often passing polygraph tests and creating armies of supporters. Watch a taped interview of James Earl Ray. His facial expressions are soft wax, the eyes devoid of content, the voice deferential and without emotion or an apparent need to convince the listener.

Why the digression? Because on my Monday-morning trip over to St. Mary Parish, I realized how severe my limitations were when it came to discerning truth from falsehood and good from evil in my fellow human beings.

Three miles from Croix du Sud Plantation, I saw a Saab convertible on the left shoulder of the road and a woman changing a tire. She had already removed the lugs and lifted off the flat, but she was having trouble raising the jack high enough to fit the spare on the studs. I pulled the cruiser onto the shoulder and turned on the light bar and crossed the road. Varina Leboeuf was still squatting down in the gravel and struggling with the tire and did not look up at me. Her father was sitting in the passenger seat, smoking a cigarette, making no attempt to hide his glower. I turned the handle on the jack and raised the frame of the Saab another two inches. I could feel Jesse Leboeuf's stare taking off my skin. "Your old man fires up a smoke right after having a heart attack?" I said.

Varina pushed the spare tire onto the studs and started twisting the lugs on. "Ask him that and see what you get," she said.

"Did y'all just come from your husband's home?"

"It's none of your business."

"Is Alexis Dupree there? Or your husband?"

"Both of them are. And I do not consider Pierre my husband."

"I thought you couldn't stand to be around Alexis."

"My father needed to talk with him."

I leaned down so I could speak to her father through the driver's window. "Is that right, Jesse?" I said.

"I don't like you calling me by my first name," he replied.

"Okay, Mr. Jesse. In the past, you gave me the impression that you didn't want any truck with the Dupree family. Did you change your mind about them?"

"That old Jew owes me money. I aim to get it from him," he replied.

"How is Pierre doing?" I asked Varina.

"Not feeling very well. It couldn't happen to a more deserving guy. Do you know why I had a flat? My goddamn husband put recaps on my Saab so he could save two hundred bucks." She stood up. There was a smear of grease on her cheek. "What's your problem of the day, Dave?"

"Everything. You, your father, your husband Pierre, your grandfather-in-law Alexis. But right now my big problem is mostly you and your involvement with my friend Clete Purcel."

"Well, you arrogant fuck."

"I always liked you. I wish you hadn't tried to hurt my friend."

"You have no right to talk about my private life. I thought Clete had some class. I can't believe he discussed our relationship with you."

A diesel truck passed, blowing dust and exhaust fumes in its wake, its weight causing the Saab to shudder on the jack. When I looked back at her, her eyes were moist.

"Why couldn't your father call up Alexis Dupree rather than come out to his house?" I said.

"Because I confront people to their face, not over the telephone," Jesse Leboeuf said from the front seat. "You leave my daughter alone."

"I'll catch y'all later," I said.

Varina was breathing hard through her nose, her face pinched, not unlike a child's. "You don't know how mad you can make people," she said. "I had tender feelings for you once, whether you knew it or not. But you're a shit, Dave Robicheaux."

I got in the cruiser and drove down the two-lane toward Croix du Sud Plantation. In the rearview mirror, I saw Varina drop the flat tire in the trunk and throw the jack on top of it and slam the hatch, then stare down the road in my direction. If she and her father were acting, their performance had reached Oscar-level standards.

• • • •

A BLACK MAID wearing a gray uniform and a frilled white apron let me in and went to fetch Alexis Dupree while I stood in the foyer. When he emerged from the back of the house, he was squinting, as though he didn't quite recognize me.

"I'm Dave Robicheaux from the Iberia Parish Sheriff's Department," I said.

"Oh, yes," he replied. "How could I forget? Are you here about my grandson?"

"Yes, sir, I understand he was assaulted in a restaurant in New Orleans. He left the scene without giving any information to the New Orleans police."

"If I recall, your last visit here wasn't a very pleasant one, Mr. Robicheaux. I don't always remember things with great clarity. What was the issue?"

"I called my daughter a pet name. You thought I used the word 'Waffen.'"

"Pierre left the restaurant in New Orleans to get medical care. In regard to his not reporting the matter, any involvement with the New Orleans Police Department is a complete waste of time."

"May I speak with him?"

"He's sleeping. He was beaten badly."

I waited for Alexis Dupree to ask me to leave, but he didn't. This was my third encounter with him. On each occasion I had felt as though I were speaking to a different individual. He was the patrician and the veteran of the French Resistance whose mind hovered on the edges of senility; the irascible victim of the Holocaust; the avuncular patriarch whose bones were weightless as a bird's. Or perhaps the problem lay in my perception. Perhaps Alexis Dupree was just old, and I should not have been surprised by his mercurial behavior.

"I'm having a glass of lemon and tea in the library. Sit with me," he said.

Without waiting, he walked into an oak-paneled study furnished with a big wood desk and tan leather chairs and a liquor cabinet. Against the far wall, by the French doors, was a stand with a large Oxford dictionary on it. On the walls was a collection of photographs that had been taken all over the world: an indoor-cycling racetrack in Paris, the canals of Venice at night, the Great Wall of China, a decayed Crusader castle on the edges of a desert, Italian soldiers marching through a destroyed village, ostrich plumes stuck in the bands of their campaign hats. One photograph in particular caught my eye. In it, a dozen men and women who looked like partisans were facing the camera. They wore trousers and berets and bandoliers stuffed with large brass cartridges. Their weapons seemed to be a mix of Mausers and Lee-Enfields and Lewis guns. Behind them was a chalklike bluff, grooved by erosion, and on top of it, buildings pocked from shellfire. The photograph was inscribed "To Alexis" and signed by Robert Capa.

"You knew Capa?" I asked.

"We were friends," Dupree said. "That photo was taken in the front lines outside Madrid, just before the city fell. But I met Robert much later, after World War Two. I worked for both British and American intelligence. Robert stepped on a mine in Indochina in 1954." He gestured for me to sit down. "It was a grand time to be around, actually. Our ideological choices were clearly defined. We never had any doubt about who was right in the struggle."

"You were in the Resistance?"

"We called it *le maquis*. The underbrush."

"You were also in Ravensbrück?"

"Why do you ask of these things?"

"Because I was in Vietnam. I saw the tiger cages and some other things on a prison island both the French and the Imperial Japanese once used. I had no experiences like yours, but I saw a bit of what Orwell called 'the bloody hand' of an empire at work."

"I believe you have the wrong idea about my experience. I don't look upon myself as a victim. I survived in the camp because I worked. I did as I was told. I didn't show disrespect. Each day I imposed a soldier's discipline upon myself and never complained about my situation or my physical state. Nor did I beg. I would die before I begged. I learned that begging always breeds contempt and ensures one's victimization."

"I see," I said. But his account did not square with a detail Pierre

Dupree had mentioned. I tried not to let the discrepancy register in my face. "Was Capa a Communist?"

"Because I admired and respected Robert, I never asked him."

"The Italian troops with plumes in their hats? That photo was taken in Ethiopia, wasn't it?"

"It could have been. I wanted to be a photojournalist, but the war intervened," he said. "I hope my own unfulfilled aspirations have a second and more successful outcome in my grandson's life."

"Jean-Paul Sartre was in the Resistance. Did you know him?"

"No, Mr. Sartre was not in the Resistance. He was a writer who resisted. He was not a resister who wrote. Do you know who said that? His friend Albert Camus."

"I didn't know that," I replied.

I was learning quickly that Alexis Dupree was as elusive as a butterfly floating on the wind stream. As I looked at him sitting behind his desk, I was overcome with a sensation that even today I cannot adequately explain. His stoicism was laudable. He was distinguished-looking, handsome for a man his age. But there was an aura about him that made words stick in my throat when I tried to speak to him in a normal voice. Maybe it was a combination of things that in themselves were superficial: the odor of Vick's Vapo-Rub in his clothes, the discolorations like tiny purple carcinomas in his arms and high up on his chest, the dark luminosity of his eyes. For some reason, each moment I spent with him made me feel that I had been diminished.

Let me put it another way. Have you ever found yourself in the company of someone you are afraid to be compassionate toward? When you shake hands with him, his guile is like a smear on your skin. You find yourself unconsciously praying that he is a better person than you think he is. You actually fear the revelation he may make about himself, thereby forcing you to realize you have walked into his web. It's not unlike picking up a hitchhiker who settles himself into the passenger seat and then gives you a look that turns your viscera to ice water.

Had Alexis Dupree seen the red glow of the gas ovens roaring at night and smelled the odor from the tall brick chimney atop the building where his friends and siblings and parents died? Had he lined up among the other skeletons in striped uniforms and caps, pinching color into his cheeks so he would make it through the selections? Had he watched an SS officer point a Luger to a child's temple while the child wept and trembled and held his father's head down in a barrel of water? Was indeed the inside of this man's head a repository of images that would drive most of us mad?

"You have a peculiar expression on your face, Mr. Robicheaux," he said.

"Sorry," I replied. "I'd really like to see your grandson, sir, and then I can be on my way."

"He's heavily medicated. Another time, perhaps. Here, drink your tea."

"Mr. Dupree, your grandson told me you survived Ravensbrück only because you were used in a medical experiment."

"That's not true. There were no medical experiments at Ravensbrück. This is the kind of drivel that was manufactured after the war."

"I beg your pardon?"

"Believe whom you will. I was there. Let me check on Pierre. He'll see you if he can. In the meantime, please finish your tea."

I had the feeling I was being both indulged and told to leave. He walked through the dining room and up a spiral staircase. While he was gone, I got up and gazed through the French doors at the bayou and at the camellias blooming in the side yard. Then I noticed a thick gilt-edged book, bound in soft maroon leather, inserted horizontally on a shelf immediately below the Oxford dictionary on top of the podium. It was not the shelved book itself that was unusual. It was the wispy strands of hair protruding from the bottom pages that caught the eye.

I could hear Alexis Dupree speaking to someone upstairs. I picked up the book and set it on top of the dictionary and opened the cover. The pages were filled with a flowing calligraphy, written with a traditional fountain pen. Some of the entries were in French, some in Italian, a few in English and German. From what I could read of the content, most of the entries were observations on Nordic mythology and Florentine art and the Gypsies of Andalusia and the ethnicity of primitive people in the Balkans. I flipped to the back pages and discovered at least two dozen locks of hair, of every possible color and shade, either Scotch-taped to the paper or inserted in tiny plastic pouches. I felt my throat clotting and a burning sensation in my eyes and wondered if my imagination was running away with me. I closed the book and replaced it on the shelf below the dictionary, just as Alexis Dupree descended a spiral staircase at the far end of a hallway.

He reentered the study and shut the door behind him. "Pierre is just coming out of the shower. Give him a minute or two, and he'll see you," he said. "Be kind to him, Mr. Robicheaux. He's had a rough go of it."

"You mean the beating he didn't report?"

"No, his career as a painter. His talent is ignored because he's clearly influenced by the great painters of the late nineteenth and early twentieth centuries. The art world is controlled by a handful of people in New York. Most of them are idiots who think a screened-in piece of ham swarming with flies constitutes expression. There are many fraudulent aspects to American life, but the art world is probably the most egregious."

Through the French doors, I saw a man with bobbed white hair, wearing a black suit and a lavender Roman collar, cutting across the lawn toward a huge blue SUV parked among the oak trees. I had seen him before but could not remember where. Alexis Dupree walked to the podium and rested his hand on the open dictionary. He smiled at me. "Were you looking up a word?" he asked.

"No," I replied.

He lowered his hand to the journal bound in maroon leather and straightened it so its cover was flush with the edge of the shelf. "I thought you might have used my dictionary and accidentally brushed against my travel diary."

"Maybe I did. I'm clumsy that way."

"Oh, I don't think you're clumsy at all, Mr. Robicheaux. Why don't you go upstairs and talk with Pierre, then I'm sure you'll need to get back to your office and resume protecting and serving. That's what you call it, don't you, 'protecting and serving'?"

"The man I saw cutting across the lawn, he's a televangelical minister, isn't he?"

"Could be. They're busy little fellows in this area, scurrying here and there, saving people from themselves. You're an observant and obviously educated man, Mr. Robicheaux. What I'd like to ask, if you wouldn't mind, is how did you end up in a place like this, obsessing over issues that absolutely no one else cares about? It must be a very unpleasant way to live."

"I'll have to give that one some thought, sir. I'll get back to you on it. I'd like to talk to you about your travel diary one day. I'll bet you've picked up all kinds of things over the years."

One of the few gifts of age is that, with impunity, you can treat an elderly son of a bitch for exactly what he is.

PIERRE DUPREE WAS propped up in a bed that had been pushed against the window so he could have a full view of the lawn and the camellias and the rosebushes and the oaks hung with Spanish moss and a tennis court whose canvas windscreens were stained with mold and whose clay surface was blown with dead leaves. Indian summer was still with us, but the tennis court seemed to have the marks of year-round winter, and I wondered if Pierre Dupree ever brooded upon concerns of this kind.

The blisters on his forehead and nose and chin were shiny with salve, his black hair thick with it in the places his scalp had been burned, the back of his neck yellow and purple with bruising. Through the window I could see the minister's SUV at the end of the driveway, waiting to pull onto the state road.

"The last time I was here—" I began.

"I want to apologize for that," Pierre interrupted. "I said some things I regret. I not only regret them, they were not true."

"Calling me white trash?"

"I'm truly sorry, Mr. Robicheaux. That's an unforgivable thing to say to someone."

"A detective at NOPD called me about the assault on you and your friends in the restaurant. Your grandfather says you don't have much confidence in the system, so you didn't report it and apparently wrote it off. That's an extremely forgiving attitude, don't you think?"

"Do you know what the media would do with that story? Three grown men beaten into pulp by one young woman? I have a hard time explaining it to myself."

"What do you think provoked her?"

"She said she was from the Guggenheim in New York. Then she went crazy."

"She didn't like your paintings?"

"Did you come here to bait me?"

"A minister just left your home. That was Amidee Broussard, wasn't it? I've seen his television broadcast several times. He knows how to deliver the vote," I said.

"Excuse me?"

"Abortion, gay marriage, that sort of thing, it works every time."

Pierre removed a pill from a bottle on his nightstand and put it on his tongue. He flinched when he shifted himself in bed, and I realized he had probably been hit in places that would hurt for a long time. "Would you pour me a glass of mineral water, please?"

I filled a glass from a green bottle on the nightstand and handed it to him. His show of dependence and his desire to make me into a caretaker seemed more thespian than real, and I wondered if anything in the Dupree manor went deeper than the cheap facade on a stage set. He turned his head on the pillow and gazed wistfully out the window, like a caricature of royalty in exile. I waited for him to speak, but he didn't.

"Why not come clean on this stuff and put it behind you?" I said.

He nodded slightly, as though ending a philosophic debate with himself. "I insulted her. That's why she attacked me. I called her a kike."

"Even though your grandfather is a holocaust survivor?"

"That's why I did it. I get tired of hearing *Gran'père*'s constant replay of his ordeal. Did you know my mother?"

"No, I did not."

"She was a suicide. She jumped from a passenger liner off the Canary Islands."

This time it was I who didn't speak. I didn't want to hear about the fortunes or misfortunes of his family. For a lifetime, I had witnessed the damage the Duprees and their relatives and their corporate partners had done to the poor and the powerless. Worse, their arrogance and imperious behavior had always existed in inverse proportion to the defenselessness of the working people they exploited and injured.

"Do you know who my father is?" he asked.

"No, I never knew him."

"Yes, you do."

"I'm afraid I don't understand."

"You know my father. He's still alive. You were just talking with him downstairs. Alexis Dupree is both my grandfather and my father. My mother was his daughter."

I searched his face, his eyes, his body language, looking for the blink, the tic in the cheek, the stiffness in the lips, the twitch in the hand that signals a lie. I saw none of those things.

"Maybe you should be telling these things to a clinician," I said. "I'm here for only one reason. Dana Magelli, my friend at NOPD, called to find out why somebody of your background would allow himself and his friends to be assaulted and not call 911. I don't think you've provided an adequate answer. What are the names of the two men who were with you at the restaurant?"

"Ask them when you find them. I'm not interested in talking about this anymore."

"This kind of doodah isn't working for you, pòdna," I said, my anger growing. "I think you were in business with Bix Golightly and Frankie Giacano and Waylon Grimes. It had something to do with stolen or fraudulent paintings. You're also involved in something far bigger and more important. Bix and Frankie and Waylon are worm food now, but in reality, they were never players. What are you and your wife and your father-in-law and that televangelical huckster up to, Pierre? The bunch of you always give me the feeling you have Vitalis oozing out your pores."

As I laughed openly at him, I saw his face cloud and his eyes darken, as though the needle of a phonograph he'd been playing had jumped off the record. Then he bit his bottom lip, refocusing. "I hurt her fingers," he said.

"Whose?"

"You asked me what provoked the woman. I clutched her fingers in mine and squeezed until I thought they would break. I made fun of her while I did it. I also enjoyed it. Ask yourself what kind of man would do that to a woman. That's why I didn't call the police."

"Then you had a conversion while you were lying in sick bay?"

"I just told you the dirtiest secrets in the history of my family. You think I do it to extract sympathy? I told all this to Reverend Broussard. My grandfather stole my childhood and destroyed my mother. All these years I've defended him. You know why? He's the only family I had."

A good liar always threads an element of truth inside his deception. I didn't know if that was the case with Pierre Dupree. His hands seemed unnaturally large on top of the sheet. They were broad and thick and not the hands of an artist or a musician or a sculptor who worked with clay. They were the hands of a man who had almost broken a woman's fingers. I did not believe that Pierre Dupree told lies simply to deceive others. I believed he told lies to deceive himself as well. I believed he was a genetic nightmare and a validation of Hitler and Himmler's belief that pure evil could be passed on through the loins.

I DROVE OUT of the Dupree enclave onto the two-lane and headed back toward New Iberia. To the south, there were clouds that resembled black curds of smoke from an industrial fire, and I wondered if cleanup crews out on the salt were burning off some of the two million gallons of oil from the blowout or if those clouds were just clouds, swollen with rain and electricity and a smell that in summertime is like iodine and seaweed and small baitfish. As I neared New Iberia, the sun went behind the clouds and the wind came up and the cane fields and the corridors of live oaks and the light winking on Bayou Teche turned the world into the Louisiana of my youth. Wilderness enow, the poet wrote. But that's all it was, a dream, like the lyrics in Jimmy Clanton's famous song from the year 1958.

• • •

TEN MINUTES LATER, I parked the cruiser in front of Clete Purcel's office on Main and went inside. Behind the reception desk, Gretchen Horowitz was eating take-out Chinese with chopsticks. Three loungers were sitting on the folding chairs, smoking, grinding out their cigarettes on the floor, and picking at their fingernails. "Where's Clete?" I said.

"Not here," Gretchen said, poking a tangle of noodles into her mouth, not bothering to look at me.

I reversed the "open" sign on the door so that it read "closed" to the outside world. I dropped the blinds on the door and the big glass window in front. "You three dudes beat it," I said.

They didn't move. One of them was hatchet-faced and had the crystalline-clear eyes of either a meth addict or a psychopath. Another had a rattail haircut and rings in his eyebrows and a dark blue tattoo of a penis and testicles on his throat. The third man was dressed in bib overalls and had the gargantuan proportions and body odor of an elephant in rut. His arms were wrapped with one-color ink from the wrist to the armpit, a form of tattooing that is painful and prolonged and inside the system is called "wearing sleeves." There were no words inside his tats, but the message to the viewer on the yard was clear: "If you want to finish your time, don't fuck with me."

I opened my badge holder. "I don't think y'all are from around here. If you're Nig Rosewater and Wee Willie Bimstine's bail skips, I recommend you get your ass back to New Orleans. Regardless, get out of the office and don't come back until you see me leave."

"What if we don't?" the large man said.

"We'll make you take a shower," I said.

After they were gone, I locked the door.

"What do you think you're doing?" Gretchen said, poking at her noodles.

"Bringing you up-to-date."

"You got accepted by the Premature Ejaculators Society?"

"Number one, you don't tell an Iberia Parish sheriff's detective to fuck himself."

"Oh, gee, I feel terrible about that."

I dragged a metal chair over to the desk and sat down. She kept eating, never looking up.

"I'm not sure who you are, Gretchen. Maybe you're more snap-crackle-and-pop than substance. Maybe you've been knocked around a bit. Or maybe you've been over on the dark side. It doesn't matter. The people who live inside Croix du Sud Plantation may look like the rest of us, but they're not. I cannot tell you what they are, but I can tell you what they are not. The three dudes I just kicked out of here are recidivists who will never figure out they serve the interests of people who want to keep the rest of us distracted. Does any of that make sense to you?"

She squeezed her eyes shut, as though trying to work her way through my question. "I've got it. You shut down your friend's office and run his clients out of town because you have access to knowledge that nobody else does?"

"You're an intelligent woman. Why don't you stop acting like a juvenile delinquent? I just finished talking with Alexis Dupree. While he was in another room, I looked in a journal that he's evidently kept over the years. There were at least two dozen locks of hair between the last pages."

She had been stirring the noodles in the box, but her hand slowed and stopped, and she blinked once and then looked at nothing. "Did you say anything to him?" she asked.

"No. But I think he knows I saw the locks of hair."

"What was the name of the place he was in?"

"Ravensbrück," I said.

"Didn't they cut the hair off the people they killed?"

"Yes, particularly in the women's camps," I replied.

"Maybe he's just an old man on the make. Maybe he's a trophy-sex addict."

"It's possible," I said. "What are the other possibilities?"

"He's a pedophile?"

"We would have heard about it."

"Did the hair look old?"

"Yeah, most of it."

She wrapped her uneaten food in the plastic bag in which it had been delivered and set it in the bottom of the wastebasket. "I told Clete the old man made me feel funny, like his fingers were crawling all over me." She was studying the floor. Then she looked me full in the face. "He was one of them?"

"One of what?"

"He's not a Jew? He was one of the Nazis who worked in those camps? He herded all those children and women and sick people into the gas chambers? That's what you're saying?"

"Pierre says Alexis is not only his grandfather but his father as well," I said. "So tell me who's lying and who's evil and who's telling the truth. This is the wasp's nest you threw a rock in."

I heard a key turn in the front-door lock and the blinds rattle against the glass when the door swung open. "What's going on in here?" Clete said, a double-folded manila envelope in his hand.

"Gretchen was eating some noodles. I kicked three of your clients out. Both of us think Alexis Dupree may have been a Nazi, not a Jewish inmate in a death camp," I said. "Outside of that, it's been a pretty dull day."

CHAPTER
17

Clete and I went into his inner office, and I told him about my visit to the Dupree plantation. "So you think the old man is actually a war criminal?" he said.

"It's possible. He claimed he survived Ravensbrück because of his inner discipline and the fact that he did everything his warders told him to do. Listening to him tell it, I had the feeling that those who died brought their deaths upon themselves. He also said he was a friend of Robert Capa. But he didn't know if Capa was a Communist. On his wall, he has a photo of Italian troops in what I think was the Ethiopian campaign. They used chemical weapons on people who fought with spears and bows and arrows. Why would a victim of the fascists want a photo like that on his wall?"

I could tell I was losing Clete's attention. "I know that look. What have you done now?" I said.

"Hang on," he said. He sent Gretchen on an errand, then closed the door and untaped the double-folded manila envelope he had been holding and removed two memory cards. "I creeped Varina's apartment in Lafayette and her house on Cypremort Point. You were right about the teddy bear on the couch. It's a nanny-cam. She had another one on a shelf in Lafayette."

"You broke into her home and her apartment?"

"Not exactly. I showed my PI badge to the apartment manager in Lafayette."

"How did you get into the house on Cypremort Point?"

"The key was in a flowerpot."

"How'd you know it was there?"

"She showed me. In case I wanted to let myself in if her old man wasn't there." He saw my look. "So I took advantage of her trust. It doesn't make me feel good," he said. "You want to watch this stuff or not?"

"No, I don't. I don't think you should watch it, either."

"Maybe I'm on tape. You think I should ignore that?" he said, uploading the first card into his computer.

"Don't give power to it."

"To what?"

"Evil."

"You think Varina is evil?"

"I don't know what she is. Just stay away from her. Stay away from the shit on that card, too."

"What am I supposed to do with it?"

"Give it back to her. Treat it with contempt. Let her live in her own deceit."

"Maybe I can have a second career as the model on the covers of bodice-buster novels. Will you lighten up? You make me feel awful, Dave."

"What can I say?"

"Try nothing," he replied.

He began clicking the keys on his computer, his huge shoulders stressing the fabric in his sport coat, his porkpie hat pulled down on his eyes, as though, unconsciously, he wanted to shield them. The first image on the monitor was that of Varina in the nude, her back to the camera, as she approached a naked man lying on the couch, one hand tucked behind his head, his chest hair like a black fan spread across his sun-browned skin. The figure was not Clete.

"Adios," I said.

"Come on, Dave. I went this far with it. I don't want to look at it by myself. I already feel like a pervert."

Then I said something I never thought I would say to Clete Purcel: "I can't help you with this one, partner."

My cell phone vibrated in my pocket. I looked at the caller ID. Helen Soileau. "Where are you?" she said.

"In Clete's office."

"What are those sounds in the background?"

"Turn the speaker off, Clete," I said.

"What the hell are you guys doing?" she asked.

"Nothing. I was just leaving."

"You know anything about hammerhead sharks?" she asked.

"They eat stingrays and their own young. The males bite the females until they mate."

"I mean where they live or feed or whatever."

"They go where they want. Why are you asking about hammerhead sharks?"

"The pictures are just coming in on the Internet from Lafourche Parish. We found out what happened to Chad Patin," she said.

A SPORT FISHERMAN had been trolling with outriggers southwest of Grand Isle when he foul-hooked what he thought was a sand shark. The drag began to accelerate and sing with such velocity that smoke was rising off the reel. To keep from breaking the line, the mate reversed the vessel in the same direction the shark was running. From the stern, you could see a long torpedo-shaped shadow appear briefly beneath a swell, then a dorsal fin slicing through a wave and dipping below the surface again, bubbles trailing after it. For just a moment the line went slack, as though it had been severed, and the mate throttled back the engine and let the boat drift. The slick spots between the waves were undisturbed, the water glistening with a fine sheen like baby oil, the exhaust pipes of the boat gurgling just below the surface. Overhead, pelicans drifted on the breeze, making a wide turn, the way they always do before they cock their wings and plunge down into a wave. However, they seemed to lose interest. Suddenly, a school of baitfish were skittering across a swell, as though someone were flinging handfuls of silvery dimes on the water.

The hammerhead burst to the surface, the line tangled in its gills, streaming blood, its side striped with lesions cut by the steel leader. Its back had been tanned by the sun, giving it the coloration of a sand shark. Its belly was as white as a toadstool that had never seen sunlight. Its eyes, set on the sides of its anvil-like head, gleamed disjointedly, similar to those inside a cubist painting. From nose to tail, it was at least eleven feet long.

All of this was on the sportsman's cameraphone, along with images of the sportsman and another mate gaffing the shark in the gills and in its mouth and clubbing it with a mallet and finally dragging it high enough on the gunwale to hit it in the head with a hatchet. The sportsman rolled the hammerhead on its back and inserted a knife in its anus and split its belly open. The contents that spilled out on the deck were not what he was expecting to find.

A hammerhead has a small mouth for a shark of its size and takes a while to consume its prey. Evidently, this one had managed to eat and swallow everything it had been provided. The dismemberment of the prey looked like it had been done with a saw. The details are not pleasant to narrate. Only two details of the shark's engorgement were of significance, at least from a forensic or evidentiary point of view. Glimmering among the spill on the deck were a Caucasian hand and part of a forearm. On the hand was a ring. Later, the coroner in Lafourche Parish removed the ring and found the name of Chad Patin engraved inside it. The other forensic detail of importance was the discovery of two .223 rounds in the back muscles of the victim.

Chad Patin had tried to kill me with a shotgun blast fired from the freezer truck. But as I looked at the images on Helen's computer screen, I could feel no enmity toward him. When he called me in the middle of the night from Des Allemands, begging for help, I discounted much of what he said, particularly his rant about a cabal of some kind that controlled events in the lives of those at the bottom of the food chain. Also, his mention of a mysterious figure called Angel or Angelle and his description of someone dying inside the iron maiden seemed the stuff of drug-induced psychosis. But I had been selective in listening to Chad Patin. He'd said he transported narcotics and prostitutes from Mexico into the United States. He also indicated he had abandoned his charges in a locked truck and perhaps left them to die of suffocation. Those were statements I believed. He admitted he had tried to kill me and in the same breath asked for money so he could get out of the country. In his mind, the request was perfectly reasonable. I had acted incredulously, but in reality, his point of view was one that people in law enforcement deal with every day. The real problem was not Chad Patin. The real problem lay in my discounting his story about a mysterious island where modern-day people made use of a torture instrument out of medieval Europe.

Helen was tilted back in her swivel chair, chewing on a hangnail, staring at her computer and the frozen image of Chad Patin's remains on the boat deck. "I don't get it," she said.

"Why nobody took the ring off him?" I said.

"*That* and the fact that he was dumped overboard. Didn't they learn anything after they put Blue Melton over the side in a block of ice?"

"Maybe they didn't put him in the water. Maybe he was running and somebody popped him with a couple of .223 rounds, maybe from an AR-15 or M16. He fell off the boat, and they couldn't find him in the dark."

"You buy that stuff about an island and a torture chamber on it?"

"Patin was reporting something he heard on a tape. Maybe the tape was bogus, something excerpted from a slasher film. Who knows? Somebody fried Patin's apartment with a flamethrower. That's a tough act to follow. The bigger problem for me is this person Angel or Angelle. The notion of a cabal is too much like the New World Order or the Trilateral Commission."

"You don't believe in conspiracies?"

"Not the kinds that have formal names."

"Was that a porn film I heard when I called you?"

"Not exactly."

"You and Clete were watching an old Doris Day movie?"

"Give it a break, Helen. Clete is going through a bad time."

"So am I. It's called doing my job. Does he have somebody new working in his office?"

"She's a temp."

"What's her name?"

"You made a crack about a porn film. Varina Leboeuf is probably extorting her lovers. Clete got involved with her."

"Don't change the subject. What's the name of the temp?"

I got up from my chair and opened the door to leave. "Cut Clete a little slack. He'll deliver. He always does. He's the best cop either one of us ever knew."

"I want to meet her."

"Why?"

"You know why, Pops. Believe it or not, we're on the same side. But you two guys don't get to write the rules," she said.

CLETE CALLED ME an hour later. "I'm not on those memory cards. But a lot of other guys are," he said. "A couple of them are insider contractors who got in on the big bucks rebuilding New Orleans. I recognize a couple of shysters and oil guys, and then there were a few guys I never saw before. Anyway, I don't see any big revelations. Actually, I feel like going outside and puking. I'm not up to this stuff."

"She's blackmailing people. You don't call that a revelation?"

"Maybe she's just covering her ass."

"Great choice of words. Listen to yourself."

"Maybe she's got a fetish. Who's perfect? Anyway, she left me out of it."

"I know what you're thinking."

"What?"

"You're going back for seconds is what."

"So she's a little weird. That doesn't make her the Lucrezia Borgia of South Louisiana."

"What does it take? How bad do you have to get hurt before you see what you're doing to yourself?"

"Maybe I still like her. The apartment manager in Lafayette must have told her I was in her place. But she didn't dime me."

"Most extortionists don't call the cops to report the theft of their blackmail materials."

"Dave, you're crucifying me for something I haven't done. I didn't say I was going to get it on with Varina again. I was just saying nobody is all good or all bad. Look, I'm burning this stuff and forgetting about it. I wish I'd never seen it. I wish I hadn't gotten in the sack with her. I wish I hadn't accidentally killed a mamasan and her children in Vietnam. I wish I hadn't flushed my career with NOPD. My whole life is based on the things I wish I hadn't done. What else do you want me to say?"

"I think Pierre and Varina and Alexis Dupree are a tighter unit than they let on. They might hate one another, but they're all in the same lifeboat."

"Neither of us knows that," he replied.

"Chad Patin's remains just showed up in the belly of a hammerhead shark a guy caught south of Grand Isle. Lose the charade with Varina. She knows you're a kindhearted guy, and she used you."

"Why don't you show some fucking respect?"

"You're the best guy I've ever known. I'm supposed to stand around with my hands in my pockets while other people mess up your head?"

"Say that about Patin again?"

"There were two rifle slugs in the remains. He was probably trying to escape from his abductors when they popped him. He told me about an island run by people who made a tape of a guy being squeezed to death inside an iron maiden. I think he was probably telling me the truth. Wake up, Cletus. Compared to what we're dealing with, Bix Golightly is the Dalai Lama."

"Dave?"

"Yeah?"

"You know all that stuff you hear about getting it on with a young woman so you can feel young again?"

"What about it?"

"It works fine. Until you come out of the shower the next morning and look in the mirror and see a mummy looking back at you."

• • •

CLETE HUNG UP his desk phone and gazed out the back window at the bayou. A black man seated on an inverted bucket was fishing with a cane pole in the shade of the drawbridge. Water hyacinths grew thickly along the banks, and on the far side was the old gray hospital and convent that had been converted into business offices, all of it shadowed by giant live oaks. The wind was up and the moss was straightening in the trees and the oak leaves were tumbling on the manicured lawn. Clete rubbed the heel of his hand into his eye and felt a great weariness that seemed to have no origin. He lit his Zippo lighter and placed it in the center of an ashtray and, with a pair of tweezers, held the memory cards he had retrieved from Varina Leboeuf's property over the flame.

He had left his office door open. He failed to notice that Gretchen Horowitz had returned from the errands he had sent her on. She tapped on the doorjamb before entering his office. "I wasn't deliberately listening, but I heard your conversation," she said.

He watched the second memory card curl and blacken in the flame of his Zippo. He dropped it into the ashtray. "What about it?" he asked.

"I wish you would trust me more."

"About what?"

"Everything. If you trusted me, maybe I could help."

"You're a kid and you don't know what you're talking about, no matter how much you've been around."

"I told you not to call me that."

"There's nothing wrong with being a kid. That's what we all want to be. That's why we screw up our lives, always trying to be something we're not."

"I don't like to hear you talk like that. I don't like what this woman is doing to you."

"Did you get the mail?"

"Yes."

"Did you go to FedEx in Lafayette?"

"Yes."

"Then you did your job. We're done on this subject."

"Can I have the rest of the afternoon off?"

"To do what?"

She leaned down on his desk. Her shoulders were too big for her shirt, her upper arms taut with muscle. The violet tint of her eyes seemed to deepen as she looked into his face. "Personal business."

"I think you should hang around."

"I want to buy a vehicle for myself. Maybe a secondhand pickup."

"Stay away from Varina Leboeuf," he said.

"How about taking your own advice? You're unbelievable."

He watched her walk out the front door into the brightness of the day, a cute olive-drab cap tilted on her head, her wide-ass jeans stretched tight on her bottom, her tote bag swinging from her shoulder.

THREE HOURS LATER, Alafair's cell phone rang. "Are you working on your novel right now?" Gretchen asked.

"I've finished the galleys on the first one. I've started a new one," Alafair replied.

"What's it about?"

"I'm not sure. I never am. I make it up each day. I never see more than two scenes ahead."

"You don't make an outline?"

"No, I think the story is written in the unconscious. You discover it a day at a time. At least that's the way it seems to work for me."

"I'll buy you dinner if you drive me to a couple of car lots," Gretchen said. "I took a cab to three but didn't find anything interesting. I don't want to waste the rest of the day waiting on more cabs."

"Dave says you tore up Pierre Dupree and two other guys with a blackjack."

"Shit like that happens sometimes."

"Where are you?"

Alafair picked up Gretchen at a car lot out by the four-lane. She was standing on the corner, wearing dull red cowboy boots, her jeans stuffed into the tops, cars whizzing by her. She pulled open the passenger door and got inside. "Do the drivers around here drop acid before they get in their automobiles?" she said.

"What kind of car are you looking for?" Alafair asked.

"Something that's cheap with a hot engine." Gretchen gave directions to a car lot on the edge of town.

"You know a lot about cars?" Alafair said.

"A little. But forget about that. Clete told me you were number one in your class at Stanford Law."

"There's no official rating of graduates at Stanford, but I had a four-point GPA. My adviser said if I was ranked, I'd probably be first in my class."

"You were born in a grass hut? You make me feel like a basket case. I'm sending in my application forms to the University of Texas. I think you have to be interviewed to get into the film program. I'm a little nervous about that."

"Why should you be nervous?"

"Because I've always had a tendency of sending certain kinds of signals to men when I wanted something from them. Like maybe they could get into my pants if things went right for me. I pretended to myself that wasn't what I was doing, but it was. I'd find a middle-aged guy who couldn't control where his eyes went and home in on him."

"Stop talking about yourself like that. If you have to go to Austin for an interview, I'll go with you."

"You'd do that?"

"Gretchen, talent doesn't have anything to do with a person's background or education. Did you ever see *Amadeus*? It's the story of Mozart and his rivalry with Antonio Salieri. Salieri hated Mozart because he thought God had given this great talent to an undeserving idiot. Talent isn't earned, it's given. It's like getting hit by lightning in the middle of a wet pasture. People don't sign up for it."

"If I could talk like you."

"I told you to quit demeaning yourself. You're the kind of person writers steal lines from. What kind of people do you think make movies? Most of them belong in detox or electroshock. The rest are narcissists and nonpathological schizophrenics. That's why Los Angeles has more twelve-step meetings than any other county in the United States. Can you see your local Kiwanis Club making *Pulp Fiction*?"

"I've got to write that down."

"No, you don't. You have better lines in your own head."

"I'm one of the people you just mentioned?"

"Anybody can be normal. Count your blessings," Alafair said.

She turned in to a used-car lot that, only two weeks earlier, had been a cow pasture. The car seller was a notorious local character by the name of T. Coon Bassireau. His business enterprises had ranged from burial insurance to car-title loans to storefront counseling centers that billed Medicaid to treat street people who had to be taught the names of their illnesses. He also patented a vitamin tonic that contained 20 percent alcohol and was guaranteed to make the consumer feel better. He swindled pensioners out of their savings in a Mexican biotech scam and once dumped a bargeload of construction debris in a pristine swamp. But the big score for T. Coon came in the form of deteriorating train tracks across southern Louisiana. Whenever there was a freight derailment, particularly one involving tanker cars, he and his brother, a liability lawyer, distributed T-shirts to people in the neighborhoods along the tracks. The message printed on the back read: HAVE TOXIC SMELLS IN YOUR HOUSE FROM THE TRAIN WRECK? YOU MAY BE ELIGIBLE FOR A LARGE CASH SETTLEMENT. CALL T. COON BASSIREAU. T. COON IS YOUR FRIEND. The 800 number was emblazoned in red on the front and back.

He stood proudly under the vinyl banner that stretched across his new car lot. Half a dozen American flags, their staffs speared into the ground, popped in the breeze. A battery-lit portable sign that read WE SUPPORT THE TROOPS glittered by the entranceway. T. Coon wore sideburns that flared like grease pencil on his cheeks, and a Stetson and a shiny magenta shirt with pearl snap buttons and a Stars and Bars belt buckle as big as the bronze plate on a heliograph. He rocked back and forth on the heels of his boots, a man at peace with both Caesar and God.

Gretchen walked past him without speaking and examined the two rows of junker cars and trucks T. Coon had assembled in the pasture. "You ladies want to go for a test drive?" he said. "You can do anyt'ing you want here. Just ax. For ladies like y'all, I'll lower my price any day of the week and twice on Sunday and t'ree times on

Monday." He crossed his heart. "If I'm lying, dig me up and spit in my mout'."

"Tell your mechanic to wipe the sawdust off the transmission cases," Gretchen said.

"I'm lost here," T. Coon said.

"You packed the transmission cases with sludge and sawdust to tighten up the gears. I bet you put oil on the brake linings to keep them from squeaking. The odometer numbers are a joke. I wouldn't sit on the seats unless they'd been sprayed for crab lice."

"I'm blown away by this," he said.

"There's not a car on the lot that's not a shitbox. Your tires are so thin, the air is showing through. I think some of these cars came from Florida. They're rusted with salt from the bottom up."

"This is some kind of put-on."

"Who are *you* that I should put you on?"

T. Coon's eyes shifted nervously back and forth. "I'm making a living here."

"You see that Ford truck with the chrome engine?"

"It's a hot rod. It belongs to my nephew."

"I ran the plate two days ago. It's registered in your name. You use it as a leader and claim your nephew won't sell it unless the figures are right. What are the right figures?"

"My nephew might take fifteen t'ousand."

"Give me the keys," Gretchen said.

She got in the pickup and fired it up and spun rubber on the grass and swung out on the highway, the dual exhausts throbbing on the asphalt. A few minutes later, she was back, the exposed chrome engine ticking with heat. She left the keys in the ignition and got out of the cab. "I'll give you eight. In cash, right now. It'll have to be re-primed and painted and the interior entirely redone. The only things good about it are the chop and channel jobs and the Merc engine and the Hollywood mufflers. The rest of it blows."

"I cain't believe I'm being verbally assaulted like this. I feel like I inebriated a whole bottle of whiskey and am having delusions."

She opened her tote bag and removed a brown envelope stuffed with hundred-dollar bills. "Tell me what you want to do," she said.

"Make it nine," he said.

"Make it eight."

"Make it eighty-five hunnerd. The tires are almost brand-new."

"That's why you're not getting seventy-five hundred," she said. "Stop trying to see down my shirt."

T. Coon wore a stupefied expression, like a man who had just gotten off a centrifuge. "We got to do some paperwork in my office, that li'l trailer over there. Don't look at me like that. I'll leave the door open. Jesus Christ, where you from, lady? You got your spaceship parked somewhere? You need a job? I'm serious here. I got an entry-level position we can talk about." He looked at her expression to see what effect his words were having. "Okay, I was just axing."

Half an hour later, Gretchen followed Alafair to a restaurant on the highway and bought seafood dinners for both of them. Through the window, Alafair could see a blue-black darkness taking hold in the sky and gulls that had been blown inland circling over a cane field. "I've got another favor to ask you," Gretchen said. "I don't want to embarrass you, but I'd like to live my life the way you do. Maybe you could give me a reading list and some tips on things."

"That's flattering, but why not just be your own person?"

"If I was who I started out to be, I'd be in prison or worse. I've got an advantage over other people who write novels and make movies. I lived inside a world that most people couldn't imagine. Did you ever see *Wind Across the Everglades*, the story of James Audubon trying to put the bird poachers out of business? I know those kinds of people, how they think and talk and spend their time. I know about racetracks and drug smuggling in the Keys and CIA people in Little Havana and the money that gets laundered through the pari-mutuel windows."

"I think you're probably a real artist, Gretchen. You don't have to model yourself on me. Just stay true to your own principles."

"I need you to go with me to see Varina Leboeuf."

"You want to do this because of Clete?"

"Varina Leboeuf tapes the men she goes to bed with. Clete doesn't have any judgment about women. I need to have a talk with her, but in the way you would do it, not in the way I usually do things. I need you there as a witness, too. I don't want her making up lies about me later."

Alafair was eating a deep-fried soft-shell crab. She put it down and gazed at the seagulls cawing above the cane field. The sky was completely dark now, the clouds rippling with flashes of yellow light. "Clete can take care of himself. Maybe you should leave things alone."

"You're smarter than me about almost everything, Alafair, but you're wrong about this. Most people think society is run by lawyers and politicians. We believe this because those are the people we see on the news. But the only reason we see these people on the news is because they own the media, not people like us. When things have to be taken care of—I'm talking about the kind of things nobody wants to know about—there's a small bunch that does the dirty work. Maybe you don't believe this."

"That's the way cynics think. And they think that way because it's uncomplicated and easy," Alafair said.

"Did you see *Mississippi Burning,* the story of the boys who were murdered by the Klan and buried in an earthen dam?" Gretchen said. "In the movie, the FBI outsmarts the Klan and turns them against each other and gets them to start copping pleas. But that's not what happened. Hoover sent a Mafia hit man down there, and he beat the crap out of three guys who were only too glad to turn over the names of the killers."

"What are you going to say to Varina?"

"Not much. You don't have to go. I've asked a lot of you already."

"Maybe it's better I not."

"I can't blame you. I try to stay out of other people's lives. But I don't think Clete has much chance against Varina Leboeuf. I don't think he sees everything that's involved, either."

"What's that last part mean?" Alafair asked.

"I've known a lot of bad people in Florida. They all had connections in Louisiana. Some of them may have been involved with the murder of John Kennedy. How do you think the crack got in the projects here? It just showed up one day? The money from the crack paid for AK-47s that went to Nicaragua. But who gives a shit, right?"

"This is becoming an expensive dinner."

"That's why I said you don't have to go with me."

"In for a penny, in for a pound," Alafair said.

CHAPTER
18

GRETCHEN HOROWITZ HAD never understood what people called "shades of gray." In her opinion, there were two kinds of people in the world, doers and takers. The doers did a number on the takers. Maybe there were some people in between, but not many. She liked to think she was among the not many. The not many set their own boundaries, fought under their own flag, gave no quarter and asked for none in return. Until recently, she had never met a man who had not tried to use her. Even the best of them, a high school counselor and a professor at the community college, had turned out to be unhappily married and, in a weak moment, filled with greater need than charity in their attitude toward her, one of them groping her in his office, the other begging her to go with him to a motel in Key Largo, then weeping with remorse on her breast.

That was when she tried women. In each instance she felt mildly curious before the experience and empty and vaguely embarrassed after, as though she had been a spectator rather than a participant in her own tryst. She saw a psychiatrist in Coral Cables who treated her with pharmaceuticals. He also told her that she had never been loved and, as a consequence, was incapable of intimacy. "What can I do about that?" she asked.

"It's not all bad. Eighty percent of my patients are trying to escape emotional entanglements," he replied. "You're already there. What I think you need is an older and wiser man, namely a paternal figure in your life."

"I have feelings I didn't tell you about, Doc," she said. "On a bright, clear day out on the ocean, without a problem in the world, I have this urge to do some payback. On a couple of occasions I acted on my urge, one time with a guy who owned a skin joint and asked me out on his boat. Things got pretty entangled. At least for him. Want to hear about it?"

Later that day the receptionist called Gretchen and told her that the psychiatrist was overloaded and would be referring her to a colleague.

Alafair left her car in town and rode with Gretchen down to Cypremort Point. On the western horizon a thin band of blue light was sealed under clouds as black as a skillet's lid, and waves were sliding across the darkness of the bay, smacking against the shoals. Gretchen could smell the salt in the air and the rain in the trees and the leaves that had been blown onto the asphalt and run over by other vehicles. But inside the coldness of the smell and the freshness of the evening, she could not take her eyes off the rain rings on the surface of the swells. They reminded her of a dream she'd been having since she was a child. In it, giant hard-bodied fish with the grayish-blue skin of dolphins rose from the depths and burst through the surface, then arched down into the rings they had created with their own bodies, slipping into darkness again, their steel-like skin glistening. The dream had always filled her with dread.

"You have dreams?" she asked.

"What kind?" Alafair said.

"I don't mean dreams with monsters in them. Maybe just fish jumping around. But you wake up feeling like you had a nightmare, except the images weren't the kinds of things you see in nightmares."

"They're just dreams. Maybe they represent something that hurt you in the past. But it's in the past, Gretchen. I have dreams about things I probably saw in El Salvador."

"You ever have violent feelings about people?"

"I was kidnapped when I was little. I bit the guy who did it, and a female FBI agent put a bullet in him. In my opinion, he got what he deserved. I don't think about it anymore. If I dream about it, I wake up and tell myself it was just a dream. Maybe that's all any of this is."

"What do you mean?"

"Like a dream in the mind of God. We shouldn't worry about it."

"I wish I could be like you," Gretchen said.

"There's an amphibian out there," Alafair said.

Gretchen looked through the window and saw the plane on the bay, not far offshore, floating low in the water, bobbing in the chop. It was painted white, its wings and pontoons and fuselage glowing in the blue band of light on the western horizon. A fiberglass boat with a deep-V hull and flared bow was anchored close by. The cabin of the boat was lighted, the bow straining against the anchor rope, the fighting chairs on the stern rising and falling against a backdrop of black waves. "Where is Varina Leboeuf's place?" Gretchen asked.

"Right up there about a hundred yards."

Gretchen pulled to the shoulder of the road and cut the headlights and the ignition. Through a break in the flooded cypress and gum trees, she had a clear view of the plane and the boat. She took a small pair of binoculars from her tote bag and got out of the truck and adjusted the lenses. She focused first on the amphibian, then on the boat. "It's a Chris-Craft. The bow has a painting of a sawfish on it," she said. "That's the boat Clete and your father have been looking for, the one that Tee Jolie Melton's sister was abducted on."

Alafair got out and walked around to Gretchen's side of the truck and stood beside her. Gretchen could see Varina Leboeuf on the stern and, next to her, a man with albino skin and shoulder-length hair that looked like white gold. He was wearing a shirt with blown sleeves and slacks belted high up on his stomach, the way a European might wear them. His forehead and the edges of his face were scrolled with pink scars, as though his face had been transplanted onto the tendons.

Gretchen handed Alafair the binoculars. "I'll call Clete and tell him about the boat," she said.

"We don't have service here," Alafair said.

"What do you want to do?"

"Confront her."

Gretchen took back the binoculars and looked again at the boat and at Varina and the man standing on the deck. The man was heavy-set and broad-shouldered, thick across the middle and muscular and solid in the way he stood on the deck. He looked in Gretchen's direction, as though he had noticed either her or her truck. But that was impossible. She forced herself to keep the binoculars directly on his face. He was backlit by the lights in the cabin, his slacks and shirt flattening in the wind. He leaned over and kissed Varina Leboeuf on the cheek, then boarded the amphibian.

The plane's twin engines coughed, then roared to life, the propellers blowing a fine mist back over the fuselage. Gretchen watched the plane gain speed, the pontoons cutting through the chop, the nose and wings abruptly lifting into the air. Her mouth was dry, her face hot, her breath catching in her throat for no reason.

"Are you okay?" Alafair asked.

"Yeah, sometimes I have kind of a blackout. More like a short circuit in my head. I look at somebody and can't breathe and get dizzy and have to sit down."

"How long has this been going on?"

"Since I was a child."

"What do you see through the binoculars that I didn't?"

"Just that guy with the weird face. He's like somebody from a dream. When I see a guy like that, maybe on an elevator or in a room with no windows, strange things light up in my head. I'll go on okay for a few days, then shit starts hitting the fan."

"What kind of shit?"

"I go out and look for trouble. I've got a bad history, Alafair. There's a lot of stuff I'd like to scrub out of my life. That guy with the albino skin and pink scars on his face—"

"What about him? He's just a guy. He's made of flesh and blood. Don't rent space in your head to bad people."

"He's like Alexis Dupree. These are people who are made different from the rest of us. You don't know them. Neither does Clete. But I know everything about them."

"How?"

"Because part of them is in me."

"That's not true," Alafair said. "Come on, the boat is headed for Varina's dock. Let's see who these guys are."

"I told you I wanted to deal with Varina Leboeuf the way you would. How should I handle it?"

"You don't 'handle' anything, Gretchen. You step back from bad people and let their own energies consume them. It's the worst thing you can do to them."

"See? You know stuff I never even thought about."

They got in the truck and drove down the road to the shell drive that led to Jesse and Varina Leboeuf's house. Out on the bay, the pilot of the Chris-Craft had throttled back his engine, allowing the boat to drift into the dock. As soon as the hull thumped against the tires that hung from the pilings, Varina stepped off the gunwale onto the planks, and the pilot turned the boat southward and gave it the gas.

The rain had stopped and the clouds had broken up in the west, and there was a tiny glimmer of purple melt at the bottom of the sky. Gretchen got out of the truck before Alafair did, and walked across the lawn toward Varina Leboeuf. The windmill palms were rattling in the breeze, rain dripping out of the tree limbs overhead. "I'm sorry to disturb you," Gretchen said.

"You're not disturbing me. That's because I'm going into my house now. That means I will not be talking with you, hence there is no reason for you to think you're disturbing me."

"Ms. Leboeuf, that boat you were on was used in a kidnapping, maybe even a homicide," Gretchen said. "A girl named Blue Melton was forced onto that boat. The next time anybody saw her, she was inside a block of ice."

"Then please go back to town and report all this to the authorities."

"That's not why I came out here. I wanted to ask you to leave Clete Purcel alone. He has nothing you want, and even if he did, he wouldn't use it to hurt you. Do you understand what I'm saying?"

"No, I don't know what you're saying. Are you confirming he burglarized my apartment and my father's house?"

"I'm saying he doesn't have anything in his possession that can injure you."

"I want you to take the wax out of your ears and listen carefully, you stupid little twat. If I didn't have to go inside and care for my father right now, I'd make you cut your own switch. Actually, I feel sorry for you. You look like you were injected with steroids that went to the wrong places. Now get out of here before I kick those two watermelons you call an ass down the road."

Alafair stepped forward and slapped Varina Leboeuf across the face. "Where do you get off talking to her like that, you lying whore?" she said. "You want another one? Give me an excuse. I would love to rip you apart."

Varina Leboeuf's eyes were watering, her cheek flaming. She started to speak, but her mouth was quivering, and her voice clotted in her throat.

"You're not only a liar, you're an accessory to murder after the fact," Alafair said. "By the way, how's it feel to be a porn star? I wonder if your video will make YouTube."

Varina's face looked like a balloon about to burst. The whites of her eyes had turned red as beets. "If you come here again, I'll kill you."

"I told you to give me an excuse," Alafair said. And with that, she hit Varina across the mouth, so hard the other woman's chin twisted against her shoulder.

"YOU DID WHAT?" I said.

"It was the way she treated Gretchen," Alafair replied. "She said her ass looked like a pair of watermelons."

We were sitting in the living room. Outside, the street was wet and glazed with pools of yellow light from the streetlamp. Lightning that made no sound flared and died in the clouds over the Gulf. "It was her fight, not yours. Why mix in it?" I said.

"Because I doubt she ever had a real friend or that anyone cared what happened to her."

"Varina Leboeuf could have you charged with assault."

"She won't."

"Why not?"

"The boat with the sawfish on the bow. She's hooked up with the people who kidnapped and murdered Tee Jolie's little sister."

"We don't have any proof of that."

I thought she was going to argue with me, but she didn't. "I did something dumb, Dave. Varina has confirmation that Clete took the memory cards out of her nanny-cams."

"Clete destroyed them."

"She can never be sure of that. What if there's somebody on them she doesn't want anybody to know about?"

"Don't worry about that. You did the best you could. Don't make a burden out of tomorrow," I said.

"I think I set a bad example for Gretchen tonight. She kept telling me she wanted to handle Varina Leboeuf in the way I would. A few minutes later, I slapped Varina's face into next week."

"I'm proud of you."

"Really?"

"Of course. I'm always proud of you, Alf."

"You said you wouldn't call me that anymore."

"Sorry."

"Call me whatever you want," she said.

I WAS SERIOUS when I said Alafair should have been in law enforcement. At the onset of her last semester at Stanford, her professors released her from class and gave her credit for clerking at the Ninth District Court in Seattle. The judge with whom she worked, an appointee of President Carter, was a distinguished jurist, but Alafair had an opportunity to clerk at the United States Supreme Court and would have done so, except her meddling father didn't want her living in D.C. Regardless, her career in the Justice Department was almost assured. Instead, she chose to return to New Iberia and become a novelist.

Her first book was a crime novel set in Portland, where she attended undergraduate school. Perhaps because she had an undergraduate degree in forensic psychology, she had extraordinary insight into aberrant behavior. She also knew how to use the Internet in ways that were virtually miraculous.

When she turned on her computer Tuesday morning, her Google

news alert had posted four entries in her mailbox. "Better come in here, Dave," she called from her bedroom.

The news stories originated with a small wire service in the Midwest. A man who owned rows of grain silos along railroad tracks throughout Kansas and Nebraska had died unexpectedly and left behind an eclectic collection of art that ranged from Picasso sketches done during the Blue Period to pretentious junk that the grain-elevator magnate probably bought at avant-garde salons in Paris and Rome. The heirs donated the entire collection to a university. Included in it were three Modigliani paintings. Or at least that was what they seemed to be. The curator at the university art museum said they were not only fakes, they were probably part of a hoax that had been perpetrated on private collectors for several decades.

The operational principle of the scam was the same used in all con games. The scammers would seek out a victim who either wanted something for nothing or was basically dishonest himself. The private collector would be told the Modigliani paintings were stolen and could be purchased for perhaps half of their real worth. The collector would also be told that he was not committing a crime, because the museum or private collection from which the paintings had been stolen had indirectly victimized either Modigliani or his inner circle, all of whom were poor and probably sold the paintings for next to nothing.

The scam worked because Modigliani's paintings were in wide circulation, many of them having been used by the artist or his mistress to pay hotel and food bills, and were comparably easy to forge and difficult to authenticate.

"I think this is the connection between Bix Golightly and Pierre Dupree," Alafair said. "Golightly was probably fencing Pierre's forgeries as stolen property. If you look at Pierre's paintings, you can see Modigliani's influence on him. Remember when you looked at the photo of Pierre's nude on the sofa? You said the figure in it was Tee Jolie, and I said the painting was generic and was like Gauguin's work. The painting of Tee Jolie was like a famous nude by Modigliani. Here, look."

She clicked the image of the Modigliani painting onto the screen.

"The swanlike neck and the elongated eyes and the coiffured hair and the prim mouth and the warmth in the skin are all characteristics you see in Pierre's paintings. Pierre isn't a bad imitator. But I'd bet he's both greedy and jealous. Not long ago Modigliani's painting was auctioned off at Sotheby's for almost seventy million."

"I think you're probably right," I said. "Clete broke in to Golightly's apartment the night he was killed and said there was evidence he was fencing stolen or forged artwork. When you think about it, it's the perfect scam. All you need is a buyer with sorghum for brains and too much money in the bank. Even if the buyer discovers he's been suckered, he can't call the cops without admitting he thought he was buying stolen paintings rather than forged paintings."

"What do you want to do?" she asked.

"I'll call the FBI in Baton Rouge today, but I usually don't get very far with them."

"Why not?"

"Clete and I are not considered reliable sources."

"Fuck them," she said.

"How about it on the language, Alafair? At least in the house."

"Is it okay to use it in the yard? If not, how about on the sidewalk?"

Don't buy into it, I heard a voice say. "Can you make me a promise about Varina?"

"Stay away from her?"

"No, that's not it at all. Be aware of what she is. And her father. And Alexis and Pierre Dupree and what they represent."

"Which is what?"

"They're working for somebody else. Somebody who is even more powerful and dangerous than they are."

"Why do you think that?"

"We're minions down here, not players. Everything that happens here is orchestrated by outsiders or politicians on a pad. It's a depressing conclusion to come to. But it's the way things are. We take it on our knees for anybody who brings his checkbook."

● ● ● ●

RHETORIC IS CHEAP stuff and about as useful as a thimbleful of water in the desert. When I was a boy and pitching American Legion baseball in the 1950s, a catcher from the old Evangeline League gave me some advice I never forgot, although I don't necessarily recommend that other people follow it. The Evangeline League was as rough and raw as it got. Cows sometimes grazed in the outfield, and so many of the overhead lights were burned out that sometimes the fielders couldn't find the ball in the grass. Players smoked in the dugout, threw Vaseline balls and spitters, and slung bats like helicopter blades at the pitcher. They also fist-fought with umpires and one another, came in with their spikes up, and frequented Margaret's infamous brothel en masse in Opelousas, a practice that on the team bus was called "running up the box score." My friend the bush-league catcher from New Iberia tried to keep things simple, however. His advice was "Always keep the ball hid in your glove or behind your leg. Don't never let the batter see your fingers on the stitches. When they crowd the plate, float one so close to the guy's twanger, he'll think he was circumcised. Then t'row your slider on the outside of the plate. He'll swing at it to show he ain't a coward, but he won't hit it. Then t'row a changeup, 'cause he'll be expecting the heater instead. If he gets mean and starts shaking his bat at you, don't even take your windup. Dust him wit' a forkball."

The question was where and when to throw the forkball. At the office that morning, I saw an ad for an evangelical rally at the Cajun-dome in Lafayette. The centerpiece of the rally was none other than Amidee Broussard, the minister I had seen leaving the Dupree home through the side door.

Beginning perhaps in the 1970s, Pentecostal and fundamentalist religion took on a new life and began to grow exponentially in southern Louisiana. There are probably numerous explanations for the phenomenon, but the basic causes are rather simple: the influence of televised religion that was as much entertainment as it was theology; and the deterioration of the Acadian culture in which my generation grew up. In the 1950s courthouse records were still handwritten in formal French, and Cajun French was spoken almost entirely in the rural areas of the parish; in cities like Lafayette or New Iberia, perhaps half of the population spoke French as their first language. But during the 1960s, Cajun children were not allowed to speak French on school property, and the language that Evangeline and her people brought with them from Nova Scotia in 1755 fell into decline and became associated with ignorance and failure and poverty. The fisher-people of southern Louisiana became ashamed of who they were.

My experience has been that when people are frightened and do not understand the historical changes taking place around them, they seek magic and power to solve their problems. They want shamans who can speak in tongues, even Aramaic, the language of Jesus. They want to see the lame and the blind and the incurably diseased healed onstage. They want the Holy Spirit to descend through the roof of the auditorium and set their souls on fire. And they want a preacher who can pound a piano like Jerry Lee Lewis but sing gospel lyrics written by angels. The blood of Christ and the waters of baptism and the hypnotic rant of a clairvoyant all become one entity, a religion that has no name and no walls, a faith you carry like a burning sword, one that will cause your enemies to cower.

There's an admission price in this church, but contrary to popular belief, it's not always monetary. That night Clete Purcel and I drove to the Cajundome and entered the throng working its way through the front doors. Almost all the seats had been taken. The overhead lights created an iridescent sheen above the crowd, which was buzzing like a giant beehive. When Amidee Broussard took the stage, the reaction was electric. The crowd clapped and stomped their feet and laughed as though an old friend had returned to their midst with glad tidings.

I had to hand it to him. As a speaker, Amidee was stunning. There was an iambic cadence in all his sentences. His diction and voice were as melodic as Walker Percy's or Robert Penn Warren's. He made people laugh. Then, without seeming to shift gears, he began to speak of Satan and the apocalyptic warnings in the book of John. He spoke of lakes of fire and halls of torment and sinners impaled like snakes on wooden stakes. He spoke of the sacrifice of Jesus and the scourging and the crown of thorns and the nails in his hands and feet. You could feel the discomfit growing in the crowd, like a tremolo effect across calm water. Broussard was a master at inculcating fear, anxiety, and self-doubt in his constituency. When the tension in the crowd was such that people were clenching their arms tightly across their chests, and breathing through their mouths as though their oxygen supply were being cut off, he raised his hands high in the air and said, "But his ordeal has set us free. Our sins are paid for, just like you pay off a friend's life insurance policy, just like you pay for his legal fees and hospital bills. Your friend can announce to the whole world, 'I owe no debt anywhere, because it has already been paid.' That's what Jesus has done for you."

The change in the audience was instantaneous, as if someone had turned on a huge electric fan and a cool breeze had begun to blow into their faces. At that point I thought he would begin curing the crippled and the terminally ill, hoaxes that are easily perpetrated in a controlled situation. But Amidee was much more sophisticated than his peers. Instead of claiming he possessed the power to heal, or that God healed through him, he told his audience the power was theirs to seize, and all they had to do was reach out and grab it.

"You heard me right," he said into the microphone, his silver hair and high forehead gleaming under the lights, his recessed turquoise eyes radiant in his weathered face. "It doesn't cost you money. You don't have to pledge or tithe or sign up as a church member. You've already given witness by being here. The power of the Holy Spirit is within you. You take it with you wherever you go, and every day it grows stronger. You're part of a special group now. It's that easy. If your life doesn't change after tonight, I want you to come back and tell me that. Know what? I've said that ten thousand times, and it's never happened. And why is that? Because once you're saved, your salvation can never be taken away from you."

I never saw a local audience give anyone a longer and more enthusiastic ovation than Amidee Broussard received that night.

Clete went to the restroom and rejoined me in the concourse. He was wearing his shades and seersucker suit and a Panama hat and a tropical shirt with the collar outside the jacket, and he looked like a neocolonial on the streets of Saigon. "A guy in the head said there's a big lawn party for Broussard at a place on the Vermilion River. What do you want to do?"

"Let's go."

"How do you read this dude?" he asked.

"I think he could probably sell central heating to the devil," I replied.

"He doesn't seem like a bad guy. I've heard worse."

"He's a snake-oil salesman. He's smarter and more cunning than most, but he's a fraud, just like Varina Leboeuf and the Duprees."

Clete now knew about Varina's connection to the Chris-Craft boat with the sawfish on the bow, and I saw his expression change at the mention of her name. I rested my hand on his shoulder as we walked toward the exit. "Let her go," I said.

"I already have."

"I don't think that's true. When you sleep with a woman, you always believe you've married her. You're not a one-night-stand man, Cletus."

"Why don't you tell the whole fucking auditorium?"

"Cool it back there," a man in front of us said.

Clete looked around uncertainly. "Oh, excuse me, you're talking to me? The rest of us don't have First Amendment rights because you say so? Is that what you were saying?"

The man was as big as Clete and younger, jug-eared, his face like a boiled ham, the kind of tightly wrapped man who sweats inside his clothes and never takes his coat off. "Who are you guys?" he asked.

"We're cops. That means beat it, asshole," Clete said.

I held Clete by his upper arm until the momentum of the crowd separated us from the man. His arm felt as hard as a pressurized fire hose and was humming with the same level of energy. "What's the matter with you?" I said.

"Remember when we walked a beat in the First District? That was the happiest time of my life."

"We're in the bottom of the sixth. It's not even the seventh-inning stretch yet," I said.

"Right, keep telling yourself that," he replied. "I need a drink." He took a flask from his coat pocket and unscrewed the cap with his thumb and drank it half empty before we reached the Caddy.

• • • • •

THE PARTY WAS being held inside a magnificent grove of oak trees wrapped with strings of white lights, backdropped by a brightly lit mansion on the Vermilion River that was owned by an oilman from Mississippi. Though the house had a swimming pool in back and probably cost a fortune to build, the final result was a cross between an architectural nightmare and a deliberate celebration of vulgarity and bad taste. The pillars were made of concrete and swollen in the middle like Disney dwarfs; the brickwork had the shiny uniformity of laminated siding, the kind that is rolled and glued onto cinder block. The ceiling-high windows, the most outstanding feature of Louisiana houses, were bracketed with nonoperational shutters painted mint green and bolted flatly on the brick like postage stamps. The patio was a bare concrete pad that had settled and cracked through the center and was infested with fire ants. Through the windows, a visitor could look into a series of rooms carpeted in different colors and filled with furniture that could have been painted with shellac that morning.

The five acres of front lawn were filled with vehicles, row after row of them, extended-cab pickups and the biggest SUVs on the market. The guests were the glad of heart and the curious and the voyeuristic or those who had recently discovered that salvation and prosperity and the exploitation of the earth's resources were all part of the same journey.

The serving tables groaned with bowls of white and dirty rice and étouffée and deep-fried crawfish and boiled shrimp. White-jacketed black waiters sliced pork off a hog on the spit and carved up turkeys and sirloin roasts and smoked hams swimming in pineapple rings and redeye gravy. There were beer kegs in tubs of ice and a three-table bar for those who wanted champagne or highballs. With the breeze off the river and the rustle of the moss in the trees and the smell of meat dripping into an open fire, the night could not have been more perfect. What imperfection could anyone see in the scene taking place before us? Even the Vietnamese serving girls seemed like a testimony to the richness of the New American Empire, one that indeed offered sanctuary to the huddled and downtrodden.

We found a place on a bench under a spreading oak, and Clete went straight to the drinks table and came back with a Jack on the rocks and a draft Budweiser foaming over the edges of a red plastic cup. "Guess who I just talked to in the line. The guy who was giving us trouble in the concourse. He said he didn't know we were cops and he was sorry for getting in our face. Can you figure it?"

"Figure what?"

"As soon as these guys think you're in the club, they want to kiss your ass."

We were a few feet away from a plank table where people were eating off paper plates. They glanced at us from the corners of their eyes. "Sorry," Clete said. "I've got a genetic case of logorrhea."

A couple of them smiled good-naturedly and went on eating. Clete drank from his cup and wiped the foam off his mouth with a paper napkin. "I know you worry about me, big mon, but everything is copacetic," he said.

"The only person who doesn't worry about you is you."

"Where'd all these Vietnamese girls come from?"

"A lot of them got blown out of New Orleans by Katrina."

"You ever think about going back to 'Nam?"

"Almost every night."

"John McCain went back. A lot of guys have. You know, to make peace with yourself and maybe some of the people we hurt or who were shooting at us? I hear they treat Americans pretty good today."

I knew Clete was not thinking about making peace. He was thinking about the irrevocable nature of loss and about a Eurasian girl who had lived in a sampan on the edges of the South China Sea and whose hair floated off her shoulders like black ink when she walked into the water and reached back for him to take her hand.

"Maybe it's not a bad idea," I said.

"Would you go with me?"

"If you want me to."

"You believe spirits hang around for a while? They don't take off right away to wherever they're supposed to go?"

I didn't answer him. I wasn't sure he was talking to me any longer.

"The girl I had over there was named Maelee. I told you that already, huh?" he said.

"She must have been a great woman, Clete."

"If I'd stayed away from her, she'd still be alive. Sometimes I want to find the guys who did it and blow up their shit. Sometimes I want to sit down and explain to them what they did, how they punished an innocent, sweet girl because of a guy from New Orleans who wasn't much different from them. We thought we were fighting for our country just like they thought they were fighting for theirs. That's what I'd tell them. I'd meet their families and tell them the same thing. I'd want them all to know we didn't get over the war, either. We're dragging the chain forty years down the road."

He swirled the whiskey and ice in his cup, then drained it and crunched the ice between his molars. His cheeks had the red blush of ripe peaches, his eyes aglow with an alcoholic benevolence, one that always signaled an unpredictable metabolic change taking place in his system. "There's Amidee Broussard. Check out the dude sitting with him," he said.

I tried to see through the crowd, but my angle was wrong, and I couldn't get a clear view of Broussard's table.

"Gretchen said she saw Varina on board that Chris-Craft with an albino. I don't know if I'd call this guy an albino or not," Clete said. "His face looks like a piece of white rubber somebody sewed onto his skull. You think that's the guy?"

I took a barbecue sandwich off a tray a waiter was passing around, then stood up so I could see Broussard's table. I cradled the sandwich in a napkin and ate it and tried to hide my interest in Broussard while I watched him and his friend. As a police officer, I had learned many years ago that you learn more by seeing than listening. Why? All perps lie. That's a given. All sociopaths lie all the time. That's also a given. Any truth you learn from them comes in the form of either what they don't say or what their eyes and hands tell you. A refusal to blink usually indicates deception. A drop in the register of the voice and a blink right after a denial means you tighten the screw. Evasion and begging the question and telling half a truth are indicators of a habitual liar whose methodology is to wear you down. It's not unlike playing baseball. Have you ever gone up against a left-handed pitcher who hasn't shaved in three days and looks like his wife just kicked him out of the house? You either read his sign language or you get your head torn off.

When you watch a man like Amidee Broussard, if he's deprived by distance of his ability to deceive with words, what things do you look for? You ignore the ceramic smile, the work-worn, sun-freckled hands of the farm boy and the bobbed white hair of a frontier patriarch. You look at the eyes and where they go. He was being served dinner from the kitchen rather than from the buffet tables. The black waiter who put Broussard's steak before him wore sanitary plastic mittens, although none of the other serving personnel did. After the waiter set the plate down, Broussard offered no word of appreciation, no show of recognition; he never paused in his conversation with the man who had the surreal face of someone you thought lived only in the imagination.

I dropped the rest of my sandwich in a trash barrel and began walking toward the Broussard table. A Vietnamese girl was refilling his water glass and picking up the dirty dishes from the tablecloth. There was no mistaking the direction of Broussard's eyes. They darted to her cleavage when she bent over, and they followed her hips as she walked away. His dentures looked as stiff as bone. "You think our man might be having impure thoughts?" Clete said.

Before we reached the table, we were joined by the man who had given us trouble at the Cajundome. "Hey, y'all fixing to talk to Reverend Amidee?" he said.

"Yeah, that's our plan," Clete said.

"Come on, I know him. I went fishing with him and Lamont Woolsey. Lamont had so much protective clothing on, he looked like he was wearing a hazmat suit."

"Woolsey is the guy with the latex skin?" Clete said.

"I wouldn't call it that," the man said. He looked at me and extended his hand. It was as hard and rough as brick. "I'm Bobby Joe Guidry."

"How you doing, Bobby Joe?" I said.

"I was a drunkard for fifteen years. Up until I met Amidee six months ago. Not one drink since."

"That's great. My friend has met the reverend, but I haven't. Can you introduce me?" I said.

Clete and I both shook hands with Broussard, but I don't think he saw or heard either of us. He never stopped chewing his salad and never quite took his eyes off the Vietnamese waitress. Clete and I and Bobby Joe Guidry pulled up folding chairs to his table and sat down among a group of people who seemed to share no commonalities except their faith in Amidee Broussard, a man who knew the will of God and also what was best for their country.

"You've got a collection of the biggest SUVs I've ever seen," Clete said. He'd already snagged another whiskey on the rocks, at least four fingers of it, drinking it in sips while he talked. "What kind of vehicle do you drive?"

"It's a dandy, a Chevrolet Suburban. I can fit nine people in it," Broussard said.

The Vietnamese waitress set a ketchup bottle and a bottle of steak sauce by Broussard's plate. He patted her kindly on the forearm, looking up brightly at her. "Would you take this steak back? It's still red in the middle."

"Yes, sir. I sorry. I bring it back to you all cooked, Reverend Amidee," she replied.

"That's a good girl. You give that cook a good fussing-out while you're at it," he said. He continued to look at her as she walked away, but this time he did not let his eyes drop below her waist. "A beautiful girl."

"You think we kicked enough raghead butt over there to keep the oil flowing?" Clete said.

Please don't blow it, Clete, I thought.

"What was that about ragheads?" Broussard said.

"I was talking about the price of gas. That Suburban must get the mileage of a motor home packed with concrete," Clete said.

I tried to interject myself into the conversation and stop Clete from wrecking our situation. "I think I know you," I said to Lamont Woolsey. "You're a friend of Varina Leboeuf."

His eyes made me think of dark blue marbles floating in milk, his mouth duck-billed, his nose shiny with moisture, even though the night air was cool and getting cooler. I had never seen anyone with such strange coloration or with such a combination of peculiar features, nor had I ever seen anyone whose eyes were so deeply blue and yet devoid of moral light.

"Yes, I'm familiar with Ms. Leboeuf. I don't recall seeing you while I was in her company," he said. The accent was Carolinian or Tidewater, the vowels rounded, the R's slightly bruised. That he'd chosen the word "familiar" to describe his relationship with a woman didn't seem to bother him.

"I think she was on your boat, the one that has a sawfish painted on the bow," I said.

His eyes fixed on mine, hard and so blue they were almost purple. "I don't remember that."

Take a chance, I heard a voice say. "Don't you live on an island somewhere?"

"I did. I grew up in the Georgia Sea Islands."

"You ever hear of a guy named Chad Patin? He took a shot at me."

"Why would I know someone like that?" Woolsey said.

"This guy Patin was a couple of quarts down. He told me this crazy story about a medieval instrument called the iron maiden. He said it was on an island someplace. It works like a grape press. Except people are put inside it and not grapes."

Woolsey's head swiveled on his shoulders, as though he were surveying the crowd. His hands rested on the tablecloth, as round and pale as dough balls, his chest as puffed as a peacock's. "Who are you?"

"Dave Robicheaux is the name. I'm a homicide detective in Iberia Parish."

He fingered a gold cross that hung from his neck. His eyes came back to mine. "I think you and your friend have had too much to drink."

"I don't drink," I replied.

He stretched his legs out before him, popping his knees, and smiled at me. "Maybe you should start. A snootful gives a fellow a wonderful excuse to say whatever is on his mind. He can apologize later and have it both ways."

"I never thought of it like that. You're not up to speed on iron maidens, huh?"

He scratched the back of his neck, then put on a pair of sunglasses that were tinted almost black. "No, I've met no maidens recently, iron or otherwise."

"How about a kid named Blue Melton?"

"Sorry."

"She was abducted on your boat."

"The boat you're describing is not mine, and I have no idea what you're talking about, Mr. Robicheaux."

"How about that amphibian you were on? I've always wanted to take a ride on one of those."

"This conversation is over," he replied.

The Vietnamese girl set Broussard's steak by his elbow, the meat so hot it was sizzling in its gravy. "The cook say he sorry and hope you like it," she said.

"Later, I want you to take me in the kitchen so I can meet him," Broussard said. "We don't want him to leave here with hurt feelings."

"That's white of you," Clete said.

"Your mockery is not appreciated, sir," Broussard said. "I was trying to indicate to this little girl that I was only teasing when I told her to fuss at the cook."

"That's exactly what I'm talking about. We need to do a lot more good deeds like that, particularly for the Vietnamese," Clete said, crunching his ice, lifting his index finger for emphasis. "I saw some stuff in Vietnam that takes the cake. Throwing prisoners out of the slick, going into a ville at night and cutting a guy's throat and painting his face yellow, you know, the kind of heavy shit the home folks don't want to hear about. I knew this one door gunner who couldn't wait to get back to a free-fire zone. Someone asked him how he killed all those women and children, and he said, 'It's easy. You just don't lead them as much.' You ever think about that kind of stuff while you're tanking up at the pump?"

The conversation at the table went into slow motion and then died. Amidee raised his hand and gestured at the security personnel as though cupping air with his fingers.

"Eighty-sixing us, are you?" Clete said. "Tell you what, Rev, I'm going to check up on that Vietnamese girl, and if I find your fingerprints on her, you're going to get large amounts of publicity that you don't need."

"There's some misunderstanding. I think we need to talk this out," Bobby Joe Guidry said.

"Don't interfere," Woolsey said.

"I thought we were all members of the church here. What's going on?" Bobby Joe said, trying to smile.

"Get these two men out of here," Woolsey said to the three security men who had arrived at the table.

I stood up and heard Clete getting out of his chair beside me, knocking against the table, shaking the glasses on it. I did not have to look at him to know what he was thinking or planning. The three security men had concentrated their attention entirely on Clete and were not looking at me at all. "We're leaving," I said to Woolsey and Broussard. "But you guys are going to see a lot more of us. Both of you have shit on your noses. I saw Blue Melton's body after it was defrosted and taken apart by the coroner. How do you do something like that to a seventeen-year-old girl and live with yourself?"

It was an odd moment, one that I didn't expect. Neither man looked at me, and neither spoke. They seemed to have folded into themselves like accordion cutouts made of cardboard. Clete and I walked toward the Caddy, the wind rustling the tree limbs. I heard feet crunching on the leaves behind me and assumed the security men had decided to score some points with either Broussard or us by escorting us to our vehicle. When I turned around, I was looking into the face of Bobby Joe Guidry. "I don't like what happened back there," he said.

"Oh yeah?" Clete said.

"Y'all seem like good guys. They shouldn't have treated y'all like that. I was a radio operator in Desert Storm. I know what happened out there on the highway when all that traffic got caught by our planes. You know, what the media called the 'Highway of Death.' Some of those people were probably civilians. Whole families. I saw it. It's something you don't want to remember."

"You ever go to A.A., Bobby Joe?" I asked.

"I didn't figure I needed it after I met Amidee."

"I attend the Solomon House meeting in New Iberia. Why don't you drive down and see us sometime?"

"My main issue right now is finding a job."

"I tell you what," I said. I removed a business card from my billfold and wrote on the back of it. "We have an opening for a 911 dispatcher. You might give it a shot."

"Why you doing this?"

"You look like a stand-up guy," I said.

"You're talking to the Bobbsey Twins from Homicide," Clete said.

"What the hell is that?"

"Stick around," Clete said.

"Amidee fooled me real good, didn't he?" Bobby Joe said.

"I wouldn't think of it like that," I said.

"He doesn't ask people for money," he replied. "That means somebody else is paying his freight. Any fool would see that, I guess."

Clete and I looked at each other.

CHAPTER
19

CLETE CALLED MY office at 8:05 the next morning. "Somebody got past my alarm and punched my safe and tore up my office," he said.

"When?"

"The alarm went off-line at two-seventeen this morning. The safe was done by a pro. The windows were taped over with black vinyl garbage bags. All my file cabinets and desk drawers were dumped, my swivel chair split open, and the top of the toilet tank pulled off and dropped in the bowl. Want to hear some more?"

"Who was on those videos with Varina?"

"I already told you. A few shysters and oil guys who wanted to get laid. They're not skells."

"No, you said there were some you didn't recognize. What do you remember about them?"

"They had bare asses."

"What else?"

"One guy had a British accent."

"Why didn't you mention that before?"

"Who cares about his accent?"

My mind was racing. "You didn't save any of this on your hard drive? You don't have an automatic backup system of some kind?"

"No, I told you, I burned the memory cards and opened up the

291

windows in my office to get the smell out. I should have taken your advice and never looked at it."

"I'm going to send some guys from the crime lab to your office. Leave everything just as it is."

"I'll need a copy of the report for my insurance claim, but forget about prints. The guys who did this are good."

"Did Varina ever mention a Brit to you?"

"News flash, Dave: When you're with Varina, the only person she talks about is you, all the time staring straight into your eyes. It takes about ten seconds before your flagpole wakes up and decides it's time to fly the red, white, and blue."

"You've still got the hots for her."

"Wrong. Since I met her, I feel like I've been living inside a snare drum. We've got to take these guys down, Dave. This started with Alexis Dupree and Bix Golightly. We need to go back to the source and put some hurt on that old man. You hearing me on this? The guy is probably a war criminal and a mass murderer. Why are we letting him do this kind of stuff to us?"

"I'm sending the guys from the crime lab now," I said.

"I won't be here. Gretchen can show them around."

"Where are you going?"

"I'm not sure. Did you run Lamont Woolsey yet?"

"No, I haven't had time."

"Don't bother. I called a guy I know at the NCIC. There's no Lamont Woolsey in the system. And I mean nowhere. He doesn't exist. I'll check back with you later."

"What are you up to?"

"I'm not even sure myself. How can I tell you? Alexis Dupree has locks of hair in a scrapbook. Maybe we've got John Wayne Gacy living in St. Mary Parish. You ever think of that?" he replied.

CLETE WAS RIGHT. How does a man like Alexis Dupree end up in our midst? From what I could find out about him through Google, he had been living in the United States since 1957 and was naturalized ten years later. Had he worked for both British and American intelligence? Were there any people alive who could authenticate his claim that he was a member of the French underground? The articles posted on the Internet seemed to replicate one another, and none of them contained any source except Dupree.

That afternoon I called a friend in the FBI and another friend at the INS and a friend whose drinking had cost him his career at the CIA. Of the three, the drunk was the most helpful.

"It's possible your man is telling the truth," he said.

"Telling the truth about what?" I said.

"Working with MI6 or one of our intelligence agencies."

"Maybe he was never an inmate at Ravensbrück," I said. "Maybe he was a guard there. I don't know what to believe about him."

"After the war, we gave citizenship to the scientists who built V-1 and V-2 rockets and helped Hitler kill large numbers of civilians in London. During the 1950s any European who was anti-Communist pretty much got a free pass with the INS. The consequence was we gave safe harbor to a bunch of shitbags. No matter how you cut it, you'll probably never find out this guy's real identity."

"Somebody out there knows who he is," I said.

"You don't get it, Dave. This guy is whatever somebody else says he is. Any file you find on Dupree was written by someone who created a work of fiction. You're a fan of George Orwell. Remember what he said about history? It ended in 1936. Unless you want to get drunk again, leave this crap alone."

His statement was not one I wanted to hear. I tried to dismiss his words as those of a cynic, a CIA agent who had aided in the installation of a Chilean dictator, armed state-sponsored terrorists in northern Nicaragua, and been the associate of men who operated torture chambers and were responsible for the murder of liberation theologians. Unfortunately, those who give witness to the darker side of our history are usually those who helped precipitate it and, as a result, make it easy for us to discount their stories. Sometimes I wondered if their greatest burden was their eventual realization that they collaborated with others in the theft of their souls.

"We're going to find out who this guy is. I don't care how long it takes," I said.

There was a pause, then my friend who had destroyed his liver
and two marriages and the lives of his children hung up the phone.
At quitting time, I went home in a funk and sat on a folding chair by
the bayou and stared at the current flowing south toward the Gulf of
Mexico. Clete had said that our own John Wayne Gacy was perhaps
living just down the road, ensconced in an antebellum home that
could have been a backdrop for a Tennessee Williams play. Except the
comparison was inadequate. Gacy had been a serial killer of young
men and boys whose bodies he interred in the walls and crawl spaces
of his home. Gacy may not have been psychotic, but there was no
question he was mentally ill. Supposedly, his last words to one of the
guards who escorted him to his execution were "Kiss my ass." Alexis
Dupree was totally rational and by no means mentally ill, and if he
had been a member of the SS, his crimes were probably far worse and
more numerous than Gacy's. Every time I reached a conclusion about
him, I found myself using the word "if." Why was that? In the age of
Google and the Freedom of Information Act, I had been unable to
find one incontestable fact about his life.

I tried to think about Alexis Dupree in terms of what he wasn't.
He claimed to have been a prisoner at Ravensbrück. But if he had
been a guard or a junior officer at Ravensbrück and not an inmate,
would it make sense for him to draw attention to his association
with the camp whose survivors would quickly recognize his photograph? If Alexis Dupree had been a member of the SS, he probably
worked at a camp he never made mention of, maybe one that was
liberated by the Soviets and whose records were confiscated and not
shared with the Americans or the British or the French. When the
German army began to collapse on the Eastern Front, the SS fled
west and left thousands of bodies in freight cars and in train yards
or stacked like cordwood outside crematoriums. They put on the
uniforms of the regular German army, hoping to surrender to American or British personnel rather than to the Russians, who summarily
shot them.

Alexis Dupree was a smart man. Maybe he had taken the deception one step further and tattooed a prison number on his left
forearm and played the role of survivor and veteran of the French

Resistance, composed primarily of Communists. Dupree may have been many things, but leftist was not one of them. Maybe he'd been an informer. He certainly met the standard of a self-serving turncoat. Had he been a friend of the famous combat photographer Robert Capa? Out of all the possibilities and claims about Dupree's past, I was positive that one was a lie. I also believed the photo of the Republican soldiers taken at the siege of Madrid and inscribed by Capa to Dupree was another fraud perpetrated on the world by the Dupree family. All of Capa's work had already been published, including a lost satchel of photos discovered in Mexico in the 1990s. Plus, Capa was a socialist who probably would have been repelled by an elitist like Dupree.

Where does that leave us? I asked myself. The boughs of the cypress trees were as brittle and delicate as gold leaf in the late sun. An alligator gar was swimming along the edge of the lily pads, its needle-nose head and lacquered spine and dorsal fin parting the surface with a fluidity that was more serpent than fish. The great cogged wheels on the drawbridge were lifting its huge weight into the air, silhouetting its black outline against a molten sun. Then the wind gusted and a long shaft of amber sunlight seemed to race down the center of the bayou, like a paean to the close of day and the coming of night and the cooling of the earth, as though vespers and the acceptance of the season were a seamless and inseparable part of life that only the most vain and intransigent among us would deny.

Meditations upon mortality become cheap stuff and offer little succor when it comes to dealing with evil. The latter is not an abstraction, and ignoring it is to become its victim. The earth abides forever, but so does the canker inside the rose, and the canker never sleeps.

I wondered if Clete was right: that at some point you must become willing to put hurt on an old man. Those words had an effect on me that was like a saw cutting through bone. You do not give your enemy power, and you do not let him remake you in his image. I picked up a pinecone and tossed it in a high arc into the middle of the current, as though I had fought my way through a long mental process and was freeing myself of it. But my heart was as heavy as an anvil in my chest, and I knew I would have no peace until I found the killers of Blue Melton and brought Tee Jolie back to her Cajun home on the banks of Bayou Teche.

AT THE SUPPER table, I couldn't concentrate on what Molly and Alafair were talking about. "It's going to be a big event, Dave," Alafair said.

"You mean the Sugar Cane Festival? Yeah, it always is," I said.

"The Sugar Cane Festival was a month ago. I was talking about the 1940s musical revue," she said.

"I thought you were talking about next year," I said.

Molly let her gaze settle on my face and kept it there until I blinked. "What happened today?" she asked.

"Somebody burglarized Clete's office. Probably friends of Varina Leboeuf," I said.

"What were they looking for?" she asked.

"Why put yourself in the mind of perps? It's like submerging your hand in an unflushed toilet," I said.

"Way to go, Dave," Alafair said.

"It's just a metaphor," I said.

"Next time hand out barf bags in advance," she said.

"Both of you stop it," Molly said.

"Varina is part of a cabal of some kind. Clete got ahold of some incriminating video footage that he destroyed, but Varina believes he still has it. The guy I can't get out of my head is Alexis Dupree. I think he was in the SS, and I think he worked in an extermination camp in Eastern Europe."

"How did you arrive at all this?" Molly said.

"Dupree is the opposite of everything he says about himself," I said.

"That's convenient."

"You think he's a veteran of the French underground, a man of the people? He and his family terrorized the farmworkers you tried to organize," I said.

"That doesn't mean he's an ex-Nazi."

I set my knife and fork down on the edges of my plate as softly as I could and left the table, my temples pounding. I went out on the gallery and sat down on the front steps and looked at the fireflies lighting in the trees and the leaves blowing end over end down the sidewalk. I saw a cardboard box wrapped in brown paper next to the bottom step, the wrapping paper folded in tight corners and sealed neatly with shipping tape. There was no writing on the paper. I opened my pocketknife and sliced away the tape and peeled off the paper and pulled back the flaps on the box and peered inside. The packing material was a mixture of straw and wood curlicues that smelled like shaved pine. An envelope with a rose stem Scotch-taped across it rested on top of the straw. Inside the envelope was a thick card with silver scroll on the borders, a message written in the center in bright blue ink. I stared at the words for a long time, then moved some of the straw aside with my knife blade and looked in the box again. I put away my knife and pushed the box with my foot to the edge of the walk just as the door opened behind me. "Dave?" Molly said.

"I'll be inside in a few minutes," I said.

"You have to stop internalizing all these things. It's like drinking poison."

"You're saying I bring my problems home instead of leaving them at the department?"

"That wasn't what I meant at all."

"I was agreeing with you. Clete and I met a guy named Lamont Woolsey. His eyes are so blue they're almost purple. You know who else has violet eyes? Gretchen Horowitz."

She sat down next to me, distraught, like someone watching a car accident about to happen. "What are you saying? Who's Woolsey?"

"I'm not sure. I can't think straight anymore. I don't know who Woolsey is, and I don't understand my own thoughts. I don't have any right to drop all this on you and Alafair. That's what I'm saying."

She took my hand in hers. "I don't think you see the real issue. You want Louisiana to be the way it was fifty years ago. Maybe the Duprees *are* evil, or maybe they're just greedy. Either way, you have to let go of them. You also have to let go of the past."

"In some of those camps, there were medical experiments done on children. The color of their eyes was changed synthetically."

She released my hand and stared into the dark. "We have to put an end to this. You and Clete and I need to sit down and talk. But more of the same isn't going to help."

"I didn't make any of it up."

I could hear her breathing inside the dampness, as though her lungs were working improperly, as though the smell of the sugar refinery and the black lint off the smokestacks were catching in her throat. I didn't know whether she was crying or not. I picked at my fingernails and stared at the streetlamps and at the leaves gusting in serpentine lines along the asphalt.

"What's that?" she asked, looking into the shadows below the camellia bushes.

"Somebody left a box on the step."

"What's in it?"

"Take a look."

She leaned over and pulled the box toward her by one of the flaps. She brushed away some of the packing material and tried to tilt the box toward her, but it was too heavy. Then she stood up and set it on the steps so the overhead light shone directly down on it. I could hear the bottles inside tinkling against one another. "Johnnie Walker Black Label?" she said.

"Check out the card."

She pulled it from the envelope and read it aloud: " 'Charger would want you to have this. Merry Christmas, Loot.' " She looked at me blankly. "Who's Charger?"

"That was the code name of a colonel I served under. He was a giant of a man and went naked in the bush and drank a case of beer a day and blew bean gas all over his tent. He had huge pieces of scar tissue stapled across his stomach where he'd been wounded by a burst from an AK. He was the best soldier I ever knew. He founded the Delta Force."

"You never told me about that."

"It's yesterday's bubble gum."

"Why would somebody do this? Do they think sending you a case of Scotch will get you drunk?"

"Somebody wants me to know he and his buds have access to

every detail in my life, including my military record and the fact that I'm a drunk."

"Dave, this scares me. Who are these people?"

"The real deal, right out of the furnace," I replied.

WHEN IT CAME to courage and grace under fire, Clete Purcel was not an ordinary man. He grew up in the old Irish Channel in an era when the welfare projects of New Orleans were segregated and the street gangs were made up primarily of kids from blue-collar Italian and Irish homes who fought with chains and knives and broken bottles for control of neighborhoods that most people wouldn't spit on. The pink scar that resembled a strip of rubber running through his eyebrow to the bridge of his nose had been given to him by a kid from the Iberville Projects. The scars on his back had come from the .22 rounds he took while he carried me unconscious down a fire escape. The scars across his buttocks had come from his father's razor strop.

He seldom mentioned the specifics of his two combat tours in Vietnam. He went there and came back and never made an issue of the psychological damage that had obviously been done to him. He still served tea to the mamasan he killed and who had traveled with him from Vietnam to Japan and New Orleans and Vegas and Reno and Polson, Montana, and back to New Orleans and his apartment on St. Ann Street. In terms of physical courage, he had no peer; he ate his pain and swallowed his blood and never let his enemies know he was hurt. I had never known a braver human being.

But the sense of shame and rejection that was inculcated in Clete by his father was the succubus he could never exorcise, and it was never more apparent than when he was confronted by the odium his name carried with the New Orleans Police Department. The irony was that the department was notorious for its corruption and vigilantism and its targeting of Black Panthers during the 1970s. I knew cops who investigated their own burglaries. I knew a Vice detective who put a hit on his own confidential informant. I knew a patrolwoman who murdered the owners of the restaurant she held up.

Sound like exaggeration? The hiring procedures at NOPD were so shabby, the department hired known ex-felons.

Dwelling on the moral failure of others brought no respite for Clete Purcel. No matter how elegantly he dressed, the man he saw in the mirror not only wore sackcloth and ashes but deserved them.

He had driven to New Orleans and checked in with his secretary, Alice Werenhaus, and the PI who handled some of his cases when he was out of town. Then he went upstairs to his apartment and picked up the phone and called Dana Magelli, not allowing himself to stop at the refrigerator, where almost every shelf was stocked with Mexican and German beer and chilled bottles of gin and vodka. While he waited for the call to be transferred, he could hear his breath echoing off the receiver.

"Magelli," a voice said.

"It's Clete Purcel, Dana. I need some help with that Luger you took off me."

"Bix Golightly's piece?"

"Right. Did you run the serial number?"

"Why should that be of interest to you?"

"I think Bix stole the Luger from Alexis Dupree. I think Dupree may be a Nazi war criminal."

"I should have known," Magelli said.

"Known what?"

"It's not enough that you leave shit prints all over New Orleans. Now you're branching into international affairs."

"This isn't funny, Dana. That old man has a scrapbook full of human hair in his house. Does that sound normal to you?"

There was a beat. "Where'd you get that information?"

"Dave Robicheaux saw it. Why do you ask?"

"Maybe we should talk. Where are you?"

"At my apartment."

"Stay there."

"No, I want to come down to the district."

"That's not necessary."

"Yeah, it is," Clete replied.

He shaved and showered and wet-combed his hair, trying to keep his mind empty, trying not to think about the people he was about to see and the situation he was about to place himself in. He put on a flaming-red long-sleeve silk shirt and his gray suit and a pair of black dress shoes he kept stored in velvet bags with drawstrings. Then he took his Panama hat off his closet shelf and fitted it low on his brow and walked down the stairs into the breezeway and told Alice Werenhaus she could go home early.

"You're bringing a guest here?" she asked. "Because if you are, you don't have to hide your behavior from me."

"No, it's just a fine afternoon, and you deserve some time off, Miss Alice."

"Is everything all right?"

"I'm raising your salary by one hundred a week."

"You pay me adequately. You don't have to do that."

"I just sold a waterfront lot I've been hiding from my ex-wife's lawyers. I'd rather give the capital gains to you than the IRS."

"Is that legal?"

"Miss Alice, tax laws are written by rich guys for rich guys. But in answer to your question, yeah, it's legal. I'm just cleaning house a little bit, know what I mean?"

"Thank you very much," she said. "You're a very good man, Mr. Purcel."

"Not really," he replied.

"Don't you dare say that of yourself again," she said.

He lifted his hat to her and walked down to the old district headquarters on Royal and Conti and entered the lions' den.

DANA MAGELLI CAME out to the reception desk and walked with Clete to his office. Clete knew almost all the personnel in the room, but they looked right through him or found other ways not to see him. Magelli shut the door. Clete gazed through the glass at the cops working at their desks or getting coffee or talking on the telephone. Then he looked out the office window at the palm trees and the motorcycles and cruisers parked at the curb. He also looked at the Crescent City logo painted on their immaculate white paint jobs. He wondered at what exact point he had taken a wrong turn into the cul-de-sac that had become his life. "You look sharp," Dana said.

"What were you going to tell me about the Luger?" Clete asked.

"It was issued in 1942 to a junior German submarine officer by the name of Karl Engels. But this guy Engels didn't stay in the navy. He transferred into the SS."

"You can run numbers on German ordnance issued in 1942?"

"How about that?"

"You went through the CIA or the National Security Agency or something?"

"No, a reference librarian up St. Charles. She could find the street address of the caveman who invented the wheel."

Clete was sitting in a chair by the window, his hat crown-down on Dana's desk. He put his hand inside his shirt and scratched a place on his shoulder. "What happened to Karl Engels?"

"My reference friend went through a bunch of German veterans' organizations and found some records on a Karl Engels who was stationed in Paris until late 1943. And that's it."

"Why'd you have all this interest in the Luger?"

"It started out as routine. We found information in Golightly's computer that indicated he was mixed up with Dupree in a stolen-painting scam of some kind. The more I thought about the possible connection between the Luger and Alexis Dupree, the more I thought about something my wife had told me."

"Told you what?"

"We'd met Alexis Dupree two or three times at social functions. Everybody had heard about his work in the French underground. My wife is from Wiesbaden. She speaks both German and French and teaches in the language department at Tulane. She heard Dupree speaking German to someone. She said his German was perfect. She went up to him and spoke to him in French. She said he had an accent, a bad one, and it was obvious that French was not his first language."

"You think Karl Engels is Dupree?"

"That's anybody's guess."

Clete picked up his hat and smoothed the brim. He looked through the glass at the squad room and all the cops at their desks. "I need to get something off my chest," he said. "Out there, I'm the Invisible Man or the spit on the sidewalk, take your choice. I've got no beef about y'all's attitude toward me. I took money from the Giacanos. I also did security for a mobbed-up guy out west. I haven't helped matters by knocking around a couple of your detectives. But I never braced a cop who was on the square, not in New Orleans or anywhere else."

Dana started to interrupt, but Clete stopped him. "Hear me out. I deserved to get fired and probably worse. Dave Robicheaux didn't. Y'all treated him rotten, and you've never owned up to it."

"I didn't hear Dave complain."

"That's because he's stand-up. And because he's stand-up doesn't make y'all right."

"I want to talk with you about something else," Dana said. "About the night Waylon Grimes and Bix Golightly got smoked."

"What about it?"

"I think you called in the shots-fired."

"What makes you think that?"

"I listened to the tape. Did you have a pencil between your teeth?"

"What did you want to tell me?" Clete asked.

"Maybe there was more than one shooter involved."

"Say that again."

"Bix Golightly got it with a .22. So did Waylon Grimes. But the rounds didn't come from the same gun. Here's the rest of it. Whoever popped Frankie Giacano in the Baton Rouge bus depot used the same gun that killed Waylon Grimes."

Clete had been preparing to leave Dana's office, but he leaned back in his chair and stared out the window at the fronds of the palm trees rattling in the wind, without seeming to see them. "So two killers were working together. What's the big deal in that?"

"Maybe they were, maybe not. The coroner says Waylon Grimes was dead at least an hour before Golightly died. Grimes got it in his apartment. Golightly got it in his van. Why would two killers be hanging around for an hour to clip Golightly? How would they know he'd be at Grimes's apartment? I think Golightly was followed."

"What was the motivation on the Golightly hit?"

"He was in the rackets for forty years. He had a sheet for statutory rape and child molestation in Texas and Florida. He did smash-and-grabs on old people and paid his whores in counterfeit. There's nothing this guy didn't do. The real question is how he survived as long as he did. You were at the Golightly hit, weren't you?"

"I was in the vicinity."

"Are you going to tell me what you saw?"

"What difference does it make? I've got zero credibility with both the department and the DA's office."

"What if I could get you back in?"

"In the department, with a shield?"

"It could happen."

"See you around."

"That's all you have to say?"

"No, I owe you one."

When Clete walked outside into the mix of shadow and sunlight on the buildings, he thought he could hear music from the clubs on Bourbon and smell the salt air off the Gulf and the coffee in Café du Monde and the flowers blooming on the balconies along Royal. Or maybe it was all in his imagination. Either way, it was a grand afternoon, one that presaged an even better evening and access to all the fruits the world had to offer.

CLETE HAD CALLED Gretchen the same afternoon and told her he was in New Orleans and would not be back in New Iberia until Thursday morning.

"Did you find out anything about the Luger?" she asked.

"Yeah, the guy who owned it was SS and stationed in Paris in 1943," Clete said. "That's as far as I got. You going to be okay till I get back?"

"Take it to the bank," she replied.

But when she went to bed that night with her cell phone under her pillow, she didn't feel like taking anything to the bank. Her dreams made her frown in her sleep, as though a hot red light were shining through her eyelids. She woke and opened the door and looked outside, although she wasn't sure why. The trees above the cottage were thrashing in the wind, and lightning snapped across the heavens, the thunder so loud that the surface of the bayou trembled as though the earth were shaking.

It was 12:14 A.M. when her cell phone vibrated under the pillow. She sat on the side of the mattress and opened the phone and placed it against her ear, knowing that only one person would call her at this hour. "Raymond?" she said.

"You're close. Call me Raymond's successor. I'm talking to Caruso, right?" an unfamiliar voice said.

"No, you're talking to Gretchen Horowitz."

"I've seen you around Key West. When we get our business out of the way, I'd like to hook up with you."

"I hope you're imitating a jerk. Because if you're not, you've got a real problem. Where's Raymond?"

"Swimming to Havana."

"Did you hurt Raymond?"

"Me? I don't hurt anybody. I make phone calls. If I was you, I'd listen and stop asking questions."

"I didn't catch your name."

"Marco."

"You don't sound like a Marco. How about I call you asshole instead?"

"We'll talk about that in a minute. We've got another job for you."

"I told Raymond, and now I'll tell you. I'm in the antique business full-time."

"Wrong. You're in the life, and that's where you're gonna stay. You've got three targets. Guess who they are."

She had left the blinds open, and she could see the leaves of the live oaks flickering against the sky and hear thunder rumbling in the south. Across the bayou a large, thick-haired dog had wound its chain around an iron pole and was trying to run to its doghouse, clanging the chain taut each time it tried. The dog was wet and trembling with fear. Gretchen cleared her throat before she spoke.

"I think you've got a hearing problem," she said. "I'm out. I wish I'd never been in. But I'm out. That means don't push your luck."

"This is the threesome: Clete Purcel, Dave Robicheaux, and the daughter, Alafair. If you want to, you can clip Robicheaux's wife for a bonus. You can make it look like an accident, or you can cowboy the bunch. It's your call. But Purcel and Robicheaux and his daughter all go down."

"Who's the client?"

"It don't work that way, Gretchen."

"Don't call me again. Don't send anybody else here, either. If you do, I'll cancel their ticket, and then I'll cancel yours."

"We dropped by your mother's place in Coconut Grove. I'll put her on. Be patient with her. She's a little woozy. I don't think she's used to China white." He took the phone from his mouth. "Hey, Candy. It's your daughter. She wants your advice about something."

Gretchen heard someone fumbling with the phone, dropping it once and picking it up. "Hello?" said a woman's voice in slow motion.

"Mama?"

"Is that you, baby? I was so worried. Are you having a good time in New Orleans?"

"Listen to me, Mama. You need to get away from these guys. Don't let them give you any more dope."

"I'm in recovery now. I just shoot twice a day. Marco said you wanted some advice."

"Mama, answer by saying yes or no. Are you in Miami?"

"Of course I'm in Miami. That's where I live. That's where you bought me the house."

"You're not at the house now. You're somewhere else. I need to know where that is," Gretchen said. "Tell me where it is without them knowing. Can you do that, Mama? Tell me how long you were in a car before you got to where you are now."

Gretchen heard the sound of someone fastening his grip around the phone, scraping it against a hard surface. "That wasn't a smart move," Marco said.

"No, it's you who made the dumb move. I haven't seen my mother in over a year. You think I'm going to clip three people for someone I never want to see again?"

"Good try, kid. You want me to describe what's happening right now? Mommy is going in the bedroom with a dwarf who has a black satchel. He's gonna turn Mommy's head into a pinball machine. He's also a degenerate. Don't get the wrong idea. We keep an eye on him. But the client doesn't have parameters, Gretchen. If you don't come across for us, Mommy is going inside a big waffle iron. Or maybe they'll turn her into wood chips, feet-first. They'll send you a video. Want to call me an asshole now? You've got ten days, bitch."

He broke the connection. When she closed her phone, she felt dead inside, her face numb, as though it had been stung by bumblebees. She stared through the blinds into the darkness. The dog across the bayou was no longer running back and forth. Then she realized why. It had broken its neck running against its own chain.

CHAPTER
20

B Y SUNRISE, THE rain had stopped and the sky was filled with white clouds and the trees were dripping on the sidewalks and dimpling the puddles in the gutters, and I decided to walk to work and to think in a calmer and more reasonable way about all the problems that seemed to beset me. At eleven-fifteen I saw Clete's maroon convertible coming up the long driveway past the city library and the grotto dedicated to Jesus' mother. When I went outside, all his windows were down and he was smiling at me from behind the wheel, his eyes clear, his face pink and unlined. A long-stemmed lavender rose rested on his dashboard. "How about an early lunch at Victor's Cafeteria?" he said.

"You brought me a rose?"

"No, the gal I was with last night brought me a rose. In fact, her name was Rose."

I got in on the passenger side and sat back in the deep leather comfort of the seat. "You look good," I said.

"Maybe if I could go three days without booze, I'd rejoin the human race. I got the gen on that Luger I took off of Frankie Gee. It belonged to a guy in the SS by the name of Karl Engels. He was in Paris in 1943, then he dropped off the screen." He waited for my response. When I didn't speak, he said, "Say what you're thinking."

"It's a start."

"That's it, a start?"

"I don't know what else to say."

"No, that's not it at all. You can't wait to rain on the parade."

Once again I was using all my energies to avoid hurting his feelings and doing a poor job of it. There were few times when Clete was genuinely happy. The irreverent and sardonic humor and outrageous behavior that characterized his life were surrogates for happiness, ephemeral ones at that, and I would have given anything in the world if I could have waved a wand over him and cast out the gremlins constantly sawing at the underpinnings of his life. Then I realized I had not only fallen prey to my old arrogance and hubris—namely, that I could fix other human beings—but I had been so concentrated on protecting Clete's feelings that I had failed to make the connection between the provenance of the Luger and a detail inside the home office of Alexis Dupree.

"Jesus, Clete," I said.

"What is it?"

I rubbed my forehead like a man who has had a flashbulb popped in his face. "Dupree has a stunning collection of framed photographs on the walls of his den. One shows Italian troops marching through a bombed-out village in Ethiopia. Another one shows a Crusader castle in the desert. There's one of the Great Wall in China and one of the Venetian canals. But I kept concentrating on a photo of the defenders of Madrid that Robert Capa supposedly inscribed to Dupree. The photo I ignored was of an indoor cycle track in Paris."

"Like a racetrack for bicycles?"

"Yeah, there was one in Paris that was used as a holding area for Jews rounded up by the SS and the French police. I don't remember all the details. I think Alexis Dupree's photographs are a tribute to the Axis attempt to conquer the world."

Clete opened a packet of turkey jerky and stuck a piece in his mouth and started chewing. This was the first time I could remember his reaching for something other than a drink or a cigarette when he was agitated. "I can't believe a guy like that has been sitting under our noses all this time. He's breathing the same air we do. That's a disgusting thought. We ought to bulldoze that mausoleum of his into the bayou."

"Why blame the house for the occupant?" I said.

"Places like that are monuments to everything that's wrong in Louisiana's history. Slavery, rental convict labor, the White League, corporate plantations, the Knights of the White Camellia, elitist shitheads figuring out new ways to pay working people as little as they can. Why not put a match to all of it?"

"Then we'd be stuck with ourselves."

"That's the most depressing thing I ever heard anyone say. You should get together with Gretchen."

"What's the deal with Gretchen?"

"You got me. She woke up looking like she'd been hit by a wrecking ball. I can't figure her, Dave. One minute she's a sweet girl, the next she's the contract hitter who snuffed Bix Golightly's wick. By the way, Dana Magelli thinks two different shooters capped Waylon Grimes and Frankie Gee."

"I don't need to know about this."

"Out of sight, out of mind? That's smart."

"Cut off the head of the snake," I said.

"Alexis Dupree?"

"You got it."

"But I shouldn't be thinking about burning down his house? Streak, if you ever see a psychiatrist, you're going to end up shooting yourself."

"You don't think getting drunk every day is a form of suicide?"

"You talking about me?" he said.

"No, you never hide your feelings or pretend you're anything other than what you are. I don't have your candor. That's what I was saying."

"Don't talk like that, big mon. It makes that lead start moving around in my chest. It's still in there. I don't care what the docs say. Dave, we've got to make things like they used to be. That's what it's about. You get to a certain age, and you go back to where you started out. It's not wrong to do that, is it?"

"Thomas Wolfe already said it. You can't go home again."

"I've got to have a drink. My liver is flopping. Let's go to Clementine's. We can eat at the bar."

"I can't do that," I replied.

"Suit yourself," he said. He started his engine, the joy gone from his face, his cheeks splotched with color, as though he were coming down with a fever.

I watched him drive through the dappled sunlight, past the grotto and the city library, and turn in to the midday traffic on East Main, the starched white top and waxed surfaces of his Caddy like a tribute to a happier and more innocent time. Then I went into my office and brought up Google on my computer screen and began typing the words "Paris" and "racetrack" and "Jews" into the search window.

GRETCHEN HOROWITZ DID not contend with the nature of the world. In her opinion, no survivor did. The world was a giant vortex, anchored in both the clouds and the bottom of space, at any given time swirling with a mix of predators and con men and professional victims and members of the herd who couldn't wait to get in lockstep with everyone around them. She felt little compassion or pity for any of them. But there was a fifth group, the arms and heads and legs of the individuals so tiny they could barely be seen. The children did not make the world. Nor did they have the ability to protect themselves from the cretins who preyed upon them. She did not speculate on the afterlife or the punishment or rewards it might offer. Instead, Gretchen Horowitz wanted to see judgment and massive amounts of physical damage imposed on child abusers in this life, not the next.

Even popping a cap on them seemed too mild a fate. But to do more than summarily blow them out of their socks would give them power. The three child abusers she'd capped had it coming, she told herself. They'd dealt the play when they declared war on the defenseless. Except there had been others, two of them. She didn't like to think about the others. She told herself they were killers and sadists and contract assassins who were mobbed up all the way to New Jersey. They'd both been armed, and both of them had gotten off a shot before they went down. Gretchen's argument with herself over the others usually lasted through the night into the dawn. The woman named Caruso may have been feared in the underworld, but for Gretchen Horowitz, Caruso had never existed.

Gretchen did not do well when the center began to come apart. She was not exactly sure what the center was, but she knew it was related to predictability and not letting other people hurt you. You kept it simple, the way people in twelve-step groups did. That meant not getting involved in other people's problems. You took care of yourself, covered your own back, and drew a line in the sand that other people were told not to cross. When somebody tried to find out if you were blowing smoke, you stepped on his cookie bag. If he had another run at it, you punched his whole ticket. In the meantime, it didn't hurt to do a good deed or two. You looked out for infants and small kids and girls who fell in with the wrong guys, not just pimps and pushers but guys they had trusted and who threw them away like used Kleenex. Last, when you had a real friend, someone who was stand-up and loyal, you never let him or her down, no matter what price you had to pay.

Gretchen had often wished her mother would nod off on the tar or the mixture of cocaine and whiskey she shot. Candy Horowitz had traded off her daughter's childhood for her habit and had never felt sorry for anything or anyone except herself. With luck, the dwarf with the satchel would overload her heart and give her the peace she had never found. What more fitting way for Candy to do the Big Exit than to glide into eternity on angel wings trailing streams of China white? That was a cruel thought, Gretchen told herself. Her mother was a child, no different than the defenseless child Gretchen had been when she was molested by at least half a dozen of her mother's boyfriends. And now Candy Horowitz was in the hands of a man who talked about sticking her inside a wood chipper or a waffle iron.

Gretchen took the four-lane to New Orleans. The Ford pickup she had bought from T. Coon was a dream, the cab chopped down so the windows looked like slits in a machine-gun bunker, the body lowered on the frame, the Merc engine souped up with dual carburetors and a hot cam and milled heads. The dual Hollywood mufflers probably had been deliberately filled with motor oil in order to carbonize the filters and create a deep-throated rumble that echoed off the asphalt like soft thunder. At Morgan City, she got stuck behind two semis on the high bridge over the Atchafalaya River. Finally, when there was a narrow opening between the lanes, she double-clutched into second and floored the accelerator, passing the trucks so suddenly that both of the drivers swerved. In under ten seconds, the semis had shrunk to the size of toys in her rearview mirror.

In two hours, she was at Joe & Flo's Candlelight Hostel, not far from the Quarter, where she had rented a security locker. She removed a hatbox from the locker and got back in her pickup and drove onto the I-10. In minutes she was back on the connector to the four-lane, headed toward New Iberia, the chrome-plated Merc engine humming like a sewing machine. Far down the road, where it traversed miles of flooded woods and the swamp water was coated with a milky-green blanket of algae, she popped the top loose from the hatbox and put her right hand inside. She felt the hard, square outline of the .22 auto and the nine-millimeter Beretta. She also felt the suppressor for the .22 and the magazines and boxes of cartridges for both weapons. The contents of the hatbox were old friends. They didn't argue or contend or judge. They did as they were asked and became an extension of the will. As a retired button man in Hialeah once told her, "The objective is not the target, Gretchen. The objective is controlling the environment around you. The proper use of your piece gives you that kind of control. After that point, the personal choices are up to you."

"What did you do before you were a hitter, Louie?" Gretchen asked.

"You see *The Gang That Couldn't Shoot Straight*?"

"Yeah, Jerry Orbach played Joe Gallo."

"Remember the lion Joe kept in his basement, the one they hooked up to the chain in the car wash? I'm the one who took care of the lion. I participated in history," he said.

But neither her fingers on the oiled coldness of the guns nor her reveries about the humorous hit man from Brooklyn could relieve her of the sick feeling in her stomach. No, "sick feeling" didn't approach the systemic debilitation that seemed to be eating its way through her body. Her palms were stiff and hard and dry when she closed them around the steering wheel. Her face looked gray and unfamiliar when she looked at herself in the rearview mirror. A sour odor rose from her shirt. If she stopped and ate anything, she knew she would throw up. She had thought nothing worse than her childhood could ever happen to her again. Her choices were like multiple doors that all opened onto a furnace. She could either do as she had been told by the man who called himself Marco or become responsible for her mother's death, one that was fiendish in design. The guns she had owned and used to control her environment had become the trap that was about to rob her of her soul and the lives of her mother and Dave and Alafair Robicheaux and Clete Purcel, the best man she had ever known, one whose goodness was in every inch of his body, every touch of his hand, every kind expression of concern. His selfless affection for her seemed to have no source. He didn't want anything from her, and he didn't get mad when she got mad at him. He made no sense at all. He had an affection for her that only a father had for a daughter, a man to whom she had no known blood relation. Why had this fate been visited upon her?

When she pulled in to the motor court on East Main, a sun shower had just ended, and smoke from Clete's barbecue pit was hanging in the trees, and red and yellow leaves from a swamp maple were pasted damply on the driveway. The roast on the rotisserie had been burned into a lump of coal. She cut the engine and picked up the hatbox from the passenger seat and went inside Clete's cottage. The blinds were shut, and the air was gray and dense with an odor that was like moldy towels and dried testosterone and beer that had been sweated through the glands into the bedclothes. A bottle of peppermint schnapps and a half-empty bottle of Carta Blanca were on the breakfast table. Clete was sleeping in his skivvies on the couch, on his side, a pillow over his head. His shirt and trousers lay on the floor.

Gretchen sat down in a straight-back chair close to the couch and removed the .22 auto and screwed the suppressor on the barrel. Her scalp was tingling, her heart thudding. A tiny pool of perspiration had already formed between her palm and the grips on the .22.

Her breath was so loud and ragged in her throat that she thought it would wake him. She lowered the .22 behind her calf and touched Clete on the back. "It's me," she said.

He didn't move.

"It's Gretchen. Wake up," she said.

When he didn't move, she felt a surge of anger and impatience toward him that was irrational, as though he were the source of all her problems and deserved whatever happened to him. Her heart was pounding, her nostrils flaring with fear and angst. She clenched his shoulder with her left hand and shook it. His skin was oily and hot, beaded with pinpoints of perspiration. He pulled the pillow from his head and looked over his shoulder at her, his eyes bleary. "What's the haps?" he said.

"Are you in the bag again?"

"Yeah, bad night, bad day. I got to stop drinking," he replied. He turned over on the couch and supported himself on one elbow. "What time is it?"

"Forget about the time."

"What's going on, Gretch? What's that in your hand?"

She lifted the .22 above the level of the mattress. "This is the piece I used to clip Bix Golightly. On my sixth birthday, he asked me to come into the kitchen and help him make lemonade. My mother had just left for the grocery to buy a cake. He unzipped his pants and pushed my face against his cock. He squeezed my head so tight, I thought he would crush my skull. He told me if I was a bad girl and told my mother what we'd done, that's how he put it, what *we'd done,* he'd come back to Miami and bury me in my backyard. I never knew his full name or where he was from. Earlier this year he was at the track in Hialeah with some other gumballs. They told him I did button work for the Mob. He never made the connection between me and the little girl he sodomized. It took me a long time to catch up with him, but I did. What do you think of that, Clete?"

Clete fingered the sheet that covered his loins, his mouth gray, his lips dry-looking. "I don't think it's a big deal."

"Popping a guy?"

"No, popping a guy who makes a little girl perform oral sex on him on her birthday and threatens to murder her. What are you going to do with that piece?"

"Use it."

"On who?" he asked.

"The field is wide open."

He sat up on the side of the couch. He took the .22 from her hand. The magazine was not in the frame. He pulled back the receiver. The chamber was empty. "Did you take down Frankie Giacano or Waylon Grimes?"

"No, I didn't. Golightly and Grimes and Giacano were all supposed to catch the bus. I did Golightly, but I didn't take money for it. I don't know who clipped the others."

"Do you know who I am?" Clete asked.

"A guy who smells like he's been drinking for twenty-four hours?"

He unscrewed the suppressor from the .22 and handed both the gun and the suppressor back to her. "What else is in that hatbox?"

"A Beretta nine and a gun-cleaning kit and several extra magazines and boxes of ammo."

"I'm your old man. That's who I am," he said.

"Meaning like my boyfriend?"

"I'm your father."

She felt a sharp pain in her heart that spread through her chest and seemed to squeeze the air out of her lungs. Her brow twitched once, like a rubber band snapping, then something shut down the flow of light into her eyes. "Don't play around with me."

"I wouldn't do that," he said.

"My father died in Desert Storm."

"You went to juvie when you were fifteen, then to foster care. Your mother was in the Miami-Dade stockade. I had a blood test done on you. There was no doubt I was your dad. But you ran away from foster care before I could process the custody application. I tried to find you twice on my own, and later, I hired a PI in Lauderdale, but the trail stopped at the track in Hialeah. You were a hot walker there, right?"

"Yeah, and a groom and I worked at the concession stand," she said.

"You feel like I've deceived you?"

"I don't know what to call it. I can't begin to describe what I feel right now," she said.

"I saw you smoke Golightly. I called in the shots-fired, but I didn't dime you. After you brought me my cigarette lighter, I figured you'd run away if I told you I was in Algiers the night Golightly and Grimes got it. If you ran away again, I knew I would never find you. You got a rotten break as a kid, Gretchen. In my view, you're not responsible for any of the things you did. If anybody is responsible, it's me. I was a drunk and a pill addict working Vice. I took juice from the Mob, and I took advantage of your mother. Candy was mainlining when she was nineteen, and instead of helping her, I made her pregnant. If you told me you didn't want a son of a bitch like me for a father, I'd understand."

"You're not a son of a bitch. Don't say that."

He reached down on the floor and picked up his trousers, then stood up from the couch with his back to her and put them on. "Why are you crying?" he said.

"I'm not. I don't ever cry."

"Our supper is probably burned up. Let's go to the Patio for some étouffée. A guy couldn't have a better daughter than you. You have character and you're not afraid. Anybody who says different is going to have to answer to me."

Her hands were propped on her knees, and her head was bent forward so he could no longer see her face. She pushed the wetness out of her eyes with the back of her wrist. "There's a hit on you. You and Dave Robicheaux and Alafair and maybe Mrs. Robicheaux. They've got my mother, Clete. I was offered the choice of doing the hit or letting my mother be tortured to death."

"Who gave you the contract?" he asked.

"A guy named Marco. He's not important. The contract can come from anywhere or anybody. It gets processed through Jersey or Miami or San Diego. The middle guys do business through drop boxes and electronic relays. Right now they're shooting up my mother with some high-grade smack that could kill her."

She waited for him to speak. Instead, he sat down on the couch and stared at the floor. "Where'd they grab Candy?"

"Probably at her house in Coconut Grove. Are you going to tell
Dave Robicheaux and Alafair?" she asked. "I can't stand the thought
of that. Alafair stood up for me. She hit Varina Leboeuf in the face."
He lifted his eyes to hers. There was a level of sadness in them that
seemed to have no bottom.

AT THE DEPARTMENT I had started my Internet search into the history
of the cycle track in Paris in hopes of discovering a connection with
the Nazi SS officer Karl Engels. Some of the search was easy, some of
it elusive, some of it a dead end. The name of the racetrack in Paris
was Vel' d'Hiv, a place that had become infamous as the first stop
for French Jews on their way to a camp at Drancy and the freight
cars that would take them to Auschwitz. Many of the photos were
horrific, the eyewitness accounts so gruesome and cruel that you
wondered if there was not a demonic agent at work in human beings.
There was nothing to link the name of Karl Engels with the cycle
track in Paris or the camp at Drancy or the chimneys at Auschwitz.

When I got home that night, I continued the search on our home
computer via a different avenue. I didn't put in a search for Karl
Engels but for the people he might have known or worked under.
I brought up photos of Adolf Eichmann and Reinhard Heydrich
and the people in their entourage. I searched the lists of those who
had been tried at Nuremberg and those who had escaped justice and
fled to South America. I read seemingly endless accounts of their
backgrounds. Most of them had come from middle-class homes and
been raised by Lutheran or Catholic parents. Their previous lives,
before their admission to the SS, had been characterized by medi-
ocrity and failure. That they would pose before cameras in front
of the barbed wire holding their victims was mind-numbing. That
they would allow themselves to be photographed shooting unarmed
people on their knees or a woman with a child in her arms would
probably be incomprehensible to a sociopath. The world these men
created might exist today only in cyberspace, but to visit it even as a
virtual reality makes the stomach crawl.

By eleven P.M. my eyes were burning, and I was ready to give it up. Then I looked again at a photo I had not lingered on, possibly because of the way the individuals were dressed. The photo showed Heinrich Himmler and three other men talking, all of them wearing business suits. They looked like men who might have gathered at a piece of cleared land in anticipation of a shared business venture. They did not look evil or cunning or remarkable in any fashion. In the cutline, Himmler and two of the other men were named; the fourth man was not. His face was turned at an angle, his posture both confident and regal. There was a dimple in his chin, a pleasant smile on his mouth. The profile was a replica of Alexis Dupree's.

I went back to the firsthand accounts given by survivors of Auschwitz. Many of them mentioned a junior SS officer who was singularly cruel and took obvious delight in conducting the selections. Some called him "the light bearer" because of the way his eyes brightened when he let his riding crop hover above an inmate's head, asking innocuous questions about his place of birth or the work he did, just before touching him on the brow and condemning him to the ovens.

Other inmates were less poetic in their choice of terms for the light bearer. They simply called him Lucifer.

"Why don't you come to bed?" Molly said.

"I found a guy who might be Alexis Dupree. He was an SS officer by the name of Karl Engels. Look at this photo. That's Himmler on the left. The guy on the far right looks like Dupree. At least the profile does."

She rested her hand on my shoulder as she gazed at the screen. Then she sat down next to me and looked more closely. "He even has the dimple in his chin, doesn't he?"

This was the first time Molly had agreed with me about the darker possibilities of Alexis Dupree's background. "The root of the name Engels means 'angel.' The guy who tried to kill me in Lafayette, Chad Patin, said this island where there's an iron maiden is run by someone named Angel or Angelle."

"So Alexis Dupree is the guy running things?"

"You don't think that's possible?"

"Too big a stretch," she replied.

I couldn't argue with her. Dupree was close to ninety and did not have the emotional stability it would take to run a well-organized criminal enterprise. And even if he were Karl Engels, there was no way to confirm that Karl Engels was the man known as the light bearer at Auschwitz.

"Look at it this way," Molly said. "You were right about Alexis Dupree, and I was wrong. He's probably a war criminal. He's also at the end of his days. The fate that's waiting for him is one we can only imagine. I think he'll find that hell is just like Auschwitz, except this time he'll be wearing a striped uniform."

I hadn't thought of it in those terms. That night I opened the bedroom window and turned on the attic fan and let the breeze blow across the bed. As I fell asleep, I could hear the wind in the trees and the squirrels running on the roof and a dredge boat deepening the main channel in the bayou. I slept all the way to morning without dreaming.

IT WAS LATE the next afternoon when Clete showed up at the house, just after a sun shower and the return of Gretchen Horowitz from New Orleans. He was chewing breath mints and had shaved and combed his hair and put on shades and a crisp Hawaiian shirt to hide his dissipation and the increasing pain his hangovers caused him. But when he came into the house and removed his shades, the skin around his eyes was a whitish-green, the lids constantly blinking, as though someone had shone a flashlight directly into the pupils. "Where are Molly and Alafair?" he asked.

"At Winn-Dixie," I said.

"I've got to tell you something."

"It can't be that bad, can it?"

"You got anything to drink? I feel like I'm passing a gallstone."

I poured him a glass of milk in the kitchen and put a raw egg and some vanilla extract in it. He sat at the breakfast table and drank it. The windows were open to let in the coolness of the evening, and fireflies were starting to spark in the trees. None of that did anything to relieve the turmoil that was obviously roiling inside Clete Purcel.

He told me everything about Gretchen Horowitz's confession to him—the hit on Bix Golightly, her career as an assassin, the kidnapping of her mother, and the contract Gretchen was supposed to carry out on me and my family.

At first I felt only anger. I felt it toward Gretchen and toward Clete and toward myself. Then I felt incurably stupid and used. I also felt a nameless and abiding fear, the kind that is hard to describe because it's irrational and goes deep into the psyche. It's the sort of fear you experience when someone unexpectedly turns off a light in a room, plunging it into darkness, or when the airplane you are riding on hits an air pocket and drops so fast that you cannot hear the sound of the engines. It's the kind of fear you experience when an atavistic voice inside you whispers that evil is not only real but it has become omnipresent in your life, and nothing on God's green earth can save you from it.

After he finished telling me things he probably never guessed he would say to his best friend, he got up from the breakfast table without looking at me and went to the cabinet and poured more milk in his glass and added more vanilla extract, shaking the last few drops out of the tiny bottle. "Have you got anything stronger?" he asked.

"No, and I wouldn't give it to you if I did."

"If you slugged me, I'd consider it a gift," he said.

"You think Gretchen's mother is being held in Miami?" I asked.

"I doubt it." He tried to meet my stare, but his gaze broke. "You want to go to the FBI?"

I looked at him for a long time, and I didn't do it to make him feel uncomfortable. I knew there had to be an answer to the problem, but I didn't know what it was. The moment we brought in the FBI, they would pick up Gretchen Horowitz, and the contract for our death would go to someone else. In the meantime, there was a strong chance that Clete Purcel would go down for aiding and abetting. When all that was done, we would still be on our own. Sound like exaggeration? Ask any victim of a violent crime or any witness for the prosecution in a trial involving the Mob what his experience with the system was like. Ask him how safe he ever felt again or how often he slept soundly through the night. Ask him what it was like to be afraid twenty-four hours a day.

"I need to tell Molly and Alafair and see what they think," I said.

I saw him trying to control his emotions. His throat was prickled with color, the whites of his eyes full of tiny pink vessels, the skin around his mouth as sickly-looking as a fish's belly. My guess was he couldn't begin to sort through the shame and embarrassment and guilt he was experiencing. Nor could he help wondering if he would ever stop paying dues for the mistakes he had made years ago.

"Whatever y'all want to do is jake with me," he said.

"Gretchen has no idea where the contract came from?"

"You know how it works. They use people who are morally insane to carry out the job, then half the time they dispose of them." He paused as though he couldn't deal with the content of his own statement. "Gretchen didn't choose the world she was born into. She was tortured with cigarettes when she was an infant, all because her father wasn't there to protect her. On her sixth birthday, she had to perform oral sex on Bix Golightly. Does anyone in his right mind believe a kid like that will grow into a normal adult? I think it's amazing she's the decent person she is."

His eyes were shiny, his voice so wired that some of his words were almost inaudible.

"Let's take a walk," I said.

"Where?"

"To get some ice cream."

"Dave, I'm truly sorry for this. Gretchen is, too."

"Don't tell me about Gretchen's problems, Clete. I'm not up to it."

"I'm just telling you, that's all. She's human, too. Give her a break."

"That might be hard to do," I said.

He looked at me, surprised and hurt.

I could see the light failing in the trees and hear the frogs croaking on the bayou, and I wanted to walk into the yard and wrap myself and Molly and Alafair and Clete inside the gloaming of the day and forget everything taking place around us. Instead, I said, "We'll get through it. We always do."

"I forgot to tell you something. While I was getting dressed to come over, I had the television on. There was a clip about a British oil guy who's giving a talk in Lafayette. There was a shot of him with Lamont Woolsey, that albino who hangs out with the televangelist."

"What about the oil guy?"

"I've seen him before. He was on the Varina Leboeuf video," he replied. "After he finished pumping her, he was combing his hair, still in the nude. He looked straight into the camera. The words 'narcissist' and 'real bucket of shit' come to mind. Think we should dial him up?"

CHAPTER
21

I CALLED THE department and had a cruiser placed in front of my house. It would be manned and unmanned at different times of the day. It would be replaced by another cruiser parked in a different spot. Anyone watching our house could not avoid concluding that there was a police presence there twenty-four hours a day.

Then I drove to the Winn-Dixie and found Molly and Alafair and followed them back home. The three of us sat down in the kitchen, and I told them everything Clete had told me. Alafair started opening her mail, seemingly more concerned with it than the discussion. Molly opened a can of cat food and brought Snuggs and Tripod in and fed them on a piece of newspaper and then filled a bowl of water and set it beside the cat food. Snuggs's tail flipped from side to side on the paper while he and Tripod ate.

"Clete's sorry for this, and so am I," I said.

"Clete's a mess. He'll never change. The question is what do we do about it," Molly said. "Have you talked to Helen?"

"Not yet," I replied.

"When are you going to do that?" she asked.

"First thing in the morning."

"Don't blame yourself for this, Dave. You thought you were helping Clete. It's time he becomes responsible for his choices."

"I don't think choice enters into it. He didn't have a lot of alternatives."

"Helen is probably going to have something to say about that," Molly said.

I didn't want to think about my conversation with Helen Soileau. She had given great latitude to Clete and me, and I was about to repay the favor by telling her that Clete's daughter had been ordered to kill the department's senior homicide investigator as well as his family.

"Somebody thinks Clete and I have information that, in reality, we don't possess," I said. "I don't think this contract is about revenge or that it came from the Duprees or Varina Leboeuf. I believe the guys behind it are people we never met."

"Gretchen was getting off her leash," Alafair said. Molly and I looked at her. She went on, "This is how the people she works for are getting rid of her. In the meantime, they use her to cause a lot of trouble for Clete and Dave and keep all of us running in circles for a long time."

"Who?" I said.

"Somebody who's about to lose a great deal of money," she replied.

This is what happens when your kid graduates with a degree in forensic psychology.

"Remember what Tee Jolie told you originally?" Alafair said. "She said she knew dangerous men who were talking about centralizers."

"Yeah, they're used inside the drill casing on a rig. Everybody knows that," I said. "That's part of the suit against two or three companies responsible for the blowout."

"I think this is about oil, all of it," she said.

That was my kid.

"They're underestimating Gretchen Horowitz," she went on. "I think they've made an enemy with the wrong person."

"Don't let Gretchen Horowitz anywhere near this house," Molly said. "If I see her, I'm going to pull her hair out. Please tell her that for me."

And this is where we ended up, arguing among ourselves, letting the evil of others invade our home and family.

It was dark in the trees, and the electric lights in the park were shining on the surface of the bayou, which was high and muddy and filled with broken tree branches. In the quiet, I could hear geese honking overhead and smell gas pooling in the yard. The wind had shifted out of the north, and inside it was a tannic coldness that only minutes ago had not been there.

I drove to Clete's motor court. Gretchen's hot-rod truck was gone, and I was glad I did not have to see her. Her childhood had been terrible, but that was true of many people who had not become contract killers. This kind of conclusion about human behavior is one that almost every man and woman in law enforcement eventually comes to, although the reason behind it is ultimately pragmatic. If a cop begins to think of morality in relative terms, he will quickly find himself in a quandary. Prisons are bad places. We put away eighteen-year-old kids who weigh 120 pounds soaking wet and leave them to their fate. In other words, does a kid like that deserve to be spread-eagled and split apart and forced to his knees in the shower by any swinging dick who wants an easy bar of soap? Did the kid deal his own play? Is he receiving the same treatment a rich kid would? Does the system serve and treat everyone equally? Does anyone in his right mind believe that?

I've seen five people executed, three by electrocution, two by injection. I did not refer to them as inmates or killers. When you watch them die, they become people. Maybe they deserve an even worse fate than the one you are witnessing. But when you see it take place, when you smell the stink in their clothes and see the sheen of fear in their eyes and the jailhouse iridescence on their skin and the nakedness of their scalps where the hair has been shaved away, they become human beings little different from you and me, unless something in us has already died and made us into people we never wanted to be.

I guess what I'm saying is that deep down inside, I believed Clete's protective feelings for his daughter were justified, that with a different shake of the dice, I could have turned out just like her.

When he opened his door, he was eating a cheese and lettuce and tomato sandwich, his jaw packed like a baseball.

"What was the Brit doing in Lafayette?" I said.

"Telling people that sweet crude tastes like chocolate syrup," Clete replied.

I went inside the cottage and sat down. I felt as though I'd aged a decade in the last hour. "Where's Gretchen?"

"Search me."

"That's not a good answer."

"I've thought some things over," he said. "I'm going to do whatever it takes to protect her, but maybe it's too late. Maybe she's too damaged, and so am I. Same with you, Streak. You're sober, but you've got more of me in you than you want to admit. We don't fit in, and everybody knows it except us. Maybe we should have bought it in the shootout on the bayou."

I propped my elbows on his breakfast table and rested my head on the heels of my hands. I felt that something had torn loose behind my eyes and that I couldn't see Clete or the room correctly. "Who's playing that song?"

"What song?" he said.

"Jimmy Clanton's 'Just a Dream.' You don't hear it?"

"No, I don't hear anything except that workboat deepening the channel in the bayou. You coming down with something?"

VARINA LEBOEUF WAS good at whatever she did, whether in love, war, or deception. Her suitors had never been unintelligent men, yet most of them, no matter how bad they got hurt, came back for more, and I never heard one of them say he regretted his choice. When the phone rang on my kitchen counter at eleven-ten that night, she was at her best. "You have to help me," she said. "I know this is outrageous, but I also know your capacity for forgiveness, and I know you never turn away a person who genuinely needs your help and understanding."

I tried to think of an adequate response.

"Hello? Are you there?" she said.

"Yeah, I'm here, and it's really late," I said.

"My father is drunk and believes you sent the Horowitz woman to our house. He says he saw her parked down the road this afternoon."

"Why would I send Gretchen Horowitz to your house?"

"He's getting more and more irrational. He resents you because you're educated and you were given advancements at the department that he thought should be his. He believes you and the black female deputy conspired to degrade him in front of his peers."

"Where is he now?"

"I don't know. He has a gun. I don't want him hurt. He called you a nigger-lover before he left. I'm afraid of what he's going to do."

"Call 911 and make a report."

"Dave, if he gets into it with a black deputy, somebody is going to be killed."

"Frankly, I don't care what happens to your father, Varina. He's an ignorant, stupid man, a racist, and a bully who molested black women and jailed and beat their men. His sin lies not in his ignorance and stupidity but in his choice to stay ignorant and stupid. I'm going to hang up now so you can call 911. Take my number out of your Rolodex."

"He's a sick old man. What's the matter with you?"

"Nothing. Thanks for asking, though."

I was lowering the telephone receiver to the cradle when I heard her voice again, as though her intentions, whatever they were, had taken on a new direction and were shifting into overdrive. "Clete Purcel betrayed my trust and stole something from my home and my apartment. I think you know what that is."

I put the receiver back to my ear. "Clete doesn't always confide in me."

"Stop lying. I had some things on video I'm not proud of. But I never used that material against anyone. I've had two men try to extort me. One man named me as the third party in a divorce suit. So I decided to get some insurance. That's all."

"You had someone burglarize Clete's office."

"That's ridiculous."

"Your father carries a key chain with a fob on it that resembles a sawfish. I think Alexis Dupree gave the fob to him. I also think Alexis Dupree is a Nazi war criminal and your father admired him as a kindred spirit. Except your father finally realized that in Dupree's eyes, he was a throwback walking around with a Styrofoam spit cup in his hand. Where is Tee Jolie Melton, Varina? Why did y'all have to murder Blue?"

"I'd get mad at you, Dave, but objectively speaking, you're not worth the effort. Good God, what did I ever see in you?"

I CALLED CLETE at six A.M. and woke him up. "Where's Gretchen?" I said.

"I think she flew to Miami," he replied.

"Varina Leboeuf claims her father saw her at Cypremort Point yesterday."

"That's possible."

"What's she up to, Clete?"

"She wants to find her mother."

"I'm going to have a talk with Helen about Gretchen this morning."

I heard him exhale against the receiver. "Is there another way to do this?" he asked.

"No."

"A PI friend of mine in Lafayette found the British oil guy. His name is Hubert Donnelly. He and Lamont Woolsey are staying at a motel on Pinhook Road in Lafayette."

"After I talk with Helen, I'll call you back."

"Gretchen is still my daughter, no matter what happens."

"I don't know how I should take that."

"Any way you want," he replied. Then he hung up.

I ate breakfast in the kitchen with Molly while Alafair worked on her new novel in her bedroom. The windows were open, and the morning was cool and fresh and smelled of humus and night damp and the flowers opening in the shadows. I heard Alafair clicking on the old Smith Corona I gave her when she was eight years old. She wrote in a strange fashion, one I never quite understood. She woke in the middle of the night and wrote with a pen in a notebook, typed the words on the Smith Corona in the morning, and then retyped them onto her computer. When I asked her why she did it that way, she replied, "It's never any good unless you're sure that not one period or comma is out of place and not one word is used that can be taken out."

"Who was that on the phone last night?" Molly asked.

"Varina Leboeuf. She said her father was drunk and out to get me. I didn't take her seriously. That whole bunch at Croix du Sud Plantation are a tangle of vipers. Their schemes are coming apart, whatever they are, and Varina is trying to save herself."

"Why would her father have it in for you?"

"Years ago someone taught him to hate himself so he'd blame his lot in life on people of color or people who disagree with him. It's a fine morning. Let's not talk about these guys."

"We have to."

"No, we don't. It's like reading the Bible," I said. "We know how the last chapter ends. The good guys win."

"You skipped over the part where a lot of the earth gets wiped out."

"No story is perfect," I said.

We both laughed, in the way we used to laugh when we didn't have any cares. We divided a hot cinnamon roll and drank the rest of the coffee and hot milk on the stove. Then we went outside and walked down to the edge of Bayou Teche with Snuggs and Tripod flanking us. The air was cold and wonderful rising off the water, the light as soft as pollen on the tree limbs above us. There was no sound at all on the bayou, not even on the drawbridge at Burke Street. Molly took my hand in hers without speaking, and we watched the bream feeding among the lily pads, which were turning brown and curling stiffly along the edges. I wondered how many weeks we might have before the gray, rainy days of the Louisiana winter set in, laying bare the water oaks and the pecan trees, smudging the windows with fog that could be as cold and wet as seepage in the grave.

WHEN I WENT to the department, I learned that Helen's half sister, Ilene, had almost died in an auto accident in Shreveport and that

Helen had gone to be by her side. I had been prepared to tell her everything I knew about Gretchen Horowitz and the kidnapping of Candy Horowitz and the contract on me and my family and Clete, and like the guilt-ridden man who finds the church house closed, I found myself with nowhere to take my story.

I called Clete at his office. "What's the status of the Brit and Lamont Woolsey this morning?" I said.

"Funny you asked. I just called Lafayette. The Brit is addressing a chamber of commerce luncheon on Pinhook Road," he replied. "Dig this. They're serving oysters on the half shell that they had flown in from Chesapeake Bay. There's nothing like being safe."

THE RESTAURANT WAS located in the older section of Pinhook, where the oak trees had been spared the chain saw and whose gnarled, thick limbs arched over the two-lane and created a leafy, windblown arbor that was truly grand to stand under, particularly when the morning was still fresh and the sunlight cool and filtering through the canopy. It was the kind of moment that made you believe Robert Browning was correct and the naysayers were wrong, that in truth God was in His heaven and all was right with the world.

Unfortunately, all was not right with the world. Giant tentacles of oil that had the color and sheen of feces had spread all the way to Florida, and the argument that biodegradation would take care of the problem would be a hard sell with the locals. The photographs of pelicans and egrets and seagulls encased in sludge, their eyes barely visible, wounded the heart and caused parents to shield their children's eyes. The testimony before congressional committees by Louisiana fisher-people whose way of life was being destroyed did not help matters, either. The oil company responsible for the blowout had spent an estimated $50 million trying to wipe their fingerprints off of Louisiana's wetlands. They hired black people and whites with hush-puppy accents to be their spokesmen on television. The company's CEOs tried their best to look earnest and humanitarian, even though their company's safety record was the worst of any extractive industry doing business in the United States. They also had a way of chartering their offshore enterprises under the flag of countries like Panama. Their record of geopolitical intrigue went all the way back to the installation of the shah of Iran in the 1950s. Their even bigger problem was an inability to shut their mouths.

They gave misleading information to the media and the government about the volume of oil escaping from the blown well, and made statements on worldwide television about wanting their lives back and the modest impact that millions of gallons of crude would have on the Gulf Coast. For the media, their tone-deafness was a gift from a divine hand. Central casting could not have provided a more inept bunch of villains.

Clete and I had seated ourselves in the middle of the banquet room with a clear view of the podium and the long linen-covered table where the guests of honor were seated. On each table was a silver bowl filled with water and floating camellias. Clete ordered a Bloody Mary and a cup of crawfish gumbo, then leaned toward my ear and pointed at the front of the room. "There's the albino. You see that cocksucker who just came in? That's Donnelly. Watch him. He's going to work the room."

"How do you know?" I said, trying to ignore the stares we were getting from other tables.

"I saw him on tape with Varina." I looked at Clete, waiting for him to explain. "You didn't want to watch the tapes," he said. "Good for you. But *I* did watch them. Believe me when I tell you this guy has got one agenda—getting his hammer polished."

Donnelly was eating strips of lobster with his fingers, dipping them gingerly in oil before he placed them in his mouth. His nails were like pink seashells, his hair freshly clipped and stiff and silver on the tips. He looked youthful and healthy, his skin glowing with tan. His only physical imperfection was in the flesh that sagged under his jaw, as though he couldn't hide the sybarite that lived inside him.

Donnelly wiped his fingers on a napkin and rose from his chair and began shaking hands and introducing himself to the people around him, moving from one table to the next, until he was standing directly in front of ours. His eyes were bluish-gray, his hand soft inside mine when I took it. "It's nice meeting you. I hope both you gentlemen enjoy my little talk," he said.

"I'm looking forward to it," I replied.

Then I realized he was not actually seeing or hearing me. His eyes were fixed on the people behind me, or on the wall, or in neutral space, but not on me or on Clete. He saw them in a collective fashion, as part of a purpose, but he didn't see the individual whose hand he was shaking. It was strange to find myself extending my hand to a man who I was convinced did not care whether I lived or died, and I wondered how such a man took in so many people, and I wondered why I was actually holding his hand in mine.

I heard Clete drain his Bloody Mary down to the ice, then set the glass heavily on the table. "I've seen you in the movies," he said before Donnelly could get away.

"Beg your pardon?"

"Have you ever done any character roles? Maybe a low-budget independent film. I'm sure I've seen you in one," Clete said.

"I'm afraid I have no experience of that kind," Donnelly said. "You must be thinking of someone else."

"A romantic comedy, maybe," Clete said. "I'm sure of it. It'll come to me. Just give me a minute. You ever do any film work in Tijuana?"

"It's been such a pleasure meeting you," Donnelly said.

"Do you have a big mole on your left rear cheek?" Clete asked.

Donnelly kept moving, but the back of his neck was flaming.

"Have you lost your mind?" I said to Clete.

"I found a bug in my office this morning. I wanted to send him a message," Clete said.

"Why didn't you tell me?"

"Because I can't prove who put it in there. Now lighten up." He snapped his fingers for the waiter and ordered another Bloody Mary.

Donnelly sat back down and cleaned his hands with a hand wipe. Later, two men in navy blue suits, shades, and shined black shoes entered the room and stood by the door. They looked like they were wearing makeup, perhaps to cover a serious bruising. Clete touched me on the arm. "Check it out," he said.

"I see them. You think they're the guys Gretchen busted up?"

He pulled the celery stick out of his second drink and began chewing on it, making loud crunching noises. "See the guy with the greased hair and the bump on his nose and the scalp job around his ears? He's got to be one of them. She said the second guy was fat. She broke off some of his teeth up front. Maybe we should forget about the Brit and the albino and tune this pair up."

"No, we don't get into it with anybody."

"Whatever you say. Waiter, I need a refill."

Hubert Donnelly went to the podium and smiled politely while he was introduced. Then he launched into a long presentation of all the remedial measures his company and others were undertaking in order to undo the damage they had done. His tone was confessional and humble and filled with references to the men who had died on the rig. A medieval penitent on the road to Canterbury could not have been more contrite. The audience was made up of business-people who had a vested interest in the drilling industry and should have been receptive to the emotional nature of his delivery. In this instance, local rage trumped both unctuousness and long-term profit, and Donnelly's mojo was not sliding down the pipe.

He loosened his tie and put aside his prepared remarks. I began to realize the level of my own naïveté about the intelligence and complexity of the enemy. Donnelly wasn't an oil executive or a geologist. I wasn't sure which company he worked for or why he was here. He kept referencing electronic technology and talking about oceanic grids and the Atlantic community of nations that depended on oil from the Persian Gulf. He wasn't talking about a business anymore but a nongovernmental empire that encompassed most of the world and drove the engines in it, all of it maintained by corporate interests that could never be compartmentalized or separated one from the other. Flags and national borders were an illusion, he said. The issue was energy, and it had been the issue since 1914. His teeth were small and crooked and looked crowded inside his mouth. He began talking about T. E. Lawrence. I doubted that more than three or four people in the room were listening.

Clete stirred the ice in his drink with a fresh celery stick. "I think our man is losing it," he said.

"I'm not sure about that," I said.

People were looking at their watches and trying not to yawn. When Donnelly finally sat down, he might have just climbed from the wicker basket of a hot-air balloon. Later, Clete and I followed him and Woolsey into the parking lot. Clete had stuck an unlit cigarette in his mouth and was snapping and unsnapping the top of his Zippo. The two men in shades and navy blue suits were leaning against a Buick out in the sunlight, watching us, seemingly indifferent to the heat radiating off the metal.

As I looked at Donnelly and Lamont Woolsey and their hired security men, I experienced a strange sensation I couldn't quite define. I felt that I was part of a grand folly, not only here, outside the restaurant, but in every aspect of my professional life, in the same way that the survivors of Flanders Fields and the Battle of the Somme had come to think of their war as the Grand Illusion. I also felt I had just listened to a cynic tell the truth in a way that was so candid, it would never be recognized as such nor have any influence on anyone or anything.

"You got a minute, Mr. Donnelly?" I said, opening my badge holder.

"What is it?" he said, turning around, the dappled shade of the live oaks sliding back and forth on his face.

"You're an intelligent man. Why do you work for a collection of shits?" I said.

"Whom do you think *you* work for, Mr. Robicheaux?" he said.

"That's a valid question."

"Will you answer it?" he said.

"Mr. Woolsey was on a boat that was used in the abduction of a homicide victim. Is this the kind of guy you associate with?"

"Do I need an attorney?"

"That's up to you."

"I think we're finished," he said.

"No, we're not."

"Then please tell me why you're following me."

"Who are you?" I said.

"What difference does it make? Do you think harassing me and Lamont Woolsey is going to stop oil drilling in the Gulf of Mexico?"

"What did Blue Melton know about y'all that was so important you had to kill her? She was seventeen years old. Does that weigh on you at all, Mr. Donnelly?"

"I've killed no one. You have no right to say that."

"Get your nose out of the air, bud," Clete said. "As we speak, Varina Leboeuf is selling your snooty ass down the drain."

"Tell me, Mr. Purcel, if what you say is true, why are you staging this little show for us? I don't wish to offend you gentlemen, but don't you think it's time to grow up? An oil company doesn't deliberately destroy its own drilling apparatus. It was an accident, a blip that is nothing compared to the daily environmental and human cost in the Middle East. I don't hear you objecting to the things that go on over there. The Saudis cut off people's heads."

Clete lit his cigarette, the smoke drifting out of his mouth, his eyes focused on nothing. "This is our state, Jack. You and your friends are tourists," he said.

"I have news for you, friend," Donnelly said. "The sidewalks you stand on are paid for with money you borrow from foreigners."

Donnelly and Woolsey got in the backseat of the Buick. The two security men looked at us from behind their shades, their expressions flat. The wind blew the coat of the man with the bump on his nose, exposing the strap of a shoulder holster. Then all of them drove away, leaving Clete and me in the parking lot, leaves swirling around our shoes.

"How did that just happen?" Clete said.

"We came on their turf. It was a mistake," I said. "Take a look across the street."

"At what?"

"The guy in the pickup truck. It's Jesse Leboeuf," I said.

"What's he doing here?"

"I hate to guess," I replied. I began punching in a 911 on my cell phone, but Leboeuf pulled into the traffic before I had finished.

WHEN I GOT back to the department, I asked Wally, our head dispatcher, if he had received any reports on Jesse Leboeuf. Wally had been with the department for thirty-two years and still lived with his mother and never answered a question directly if there was a chance of turning it into a two-cushion bank shot. A conversation with Wally was as close to water torture as it comes. "You mean the Breat'alyzer test or causing a disturbance on Railroad Avenue?" he said.

"His daughter told me he was drunk. I guess she knew what she was talking about," I said, determined not to take the bait.

"I t'ink he got a free pass on the Breat'alyzer."

"Really? Thanks for the feedback."

I started toward my office.

"Down on Railroad, it was a li'l different," he said.

"That's right, you did mention something about Railroad Avenue. Leboeuf got into it with somebody?"

"You could say that. A new black pimp was working the corner wit' a couple of rock queens. They were both white. Leboeuf t'ought he'd straighten him out."

"No kidding?"

"A kid wit' a slingshot fired a marble into the back of Leboeuf's head."

"It couldn't happen to a more deserving guy."

"You know what I t'ink?"

"What's that, Wally?"

"Pretty sad, an old man full of hate like that, carrying it around all these years."

"Don't waste your sympathies."

"He had a t'row-down on him."

I stopped. "Say again?"

"He was carrying a drop. He's retired. He don't have no business doing that. He don't like you, Dave. I wouldn't want a man like that mad at me, no."

I went to my office and called Varina at her father's home on Cypremort Point.

"Oh, you again. How nice of you to call," she said.

"Your father is obviously having some kind of breakdown. Either get him under control or we'll lock him up," I said.

"He's taking a nap now and he's fine, no thanks to you."

"I saw him earlier today in Lafayette. I think he was following me."

"Don't flatter yourself. He had a medical appointment there," she said.

"Think back, Varina. My family and I have done nothing to harm you. I tried to be your friend. Alafair popped you in the mouth, but only after you verbally abused her friend. Isn't it time to man up, or woman up, or whatever you want to call it, and stop blaming others for your problems?"

"I can't express how I feel about you," she replied.

So much for the Aquinian advice about erring on the side of charity, I thought.

HELEN CALLED ME from outside the IC unit in Shreveport where her half sister was hospitalized and asked how everything was going in the department. Obviously, she was asking how everything was going with me and Clete and Gretchen Horowitz and my circular and unproductive investigation into the murder of Blue Melton. I didn't know what to tell her. I didn't want to deceive her, nor did I want to add to her troubles while she was already dealing with her half sister's near-fatal injuries. "We're doing okay," I said. "When do you think you might be coming back?"

"Two or three days, I think. I get the sense you want to ask me or tell me something."

"Jesse Leboeuf has been on a drunk and might try to square an old beef or two."

"If you have to, put him in the jail ward at Iberia General. I'll have a talk with him when I get back."

"The situation with Gretchen Horowitz has gotten a little more complicated."

"In what way?"

"She told Clete she was given a contract on me and Alafair. She was also told to clip Clete."

"You and Clete clean this shit up, Pops. I don't want to hear that girl's name again."

"Clean it up how?"

"I don't care. Just do it. I'm too old for this kiddie-car stuff, and so are you. What else is going on?"

"Kiddie-car stuff?"

"Yeah, because I have a hard time taking this girl seriously. If she wants to be Bonnie Parker, she's picked a pretty small stage to do it on. Anything else on your mind?"

"I think Alexis Dupree was an SS officer at Auschwitz. I think his real name is Karl Engels."

"You've got evidence to that effect?"

"Nothing that's going to put him in handcuffs."

I could hear her breathing in the silence. "Okay, stay with it," she said. "One way or another, the Duprees are mixed up with Tee Jolie's disappearance and the murder of her sister. Let's use whatever we can to make life interesting for them."

"I've got to be honest with you, Helen. Gretchen Horowitz is the real deal. She's not to be taken lightly."

"Look, sometimes I turn a deaf ear to you and pretend you create problems that in actuality are already there. You're bothered by injustice and can't rest till you set things right. In other words, you're an ongoing pain in the ass. In spite of that, I don't know what I'd do without you. Say a prayer for Ilene. She might not make it."

"I'm sorry, Helen."

"Don't let me down, bwana," she said, and hung up.

CHAPTER
22

THAT NIGHT IT rained again, the way it always does with the advent of winter in Louisiana, clogging the rain gutters on the house with leaves, washing the dust and black lint from the sugar mills out of the trees, sometimes filling the air with a smell that has the bright clarity of rubbing alcohol. These things are natural and good, I would tell myself, but sometimes the ticking of the rain on a windowsill or in an aluminum pet bowl can take on a senseless, metronomic beat like a windup clock that has no hands and that serves no purpose except to tell you your time is running out.

I have never liked sleep. It has always been my enemy. Long before I went to Vietnam, I had nightmares about a man named Mack. He was a professional bourré and blackjack dealer in the gambling clubs and brothels of St. Landry Parish. He seduced my mother when she was drunk and blackmailed her and made her his mistress while my father was working on a drill rig offshore or fur-trapping on Marsh Island. Mack drowned my cats and held his fingers to my nose after he was with my mother. I hated him more than any man I had ever met, and in Vietnam I sometimes saw his face superimposed on those of the Asian men I killed.

Mack lived in my head for many years and dissipated in importance only after I began to assemble a new collection of specters and demons—the shadowy figures who came out of the trees and used

340

our 105 duds to booby-trap a night trail, the suspended corpse of a suicide dancing with maggots that Clete and I cut down from a rafter, the discovery of a child inside a refrigerator that had been abandoned in a field not far from a playground, a black man strapped in a heavy oak chair, his face and nappy hair bejeweled with sweat just before the hood was dropped over his face.

It's my belief that images like these cannot be exorcised from one's memory. They travel with you wherever you go and wait for their moment to come aborning again. If you are rested and the day is sunny and cool and filled with the fragrances of spring, the images will probably remain dormant and seem to have little application in your life. If you are fatigued or irritable or depressed or down with the flu, you'll probably be presented with a ticket to your unconscious, and the journey will not be a pleasant one. One thing you can count on: Sleep is a flip of the coin, and you are powerless inside its clutches unless you're willing to drink or drug yourself into oblivion.

It was 11:07 P.M., and I was reading under the lamp in the living room. The kitchen was dark and I could see the message light on the machine blinking on and off, like a hot drop of blood that glowed and died and then glowed again. Molly and Alafair were awake, and I could have gotten up and retrieved the message without disturbing anyone, but I didn't want to, in the same way you sometimes hesitate to answer the door when the knock is more forceful than it should be, the face of your visitor obscured by shadows.

"Did you drop your pills in the bathroom sink?" Molly said behind my chair.

"Maybe. I don't remember," I replied.

"Over half of them are gone. They have morphine in them, Dave."

"I know that. That's why I try not to use them."

"But you've been taking them?"

"I was taking them two or three times a week. Maybe not even that much. I haven't felt a need for them in the last few days."

She sat down across from me, the capped plastic bottle in her hand. She held her eyes on mine. "Can you go without them altogether?"

"Yeah, toss them out. I should have done that already." But my words sounded both hollow and foolish, like those of a man standing in a breadline and pretending he doesn't need to be there.

"It's late. Let's go to sleep," she said.

I closed my book and looked at the title. It was a novel about British soldiers in the Great War, written by an eloquent man who had been gassed and wounded and had seen his best friends mowed down by Maxim guns, but I could remember hardly anything in it, as though my eyes had moved across fifty pages and registered almost nothing. "Maybe you and Alafair should visit your aunt in Galveston," I said. "Just for a few days."

"We're not going anywhere."

I stood up and pulled the tiny chain on the reading lamp. Through the doorway, I could see the reflection of the red light in the window glass above the sink. The driveway was completely black, and in the window glass, the red light was like a beacon on a dark sea. "Tee Jolie is out there somewhere," I said.

"She's dead, Dave."

"I don't believe that. She brought me the iPod in the recovery unit in New Orleans. I talked to her on the phone. She's alive."

"I can't have this kind of conversation with you anymore," Molly said.

She went back in the bedroom and closed the door. I sat for a long time in the dark, the message machine blinking in sync with my heart, daring me to push the play button. Maybe with a touch of the finger, I could be back on the full-tilt boogie, free of worry and moral complications, delighting in the violence I could visit upon my enemies, getting back on the grog at the same time, surrendering myself each day to the incremental alcoholic death that preempted my fear of the grave.

The rain seemed to rekindle its energies, thudding as hard as hail on the roof. I walked into the kitchen and stood at the counter and pressed the play button with my thumb.

"Hi, Mr. Dave," the voice said. "I hope you don't mind me bothering you again, but I'm real scared. There ain't nobody here except a nurse and a doctor that comes sometimes 'cause of a problem I got. I need to get off this island, but I ain't sure where it is. The people that owns it has got a big boat. One of the men here said we was sout'east of the chandelier. That don't make no sense. Mr. Dave, the man I'm wit' is a good man, but I ain't sure about nothing no more. I don't know where Blue is at. They say she's all right, that she went out to Hollywood 'cause her voice is good as mine is and she's gonna do fine out there. The medicine they been giving me makes me kind of crazy. I ain't sure what to believe."

On the machine I heard a door slam in the background and another voice speaking, one I didn't recognize. Then the recording ended.

The Chandeleur Islands, I thought. The barrier islands that formed the most eastern extreme of Louisiana's landmass. That had to be it. I woke Molly and asked her to come into the kitchen. She was half asleep, her cheek printed by the pillow. "I thought I heard a woman's voice," she said.

"You did. Listen to this."

I replayed Tee Jolie's message. When it was over, Molly sat down by the breakfast table and stared at me. She was wearing a pink nightgown and fluffy slippers. She seemed dazed, as though she couldn't extract herself from a dream.

"You're not going to say anything?" I asked.

"Don't get anywhere near this."

"She's asking for help."

"It's a setup."

"You're wrong. Tee Jolie would never do anything like that."

"When will you stop?"

"Stop what?"

"Believing people who know your weakness and use it against you."

"Mind telling me what this great weakness is?"

"You're willing to love people who are corrupt to the core. You turn them into something they're not, and we pay the price for it."

I took a carton of milk out of the icebox and walked down to the picnic table in the backyard and sat down with my back to the house and drank the carton half empty. I could hear Tripod's chain tinkling as he dragged it down the wire stretched between two live oaks. I reached down and picked him up and set him on my lap. He rubbed his head against my chest and flipped over on his back, waiting for me to scratch his stomach, his thick tail swishing back and forth. A tug passed on the bayou, its green and red running lights on, its wake slapping against the cypress roots. I longed to pour a half pint of whiskey into the milk carton and chugalug it in one long swallow, until I pushed all light out of my eyes and sound from my ears and thoughts from my mind. At that moment I would have swallowed broken glass for a drink. I knew I would not fall asleep before dawn.

At 6:13 A.M., just as I finally nodded off, the phone rang. It was Clete Purcel. "Gretchen's back from Miami," he said.

"So what?" I said.

"She says she found her mother."

"Keep her away from Molly and Alafair and me."

I hung up the phone, missing the cradle and dropping the receiver on the floor, waking my wife.

JESSE LEBOEUF HAD never thought of himself as a prejudiced man. In his mind, he was a realist who looked upon people for what they were and what they were not, and he did not understand why that was considered bad in the eyes of others. People of color did not respect a white man who lowered himself to their level. Nor did they wish to live with whites or be on an equal plane with them. Any white person who had grown up with them knew that and honored the separations inherent in southern culture. Saturday-night nigger-knocking was a rite of passage. If anyone was to blame for it, it was the United States Supreme Court and the decision to integrate the schools. Shooting Negroes with BB guns and slingshots and throwing firecrackers on the galleries and roofs of their homes didn't cause long-term damage to anyone. They had to pay some dues, like every immigrant group, if they wanted to live in a country like this. How many people in those homes had been born in Charity Hospital and raised on welfare? Answer: all of them. How would they like living in straw villages back in Africa, with lions prowling around the neighborhood?

But when Jesse reviewed his life, he stumbled across an inalterable fact about himself that he didn't like to brood upon. In one way or another, he had always needed to be around people of color. He not only went to bed with Negro girls and women as a teenager, he found himself coming back for more well into his forties. They feared him and shrank under his weight and cigarette odor and the density of his breath, while their men slunk away into the shadows, the whites of their eyes yellow and shiny with shame. After each excursion into the black district, Jesse felt a sense of power and control that no other experience provided him. Sometimes he made a point of drinking in a mulatto bar near Hopkins just after visiting a crib, drinking out of a bottle of Jax in the corner, looking nakedly into the faces of the patrons. His sun-browned skin was almost as dark as theirs, but he always wore khaki clothes and half-top boots and a fedora and a Lima watch fob, like a foreman or a plantation overseer would wear. The discomfort Jesse caused in others was testimony that the power in his genitals and the manly odor in his clothes were not cosmetic.

It ended with affirmative action and the hiring of black sheriff's deputies and city police officers. It had taken Jesse thirteen years and three state examinations and four semesters of night classes at a community college to make plainclothes. In one day, a black man was given the same pay grade as he and assigned as his investigative partner. The black man lasted two months with Jesse before he resigned and went to work for the state police.

Jesse became a lone wolf and was nicknamed "Loup" by his colleagues. If an arrest might get messy or require undue paperwork, the Loup was sent in. If the suspect had shot a cop or raped a child or repeatedly terrorized a neighborhood and barricaded himself in a house, there was only one man for the job; the Loup went in carrying a cut-down twelve-gauge pump loaded with pumpkin balls and double-aught bucks. The paramedics would have the body bag already unzipped and spread open on the gurney, ready for business.

Jesse knew a trade-off had been made without his consent. He was a useful tool, a garbage collector in a cheap suit, a lightning bolt that stayed in the sheriff's quiver until a dirty job came along that no one wanted to touch. In the meantime, black law officers, some of them female, had replaced him as a symbol of authority in the black neighborhoods, and Jesse Leboeuf had become one more uneducated aging white man, one who no longer had sexual access to the women whose availability he had always taken for granted.

At 5:46 A.M. Saturday, he drove his pickup truck down East Main through the historical district. The street was empty, the lawns blue-green in the poor light, the caladiums and hydrangeas beaded with dew, the bayou smoking just beyond the oaks and cypress trees that grew along the bank. Up ahead he could see the Shadows, and across the street from it, the plantation overseer's house that had been converted into a restaurant. Jesse had never been impressed by historical relics. The rich were the rich, and he wished a pox on every one of them, both the living and the dead.

He peered through his windshield at a modest shotgun home with a small screened gallery and ceiling-high windows and ventilated green storm shutters. No lights were on in the house. A rolled newspaper lay on the front steps. Two compact cars and a pickup truck were parked in the driveway and under the porte cochere, their windows running with moisture. He went around the block and this time pulled to the curb, under the overhang of a giant live oak, two houses up from the home of the homicide detective who Jesse believed had besmirched his reputation and humiliated him in front of his peers.

He cut the engine and lit an unfiltered cigarette and sipped from a pint bottle of orange-flavored vodka. The cigarette smoke went down into his lungs like an old friend, blooming in his chest, reassuring him that his heart problems had nothing to do with nicotine. He'd acquired several drops over the years, but nobody had seen the one he had on him now. It was a five-chamber .22 revolver he had taken off a New Orleans prostitute. He had burned the serial numbers with acid and reverse-wrapped the wood grips with electrician's tape and coated the steel surfaces with a viscous layer of oil. The possibilities of lifting a print from it were between remote and non-existent. The challenge was to arrange the situation. It couldn't be in the home; it would have to be someplace else, where there would be no adult witness.

He took another drink from the bottle and another deep puff off his cigarette, letting the exhaled smoke drift through his fingers. He saw himself squeezing the trigger of his .38 snub, the flash leaping from the muzzle and either side of the chamber, the bullet catching the target unaware, pocking a single hole in the middle of the forehead, the facial muscles collapsing as the brain turned to mush. Then he would wrap the drop in his victim's hand and fire a round into a wall. It was that easy. In his lifetime, he had never seen a cop go down for an execution if there were no witnesses and it was done right.

The street was completely silent, the lawns empty, the Victorian and antebellum homes overhung by trees dripping with Spanish moss. The setting was like a replication of everything that he secretly hated. Was he being silently mocked for the fact and circumstances of his birth? He had picked cotton and broken corn and mucked out cow stalls before ever seeing the inside of a school. He wondered if anyone in those houses had seen the tips of a child's fingers bleed on a cotton boll.

He looked at the shotgun house again. *Wrong time, wrong place,* he thought. Down the bayou in Jeanerette, there was another person he might visit, someone who deserved an experience he hadn't given a woman in a long time. He wet his lips at the prospect. As he pulled away from the curb, he thought he heard the deep-throated rumble of dual exhausts echoing off a row of buildings, the kind of sound he associated with hot rods and Hollywood mufflers. Then the sound thinned and disappeared over on St. Peter Street, and he gave it no more thought.

JESSE TOOK THE back road into Jeanerette and crossed the drawbridge by a massive white-pillared home surrounded by live oaks whose leaves trembled simultaneously when the wind gusted. The eastern sky was black with rain clouds, the moon still up, the surface of the bayou coated with fog as white and thick as cotton. Catin Segura's home was not hard to find. It was the last one on the block, down by the water, in a neighborhood of small wood-frame houses. Her cruiser was parked in the gravel driveway, and she had put new screens on her gallery and planted flowers in all the beds and window boxes and nailed a big birdhouse painted like the American flag in a pecan tree. A tricycle rested on its side in the yard. A plastic-bladed whirligig fastened to a rain gutter was spinning and clicking in the breeze. Other than the whirligig, there was no movement or sound anywhere on the short block where Catin lived with her two children.

Jesse had one more drink and capped his bottle and rolled down his windows. He lit another cigarette and draped one arm over the steering wheel and thought about his alternatives. There were two or three ways to go. He could get rough with her in a major way and teach her a lesson in the bedroom that she would never forget and probably would be afraid to report. Or he could park one in her ear with his .38 snub and put the drop in her hand and tack a small holster for it under the breakfast table. He could take a flesh wound if he had to. He drew in on his cigarette and heard the paper crisp and burn. He took the cigarette from his mouth, holding it with his thumb and three fingers, exhaling through his nostrils, his thoughts coming together, an image forming before his eyes. He dropped the cigarette out the window and heard it hiss in a puddle of water. He reached into his glove box and removed a pair of handcuffs and the clip-on holster that contained his .38 snub. Then he got out of the truck and put on his coat and took his old fedora from behind the seat and put it on his head and threaded the handcuffs through the back of his belt. He worked a crick out of his neck and flexed his shoulders and opened and closed his hands. "Tell me how your life is going one hour from now, you black bitch," he said under his breath.

The screen door on the gallery was latched. He slipped a match cover between the jamb and the door and lifted the latch hook free of the eyelet and stepped inside. As he tapped on the inside door, he heard the same rumble of twin exhausts that he had heard in New Iberia. He looked down the street and caught a glimpse of a pickup painted with gray primer, its windows no more than one foot high. The vehicle went through the intersection, the driver easing off the accelerator and depressing the clutch to prevent the dual exhausts from waking up the neighborhood.

Catin opened the door on the night chain. Through the crack, he could see her slip showing where she had belted her bathrobe. He could also see the black sheen and the thickness of her hair and the way it curled on her cheeks, like a young girl might wear it. Her skin had the color and tone of melted chocolate; it didn't have the pink scars that black women often got from shucking oysters or fighting over their men in the juke. "What are you doing on my gallery?" she said.

"I came to apologize," he replied.

Her eyes went away from his face and focused on the latch hook that he had worked loose with his match cover. "I already forgave you. There's no reason for you to be here."

"I want to make it right, maybe do something for your kids."

"Don't you talk about my children."

"I can get them into a private school. My daughter's church has got a scholarship fund for minority children."

"I think you've been drinking."

"Getting to the end of the road isn't much fun. People deal with it in different ways."

"Go home, Mr. Jesse."

"I'm talking about death, Miss Catin."

"It's Deputy Segura."

"You know why each morning is a victory for an old person? It's 'cause most old people die at night. Can I have a cup of coffee? It's not a lot to ask."

He noticed the pause in her eyes and knew he'd found the weak spot. He could see into the house's interior now, a bedroom door that opened on two small beds, the covers tucked tightly in, the pillows fat and unmarked by the weight of anyone's head. The children were not home. He could feel a tingling in his hands and a stiffening in his loins.

"I can call a cab for you or have a cruiser drive you home," she said.

"You said you was a Christian woman."

"I am."

"But you'll turn me from your door?"

Her eyes were lidless, her face absolutely still.

"What do you think I'm gonna do? I'm an old man with congestive heart failure," he said.

She slid the night chain off the door and pulled it wide. "Sit at the dining room table. I'll start the coffee. There's a sweet roll on the plate."

He removed his hat and set it crown-down on the table and sat in a straight-back chair. "You have two, don't you?"

"Two what?"

"Children. That's what I always heard. You're a single mother. That's what they're calling it, aren't they?"

She was at the stove. She looked sideways at him. "What was that?"

"They use the term 'single mother' these days. That's not how we used to put it."

"I changed my mind. I want you to leave."

"Your robe isn't tied tight. You got a piece of string wrapped around your waist so it hikes up your slip and don't let it show below your hem. My mother learned that trick from a nigra woman we picked cotton with. Where's your children at?"

"I told you to leave."

He didn't move.

"Don't smoke in here," she said.

He blew out the paper match he had used to light his cigarette and dropped it in the flower vase on the table. "You came out to my house with Dave Robicheaux and treated me like I was dirt. Now I'm in your house."

"You stay back."

"You ever have a white man in your house?"

"Don't you dare put your hand on me."

"'Fraid my color is gonna rub off on you?"

"You're a sick man. And I pity you."

"Not as sick as you're fixing to be."

He hit her across the face with the flat of his hand. His hand was large and square and as rough-edged as an asbestos shingle, and the blow knocked the light out of her eyes and the shape out of her face. He grabbed her around the neck with his left arm and turned off the burner on the stove with his right hand. Then he pinched her chin and forced her to look into his face. "Where's your piece?"

Her left eye was red and watering where he had struck her. "You're going to prison."

"I doubt it. When I get finished with you, you'll think twice about the story you tell."

She spat in his face. He picked her up in the air, locking his hands behind her back, crushing her ribs, and slung her across the table. Then he wiped her saliva off his skin with a paper towel and lifted her to her feet and slammed her down in the chair where he had been sitting. "Want to answer my question? Where's your piece?"

She was bleeding from one nostril, her face trembling with shock. "You're a man and twice my size. But you're afraid of me."

He wrapped his fingers in the back of her hair and slowly raised her up from the chair, twisting her hair to get better purchase, making tears run from her eyes. He pulled his handcuffs from the back of his belt and bent one arm behind her and fitted a cuff on her wrist and pushed the steel tongue into the lock, then crimped the second cuff on her other wrist and squeezed the mechanisms so tight that the veins on the undersides of both wrists were bunched like blue string.

"You gonna yell?" he asked.

"No."

"That's what you say now." He wadded up three paper towels and pushed them into her mouth. "See, that takes away all temptation."

He walked her into her bedroom and opened a pocketknife and cut her robe down the back and her slip down the front and peeled both of them off her. Her eyes were bulging, sweat beading on her forehead, her breath starting to strangle on the paper towels that had become so soaked with saliva, they were slipping down her throat. He fitted his hand on her face and shoved her on the bed.

"Think this is tough?" he said. "Wait till we get to the main event."

Then he began to hurt her in ways she probably did not know existed. But Jesse Leboeuf had a problem he was not aware of. He'd always considered himself a cautious man. As a lawman, he had taken risks only when necessary and had never felt the need to prove himself to his colleagues. In fact, he looked upon most displays of bravery as theatrical, as confessions of fear. When the Loup went after a barricaded suspect with a cut-down Remington pump, he had no doubt about the outcome: Only one man would walk out of the building. Most perps, particularly the black ones, would drop their weapons and beg right before he pulled the trigger. The equation had always been simple: He was better than they were and they knew it, and as a result, he lived and they died. People could call it bravery if they wished; Jesse called it a fact of life.

He had shut the bedroom door and made sure the windows were down and the shades pulled all the way to the sills. He had turned on a floor fan to keep the room cool. He was environmentally safe and comfortable and sealed off from the outside world and could do whatever he wanted and take all the time in the world doing it. All these were unconscious conclusions that he considered a done deal.

Until he heard the doorknob twist behind him and the door scrape across the throw rug that had knotted under his boot when he shoved Catin Segura into the room. He rose naked from the bed, his body hair glistening with sweat, his mouth and throat choked with phlegm. "Who are you?" he said.

The figure was wearing a hooded jacket and a face mask made of digital camouflage and was pointing a Sig Sauer P226 at him, a sound suppressor screwed onto the barrel. His eyes drifted to Catin's dresser, where he had placed his .38 snub in its clip-on holster. The .38 was under five feet from where he stood, but the distance could have been five miles. There was salt in his eyes, and he tried to wipe them clean with his fingers. His erection had died, and a vinegary stench was rising from his armpits. He heard the roof creak in the wind.

"The woman invited me here. Ask her," he said. "Me and her go back. We got us an arrangement."

He realized he had started to raise his hands without being told and that a kettledrum was pounding in his head. What were the right words to say? What argument could he make to save his life? What verbal deceit could he perpetrate on the person aiming the silenced P226 at his sternum? "That's military-issue. I was a serviceman myself. United States Air Force," he said.

The figure moved toward the bed and, with a gloved hand, removed the wadded-up paper towels from Catin Segura's mouth.

"I know who you are," Jesse Leboeuf said. "You're the one that was out at the Point. You got no reason to kill me, girl."

He tried to hold his eyes on the masked figure, but they were burning so badly that he had to press his palms into the sockets. Red rings receded into his brain, and sweat ran down his chest and stomach and pubic hair and phallus onto the floor. *Reach out and take death into your arms and pull it inside your chest,* he heard a voice say. *It cain't be as bad as they say. A flash, a moment of pain, and then blackness. Don't be afraid.*

"Kill him," Catin Segura said.

"She tole me to do all this. The handcuffs, all of it," he said. "We need to talk this out. I'm gonna put on my pants, and we'll sit down and talk. You got to let me give my side of it."

"He's lying," the woman said from the bed.

"It's her that's lying. It's their nature. It's the way they was raised. I'm not being unfair. I'm not afraid. I know you're probably a good person. I just want to talk."

But he was terrified and acted it. He ran for the bathroom, where he had not locked the window, slipping on the rug, slamming into the doorframe, trying to right himself with one hand and reach a spot that was beyond the shooter's angle of fire. His flab and his genitalia jiggled on his frame; his breath heaved in his chest; his heart felt like it was wrapped with wire. He heard a sound that was like a sudden puncture and the brief escape of air from a tire, just as a round cored through his left buttock and exited his thigh, slinging a horsetail of blood across the wall. He tried to grab the windowsill with one hand and mount the toilet seat so he could knock the screen out of the window with his head and leap to the ground. Then he heard the *phitt* of the suppressor again. The round hit him with the bone-deep dullness of a ball-peen hammer thudding between his shoulder blades, the bullet punching an exit hole above his right nipple. He fell sideways and tumbled over the edge of the bathtub, bringing the shower curtain down on top of him, his legs spread over the tub's rim as though they had been fitted into stirrups.

The figure stood above him, aiming with both hands, arms outstretched. The suppressor was pointed directly at his mouth. Jesse tried to look through the slits in the mask at the shooter's eyes. Were they lavender? If he could only explain, he thought. If someone could reach back in time and find the moment when everything went wrong, if someone could understand that he didn't plan this, that this was the hand he was dealt and it was not of his choosing. If others could understand that, they could all agree to go away and let the past be the past and forget about the injuries he had done to his fellow man and let him start all over. If he could just find the right words.

"None of y'all know what it was like," he said. "I broke corn when I was five. My daddy worked nights eleven years to buy ten acres."

He tried to make himself stare into the suppressor, but he couldn't do it. He saw a soapy pink bubble rise from the hole in his chest. The tears in his eyes distorted the room as though he were looking at the world from the bottom of a goldfish bowl. "Tell Varina—"

His lung was collapsing, and he couldn't force the words out of his mouth. The figure stepped closer, then squatted next to the tub, gripping the rim with one hand, holding the P226 with the other.

Jesse waited for the round that would rip through his brain and end the bubbling sound in his throat, but it didn't happen. He shut his eyes and whispered hoarsely at the masked face. It was a phrase he had learned from his French-speaking father when the father talked about Jesse's baby sister. Then the words seemed to die on his lips. For just a moment, Jesse Leboeuf thought he heard black people laughing. Oddly, they were not black people in a juke joint, nor were they laughing at him behind his back, as they did when he first wore a policeman's uniform. They were in a cotton field in North Louisiana at sunset, and the sky and the earth were red and the plants were a deep green and he could smell rain and see it blowing like spun glass in the distance. It was Juneteenth, Emancipation Day, and all the darkies in the parish would be headed into town soon, and he wondered why he hadn't chosen to celebrate the occasion with them. They had always been kind to him and let him ride on the back of the flatbed when they drove to town, all of them rocking back and forth with the sway of the truck, their bodies warm with the heat of the day, smelling slightly in a good way of the sweat from their work, their legs hanging down in the dust, the children breaking up a watermelon in big meaty chunks. Why hadn't he gone with them? It would have been fun. He opened his eyes one more time and realized a terrible transformation was taking place in him. He was no longer Jesse Leboeuf. He was dissolving into seawater, his tissue and veins melting and running down his fingertips and pooling around his buttocks. He heard a loud sucking sound and felt himself swirling through the chrome-ringed drain hole at the bottom of the tub. Then he was gone, just like that, twisting in a silvery coil down a pipe to a place where no one would ever celebrate Juneteenth.

CHAPTER
23

Catin Segura called in the 911 herself. The first emergency personnel to arrive were the Acadian Ambulance Service, followed by deputies from Iberia and St. Mary Parish. Because it was Saturday, many of the neighbors had slept in and seen nothing unusual. When I arrived, the paramedics were already in the bedroom with Catin. There was blood on the sheets and the pillowcase. Her face was dilated with bruises, both wrists scraped raw by Leboeuf's handcuffs. Through the bathroom door, I could see his bare feet and legs extending over the edge of the tub. No brass had been found in the bedroom or the bathroom.

"How'd Leboeuf get in?" I asked her.

She told me. Then she looked at the two paramedics. "Can you guys give us a minute?" I asked.

They went out of the room, and she told me what Leboeuf had done to her. Her eyes were dulled over, her voice hardly audible, as though she did not want to hear the things she was saying. Twice she had to stop and start over. "It's his smell," she said.

"What?"

"It's on my skin and inside my head. I'll never be able to wash it off me."

"No, this man is dead and has no power over you, Catin. He died the death of an evil man and took his evil with him. Eventually, you'll think of him as a pitiful creature flailing his arms inside a furnace of his own creation. He can't touch you. You're a decent and fine lady. Nothing Leboeuf did can change the good human being that you are."

Her eyes never blinked and never left mine. A St. Mary crime-scene investigator and a female deputy from Iberia Parish were waiting in the doorway. I asked them for a few more minutes. They stepped outside on the gallery. "The shooter never spoke?" I said.

"No," Catin replied.

"You have no idea who the shooter was?"

"I already told you."

"Leboeuf took two rounds, then fell into the tub?"

"I can't keep it straight in my head. It was something like that."

"My guess is Leboeuf was still alive after he fell into the bathtub. But there was no coup de grâce. How do you explain that?"

"I don't know. My children stayed overnight with their grandmother. I want to see them," she said.

"I'll take them up to Iberia General to see you. First you have to help me, Catin."

"Leboeuf said something in what sounded like French. I don't speak French. I don't care what he said or didn't say. There's something I left out. I told the person in the mask to kill him. I wanted him to suffer, too."

I looked over my shoulder at the doorway. "That has no bearing on what occurred. You roger that, Cat?"

She nodded.

"You called the shooter a person, not a man," I said. "Was the shooter a woman?"

She looked at the water spots in the wallpaper and on the ceiling. "I'm tired."

"Who took the cuffs off you?"

"The person did."

"And you called 911 immediately?"

"Jesse Leboeuf was left on the street when he should have been in a cage. The department didn't save my life," she said. "The shooter did. I hope Jesse Leboeuf is in hell. It's a sin for me to think that way, and it bothers me real bad."

I pressed her hand in mine. "It's the way you're supposed to feel," I said.

I waved to the paramedics to come back in the bedroom, then I picked up Jesse Leboeuf's coat and shirt and underwear and hat and half-top boots and holstered .38 snub-nose and stuffed them in a plastic garbage bag. I didn't hand them over to the crime-scene investigator. I went into the kitchen, where I could be alone, and removed his wallet from his trousers and thumbed through all the compartments. In it was a color photograph of Leboeuf with a little girl on a beach, the waves slate-green and capping behind them. The little girl had curly brown hair and was holding an ice-cream cone and smiling at the camera. Deeper in the wallet, I found a folded receipt for airplane fuel. The name of the vendor was the same as the boat dock whose phone number we had pulled from Jesse Leboeuf's telephone records. Written in pencil on the back were two navigational coordinates and the words "Watch downdrafts and pilings at west end of cove."

I put the gas receipt in my shirt pocket and replaced the rest of Leboeuf's belongings in the bag. The female deputy from the Iberia department was watching me. "What are you doing, Streak?" she asked.

"My job."

Her name was Julie Ardoin. She was a small brunette woman with dark eyes who always looked too small for her uniform. Her husband had committed suicide and left her on her own, and when she was angered, her stare could make you blink. "Good. You gonna handle the notification?" she said.

I CALLED MOLLY and told her I wouldn't be home until noon, then drove down to the Leboeuf home on Cypremort Point. Theologians and philosophers try to understand and explain the nature of God with varying degrees of success and failure. I admire their efforts. But I've never come to an understanding of man's nature, much less God's. Does it make sense that the same species that created Athenian democracy and the Golden Age of Pericles and the city of Florence also gifted us with the Inquisition and Dresden and the

Nanking Massacre? My insight into my fellow man is probably less informed than it was half a century ago. At my age, that's not a reassuring thought.

When I pulled in to Varina Leboeuf's gravel driveway, the tide was coming in and the sky was lidded with lead-colored clouds and waves were breaking against the great chunks of broken concrete that Jesse Leboeuf had dumped on the back of his property to prevent erosion. Varina opened the inside door onto the screened veranda and walked down the stairs toward my cruiser. I got out and closed the car door behind me and stared into her face. I could hear wind chimes and leaves rustling and the fronds of a palm tree clattering, and smell the salt in the bay, all the indicators of life that were ongoing and unchanged among the quick but that were gone forever for Varina's father.

I wanted to state what had happened and get back to town. I wished I had violated protocol and telephoned. I wanted badly to be somewhere else.

I had lost the respect I once had for Varina; I had come to think of her as treacherous and dishonest. I bore her even greater resentment for her seduction and manipulation of a good man like Clete Purcel. But I resented her most because she reminded me in some ways of Tee Jolie Melton. Both women came out of an earlier time. They were alluring and outrageous and irreverent, almost childlike in their profligacy, more victim than libertine. That was the irony of falling in love with my home state, the Great Whore of Babylon. You did not rise easily from the caress of her thighs, and when you did, you had to accept the fact that others had used her, too, and poisoned her womb and left a fibrous black tuber growing inside her.

Varina wasn't over ten feet from me now, her hair blowing over her brow, her mouth vulnerable, like that of a child about to be scolded. I looked at the waves cresting and breaking into foam on the chunks of concrete, the petals on the Japanese tulip tree shredding in the wind.

"My father isn't here. He went fishing," she said. "He made a ham-and-egg sandwich and was eating it when he drove out at daybreak. I saw him."

"No, that's not where he went."

"He put his poles and tackle box and a shiner bucket in the back of the truck. He wasn't drinking. He went to bed early last night. Don't tell me he's drunk, Dave. I know better. He's going to be fine."

"Your father is dead."

She started to speak, but her eyes filmed and went out of focus.

"Maybe we should go inside," I said.

"He was in an accident? He's dead in an accident?" she said, turning her head away as though avoiding her own words.

"He was shot to death in Jeanerette."

She placed one hand on the rope of a swing suspended from an oak limb. The blood had drained from her face. She was wearing a yellow cowboy shirt with the top snap undone. She began pushing on it with her thumb, knotting the fabric, unable to snap the brad into place, her eyes fastened on mine. "He went to a bar?"

"He was in the home of an Iberia Parish deputy sheriff. I think you know who I'm talking about."

"No, I don't. He was going fishing. He'd been looking forward to it all week."

"He raped and sodomized Catin Segura. He also beat her severely. A third party came into the house and shot and killed him."

"My father isn't a rapist. Why are you saying all this?" Her breath was coming too fast, she was like someone verging on hyperventilation, the color in her face changing.

"Do you have any idea who the shooter was?" I asked.

"I have to sit down. This is a trap of some kind. I know you, Dave. You were out to get my father."

"You don't know me at all. I always believed in you. I thought you were stand-up and honorable. I believed you beat the male-chauvinist oil bums around here at their own game. I was always on your side, but you never saw that."

She was crying now, unashamedly, without anger or heat. There was a red dot on her chest where she had almost cut herself trying to snap her shirt. "Where is he?" she said.

"At Iberia General. Catin is at Iberia General, too. She has two children. I promised to take them to see her. It will probably be years before Catin overcomes the damage that's been done to her. Would it hurt if you talked to her?"

"Me?"

"Sometimes the Man Upstairs gives us a chance to turn things around in a way we never see coming. Do Catin and yourself a favor, Varina."

"You want me to go in there and talk to the woman who claims she was sodomized by my father?"

"I saw her at the crime scene under an hour ago. What happened to that woman is not a claim."

I was not sure she was hearing me anymore. She looked as though she were drowning, her eye shadow running, her cheeks wet. She started walking toward the kitchen entrance of her house, trying to hold her back straight, almost twisting her ankle when she stepped in a depression. I caught up with her and put my arm around her shoulders. I thought she might resist, but she didn't.

"Listen to me. Cut loose from that fraudulent preacher, the Duprees, Lamont Woolsey, the rackets they're involved in, the whole nefarious business. There's still time to turn it around. Say 'full throttle and fuck it' and get this stuff out of your life forever."

Then she did one of the most bizarre things I had ever seen a bereaved person do. She went up the steps into her kitchen and took a half-gallon container of French-vanilla ice cream out of the freezer and sat at the same table where she had gotten Clete Purcel loaded and began eating the ice cream with a spoon, scraping its frozen hardness into curlicues, as though she were the only person in the room.

"Will you be all right if I leave?" I asked.

She looked at me blankly. I repeated my question.

"Look in the garage. You'll see his spinning rod and ice chest and tackle box are gone. He was going to stop for shiners. He was going after sac-a-lait at Henderson Swamp."

I put my business card on the table. "I'm sorry for your loss, Varina."

She rested her forehead on her hand, her face wan. "He was poor and uneducated. Nobody ever helped him. All y'all did was condemn him. You should have helped him, Dave. You grew up poor. Your

parents were illiterate, just like his. You could have been his friend
and helped him, but you didn't."

"Not everyone who grew up poor took out his grief on people
of color. Your father wanted to do payback on me and probably
took Catin as a second choice. That doesn't make me feel too good,
Varina," I said. "Jesse victimized black women for decades. This time
he got nailed. That's the sum total of what happened. If you want
to hear the truth, visit Iberia General and talk to Catin and cut the
bullshit."

"How can you talk to me like this? I just lost my father."

"Your father dealt the play. Unless you accept that fact, you'll
carry his anger the rest of your life."

"I wouldn't go in that woman's hospital room at gunpoint."

"Good-bye, Varina," I said.

I went outside and closed the screen door softly behind me and
walked to the cruiser. I thought I heard her crying, but I had decided
that Varina Leboeuf could not be helped by me or probably anyone
else. I was glad that I was alive and that I owned my own soul and
that I didn't have to drink. To others, these might seem like minor
victories, but when you are in the presence of the genuinely afflicted,
you realize that the smallest gifts can be greater in value than the
conquest of nations.

I went to an A.A. meeting and to Mass that afternoon. Molly and
I and Alafair had supper at home, and later, I drove to Clete's cottage at the motor court. I knocked on the door, then realized he was
down the slope, standing under the oaks by the bayou's edge, fishing
in an unlikely spot with a cane pole. I knew he had heard the sound
of my pickup and that certainly he had heard me walk up behind
him. But he continued to study his bobber floating on the edge of
the current, the bronze glaze of the late sun flashing on the ripples.
A mosquito was drawing blood from the back of his neck. I wiped it
off his skin with my hand. "Got a reason for ignoring me?" I asked.

"I saw the news about Leboeuf, and I know what's coming," he
replied.

"Where is Gretchen?"

"I haven't seen her today."

"I need to bring her in."

"Then do it."

"She got her mother loose from those guys in Florida?"

"Yeah, I told you."

"How did she pull it off?"

"How do you think?" he said.

"She popped somebody?"

"Gretchen hasn't done anything that we haven't. We've probably done worse. Remember those Colombians? How about the time we went after Jimmie Lee Boggs? How about the way we nailed Louis Buchalter? Tell me you didn't enjoy being under a black flag."

I didn't want to think about the years Clete and I had stayed high on booze and racetracks and the smell of cordite and, in my case, rage-induced blackouts that allowed me to do things I would never do in a rational state of mind. I did not want to say any more about his daughter; nonetheless, I did. "I think Gretchen may have been lying to you, Clete."

He started to turn around but lifted his bobber out of the water and threw it and his sinker and hook farther out in the current. There was only a tiny thread of worm on the hook. "Lying about what?" he said.

"She claims she didn't clip Waylon Grimes and Frankie Giacano. She told you she only clipped Bix Golightly, a guy who molested her and had it coming."

"He didn't just molest her. He forced his dick into her mouth."

"I know that. But doesn't it seem too convenient that Grimes and Frankie Gee get capped by somebody else? How about the abduction of her mother? Now the mother is free, and as soon as Gretchen is back in New Iberia, Jesse Leboeuf gets his eggs scrambled. In every situation, Gretchen is the victim."

"Right or wrong, she's my daughter. Of all people, you should understand that."

"Alafair doesn't do contract hits for the Mob."

He broke his cane pole across his knee and flung both pieces into the bayou and watched them drift upstream and disappear inside the band of bronze sunlight still shimmering on the surface. He continued to stare at the sunset on the water, his huge back rising and falling in the shadows.

"You all right?" I said.

"You piss me off sometimes, Dave."

"Jesse Leboeuf ate two rounds before he fell into Catin Segura's bathtub. He said something to the shooter before he died. The shooter could have put one in his mouth or through his forehead but evidently decided not to. For whatever reason, the shooter showed mercy. If Gretchen popped him, maybe she had to. His piece was on the dresser. But she didn't shoot him a third time, which is what a contract hitter would have done."

"What did Leboeuf say?" Clete asked.

"Catin doesn't speak French."

"You think the shooter was Gretchen?"

"Who else?"

"Give her a chance. Let me talk to her before you bring her in."

"No dice."

"I don't know where she is. I'm telling you the truth."

I believed him. Clete had never lied to me, at least not deliberately. I unfolded the gas receipt I had taken from Jesse Leboeuf's wallet. "Leboeuf had this receipt for aviation fuel on him when he died. There're some landing coordinates written on it. The coordinates are southeast of the Chandeleur Islands. I think that's where Tee Jolie is."

Clete rubbed the spot where the mosquito had bitten him. "I don't like the things you said about Gretchen. Alafair had a loving home. Gretchen had guys shoving their cocks down her throat. That was a lousy crack you made."

"You're right. I'm sorry. You want in or out?"

He folded his arms and cleared his throat and spat. "You know anybody with a seaplane?" he asked.

"Yeah, Julie Ardoin."

"The one whose husband killed himself? She's kind of a pill, isn't she?"

"How many normal people does either of us know?" I replied.

JULIE'S HUSBAND HAD been an offshore pilot and an untreated drug addict and, finally, a Saran-wrapped fundamentalist fanatic who tried to cure his addiction with exorcism and tent revivals. The night he did the Big Exit, he parked his car in the yard and came in the house and told his wife he had a surprise for her, namely that he was clean and had found a cure. He retrieved a double-barrel shotgun from his car trunk and reentered the house and sat down in his favorite chair and told his wife to open her eyes. The butt of the shotgun was propped on the floor between his legs and the twin muzzles under his chin. He was grinning from ear to ear, as though he had found the secret to eternal wisdom. "Keep it between the ditches, baby cakes," he said. Then he depressed both triggers.

He left her with a Cessna 182 four-seat amphibian that she learned to pilot and used to pay off his debts. It was bright red and sleek and ideal for landing on freshwater lakes in the wetlands and even out on the salt if the wind wasn't too bad. Julie kept to herself and never discussed her husband's suicide, but sometimes I would see her blank out in the middle of a conversation, as though a movie projector had clicked on behind her eyelids and she was no longer with us.

Clete and I met her at New Iberia's small airport early Sunday morning. I had convinced Molly and Alafair to visit Molly's family in Beaumont for the day. I told Julie I would pay for her fuel and flight time if I couldn't put it on the department. I watched Clete load his duffel bag into the baggage compartment behind the cabin area. The muzzle of his AR-15 and my cut-down Remington pump were sticking out of the bag. "How hot is this going to be, Dave?" she asked.

"It's a flip of the coin," I said.

"I think I know that island," she said.

"You've been there?"

"I think Bob may have flown there." The wind was blowing hard out of a gray sky, flattening her khakis and blue cotton shirt against her body. "He got mixed up with a televangelist here'bouts. His name is Amidee Broussard. Bob took him on a couple of charters. You know who I'm talking about?"

"I sure do."

"What are we into, Streak?"

"I haven't figured it out. It involves the Dupree family in St. Mary Parish and maybe Varina Leboeuf. It may involve some oil guys, too. Maybe Tee Jolie Melton is on that island. Maybe these are the guys who killed her sister."

"Does Helen know about this trip?"

"She's got enough to worry about as it is."

"Tee Jolie Melton is a singer, right? Why would she be with the Duprees? They wouldn't take time to spit on most of us."

"What the Duprees can't have, they take."

"Tell your friend to ride in back."

Clete was on the edge of the tarmac, locking up his Cadillac. "You have a problem with Clete?" I asked.

"I need to balance the weight. I don't need a freight car in the front seat," she replied.

Clete opened the cabin door of the plane and threw a canvas rucksack of food inside. "Let's kick some butt," he said.

We took off buffeting in the wind and flew through a long stretch of low clouds full of rain and popped out on the other side into a patch of blue with a wonderful overview of Louisiana's wetlands, miles and miles of marsh grass and gum trees and rivers and bayous and flooded woods and sandspits covered with white birds. Through the side window, I could see the plane's shadow racing across an inaccessible lake that was lime green with algae; then the shadow seemed to leap from the water's surface and continue across a dense canopy of willows and cypresses that had turned gold with the season. From the air, the wetlands looked as virginal as they had been when John James Audubon first saw them, untouched by the ax and the dredge boat, thousands of square miles that are the greatest argument for the existence of God that I know of.

At the edge of the freshwater marsh, the canals that had been dug in grid fashion from the Gulf were now bulbous in shape, like giant worms that had been stepped on. I didn't want to look at it, in the same way that you don't want to look at people throwing litter out of a car window, or at pornography, or at an adult mistreating a child. This was even worse, because the injury to the wetlands was not the result of an individual act committed by a primitive and stupid person; it had been done collectively and with consent, and the damage it had caused was ongoing, with no end in sight. Eventually, most of the green-gray landmass below me would probably turn to silt and be washed away, and there would be no Ionian poet to witness and record its passing, as there had been for the ancient world.

I looked straight ahead at the darkening horizon and tried not to think the thoughts I was thinking. We crossed Lafourche and Jefferson parishes and flew over Barataria Bay and then crossed the long umbilical cord of land extending into the Gulf known as Plaquemines Parish, the old fiefdom of Leander Perez, a racist and dictatorial politician who ordered a Catholic church padlocked when the archbishop installed a black man as pastor. In the distance, I could see the smoky-green waters of the Gulf and, on the horizon, a line of blue-black thunderheads forked with lightning.

Clete was sleeping with his head on his chest. I could feel the airframe shuddering in the updrafts. "That's Grand Gosier Island," Julie said. "I'm going down on the deck. Hold on to your ass."

CHAPTER
24

WE MADE A wide turn east of the national wildlife refuge, rain hitting the windshield, the wings wet and slick and bright against a sky growing blacker by the minute. In the distance, I could see an island with a biscuit-colored apron of beach around it and a cove on the near side and a compound with palm trees in it. My ears began popping as we started our descent. "Anybody want a ham-and-onion sandwich?" Clete said.

"Tell him to shut up unless he wants to walk," Julie said, her eyes fixed on the cove and the waves sliding across a sandbar at the entrance and capping inside it.

We leveled out at about one hundred feet above the water, the rain hitting as hard as pellets on the windshield and cabin roof, a downdraft pounding us so violently that for a moment I didn't hear the engine. Up ahead I could see a strip of beach and pilings sticking out of the surf and what appeared to be a fortress with ten-foot walls around it. The tapered trunks of palm trees extended above the walls, beating in the wind. Our plane dipped down toward the water, then suddenly, the pontoons smacked the surface, and a dirty spray of foam blanketed the windshield and whipped back in strings across the side windows. A piling that probably once supported a dock or jetty missed the starboard wing by under six feet.

"Wow!" Clete said. "What do you do for kicks on your days off?"

Julie had cut the engine and was opening and closing her mouth, as though clearing her ears. "Would you mind?" she said.

"Mind what?" Clete said.

"Removing your onion breath from my face."

"Sorry," he said.

The rain was dancing on the chop and drumming on the wings and roof. The wind had pushed us into the shallows almost to the beach. There were wheels built into the pontoons, and I wondered why Julie didn't take us onto the sand, but I did not want to ask. I suspected she was feeling less and less sure about the wisdom of our mission, and I couldn't blame her. The walls around the house, like the house itself, were built of stucco and painted magenta. The glass from broken bottles was strewn along the top of the walls, but the security measure was of no value. The walls had been breached and reduced to rubble in several places, probably by Hurricane Katrina, exposing the cinder blocks inside. The interior of the compound was littered with flotsam and tangles of seaweed and shrimp nets and rotting tarps and hundreds of dead birds. The entirety of the beach was dotted with tar balls.

Clete and I put on our raincoats and hats and dropped down in the shallows up to our knees. Clete pulled his duffel bag from the baggage compartment and slung it over his shoulder. Through the rain, I could see a boat with two outboard engines and a small cabin moored on the south side of the island.

"I'll come with you," Julie said.

"Better stay here," I said. "We might have to get out of Dodge sooner than we planned."

"I thought I'd ask. Suit yourself," she said, her voice almost lost in the rain.

I smiled at her and tried to indicate I appreciated her gesture, but Julie was not the kind of person you made a show of protecting, not if you wanted to retain her friendship.

Clete and I walked out of the surf onto the sand. The smell from the dead birds was eyewatering. Clete looked over his shoulder at the plane and at the silhouette of Julie Ardoin inside it. "She's cute," he said.

"Will you concentrate on the objective?"

He blew his breath on his palm and smelled it. "You got any mints?" he said.

"I can't believe you."

"What did I do wrong? I just said she's cute. I take that back. She's more than cute. I bet she's heck on wheels. Is she getting it on with anybody?"

"When will you grow up?"

"I was just asking. When she yelled at me, my johnson started doing jumping jacks. That only happens with a very few women. It's not my fault." He pulled the Remington from the bag and handed it to me, then slung the AR-15 upside down on his right shoulder. "Oops, at ten o'clock," he said.

"What?"

"A campfire. By that boat. I saw somebody look at us from behind that tree."

Beyond the angle of the wall, I could see the salt-eaten, sun-scalded, wind-polished trunk and root system of a thick tree, one that had probably floated from the Mississippi or Alabama or Florida coastline. Clete and I worked our way along the edge of the wall until we reached a berm that sloped down to the beach and a polyethylene tent staked into the sand with aluminum pins. The rain had slackened, but the wind was blowing hard, popping the tent.

The barrel of the shotgun was cradled across my left arm; there was no round in the chamber. "My name is Detective Dave Robicheaux of the Iberia Parish Sheriff's Department," I said. "I need to see y'all's hands out here in the light. Do it now."

Clete moved left, unslinging his rifle. He had jungle-clipped two magazines together with electrician's tape, so when one magazine was empty, he could release it and insert the second one in the frame with hardly any interruption in his rate of fire. Water was dripping off his hat brim; his face looked as taut as a bleached muskmelon. He held up two fingers.

"Did you hear me?" I called out.

There was no answer.

I moved around to the front of the tent so I could see through the flap. The campfire had flattened in the wind and smelled from a can of beans that had boiled over and burned in the ashes. I could smell another odor, too.

The boy and the girl inside looked like they were in their late teens or early twenties. It wasn't their age that defined them. They were tanned from head to foot, as though they had never lived anywhere except under a blazing sun. Their eyes were lustrous and too big for their faces, like the eyes of anorexics or survivors of famines. The girl was sitting barefoot on an air mattress and wearing cutoff blue jeans and a halter. She pulled a shirt over her left arm, covering a tattoo, then took a hit off a pair of roach clips, even though I had already identified myself as a sheriff's detective. They said their names were Sybil and Rick and that they were from Mobile and were taking refuge from the storm. Rick wore sandals without socks and a Speedo swimsuit and a Gold's Gym T-shirt that exposed the bleached tips of the hair under his arms. He and Sybil climbed out of the tent, smiling broadly, neither of them showing any reaction to the cold wind.

"Who's up in the house?" I asked.

"They come and go, man. They've got this big fucking yacht you wouldn't believe," Rick said. His hair was black and oily and as thick as carpet weave; it hung in rings on his shoulders and resembled a seventeenth-century wig on his narrow head. "If the yacht is anchored on the other side of the island, that means they're here, no fucking mistake about it."

"That's what we were doing when y'all came," Sybil said. She opened her mouth wider than necessary when she spoke, and huffed out her breath instead of laughing.

"Doing what?" Clete asked.

"What Rick just said. We were fucking," she replied.

Clete looked at me.

"Why are y'all in a tent and not on your boat?" I asked.

"I got seasick and puked," Sybil said. She huffed out her breath. "I always get seasick when it rains, and then I puke. I got to brush my teeth."

"Who owns this place?" I said.

Rick turned to Sybil. "What's the name of that old dude?"

"I can't remember." She felt her head. "My hair's wet. This weather sucks. Where'd y'all say you're from?"

"New Iberia, Louisiana. I'm with the sheriff's department there."

"This isn't Louisiana, man," Rick said.

"Then where are we?" Clete asked.

"Fuck if I know," Rick replied.

Sybil combed her hair with her fingernails. The wind puffed the sleeves of her shirt, and I saw the tattoo of tangled barbed wire wrapped around her upper left arm. More important, I saw a red swastika tattooed like a clasp in the center of the wire.

"Is the old dude named Alexis Dupree?" I said.

"I don't know, man. He's just a kindly old dude, maybe a little weird, but there's a lot of that going around these days," Rick said. "Y'all want to eat some hot dogs? They're a little bit scorched, but they're not bad with mustard."

"I tell you what, you guys sit tight while my friend and I look around," I said. "By the way, Miss Sybil, I like your tattoo. Where'd you get it?"

She began fooling with her hands, examining them as though she had just discovered them. "I used to have this biker boyfriend that was kind of nuts on the subject of Nazi memorabilia and shit, so I told him I had a surprise for him on his birthday, but he got real pissed off 'cause he thought he was gonna get a blow job instead."

"Yeah, that's fucked up, isn't it, man?" Rick said, pointing a finger at me to emphasize his disappointment with the world.

"Like Dave says, hang loose. We'll be back and chat you up on some of this stuff," Clete said. "Go easy on the stash."

"That's not gonna be a problem, is it? Because if it is, we'll get rid of it," Rick said. He smiled vacantly. "Actually, we're in recovery now, so maybe we shouldn't be smoking it, huh?"

"A big ten-four on that," Clete said.

I heard Clete say "Jesus, God" under his breath, then we walked back up the berm and entered the compound and found ourselves surrounded by the stench of dead birds; their feathers ruffled every time the wind gusted. Clete choked and held a handkerchief to his mouth. "You see the tracks inside that girl's thighs?" he said.

"Yeah," I said, my eyes on the house.

"Think she and her boyfriend were coming here to shoot up?"

"Probably. Maybe Alexis Dupree has acolytes in the drug culture."

"Those palm trees aren't from the Gulf Coast."

He was right. They had probably been transplanted from South Florida. They hadn't rooted properly, and their fronds were yellow and frayed by the wind. The entire compound reeked of contrivance and artifice, a shabby attempt to create a Caribbean ambiance in an inhospitable environment where fresh water had to be brought in by boat and pumped into a tank that stood on steel stanchions behind the house. It was like a movie set. It was the kind of place that seemed indicative of the Duprees, people who not only had chosen to be first in Gaul rather than second in Rome but were satisfied to have one eye in the kingdom of the blind.

"How do you want to play it?" Clete said.

"Let's knock on the door and see who's home," I replied.

"This place gives me the creeps."

"It's just a building."

"No, it's got something really bad inside it. I can feel it. Maybe it's that stink. You see the eyes of those kids? They haven't even started their lives, and they're already zombies." He wiped his mouth with his handkerchief.

I knew Clete wasn't thinking of our new friends Rick and Sybil. He was thinking of Gretchen and his failure as a father. "I bet you five years from now, those kids will be fine," I said.

"Yeah, they'll probably be running Goldman Sachs. Give it a break, Streak. And screw knocking on the door."

It was made of heavy oak and had three rusted strips of iron bolted across it. Clete used the butt of his rifle to break a pane out of a frosted viewing panel next to the jamb. He reached inside, careful not to cut himself, and twisted the deadbolt free. I pushed the door back on its hinges and walked in ahead of him. The vast tomblike emptiness of the house was stunning. The high ceilings and huge rafters and peaked skylights operated by pulleys and chains had the look of an abandoned cathedral. Our footsteps echoed throughout the entirety of the building.

"What the hell is this place?" Clete said.

"Whatever it is, it was gutted," I said.

"Listen," he said.

I could hear wind blowing through a broken door or window, and perhaps the flapping of birds taking flight, but nothing else.

Clete walked ahead of me, his AR-15 slung over his shoulder. Then he froze and made a fist with his right hand, the infantryman's signal to stop in your tracks. This time I heard it, tinkling sounds mixed with a frenetic flapping of something alive and trapped in an enclosure.

We walked out of the main room and down a corridor into a kitchen. The cabinets and shelves and drawers and refrigerator were empty. I clicked on a light switch, but there was no power. Through the back window, I saw the crumbled brick shell of what probably was a lighthouse. Then I felt a puff of air through a side hallway and heard the tinkling and flapping sounds again. Clete unslung his rifle and moved down the hallway ahead of me, his hat and raincoat dripping, his silhouette massive against the light. He stepped down onto a bare concrete pad inside a room that had a barred window inset in one wall, the glass broken by a pelican that had flown directly into it and lay dead between the glass and the bars. Three concrete steps led down into a room that had been constructed beneath the level of the main floor. There was no mistaking where the sounds had come from.

Clete went down the steps first. At the far end of the lower room was another barred window, this one at ground level and as narrow as a gun slit. Like the room above it, the floor was concrete, but it was covered with gray sand that had seeped through the cracks in the walls.

Clete stared in disbelief. "It's Didi Gee's fish tank. Don't tell me it isn't. I saw it too many times. Jesus Christ, I told you this place gave me the willies."

A huge aquarium rested on a stone block. Almost all the water had evaporated from it, and five piranhas were flapping violently in the soup at the bottom, scissoring and skittering across it, smacking their noses into the glass.

An iron bar ran across the top of the ceiling, and at least a dozen oiled and shiny steel chains hung from it, either a hook or a manacle attached to each. Clete touched one of the hooks, then wiped his hand on his handkerchief, swallowing drily. I walked closer to the chains and took my ballpoint from my shirt pocket and speared one of the links and lifted the chain against the light. The end of the hook was encrusted with matter that resembled dried jelly. Higher up on the chain, a strand of auburn hair glowed against the light.

I took a penlight from my pocket and shone it at the bottom of the far wall. "Take a look," I said.

A rusted outline slightly larger than the size of a coffin was stenciled into the concrete floor. There was a long orange horizontal strip of rust on the wall, as though a heavy iron object had rested against it. The floor was speckled with what looked like dried blood. "I think this is where the iron maiden was," I said. "I think the lid was pushed back against the wall. The victims were lowered into it, and the lid was shut on top of them. You see those three pools? That's where the drain holes were."

"Alexis Dupree?"

"Who else could create something like this?" I said.

"This operation isn't being run by a bunch of geeks. Didi Gee stuck people's hands in his fish tank, but the object was money, not payback. The people behind this stuff don't have a category. You know what our problem is, Dave? We keep playing by the rules. These guys need to be naped off the planet."

"So we drop a hydrogen bomb on Jeanerette, Louisiana?" I said.

"What do you want to do with the piranhas?"

"We have to put them under," I said.

"Maybe those kids can dump them in an ice chest full of fresh water and take them somewhere."

"They'll get cut to pieces."

"I got to ask you something," Clete said.

"Go ahead."

"Who's more messed up, my daughter or kids like those two out there?"

"I don't know, Clete. What does it matter? Young people make mistakes. Some come out of it, some don't. Stop beating up on yourself."

"I want your promise on something. You don't jam Gretchen. She deserves a better life than the one I left her with. You cut her some slack or we go our separate ways. I want your word."

He had never spoken like that to me in all the years I had known him.

"I was never big on loyalty oaths," I said.

"I want your word, Dave."

"I can't give it to you."

I saw a great sadness come into his eyes. "All right, let's get those two down here and see what they have to say. Blow the shit out of those fish first. Yeah, lock and load, Dave, paint the fucking wall."

When we went back outside, the sky was a bright metallic gray, the wind blowing a dirty chop on the cove where we had set down, the plane rocking in the swells that swirled across the pilings of a submerged jetty. I could see Julie Ardoin in the cabin. I waved at her to indicate we would be along in a few minutes. Sybil and Rick were squatting on the sand, rolling up their tent. Rick had a joint between his lips.

"I fixed y'all sandwiches from our wieners," Sybil said. "They're a little bit sandy, though."

"That's nice of you, but I want y'all to come into the house and check out a room we found," I said.

"Is someone home there?" she replied. "I don't know if we should go in there if nobody's home."

"Have you been in that house before, Miss Sybil?" I asked.

"No, sir," she replied.

I continued to look directly into her face.

"Maybe once," she said.

"Who'd you see in there?" I asked.

"Just that old man. He was nice. He said I looked like a model, somebody named Twiggy."

"Did y'all meet somebody named Angel or Angelle?" I said.

"That last one, I heard that name."

"You heard the name Angelle?" I said.

"Yeah, I *think* I did, but with all kinds of shit happening, I mean, you can't always be sure."

"I'm not reading you, Miss Sybil. What kind of shit?"

"We were inside the house once, talking to the old dude," Rick said, his pupils dilated into big drops of black ink. "Then somebody started screaming. The old guy said it was a crazy person he was taking care of. We hauled ass. I mean, fuck, man, who wants to have lunch with crazy people screaming and probably throwing food and shit at the table? We didn't come all the way out here for *that*."

"So why'd y'all come back?" I said.

"He gave us some crystal," Sybil said.

"That's why you had a swastika tattooed on your arm?" I said. "You wanted to score meth from the old man?"

"No, I told you. It was for my boyfriend's birthday, except that's not what he wanted. What does my tattoo have to do with the old guy?" She squeezed her eyes shut in consternation and exhaled loudly, letting her mouth remain open, as though silently laughing.

"You made these sandwiches for us?" I said.

"I got to make a confession. I think a crab was eating on one of the wieners," she said. She scratched at a scab on her tattoo. "I'm sorry for probably telling you some lies today. I say things I kind of make up and they seem real, but later, they don't."

What can you say to kids like these? You might as well fill reams of paper with all the wisdom of the ancient and the modern world and pack them down a ship's cannon with a plunger and stand back and ignite the fuse and blow six thousand years of knowledge into confetti and watch it float away on the next wave.

"There's a torture chamber in that house. You could have been hung up in it. Don't come back here," I said.

"Wow, that's seriously fucked up, man," Rick said.

Clete and I walked past the dead birds in the compound, not speaking, our weapons across our shoulders, our raincoats flapping in the wind, the sun cold and gaseous in the pewter-colored sky.

Clete stopped. "We didn't take the sandwiches she fixed," he said.

"Forget it."

"It'll hurt her feelings. What's the harm? I'll see you at the plane."

I waded out into the water and climbed into the cabin of the Cessna. I could think of only a few instances in my life when I had felt as depressed as I did then.

"What's in that house?" Julie said.

"Pure evil."

"Like what?"

"Nothing anyone will believe."

"What's your podjo doing?"

"He was worried we hurt a young woman's feelings."

"That's why he went back?"

"Clete is a cross between Saint Francis of Assisi and Captain Bly. But you never know who's coming out of the jack-in-the-box."

I saw her watching him through the windshield as though seeing him for the first time, her thoughts hidden.

"I'm going to tell you something that maybe I have no right to say, but I'll say it anyway," I said. "When people kill themselves, particularly when they bail off buildings or leave blood splatter on the ceiling, it's usually because of a chemical assault on the brain. They can free themselves of their rage only by creating a legacy of guilt and shame and depression that is equal to their own suffering and that other people will buy into. In their fantasy, they survive their death and witness the discovery of their remains by the people they want to injure. Don't let that be your fate, Julie. The world belongs to the living. Let the dead stay under their headstones."

"Boy, you know how to say it, don't you?"

"I think you're a nice lady, too good to carry the weight of a guy who decided to mess you up as bad as he could," I said.

"You're the only person who ever had the guts to talk to me like that." She looked in Clete's direction again. "Something happen between you and your friend?"

"I let him down. Or at least he thinks I did."

"How?"

"It doesn't matter. He's my friend. You don't let your pals down. Right or wrong, you brass it out. Right?"

"You're a funny guy, Dave. Here he comes now. He's smiling. I bet he's forgotten all about it."

Clete climbed into the cabin and sat down heavily in the backseat, a smear of mustard on his cheek. His face was flat, his eyes empty when he looked at me. "Let's blow this dump," he said.

CHAPTER
25

I CALLED IN sick Monday and spent the early-morning hours raking leaves in the backyard. I piled them in stacks by the water's edge and soaked them with kerosene and set them ablaze and watched the curds of smoke rise through the trees and break apart in the wind. I felt like a man coming off a bender, wanting to invest the rest of his life in garden chores and fixing his roof and oiling his fishing tackle and sanding the barnacles off a boat he left half filled with rainwater for the last year. I wanted to take every misadventure and wrong choice in my life and set it on fire with the leaves and watch it burn into a pile of harmless ash.

I wanted to be rid forever of martial thoughts and the faces of the men I had killed and the images of dead children and animals in third-world villages. I wanted to slip through the dimension into a place where moth and rust did not have their way, where thieves did not break in and steal. I felt sickened by my own life and the evil that seemed to pervade the earth. I wanted to find a gray-green tree-dotted tropical stretch of land on the watery rim of creation that had not been stained by war and the poisons of the Industrial Age. I was convinced that Eden was not a metaphor or a legend and that somehow it still lay within our grasp if only we could find the path that led back into it. If it had existed once, it could exist again, I told myself. I wondered if the dead who seemed to wander the earth were not seeking it, too, over and over, feeling their way through the darkness, searching for the place that lay somewhere between the Tigris and the Euphrates rivers.

I guess these were strange thoughts to have on the cusp of winter, inside the smoke of a leaf fire that contained both the fecund smell of the earth and a petrochemical accelerant, but could there be a more appropriate season and moment?

I did not hear the footsteps of the person standing behind me while I heaped layer upon layer of blackened leaves onto the flames, my face hot, my eyes stinging with humidity.

"I hear you're looking for me," Gretchen said.

I stepped back from the fire and turned around and propped the bottom of the rake on the ground. "That's one way to put it."

"I'm not staying with Clete. I've got my own place. What do you want?"

"Did you have to pop somebody when you rescued your mother?"

"I scared a couple of guys, but no, I didn't hurt them. You can check out my mother. She's holed up in Key Largo, coked to the eyes. Something else you want to know?"

"Yeah, after you put two rounds into Jesse Leboeuf, he said something to you in French. Remember what it was?"

"I'm here about Clete, Mr. Robicheaux. He has to choose between me and you, and it's tearing him up. I don't want him taking my weight."

"Then tell me what Leboeuf said before he died."

Her eyes followed a speedboat that had just roared past us, splitting the bayou with a frothy yellow trough, the wake sliding through the cypress roots.

"They're going to send people after you," she said.

"Answer the question. Why not get your old man off the hook? The Leboeuf shooting was probably justified. You stopped a rape in progress. Leboeuf was armed and a threat to both you and Catin Segura. You can skate."

She was breathing through her nose, her nostrils white around the edges. "You want me to confess to snuffing a cop in a place like this?"

"You probably saved Catin's life. If you'd wanted to summarily execute Leboeuf, you would have parked a third round in him while he was lying in the bathtub. That means you have a conscience."

"Roust me if you want. Tell my landlord I have AIDS. Do all the dog shit you guys do when you can't make your case, but lay off Clete."

"You've got it turned around, Miss Gretchen. Clete saw you put three rounds in Bix Golightly's face. You made him a witness to a homicide and an accessory after the fact. You've done a major cluster-fuck on your father. You just haven't figured that out yet."

Her breathing had grown louder, the blood draining from around her mouth. "The guys who kidnapped my mother are pretty dumb, but they were smart enough to know the difference between coopera-tion and going over a gunwale with cinder blocks wired around their necks. The contract came down from a guy who talks like he has a speech defect, like he can't pronounce an R. Did you see *Lawrence of Arabia?* Remember how Peter O'Toole dressed? The guy who sounds like Elmer Fudd wraps himself up like Peter O'Toole because he's afraid of the sunlight. Know anybody like that?"

"The albino, Lamont Woolsey?"

"God, you're smart," she said.

CLETE PURCEL WAS not a fan of complexities. Or rules. Or concerns about moral restraint when it came to dealing with child molesters, misogynists, rapists, and strong-arm robbers who jackrolled old people. Clete wasn't sure which category Lamont Woolsey fit into, but he didn't care. The chains and hooks and manacles and piranha tank and dried blood in the room we found on the island southeast of the Chandeleurs gave Lamont Woolsey the status of crab bait.

Woolsey had used a credit card to pay for his stay in a hotel on Pinhook Road in Lafayette. It took Clete's secretary, Alice Werenhaus, ten minutes to get the billing address. It was uptown in New Orleans, right off Camp Street, one block from the old home of the Confeder-ate general John Bell Hood. Clete called me from his cottage. "I'm going to dial him up, Dave. He's going to know it's our ring, too," he said.

"Be careful. Dana Magelli doesn't want us wiping our feet on his turf anymore," I said.

"Dana's okay. People give him a bad time because he's Italian. That's the advantage of being Irish. Nobody expects much from a pagan race."

"Who told you that?"

"I did. You don't think I read? You don't think I have a brain? Listen, I wasn't fair to you on the island. I didn't mean what I said about going our separate ways. That's never going to happen. *Diggez-vous,* big mon? The Bobbsey Twins from Homicide are forever. You copy that?"

"You got it, bud."

"We wrote our names on the wall, didn't we?"

"Five feet high."

"You ever miss the greaseballs?"

"That's like missing bubonic plague."

"Be honest. It was like being in the middle of a Dick Tracy comic strip. Who could invent guys like Didi Gee and No Duh Dolowitz? How about the broads? I used to think getting laid on the ceiling was a physical impossibility. After every Mardi Gras, I'd have to send my flopper to rehab."

"Watch out for Woolsey, Clete. Most of the greaseballs were family men and had parameters. These guys don't."

"That's the point. These cocksuckers ran up the black flag. Not us," he said.

CLETE HAD A working relationship with skells of every stripe. One of the most resourceful was a totally worthless human being by the name of Ozone Eddy Mouton, who had cooked his head by shooting up with paint thinner and sniffing gas tanks and airplane glue and drinking dry-cleaning fluid in Angola. For a long time Ozone Eddy worked as a stall for a bunch of street dips in the Quarter, then upgraded as a money washer at the track, which cost him an ice pick through both kneecaps. On his last bust, the judge took mercy on him and gave him probation, contingent on his attendance at twelve-step meetings.

The lowest of the low-bottom groups in Jefferson and Orleans parishes was the Work the Steps or Die, Motherfucker meeting, a collection of outlaw bikers, prostitutes, street bums, wet-brains, and violent offenders known in Angola as "big stripes." After six weeks of dealing with Ozone Eddy, the Work the Steps or Die, Motherfuckers held what is called a group-conscience meeting, and Eddy was told to hit the bricks and never come back unless he wanted his head shoved up a Harley-Davidson exhaust pipe.

That was when he teamed up with No Duh Dolowitz, the Merry Prankster of the Mafia. No Duh and Ozone Eddy became legendary as architects of mayhem from Camden to Miami. They shot a paintball into the mouth of a right-to-work politician at a Knights of Columbus dinner. At a tar roofers' convention in Atlantic City, they put cat turds among the breakfast sausages and flushed twenty-five M-80s down the plumbing and blew water out of the commodes all over the hotel. They freeze-wrapped the severed parts of a stolen cadaver and submerged them in the punch bowls at a bridal shower for the daughter of a Houston button man. They arranged for a busload of dancing transvestites to show up on a middle-school stage at a charitable event in Mississippi. I always thought their masterpiece was the night they hauled away a corrupt judge's sports car from his driveway and returned it to the same spot before dawn, compacted into a gleaming block of crushed metal not much larger than a footlocker.

Ozone Eddy was to New Orleans what mustard gas was to trench warfare; you tried to stay upwind from him, but it was not an easy task.

MONDAY EVENING EDDY drove his car down a narrow street a couple of blocks from Audubon Park, the air as dense as a bruise, the trees throbbing with birds. He backed his vehicle into the driveway of a white one-story Victorian home that was elevated high above the lawn and had square pillars on the gallery, then he got out and mounted the steps and tapped on the door. The man who answered had a face that looked like it had been poured out of a pitcher of cream, the eyes the most brilliant blue Ozone Eddy had ever seen. The man was holding a book in one hand; behind him, a reading lamp burned inside a flowery shade. "Glad I caught you. I'm returning your tire," Eddy said.

"What tire?"

"The one I borrowed. I got mine fixed, and I'm returning yours. I'm about to put it back on. I thought I'd tell you so you'd know what was going on."

"Who are you? What are you talking about?"

"I ran over a nail and didn't have a spare tire. I saw you had the same size tire as me. So I took yours and got mine fixed. Now I'm putting yours back on. Why are you making that face?"

"Your hair. It's orange. Say that about my tire again."

"I hate to tell you this, but you look like you haven't seen sunlight in five hundred years. You got a vampire coffin in there? What's with this about my hair? I just told you about your tire. You want it back or not?"

Lamont Woolsey walked down the steps and stared at his SUV. One corner of the frame was almost flush with the concrete. "You left it on the rim?"

"What if a neighborhood kid came by and pushed your SUV on top of himself? Besides, I needed the jack to change my own tire. Want to give me a hand? I'm late for my bridge club."

"I told you what would happen," a woman said from the passenger seat of the car. "Leave him his tire and forget it."

"Who's that?" Lamont asked.

"That's Connie Rizzo, my cousin. She lives in your neighborhood. I was trying to do the right thing. Instead, how about you jam your bad manners up your nose?"

Lamont pushed Eddy in the chest with one finger. Eddy was surprised by the force and power in the man's thrust. "You want trouble?" Lamont said, and speared him in the sternum again.

The woman got out of the van. She was dark-haired and lovely and had youthful skin and a bright red mouth. She wore a beige T-shirt and baggy strap overalls spotted with paint. "Keep your hands to yourself, you freak," she said.

"Did you people get loose from an asylum?" Lamont said.

"No, but I think you escaped from the circus," she said. "You lay off Eddy. You want to push people around, try me."

"You're cute," Lamont said.

"Think so? Try this," she said. She pulled a can of oven cleaner from her overalls and squirted it in his eyes and nose and mouth, stepping back as he flailed his arms, a steady stream flowing into his face.

In under thirty seconds, Lamont Woolsey was in the trunk of Eddy's car, his wrists tied behind him with plastic ligatures, a black bag pulled down over his head, snugged tight with a drawstring under the chin.

THE STARS WERE out when Clete parked his Caddy behind Ozone Eddy's tanning parlor on Airline. He went through the back door into the cluttered room that Eddy called his office. Eddy and a woman Clete didn't know were drinking coffee at a desk while the albino sat shirtless in a heavy chair, his arms secured behind him, his forehead knurled, his skin like white rubber. "What kept you?" Eddy said.

"What *kept* me? What happened to him?" Clete said.

"You wanted him brought here. So we brought him here," Eddy said.

"I didn't tell you to boil his face off. Who's *she*?"

"Connie. I pieced off the job. You got any weed on you?"

"Where's his shirt?" Clete said.

"He puked on it," Eddy replied. "Actually, he puked inside the bag we put over his head, and it drained on his shirt. What's with the attitude?"

"I said get him in here. That I'd talk to him when you got him here. That doesn't mean you turn him into a boiled shrimp," Clete said.

"You were gonna put an albino in a tanning bed, but you're lecturing us on abusing people?" the woman said.

"Get her out of here, Eddy," Clete said.

"You weren't so choosy that New Year's Eve when you tried to grab my ass in the elevator at the Monteleone," the woman said.

Clete tried to think straight, but he couldn't. Lamont Woolsey was looking at him from under his brow, his face sweaty, his body starting to stink, his slacks streaked with grease and dirt from the car trunk.

"What's your fucking problem?" Eddy said.

"You don't hurt people when you don't have to," Clete said.

"The guy's a geek," Eddy said.

"Beat feet, Eddy, and take her with you," Clete said. "I'll lock up."

"If you haven't noticed, this is my salon, my office, my girlfriend."

"You forget what happened here tonight, and with luck, you won't get melted into soap," Clete said.

"You don't throw me out of my own place."

"What did you say? Melted into soap?" the woman said.

"Did you frisk this guy?" Clete asked.

"What do you think?" the woman said. "I told Eddy to leave this shit alone. I also told him you were a masher. What was that about the soap?"

"I'm going to bet Woolsey here had a fob on a key ring that looked like a dolphin," Clete said.

The woman and Ozone Eddy glanced at each other. "What about it?" she said.

"That fob means Woolsey has ties to a Nazi war criminal," Clete said. "I've been in a dungeon operated either by him or by his friends. There were chains and steel hooks in that room that had pieces of hair and human tissue on them."

"Are you drunk?" the woman said.

"Tell her," Clete said to Woolsey.

A blue vein pulsed in Woolsey's scalp. His lifted his eyes to the woman's. They were electric, the pupils as tiny as pinheads. A solitary drop of sweat rolled off the tip of his nose and formed a dark star on his slacks. "I was a dance instructor at an Arthur Murray dance studio. I'd like to take you dining and dancing some night," he said. "You have a nice mouth. Your lipstick is too bright, but your mouth is nice just the same."

The certainty had gone out of the woman's face.

"Where's the bag for his head?" Clete said.

"I threw it in the trash. I told you. It had puke on it," Eddy said.

"It's not important," Clete said. "Come on, Lamont. We're going to take a ride."

"That stuff about the steel hooks, that was a put-on, right?" the woman said.

"Keep telling yourself that," Clete said.

He pulled Woolsey from the chair and walked him through the back door to the Caddy. Woolsey's arms felt as hard as fence posts. "You lift?" Clete said.

"Occasionally."

"Impressive. The credit card you used in Lafayette was only three weeks old. Otherwise, you're off the computer."

"That's not hard to do. But you're definitely in the computer, Mr. Purcel. We know everything about you and everything about your family and everything about your friends. Think about that."

Clete shoved him into the backseat and handcuffed him to the D-ring inset in the floor. "Open your mouth again, and you'll have that bag full of puke pulled over your head."

"You're a stupid man," Woolsey said.

"You're right about that," Clete said. "But check out our situation. I'm driving the car and you're hooked up like a street pimp. I know where we're going and you don't. Your face is fried and you don't have a shirt to wear and your slacks look like you took a dump in them. You're not in Shitsville because of bad luck, Mr. Woolsey. You're in Shitsville because you got taken down by a guy who has hair like Bozo the Clown and a brain the size of a walnut. How's it feel?"

CLETE DROVE UP the I-10 corridor toward Baton Rouge, then took an exit that accessed a dirt road and a levee bordering a long canal and a flooded woods thick with cypress and gum and persimmon trees. In the moonlight he could see three fishing camps farther up the canal, all of them dark. Clete pulled into a flat spot below the levee and cut the engine. In the quiet he could hear the hood ticking with heat, the frogs croaking in the flooded trees. He went to the back of the Caddy and popped the trunk and pulled a long-sleeve dress shirt from an overnight bag.

"I'm going to unhook you, Mr. Woolsey," he said. "I want you to put on this shirt. If you get cute with me, I'll pull your plug."

"Where are we going?"

"Who said we're going anywhere? See that cypress swamp? That's where the Giacano family used to plant the bodies of people they considered a nuisance."

"I'm not awed by any of this, Mr. Purcel."

"You should be. When the Giacanos clipped somebody, they did it themselves, up-front and personal. Or they did it up front and impersonal. But they did it themselves. You use the telephone. Like the hit you put on me and Dave Robicheaux."

Woolsey was slipping on the shirt in the backseat, working it over his shoulders, one cuff hanging from his wrist. "Somebody has been telling you fairy tales."

Clete cleared his throat. "This gun I'm holding is called a 'drop' or a 'throw-down.' When cops accidentally cap an unarmed man, the throw-down gets put on his body. Because the throw-down has its numbers burned off and no ballistics history associated with the cop, it's a convenient weapon to carry when dealing with troublesome people who need a bullet in the mouth. Are you getting the picture?"

"I think so. But speak more slowly, please. You're probably too intelligent for a man like me."

"Here's the rest of it. I wasn't going to put you in a tanning bed. Why? Because, number one, it doesn't work. People who are scared shitless tell any lie they think their tormentor wants to hear. Number two, I don't take advantage of somebody's handicap. So what does that mean for you? It means you take the contract off me and Dave, and you stay the fuck away from us. If you don't, I'll visit you at your pad and break your teeth out with a ball-peen hammer. Then I'll stuff my drop down your throat and blow one into your bowels. That's not a threat; it's a fact." Clete took a breath. "One other thing, Mr. Woolsey. No payback on Bozo the Clown and his girlfriend. They're gumballs and are not accountable."

"I look like a vengeful man?"

"Hook yourself up."

"That's it?"

"That's it."

"I don't understand you."

"You don't have to. Just don't fuck with me or Dave Robicheaux again," Clete said.

Lamont Woolsey seemed to think about it in a self-amused fashion, then slipped the tongue of the loose manacle through the D-ring and squeezed it into the locking mechanism.

Clete stuck a green-and-white peppermint stick in his mouth, glanced once at Woolsey in the rearview mirror, and floored the Caddy back onto the levee, his tires sprinkling dirt and gravel into the canal.

THE TRAFFIC WAS thin as Clete drove down I-10 along the edge of Lake Pontchartrain and passed the airport and the cutoff that led to New Iberia. Woolsey was staring out the window like a hairless white ape being transported back to the zoo. Thinking derogatory thoughts about Woolsey brought Clete no consolation. His mockery of Woolsey was, in reality, a bitter admission of his own failure. Woolsey had been taken down by a moral imbecile, but Clete had willingly formed a partnership with one. And Eddy being Eddy, he had immediately factored in his girlfriend, who had almost blinded Woolsey with oven cleaner. On top of that, the two of them had probably told Woolsey he was going to be baked alive in a tanning bed, which Clete had never planned to do.

The shorter version was Clete had empowered Ozone Eddy and his girlfriend to torture a man in Clete's name. Now he was operating a jitney service for the man who had put a hit on him and his best friend. How bad could one guy screw up?

He looked at his passenger in the rearview mirror. "What do you get out of all this, Mr. Woolsey?"

"Enormous sums of money. Want some?"

"You connected to the oil spill?"

"Not me. I'm an export-import man. One of our biggest clients is Vietnam. Some people say it's the next China. Want to get in on it?"

"I already did. Two tours."

"Shooting gook and dreaming of nook? Boys will be boys and all that? I bet y'all had some fun."

"Take a nap. I'll tell you when you're home," Clete said.

"Touch a nerve?"

"Not a chance," Clete said.

He turned off I-10 and drove up St. Charles Avenue into the Garden District and pulled into Lamont Woolsey's driveway. Woolsey's SUV still rested lopsidedly on one of the back rims. The light was burning on the elevated gallery. An Asian girl in a print sundress was standing under it.

"There's our loyal Maelee," Woolsey said.

"What'd you say?" Clete asked.

"My sweet young Vietnamese girl. They're a loyal bunch. And Maelee is as lovely and fragrant as they come."

"Her name is Maelee?"

"That's what I said. Do you know her?"

Clete didn't answer. For a moment he saw a young woman swimming next to a sampan on the edge of the China Sea, her face dipping into a wave.

But the person on the gallery was not a woman. She was a girl, her bare shoulders brown and warm-looking in the light, the flowers on her dress as vibrant as flowers in a tropical garden.

"Is that you, Mr. Lamont?" the girl said. "I was worried. You were gone so long without telling me."

"See, they're loyal," Woolsey said. "The French taught them manners."

"Why don't you show some appreciation and answer her?"

"Unlock my handcuffs."

"I've seen her before," Clete said. "She was the one who waited on Amidee Broussard after his speech at the Cajundome in Lafayette. He sent his steak back."

"Correct-o. You must have had your eye on her."

"What's she doing here?"

"Amidee knew I needed a maid and drove her over. I've given her the cottage in back. She seems quite happy with her new situation. Something wrong?"

Clete pulled back the seat in the Caddy and fitted the handcuff key into the lock on Woolsey's wrist. He could smell onions on Woolsey's breath and the dried talcum around his armpits. He stepped back while Woolsey got out of the car. Woolsey's lips looked purple in the gloom, his eyes dancing with light.

"Yeah, there is something wrong," Clete said. "Neither of you guys has any business around a young girl like that."

"What's really bothering you, Mr. Purcel? You still dream about the little flower girls? It's no fun keeping one's wick dry, is it? You said you knew a woman named Maelee. She was Vietnamese?"

"She was Eurasian."

"A taste of two worlds in one package? Yum-yum."

The crow's-feet at the corners of Clete's eyes had gone flat, but his eyes remained placid and bright green and showed no emotion. "I know a couple of Quaker ladies who work with refugees. They'll be here tomorrow to talk with the girl and take her somewhere else if she wants to go."

"What is it you're really after, Mr. Purcel? Your history with women is well known. You can't keep your eyes off Maelee, can you? Would you like to go in the cottage with her? She won't mind. She was very accommodating with Amidee. Last night I tried her myself. I highly recommend her."

"I think we're square on the damage Ozone Eddy and his girl-friend did to your face," Clete said. "That means we're starting with a clean slate. Is that okay with you?"

"Whatever you say. I'm going to go inside now and have a shower and a hot dinner. Then I'm going to bed down Maelee. I've earned that, and she knows it. We're a colonial empire, Mr. Purcel, although you don't seem to know that. Everyone benefits. The dominant nation takes the things it needs. Our subjects are only too happy to receive what we give them. It's win-win for everyone."

"A fresh slate also means all bets are off. For you, that's not good, Mr. Woolsey," Clete said.

"Time for you to be gone. Unless I missed something. Are you thinking of sloppy seconds?"

Clete huffed an obstruction out of his nostrils and brushed at his nose with the back of his wrist. "I didn't want to do this."

"Do what?"

"I mean in front of the girl I didn't want to do it. I feel bad about that. She probably feels sorry for you and doesn't understand that you're a piece of shit out of choice, not because your mother thought she'd given birth to a sack of Martha White's self-rising flour. By the way, I want my shirt back." He paused. "Look, my real problem is I can't get anyone over here tonight to look in on the girl, so that means we have to work things out right now, here, in your driveway. Are you hearing me? I said take off my shirt. Don't make me ask you again. I'm sorry I sicced Ozone Eddy and his broad on you. Nobody deserves that, not even you. We're straight on that, right? I'm glad we have that out of the way. Now give me back my threads. That's not up for debate. You're starting to upset me, Mr. Woolsey."

"You're a ridiculous man."

"I know," Clete said. "What's a fellow going to do?"

Clete put his entire shoulder into his punch and sent Woolsey crashing into the side of his SUV. He thought it was over and hesitated and eased up when he swung again. But his estimation of Woolsey was wrong. Woolsey righted himself and slipped the second blow and caught Clete squarely on the jaw, snapping his head sideways. Then he hooked his arm behind Clete's neck and drove his fist into Clete's rib cage and heart again and again, his phallus pressed against Clete's thigh, his smell rising into Clete's face. "How do you like it, laddie? How does it feel to have your ass kicked by a freak?" he said.

Clete brought his knee up into Woolsey's groin and saw the man's mouth open like that of a fish slammed on a hard surface. Clete hit him in the side of the head and managed to hook him once in the eye, but Woolsey wouldn't go down. He lowered his head, turning his left shoulder forward as a classic open-style fighter would. He slammed his fist into Clete's heart, then hit him in the same spot a second time, and glazed Clete's head with a blow that almost tore his ear loose.

Clete stepped back and set himself, crouching slightly, raising his left hand to absorb Woolsey's next punch, then drove his fist straight into Woolsey's mouth. Woolsey's head hit the SUV, and he went down as though his ankles had been kicked from under him.

But the engines that drove the rage and violence living inside Clete Purcel were not easily turned off. Like all of his addictions—weed and pills and booze and gambling and Cadillac convertibles and fried food and rock and roll and Dixieland music and women who moaned under his weight as though it only added to their pleasure—bloodlust and the wild release of confronting the monsters that waited for him nightly in his dreams were a drug that he could never have too much of.

He stomped Woolsey in the head, then grabbed the outside mirror and the roof of the SUV for support and brought the flat of his shoe down on Woolsey's face, over and over, hammering Woolsey's head into the door, reshaping his nose and mouth and eyes, whipping strings of blood across the side of the SUV. At that moment Clete genuinely believed that a helicopter was hovering immediately overhead, flattening all the flowers and banana fronds and elephant ears and caladiums and windmill palms that grew in Woolsey's yard.

Then the flame that had consumed him shrank into a bright red dot in the center of his mind and died. For just a moment he saw nothing but darkness around him. The thropping sounds of the helicopter blades rose into the sky and disappeared. He felt a sharp pain in his chest, like a shard of glass working its way through the tissue around his lungs. His hands throbbed and seemed too large for his wrists, but he had no awareness at all of his surroundings. He blinked several times and saw Woolsey lying at his feet and the girl standing on the gallery, her hands trembling with shock.

Clete bent over and tore his shirt from Woolsey's torso and threw it in the flower bed. "Okay," he said, trying to catch his breath. "We got that issue off the table. Next time I tell you to take off my threads, take off my threads. That shows a definite lack of class and a definite lack of mutual respect."

"Oh, sir, why have you done this?" the Vietnamese girl said.

"It's a problem I've got, Maelee. I don't like guys like Woolsey pretending that they're Americans and they speak for the rest of us. You're a nice kid, and you don't have to put up with the Michelin man here. Some nice ladies are coming to see you tomorrow. In the meantime, stay away from Woolsey. This is my business card. If he lays a hand on you or tries to make you do something you don't want to, you call that cell phone number."

He started up the Caddy and headed down St. Charles, coughing blood on the steering column and dashboard, the streetcar clanging down the neutral ground toward him, the conductor's eyes cavernous, his face skeletal under the lacquered-billed black cap he wore.

CHAPTER
26

Morning had never been a good time for Gretchen Horowitz. Others on the South Florida coast might wake to birdsong and tropical breezes and sunlight on blue-green water, but for her, the dawn brought with it only one emotion—a pervasive sense of loss and personal guilt and an abiding conviction that there was something obscene and dirty about her physical person. As a little girl, she had bathed herself from head to foot with a washcloth until the water in the tub turned cold and gray, but she had never felt clean. Afterward, she had scrubbed the tub on her knees, rinsing the porcelain surface repeatedly, in fear that the germs she had washed off her skin would be there the next time she bathed.

In middle school she learned there were ways to deal with problems that no educational psychologist would go near. Right after homeroom, the first stall in the girls' bathroom was the place to be, provided you needed a few pharmaceutical friends such as rainbows, black beauties, Owsley purple, or a little sunshine that glowed inside your head all day, no matter what kind of weather the rest of the world was experiencing. The school day slipped by like a vague annoyance, white noise on the edge of a drowsy interlude before the bell sounded at three o'clock. Her weekday afternoons and evenings took care of themselves and did not require that she think about any issue outside of her head. She sacked groceries at a Winn-Dixie or sat in a movie theater by herself or hung out at the public library or smoked a little dope with a high school football player in the back of his car. When it was dark, she got under the covers in her bedroom and tried not to hear the sounds her mother made when she feigned climax with her johns. It was easy.

But sunrise was a curse, a condition, not a planetary event. The feeling that came with it could not be described as pain, because it had no sharp edges. In fact, the feeling she woke with was one she somehow associated with theft. As the sun broke on the horizon, her sensory system remained trapped inside her sleep, and her skin felt bloodless and dead when she touched it. Her soul, if she had one, seemed made of cardboard. As the darkness faded from her room, she was able to see her school clothes on their hangers in her closet and the absence of anything of value on her dresser and the hairbrush on her nightstand that always looked unclean. She waited for the daylight to burn away the shadows in the room and, in some fashion, redefine its contents. Instead, she knew the shadows were her friends, and the day ahead held nothing for her except glaring surfaces that made her think of glass from a broken mirror. She also knew she was unloved for a reason, and the reason was simple: The girl named Gretchen Horowitz was invisible, and not one person on earth, including the high school football player who placed her hand down there whenever they were alone, had any idea who she was, or where she came from, or what her mother did for a living, or what had been done to her by men even cops were afraid of.

Gretchen Horowitz owned the name on her birth certificate and nothing else. Her childhood was not a childhood and did not have a category. Her umbilical connection to the rest of the human family had been severed and tied off a long time ago. Reverie was a fool's pursuit and filled with faces she would change into howling Greek masks if she ever saw them again. And morning was a bad time that passed if you didn't let it get its hooks into you.

Tuesday at nine A.M. she drove to Lafayette and bought a video camera, a boom pole, a lighting kit, and a Steadicam. Then she bought a take-out lunch at Fat Albert's and drove into the park by the university to eat. There was a muddy pond with ducks in the park, and swing sets and seesaws and a ball diamond and picnic shelters, and dry coulees among the live oaks where children played in the leaves. It was 11:14 A.M. when she sat down at a plank table in the sunshine and began eating her lunch. In forty-six minutes the morning would be over, and she would step over a line into the afternoon, and that would be that.

At first she paid little attention to the family who had walked from the street onto the park grounds and sat down at a table by the pond. The man had a dark tan and black hair and wore denims and work shoes. His wife had the round face of a peasant and wore a cheap blue scarf on her head and carried a calico cat on her shoulder, a harness and leash on its neck. She had no makeup on her face and seemed to be seeing the park for the first time. It was the child who caught Gretchen's eye. His hair was blond, his smile unrelenting, his cheeks blooming with color. When he tried to walk, he kept falling down, laughing at his own ineptitude, then getting up and toddling down the slope and falling again.

The family had brought their lunch in a paper bag. The woman placed a jar of sun tea and three peanut-butter-and-jelly sandwiches on a piece of newspaper and cut two of them in half and quartered the third for the child. She had smeared jelly on her hands, and she tried to wipe them clean on the paper bag, then gave it up and said something to her husband. She walked through the live oaks toward the restroom, the leaves gusting out of the coulee in the shade. The husband yawned and rested his head on one hand and stared vacantly at the ball diamond, his eyes half lidded. In under a minute, he had put his head down and was asleep. Gretchen looked at her watch. It was eight minutes until noon.

She finished her lunch and looked at the university campus on the far side of the curving two-lane road that separated it from the park. A marching band was thundering out a martial song on a practice field. The sun was as bright as a yellow diamond through the oak trees, and its refraction inside the branches almost blinded her. She looked back at the table by the pond where the man and his little boy had been sitting. The child was gone.

She stood up from the bench. The mother had not returned from the restroom, and the husband was sound asleep. The wind was cold and blowing hard, the surface of the pond wimpling in the sunlight like needles that could penetrate the eye. The ducks were in the reeds along the bank, engorged with bread scraps, their feathers ruffling, surrounded by a floating necklace of froth and Styrofoam containers and paper cups. Beyond the plank table where the husband was sitting, Gretchen saw the little boy toddling down the slope toward the water's edge. She began running just as he fell.

He tumbled end over end down the embankment, his zippered one-piece outfit caking with mud, his face filled with shock. Gretchen charged down the embankment after him, trying to keep her balance, her feet slipping from under her. She was running so fast, she splashed into the water ahead of the little boy and grabbed him up in both arms before he could roll into the shallows. She hefted him against her shoulder and walked back up the embankment and looked into the horrified face of the mother and the blank stare of the father, who had just lifted up his head from the table.

"Oh my God, I fell asleep," he said. He looked at his wife. "I fell asleep. I ain't meant to."

The woman took the child from Gretchen's arms. "T'ank you," she said.

"It's all right," Gretchen said.

The mother bounced the baby up and down on her chest. "Come play wit' your cat," she said. "Don't be crying, you. You're okay now. But you was bad. You shouldn't be walking down by the water, no."

"He wasn't bad," Gretchen said.

"He knows what I mean. It's bad for him to be by the water 'cause it can hurt him," the mother said. "That's what I was saying to him. His father ain't had no sleep."

"Why not?" Gretchen said.

"'Cause he works at a boatyard and he ain't had no work since the oil spill," the mother said. "He cain't sleep at night. He worries all the time. He's that way 'cause he's a good man."

"Drink some tea, you," the husband said. There were carpenter's bruises on his nails, purple and deep, all the way to the cuticle. "If it ain't been for you, I cain't t'ink about what might have happened."

"It didn't. That's what counts," Gretchen said.

He looked into space, his eyes hollow, as though he were watching an event for which there would have been no form of forgiveness if he had let it occur. "How long I been asleep?"

"Not long. Don't blame yourself," Gretchen said. "Your little boy is fine."

"He's our only child. My wife cain't have no more kids."

"Where's your car?" Gretchen said.

"We sold it. We rode the bus here," the mother said.

"Tell you what," Gretchen said. "I'd like to take your picture on my video camera. Will you let me do that? I make movies."

The mother gave her a coy look, as though someone were playing a joke on her. "Like in Hollywood or somet'ing?"

"I'm making a documentary on the 1940s musical revue in New Iberia." She could tell neither of them understood what she was talking about. "Let me get my camera. After you eat, I'll drive you home."

"You ain't got to do that," the man said.

It was two minutes to noon. The feelings Gretchen had had all morning were gone, but their disappearance was not related to the time of day. She got her video camera from the pickup and focused the lens on the man and woman and child, then showed them the footage. "See? You all are a wonderful family," she said.

"I ain't dressed to be on that," the woman said.

"I think all of you are beautiful," Gretchen said.

The man and woman seemed embarrassed and looked at each other. "T'ank you for what you done," the man said.

There was an emotion inside Gretchen that she could not understand. She did not know the name of the family, yet she did not want to ask it. "That's such a cute little boy," she said.

"Yeah, he's gonna be somet'ing special one day, you gonna see," the mother said.

"I bet he will," Gretchen said.

"You're a nice lady," the woman said.

And so are you, Gretchen thought, *and your husband is a nice man, and your little boy has the loveliest smile on earth.*

These are the things she thought, but she did not say them, nor did she steal the man and woman's dignity by trying to give them money when she drove them to their house in a poor section of Lafayette. Inside herself, she felt cleansed in a way she could not explain, and worries about the sunrise and fear of her own memories seemed like silly pursuits that weren't worth two seconds of her time.

Or was she fooling herself?

She wasn't sure. But something had dramatically changed in her life. She just didn't know why.

TUESDAY AFTERNOON DANA Magelli called me at the department. "Where's Purcel?" he asked.

"Haven't seen him. What's up?" I replied.

"Last night somebody kicked the shit out of a guy named Lamont Woolsey. Know him?"

"An albino who talks like Elmer Fudd?"

"He's missing a few teeth, so it's hard to say who he sounds like. His face looks like a car tire ran over it. He says he doesn't know who attacked him or why. The neighbors say a guy driving a Caddy convertible did it. A guy wearing a short-brim hat. Sound like anybody you know?"

"If I understand you correctly, the guy isn't filing charges."

"That doesn't mean Purcel can come into New Orleans and wipe his feet on people's faces any time he wants."

"Anything else?" I asked.

"Yeah, somebody snatched Ozone Eddy Mouton and a female employee out of Eddy's tanning parlor. Guess what. The people who saw Purcel stomp the albino's face say a guy with orange hair was in the albino's driveway earlier. Sound like coincidence to you?"

"Woolsey is mixed up in at least one homicide, Dana. Run him and you'll find a blank. How many high rollers can stay off the computer?"

"You listen to me, Dave. If Ozone Eddy and his employee are found in a swamp, Clete Purcel is going to jail as a material witness, and this time I'll make sure he stays there. By the way, when you see

Purcel, tell him the Vietnamese girl was traumatized by what she saw."

"What Vietnamese girl?"

"She works for Woolsey. Or did. Some Quaker women picked her up this morning. Her name is Maelee something."

"That was the name of Clete's girlfriend in Vietnam."

"I'm not making the connection," Dana said.

"She was a Eurasian girl who lived on a sampan. Clete wanted to marry her. The VC murdered her."

There was silence on the phone.

"You there?" I said.

"I didn't know that about Purcel. You think Woolsey is hooked up with intelligence people?"

"I think he has connections to corporations of some kind," I said. "Maybe a drilling company. Maybe all of this is related to the oil blowout."

"Keep Purcel out of the city. I'll see what I can find out about Woolsey on this end. Why would a meltdown like Ozone Eddy be in Woolsey's driveway?"

I didn't have an answer. Dana was a good man who followed the rules and believed in a broken system and probably would never be recognized for the heroic and steadfast and decent police officer that he was. But dwelling on Dana's decency would not help me with another problem I had been confronted with. Helen Soileau had just returned from Shreveport, where she had stayed almost constantly by the bedside of her half sister. I opened her office door and leaned inside. "It's good to have you back," I said.

She was standing behind her desk. "I want all your notes on the Jesse Leboeuf shooting," she said.

"I don't think they'll be very helpful."

I could see lights of impatience and irritability flicker in her eyes. "Who's your prime subject, Dave?"

"Gretchen Horowitz."

"An out-and-out execution?"

"No, she stopped a rape and probably a murder. If you ask me, Jesse got what he deserved."

"You questioned Horowitz?"

"Yep, but I got nowhere. Here's what interesting. Before he died, Jesse said something to the killer in French. Catin Segura heard it but says she doesn't speak French."

"Catin has no idea who the shooter was?"

"You'd better ask her."

"I'm asking you."

"The damage Jesse did to her was off the scale."

"Where's Catin now?"

"Back home with her kids. You want me to call her and tell her to come in?"

I saw Helen's eyes searching in space. "No," she said. "I'll talk to her at her house. No evidence at the scene or eyewitness account puts Horowitz there?"

"Nothing."

"I passed by your door when you were on the phone. Was that Dana Magelli you were taking to?"

"Yeah."

"And?"

"Maybe Clete busted up a guy named Lamont Woolsey in the Garden District last night."

"I just don't believe it," she said.

"It's the way it is, Helen."

"Don't tell me that," she said, turning her back to me, her hands on her hips. The muscles in her upper arms looked like rolls of quarters.

"Helen—"

"Don't say any more. Just leave. Now. Not later. Right now," she said.

AT QUITTING TIME, I drove to Clete's cottage. The air was damp, the sky plum-colored, and stacks of raked leaves were burning and blowing apart in the wind on the far side of the bayou, the ash glowing like fireflies. I didn't want to accept that winter was upon us and soon frost would speckle the trees and the cane fields that were already being turned into stubble. I was bothered even more by the fact that dwelling too much on the cycle of the seasons could turn one's heart into a lump of ice.

Clete was barefoot and wearing unpressed slacks and a strap undershirt and was watching the news on television in his favorite deep-cushioned chair. He poured from a pint bottle of brandy into a jelly glass and added three inches of eggnog from a carton. There was a wastebasket by his foot. A roll of toilet paper was tucked between his thigh and the arm of the chair. "Get yourself a Diet Doc," he said, barely looking at me.

"I don't want a Diet Doc."

"Rough day?"

"Not particularly. What's with the toilet paper?"

"I get the sense Helen is back on the job."

"Helen's not the problem. Magelli called. He says you busted up Lamont Woolsey."

"Woolsey dimed me?"

"No, the neighbors saw you kick his face in."

"Things got a little out of control. Magelli say anything about Ozone Eddy Mouton and a broad named Connie?"

"He said Eddy and a female employee were kidnapped."

"It gets worse. On the five o'clock news, there was a story about a pair of bodies found in the trunk of a burned car in St. Bernard Parish. One victim was male, one female. No ID yet. I screwed up real bad on this one, Streak."

"Maybe it's somebody else."

"A hit like that? Even the Giacanos didn't kill like that. It's Woolsey." Clete coughed and wadded up a handful of toilet paper and pressed it to his mouth. Then he compressed the paper tightly in his hand and lowered it into the wastebasket and took a drink of eggnog and brandy from the jelly glass. I sat down on the bed and pulled the wastebasket toward me. "You coughing up blood?" I said.

"No, I had a nosebleed."

"How long has this been going on?"

"Woolsey went down hard. He got off a couple of good shots. I'm fine."

"I'm taking you to Iberia General."

"No, you're not. Whatever is in my chest is going to stay in my chest. Listen to me, Dave. At a certain point in your life, you accept the consequences of your choices, and you play the hand out. I'm not going to have anybody cutting on me or sticking tubes down my throat or injecting radium into my bloodstream. If I catch the bus with an eggnog and Hennessy in my hand, that's the way it flushes."

"Hospitals are bad, and eggnog and booze are good. Do you know how dumb that sounds?"

"That's the only way I know how to think."

"It's not funny."

He got up from his chair and took a long-sleeve scarlet silk shirt off a hanger and put it on, then sat on the side of his bed and began pulling on his socks.

"What are you doing?" I said.

"Taking you and Molly and Alafair to dinner. Enjoy the day, Dave. It's all we've got."

"I don't like to hear you talk like that."

"We're running out of time, big mon. I'm talking about with the Duprees and Woolsey and this phony preacher and Varina and whoever the hell else they're mixed up with. Look at what they did to Ozone Eddy and his broad. They hate our guts. Gretchen tore Pierre Dupree apart with a blackjack. You and I have been rubbing shit in their faces from the jump. It's a matter of time before they get even. How about those locks of hair the old man keeps in his study?"

"You're preaching to the choir, Cletus."

"You're not hearing me. Helen doesn't listen. She thinks like an administrator. Administrators don't believe in conspiracies. If they did, they'd have to resign their jobs. That's the problem. In the meantime, we're waiting for Bed-Check Charlie to come through our wire and park one in our ear, if not worse."

"What are you suggesting?"

He didn't answer right away. He poured more brandy into his glass, swirling it, watching the eggnog turn brown before he drank it. "Burn them out."

"You and I? Like the White League?"

"They're going to kill us, Dave."

"No, they won't."

"They almost got us in the shootout on the bayou. I dream about it every second or third night. You know what's worst about the dream? We were supposed to die there. That paddle wheeler was real. Both of us were supposed to be on it, and that son of a bitch is still out there, waiting for us in the fog. But this time they're going to take everybody. You, me, Alafair, Molly, and Gretchen, all of us. That's what I see in the dream."

I could feel a cold wind on the back of my neck. I turned around to see if the door was open, but it wasn't.

"You okay?" Clete said.

No, I wasn't okay. And neither was he. And I had no way to set things right. Also, at that moment I had no way of knowing that Gretchen and Alafair and, in her sad way, Tee Jolie would write the fifth act in our Elizabethan tale on the banks of Bayou Teche.

GRETCHEN HAD RENTED a cottage in the little tree-shaded town of Broussard, located on the old two-lane highway midway between New Iberia and Lafayette. On Wednesday morning she looked out her front window at a scene she had trouble assimilating. Across the street, Pierre Dupree was walking a child through the side door of a Catholic church. The child could not have been over eight or nine years and wore metal braces on both of his legs. Gretchen took a cup of coffee out on her gallery and sat down on the steps and watched the church. A few minutes later, Dupree came back outside with the little boy and escorted him to a playground and placed him on a swing and began pushing him back and forth. Dupree seemed to take no notice of anyone around him or the fact that he was being watched.

Ten minutes passed, and Dupree strapped the little boy in the front seat of his Humvee. Gretchen set down her coffee cup and walked out onto the swale and leaned on one arm against the live oak that shaded the front of her cottage. Still Dupree did not notice her. He pulled out on the street and drove toward the only traffic signal in town. Then she saw his face reflected in the outside mirror as his brake lights went on. He made a U-turn in the filling station at the intersection and drove back toward her, turning in to her driveway, the shadows of the live oak bouncing on his windshield. He opened the door and got out. "I didn't realize that was you," he said.

"Who else do I look like?" she asked, her arm still propped against the tree trunk.

"If you don't want to talk to me, Miss Gretchen, I understand. But I want you to know I hold no grudge against you."

"Why is it I don't believe that?"

"I guess I'm a mighty poor salesman."

The little boy was looking out the passenger window at her, his head barely above the windowsill. She winked at him.

"This is Gus. He's my little pal in Big Brothers," Pierre said.

"Been at it long?" Gretchen said.

"Just of recent. I was enrolling Gus in the Catholic school here. I'm endowing a scholarship fund."

She nodded and tucked her shirt into her jeans with her thumbs. "How you doin', Gus?" she said.

"Fine," the little boy replied. He had a burr haircut and eyes that were mere slits, as though his face had not been fully formed.

"I blame myself for what happened in the restaurant in New Orleans," Pierre said. "I got involved in some business dealings that had consequences I didn't foresee. That's my fault and not yours. I think you're quite a woman, Miss Gretchen. I'd like to know you better."

"You're serious?"

"How many times does a guy meet a one-woman army?" He held his gaze on hers. "At least think about it. What's to lose? You've already shown what you can do if a fellow gets out of line."

Something was changed about him, she thought, though she couldn't put her finger on it. Maybe it was his hair. It looked freshly washed and blow-dried. Or was it his eyes? They were free of scorn and arrogance. Also, he seemed genuinely happy.

"Is Mr. Dupree treating you all right, Gus?" she said to the little boy.

"We went to the carnival in Lafayette. We went to the zoo, too," Gus replied.

"How about it?" Dupree said.

"How about what?" she said.

"Having lunch with me and Gus. Then I have to get him back home. It's a beautiful day." Again, his eyes lingered on hers. They were warm and seemed free of guile. "Have you ever modeled?"

"Sure, steroid ads when I rode with Dykes on Bikes."

"Stop it," he said.

He waited for her to speak, but she didn't. She gazed down the street, her chin raised slightly, her pulse fluttering in her throat.

"I'd love to get you on canvas," he said. "Come on, have lunch and we'll talk about it. I'm no Jasper Johns, but I'm not bad at what I do."

"Sorry, no cigar," she said.

"I'm disappointed. Keep me in mind, will you? You're a pistol, Miss Gretchen."

Her face and palms were tingling as she watched him drive away, the paint job on his Humvee as bright as a yellow jacket in the sunlight. *Dammit,* she thought. *Dammit, dammit, dammit.*

CHAPTER
27

AFTER SUPPER ON Wednesday evening, Alafair received a call on her cell phone from Gretchen Horowitz. "Take a ride with me," she said.

Alafair shut and opened her eyes and wondered how she could hide the reluctance she felt in her chest. "Now?" she said.

"I need your advice."

"About what?"

"I don't want to talk about it on the phone."

"I was thinking of taking a walk in a few minutes."

"Your father doesn't want you around me?"

"It creates certain kinds of conflicts for him, Gretchen. Be realistic."

"I bought a whole bunch of film equipment. I'm going to make the documentary on the 1940s music revue."

"That's not why you called."

"I'll be parked by the drawbridge on Burke Street. If you don't feel like talking with me, don't worry about it."

"Gretchen—"

Minutes later, Alafair walked past the Shadows and the old brick building that had been a Buick agency and was now a law office. She turned up the street that fed onto the drawbridge and saw Gretchen's chopped-down pickup parked by the corner, its exposed chrome-plated engine gleaming in the twilight. Gretchen got out on the sidewalk. "Thanks for coming," she said.

"What's the trouble?" Alafair said.

"Something happened today. I'm a little mixed up about it. You want a drink?"

"No. Tell me what it is."

"I saw Pierre Dupree take a crippled child into the Catholic church in Broussard this morning. He saw me watching him and pulled into my driveway. He invited me to lunch."

A pleasure boat loaded with revelers emerged from under the bridge and passed the old convent and hospital on the opposite side of the bayou. They were holding balloons and smiling, and their expressions seemed garish and surreal among the balloons. "You're not going to say anything?" Gretchen asked.

"Did you go with him?"

"No."

"I think you made a wise choice," Alafair said.

Gretchen folded her arms on her chest and looked at the diners eating and drinking in the courtyard behind Clementine's. There were white cloths and candles that flickered inside glass vessels on the dining tables, and the candles made shadows on the banana plants that grew along the restaurant's walls.

"I called the church," Gretchen said. "Pierre—"

"*Pierre?*"

"That's his name, isn't it? He not only paid for the crippled boy's tuition, he set up a scholarship fund."

"Don't be taken in by this guy," Alafair said.

"He had no way of knowing I'd see him at the church with the little boy."

"I think something else is going on with you, Gretchen. You're having second thoughts about your own life, and you want to believe that people can be redeemed. Pierre Dupree is no good."

"Where do you get all this knowledge about what goes on in other people's heads?"

"Sometimes I want to believe certain things for reasons I don't want to accept," Alafair said.

"You're talking about me, not you, right? Don't start that twelve-step psychobabble with me."

"If you want to have lunch with him, do it," Alafair said.

Gretchen's face was flushed, her eyes moving from the bayou to the diners in the courtyard to the drawbridge, without seeming to see any of it. "You're supposed to be my friend. I came to you for advice, nobody else."

"Some people have to work at being assholes. That's not true of Pierre Dupree. He was born one."

"Explain to me how he knew I'd see him with the crippled boy."

"He's afraid of you. He knows what happened to Jesse Leboeuf. He doesn't want to end up in a bathtub with a bullet in his brisket."

"You're saying I killed Leboeuf? You know that for a fact?"

"No, I don't know anything. I don't want to, either."

"That's a chickenshit attitude."

"What other attitude can I have? You ask me for advice, then you argue about it."

"The 1940s revue is this weekend. I thought you'd be there with me."

"I'm trying to make some headway on my new novel."

"You and Clete are the only two people I ever thought of as friends."

"I think Pierre Dupree will hurt you. You're not being honest with yourself. You're about to let a bad man use you. The worst thing we can do to ourselves is to help other people injure us. The feeling of shame never goes away."

"Anything else you want to say?"

"Yeah, I think it's going to rain."

Gretchen widened her eyes, her face hot and bright in the sunset. "I won't call you again," she said. "I'm really angry right now and having thoughts I don't like to think."

THAT SAME EVENING Clete had a caller he did not expect. When he opened the cottage door, he had to look down to see her face. She was holding a pot of soup with two hot pads. "I put too much in. It's sloshing over the sides. Where can I put this down?" she said.

She went past him without waiting for him to answer. It was Julie

Ardoin, the pilot who had flown him to the island southeast of the Chandeleurs. She set the pot heavily on the stove and turned around. "Dave said you were sick. So I took the liberty," she said.

"Dave exaggerates. I had a nosebleed," Clete said.

"Can I sit down?"

"Yes, ma'am, I'm sorry," he said, pulling a chair out from the breakfast table.

"I'm not a 'ma'am,'" she said.

"You want a drink or a beer?"

She looked around at the general disarray that characterized his room. She wore makeup and jeans and a short-sleeve embroidered shirt spotted with rain. Her hair was damp and shiny under the light. "I had another reason for coming here."

"Yeah?" he replied.

"I know you and Dave had words on the island. He thinks the world of you. He'd do anything for you. I figured you ought to know that."

"You came out in the rain to tell me that?"

"What, you think I'm minding y'all's business or something?"

"No, I meant that's a kind thing to do. Excuse the way the place looks. I was just cleaning up when you knocked." He picked up the wastebasket and opened a cabinet under the sink and put it inside.

She glanced at his raincoat and hat on top of his bed. "You fixing to go out?"

"I'm moving my boat from East Cote Blanche Bay, but it can wait. What all did Dave tell you?"

"Just that you were sick and he was worried about you."

"Out of nowhere he said that?"

"Not exactly. I asked him how you were getting along."

"Yeah?"

"You want to try the soup?"

Clete sat down across from her. "I ate a little bit ago. Let me get you a Dr Pepper. I keep some iced down for Dave."

"I need to get back home pretty soon. There's something you did at the island that I thought was out of the ordinary."

"Like what?"

"The hippie girl, Sybil. She made some sandwiches for y'all, but you forgot to take them. You went back for the sandwiches so her feelings wouldn't be hurt."

"It wasn't a big deal."

"So that's why I asked Dave how you were doing. Some people you ask about, some you don't. Do I make you uncomfortable?"

"No," he said. He coughed softly into his palm and lowered his hand beneath the tabletop.

"Because you look like it," she said.

He searched the room for the right words. "I'm an awkward guy. I have a way of messing up things. I've got a bad track record with relationships."

"You ought to check out mine. I got married the first time when I was sixteen. My husband played for Jerry Lee Lewis. Does that tell you something?"

"I'm over the hill. I break the springs in bathroom scales. My doc says there's enough cholesterol in my system to clog a storm drain."

"You look okay to me."

"I really like the way you pilot a plane."

"Give me a monkey and three bananas, and I'll give you a pilot. Ever hear that one?" she said.

"I know better than that. I was in Force Recon. I learned to fly a slick, and I learned enough to keep a fixed-wing plane in the air if the pilot got hurt." When she didn't reply, he said, "You hang out with old guys?"

"You're not old."

"Tell my liver that."

"I heard maybe you and Varina Leboeuf were an item."

"Where'd you hear that?"

"It's a small town."

"We're talking about the past tense. Anything bad that came out of that is on me, not her. Your husband took his life, Miss Julie?"

"I'm not a 'miss,' either. And we're not on the plantation. Why do you ask about my husband?"

"Because it's rough when you lose somebody that way. Sometimes a person reaches out for anybody who's available and doesn't think things through. I've got a sheet longer than most perps'. I capped a federal informant. There are some government guys who've got it in for me because I fought on the leftist side in El Salvador."

"Who cares?"

"The government does."

"I don't," she said.

"Streak said you're stand-up. That's his ultimate compliment."

"I hope you like the soup."

"Hey, don't go off," he said.

"Take care of yourself. Watch out for your cholesterol and give me a call if you really dig that old-time rock and roll."

She opened the door and went outside, splashing through a puddle, getting into her car. He followed her, the rain blowing in his face. "I need to return your pot. Where do you live?" he said.

She rolled down the window and grinned as though the issue were of no consequence, then drove away.

If she had wanted to set the hook, she had done a proper job of it, he thought.

CLETE PURCEL'S DEEDS for the rest of the night and the early hours of the following day were not of a rational kind. Even to him, his behavior was bizarre. It had nothing to do with Julie Ardoin's visit to his cottage, or his addictions, or his abiding need to find approval in the eyes of his father. The concerns that had beset Clete for most of his life had disappeared, only to be replaced by the conviction that every tick of the second hand on his wristwatch was an irrevocable subtraction from his time on earth.

He knew that death could come in many ways, almost all of them bad. Those who said otherwise had never smelled the odor of a field mortuary in a tropical country when the gas-powered refrigeration failed. Nor had they lain on a litter next to a black marine trying to hold his entrails inside his abdomen with his fingers. They had never heard a grown man cry out for his mother in a battalion aid tent. Death squeezed the breath from your chest and the light from your eyes. It was not kind or merciful; it lived in bedsheets that stuck to the body and wastebaskets filled with bloody gauze and the hollow-eyed stare of emergency room personnel who went forty-eight hours without sleep during Hurricane Katrina. It invaded your dreams and mocked your sunrise and stood next to your reflection in the mirror. Sex and booze and dope brought you no respite. When you lived in proximity to death, even a midday slumber was filled with needles and shards of glass, and the smallest sounds made the side of your face twitch like a tightly wound rubber band.

Once you understood that the great shade was your constant companion, a change took place in your life that you did not share with others. Sometimes you quickened your step when you walked through woods in the late fall; at other times indistinct figures beckoned to you from the edge of your vision, their voices as soft as the rustling of leaves, asking you to pause in your journey and rest with them awhile. Just when you thought you were onto their tricks, you discovered the joke that death had played upon you. While you were trying to avoid the natural cycle of the seasons, you empowered evil men to perpetrate upon you the greatest theft of all, enticing you into a manufactured crusade, taking you from your loved ones, robbing you of choices that should have been yours, separating you without warning from the gold-green cathedral given to you as your birthright.

These were the kind of reflections that lived behind the calmness of Clete's intelligent green eyes. And these were what made him the brave man he was. He saw the truth but never pushed the burden onto someone else.

He drove his Caddy in the rain to the boatyard on East Cote Blanche Bay where he kept his eighteen-footer and his Evinrude seventy-five-horsepower engine. He went into the tin-roofed shed where his boat was moored to a post and winched it up on a trailer and hooked the trailer to his Caddy. The bay was chain-ringed with raindrops, the branches of the gum and willow trees along the shore flattening in the wind. He filled two five-gallon plastic containers with gasoline and hefted them inside the boat. Then he opened a steel lockbox he rented from the owner and removed two road flares, an entrenching tool, a KA-BAR knife attached to a web belt, a military-issue flashlight, an

AK-47 modified into a semi-auto, and a scoped '03 Springfield rifle that was heavily oiled and snugged up inside a canvas bag. Under the shed, he removed the Springfield from the bag and opened the bolt and placed his thumb in the empty chamber and closed the bolt. He wiped the excess oil from the stock and the steel surfaces of the rifle and placed it and a box of .30-06 rounds in the bag and put the bag in the trunk of the Caddy.

By 4:15 A.M. he had off-loaded his boat into Bayou Teche and, with no lights on, had gone downstream ten miles to the back of Croix du Sud Plantation. The rain had stopped and the moon was up, and an elevated carriage lamp glowed inside the humidity in the backyard. When the wind blew, the yard was filled with moving shadows and rainwater that shone like crystal sprinkling from the trees. Clete had cut his engine upstream and allowed his boat to float silently through the shallows, past the cypress and oak trees and flooded canebrakes that bordered the back of the Dupree property. He picked up his anchor and lowered it over the gunwale and let the rope slide through his palm until the anchor sank in the mud and the rope tightened and the stern swung around and hung stationary in the current.

Someone turned on a light in the kitchen. Clete removed the Springfield from its canvas bag and opened the bolt and began thumb-loading a handful of soft-nosed rounds into the magazine. After he had locked down the bolt, feeding a bullet into the chamber, he set the safety and wiped his hand free of oil on his shirt and looked through the telescopic sight into the kitchen. The clarity of detail inside the lenses was stunning.

Alexis Dupree was eating a piece of cobbler and drinking a glass of milk at the kitchen table. He was wearing a striped robe, one that, paradoxically, might be confused with the striped pattern on the work uniforms of the inmates in Dachau and Buchenwald. His eyes were deep-set, his jowls flecked with tiny veins, his throat as coarse and wrinkled as a turtle's. Hair grew out of his nose. His eyebrows looked feral; he scratched at a dark, crusty mole inside one sideburn. His tall frame had the stiffness of coat hangers. He ate with small bites, as though the process of eating were a joyless activity and should be undertaken only with measure and control. He gazed through the window at the backyard and at the giant trees that swelled with wind and scattered leaves on the bayou, and dabbed at a smear of cobbler on his chin.

Clete wondered if Alexis Dupree saw things inside the darkness that others did not. Had Dupree not only looked into the abyss but immersed himself in it, exchanging his soul for the black arts he unleashed on helpless people behind barbed wire? Or had he been little more than a cipher, a mindless bureaucrat carrying out the orders of other people, a man with the wingspan of a blowfly rather than a condor?

A flip of the safety mechanism, a squeeze of the trigger, and Clete could make all these questions moot. How would the world be the less? One squeeze, one bullet, and a few of Dupree's victims would not have to wander the earth seeking justice.

Just do it and think about it later, Clete told himself.

Then he saw Pierre Dupree enter the kitchen, followed by a woman who remained in the background, her face obscured by the knives and skillets and cooking pans that hung from an iron rack suspended above a butcher block. Pierre was dressed in slacks and a snow-white shirt, and the woman wore a maroon skirt cinched with a gold belt. Clete suspected they were going on a trip or they would not have been up this early. He could not see the woman's face or even the color of her hair, and he wondered who she could be.

He realized he had devoted too much attention to the scene and the people in the kitchen. In the corner of his vision, he saw the shape of a man by the gazebo on the left side of the backyard. Clete shifted his position in the boat and looked through the telescopic sight at the gazebo and the shadows in the yard, but the man who had been standing on the lawn seconds ago had disappeared. The wind gusted out of the north, blowing hundreds of unraked leaves across the Saint Augustine grass. While all the other shadows in the yard swayed back and forth, one remained starkly immobile. Then the figure lit a cigarette, the flame from his lighter flaring on his face.

There was no mistaking the bump on his nose, the greased hair, or the scalp job around his ears. He was one of the men Clete had seen in Lafayette with Lamont Woolsey and the British oilman Hubert Donnelly.

Clete's eyes were beginning to burn in the humidity. He lowered the rifle and wiped his eyes clear on his sleeve, then raised the telescopic sight again and scanned the area around the gazebo. The man with the bump on his nose was gone. His disappearance made no sense. Clete had a view of the entire yard, which was terraced like three stair steps, with gardens on each step. The gazebo and the latticework on it were silhouetted against the moonlit reflection of the house. In no more than three or four seconds, the Duprees' sentinel had walked either to the house or out to a sugarcane field, neither of which seemed possible.

Clete moved the telescopic sight back onto the kitchen. Pierre Dupree was seated with his grandfather, dipping a powdered beignet into a cup of coffee, a napkin tucked into his collar. Clete could not see the woman. Then he realized she had gone out the French doors and was standing on a patio overhung by the limbs of a live oak. The light from the kitchen fell across her hips and lower back and calves but not her upper body or face. She turned briefly, and Clete caught sight of her hands and her broad, laminated gold belt and the plate and fork she was eating with. Fog had started to form on the bayou and drift through the trees, wrapping around her, almost as though she enjoyed a symbiotic relationship with it.

Downstream he heard the drawbridge closing, then the droning sounds of a tugboat pushing a huge barge against the tidal inflow, the wake slapping loudly in the trees along the bank. The woman walked out in the mist and gazed at the tug and barge passing beyond the tree trunks. Did the boat represent escape? Was it a reminder of a working-class world she had abandoned for the ambience the Duprees could provide her? Did she long for a better and simpler world than the one she lived inside? Was she Tee Jolie Melton? Or Varina Leboeuf? Or someone else?

Clete would not learn the answer to his questions, at least not that night. The woman went back into the house and fastened the French doors and disappeared into the room beyond the kitchen.

Clete pulled up the anchor and let the boat drift south of the Dupree property before he fired up his engine. He worked his way upstream toward New Iberia, the running lights off, keeping to the far side of the bayou so he would not be seen from the Dupree home.

He rounded a bend and angled his boat toward a spot at the extreme end of the Dupree property, then cut the gas feed and tilted the propeller out of the water. His bow slid up on the mudflat between two cypress trees, and he stepped into the shallows and pulled the boat's hull farther up the bank. Through the trees, he could see the lights in the Dupree kitchen and a porch light that someone had turned on. He lifted the five-gallon gasoline containers out of his boat and set them on the mudflat, then retrieved his E-tool and dug a loamy hole on the edge of a wild blackberry bush spiked with thorns. He wrapped the containers and the road flares inside a plastic tarp and buried them in the hole, sweating inside his clothes, his breath coming hard in his chest. He spat in his palm and looked at it, then rubbed his palm clean on his pants and tried not to think about the pink tinge in his saliva.

He stared through the darkness at the house, his head as light as a helium balloon. "Tomorrow or the next day or the day after that or maybe a month down the road, I'm going to get you," he said.

To whom was he speaking? The Duprees and their hired gumballs? Or the men who would probably try to kill Gretchen? No, Clete's real enemy had been with him much longer. He had seen him the first time he lay in a battalion aid station in the Central Highlands, dehydrated from blood expander, his face white from the concussion of a grenade, his neck beaded with dirt rings, his utilities fouled by his own urine. A corpsman had closed off an artery with his thumb, and suddenly the light had come back into Clete's eyes and air had flowed into his lungs, as cool as if it were blowing across open water. That was when he saw the cloaked and hooded figure with the white face and thin lips and sunken cheeks.

The figure smiled and leaned over and pressed his mouth to Clete's ear, as though no one else were in the tent. His breath smelled like nightshade and lichen on damp stone and ponded water gone sour in a forest whose canopy seldom admits light. *I can wait,* the hooded figure whispered. *But no matter where you go, you're mine.*

CHAPTER 28

IF YOU HAVE met the very rich, and by the very rich, I mean those who own and live in several palatial homes and have amounts of money that people of average means cannot conceive of, you have probably come away from the experience feeling that you have been taken, somehow diminished and cheapened in terms of self-worth. It's not unlike getting too close to theatrical people or celebrity ministers or politicians who have convinced us that it is their mandate to lead us away from ourselves.

If you are around the very rich for very long, you quickly learn that in spite of their money, many of them are dull-witted and boring. Their tastes are often superficial, their interests vain and self-centered. Most of them do not like movies or read books of substance, and they have little or no curiosity about anything that doesn't directly affect their lives. Their conversations are pedestrian and deal with the minutiae of their daily existence. Those who wait on them and polish and chauffeur their automobiles and tend their lawns and gardens are abstractions with no last names or histories worth taking note of. The toil and sweat and suffering of the great masses are the stuff of a benighted time that belongs in the books of Charles Dickens and has nothing to do with our own era. In the world of the very rich, obtuseness may not quite rise to the level of a virtue, but it's often the norm.

421

What is most remarkable about many of those who have great wealth is the basic assumption on which they predicate their lives: They believe that others have the same insatiable desire for money that they have, and that others will do anything for it. Inside their culture, manners and morality and money not only begin with the same letter of the alphabet but are indistinguishable. The marble floors and the spiral staircases of the homes owned by the very rich and the chandeliers that ring with light in their entranceways usually have little to do with physical comfort. These things are iconic and votive in nature and, ultimately, a vulgarized tribute to a deity who is arguably an extension of themselves.

The British oil entrepreneur Hubert Donnelly could be called an emissary for the very rich, but he could not be called a hypocrite. He came in person to my office at nine A.M. on Thursday. If he was a lawbreaker, and I suspected he was, I had to grant him his brass. He came without a lawyer into the belly of the beast and laid his proposal on my desk. "I want you and Mr. Purcel to work for us," he said. "You'll have to travel, but you'll fly first-class or on private jets and stay at the best hotels. Here's the starting figure."

He placed a slip of paper on my desk blotter. The number 215,000 was written on it.

"That's for the probationary period," he said. "After six months or so, you'll get a significant bump."

"That's a lot of money," I said.

"You'll earn it."

"A guy like me would be a fool to pass it up."

"Talk it over with your family. Take your time."

He wore a dark blue suit and a shirt as bright as tin. His grooming was immaculate. I couldn't keep my eyes off the pits in his cheeks and the way his skin sagged under his jaw.

"You already know this is a waste of time, don't you?" I said.

"Probably."

"You're here anyway."

"One toggles from place to place and carries out his little duties. I'm sure you do the same."

"Have you chatted up Lamont Woolsey of late?"

"He and I are not close."

"I hear somebody stomped his face in."

"Woolsey has a way of provoking people."

"Ever hear of a guy by the name of Ozone Eddy Mouton?"

"No, I can't say that I have."

"A couple of people were found incinerated inside a car trunk in St. Bernard Parish. I hear even their teeth were melted by the heat."

He didn't blink. I watched his eyes. They had a translucence about them that was almost ethereal. They were free of guilt or worry or concern of any kind. They made me think of blue water on a sunny day or the eyes of door-to-door proselytizers who tell you they were recently reborn.

"If you worked for us, you would be free of all these things," he said. "Why not give it a try? You seem to have the benefits of a classical education. As a soldier, you walked in the footprints of the French and the British, and you know how it's all going to play out. Do you always want to be a beggar of scraps at the table of the rich? Do you enjoy being part of a system that instills a vice like gambling in its citizenry and placates the poor with bread and circuses?"

"The guys who died on that rig are going to find you one day, Mr. Donnelly."

"When all else fails, we whip out our biblical dirge, do we?"

"Maybe you'll have better luck dealing with the dead than I. They go where they want. They sit on your bed at night and stand behind you in the mirror. Once they locate you, they never rest. And you know what's worse about them?"

He smiled at me and didn't reply.

"When it's your time, they'll be your escorts, and they won't be delivering you to a very good place. The dead are not given to mercy."

He did something I didn't expect. He leaned forward in his chair, his elbows splayed on my desk. "I was once like you, determined to impose my moral sense on the rest of the world. I was in Sudan and Libya and Turkistan and Rwanda and the Congo. I was repelled when I saw peasants buried up to their necks and decapitated by earth graders, and women disemboweled with machetes on the roadside. But I learned to live with it, as I'm sure you and Mr. Purcel did. Don't rinse your sins at the expense of others, sir. It's tawdry and cheap stuff and unworthy of a good soldier and a knowledgeable man."

"Clete Purcel and I have nothing you want."

"When you cross the wrong Rubicon, you enter a harsh and unpredictable environment, Detective Robicheaux. It's not a country where you can depend on the kindness of strangers or those who seem to be your friends. Do you get my drift?"

"No, not at all," I replied.

"That's too bad. I thought you were a more perceptive man. Good-bye, sir," he said.

GRETCHEN HOROWITZ DID not deal well with emotions that involved trust or deconstructing her defense system. Her program had always been simple: Number one, you didn't empower others to hurt you; number two, when people didn't heed your warning signs, you taught them the nature of regret; number three, you didn't let a man get in your head so he could get in your pants.

Her ongoing conversation with herself about Pierre Dupree was causing her problems she had never experienced. The more she thought about him, the more power she gave him. The more she shut him out of her thoughts, the more she lost confidence in herself. Since she was sixteen, she had never run from a problem. She could also say she had never been afraid, or at least she had never let fear stop her from doing anything. Not until now. She was obviously losing control, something she'd believed would never happen to her again. She felt weak and agitated and ashamed, and she felt unclean and refused to look directly at herself in the mirror. Had she secretly always wanted to be in the arms of a large and powerful and handsome man who was rich and educated and knew how to dress? In this case, the same man who had almost broken her fingers in his palm. Did another person live inside her, someone whose self-esteem was so low that she was attracted to her abuser?

She felt her eyes filming, her cheeks burning.

There was no harm in listening to what he had to say, was there? You kept your friends close and your enemies closer, right?

Don't think thoughts like that, she told herself. *He wants you in the sack.*

So I won't let that happen.

Who are you kidding, girl?

He did a good deed for the little cripple boy. I didn't make that up. There was no way he could know I'd see him taking the little boy into the church.

He's a con man. He's probably having you surveilled. Tell somebody about this. Don't act on your own. You're about to sell out everything you thought you believed in.

She went into the bathroom and washed her face and sat down on the stool, her head spinning. She could not remember when she'd felt so miserable.

Pierre Dupree was not her only problem, and she knew it. The man named Marco had given her ten days to kill Clete Purcel and Dave and Alafair Robicheaux. Gretchen's mother was no longer a hostage, but that would not change what was expected of her. She would either deliver or get delivered, along with Clete and his best friend and Alafair. Though her enemies knew where she was, she had no idea where they were, just as Clete had warned her. How could all of these things be happening right when she thought she might be beginning a new life, one that offered a chance at a career in film-making?

These were her thoughts when she glanced through the front screen and saw Pierre Dupree pull into her driveway early Thursday afternoon and begin fishing something out of a paper sack. Why was it that everything about him had become a mystery? Even his arrival at her cottage seemed unreal, like part of a dream that had detached itself from her sleep and reappeared during her waking hours. Leaves were drifting down on top of the Humvee, the sunlight on his tinted windows like a yellow balloon wobbling inside dark water. She could hear the heat ticking in the engine and the sprinkler system in the neighbor's yard bursting to life.

Dupree leaned down and picked up a bouquet of mixed roses

and opened the door of his Humvee. As he walked up on her porch, he was so tall that he almost blocked out the trees and the sky and the church steeple across the street. Even though it was not yet two P.M., his beard had already darkened, as though he had shaved in the predawn hours; a strand of black hair hung down over his forehead. There was a dimple in his chin and a dent in the skin at the corner of his mouth, as though he wanted to smile but did not want to be presumptuous. In his left hand, he carried a box wrapped in gold foil and red felt ribbon.

"I was on my way back from the airport in Lafayette and stopped and bought these for you," he said.

She had rehearsed a reply, but she couldn't remember what it was.

"Miss Gretchen, I don't blame you for being suspicious of me," he said. "I simply wanted to drop these by. If you like, you can give them to someone else. It's just a small gesture on my part."

"Come in."

Had she said that?

"Thank you," he said, stepping inside. "You have such a nice spot here. It looks so comfortable and restful. I hope I'm not bothering you."

"It's all right. I mean the place is all right. I rented it. The furniture came with it."

"Can I put the flowers in some water?" he asked. He was peering into the back of the house, but he was so close she could smell the heat that seemed to exude from his skin. "Miss Gretchen?"

"Can you what?"

"Put these in a vase. They'll go well on the dining room table, don't you think? You know, add a splash of color? Here. You like dark chocolate? You're not on a diet, are you?"

She couldn't keep up with what he was saying. Her face was hot, her ears pinging as though she were deep underwater, her air tanks empty, the pressure breaking something inside her head. "There's a glass jar in the cabinet," she said.

He walked through the dining room and began filling the jar at the sink, his back to her, his shoulders as broad as an ax handle inside his dress shirt. "I went on a private plane to Galveston early this morning and dissolved my business connections with a company I never should have been involved with," he said. "I also settled some financial affairs with my ex. I'm going back to painting full-time. I'm getting rid of my ad business as well."

He turned around, drying his hands on a paper towel. He crumpled the towel and set it absentmindedly behind him on the drainboard. Then he picked up the towel and began looking for a place to put it.

"Under the sink," she said.

"Are you going to the musical revue in New Iberia this weekend?"

"I'm making a documentary of it."

"That's wonderful. My ex is sponsoring one of the bands, a western swing group of some kind." He continued to gaze into her face, his eyes locked on hers. "You're not a fan of my ex?"

"She said some ugly things to me."

"What did you do about it?"

"Nothing."

"That doesn't sound like you."

"I didn't have to. Alafair Robicheaux did. She popped her in the mouth. Your ex is a cunt."

"Good Lord, Miss Gretchen."

"I don't like people calling me 'miss,' either."

"That's what Varina says. She hates that word."

"Good for her. She's still a cunt. Are you holding your breath?"

"No. Why?"

"Because your face is red. Men do that when they want to seem innocent and shy."

"I grew up here. Most women here don't use that kind of language."

"You're saying I'm not as good as they are?"

"No, it's the other way around. I admire you tremendously."

"Oh yeah?"

"You know how to put the fear of God in a man. On top of it, you're beautiful."

"Beautiful?"

"I'm going to be a little personal here. Let's put the nonsense aside. You're an extraordinary woman, the kind every man wants to be with. You radiate a combination of power and femininity that's rare. I'm very drawn to you."

"Yeah, that *is* a little personal," she replied. She could feel the blood rising in her chest, her breasts swelling. "What do you think you know about me?"

"I don't understand."

"My background. Who do you think I am? What do you think I do for a living?"

He shook his head.

"You don't know?" she said.

"I don't care what you do for a living."

"I have an antique business. I've done other things as well."

"I don't care about your history. You are what you are. You have the statuesque physique of a warrior woman and the eyes of a little girl."

"Why are you here today?"

"To bring you these small gifts."

"Don't lie."

"I'm here to do whatever you want."

He touched her on the cheek with his fingertips. She was breathing through her nose, her nipples hardening. She searched his eyes, her cheeks flaming. "Call me later," she said.

"What's your number?"

"I just got my phone. I don't remember what it is. Call information."

"You don't have a cell phone?"

"I lost it."

"You still don't trust me, do you? I don't blame you."

She wet her lips. She couldn't take her eyes off his. Her cheek seemed to burn where he had touched her. "You called me a kike while you almost broke my fingers."

"I'll be ashamed of that for the rest of my life."

"I have to go into the bathroom."

"Do you mean for me to stay? I don't want you to do something you'll regret later. I'm going to leave and let you make some decisions while I'm not around."

"I didn't say you had to leave."

"No, I don't want to be a source of anxiety or guilt or conflict for you. I'd better go. I'm sorry for any offense I may have given you."

After he walked across the gallery and out the screen door and across the grass to the Humvee, oak leaves tumbling out of the sunlight onto his hair and dress shirt, she was so weak that she had to hold on to the doorjamb lest she fall down.

"WHAT'S THE MATTER?" Clete asked her. He was sitting in his swivel chair behind his office desk, one corner of his mouth downturned, his eyes veiled.

"I feel pretty stupid," she answered. "No, worse than that. I hate myself."

"Over what?"

"Pierre Dupree. He was just at my house," she said.

Clete showed no expression. "Want to tell me about it?" he said.

She talked for ten minutes. His eyes looked into space while he listened. Through the window, she could see the bayou and, on the far side of it, a black man cutting the grass in front of the old convent. The grass had already started to turn pale with the coming of winter, and the flowers in the beds looked wilted, perhaps from an early frost. The cold look of the shade on the convent walls disturbed her in a way she couldn't articulate. "I don't understand my feelings," she said. "I feel like something died inside me."

"Why? You didn't do anything wrong," Clete said.

"I liked it when he flattered me. I didn't want him to go. If he'd stayed longer, I don't know what would have happened. That's not true. I would have let him—"

"You don't know what you would have done, so stop thinking like that," he said. "Listen, it's natural to feel the way you do. We want to believe people when they say good things about us. We also want to believe they're good people."

"Something happened to me in the park in Lafayette. A little boy almost fell into the pond. His father was supposed to be watching him, but he had fallen asleep. Maybe I saved the little boy from drowning. Then I drove the family home. They're real poor and having a hard time. I felt different about myself afterward. There was something about the family that made me feel changed inside. Or maybe it was because I helped them that I felt changed inside, I'm not sure."

Clete put a stick of gum in his mouth and chewed. "Then Dupree shows up, and you don't know if you're supposed to forgive him or kill him?"

"That pretty much says it."

"Don't trust him. He's no good."

"He says he's changed."

"He had a woman at his house in the early A.M. today."

She stared at him. "How do you know?"

"I was looking through his kitchen window with a telescopic sight at four this morning. The woman had a gold belt on. I couldn't see her face. I don't know who she was. She left with Dupree."

"She was at his house all night?"

"That's what it looked like."

"What were you doing there?"

"I was thinking about taking out the old man. I was thinking about taking out Pierre, too. Right now I wish I had."

"You're not like that."

"Don't bet on it," he said.

"I think maybe I should leave town, Clete."

"Where will you go?"

"It doesn't matter. I'm causing trouble between you and your best friend. I made Alafair mad, too. If I stay here, eventually I'll be arrested. I feel like my life is permanently messed up, and there's no way out."

"You're worried because of the Jesse Leboeuf shooting?"

She nodded.

"Leboeuf was in the act of raping a female sheriff's deputy. Whoever popped him probably saved her life. Don't look out the window, look at me. Jesse Leboeuf was a bucket of shit, and everybody around here knows it. End of story."

"You think Pierre was lying to me, all those things he said to me?"

She could see Clete trying to think his way around her question. "You're beautiful and a great person on top of it," he said. "He's not telling you anything that anyone with eyes doesn't already know. Don't go near the bastard. If I see the guy, he's going to have the worst day of his life."

"I don't want to hurt people anymore. I don't want to be the cause of them getting hurt, either."

"I let you down, Gretchen. There's nothing worse than for a girl to grow up without a father. I'll never forgive myself for letting that happen. This guy isn't going to get his hands on you."

She stared emptily at the floor. "How do you think all of it is going to play out?"

"The guys who are behind all this think Dave and I know something we don't. The same people think you're a threat to them. If they have their way, we're going to be bags of fertilizer."

He took a Kleenex from a box on his desk and spat his gum in it and put the Kleenex in the wastebasket.

"Do you have bleeding gums?" she asked.

"Yeah, sometimes. I never brushed enough."

"What are you hiding?"

"You're worse than Dave. Look, the Bobbsey Twins from Homicide are forever. Now you're one of us. That means you're forever, too."

"No, I'm not one of you. I killed people for money, Clete."

He leaned forward on the desk, pointing his finger. "You did what you did because men molested and raped you as a child. You're my baby girl, and anyone who says you're not a wonderful young woman is going to have his voice box ripped out. Are we clear on this? Don't let me hear you running yourself down again. You're one of the best people I ever knew."

She felt a lump in her throat that was so large, she couldn't swallow.

FROM THIS POINT on in my narrative, I cannot be entirely sure of any of the events that transpired. It started to rain hard Thursday night, the kind of winter rain that in Louisiana is always followed by a cold front, one that descends out of the north as hard as a fist and limns the tops of the unharvested cane with frost and flanges the edges of the bayou with ice. It was the kind of weather I looked forward to as a boy, when my father and I hunted ducks down at Pecan Island, rising out of the reeds together, our shotguns against our shoulders, knocking down mallards and Canadian geese whose V formations were stenciled against the clouds as far as the eye could see. But those days were gone, and when Molly and I went to sleep at ten P.M. that Thursday, my dreams took me to places that seemed to have nothing to do with southern Louisiana and the barking of retrievers and the sounds the geese made when they plunged through the sheet of ice that surrounded our duck blind.

In the dream I saw a long stretch of clear green water in the Dry Tortugas, the pink and gray mass of old Fort Jefferson in the background, and down below a horseshoe-shaped coral reef that formed a bowl in which a cloud of hot blue water floated like ink poured from a bottle. The reef was strung with gossamer fans, and inside them I could see lobsters hiding in the rocks and the shadows of lemon sharks moving across the whiteness of the sand.

Then the water began to recede from the cusp of beach that surrounded the fort, exposing the ragged and crumbling foundation under it, the water dropping steadily as though someone had pulled a plug from a drain hole in the bottom of the ocean. The boat I was standing on descended with the water level until the keel settled on the seabed. I had expected to see coral-encrusted cannons and spent torpedoes and the wrecks of ancient ships and an undulating landscape that had the softly molded contours of a sand sculpture. I was mistaken. I was surrounded by a desert, and in the distance I could see the curvature of the earth dipping off the horizon into a hard blue sky unmarked by either clouds or birds. The sand was salted with volcanic grit and dotted with big lumps of basaltic rock and glimmering pools of a viscous green liquid that could have been chemical waste. There was no sign of life of any kind, not even the lobsters and the lemon sharks I had seen moments earlier inside the coral horseshoe. The only human edifice in sight was Fort Jefferson, the place where Dr. Samuel Mudd was imprisoned for his role in the assassination of President Lincoln. The flag that flew above it had frayed into sun-faded strips of red and white and blue cheesecloth.

I sat up in bed and was glad to hear the rain hitting the trees and our tin roof and running through the gutters into our flower beds and out into the yard. I hoped the rain would pour down during the entirety of the night and flood our property and clog the storm sewers and overflow the curbs and wash in waves through the streets and down the slope of the Teche until the oaks and cypresses and canebrakes along the banks seemed to quiver inside the current. I wanted to see the rain wash clean all the surfaces of the earth, as it did in Noah's time. I wanted to believe that morning would bring a pink sunrise and the hanging of the archer's bow in the sky and the appearance of a solitary dove flying toward a ship's bow with a green branch in its beak. I wanted to believe that biblical events of aeons ago would happen again. In short, I wanted to believe in things that were impossible.

I was on the way to the bathroom when the phone rang. I picked it up in the kitchen. Through the window, I could see a heavy coat of white fog on the bayou's surface, and I could see Tripod and Snuggs inside the hutch, rain sluicing off the tarp I had stretched over the top.

"Guess who this is, Mr. Dave," the voice said.

"I don't know if I'm up to this, Tee Jolie," I replied.

"I done somet'ing wrong?"

"We went to the island southeast of the Chandeleurs. Nobody was home."

"What you mean? Where you t'ink I'm at now?"

"I have no idea."

"I can see the palm trees and the water t'rew the window."

"You sound pretty stoned, kiddo."

"You make me feel bad. I cain't he'p what they give me."

"*Who* gives you?"

"The doctor and the nurse. I almost bled out. You heard from Blue?"

"No, I haven't. Blue died of an overdose. Her body was frozen in a block of ice and dumped overboard south of St. Mary Parish. I saw her body on the coroner's table. The last thing she did was put a note in her mouth telling us that you were still alive. You have to stop lying to yourself, Tee Jolie."

"Blue don't use drugs. At least not no more. I seen her on a video. She was waving at me on a boat. Out on the ocean in California."

"Where is Pierre Dupree?"

"I ain't sure. I sleep most of the time. I wish I was back home. I miss St. Martinville."

"You have to find out where you are and tell me."

"I done tole you. I can see the walls outside and the palm trees and the waves smashing on the beach."

"You're in a place that looks like a fort? That's made out of stucco?"

"Yes, suh."

"There's a wall around it with broken glass on top of the wall? Some of the wall has crumbled down, and you can see cinder blocks inside it?"

"That's it. That's where I'm at."

I was at a loss. "Listen to me. You're not where you think you are. I went to the island southeast of the Chandeleurs, but the house was deserted. You have to find out where you are now and call me back."

"I got to go. They don't want me on the phone. They say I cain't have no excitement."

"Do you know Alexis Dupree?"

"I ain't said nothing about Mr. Alexis."

"Is he there?"

"I cain't talk no more."

"Did he do something to you?"

"Good-bye, Mr. Dave. I ain't gonna call no more. Take care of yourself. Hey, you gonna see me on TV out in California one day. You gonna see me and Blue both. Then tell me I been lying, you."

After I had hung up the phone, I stared at it. I tried to think back on the things Tee Jolie had told me. Obviously, she was deluded, hyped to the eyes with coke or brown skag, inside a chemically induced schizophrenia. But I believed she had told the truth about one thing: I probably would not be hearing from her again.

● ● ●

I DIDN'T TELL Molly or Alafair about Tee Jolie's phone call. I didn't tell anyone except Clete. I no longer trusted my own perceptions, and I wondered if I wasn't experiencing a psychotic break. Since my return to the department, my colleagues had treated me with respect but also with a sense of caution and a degree of fear, the kind we express around drunk people or those whose mortality has begun to show in their eyes. It's not a good way to feel about yourself. If you've visited the provinces of the dead, you know what I'm talking about. When you hover on the edge of the grave, when you feel that the act of shutting your eyes will cause you to lose all control over your life, that in the next few seconds you will be dropped into a black hole from which you will never exit, you have an epiphany about existence that others will not understand. Every sunrise of your life will become a candle that you carry with you until sunset, and anyone who tries to touch it or blow out its flame will do so at mortal risk. There's a syndrome called the thousand-yard stare. Soldiers bring it back from places that later are reconfigured into memorial parks filled with statuary and green lawns and rows of white crosses and copses of maple and chestnut trees. But the imposition of a bucolic landscape on a killing field is a poor anodyne for those who fear their fate when they shut their eyes.

It was 7:46 Friday morning, and I was sitting at Clete's breakfast table, watching him cook at his small stove. "Tee Jolie told you she could see palm trees and ocean waves outside her window?" he said.

"She said she could see the stucco wall with the exposed cinder blocks where the wall crumbled. I mentioned the broken glass on the top of the wall and asked if she was in the house that looked like a fort. She said that's where she was."

"It sounds like you gave her the details rather than the other way around, Dave."

"That's possible. But she told me she was looking at palm trees and the ocean hitting on a beach."

"What else did she say?"

"She didn't know where Pierre Dupree was. When I mentioned the old man, she sounded frightened."

"That guy should have been put on the bus a long time ago," Clete said. He scraped a pork chop and two eggs out of the frying pan and slid them off the spatula onto a plate. "You sure you don't want any?"

"You know how much grease is in that stuff?"

"That's why I've never had problems with arthritis. The grease in your food oils your joints and your connective tissue. Nobody in my family has ever had arthritis."

"Because they didn't live long enough," I replied.

He sat down across from me and filled my coffee cup and started eating, mopping up the egg yolk with a piece of toast dripping with melted butter. He didn't lift his eyes when he spoke. "Are you sure you weren't having a dream?"

"No, I'm not sure. I'm not sure about anything these days," I replied.

"After the shootout on the bayou, I started having all kinds of weird dreams and hearing voices in my sleep," he said. "Sometimes I see things when I'm awake that aren't there."

"Like what?" I asked.

"After I busted up Lamont Woolsey, I was hauling ass down St. Charles, and I saw the streetcar coming toward me on the neutral ground. The guy at the helm didn't look like any streetcar conductor I ever saw. Know what I mean?"

"No," I replied.

"The guy's face was like a death's-head. I grew up here. The streetcar was a dime when I was a kid. I loved to ride the car downtown and transfer out to Elysian Fields and sometimes go to the amusement park on the lake. I never thought about the streetcar as something you had to be afraid of."

"It doesn't mean anything," I said. "You worked over Woolsey because he was sexually abusing the Vietnamese girl, and that made you think about the Eurasian girl back in Vietnam and what the VC did because she was in love with a GI. You were blaming yourself again for something that wasn't your fault."

"Why are you always fussing at me about my health?"

"I'm not sure that's the case."

"You kill me, Streak."

"Where's Gretchen?"

"I don't know. But if I catch Pierre Dupree around her, I'm going to turn him into wallpaper."

"Did you know a woman's panties are lying on your rug?"

"Really?" he said. His jaw was swollen with meat and eggs and bread and looked as tight as a baseball. "Want to go to the 1940s revue tonight with me and Julie Ardoin? They're going to blow the joint down."

CHAPTER
29

THE PERFORMANCE WAS scheduled to begin in the Sugar Cane Festival Building inside City Park at eight o'clock Friday evening. In that same building, in 1956, I had listened to Harry James perform with Buddy Rich on drums, Willie Smith on alto sax, and Duke Ellington's arranger Juan Tizol on valve trombone. The band had worn summer tuxes, and James had worn a bloodred carnation in his lapel. For us down here in our provincial Cajun world on the banks of Bayou Teche, the people playing horns and reed instruments on the stage were magical creatures that had descended from the ether. Their black trousers had razor creases, and their dress shoes gleamed, and their trombones and cornets had the brightness of liquid gold. The female singer sang Elvis Presley's "Heartbreak Hotel" to a swing arrangement, then the orchestra went right into "One O'Clock Jump." For two hours we were dancing at the Savoy or the Trianon or the Hollywood Palladium, James's trumpet rising like a bell into the rafters, Buddy Rich's drums rumbling in the background, the saxophones creating a second melody that was like an ocean wave starting to crest on a beach, all of it building into a crescendo of sound and rhythm that was almost sexual, that left us dry-mouthed and with a sense of longing we couldn't explain.

Now we were over a half century down the road, almost to the winter solstice and the re-creation of Saturnalia, probably no wiser than our antecedents, our fears of mortality and the coming of night no less real. The live oaks in the park were wrapped with strings of tiny white lights; the Sugar Cane Festival Building was hung with wreaths and thick red ribbons tied in big bows; and families who were undaunted by cold weather were barbecuing under the picnic shelters, the blue smoke of their meat fires hanging as thick as fog in the damp air. Above the wide sweep of the oaks in the park, the sky was black and bursting with stars. The night could not have been more beautiful.

Alafair and Molly and I parked down by the duck pond and joined the crowd entering the building. "There's Gretchen Horowitz," Alafair said.

"Pretend you don't see her," I said.

"That's a cheap way to act," she replied.

"Leave her alone," I said, putting my hand on her forearm.

"You're not going to tell me what I should and shouldn't do, Dave."

"Will both of you stop it?" Molly said. She stared through the crowd at Gretchen's hot-rod pickup, which was parked on a concrete pad at the rear of the building. "What's she doing, anyway?"

"Unloading her film equipment. She's making a documentary," Alafair said. "I was going to help her with it."

"You think she has any talent?" Molly said.

"I think she's an artist. She has the love of it. What she doesn't have are friends who are willing to help her," Alafair said.

"You're talking about me?" I said.

"No, I'm talking about myself. I gave her the impression that I might help her with her documentary. But I ended up telling her I was busy with my new novel. She got pretty mad about it."

"At you?" I said, watching Gretchen pull a boom pole from her truck.

"Of course."

"I'll meet y'all inside," I said.

"Don't," Alafair said. This time it was she who grabbed my arm.

"Gretchen needs to think about relocation. I think southern California is a fine place to visit this time of year," I said.

"If you do this, Dave, I'll move out of the house," Alafair said.

"Clete is my best friend," I said. "But he has to get Gretchen Horowitz out of New Iberia. She also needs to understand that members of our family don't have the answer to her problems, all of which are connected to killing people."

"Lower your voice," Molly said.

"There's Pierre Dupree," Alafair said.

He had moved out of the crowd and was walking toward Gretchen's pickup, wearing a pin-striped suit with a western shirt and buffed needle-nosed cowboy boots. In the background, through the trees, I could see Clete Purcel parking his maroon convertible by a picnic shelter. He and Julie Ardoin got out, and the two of them headed toward the building.

"Does Clete know Pierre is trying to put moves on Gretchen?" Alafair said.

"Yep."

"What's he plan to do about it?" she asked.

"Turn Pierre Dupree into wallpaper. Maybe that was just a metaphor," I replied.

"I'm going over there," Alafair said.

"For what?" I said.

"Pierre is evil. Gretchen is fighting a war in her head about forgiveness while this lying piece of shit is giving her a line."

"Stay with Molly, Alf. I'm asking you, not telling you," I said. "Please trust me on this."

"You said you weren't going to call me that again."

"I'm just not much good at keeping certain kinds of promises."

Her eyes studied mine, and I knew she wasn't thinking about pet names. "I've got a bad feeling, Dave."

"About what?"

"All of this," she said.

AT FIRST GRETCHEN tried to ignore him, to pretend that either his presence or his absence was of no concern to her. But even as she reached back into the cab of her pickup to retrieve her Steadicam, his shadow seemed to loom above her and block out the lights of the building and invade her thoughts and reduce her in size and importance, as though he knew the location of every weakness in her body and soul. "I hoped you'd be here," he said.

"I said I would be, didn't I?" she replied.

"You sure did. Is this your equipment?"

"Whose does it look like?"

"You have to remember, film isn't my medium." He was smiling, his collar unbuttoned, the black hair on his chest showing.

"You see movies, though?" she said.

"Sometimes."

"You ever see *The Anderson Platoon*? It was about an American patrol in Vietnam. But it was done by the French. It's one of the best documentaries I ever saw. It made me think of Robert Capa's work."

"Who?"

"He was one of the greatest combat photographers who ever lived."

"I was never that keen on motion pictures and photography. I'm a painter."

"You don't like movies?"

He grinned and shrugged. "Sit with me."

"I'm working."

"How about a drink afterward?"

"I don't know if that's a good idea, Pierre."

"Give me a chance to prove myself."

She began fitting on the harness of the Steadicam, avoiding his eyes and the way he seemed to deliberately block out the light from the building, like a dark cloak trying to wrap itself around her. She realized he was not looking at her anymore. "There's your employer," he said.

"Pardon?"

"Mr. Purcel. There in the crowd, going into the building. He's with Julie Ardoin." He sucked his teeth.

"Why do you make that sound?"

He tried to smile like a gentleman who doesn't want to be unkind.

"Sorry, I'm not good at facial sign language," Gretchen said.

He blew out his breath. "I don't think Mr. Purcel is a very good judge of character."

"I don't know what you're trying to say."

"Julie Ardoin is a pilot. She used to do some work for my ex and her father, Jesse Leboeuf. The expression 'under the radar' comes to mind."

"She's dirty?"

"Because of the mistakes I've made in my life, I don't have the moral authority to speculate about others. That said, I knew Julie's husband for twenty years. He was a good man and would put his hand in a fire for a friend. His brains ended up on Julie's ceiling. The coroner put his death down as a suicide. I don't think that's what happened. I think your employer is walking into a spiderweb."

"What kind of work did this woman do for Varina Leboeuf? Don't jerk me around, Pierre."

"They were running coke out of Panama. Guns were involved in the deal. I don't know the details. I don't want to talk about this anymore. I've changed my life, and the misdeeds of other people aren't my business. But I think your friend is about to get hurt. I'll be inside. Let me know if you want to have a drink later."

He walked away, his cowboy boots clicking on the concrete dance pad, his coat flapping open in the breeze, his handsome face turned into the barbecue smoke blowing from the picnic shelters. The back of his neck looked as graceful as a swan's, shiny with aftershave. Gretchen felt as though someone had dropped a handful of thumbtacks inside her head.

GRETCHEN WAS STARING at Pierre Dupree's back when I walked up behind her. "How are you tonight?" I said.

"How am I?" she replied. "I was doing fine. Until two seconds ago."

"Yeah, I think I picked up on that. I want you to understand something, Miss Gretchen. Outside of Clete Purcel, there's probably no one in your life who supports you more than my daughter. She believes you have a great talent, and she thinks you're a decent and good person. If she's not helping you out tonight, it's not because she didn't want to. She planned to work on her novel, but my wife and I insisted she come with us."

"Why do you think you have to explain this to me? You think I'm going to hurt her?"

"No, I don't believe that at all."

"You make a poor liar."

"I'd appreciate it if you wouldn't talk to me like that."

"Bugger off."

I looked at the crowd. I could no longer see Alafair and Molly. "Do you know martial arts?" I asked.

"Why do you want to know?"

"I was just curious. It's part of a mystique these days. A female killer leaving body parts scattered across entire continents, that sort of thing. You never can tell."

"Why should I kick somebody in the crotch when I can shoot him between the eyes?"

"That's pretty clever."

"It was meant as a joke," she said. "You don't like me, Mr. Robicheaux. It's in your eyes and your tone of voice. You think I'm the serpent in the garden. But you're wrong."

"Oh?"

"This place was corrupt long before I got here," she said.

She hefted the rest of her equipment and went inside the building.

THE FIRST MUSICIAN to take the stage was not a re-creator of 1940s music but a Louisiana legend from the 1950s by the name of Dixie Lee Pugh. He had grown up in a backwater shithole on the Mississippi and at age seventeen had become a piano player in a hot-pillow joint across the river in an area known as Natchez Under-the-Hill. Notice that I did not say Dixie Lee was born in a shithole on the Mississippi. Dixie Lee was not born; he was shot out of the womb like a rocket and, ever since, had been ricocheting off every concrete and steel surface in the Western world.

Three fifths of his stomach had been surgically removed. He had not only failed at rehab but had been kicked out of the Betty Ford

Center his first day in the program. He used to tell me his life's ambition was to live to 150 and get lynched for rape. None of his outrageous behavior could equal the night he first performed at the Paramount Theatre in Brooklyn. The host was Alan Freed. Dixie Lee thought he was supposed to close the show, but Freed believed the honor should go to a famous black rocker who had influenced and changed the genre forever. Dixie Lee was told that next time out he would close, but tonight belonged to the older rocker. So he took his place at the piano and went into his signature song, pounding and riffling the keys and screaming into the microphone, the modus operandi for which he was famous. In the middle of the song, he rose to his feet and pulled a pop bottle full of kerosene from inside his jacket and sloshed it all over the piano. When he threw a match on it, the flames exploded in a red-yellow cone and almost took his face off, then dripped onto the keys and ran down the piano legs onto the stage. Dixie Lee was undaunted. He leaned into the fire and thundered out the rest of his song, his coat sleeves burning, his hair singeing, the sprinklers in the ceiling raining down all over the theater.

The kids in the audience went crazy, screaming and jumping up and down for more. A cop hosed down Dixie Lee with a fire extinguisher, but not before he finished the song. When Dixie Lee walked off the stage with smoke rising from his clothes and extinguisher foam sliding down his scorched face, he turned and said to the black rocker, "Follow that, son of a bitch."

"He was your roommate at SLI?" Alafair said.

We were sitting at the rear of the audience, but I could see Gretchen Horowitz below the far corner of the stage, focusing her camera on Dixie Lee. "In 1956," I said. "Just before he appeared on *The Steve Allen Show*."

"Did you tell Gretchen that?" she said.

"No, why should I?"

"She'd probably like to interview him."

"She's dangerous, Alafair. That's the truth, not an opinion."

"Down inside she's a little girl, Dave."

Alafair was probably right. But the majority of people we send to the injection table go out like children. The irony is that most of them die with dignity, and some die with much more courage than I would expect of myself. They killed other people, and yet in most instances they cannot adequately explain their behavior to themselves or to others. That's the way they leave the earth, apologizing briefly to the family of the victim, unresisting, sick and gray with fear, their story, whatever it is, dying with them.

Alafair's suggestion had not been a bad one. What was there to lose in doing a good deed for a woman who might be salvageable? I got up from my seat and walked down the aisle to the spot in the shadows where Gretchen was filming Dixie Lee. His fingers were flying up and down on the keys, strands of his wavy dyed-gold hair hanging in his eyes, his cheeks puffed like a blowfish's, his blue suede stomps pounding up and down under the piano, his adenoidal accent rising like notes from a clarinet into the rafters. "Dixie Lee is an old friend of mine, Miss Gretchen," I said. "I bet he'd be happy to give you an interview."

"Meaning you'll introduce me?" she said.

"I'd love to."

"Why?"

"Because Dixie Lee Pugh is probably the best white blues musician in America, and everybody in the business knows it. No one has ever given him the credit he deserves."

She lowered her camera and looked past me into the recesses of the audience. "You know a broad named Julie Ardoin?"

"Yeah, she's in the department."

"What else is she into?"

"Excuse me?"

"Somebody told me she transported coke for Varina and Jesse Leboeuf," she said.

"I don't believe that."

"Somebody told me maybe she killed her husband."

"Who's the somebody?"

"Is it true or not?"

"Both stories are ridiculous."

"I got it. You've never had dirty cops here. Those black kids selling dope in their front yards don't have to piece off their action."

446 James Lee Burke

"I think your source for this nonsense is Pierre Dupree. Maybe it's time to wise up."

She looked around as though she could hardly contain her irritation. "I'd really appreciate you leaving me alone," she said.

"You don't want the intro to Dixie Lee?"

She brushed at her eyebrow with her thumb, quizzical, as though asking herself a question. I started back toward my seat. "Mr. Robicheaux?" she said behind me.

I stopped and turned around.

"Are you sure this Ardoin broad is straight up?" she said. "I mean really sure? Like you're willing to bet Clete's life on it?"

I SAT BACK down as my cell phone vibrated. It was a missed call. I called the number back, but it went to voice mail.

"Who was that from?" Molly said.

"Catin Segura."

"She called the house earlier. I didn't pick up in time. I left a note by the phone. You didn't see it?"

"No. What did she say on the message machine?"

"She just left her name and asked you to call her. I'm sorry, I thought you saw the note."

"Did it sound urgent?"

"I couldn't tell."

"I'll be back in a minute," I said.

"Where are you going?"

"To find Clete."

It didn't take long. He and Julie Ardoin were sitting a short distance away from the beer concession. Clete had placed a large red plastic cup foaming with beer between his feet and was adding to it from a silver hip flask. I sat down next to him and rested my hand on his shoulder. Julie was smiling brightly into my face, a purple and gold LSU cap tilted sideways on her head. "Hi, Dave," she said.

"What's happenin', Julie?" I said.

"A little of this, a little of that," she said, lifting her beer cup.

"See what Clete is doing? We used to call those B-52s. Sometimes we called them depth charges. They're guaranteed to eat holes in your stomach and give you a hangover from hell."

"No gloom and doom tonight, Streak," Clete said. He had a program in his hand. He wiped at his mouth with the back of his wrist and then studied the program. I saw a smear of blood no bigger than a cat's whisker on his wrist. "This next band is going to do some western swing," he said. "Bob Wills and Spade Cooley stuff. Did you know Commander Cody got a lot of his style from Spade Cooley?"

"Are you going to drink that?"

"No, I'm going to wash my socks in it," he replied.

"You want me to get you a cold drink, Dave?" Julie said.

"No, thanks. Y'all going anywhere later?"

"Haven't thought about it," Clete replied. "Maybe to Mulate's for some fried shrimp. What's up?"

"Nothing. You know Varina Leboeuf very well, Julie?" I said.

"I know her around. Like everybody does," she replied.

"What's that mean?" I asked.

"It doesn't mean anything. It means I know her around."

"You like her?" I said.

"What's with the attitude, big mon?" Clete said.

"I don't have an attitude. It was just a question," I replied.

"Dave, if I want to drink boilermakers, that's what I'm going to do. If they're bad for me, that's the breaks. If they give me a headful of snakes in the morning, they're my snakes."

"Dave is just trying to be a friend," Julie said.

"Yeah, but it's a grand evening, and we don't need anybody hanging crepe," he said.

"Somebody said you did some work for Varina Leboeuf," I said to Julie.

"Whoever told you that is *full* of shit," she replied.

"Where'd you hear this?" Clete said.

"Guess," I said.

I held my eyes on his. His gaze left mine and went to the front of the building, where Gretchen was standing by the corner of the stage. "We'll talk about this later," he said.

"Why don't we talk about it now?" I said.

"Dave, what the hell is the matter with you?" he said.

"I've known you a long time, Julie," I said. "I always liked you. I didn't set out to offend you. I have some concerns about a story I heard."

"No problem. Just remind me not to fly you out to any more islands, because I feel like an idiot for thinking you were a friend."

"You know Pierre Dupree very well?" I asked.

I saw Clete shake his head. "Dave?" he said.

"What?" I said.

He was wearing a tan suit and a knit tie and penny loafers and a shiny light blue shirt with stripes in it, his Panama hat resting on one knee. His face was as red as a Christmas tree bulb. I could see the wisp of blood in the hair on his wrist and his holstered .38 inside his coat. "Nothing. What's the point?" he said.

He upended his boilermaker and drank it all the way to the bottom, his eyes as devoid of expression as green marbles. He crushed the cup under his shoe and stared straight ahead, his pulse beating visibly in his throat, his big hands resting on top of his thighs, like a man too tired to get angry anymore.

I WALKED BACK toward the stage just as Dixie Lee Pugh was leaving and the western swing band was filing out from the wings. Gretchen Horowitz was sliding the strap of an equipment bag over her shoulder. "Do you want to meet Dixie?" I said.

"I need to see Clete first," she replied.

"I just talked to him. I don't think he's in the mood for any more consultations."

"You told him what Pierre said?"

"Yeah, I did."

"You named me as the source without giving me the chance to talk to him first?"

"Not exactly. But Clete is the closest friend I ever had. He's also the best man I've ever known."

She squeezed her eyes shut, then reopened them. "I can't believe you. I see you, but I can't believe someone like you exists. Is your wife doing some kind of penance for something she did in a former life?"

I stepped closer to her, my mouth three inches from her ear. "You need to understand something, Miss Gretchen. If not for me and your father, Sheriff Soileau would have you in a cage full of people like yourself. As it stands, I may have to resign from the department. Plus, I may have to deal with some serious problems of conscience. This isn't your fault, it's mine. But I don't want to listen to any more of your insults."

I stepped away from her. Her face was white. Dixie Lee Pugh walked toward us, his hand outstretched. "What's shakin', Dave?"

"I'd like to introduce you to Gretchen Horowitz. She wants to interview you for her documentary," I said.

"You're looking at the boogie-woogie man from *la Louisiane,* darlin'," he said. "Where'd you get those eyes, girl? They look like violets."

"They came out of my mother's womb with the rest of the unit," she replied.

"Did Dave tell you we were roommates in college?" Dixie Lee replied.

"You have my sympathies," she said. She walked down the side aisle toward the rear of the building, her equipment bag swinging on her rump.

"She runs a charm school?" Dixie Lee said.

"I gave her a bad time before you walked up. She's not to blame," I said.

His eyes were roving over the crowd, alighting on a familiar face here and there, his paunch resting on his belt. I wondered if he was remembering the glory years and the teenage girls who had fought to touch his shoes when he sang onstage at the Louisiana Hayride, the appearances on *American Bandstand,* the popping of flashbulbs when he descended the steps from an airliner with his new bride at Heathrow Airport.

"Let's get some ice cream," he said.

"Ice cream?"

"I've been clean and sober three years now. There's a truck outside. Look up in the balcony. They're all eating ice cream. It's free."

"I'm happy for you, Dixie."

"What was the deal with the photographer?"

"Somebody stole her childhood, so she lives every day of her life full of rage."

"She was molested?" he said, his gaze coming back on mine.

I nodded.

"I'd say she's ahead of the game."

"How do you mean?"

"If that happened to me, I think I'd be killing people. Instead, this gal is making films. Sounds like she's done all right, don't you think?"

The western band's first number was "Cimarron." I was about to rejoin Alafair and Molly and take a pass on Dixie Lee's invitation when something in our conversation began to bother me, like a piece in a mosaic that is cut wrong and doesn't fit no matter which way you turn it. I looked up at the balcony again. It was filled with children eating ice cream from paper bowls with plastic spoons. They were not eating Popsicles or soft ice cream from a mechanical dispenser. They were eating ice cream that had been hand-scooped from hard-frozen containers, the kind that neighborhood vending trucks didn't carry.

"You said there's a truck outside and the ice cream is free?" I asked.

Either Dixie Lee didn't hear my question or he didn't consider it worth answering. His deep-set eyes were looking at the crowd and at the tinseled confetti someone was throwing out of the balcony into the beam of the spotlight.

"What kind of truck?" I said.

"A freezer truck. Who cares?" he said. "Look at the women in this place. Great God Almighty, tell me this world ain't a pleasure. Pull your tallywhacker out of the hay baler and join the party, Dave."

● ● ●

I WENT OUTSIDE into the coldness of the night and the brilliance of the stars and the smell of barbecue smoke and crawfish boiling in a cauldron of cob-corn and artichokes and whole potatoes, and I saw a tan-colored freezer truck parked between the Sugar Cane Festival Building and the picnic shelters. There were rows of latched freezer compartments on either side of it, and against the background of the tiny white lights strung in the oak trees, its surfaces looked armored and hard-edged and cold to the touch, like a tank parked in the middle of a children's playground. It was the same kind of truck the Patin brothers used when they tried to blow my head off. The driver was wearing a brown uniform and a cap with a lacquered bill and a scuffed leather jacket, and he was scooping French-vanilla ice cream out of a big round container on a picnic table and placing it in paper bowls for a line of children. His head and face reminded me of an upended ham, his eyes serious with his work, his mouth a tight seam. But when he looked up at me, he smiled in recognition. "I'll be darned. Remember me?" he said.

"You're Bobby Joe Guidry," I replied. "You were in Desert Storm."

"That's me."

"Clete Purcel and I met you at that outdoor dinner for Amidee Broussard. I told you to check out a dispatcher's job with the department."

"That's right. But the job didn't offer enough hours. Everything worked out okay, though. I just started driving for this offshore supply company. I'm going to meetings, too. You helped me out a lot."

"You deliver food for deepwater rigs?"

"Yeah, every kind of frozen food there is. I drive to Morgan City and Port Fourchon, mostly."

"How'd you get on with the company?"

"A lady in your department gave me a number and told me to call them up. She told me to use her name."

"Which lady, Bobby Joe?"

"Miss Julie. I saw her inside the building just a few minutes ago."

"What's her last name, podna?"

"Ardoin. I heard her husband wasn't any good, but to my mind, Miss Julie is a fine lady."

"What did you hear about Miss Julie's husband?"

"He got in with the wrong guys and was flying coke and weed into the country. That's why he killed himself. Maybe it's just one of those stories, though."

"I never heard those stories, Bobby Joe."

"You probably wouldn't. He flew out of Lake Charles and Lafayette. Better get some of this ice cream. It's going fast," he said.

When I went back into the building, the western swing band was blaring out "The San Antonio Rose," the horns so loud that the floor was quaking under our feet.

CHAPTER
30

I SAT DOWN next to Molly. Alafair's chair was empty. I looked around and couldn't see her anywhere. "Where's Alf?" I said, my voice almost lost inside the volume of Bob Wills's most famous song.

"She went to find Gretchen Horowitz," Molly said.

I tried to think and couldn't. Everything happening around me seemed fragmented and incoherent but part of a larger pattern, like a sheet of stained glass thrown upon a flagstone. A truck like the one from which a man had blown out my windshield was parked outside the building, and its driver had just told me he'd gotten his job from the same woman Gretchen Horowitz had warned me about. Could Clete and I have been wrong all this time? Had Julie Ardoin been a key player in all the events that had transpired over the last two months? Were we that blind? And now "The San Antonio Rose" was thundering inside my head, the same song Gretchen Horowitz had been whistling after she pumped three rounds into Bix Golightly's face.

I got up and worked my way around the back of the crowd toward the beer concession. I could see Clete sitting at the end of a row, but there was no sign of Alafair or Gretchen or Julie Ardoin. I sat down next to him and scanned the audience. "Have you seen Alf?" I asked.

"Yeah, she and Gretchen were just here. They went to the ladies' room," he replied.

"Where's Julie?"

"She went with them."

"Clete, I just ran into that guy Bobby Joe Guidry, the Desert Storm vet."

"Yeah, yeah, what about him?" he said irritably, trying to concentrate on the band.

"The company Guidry works for is supplying the ice cream for the concert. It's the same company that owned the truck used by the guys who tried to kill me in Lafayette."

"The truck was stolen, right? What's the point? A guy who works for the same company is scooping ice cream outside? Big deal."

"Guidry says he got his job through Julie Ardoin. She told him to call the company and use her name."

"Julie is on the Sugar Cane Festival committee. She helps with all the events connected with the building."

"No, it's too much coincidence. Guidry says her husband was flying dope into the country."

"That's not exceptional," he said. "Most of the guys who do that stuff are either crop dusters or helicopter pilots who get tired of landing on rigs in fifty-knot gales. For fuck's sake, let's listen to the band, okay?"

"Think about it, Cletus. When we landed in that harbor off the island, she came in like a leaf gliding onto a pond."

"Yeah, because she's a good pilot. You want somebody from the Japanese air force flying us around?"

"You're not going to listen to anything I say, are you?"

"Because nothing you say makes sense," he replied. "You've got me worried, Dave. I think you're losing it."

"I've got *you* worried? That's just great," I said, and punched him in the top of the chest with my finger.

I saw the pain flicker in his face and wanted to shoot myself. "I'm sorry. I wasn't thinking," I said.

"Forget it, big mon. I'm right as rain. Now let's listen to the music."

I propped my hands on my knees, then squeezed my temples and closed my eyes and reopened them and stared at a spot between my shoes. I felt as though I were drowning. I felt exactly as I had when a black medic straddled my thighs and tore a cellophane wrapper from a package of cigarettes with his teeth and pressed it over the red bubble escaping from the hole in my chest, my lung filling with blood, my body dropping from beneath his knees into a black well. When I raised my head, the audience and the western band were spinning around me.

"Speak of the devil," Clete said, "here she comes."

"Who?"

"Who else? Every time I think of that woman, I want to unscrew my big boy and mail it to the South Pole in hopes the penguins will bury it under a glacier."

Varina Leboeuf was not merely passing by. She was headed right toward us. "I'm glad I found you," she said.

"Yeah, what's the haps? I thought Halloween was over," Clete said.

"You asshole," Varina said.

"I hear that a lot—mostly from skells and crack whores. I'm sorry for whatever harm I caused you, Varina, but how about giving us a break here?"

"You don't know who your friends are," she said.

"You had my office creeped," he said.

She clenched her jaw, her mouth tightening. "Is everything all right?" she said.

"Why shouldn't it be?" Clete said.

"Because I saw Alafair and Gretchen outside," she said. "I think they were with Julie Ardoin."

"They went to the restroom," Clete said.

"No, they didn't. They were outside."

"Why would they be outside? So what if they were?" Clete said.

"You're not listening to me. Two men were out there. I know them. They work for Pierre. I think they're involved with stolen paintings or something. They're the ones Gretchen beat up."

"Sit down and say all that again," I said.

"I'm trying to help out here. Don't be angry at me," she said.

"I'm not angry at you. I can't hear you. There's too much noise. Sit down," I said.

"Did Julie Ardoin ever work for you?" Clete said.

"Of course not. Why would she work for me? I hardly know her. Her husband used to fly Pierre around, but I never spent any time with Julie. I have to go."

I took her by the arm and pulled her down to Julie Ardoin's empty chair. "Are you telling us Alafair and Gretchen are in harm's way?" I said.

"God, you're an idiot. Do I have to write it on the wall?" she said. She walked away from us, her southwestern prairie skirt swishing on the backs of her legs.

"She's wearing a gold belt," Clete said.

"So what?"

"So was the woman I saw with Pierre Dupree at Dupree's house." My head was splitting.

I WENT BACK to my seat. Molly was still sitting by herself. "You didn't see Alf?" I said.

"No. She wasn't with Clete?" she said.

"She and Gretchen went to the restroom with Julie Ardoin. I thought maybe she came back here."

"She's fine. Stop worrying. Come on, Dave, enjoy yourself."

"Varina Leboeuf said some gumballs who want to hurt Gretchen were outside, and so were Alafair and Gretchen."

"Varina likes to stir things up. She's a manipulator. She wants to stick pins in Clete for dumping her. Now sit down."

"I'll be back."

"Where's Clete?"

"Looking for Gretchen."

"I'm coming, too."

"No, stay here. Alafair won't know where we are if she comes back and you're gone."

Maybe I was losing it, as Clete had said. I didn't know what to believe anymore. Would a couple of goons try to do payback on Gretchen Horowitz at a music festival attended by hundreds of people? Was Varina Leboeuf telling the truth? Was she a mixture of good and evil rather than the morally bankrupt person I had come to regard her as? Did she have parameters I hadn't given her credit for?

Clete and I had thrown away the rule book and were paying the price. We had protected Gretchen Horowitz and, in the meantime, had accomplished nothing in solving the abduction of Tee Jolie Melton and the murder of her sister, Blue. The greatest irony of all was the fact that our adversaries, whoever they were, thought we had information about them that we didn't. Ultimately, what was it all about? The answer was oil: millions of barrels of it that had settled on the bottom of the Gulf or that were floating northward, like brownish-red fingers, into Louisiana's wetlands. But dwelling on an environmental catastrophe in the industrial era did little or no good. It was like watching the casket of one's slain son or daughter being lowered into the ground and trying to analyze the causes of war at the same time. The real villains always skated. The soldier paid the dues; a light went out forever in someone's home; and the rest of us went on with our lives. The scenario has never changed. The faces of the players might change, but the original script was probably written in charcoal on the wall of a cave long ago, and I believe we've conceded to its demands ever since.

At the moment I didn't care about the oil in the Gulf or Gretchen Horowitz or even Tee Jolie Melton. I didn't care about my state or my job or honor or right and wrong. I wanted my daughter, Alafair, at my side, and I wanted to go home with her and my wife, Molly, and be with our pets, Tripod and Snuggs, in our kitchen, the doors locked and the windows fastened, all of us gathered around a table where we would break and share bread and give no heed to winter storms or the leaves shedding with the season and the tidal ebb that drained the Teche of its water.

The acceptance of mortality in one's life is no easy matter. But anyone who says he has accepted the premature mortality of his child is lying. There is an enormous difference between living with a child's death and accepting it. The former takes a type of courage that few people understand. Why was I having these thoughts? Because I felt sick inside. I felt sick because I knew that Clete and I had provoked a group of people who were genuinely iniquitous and who planned to hurt us as badly as they could, no matter what the cost. This may seem like a problematic raison d'être for the behavior of villainous individuals, unless you consider that there are groups of people in our midst who steal elections, commit war crimes, pollute the water we drink and the air we breathe, and get away with all of it.

I went outside through the front door and circled around the side of the building. The air was cold, the wind biting, and in the north the sky piled with clouds that looked as though they contained both snow and electricity. Bobby Joe Guidry was latching the doors on the freezer compartments of his truck.

"Did you see Miss Julie with a couple of young women?" I asked.

"I didn't see Miss Julie," he replied. "There were a couple of young women here, though."

"What did they look like?"

"One had long black hair. The other one looked kind of AC/DC, know what I mean? Her eyes were purple."

"That's my daughter, Alafair, and her friend."

"Sorry."

"Where did they go?"

"I gave them ice cream and they went back inside. The one with the black hair is your daughter, Mr. Robicheaux?"

"Yeah, why?"

"Two guys were eyeballing them. One guy had grease in his hair and a bump on his nose. The other guy was fat. His suit looked like he got it out of a laundry bag. I didn't like the looks of them. They were hanging around a long time, smoking cigarettes out there in the trees. I started to go over there and ask them what they were doing."

"Why?"

"Because I heard one of them say something when he walked by. He said, 'Maybe get them on the amphib and throw one of them out.' Then they laughed. When your daughter and her friend showed up, they stopped talking. They just smoked cigarettes and watched everything from under the tree. I didn't know that was your daughter, Mr. Robicheaux. I would have come got you."

"Where'd the two guys go?"

"Through the back door right after your daughter and her friend went inside," he replied.

I wrote my cell phone number on the back of a business card and handed it to him. "If you see these two guys again, call me."

"I feel bad about this, Mr. Robicheaux. When I came back from Iraq, I gave up hunting. I promised to do a good deed every day for the rest of my life. I also made a promise that I'd be a protector for people who didn't have anyone to look after them."

"You did fine, Bobby Joe."

"Does that business about an amphibian mean anything to you?" he asked.

I FOUND CLETE up by the stage. The band had just finished playing "Ida Red" and was giving up the stage to a full orchestra, one dressed in summer tuxes irrespective of the season, just like Harry James's orchestra. Clete was shielding his eyes from the glare of the spotlights while he searched the crowd for any sign of Gretchen and Alafair and Julie Ardoin. I told him what Bobby Joe Guidry had said. "You think those two asswipes were talking about the seaplane you saw behind Varina's place? They were talking about throwing somebody out of a plane?" he asked.

"That's what Guidry said."

Clete's face was pale, his eyes looking inward at an image he obviously didn't want to see. "I saw that once."

I could hardly hear him above the noise of the audience. "Say again?"

"Some intelligence guys brought two VC onto the Jolly Green. They were roped up and blindfolded. The guy who was the target had to watch the other guy get thrown out the door. We were probably five hundred feet over the canopy."

"Clean that stuff out of your head. You think Julie Ardoin is in on this?"

"Nobody could take down Gretchen unless she trusted the wrong person."

"You're saying Julie is dirty?"

"I don't know, Dave. Look at my history. I've trusted the wrong women all my life."

"Where do you want to start?" I said.

His eyes swept the balcony and the crowd and the beer concession. "I don't have any idea. I've made a mess of things, and I can't sort anything out."

"Follow me," I said.

We began at the women's restroom. I banged on the door with my fist and hung my badge holder inside. "Iberia Parish Sheriff's Department," I said. "Excuse us, ladies, but we need to come inside."

I pushed open the door. There was immediate laughter. "Boy, you guys are hard up!" a woman yelled.

"We're looking for Alafair Robicheaux and Gretchen Horowitz and Julie Ardoin," I said. "They may be in danger. We need your help."

The laughter and smiles died. "I know Julie and Alafair," a woman at a lavatory said. "They ain't in here, suh."

"How about in the stalls?" I said.

"They ain't in here," the woman repeated.

Regardless, I went from stall to stall, knocking on each door or pushing it open. Clete was looking from side to side, his face burning. "Has anyone in here seen Alafair Robicheaux or Julie Ardoin this evening?" I shouted out.

"By the ice-cream truck," another woman said.

"Was anyone with them?"

"I wasn't paying attention," she replied.

The room smelled of perfume and urinated beer. Toilets were flushing. Everyone in the room was staring at me, the frivolous moment gone, a deadness in every person's face, as though a cold wind had blown through the windows high up on the wall. "Thanks for your help, ladies. We apologize for bothering y'all," I said.

We went back out in the concourse and climbed the stairs to the balcony and then went back downstairs and through the crowd again. The orchestra had just finished pounding out Louis Prima's "Sing, Sing, Sing." No one I recognized or spoke to had seen Alafair or Julie Ardoin, at least not in the last twenty minutes. I saw Clete opening and closing his hands at his sides, a bone flexing in his cheek. "This is a pile of shit," he said.

"They weren't abducted by a UFO. Somebody saw them," I said.

"Except we can't find that somebody," he said.

"Where haven't we looked?"

"Behind the stage?" he said.

"It's Grand Central Station back there," I said.

"No, I chased a bail skip in there once. He was at a picnic and tried to hide in a room full of paint buckets and stage costumes."

"How do we get in?"

He thought about it. "There's a back door."

We went back outside into the cold and the damp, musky smell of leaves that had turned from green to yellow and black inside pools of water. We scraped open a heavy metal door in the back of the building just as the orchestra went into Will Bradley and Freddie Slack's boogie-woogie composition "Beat Me Daddy, Eight to the Bar."

"God, that gives me the willies," Clete said.

"What does?"

"That song is on your iPod, the one you said Tee Jolie Melton gave you."

We were inside a dark hallway, one that smelled of dust and Murphy Oil Soap. "That's right, Tee Jolie gave it to me. You believe me now?" I said.

"I'm not sure. I got a feeling this isn't real, Dave."

"What isn't?"

"Like I said before. We were supposed to die in the gig on the bayou. The real surprise is maybe we did die. We just haven't figured it out yet. I've heard stories about people's souls wandering for a long time before they're willing to let go of the world."

"We've got one issue here, Cletus: to find Alafair and Gretchen and bring them home. Come on, podna, lock and load. Let go of all this other stuff."

His pupils were dilated, his skin stretched tight on his face. He coughed into his palm and wiped it inside his pocket. He pulled his .38 snub from his shoulder holster and let it hang loosely from his right hand. Through a curtain, we could see the orchestra kicking into overdrive. The pianist's fingers were dancing on the keys, the double-pedal beat of two bass drums building into a throaty roar the way Louie Bellson used to do it, the sound of the saxophones slowly rising in volume like a living presence, starting to compete and blend in with the stenciled clarity of Freddie Slack's piano score, all of it in four-four time.

"I'm going to kill every one of them, Streak," Clete said.

I started to argue with him, but I didn't. Though bloodlust and fear and a black flag had served us poorly in the past, sometimes the situation had not been of our choosing, and we'd had little recourse. Ethics aside, when it's over, you're always left with the same emotion: You're glad you're alive and the others are dead instead of you.

At the end of the hallway was a narrow space through which I could see people dancing in a cleared area below the stage. All of them were having a good time. A young dark-haired woman in a sequined evening dress was dancing with her eyes tightly shut, her arms pumped, the back of her neck glazed with sweat. She was drunk and her bra strap was showing, and her lipsticked mouth was partially open in an almost lascivious fashion. All of her energies seemed concentrated on a solitary thought, as though she were reaching an orgasmic peak deep inside herself, totally indifferent to her surroundings. The trombone players rose to their feet, the blare of their horns shaking the glass in the windows. I didn't care about the band or the secret erotic pleasure of others. I wanted my daughter back.

Clete Purcel was staring at his left palm. In it was a bright scarlet star that looked like it had been freshly painted on his skin.

I thought he had coughed the blood into his hand. Then I saw him raise his eyes to the plank ceiling above our heads. I slipped my army-issue 1911-model .45 automatic from the leather holster clipped onto my belt. I heard the members of the orchestra pause in the middle of the melody and shout in unison:

When he jams with the bass and guitar,
They all holler, "Beat me Daddy, eight to the bar."

A two-tiered staircase made of rough-hewn lumber led through an opening in the ceiling. I went ahead of Clete, my .45 held upward. A line of blood drops preceded me up the steps, like red dimes that had spilled from a hole in someone's trouser pocket. I walked up the last three steps, my left hand on the rail, peering into the darkness. I slipped a penlight out of my coat pocket and clicked it on. The room was stacked with storage boxes and paint cans and Christmas decorations and papier-mâché figures used in the Mardi Gras parade. I shone the light along the boards toward the rear of the room and saw a pool of blood next to a pile of boxes that must have filled a fifteen-inch radius. On the edge of the blood, I saw the gleam of a gold chain and a tiny stamped religious icon.

Clete was standing behind me and had not seen the blood nor its thickness and amount. "Cover my back," I said.

"What is it?" he asked.

"Stay on my back, Clete. Please," I said.

I stepped forward and shone the light directly on the blood and the gold chain and Star of David. Then I went past the boxes and raised the penlight and moved its small beam across the face of Julie Ardoin. Her throat had been cut and her nails and nose broken; her forearms were sliced with defensive wounds. She had bled out, and her face was white and stark and had the surprised and violated expression that the dead forever stamp on the inside of our eyelids.

I heard Clete's weight on the boards behind me. He still had not seen the body. "That's Gretchen's chain and medal," he said.

"It's not Gretchen, Clete."

"Who?" he asked.

"It's Julie. Call it in. Don't look."

He almost knocked me down getting to the body. Downstairs, the orchestra had gone into a thunderous drum and horn and saxophone finale that deafened the ears and left the audience screaming for more.

CHAPTER
31

I CALLED IN the 911 myself and took Clete by the arm and walked him away from the enclosure of boxes where Julie had probably died. I could find no electric switches on the walls, but there was a single lightbulb hanging from the ceiling, and when I twisted the bulb, it lit the room in all its starkness. Clete was breathing deep down in his chest, opening and closing his eyes. "I'm going to take Gretchen's Star of David," he said.

"Don't touch it. There might be prints on it."

"No, the chain isn't broken. She dropped it there for me to find," he said.

I didn't argue. I had seen few instances in my long relationship with Clete Purcel when the world had gotten the upper hand on him and been able to do him serious injury. In this instance, he looked devastated, not only by the murder of his lover but by the simultaneous abduction of his daughter, both of which I was sure he was blaming on himself.

I looked around and tried to reconstruct what had happened. The loft we were standing in had a second set of steps by the far wall, and it led down to a second side exit. The loft had worked as a kind of bridge for the abductors. They had forced Alafair and Gretchen and Julie into the first-floor hallway, up the steps, down the other side, and out the door and into the park, where Alafair and Gretchen were likely taken away in a vehicle.

I said all these things to Clete, but I wasn't sure he was hearing me. "Come on, Cletus. We've got to get our girls back."

"Julie fought with them, didn't she?" he said. "Downstairs in the hallway, she fought back. Julie didn't take shit off anybody. She told them to fuck off, and they broke her nose and brought her up here and cut her throat."

"That's the way I would read it."

"It's Pierre Dupree."

"We don't know that yet."

"He got to Gretchen. She never had a boyfriend, and he got to her. He wants payback, Dave. Julie was in the way. Dupree has got long-range plans for Gretchen, that son of a bitch."

"Maybe, but we're not sure of any of this," I said.

"He's got plans for Alafair, too. Don't lie to yourself."

"I'm not. What I'm saying is we have to think."

"They couldn't nail us at the gig on the bayou, so they're going to kill our kids," he said.

"You're losing it, Clete. The guys who tried to clip us behind my house were cremated. We're dealing with an entirely separate bunch."

"The hell we are," he said. "If there're two drunks on a ship, they'll find each other. If there're two scum-sucking bottom-feeders in the state of Louisiana, they'll be in the same pond in twenty-four hours."

"Bobby Joe Guidry said the two gumballs were talking about an amphibian."

"Forget all the international intrigue and stuff about mysterious islands. These bastards are homegrown."

"Yeah, but where does that leave us?"

"I'll let you know," he said, taking off his coat. He knelt down and placed it over Julie Ardoin's face. When he stood up, there was a tear in the corner of his eye. He coughed before he spoke again. "We pick up Pierre Dupree, but this time out, it doesn't make the jail."

"What if we're wrong?"

"You want to wait around here for Helen and the coroner? Wake up. Nobody wants to screw with St. Mary Parish. There's an old man in that plantation house who probably stuck whole families in ovens. Blue Melton floated up on the beach in a block of ice, and nobody could care less. You know how many unsolved female homicides there are in this state? You know what Alafair and Gretchen might be going through while we're playing pocket pool up here?"

My head felt like a piece of ceramic about to crack. "You're sure it's Dupree?"

"Take it to the bank."

"We're leaving something out. I just can't put my hand on it."

"Like what?" he said.

"I told you, I don't know. It's something about a song. I can't remember."

"Bad time for a memory blackout," he said.

I heard footsteps on the stairs behind me. Clete and I turned around. Varina Leboeuf had climbed the steps and was standing halfway inside the loft, as though partially disembodied, her hair sparking with confetti, her face as heartbreakingly beautiful as it was when she was a young girl. "What are you two doing up here?" she said.

"What are *you* doing here?" Clete replied.

"I was talking to the ice-cream man. He told me y'all were looking for Alafair."

"Why would you be talking to the ice-cream man about Alafair?" I asked.

"Pierre and his father own part of the frozen-food company. They deliver to offshore rigs. What's going on?" When we didn't answer, she glanced at the loft floor. "Where'd this blood come from?"

"There's a lot more of it behind those boxes," Clete said. "It belongs to Julie Ardoin. Take a look-see if you like."

Her face seemed to wrinkle like a flower exposed to heat. "She's been murdered?"

"Her throat was cut almost to the spine," Clete said.

Varina pressed her hand to her mouth. I thought she was going to fall backward to the floor below. Clete reached down and helped her the rest of the way up the steps. She looked steadily into his eyes, as though reaching back into an intimate moment they shared. "I wish you'd killed him," she said.

"Killed who?" Clete asked.

"Lamont Woolsey. I wish you would kill Amidee Broussard, too."

"What do Broussard and Woolsey have to do with this?" I said.

"They're evil. They use young girls. They deceive people with religion. It's white slavery. That's what it's called, isn't it? Is Julie behind those boxes?"

"She told me she hardly knew you," I said.

"That's not true. I want to see Julie."

"This is a crime scene. You need to leave, Varina," I said.

"Why were you down in the hallway?" Clete said.

"I sponsored the western band. I was going to write them a check," she said.

"Where's Pierre?" he asked.

"I have no idea. We've settled all our business affairs. I hope I never see him again," she replied. "I think I'm going to be sick."

She turned and descended the steps, her small hand tightly gripping the rail, the hem of her prairie skirt bouncing on her calves. Clete stared into my face. "Can you read that broad?" he said.

"Not in a thousand years," I replied.

I TOLD MOLLY what had happened and asked her to go home and wait by the phone. It was a foolish request. "I'm not going anywhere," she said. "Where is Pierre Dupree?"

"I don't know. I can't find him," I said.

"Why would they want Alafair?" she said.

"They were after Gretchen. They only took Alafair because the two of them were together."

"Who is 'they'?" she said.

"Clete thinks this is all about payback. I don't agree. I think Gretchen knows too much, and some people in Florida and probably here want her off the board."

We were standing at the rear of the audience. The swing orchestra had been called back for an encore and was playing "The Boogie-Woogie Bugle Boy from Company B."

"Dave, this isn't happening," Molly said.

"But it is. They've got my little girl."

"She's my 'little girl,' too. I didn't believe you before. I wish I had," she said.

"Believe what?"

"That you were dealing with something that's diabolic. I wish I had believed every crazy story you told me."

"Have you seen Varina Leboeuf in the last few minutes?" I asked.

"She was going out the front door. She stopped and put her hand on me and said, 'I'm so sorry.' I didn't know what she meant. You think she's involved?"

"I gave up trying to figure Varina out. She reminds me of Tee Jolie in some ways. I'd like to believe in her, but faith has its limits."

"Forgive me for saying this, but I hate both those women," Molly said.

Up on the stage, three female singers imitating the Andrews Sisters went into the chorus of a song that, with the passage of time, had somehow made the years between 1941 and 1945 a golden era rather than one that had cost the lives of thirty million people.

Clete and I waited outside in the cold while at least eight emergency vehicles began to turn in to both the north and south entrances of the park and thread their way through the oak trees. Clete wore no coat and was starting to shiver. I used my cell phone to call the St. Mary Parish Sheriff's Department and ask that a cruiser be sent to the Croix du Sud Plantation.

"What are we supposed to be looking for?" the deputy asked.

"We have a homicide and a double abduction in New Iberia," I replied. "I want y'all to find out who's home and who isn't at the Dupree place."

"What would the Dupree family know about an abduction?"

"I'm not sure. That's why we're requesting your assistance."

"You'd better talk with the sheriff about this."

"Where is he?"

"Duck hunting at Pecan Island. Problem is, I'm not supposed to give out his private number."

"What does it take to get you to do your job?" I said.

I didn't get to hear his reply. Clete Purcel tore the phone out of my hand. "You listen, you little piece of shit," he said. "You go out to Croix du Sud and knock on their door and look in their windows and crawl under the house if you have to. Then you call us back and tell us what you find. If you don't, I'm going to come over there and kick a telephone pole up your ass."

Clete closed the phone and handed it back to me. He looked at my expression. "*What?*" he said.

"We need these guys on our side. I thought I was making some progress," I replied.

"With St. Mary Parish? Progress for those guys is acceptance of the Emancipation Proclamation," he said.

"Bring your car around. You're going to catch pneumonia."

"You coming?"

"You've got to give me a minute, Clete."

He looked at his watch. "We need to do this together, Streak. Don't depend on the locals. We're the guys with the vested interest. We take Pierre Dupree into Henderson Swamp."

His skin was prickled, and he was jiggling up and down, but it wasn't because of the cold. His eyes were wider than they should have been, his breath sour. He rotated his head on his neck and straightened his back, his shoulder rig tightening across his chest. When I touched his back, I could feel his body heat through the fabric.

An ambulance pulled to the rear of the Sugar Cane Festival Building, and two paramedics got out and removed a gurney from the back. Three cruisers pulled in behind the ambulance, the light from their flashers bouncing off the buildings and the oak trees. I looked for Helen Soileau but didn't see her. A moment later, my cell phone vibrated in my pocket. I was surprised. It was the deputy Clete had threatened. "Robicheaux?" he said.

"Go ahead," I said.

"I had a deputy do a check at the Dupree place. Nobody is home.

The only light on is the porch light. The deputy walked around back. Nobody is home."

"You're sure?"

"What did I just say?"

"One of the abduction victims is my daughter. If I don't get her back, I'm going to be looking you up," I said. I broke the connection. I looked at Clete. "That was St. Mary Parish. Nobody is home at Croix du Sud."

"I don't buy it," he said.

"Because you don't want to," I said.

"No, I scoped the place out. There was a guard standing in back by the gazebo. I took my eyes off him for two seconds and he was gone, and I mean *gone*. There was no way he could have entered the house or walked around the side without me seeing him. He never moved ten feet from that gazebo."

"So what are you saying?"

"There's got to be a subterranean entrance somewhere close to the gazebo. You ever hear stories about tunnels or basements in that place?"

"No. But the house is over a hundred and fifty years old. There's no telling what's under it."

"I'm going out there. You coming or not?"

I knew what would happen if I stayed at the Sugar Cane Festival Building. I would have to take charge of the crime scene and wait on the coroner and coordinate with Helen and make sure all the evidence was bagged and tagged and the scene secured and the body removed and taken to Iberia General. Then I would have to send someone, if not myself, to notify Julie's family. In the meantime, word would leak out that a woman had been murdered in the building, and the next problem on my hands would be crowd control. While all this was taking place, my daughter would be in the hands of men who had the mercy of centipedes.

A deputy got out of a cruiser holding a video camera and a Steadicam. "I found these by the entrance to the park, Dave. They'd already been run over. Does this have anything to do with Alafair being kidnapped?"

"Give them to the tech. We need any prints we can lift off them," I said. Clete was already walking toward his Caddy. "Wait up!" I said.

WE HEADED OUT of the park and, in some ways, I suspected, out of my career in law enforcement. At a certain age, you accept that nothing is forever, not even the wintry season that seems to define your life. I began dialing Molly's cell number to tell her where I was.

"Don't tell anyone where we're going, Dave," Clete said.

"That makes no sense."

"If nobody is at the Dupree place, if I'm all wrong, we come straight back. But if we can get our hands on Pierre or Alexis or any of their hired help, we can get the information we need. We can't blow this one, partner. Rules are for people who want to feel good about themselves in the morning. They're not for people who want to save their children's lives."

Clete had turned on the heater but was still shivering. I took off my coat and put it over his shoulders.

"What are you doing?" he said.

"I've got a corduroy shirt on. I don't need it," I replied.

"I'm not cold. My malaria kicks into gear sometimes."

"You've got to go to the VA."

He coughed deep in his chest and tried to pretend he was clearing his throat. "I've got to tell you something, big mon. I haven't done right by you. Because of me, you protected Gretchen and have probably gotten yourself in a lot of trouble with Helen."

"I'm always in trouble with Helen."

"When this is over, we're all going down to the Keys. I'm going to pay for everything. It's going to be like it used to be. We're going to fish for marlin in blue water and fill up the locker with kingfish and dive for lobsters on Seven Mile Reef."

"You bet," I said.

He was looking straight ahead, the soft green glow of the dashboard lighting his face, hollowing his eyes. "I got this sick feeling in my stomach," he said. "Like everything is ending. Like I've been full of shit for a lifetime but I never owned up to it."

"Don't say that about yourself."

"Gretchen paid the tab for my mistakes. When you steal a little girl's childhood, you can never give it back."

"You've tried to square it for years. Don't blame yourself, Clete."

"I've got an AK in the trunk."

"Yeah?"

"It's modified, but it's untraceable. No matter what else happens, the guys who killed Julie are going down."

"Can't let you do that, podna."

"You know I'm right. Don't pretend you don't."

I kept my eyes straight ahead. We were speeding down the two-lane toward Jeanerette, the bayou chained with fog under the moon, the Angus in the fields clustered under the live oaks. I waited for him to say something, but he didn't. Instead, he clicked on the FM station from the university in Lafayette. The DJ was playing "Faded Love" by Bob Wills. I stared at the radio, then at Clete.

"You said Gretchen was whistling 'The San Antonio Rose' the night you saw her clip Bix Golightly?"

"Do you have to put it that way?"

"Does it make sense that a girl from Miami would be whistling a Western tune written seventy years ago?"

"I asked her about that. She said she heard it on a car radio, and it stuck in her head." He was looking at the road while he spoke.

"She heard it on a car radio in Algiers?"

"Yeah."

"And she didn't do the hit on Waylon Grimes?"

"No."

"Was the car playing the song not far from Grimes's place?"

He looked at me. "I'm not sure. I didn't ask."

"Varina Leboeuf is big on Western art and music and clothes. She collects Indian artifacts from the Southwest."

"You think she did the hit on Grimes? Maybe on Frankie Gee at the bus depot in Baton Rouge?"

"I don't know. On this one, I've been in the dark since Jump Street, Clete."

"Join the club," he said. We came around a bend covered with shadows; he clicked on his brights. "I don't believe it."

"Pull over," I said.

"What'd you think I was going to do? Run her down?"

"It's a thought," I replied.

Parked by the side of the road was a Saab convertible, its frame mashed down on a collapsed rear tire. Varina Leboeuf stood next to the Saab, drenched in the glare of Clete's high beams. Behind her, inside a stand of persimmon trees and water oaks, was a cemetery filled with whitewashed brick and stucco crypts, most of them tilted at odd angles, sinking into the softness of the mold and lichen and wet soil that seldom saw daylight.

I got out on the passenger side. The headlights were in her eyes, and it was obvious she could barely make out who I was. "You sure have bad luck with tires," I said.

"Yeah, and I told you why. My ex-husband has tried to screw me out of every dime he could," she said.

"Want a lift?"

"No, I was just about to call AAA," she replied.

"The AAA service in this area not only sucks, it's nonexistent," I said. "You're headed for Croix du Sud?"

"No, I'm not. If it's any of your business, I'm supposed to meet friends at the Yellow Bowl for supper. I wanted to cancel, but I couldn't reach them."

"Hop in," I said.

"I don't like the way you've treated me, Dave."

"Get in front, Varina," Clete said. "Dave can ride in back. It's time for a truce, isn't it?"

While I got in back and Varina got in front, Clete stepped outside the Caddy and removed my coat from his shoulders and tossed it to me.

"You need this," I said.

"I've got a blanket in the trunk," he replied.

• • •

Clete popped the hatch on the trunk, blocking the view of anyone looking through the back window. He strapped his Marine Corps KA-BAR knife high up on his left calf and pulled his trouser leg over it. Then he lifted a blanket out of the trunk and draped it over his shoulders and picked up his pistol-grip AK-47 and held it in his left hand and covered it with the blanket. When he got back in the car, he tightened the blanket around him and looked into Varina's face and smiled. "We want to talk to Pierre. Want to help us with that?" he said.

"No," she said, staring wanly through the windshield.

"Why not?" he asked.

"Because I don't know or care where he is."

"Think Pierre is capable of kidnapping or hurting our daughters?" Clete said.

"He's a sick man, if that's what you're asking."

"How about his grandfather? Does he qualify as sick?" Clete said.

"Why ask me?"

"Because you lived with him. Is Alexis Dupree a sadist?" Clete asked.

"I'm really tired, Clete," she said. "I'm sorry about what's happened. I wish I never met the Dupree family. I don't know what else to say."

Clete dropped the gearshift into drive. "You're quite a gal," he said.

She stared uncertainly at the side of his face as the Caddy inched off the road's shoulder onto the asphalt, gravel clicking under the tires.

WE PASSED ALICE Plantation and entered a tunnel of magnificent live oaks that arched over the road, then passed another Greek-columned antebellum home and clanked across the drawbridge and passed a community of trailers leaking rust into the ground and entered the village of Jeanerette, Louisiana, where approximately one-third of the population eked out an existence below the poverty line.

"How'd you like living over here, Varina?" Clete said.

"I hated it," she replied.

"Where do you want out?"

"Every place is closed," she said. "At eight o'clock the whole town turns into a mausoleum. A 747 could crash on it and nobody would notice."

"We don't have time to take you to the Yellow Bowl," he said.

"I'll go with you to Pierre's and borrow one of his cars."

"Suit yourself," he said. "Tell me something—does Pierre have a basement in that dump?"

"There's a dank hole down there. It has water in it most of the time. Why?"

"No reason," he said. "I've always wondered what it would be like to live in a place like that. A guy who owned it in the nineteenth century was a business partner of the guy who created Angola pen. Something like two thousand convicts died when this guy rented them out as slave labor. It's the kind of history that makes you proud to be an American."

"Yes, I know all about that," she said. "But I'm a bit tired of feeling guilty about things I didn't do. Maybe people make their own beds."

"I wish I had that kind of clarity," he said. "It must be great."

I could see the color climbing in the back of Varina's neck. As though she could read my thoughts, she turned and looked at me. "Are you just going to sit there?" she asked.

"Excuse me?"

"Would you be gentleman enough to tell your fat fuck of a friend to shut up?"

I don't know if the word "entitlement" would apply to Varina's behavior, or "arrogance" and "narcissism." She possessed the same surreal mentality common among higher-class women in southern society of years ago. The self-centeredness and disconnection from reality were so egregious that it often made you wonder if you had the problem, not the spoiled bunch who believed the sun rose and set upon their anointed brows. But Varina did not come from that class of people. Her father had been from the red-clay country of North Louisiana and knew the world of sweat and cotton poison and trysts with black girls taken from the field into a barn. Maybe these contradictions were the source of the mystery that lived in her eyes and hovered around her mouth. Most men wish to be beguiled. And nobody was better at it than Varina. No matter how all this played out, I believed she would remain glamorous and seductive, beautiful and unknowable, to the very end.

When I didn't answer her question, she looked back at the road, then out the side window. Once again, she seemed wan and distant, and I wondered if her statement about people making their own beds was intended to apply to herself rather than to others.

We drove through the far end of town, the lawns stiff with frost, the houses dark, the moon shining on a backdrop of post-harvest sugarcane fields that were frozen and spiked with stubble and splintered cane. Clete depressed his turn indicator as we approached Croix du Sud. As we turned in to the driveway and passed through the open gates, I could see the blinking red reflection of the left rear light dancing on the stone pillars at the entrance and the deep green waxy leaves of the camellia bushes planted along the driveway, perhaps like a warning of things to come.

The house was dark except for the light on the porch.

"Pull around back," Varina said.

"Why?" Clete said.

"Pierre leaves a key above the door. I'm going to take one of his cars."

I felt my cell phone throb against my thigh. I opened it and looked at the caller ID. Clete drove past the carriage house and stopped at the edge of the concrete parking pad, the headlights burrowing through the darkness onto the bayou's surface, where a single-engine pontoon plane was moored inside the fog. The call was from Catin Segura, the female deputy Jesse Leboeuf had beaten and raped. "I lied to you, Dave," she said.

CHAPTER
32

C LETE GOT OUT of the Caddy, letting the blanket slip off his shoulders onto the edge of the seat.

"Lied about what?" I said into the phone.

"I told you Jesse Leboeuf said something when he was dying in my bathtub," Catin replied. "I told you I didn't know what he said because I don't talk French."

"You mean you do speak French?"

"No, not at all. But I wrote down what the words sounded like."

"Why didn't you tell me that?"

Varina had also gotten out of the car and was walking around to the other side, where Clete was standing with one hand on the half-closed driver's door, his face as cold-looking in the wind as a bluish-white balloon.

"Are you there?" Catin said.

"Yeah, go ahead," I said, getting out of the car.

"I thought what Leboeuf said might give away who the shooter was. I didn't want to give up the person who saved my life."

"Don't worry about it. What are the words?"

"Jam, mon, tea, orange."

"Say them again?"

She repeated them slowly. Though she had written down the words phonetically, if I was correct in my perception, they weren't far off the mark. The words Jesse had probably spoken were *"J'aime mon 'tit ange."*

"What do the words mean, Dave?"

"'I love my little angel,'" I replied.

The moon broke from behind the clouds, and suddenly the lawn was printed with shadows and shapes that had not been there seconds ago. The leaves of the water oaks were scattered on the grass, each leaf dry and crisp and limned with silver, sculpted like a tiny ship. I removed the phone from my ear and looked at Varina. *"Qui t'a pres faire, 'tit ange?"* I said.

"What did you say?" she asked.

"I said, 'What are you doing?' or 'What are you up to, little angel?' You don't speak French, Varina? You didn't learn it from your father? You didn't study it at LSU?"

"You think you've figured it all out, huh?" she said.

I put the phone back to my ear, then felt someone screw the muzzle of a revolver into the back of my neck. "Whoa, hoss," said the man holding the gun. He reached out with his other hand and pulled my cell phone from my palm and closed it. His hair was thick with grease and combed straight back. There was a purple bump on his nose, and his eyes were wide-set and misaligned, as if he possessed two optical systems instead of one.

He was not alone. Four other men came out of the shadows, all of them armed, one with a Taser. One of them was a fleshy man we had seen once before, in the company of the man whose eyes looked like they had been cut out of paper and glued haphazardly on his face.

The man with the Taser pulled Clete's .38 from its holster and threw it into a wall of bamboo that bordered the driveway. Then he pushed Clete against the side of the Caddy and told him to spread his legs.

"He has a gun strapped on his right ankle," Varina said.

"She'd be the one to know. I porked her once," Clete said. "While I was drunk."

"You and Dave brought this on yourselves," Varina said. "And you're foolish if you think anyone cares."

The man with the Taser ran his free hand under Clete's armpits and down his sides. Then he felt Clete's crotch and inside his thighs and pulled up Clete's right trouser leg and unstrapped the hideaway .25-caliber auto.

"You put your hand on my dick again, I'm going to break your nose, Taser or no Taser," Clete said.

The man straightened his back and smiled. "You're not my type," he said.

The man with the greased hair crushed my cell phone under his foot and removed my .45 from my clip-on holster, then told me to spread myself against the side of the car.

"I'm clean," I said.

"I believe you. But you know the drill. We're all pros here, man. Don't make it harder than it needs to be." His breath made the side of my face wrinkle as he moved his hands down my sides. "You don't like garlic shrimp with tomato sauce? That makes two of us. Remind me never to eat around here again."

"Where's my daughter?" I said to Varina.

"Out of my hands," she replied.

"Don't lie."

"Dave, do you think you're going to change anything?" she said. "There are billions of dollars at stake, and you and your rhinoceros of a friend who keeps his brains stuffed in his penis come along and fuck up everything for everyone. I tried to warn you, but you wouldn't listen."

"Yeah, we're pretty stupid, all right, because neither Clete nor I had any idea what we stumbled into. Is my daughter alive?"

"Maybe. But I haven't been downstairs, so I can't say," she replied.

"Downstairs?" I said.

"You asked for this. It's all on you. Just the same, I feel sorry for y'all and your daughters," she said.

"You think you can make us all disappear?" I said. "That nobody is going to know we came here?"

"Do you know how many convicts are buried in this yard?" she replied. "You see any monuments to them? Have you ever read any news accounts about their deaths?"

"Those men died over a hundred years ago," I said.

"How about the eleven who died in the blowout? How about all the soldiers blown apart by IEDs so people can have cheap gas? You see a lot of national hand-wringing about them?" she said.

On the edge of my vision, I saw an erect figure walk out of the shadows. He was wearing a velvet smoking jacket and a Tyrolean hat and an immaculate white shirt. "Oh, welcome, welcome, welcome to our egalitarian heroes," Alexis Dupree said. "I hope you'll enjoy the rest of your evening. Do you want to chat with your little friend Tee Jolie, Mr. Robicheaux? I know she'll be happy to see you. Your daughter will be, too."

"Get finished with this," Varina said. She hugged her arms around herself. "I'm cold."

The man with greased hair pushed the muzzle of his revolver into my ear. In the distance, I heard a freight train blowing down the line and thought I felt the heavy rumble of the freight and tanker cars through the earth. That was not what I felt at all. A ten-by-eight-foot square of lawn was lifting from the ground by the gazebo, like a doorway to a subterranean kingdom that even Dante could not imagine.

THE SUBSTRUCTURE OF the plantation home had been entirely reengineered. The ceiling was high and beamed with oak, the floor done with terrazzo and spread with throw rugs with Mediterranean colors and designs. But the walls were not walls; they were giant plasma screens that showed tropical sunsets and beaches dotted with palm trees and waves sliding onto beaches as white as granulated sugar. The main room contained conventional burgundy leather chairs and couches and a bar and a glass-topped table. There were other rooms in back, some with doors, some without. "Is my daughter back there?" I said.

"Perhaps," Alexis said. "How do you like our visual display? Here, look in this side room. You seemed to admire my collection of wartime photography. Would you like to see some movie footage from the last century?"

He pushed open a door that gave onto an office. There were four separate screens on two walls, all of them showing black-and-white images of German troops razing a village, Stukas dive-bombing a city, Jewish shops being destroyed during Kristallnacht, families climbing down from boxcars, the children terrified, all of them being herded through a barbed-wire corridor into a prison camp.

"People know where we are," I said.

"No, they don't," a voice said behind me.

Pierre Dupree had come out of a room in back and was combing his hair as he walked. "Friends of ours are within two feet of your wife," he said. "One of them stole the cell phone out of her purse. You didn't call her, Mr. Robicheaux."

"Where's Gretchen?" Clete said.

"Preparing herself," Dupree said.

"For what?" Clete said.

"An excursion into the Middle Ages. We're going to find out how much you know, Mr. Purcel, and the names of the people to whom you passed on information that isn't your business. Believe me, before this is over, you'll beg to give us information."

"Get on with it, Pierre," Varina said.

"I'll make it easy for you. What do you want to know?" Clete said.

"Where are your files? Who have you told?" Pierre said.

"Told *what*?" Clete said.

"Unfortunately, that's exactly the reaction we expected from you," Pierre said. "Maybe you're even telling the truth. But we have to be sure, and that's not good news for Gretchen and Alafair."

"You plan to kill them anyway, you motherfucker," Clete said.

"Not necessarily. Things haven't been that bad for Tee Jolie. Do you want to see her?" Pierre said.

"No, we don't," I said.

"That's strange," he said. "I found the cell phone she was using to call you. I thought you two were quite close. Come on, Mr. Robicheaux. Say hello. I'm not taunting you or being cruel. I think she's quite happy with the way things are. At first she was a little resistant about the abortion, but that's all past history."

"You made her have an abortion?" I said.

"I didn't *make* her do anything. She's a nice girl. You're an incurable romantic when it comes to her kind."

"Where are Gretchen and Alafair?" Clete said, starting toward Pierre.

A man with tattoos of a kind we had seen before stepped forward and touched the Taser to the back of Clete's neck. Clete went down as though he had been blackjacked across the temple. I knelt beside him and cradled his head in my hands. His eyes were crossed, and his nose was bleeding.

I looked up at the man with the Taser. He was thin and had black hair and was unshaved and wore jeans with suspenders and a lumberjack shirt. He smelled of the woods and the cold; he smelled like a hunter. There was a long tattoo of Bugs Bunny eating an orange carrot inside his left forearm. "I'm going to square this, buddy," I said.

"I don't blame you for being pissed, but if I was you, I'd go with the flow," he said. "It might work out for you. I carried a badge before I did this."

"That's enough, Mickey," Pierre said.

Clete sat up and wiped the blood from his nose on his sleeve. He was slack-jawed and closing and opening his eyes. The back of his neck looked like it had been stung by a jellyfish. From aboveground we heard the sound of a diesel engine cranking to life.

"That's the truck your vehicle is being loaded onto, Mr. Purcel," Alexis said. "In five minutes it will be off the property. Before morning your vehicle will be crushed into a ball of tinfoil, and so will you."

Pierre walked toward the rear of the basement and rested his hand on a doorknob. "Bring them here," he said. "I think Mr. Robicheaux deserves a degree of closure. Come on, Mr. Robicheaux. Talk with her. See what she has to say about her situation."

"With who?"

"The girl of your dreams. Tell me if you think she's been worth it," he said.

He pushed open the door slowly with the flat of his hand, exposing a room whose walls contained floor-to-ceiling plasma screens filled with scenes filmed through the windows of the stucco house on an island southeast of the Chandeleurs. Even the sound of the surf on the beach and the wind in the palm trees was being pumped through a speaker system.

Tee Jolie Melton was lying on a white brocade couch, wearing a blue evening gown and jewelry around her neck that looked like diamonds and rubies, although I doubted that was what they were. Her head was propped on a tasseled black satin pillow, the twists of gold in her hair still as bright as strings of buttercups. She seemed to smile in recognition. There were scabbed tracks on her forearms. She turned on her hip so she could see me better, but she didn't try to get up. "That's you?" she said.

"It's Dave Robicheaux, Tee Jolie," I said.

"Yeah, I knowed it was you, Mr. Dave. I knowed you'd be along someday."

"What'd they do to you, kiddo?"

"They ain't done nothing. It's just medicine."

"It's heroin."

"I couldn't deliver the baby, see, 'cause I ain't right inside. Don't be mad at Pierre. Don't be mad at me, either. Everyt'ing is gonna be all right, ain't it?"

"We'll be back later, darlin'," Pierre said. "Mr. Robicheaux and I need to talk over some business." He closed the door and slipped an iron bolt into a locked position. "She's a sweet girl."

"You turned her into a junkie," I said.

"She injected herself. So did her sister," he replied. "You know your problem, Mr. Robicheaux? You won't accept people as they are. You're only interested in them as abstractions. The flesh-and-blood reality isn't to your liking. It's you who is the elitist, not I."

The door at the bottom of the stairwell that led from aboveground opened, and a man carrying an AK-47 with a banana magazine came inside and closed the door. "This was between the seat and the door of the convertible," he said.

"Purcel had an automatic weapon in the front seat?" Pierre said.

"Yeah, it was covered by a blanket," the man said.

"You were riding in the front seat and didn't see it?" Pierre said to Varina.

"Oh, I've got it. His having a gun is my fault," she said.

"I didn't say that," he replied. "I was trying to understand how he got an AK-47 into his car without you seeing it. It's not an unreasonable question."

"I don't know how it got there. He went to the trunk for a blanket. Maybe the gun was in the trunk."

"This is foolish talk," Alexis said. "The two of you are nattering magpies."

"Shut up, you pitiful old fuck," Varina said.

I saw Clete looking at me, the light in his eyes intensifying. It wasn't hard to read the message: *Divide and conquer.*

"Lamont Woolsey gave you guys up," I said.

Varina and Pierre and Alexis all turned and stared at me.

"Woolsey thinks he's going down for the hit on Ozone Eddy Mouton and his girlfriend," I said.

"Who is Ozone Eddy?" Pierre said, a laugh starting to break on his face.

"I guess you're not up-to-date," I said. "Your buddy Woolsey had Ozone Eddy and his girlfriend burned to death in the trunk of an automobile after Clete stomped Woolsey's face in. Woolsey doesn't like the idea of being a tube of lubricant at Angola. So he told me a few things about your operation. I've got it on tape, if you want to hear it."

"I spoke with him this afternoon," Pierre said. "He's fishing in the Bahamas. He seemed quite relaxed to me."

I took a chance. "You guys made a lot of money off forged artworks. Then y'all invested it in Varina's electronic security service and offshore well supply. You should have been multimillionaires many times over. Too bad it turned to shit on you."

I could see the pause in their eyes, the doubt, the glimmer of uncertainty and calculation that characterizes the thinking of all manipulators.

"Somebody has to take the fall for the blowout," I said. "A lot of people thought the issue was the centralizers down in the hole. That was never it at all, was it? The electronic warning system failed. That's your area, isn't it?"

"Show him," Alexis said.

"Show me what?" I said.

"Dave, I didn't want this to happen," Varina said.

"Yeah, you did, Varina. None of these guys had the brains or charm to run an operation like this. You were always a winner. Men loved and admired you, and women were jealous of you. You could have been anything you wanted. Why'd you throw in with a bunch of losers like these guys?"

"Show him," Alexis Dupree repeated, his voice sharpening, the blood draining from around his mouth.

"You've made *Gran'père* angry," Pierre said. "That's not good for you or your friend or Alafair and Gretchen, Mr. Robicheaux. *Gran'père* doesn't have parameters. He has appetites of the most unusual kind."

He opened a wood door that gave onto a barred cell. The floor was spread with a rubber tarp. A cast-iron sarcophagus had been set horizontally at the rear of the room, its hinged lid open and resting against the wall. At the bottom of the sarcophagus were slits that I suspected were drains. The inside of the lid was patterned with rows of spikes shaped like stalactites. Alafair and Gretchen were sitting in the corner, wrists and ankles fastened behind them with ligatures, mouths taped. Gretchen was bleeding from a cut at her hairline. I saw Alafair's mouth working, as though trying to loosen the adhesive on her cheeks.

"You gutless sack of shit," I said to Pierre.

"You might be formally educated, but you're a coarse man, Mr. Robicheaux," he said. "As *Gran'père* would say, we can scrub everything out of the lower classes except the genes. Gretchen is going to go first. It's a nasty business. You can watch it or not. If you choose not to watch, believe me, you will hear it. Where's the tape you made of Lamont's confession?"

"In Clete's office," I said.

"Why is it I don't believe anything you say? What you don't understand, Mr. Robicheaux, is that we don't have anything to lose at this point. Do you think we plan to spend years in litigation while every cent we have is taken away from us? Do you think we plan to sell this beautiful historical home to pay years of legal fees because of you and your friend?"

"There's no way you can get away with this, Dupree," Clete said. "You think Helen Soileau won't figure out where we are?"

"Would you like to talk to her?" Pierre said.

"Can you stop talking, Pierre?" Varina said. "Just for once, please stop talking. I would take a vow of celibacy if you would take a vow of silence."

"My, my, daddy's little angel. If you're an angel, you're Lucifer in female form," Pierre said. "Think back, Varina. Who led these men into our lives again and again? You put your lovers on video while you were screwing. That's like robbing a bank and leaving your driver's license inside the vault. Oh, I forgot. You didn't have to compromise our security situation. Your idiot of a father did that when he told his minions our operation was run by his *petit ange.*"

"Don't speak of my father like that," Varina said.

"You asked if I wanted to talk to Helen Soileau," I said to Pierre.

"I insist that you do," he said. "Maybe you'll finally understand how self-deluded you are and how minuscule your importance is. However, I don't know if you'll be up to the shock. What do you think?"

"What are you saying?" I asked.

"You're uneducable, Mr. Robicheaux," he said.

"This isn't necessary, Pierre," Varina said.

"Stop hectoring the man and let him have a little fun," Alexis said.

"Excuse me for saying this, Alexis, but I hate both of you," she said. "When this is over, I'm going to—"

"What?" Alexis asked.

"I'm not sure," she replied. "Look at it this way. How much longer do you have to live? Think of me having a glass of champagne at your graveside. Think of me living in this house. Your grandson is incompetent and can't run a business by himself or paint his way out of a paper bag. How long do you think it will be before I own everything in your possession?"

"The only woman I've ever known like you was Ilse Koch," Alexis said.

"Who's that?" she asked.

"The Bitch of Buchenwald, you silly girl," he replied.

"What did you mean about Helen?" I said to Pierre.

He removed a remote control from his coat pocket and clicked a button several times. There was a bank of television monitors at the top of the wall by the entrance, most of them showing the grounds and the bayou and the two-lane highway in front of the plantation. The image on one of them changed to a scene inside a kitchen.

"That place you're looking at, Mr. Robicheaux, is just beyond Tee Jolie's bedroom," Pierre said. "The figure on the floor is Helen Soileau. She's quite unconscious right now, and I don't think she can feel very much pain. I also doubt that she's aware of her surroundings, so don't be too alarmed by what you're about to watch."

"What did you do to her?" I asked.

"She was chloroformed, that's all," he replied. He took a small walkie-talkie from his pocket and pushed a button and spoke into it. "Put her inside, fellows." Then he turned to me. "Watch now. You should enjoy this, since I suspect she's a pain in the ass to work for. It's oopsy-daisy time for the lady from Lesbos."

Helen was bound hand and foot and lying on her side, and I couldn't see her face. Two men walked in front of the camera and lifted her into the air and opened the top of a deep-freeze chest and set her inside. One of them looked back at the camera, then shut the lid.

"I give her about fifteen minutes," Pierre said. "How much did you tell her about us, Mr. Robicheaux?"

"She never believed what I said about you," I replied. "No one will. You're killing people for no reason."

"It's getting late," Alexis said. "Start with the girls, Mickey. Be fast about it, too. I'm tired."

"I want to do the one called Gretchen," the fleshy man said.

"Oh, that's right, Harold, she broke out your front teeth, didn't she?" Alexis said. "By all means."

"Look, you guys, it's obvious you make use of people inside the system," Clete said. "That's me and Dave. Maybe we can work something out. Look at our record. I don't know how many guys we've cowboyed. You don't believe me, check my jacket."

"You're not in a seller's market, Mr. Purcel," Alexis said.

"Dave already said it," Clete replied. "What's the percentage in snuffing people nobody believes?"

"And Sheriff Soileau?" Alexis said, an amused gleam in his eye.

"That's the breaks, I guess," Clete said.

"I knew others like you," Alexis said. "When we locked them inside the showers, we told them we were creating a special dispensation for those who could prove their mettle. They beat and strangled one another while we watched through a peephole, and after a few minutes we dropped the gas containers through the air vents in the roof."

"Shut up and get this over with," Varina said.

"Maybe you'll be part of the entertainment. That would be quite a surprise, wouldn't it?" Alexis said to her. "Did you know that Caligula did that to his dinner guests?"

"*What?*" she said angrily.

"I wanted to see if you were paying attention," Alexis said.

The fat man and the man with greased hair were putting on rubber boots and long rubber gloves. The fat man was looking with anticipation at the cell where Alafair and Gretchen lay bound in the corner.

"Pierre?" said the man with the greased hair.

"What is it?"

"I got a problem. I ate some garlic shrimp for supper. I'm about to download in my pants."

"Then go to the bathroom. We'll wait."

"Thank you, sir."

The man with the greased hair lumbered toward a bathroom in the rear of the building, duck-footed, clutching his stomach.

"Make sure you close the door and turn on the ventilator," said the man with the Bugs Bunny tattoo.

"That isn't funny, Mickey," Pierre said.

"Sorry, sir."

It was Clete Purcel who seemed to reveal a side that no one had ever seen in him. "I can't take this, Dave. I'd thought I'd be up to it, but I'm not. I got to sit down."

"Act with some dignity, Mr. Purcel," Pierre said.

"It's my chest. I've got some lead in there. I think it's next to my heart. I need a chair. I can't stand up."

"Don't listen to him," Varina said.

Clete gagged and spat blood on his hand. "I'm going to hit the deck if I don't sit down."

"Get him a chair," Alexis said.

"Don't get near him! Don't trust this man!" Varina said.

Clete swayed from side to side, then fell against the wall. Mickey held him up and slapped his cheek. "Hang on, big man," he said. "You were in the Crotch, right? Time to man up."

Clete bent over, his hands on his thighs, as though about to be sick. "I'm going down, Dave. You'll be on your own. I'm sorry," he said.

He crumpled to one knee, his shirt splitting down his spine, his love-handles hanging over his belt, his giant buttocks spreading like an elephant's.

"This man is pitiful," Alexis said.

"I didn't sign on for this," Clete replied, shaking his head.

"This is the legendary New Orleans badass who capped our guys in the shootout on the bayou?" Mickey said. "What a joke."

With his left hand, Clete pulled his trouser leg up and unsnapped the KA-BAR strapped on his calf. He pulled the blade from its scabbard. "Chug on this, bubba," he said.

CHAPTER
33

CLETE CLENCHED ONE arm around the throat of the man who had Bugs Bunny on his forearm, and drove the knife into his chest not once but twice, holding him up, using him as a shield. "Dave! The AK!"

He didn't have to tell me. I was already running for it. It was propped against the wall by the stairwell, painted with green and black tiger stripes, the banana-shaped magazine dull gray, nicked silver on the edges with wear. As I ran toward the stairwell, I was trying to count inside my head the number of men in the room. How many were there?

There was a fat man who wanted to personally crush Gretchen Horowitz inside the iron maiden because she had broken his teeth. There was the man whose hair was scalped around the ears and layered with grease on top, and another man who had found the AK-47 in Clete's convertible and brought it inside. There was the man who had Tasered Clete, although he was already a casualty, his feet kicking uselessly, his mouth trying to suck oxygen into his lungs after both of them had already been punctured by Clete's knife.

In the kitchen were two men who had lowered Helen Soileau into the deep freezer.

How many others were on the property, either inside or aboveground? I couldn't remember the number I had seen. Was Pierre Dupree armed? Or Alexis? Or Varina?

490

I had no way of knowing.

I would like to describe the next few minutes in a precise fashion, but I cannot. There are experiences in your life that you never quite sort out. You relive them many times in your dreams but always through a broken lens. Think of the syndrome in this way, and tell me if any of it sounds familiar. You are a man or woman who never uses profanity, but you remember yourself screaming obscenities, none of it with any syntax and none of it making any sense. You remember the buck of a weapon in your hands, but you do not remember aiming it; instead, you remember with a sinking of the heart that you did not care who was in front of it, that you would have shot your father or your brother or your son if he had been in your line of fire. You gloried in the fact that you were alive while others died and that your enemy seemed to deconstruct in a bloody mist before your eyes.

I know I pulled back and released the bolt on the AK-47 and prayed that the magazine was loaded. I know I pulled the trigger as soon as the round chambered, and I saw a man in overalls— I think the man who found the AK—grab his stomach and bend over as though someone had punched him in the solar plexus inside a crowded elevator. I saw Clete drop the man he had stabbed and pick up the Taser and use it on Pierre Dupree, or try to use it, I couldn't be sure. I saw the kitchen door open and a man's face appear briefly against a backdrop of pots and pans hanging from a wall, and I know I started firing at him and saw the door close again and the rounds pock through a metal surface that had been oversprayed with black paint.

I saw the fat man whose name was Harold unlock the door to Gretchen and Alafair's cell and go inside. I saw the man with the intestinal problem emerge from the bathroom, his fly unzipped, his belt unbuckled, a nickel-plated .357 in his hand. I lifted the AK-47 and fired two or perhaps three rounds at him and saw a spurt of blood fly from his shoulder and whip across the doorjamb. He righted himself with one hand propped behind him and began firing at me as fast as he could pull the trigger of his revolver. I saw Clete fall back against the wall and couldn't tell if he was hit. Pierre

Dupree was crouched in a ball, trembling from either fear or the shock of the Taser or both. I had no idea where Alexis Dupree or Varina had gone.

I crouched behind a divan and tried to calculate how many rounds I had fired, but I couldn't. The plasma screens in the walls were exploding, the tropical sunsets and the iridescent spray of waves and the groves of coconut palms cascading in sheets of glass on the terrazzo floor.

I had hit the man in the bathroom at least once, but he had gotten behind the protection of the wall, where he had probably used a speed loader, because all at once he was back on rock and roll.

I saw Clete crawl on his hands and knees through the broken glass, the handle of his KA-BAR clenched in his right palm. He reached the far wall and inched his way to the bathroom door, looking in my direction. I saw him mouth, *Now.* I raised up above the divan and fired two rounds at the bathroom, blowing splinters out of the doorjamb, shattering the lavatory and a mirror. The man with the greased hair ducked back behind the wall, and Clete reached around the side of the door and drove the blade of the KA-BAR into his thigh, then grabbed him by his necktie and dragged him to the floor and fastened one hand under his chin and the other on the back of his head and broke his neck.

The shooter's revolver had fallen into the toilet. Clete retrieved it, shaking water from his hand, and began searching the dead man's pockets for bullets, growing more frantic as he pulled each pocket inside out. He was saying something to me, but the gunfire had taken its toll; my ears felt like they were stuffed with cotton, and I couldn't make out his words. "What is it?" I shouted.

He pointed to the cylinder of the nickel-plated revolver, then held up his index finger and silently formed the words *One fucking round.* One of the cabinet doors under the lavatory had swung open. I saw Clete pick up a plastic bottle and stick it in his trouser pocket. Then he wiped his knife clean on a towel and eased out of the bathroom door, his eyes fastened on the entrance to the kitchen, where at least two men were barricaded. My hearing had started to clear.

We had forgotten about Pierre Dupree. He had gotten to his feet and was trying to steady himself by holding on to a chair. I also realized I had misjudged him. He had not been frightened, just temporarily traumatized by the shock of the Taser. There was glass in his hair and on his shoulders, and blood was running from his right ear. "Give it up," he said. "This property is sealed. Even if you get to the yard, you'll be killed. I'll make a deal with you. We can work this out so everyone wins."

"Tell the fat guy to come out of the cell," I said.

"All these men are trained never to surrender their weapons. Just like police officers," Dupree replied.

"Except they're not police officers. They're hired dipshits," I said.

Clete stumbled through the furniture, looking backward over his shoulder at the bullet-pocked doors to the kitchen. He inserted the blade of the KA-BAR between Dupree's thighs and raised the sharpened side into his scrotum. "Tell the blob in there to throw his piece out of the cell and to walk after it with his hands on his head."

"Or you're going to castrate me?" Pierre said.

"More like split you in half," Clete replied.

"No, you won't, Mr. Purcel. Do you know why? You don't have the courage. You're like most people who admire comic-book heroes. You think courage is about showing mercy. It's the other way around. It takes courage to give no mercy, to face life as it is, to accept that the weak wish to be ruled by the strong, that the weak would not have it any other way."

"Tell that to yourself while you're holding your guts in your hands," Clete said.

"Then do it. I've had a good life. Outside of marrying a woman who is probably the worst cunt in the history of this state, I have few regrets."

"You shouldn't use that word," Clete said.

"I shouldn't use that word? One man is dead and two others are dying, but I shouldn't use a word that perfectly describes the most hypocritical creature I've ever known? I don't think either one of you understands the culture you live in. Varina was queen of the Carnival at Mardi Gras, cheered and loved by hundreds of thousands. How about my grandfather? He gassed whole families and used children in medical experiments. He shared a mistress with Josef Mengele. But no one will ever believe your story about him. Even if people do, he'll never be punished. He's old and kindly and charming, and people will say, 'Oh, Mr. Robicheaux, all that was *so* long ago.'"

Clete looked at me. "I think he's probably right. We should cool Pierre out now and get the rest as we go."

I didn't think he meant it, but I wasn't going to take the chance. Also, we were running out of time. Helen Soileau was probably close to death from hypothermia. I hit Pierre Dupree across the face with the AK-47. His bottom lip split, and the back of his head hit the wall. I watched him slide down on the floor.

"You should have let me wax him," Clete said. He began going through Dupree's pockets. "He's not carrying."

Pierre Dupree's lack of a weapon on him wasn't the issue. We knew we had to make a choice. Did we get Helen out of the deep freeze first or deal with the fat man in Gretchen and Alafair's cell?

"Can you deal with the two guys inside the kitchen while I talk with Fatso?" Clete said.

"You've only got one round."

"He doesn't know that."

"If you miss, he'll kill the girls," I said.

"Then what do you want to do?"

"Stop talking about it and do it."

We worked our way along the wall until we reached the conventional door over the barred door of the cell. I eased the outside door back until I had a clear view of the cell's interior. The fat man had been busy while we were dealing with Pierre Dupree and the other three men. He had placed Gretchen in the sarcophagus and pulled the hinged lid partway from the wall so that its spiked weight loomed over her body and would fall upon her if anything caused him to release his grip. In his right hand, he held a small blue-black automatic with white handles. He had found the exact point of balance for the lid so that it caused the least amount of exertion in his arm and shoulder, but the strain was starting to show in his face.

"Your name is Harold?" I said.

"That's right."

He had the small mouth and cleft chin of the Irish, his face splotched like that of a man with a bloated liver. He had removed his coat, and his armpits were dark with sweat.

"Clete has your bud's .357 aimed at the side of your head. You need to ease that iron lid back against the wall," I said.

"That's not what's gonna happen," he replied. "You two lovelies are going to throw your pieces inside the cell."

I saw Gretchen raise her head from the sarcophagus. He had torn the tape loose from her mouth. She fixed her eyes on Clete but said nothing.

"Did you know she was supposed to clip you?" Harold said. "I think she planned to do it. Maybe we saved your life."

"It's not true," Gretchen said.

"We got the word on her, buddy," Harold said. "When she wasn't balling guys from the Gambino crime family, she was blowing heads for them. She pulled a train in a fuck pad in Hallandale."

I felt around the edges of the cell door and moved it slightly in the jamb. It wasn't locked. "Get a couple of cushions off the couch," I said to Clete under my breath.

"Stop whispering over there and throw your pieces to me," Harold said. "I got a bad heart. I can't hold this lid much longer. What's it gonna be?"

"Your employers have bagged ass," I said. "Why take their fall? With the right lawyer, you might skate. Angola is a bitch, Harold. Do the smart thing."

He bit down on his lip, then shook his head. Out of the corner of my eye, I saw Clete retrieve two huge leather-covered cushions from the couch.

"The problem is he's not smart," Gretchen said. "Right, Harold? But low intelligence is not your biggest problem. Did you ever see *Shack Out on 101* with Lee Marvin and Frank Lovejoy? Lee Marvin plays a Communist agent whose cover is working in a greasy spoon north of Los Angeles. Frank Lovejoy is the FBI agent who hunts him down in the last scene. Frank is holding a harpoon gun on him in the kitchen, and Lee is staring at the harpoon in this filthy apron with his mouth hanging open. Frank says, 'You know what you are, fella? You're not only a Commie, you're a slob. And you know what a slob is, don't you?'

"Lee shakes his head. He's so covered with grease and kitchen shit, you can smell the BO coming off the screen. Frank says, 'A slob is a guy who's still dirty after he takes a shower.' Then Frank shoots him through the chest with his harpoon gun. In the last frame, you see the rope on the harpoon quivering, which is a real skillful touch, because you know Lee is in his death throes on the floor, but the camera doesn't show it."

"Why should I care about a couple of dead actors?" Harold said.

"Because you're about to join them," Gretchen said.

I lifted the AK-47 and steadied it on one of the cell bars and framed Harold's face in the iron sights. Clete had already positioned himself on my right side, the cushions hidden by the wall. "Last chance, Harold. I hear hell is pretty hot even in the wintertime," I said.

"We've got your jacket, Robicheaux," he said. "You're not a cowboy. So fuck off on all this John Wayne stuff."

The timing had to be perfect. If Clete was one second too slow getting inside the cell, Gretchen would die. If I was one second too soon in squeezing off a round, Gretchen would die. If the shot wasn't clean and I didn't cut Harold's motors, Gretchen would die.

"Do it. Do it now, Dave," Clete whispered.

I was breathing through my mouth, trying to control my heart rate, my eyes stinging with sweat. As I tightened my finger on the trigger, I saw the fat man's eyes lock on mine and a strange moment of recognition swim through them, as though he had seen the entirety of his life reduced to a flip of a coin that had only one outcome: Harold had stepped through the door in the dimension.

The AK-47 long ago won great respect from anyone who ever went up against it. Unlike the early M16, which often jammed unless you burned the whole magazine, the AK was smooth-firing and had almost twice the penetrating power of its American counterpart and used a bullet that was over twice the weight of the M16 round. In semi-auto mode at close range, it was deadly accurate. I centered Harold's forehead inside the hooded sight and whispered "One, two, three" to Clete, then snapped off two rounds just as he bolted through the door, the ejected casings bouncing off the steel bars onto the floor.

I had never seen Clete move so fast. The 7.62×39mm rounds blew the back of Harold's head onto the wall, but before the lid of the sarcophagus could crush Gretchen's body, Clete threw both thick burgundy-colored leather cushions on top of her and caught the edge of the lid before its full weight had swung down.

I peeled the tape off Alafair's mouth and cut the ligatures on her wrists and ankles with my pocketknife. "Did you find Julie Ardoin?" she said.

"Yeah," I said, looking back over my shoulder through the bars, not knowing whether she had witnessed Julie's death.

"I couldn't stop it," she said. "I tried."

"It's not your fault, Alafair. They were planning to kill all of us."

"Why do they hate us so?" she asked.

"Because we're not like them," I said. "Did you see Helen Soileau?"

"No. She's here?"

"She's being held in the kitchen. Do you know how many guys might be in there?"

"No, the only guys Gretchen and I saw were the fat one and the one with the grease in his hair."

"Do you know where they might have any other guns?" I asked.

"No, they blindfolded us after they took us out of the park. I heard Varina's voice, but I didn't see her. Pierre came to the cell and watched us, but he didn't say anything."

"He did what?"

"He watched us like we were in a zoo. He was smiling. Alexis Dupree was standing behind him. Alexis said, 'They're attractive girls. Too bad they have to go up the chimney so soon.'"

"Keep Gretchen here," I said. I hit Clete on the shoulder and pointed at the kitchen area. "How many rounds did you load in the magazine?" I said.

"The full thirty."

"The two guys in the kitchen are dead as soon as we go in the door. We get Helen out of the freezer and take their guns and go aboveground."

"What about Tee Jolie?"

"First things first," I replied.

"Dave, I got to tell you something. I don't know if I'm going crazy or not. I heard that song."

"What song?"

"The one you're always talking about. The one by what's-his-name. You know, Jimmy Clanton. 'Just a Dream'? That's the title, isn't it?"

"You didn't hear that song, Clete."

"I did. Don't tell me I didn't. I don't believe in that kind of mystical mumbo jumbo, so I don't make it up. It was calling us, Dave."

I wasn't interested anymore in the year 1958 or the era that for me encapsulated everything that was wonderful about the place where I grew up. We had saved our daughters and now had the challenge of saving Helen Soileau from one of the worst fates a human being could experience—to wake inside total darkness, abandoned by the rest of the human race, the senses assaulted by a level of cold that was unimaginable.

Clete and I crunched over the broken glass down the hallway, past Tee Jolie's bedroom, until we were at the painted-over metal doors that gave onto the kitchen. I looked at the stiff shape in his trouser pocket.

"What did you take out of that bathroom cabinet?" I said.

"Mouthwash," Clete replied.

I looked at his eyes. They were flat, with no expression. "I'll go in first," I said. "Are you ready?"

He held the .357 upward. "Let's rock," he replied.

I jerked open the door and went inside fast, pointing the AK-47 in front of me, swinging it back and forth. The light inside the room was brilliant, every item on the butcher block and counters and walls and in the dry rack sparkling clean. There was nobody inside the room. At the back of the kitchen was a stairwell, and I heard someone slam a door at the top and then feet moving heavily across the floor immediately above our heads.

I set down the AK-47 on the butcher block and opened the top of the freezer. The trapped cloud of cold air rose like a fist into my face. Helen was rolled up in an embryonic position, her eyebrows and hair shaggy with frost, her cheeks gray and wrinkled as though they had been touched with a clothes iron, her fingernails blue.

Clete and I dipped our hands around her body and lifted her free of the chest and set her down on a throw rug in front of the sink. Clete found a tablecloth inside a drawer and wrapped her in it. Her eyelids looked as thin as rice paper, her nostrils clotted with frost. She was shaking so badly, I could hardly hold her wrists. She looked up at me with the expression of someone at the bottom of a deep well. So far we had seen no telephones or phone jacks in the basement of the house. "We're going to get you to Iberia General, Helen," I said. "We've put four of these bastards down so far. How many more guys are on the grounds?"

She shook her head, her eyes on mine.

"I'm sorry we didn't get here sooner," I said. "Two of Pierre's gumballs were going to kill Gretchen Horowitz and Alafair."

Her mouth opened and closed, but no sound came out.

"I can't hear you," I said.

I brushed her hair out of her eyes and leaned my ear down to her mouth. Her hair was cold and felt as stiff as straw. There was no warmth at all in her breath. Her words were like a damp feather inside my ear. "It's not Dupree," she whispered. "They're everywhere. You were right all along."

"*Who* is everywhere?"

"I don't know. I think I'm going to die, Dave."

"No, you're not," I said.

She closed one eye as though winking at me. But I realized that there was something wrong with her facial control, and the eyelid had folded of its own accord.

Clete was standing next to us, staring at the ceiling. At least three people were above us. I thought about spraying the rest of the magazine through the floor. Again I tried to remember the number of rounds I had fired. The magazine of Clete's AK-47 was a solid banana-shaped block of light metal with no viewing slit. My guess was that I had fired a minimum of ten rounds, perhaps a maximum of fifteen. But in any rapid-fire situation, you almost always let off more rounds than you remember.

"They've got one plan and one plan only, Streak," Clete said. "None of us down here ever sees sunlight again."

He walked toward the staircase that led to the first floor and gestured at me to join him. He looked past my shoulder at Helen, wrapped to the chin in the tablecloth. "We could wait these guys out, but if we do, Helen might not make it," he said.

"Let's take it to them," I said.

"We might not get out of this one, Dave. If we don't, let's write our names on the wall in big letters."

"Three feet high, all in red," I said.

"Fuckin' A, noble mon. Everybody gets to the barn, right?"

"What's in your pocket?"

"I don't remember. But Pierre Dupree is mine. You copy that?"

"The goal is to get their weapons. Shitcan the personal agenda."

He wiped his mouth on his hand and looked at me and grinned. There was blood on his teeth. I don't believe he was thinking about mortality, at least not in a fearful way. He was looking at me and I at him as though we were seeing each other as we were when we walked a beat together on Bourbon Street over three decades ago, dressed to the eyes in our blue uniforms, our shoes spit-shined, the roar of a Dixieland band coming from the open door of Sharkey Bonano's Dream Room. "I heard that damn paddle wheeler out on the bayou," he said.

"It's not there, Clete. And if it is, it's not there for us."

"How do you know?"

"Because the Bobbsey Twins from Homicide are forever," I replied.

He peeled a stick of gum with one hand, never taking his gaze off my face, a grin breaking at the corner of his mouth. " 'We don't care what people say, rock and roll is here to stay,'" he said. "That's from Danny and the Juniors, the greatest single line in the history of music."

Then he charged up the stairs, taking them three at a time, his weight almost tearing the handrail from the wall.

CHAPTER
34

CLETE HAD BEEN right. The Duprees and Varina and their employees wanted to seal us in the bottom of the house and sponge us off the face of the earth. What they had not expected was Clete Purcel coming full-throttle through the door, plunging into the darkness, knocking over a table loaded with crystal ware, creating havoc in their midst, burying himself somewhere near Alexis Dupree's study. Nor did they expect me to be hard on Clete's heels, firing first at a man unwise enough to silhouette himself against the French doors, then, from behind a couch, turning on a second man who had just emerged from the kitchen eating a po'boy sandwich with one hand and holding a semi-auto in the other.

The first man fell against the French doors. I heard something hard knock against the wood floor and guessed that it was his weapon, but I couldn't be sure. The second man was a different matter. He had left the refrigerator partially open, and I could see him clearly against the crack of white light through the door. He wore a tight-fitting olive-colored T-shirt and cargo pants with pockets all over them; his arms were round, and so were his face and his close-cropped peroxided head. He looked like a man who worked out daily but ate too much. He looked like a man who didn't have a care in the world, except vague thoughts about the next time he would get laid. I suspected he was right-handed, because his coordination broke down when he realized what was happening around him. Rather than throw his sandwich away, he tried to set it down on a table while he shifted his semi-auto from his left to his right hand, as though all the clocks in the house would stop while he adjusted to the situation.

"Put it down, bub," I said. "You can have another season to run."

Like most men who commit murder for hire, he probably concluded long ago that as the giver of death, he would never be its recipient. When he aimed at me, his mouth was full of food. He also made a childlike gesture I had seen others make in their last seconds on earth. He extended his left hand in front of him, as though it could save him from the bullets that he knew were about to explode from the muzzle of the AK-47. I know I must have fired at least three times. The first round clipped his fingers from his left hand and patterned them on his T-shirt; the second round hit him in the mouth, and the third ricocheted inside the kitchen, breaking glass and pinging off steel surfaces.

I crawled to the man who had died by the French doors and turned him over. His fingers were holding on to his Glock. I had to pick up his hand by the wrist and pull it free from its grip on the handles and the trigger guard. I searched in his pockets for a backup magazine or extra bullets but found none. I worked my way over to the kitchen entrance and took a Beretta off the man who had died with lettuce and shrimp and sourdough bread hanging out of his mouth. I found a backup magazine in one of the snap-button pockets of his cargo pants, this one a pre-AWB job that held fourteen rounds.

I could hear movement upstairs and also out on the porch and in the camellia bushes by the windows. I found a telephone that had spilled on the floor, but there was no dial tone. I suspected the Duprees had cut the phone lines. I moved along the base of the living room wall toward the staircase that led down into the basement. When I peered into the darkness, I could hear someone breathing, then I made out a shape moving up the steps toward me.

"Gretchen?" I said.

"Is Clete all right?" she said.

"He's fine." I handed her the Glock. "It probably has a full magazine, but check it. Where's Alafair?"

"With the sheriff. She found some blankets. The outside door is locked. We could hear guys talking in the yard. This is the only way out."

"I've got a Beretta with a reserve magazine that I'm going to give to Clete. How's Sheriff Soileau?"

"I think she's in a coma. Can anybody see into the house from the highway?" she said.

"I doubt it. The Duprees keep the cops on a pad, anyway."

"What if we start a fire?" she said.

"We'll have to get Tee Jolie and Helen out. A fire may also serve the Duprees' purpose better than ours. They might seal us off inside it. We're going to have to punch our way out, Gretchen."

"What happens when this is over?"

"What do you mean?" I asked.

"Am I going down for the hit on Bix Golightly?"

"I can't answer that." I wanted to tell her that perhaps it was time for her to stop thinking about herself. I'm happy I didn't.

"I just want to get one thing straight with you. I clipped Golightly, and I'm glad I did," she said. "In case I don't come out of this, I want other people to know I didn't pop him for the money. I did it because he sodomized a six-year-old girl on her birthday. He's in hell, and he'll never be able to hurt another child, and I'm glad I put him there. What do you think of that?"

"I think Bix got what he had coming, kid."

"You mean that?"

"Take care of Helen and Tee Jolie. When you and Alafair hear shooting, head up the stairs and run for the front door. We're going to kill everything in sight, got it?"

"How much ammunition do you have for the AK-47?"

"Whatever is still in the mag. I'm going to find Clete now. If you get outside and Clete and I don't get there in one piece, make sure the Duprees go down."

"What about Varina?" she asked.

"In my opinion, Varina is an adverb."

"Is this state a fresh-air mental asylum?"

"How'd you guess?" I said.

I crawled to Clete's position and gave him the Beretta and the backup fourteen-round magazine.

"I think the old man is in the study," he said. "I heard somebody knocking around in there. Why wouldn't he have blown Dodge?"

"His trophies are in there."

"Which trophies?" Clete said.

"The locks of hair from his victims. They're pressed between the pages of a travel diary."

Clete balled up a handkerchief in his hand and smothered a cough. "I feel like something sharp is moving around inside me," he said.

I WOULD LIKE to say that the events that were about to happen on the bayou were of a kind that assures us there is a semblance of justice in the world. I would like to believe that there is a resolution in the human tragedy and that order can be reimposed upon the earth in the same way it occurs in the fifth act of the Elizabethan drama that supposedly mirrors our lives. My experience has been otherwise. History seldom corrects itself in its own sequence, and when we mete out justice, we often do it in a fashion that perpetuates the evil of the transgressors and breathes new life into the descendants of Cain.

I would like to believe the instincts of the mob can be exorcised from the species or genetically bred out of it. But there is no culture in the history of the world that has not lauded its warriors over its mystics. Sometimes in an idle moment, I try to recall the names of five slaves out of the whole sorry history of human bondage whose lives we celebrate. I have never had much success.

William Faulkner was once asked what he thought of Christianity. He replied, in effect, that he thought it was a fine religion and perhaps we should try it sometime.

Were the events about to transpire on the bayou that night justified? I wish I could say. If I have found any peace of mind in this world, it lies in accepting that we know almost nothing and understand even less. A fanatical university student murders an archduke and starts a war that kills twenty million people. A man with a fifteen-dollar mail-order rifle fires from the sixth floor of a book depository and changes American history forever. And a flawed engineering system on a drilling rig kills eleven men and fouls an entire ecosystem and almost destroys a way of life. If a person had the power to retroactively undo any of these events, where would he start? The question itself suggests an alpha and an omega that numb the mind.

Clete Purcel had never thought of himself as a man of great historical significance. In my opinion, he was. He was not only the trickster of folklore, he was one of those who suffered for the rest of us. Many orthodox Jews believe in the legend of the thirty-six just men. In their view, were it not for the presence of these thirty-six just men who carry the weight of our sins, the world would be a far worse place than it is. Like the thirty-six just men, Clete was not herculean. He was made of blood and bones and sinew like the rest of us. That's the point. His courage and his nobility existed in direct measure to his acceptance of mortality.

Evil men feared and hated Clete Purcel because they knew he was unlike them. They feared him because they knew he put principle ahead of self-interest, and they feared him because he would lay down his life for his best friend. I think Ben Jonson would have liked and understood Clete and would not have been averse to saying that, like his friend William Shakespeare, Clete was not of an age but for all time.

I WENT INTO the study bent low, trying not to silhouette against the windows. I saw the shape of a tall figure by the French doors on the far side of the room. I raised the AK-47 in front of me and stood up in front of a bookcase lined with leather-bound reference books of some kind. I could hear Clete behind me. He coughed, choking, into his handkerchief. I saw the tall figure freeze, then seem to dissolve into the shadows.

"Most of your men are dead, Mr. Dupree," I said. "You have the power to put an end to this. Give it up and take your chances with the court. Who's going to put away a ninety-year-old man?"

"You'll never leave this property, Mr. Robicheaux," Alexis replied. "All your knowledge ends here. My wishes have nothing to do with it. The die has already been cast by people who are much more powerful than you and I."

"Pop him," Clete whispered.

I couldn't see Dupree well enough to shoot. Also, he was probably the best hostage we could take; I wanted to see him exposed for the genocidal criminal that he was; and last, I wanted to expose all the people who had helped him create a fiefdom out of what once was a tropical paradise.

"Drop him, Dave," Clete said.

I tried to push Clete back with one hand while I kept my eyes on Dupree or at least on the place where I thought he was standing.

"Do I have to do it?" Clete said, wheezing in the darkness.

I pushed Clete backward with one hand and moved quickly along the edge of the bookshelves, knocking into the back of Dupree's swivel chair, tripping on a telephone wire and the connections to a computer. I lifted the AK-47 in front of me as Dupree went out the French doors, his travel diary held to his chest, his regal features as sharp-edged as tin in the starlight.

I fired once through the glass and heard the round hit something in the gazebo and whine away in the distance.

"We had a chance to cut the head off the snake, big mon," Clete said. "You shouldn't have shoved me like that."

"He was no good to us dead," I replied.

"Yeah? What if we don't get out of here and he does? Did you think of that?"

Clete was on one side of the French doors, and I was on the other. The fog was white and thick and rolling on the surface of the bayou. The tide was coming in, and the pontoon plane moored to the Dupree dock was bobbing up and down in the chop. "I made the call I thought was right," I said. I looked at the handkerchief balled in his hand. "How you doin', partner?"

"I had a bad moment back there, but I'm okay now."

"You've got to have my back, Cletus."

"You saying you don't want me on point?"

"Do you have my back or not?"

He glanced at me, then looked outside at the moss frozen in the live oaks and at the flooded bamboo that rattled in the wind and at a distant sugar mill lit as brightly as an aircraft carrier. "Hear it?" he said.

"Hear what?"

"The paddle wheeler. I can hear the steam engines. I can hear the wheel churning in the water."

This time I didn't try to argue with him. "Clete, maybe there's another way to think about this. Maybe we're getting a second chance. Maybe we're putting away some of the guys we didn't get the last time out."

He gazed into my face and smiled. "I've got a suggestion."

"What?" I asked.

"Let's just do it. High and hard and down the middle. Shake and bake, snake and nape, full throttle and fuck it. On three, here comes the worst shit storm in the history of Bayou Teche."

AND THAT WAS the way we did it. We came through the French doors and across the patio in tandem. I shot a man who stood up behind a camellia bush, and I saw part of his jaw fly from his head in a bloody spray. I shot a second man who dropped his gun and limped gingerly away into the darkness, past the gazebo, pressing his palm against his thigh, as though he might have sustained a football injury rather than a bullet wound from an AK-47. I saw muzzle flashes from among the camellia and azalea bushes and from behind a restored slave's cabin and from someone firing from the corner of the carriage house. I even thought I saw a tracer round streak into the distance and die like a tiny spark behind a cane field, but I couldn't be sure. I fired until the AK-47 was empty, then I stooped over the first man I had shot and pulled a cut-down pump shotgun from his hands and fished in his pockets for the extra shells. He was still alive, his eyes as bright as polished brown marbles, his tongue moving where his jaw should have been. I could not make out the words he was trying to say.

I did something then that some would consider bizarre. I broke my religious medal from its chain and pressed it in his hand. I don't know if he had any idea what it was or if he cared, because I didn't look at him again. Someone had gotten on board the pontoon plane and started up the engine. I ran toward Clete, on the far side of the gazebo, aiming the Beretta straight out in front of him with both hands, firing at the plane taxiing into the middle of the bayou, away from the overhang of the trees.

"Let them go," I said. "There's a guy behind the carriage house. I couldn't get him."

"If anybody got on that plane, it's the Duprees," he said.

"We'll get them later," I said.

"Screw that," he said. He fired three more rounds, and I heard at least one of them hit the plane's propeller. Then the bolt on his Beretta locked open on an empty chamber. He dropped the magazine from the frame and inserted the backup magazine and chambered a round.

"Let the plane go, Clete," I said.

It wasn't really a choice now. The pilot, whoever he or she was, had given it the gas. The plane lifted off the bayou briefly, sputtered once or twice, and set back down, the fog closing as it drifted around a bend with the incoming tide. Whoever was aboard was off the playing field, at least temporarily.

Clete's face looked poached, his green eyes as big as Life Savers. I ejected a spent shell from the chamber of the twelve-gauge I had taken off the dying man and inserted three shells into the magazine, until I felt the spring come tight against my thumb. It was all going very fast now. I saw Gretchen and Alafair come out of the house. Gretchen was carrying Helen Soileau over her shoulder, and Alafair was pulling Tee Jolie Melton behind her. That was not all that was going on. Someone had started a fire inside the house, a small one certainly, with flames no bigger than the candles on a birthday cake burning in a darkened room, but it was a fire just the same.

"Who the hell did that?" Clete said.

"My bet is on Gretchen," I said.

"Good for her," he said.

"How about all the evidence in there? The computers, the paper files, the message machines, the cell phones?"

Clete's attention had wandered. "On the other side of the coulee," he said. "The door is open to the slave cabin. It wasn't open a minute ago."

I let my eyes sweep back and forth across the backyard. The wind had died, and there were no shadows moving on the grass. The man who had been behind the carriage house seemed to have disappeared. I could hear myself breathing in the silence, and steam was rising from my mouth. "I'll check out the cabin," I said. "A dead guy back there is wearing a coat that'll fit you. Maybe we're home free, partner."

"These guys don't give up that easily," he replied, his teeth chattering. "We're not finished with payback, either."

"Get the coat. You're going to come down with pneumonia."

"Pull a coat off a dead guy with bullet holes in him?"

"Just do it. Don't argue. For once in your life. I've never seen anything like it. You have a cinder block for a brain."

"What's wrong with that? It helps keep things simple," he said.

"That's what I mean. You're hopeless."

The moon was out from behind the clouds, and I could see the smile on his face. "Let's see what's going on inside Uncle Tom's cabin," he said.

We began walking across the lawn, past a stone birdbath and a Roman sundial and a dry goldfish pond scrolled with black mold. The water in the bayou had risen over the cypress knees and elephant ears and clumps of bamboo that grew along the banks. Leaves that were still yellow and red were floating on top of the water, and the caladiums someone had planted around the oaks reminded me of the ones I had seen through my window in the recovery unit on St. Charles Avenue in New Orleans.

Out in the fog, I could hear somebody grinding the electric starter on the pontoon plane. We walked down one side of a dry coulee and up the opposite slope, the leaves crackling under our shoes, the air filled with a bright, clean odor not unlike the smell of snow. The leaves had drifted in piles so thick and high they were over the tops of our shoes, and the sound of the leaves breaking made me think of squirrel hunting in the fall with my father, Big Aldous, when I was a young boy. I wondered where Big Aldous was. I wondered if he was with my mother and if they were both watching over me, the way I believe spirits sometimes do when they're not ready to let go of the earth. My parents had died violent deaths while they were young, and they knew what it meant to have one's life stolen, and for those reasons I had always thought they were with me in one fashion or another, trying to do the right thing from the Great Beyond.

The cabin was not over twenty yards ahead of us. It had been built of cypress planks and chinked with a mixture of mud and moss before the War Between the States, then restored and reroofed with corrugated tin and outfitted with an air conditioner for the guests of Croix du Sud. I had often wondered if the guests had any idea of the deprivation that characterized the lives of the historical occupants. I had the feeling they did not dwell upon questions of that sort and probably would be bored and offended if they were ever questioned on the subject.

Then a strange occurrence took place, maybe one that was the result of a cerebral accident inside my head. Or maybe I experienced one of the occasions when we glimpse through the dimension and see the people to whom we thought we had said good-bye forever. Inside an envelope of cool fire, right on the bank of the bayou, like the flame of a giant votive candle, I saw my mother, Alafair Mae Guillory, and my father, Big Aldous Robicheaux, looking at me. She wore the pale blue suit and the pillbox hat with the stiff veil she had always been so proud of, and Big Aldous was wearing his tin hat and hobnailed work boots and freshly laundered and starched PayDay overalls, his arms covered with hair as thick as a simian's. At first I thought my parents were smiling at me, but they weren't. Both were waving in a cautionary way, their mouths opening and closing without making any sound, their faces stretched out of shape with alarm.

That was when I saw Pierre Dupree walk straight at me from behind a tree, either a .32 or .25 semi-auto in his left hand, aiming into my face, his chin lifted in the air, as though even in killing someone, he could not give up the arrogant demeanor that seemed to be his birthright.

"At three o'clock, Dave!" I heard Clete shout.

I lifted the shotgun and fired, but I was too late. I saw the muzzle flash of the semi-auto like jagged fire leaping off a spark plug, but I didn't hear the report. Instead, I felt a pain high up on my cheek, similar to a heavy-handed slap that comes out of nowhere.

The burst from my shotgun had not only gone wild; there had been dirt in the muzzle, and the barrel had exploded, splitting the steel all the way down to the pump. The buckshot in the load had ripped through the canopy, scattering leaves down upon us. I fell sideways, one arm extended like a man looking for a wall to lean against. Then I crashed to the ground.

Through a red haze, I saw Clete firing at Pierre Dupree, walking toward him, the ejected nine-millimeter casings flying into the darkness, shooting one bullet after another into Dupree's chest and head and neck, then shooting him again at almost point-blank range as he lay dead and spread-eagled against the trunk of a live oak.

I sat up in the leaves and pushed myself against a tree trunk and tried to clear my vision and stop the ringing in my ears. Clete was squatted down in front of me, staring into my eyes, holding up my chin with one hand, his mouth moving, his words like the muted sounds of submerged rocks bumping together in a streambed.

I saw Gretchen moving toward me, then Alafair kneeling by my side, holding my head against her breast, saying something inaudible.

"I don't know what anyone is saying," I said.

I felt her hands touching the side of my head and stroking my eyes. Her breath was cold on my skin, and her hair smelled like leaves and pine needles. "What are you saying, Alafair? I don't understand anything you're saying."

She moved in front of me so I could see her mouth. "Can you hear me now?"

"Yes."

"I think the bullet went out the side of your cheek. I think it's a flesh wound," she said.

"Where are Tee Jolie and Helen?"

"We left them in the coulee," she said. "Some guys have got the driveway blocked. There aren't many of them left."

For reasons I couldn't explain, her words seemed unrelated to what was happening around us, perhaps because the eye sometimes registers danger before the brain does. Regardless, I knew that something had gone terribly wrong.

"Where's your gun?" I said to Gretchen.

"I dropped it in the dark when I was carrying the sheriff outside," she said.

I stared at Clete and at the gun in his hand and realized our situation had changed dramatically and unfairly, as though the fates had conspired to cheat us of what was ours and deny us the fruits of victory. The backup magazine I had given Clete had not been fully loaded, and the bolt on the Beretta was locked open, the chamber empty. I was of no help to anyone. My head was throbbing, and blood was draining down the side of my face. The trees started to spin around me, and I turned aside and vomited into the leaves.

Like an ugly black-and-white film strip out of control on the projector, our collective bête noire was in our midst. He had stepped out of the slave cabin, the Prussian imperious aristocrat confronting the mongrel mix, a Walther P38 with checkered brown grips in his right hand. I can't say that he had an amused expression, but it's safe to say it was at least one of puzzlement. He gazed at us as he would at a collection of creatures behind a wire fence on a game farm. He glanced at the dead body of the man who may or may not have been both his son and his grandson, then back at us.

"You shouldn't have done that," he said.

I could hear the trees creaking in the wind and the grinding of the starter on the pontoon plane. The propeller caught for a moment, then died. The four of us stared back at him woodenly, still unsure how we had become powerless and at the mercy of a man who not only had no mercy but who took pride in his cruelty. "I see Pierre gave you a tap, Mr. Robicheaux," he said.

"The only score that counts is the one at the bottom of the ninth," I said. "It looks to me like your grandson or son or whatever he is had a bad night. I think he's going to be dead for a long time."

"Did you do that, Mr. Purcel?" Dupree said.

"I feel bad about it, actually," Clete said. "Kind of like picking on a cerebral palsy victim."

"Where does that leave us? Let me think," Dupree said. "Is it true our little Jewish assassin here is your illegitimate daughter? Years ago I would have found a place for her. We spared many who were half Aryan. Did you know there were whorehouses at every one of the camps? I think that might have made a nice fit for you, Ms. Horowitz."

Dupree was looking intently at Gretchen, a shaft of moonlight striking half of his face, the skin under one eye wrinkling. "Would you be willing to fly away with me in order to see your life spared?"

"I guess it depends on what you have in mind. Did you ever see *The Mummy*?" Gretchen said. "It starred Boris Karloff. If there's a remake, I think you could do a better job than Boris. But wearing that mummy wrap on the set all day might be a problem. You seem to have a bulge around your ass. Do you have to wear adult diapers? I bet carrying around a couple of crab cakes all day is pretty uncomfortable."

"Where's Varina Leboeuf?" I said, trying to distract Dupree. It was not an easy task. Gretchen had gotten to him. "Is Varina on the plane?" I said. "She hates your guts, Mr. Dupree. I bet she's going to be a loose cannon."

"That's why she's handcuffed to a pipe in the utility room," he said. He glanced toward the house. "I see someone has started a fire there. How nice of you."

Through the fog, I heard the starter on the plane grind again, but this time the engine caught and I could see the fog thinning from the back draft of the propeller, the tail and fuselage standing out in relief against the water and flooded elephant ears on the far bank.

Dupree walked to a spot by the corner of the cabin so he had a clear view of us and the house and the yard and the plane. He looked at us as if placing us inside a frame, or perhaps as though he were staring at us through a peephole in a door beyond which was a shower room full of disrobed people who had been told they would be spared if they were willing to murder their fellow prisoners.

I had no doubt he was about to shoot the four of us, and Gretchen was to be first. His left hand joined his right on the Walther's grips; his tongue slid across his bottom lip. His teeth looked small and crooked inside his mouth as he raised the gun to eye level and sighted it on Gretchen's throat. "It's too bad to waste such a nice specimen," he said. "But that's the way it is."

Then Clete Purcel performed one of the bravest acts that any human being is capable of. He ran forward, his feet churning in the leaves, his arms widespread, and threw himself on Alexis Dupree, hooking his hands behind the other man's back, crushing Dupree's body against his.

I heard a single shot and saw a flash of light between their bodies. I saw Clete stagger and lift Dupree into the air, then the two of them toppling backward into the leaves. I heard the gun fire a second time and saw Clete getting to his feet, ripping the Walther from Dupree's hand, holding it by the barrel, pressing his other hand against his side, turning toward me, his mouth forming a large round O, his breath wheezing out of his throat.

"Clete!" I said. I said it again: "Clete!"

I was on my feet, and the world was tilting sideways, and I could hear a sound like a train whistle screaming inside a tunnel.

Gretchen took the Walther from Clete's hand and set the safety on it and gave it to Alafair. She put Clete's arm over her shoulder. "Sit down on the edge of the coulee," she said.

"No," he replied. "Give me the gun."

"What for?" Alafair said.

"I'm going to kill him."

"No," Gretchen said.

"Then you do it."

"What?" Gretchen said.

"Smoke him," he said. "Do it now. Don't think about it. He should have died a long time ago. Don't give this guy a chance to come back." Clete was holding on to the side of the cabin like a long-distance runner catching his breath.

"I can't do it," Gretchen said.

"Listen to me. A guy like this re-creates his evil over and over again. And nobody cares. He put thousands of people in gas ovens. He sent children to Josef Mengele's medical labs. You're not snuffing a man. You're killing a bug."

"I don't care what he did. I'm not going to do these things any-more, Clete. Not unless I have to. I'm through with this forever," she said.

Dupree was sitting up, brushing broken leaves and grains of black dirt off his hands. "Could I have a lock of your hair as a souvenir?" he said to Gretchen. "You wouldn't mind, would you? Ask Daddy if he would mind. You two are wonderful at melodrama. The little half-kike telling Daddy she's going to be a good little girl now."

Clete removed the plastic bottle from the pocket of his trousers and eased himself down on one knee, the leaves crackling under him, his face draining with the effort. The left side of his shirt was soaked with blood above the place where it tucked into his belt. He steadied himself, unscrewing the small cap on the bottle with his thumb, the bottle concealed below his thigh. "How many did you kill in that camp?" he asked.

"The people who died in the camps were killed by the Reich. A soldier only carries out orders. A good soldier serves his prince. An unfortunate soldier is one who doesn't have a good prince."

"I got it," Clete said. "You're a victim yourself."

"Not really. But I'm not a villain, either. Your government killed more than one hundred thousand civilians in Iraq. How can you think of yourself as my moral superior?"

"You've got a point there. I'm not superior to anybody or any-thing. That's why I'm the guy who's going to give you what you deserve and make sure you never hurt anyone again."

I realized what Clete was holding in his hand. "Clete, rethink this. He's not worth it," I said.

"You got to do something for kicks," he replied.

Clete pushed Alexis Dupree on his back and pinned him in the leaves with one hand. Dupree's face was filled with shock and dis-belief as he realized what was about to happen.

"*Auf Wiedersehen*," Clete said. He forced the spout on the bottle past Dupree's lips and over his teeth and pushed it deep into his mouth until the liquid Drano was pouring smoothly and without obstruction down his throat.

The consequence was immediate. A terrible odor not unlike the smell from an incinerator at a rendering plant rose from Dupree's mouth. He made a gurgling sound like an air hose bubbling underwater. His legs stiffened and his feet thrashed wildly in the leaves, and his face contorted and seemed to age a century in seconds. Then a dry click came from his throat, as though someone had flicked off a light switch, and it was over.

Clete got to his feet, off balance, and let the bottle drop from his hand. He stared up the incline at the plantation house. "That fire is spreading. Maybe we should do something about that," he said.

I had no idea what he meant. I picked up the bottle and walked deeper into the trees and scooped out a hole in the dirt with my foot and dropped the bottle into it and covered it over, my heart sick at the burden I knew Clete would carry for the rest of his life. The pontoon plane streaked past me, lifting out of the fog, banking above a sugarcane field where the stubble burned in long red lines and the smoke hung like dirty gray rags on the fields. As I walked back up the slope, I realized Clete had not gone directly to the house but to a loamy spot next to a clump of wild blackberry bushes on the bayou's edge and was dragging a heavily laden tarp from a hole, the dirt sliding off the plastic as he worked it up the slope. Two road flares were stuck in his back pockets. He fitted his hands through the grips of two five-gallon gas containers and tried to pick them up. One of them fell hard on the ground and stayed there.

"Help me," he said.

"No," I said.

"It's not over."

"Yeah, it is."

"You think I went too far with the old man?"

"What do I know?" I said, avoiding his eyes.

"He had it coming. You know he did. He was evil. The real deal. You know it."

"Yeah, I guess I do," I said. I did not let him see my face when I spoke.

"What kind of answer is that?" he said. "Come on, Dave, talk to me."

I turned and headed up to the house by myself. I could hear him laboring up the incline, dragging one of the fuel containers behind him like a mythological figure pushing a great stone up a hill.

EVEN AS I outdistanced him to the house, I knew I was selling Clete Purcel short. You should never keep score in your life or anyone else's. And you never measure yourself or anyone else by one deed, whether it's for good or bad. It had taken me a long time to learn that lesson, so why was I forgetting it now? What Clete had done was wrong, but what he had done was also understandable. What if our situation had turned around on us again? What if Alexis Dupree had been given another chance to get his hands on Gretchen Horowitz and Alafair?

For those who would judge Clete harshly, I'd have to ask them if they ever served tea to the ghost of a mamasan they killed. I'd also ask them how they would like to live with the knowledge that they had rolled a fragmentation grenade into a spider hole where her children tried to hide with their mother. Those were not hypothetical questions for Clete. They were the memories that waited for him every night he lay down to sleep.

I was on the lawn and could see the carriage house and the driveway and the towering oak trees in the front yard. I turned around and looked at Clete, still lumbering after me, the gas container swinging from his arm. "What's going on, gyrene?" I said.

He set the container down, his chest rising and falling inside his shirt. I walked back to him and removed my coat and pulled it over his shoulders. In the background I could see Alafair and Gretchen down by the coulee, helping Helen Soileau and Tee Jolie to their feet.

"It's not over," Clete said.

"You're right. It never is," I replied.

"You don't look too good."

"I'm okay. It's just a flesh wound."

"No, there's no exit wound. Alafair was wrong, Dave. You've got a big leak in you. Sit down in the gazebo. I'll be back."

"You know better than that," I said.

But the adrenaline of the last fifteen minutes was ebbing, and my confidence was fading. The yard and plantation house and windmill palms and azalea and camellia bushes bursting with flowers were going in and out of focus, like someone playing with a zoom lens on a camera.

"Hang tight, Dave," Clete said.

He went through the kitchen entrance of the house, the gasoline sloshing inside the plastic container, the road flares sticking out of his back pocket, my coat draped on his shoulders. I followed him and was immediately struck by the density of the heat stored in the house. The fire Gretchen started in the dining room had spread along the carpet and climbed up two of the walls and was flattening against the ceiling. Smoke was climbing in a dirty plume through a hole that probably was once a conduit for the exhaust funnel on a gas-fed space heater.

"Clete?" I called out.

There was no answer.

"Clete! Where are you? It's a match factory in here."

I saw a door hanging open in the hallway. The gasoline container was sitting next to the doorjamb. Downstairs I could hear metal clanging and pipes rattling and bouncing on concrete. I went down the stairs, holding on to the handrail. A solitary light was burning behind a central heating unit, and I could see shadows moving on the wall, but I couldn't see Clete. "What are you doing?" I said.

"They hung her up and beat the shit out of her," he said.

Varina Leboeuf lay on the floor, surrounded by broken plaster and pieces of water pipe Clete had torn out of the ceiling. Manacles from separate sets of handcuffs were locked on her wrists. When she looked up at me, I could hardly recognize her face.

"She says Pierre told the gumballs to do it," Clete said.

In spite of his wounds, he picked Varina up on his shoulder and labored up the stairs with her as though she were a sack of feed. "I'm going to finish up here. Take her outside," he said.

"Time to dee-dee, Cletus."

"Not yet," he replied.

I managed to get Varina Leboeuf out on the lawn while Clete went to work inside. I couldn't tell if she knew what was going on. I believed she was wicked and she used people and discarded them when they were no longer of value to her. I believed she was heartless and mean-spirited and narcissistic and understood no emotions other than her own pain or the pleasure she experienced during moments of self-gratification. I also felt I couldn't judge her. In her own mind, she thought of herself as normal and believed her misdeeds were somehow necessary. The worst irony of all was that in many ways, her perspective wasn't totally dissimilar to Tee Jolie's. They were for sale in different ways, but just the same, they were for sale.

I left her on the lawn and went back inside. Clete had traversed the entire first floor of the home and returned to the kitchen, where the gas container was resting upside down in the sink. He removed the road flares from his back pockets and stared at me, waiting to see what his beat partner from the old First District in New Orleans was going to say. The color had left his face, from either blood loss or exhaustion. I could feel the heat through the dining room wall.

"I checked the old man's study," he said. "The place is vacuumed. We'll never prove any of the things we've learned about these people. It's the right thing to do, Streak. Some of those guys might still be out there."

He waited for me to reply.

"Streak?" he said.

"Do it," I said.

He pulled the plastic cap off a flare and inverted the cap and struck the tip of the flare against the striker. When the flare burst alight, he walked into the hallway with it and tossed it into the living room. Either because of the preheated condition of the house or the influx of cold oxygen from outside, the moment of ignition produced a stunning effect. The rooms abruptly filled with the rosy coloration of a sunset during the summer solstice. The glow intensified and seemed to gather in the water-stiffened wallpaper, the oak floors, the walnut balustrades, the antique furniture, and the bookshelves lined with leather-bound collectibles. We backed out the kitchen door into the coldness of the night as the entire house lit up in a strange and sequential fashion, as though someone were running from room to room, clicking on a series of lamps with red shades.

I heard no glass break, no explosion of a gas main, no violent sounds of studs and joists and nails wrenching apart in the heat. Instead, Croix du Sud Plantation was slowly collapsing and devolving back into itself, whispering its own story on the wind, sparks stringing off the roof, the only earthly reminder of the slaves and convicts who had built and maintained it disappearing with it inside the smoke.

Clete and I walked toward the coulee to rejoin Alafair and Helen and Gretchen. Our wounds were severe, but we would survive them. We were out of step and out of sync with the world and with ourselves, and knowing this, we held on to each other like two men in a gale, the fire burning so brightly behind us that the backs of our necks glowed with the heat.

EPILOGUE

IN THE SPRING Molly and Alafair and I returned to our old haunts in Key West, and three days later, Clete Purcel joined us at the motel on the foot of the island. Key West is a fine place to visit, and it reminds me in many ways of old New Orleans, with its gingerbread houses and palm trees and genteel sense of decay and neon-scrolled pretense at vice that in reality is an illusion. At one time it was the real thing. Like South Louisiana, it originated as a displaced piece of the Spanish and French colonial world that floated across the Caribbean and affixed itself to the southern rim of the United States.

Its culture was antithetical to the Enlightenment. Its residents were pirates and slavers and mulatto and Hispanic whores and American adventurers who hoped to create personal fiefdoms in the West Indies and Nicaragua. Its veneer of Christianity disguised a pagan world that provided a home to people who could never live in a society that was Anglo-Saxon in origin and governed by the descendants of Puritans. License and lucre constituted its ethos. Those who didn't like it could take up sweet-potato farming in Georgia.

Almost year-round, the air was warm and smelled of salt and rain and tropical flowers from all over the world. The winter was not really winter at all, and therein may lie Key West's greatest charm. If one does not have to brood upon the coming of winter and the shortening of the days and the fading of the light, then perhaps one does not have to brood upon the coming of death. When the season is gentle and unthreatening and seems to renew itself daily, we come to believe that spring and the long days of summer may be eternal after all. When we see the light trapped high in the sky on a summer evening, is it possible we are looking through an aperture at our future rather than at a seasonal phenomenon? Is it possible that the big party is just beginning?

We scuba-dived off Seven Mile Reef and trolled for marlin and, in the evening, cooked redfish wrapped in tinfoil on a hibachi on the beach in front of our motel down at the southernmost point on the island. The waves were black at night and strung with foam when they capped on the sandbars, and toward dawn, when the stars went out of the sky, the sun would rise without warning in an explosion of light on the eastern rim of the world, and the water outside our motel window would be flat and calm and turquoise and blue, dimpled with rain rings, and sometimes a flying fish would be sailing through the air as though determined to begin a new evolutionary cycle.

It was grand to be there on the watery edge of my country, amid its colonial past and its ties to the tropical world of John James Audubon and Jean Lafitte and missionaries who had knelt in the sand in the belief that they had found paradise. I wanted to forget the violence of the past and the faces of the men we had slain. I wanted to forget the dissembling and prevarications that constituted the official world in which I made my living, and most of all, I wanted to forget the lies that I had told others about the events on the bayou.

They were lies of omission. The larger truth about the oil blowout on the Gulf of Mexico was not one that many people were interested in. Corporate villains are loathsome. Almost all of them avoid media exposure because they come across as corrupt, arrogant, and tone-deaf. We stare at their testimony before a congressional committee and ask ourselves how this or that gnome of a man was allowed to do so much damage to the rest of us. None of these men can function without sanction. Nations, like individuals, give up an addiction or a vice when they're ready and not until then. In the meantime, you can join Candide in his garden or drive yourself crazy proselytizing those who have no interest in your crusade, such as the street people in Mallory Square. These may not be the happiest alternatives in the world, but they're the only ones that I've been able to come up with.

Helen Soileau returned to her job, and after fighting with insomnia and nightmares for two months, she began seeing a psychotherapist. She sought out crowds and enjoyed loud parties and sometimes stayed later than she should have and went home with people whose names she wasn't sure of in the morning. She did not mind elevators, as long as there were not more than two or three people in them. Airplanes were more of a challenge. Her fear had nothing to do with heights or a loss of control. She was supposed to undergo an MRI in Lafayette, but at the last moment she could not force herself to enter the metal cylinder. She was filled with shame and depression and failure, and when she looked in the mirror, she saw a stranger created by the Duprees when they locked the woman named Helen Soileau inside the freezer.

For that reason, if for no other, I was glad the Duprees were dead and glad that Varina Leboeuf was awaiting trial in the Iberia Parish stockade. I was also glad that I could do a good deed by convincing Helen to take a leave of absence and get on the Sunset Limited and join us among the coconut palms and ficus trees on a stretch of warm beach not far from the home of Ernest Hemingway.

My face was scarred, and Clete had undergone two surgeries, one for the wound in his side and one to remove the lead fragments that had moved next to his heart. I suspect we made an odd group out on the beach, but I didn't care. Is there any worse curse than approval? Have you ever learned anything new from people who accept the world as it is? The bravest individuals I have ever known appear out of nowhere and perform heroic deeds we normally associate with paratroopers, but they're so nondescript that we can't remember what they look like after they have left the room. Saint Paul said there may be angels living among us, and this may have been the bunch he was writing about. If so, I think I have known a few of them. Regardless, it's a fine thing to belong to a private club based on rejection and difference. I'll go a step further. I believe excoriation is the true measure of our merit.

When Clete and I were with NOPD, we knew a black cross-dresser and male prostitute by the name of Antoine Ledoux who was raped repeatedly in Angola and came out a juicer and a junkie. But he got clean with the Work the Steps or Die, Motherfucker group and opened a shoeshine stand by the bus depot and freed himself of a predatory New Orleans subculture that only Tennessee Williams has written about honestly. All this happened before I was in A.A., so I asked Antoine one day how he managed to find a sanctuary from all the misery and pain that had constituted his daily life. Antoine replied, "Sometimes t'ings happen to you that ain't your fault. When you come out on the other side, you ain't never the same again. You paid your dues, and you got your own church wit' your private pew. It's the place where they cain't hurt you no more. See? It's simple."

After our third week in the Keys, I received a postcard from Tee Jolie Melton forwarded from the department. She was living in West Hollywood, with guess who as a roommate? You've got it. None other than Gretchen Horowitz. The card read:

> Dear Mr. Dave,
>
> Gretchen has got a job at Warner Bros. and is taking classes at night at film school. We are so excited. WB is the studio where Daffy Duck and Bugs Bunny were invented. I'm singing in a club and am going to make a demo. Our neighborhood is all men. Gretchen says don't worry, they're real safe. Are you okay now, Mr. Dave? You was hurt so bad.

The card was signed with the initials TJM because she had no more room on which to write. The next day I received a second card with the abbreviation "Cont." at the top rather than a salutation. It read:

> I blame myself for what happened to Blue. I go out to the ocean in Santa Monica and think I see her in the waves. I never

figured out why they did that to her. I never figured out anything. I let them put junk in my arm and abort my baby. I don't
know why I let that happen. I think it's all on me, though.
            Your friend,
                Tee Jolie

The third card arrived the following day. It read:

Dear Mr. Dave,
    I haven't give up. I'm going to make it out here. You're
going to see, you. Tell Mr. Clete Gretchen and me met John
Goodman and he looks just like Mr. Clete.
            Good-bye until I write again,
                Tee Jolie

The early mornings were grand. We ate breakfast at a buffet on the
terrace and watched the pinkness of the dawn dissolve into a hard
blue sky and a seascape flecked with foam. Throughout the day, the
view from the terrace was wonderful, the coconut palms bending
in the wind, the edge of the surf etched by starfish and conch shells,
while seagulls wheeled overhead and the clouds sometimes creaked
with thunder. As I looked at the turquoise brilliance of the water
and the channels of hot blue that were like rivers within the ocean,
I wondered if we had failed to give nature credit for its restorative
powers. Those moments were short-lived. The truth was my thoughts
about nature's resilience were self-serving, because I did not wish to
spoil the mood for everyone else by dwelling upon the sludge from
the blowout that had fouled the Gulf of Mexico from one end to the
other. Regardless of what either our government or the captains of industry had to say, I believed the oil was out there, meshed inextricably
with chemical dispersants, hanging like carpet on coral reefs and on
oyster beds and at depths that seldom experience sunlight. I started
to raise the subject with Clete on one occasion, then let it drop. Clete
was still Clete, but since the second shootout on the bayou, he had
been unduly burdened and had become more insular and detached
than any of us, gazing at images that perhaps no one else saw.

One morning after breakfast, I realized what was on his mind, and it was not the horrific death of Alexis Dupree. Clete had made friends with three Vietnamese children whose mother worked at the motel, and rather than go out on the charter boat with me, he had bought cane poles and bobbers and hooks and lead sinkers and a carton of shrimp and had taken the children fishing in the surf. He waded out with them and baited their hooks and showed them how to cast their lines above a cresting wave into the swell where schools of baitfish flickered across the surface like a spray of raindrops. To give the children better access, he carried them one by one onto a sandbar where they could throw their lines into water that was deeper and a darker blue and held bigger and more exciting fish.

He was bare-chested and wearing his Budweiser shorts that extended almost to his knees, his love handles hanging over the elastic band, his porkpie hat tilted forward on his forehead, his chest and shoulders and back tanned and scarred and hard-looking and shiny with lotion, gold curlicues of hair pasted on his skin. He was carrying an iPod, the headphones clamped on his neck, "Help Me, Rhonda" by the Beach Boys blaring from the foam-rubber earpieces.

I was looking straight at him from the deck of the motel, but I knew that in reality, Clete was no longer in Key West, Florida. Inside the driving rhythm of the Beach Boys' music and the glaze of light on the ocean, I knew he had taken flight to a place on the opposite side of the world, where a young Eurasian woman was broiling fish for him on a charcoal blazer, aboard a sampan silhouetted against a red sun as big as China.

Unfortunately, his reverie and the tranquil moment he was enjoying would not last. The day had grown much warmer, and there was a smell like brass and electricity in the air, and to the south you could see a squall line moving toward the Keys. On top of the water, I could see the pink and blue air sacs of jellyfish, and triangular rust-colored shapes that at first I thought were remnants of the sludge that had floated east from the Louisiana coast. In actuality, I was looking at the leathery backs of stingrays that had been kicked toward the shore by the storm building on the southern horizon.

Within seconds, the waves had washed the jellyfish past the sandbar, encircling it, their poisonous tentacles floating like translucent string on the surface.

I wasn't sure whether Clete knew the danger he and the children were in. I should have known better. Clete was cavalier about his own safety but never about the safety and well-being of anyone else. He picked up all three children, holding them high up on his chest, clear of the water, and waded through the jellyfish like Proteus rising from the surf with his wreathed horn, "Help Me, Rhonda" still blaring from the headphones. After he set them down on the sand, he told them all to hold hands as he led them out on the street where the ice-cream wagon had just stopped.

And that's the way we dealt with the great issues of our time. Clete protected the innocent and tried to do good deeds for people who had no voice, and I tried to care for my family and not brood upon the evil that men do. We didn't change the world, but neither were we changed by it. As the writer in Ecclesiastes says, one generation passeth away, and another generation cometh: but the earth abideth forever. For me, the acceptance of those words and the fact that I can spend my days among the people I love are victory enough.

ABOUT THE AUTHOR

JAMES LEE BURKE, a rare winner of two Edgar Awards and named Grand Master by the Mystery Writers of America, is the author of thirty-six novels and two short story collections, including numerous *New York Times* bestsellers, such as *Robicheaux*, *The Jealous Kind*, *The Neon Rain*, and *Heaven's Prisoners*. He lives in Missoula, Montana.